The Realm of Fiction: 61 Short Stories

D1240811

James B. Hall

University of Oregon

McGraw-Hill Book Company

New York   St. Louis   San Francisco   Toronto

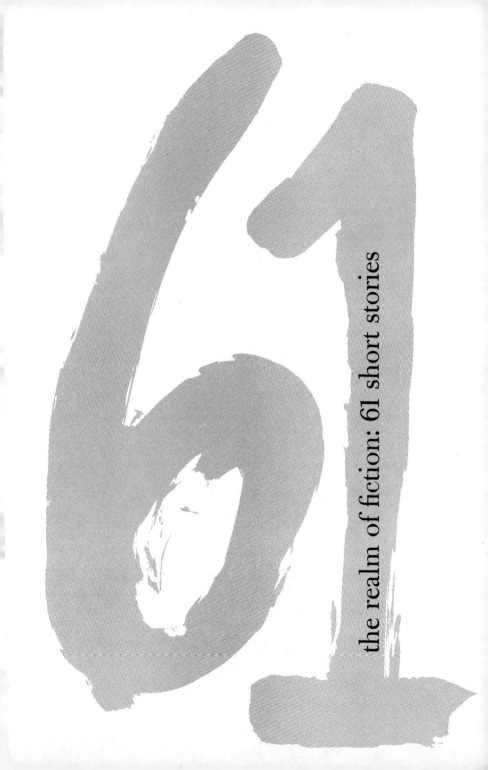

the realm of fiction: 61 short stories

The Realm of Fiction: 61 Short Stories

Sherwood Anderson, "The Egg," from *The Triumph of the Egg* by Sherwood Anderson, published by B. W. Huebsch. Copyright © 1920 by Eleanor Anderson. Reprinted by permission of Harold Ober Associates Incorporated.

Arcadii Averchenko, "The Young Man Who Flew Past," from *A Treasury of Russian Literature*, published by Vanguard Press, Inc. Translated by Bernard Guilbert Guerney. Copyright 1943 by Bernard Guilbert Guerney. Copyright © 1965 by Bernard Guilbert Guerney. By permission of Bernard Guilbert Guerney.

Isaac Babel, "The Awakening," from *An Anthology of Russian Literature in the Soviet Period from Gorki to Pasternak*, translated and edited by Bernard Guilbert Guerney. Copyright © 1960 by Bernard Guilbert Guerney. Reprinted by permission of Random House, Inc.

Samuel Beckett, "Stories and Texts for Nothing, III." Copyright © Editions de Minuit 1955, English translation by Anthony Bonner and Samuel Beckett. First published in *Great French Short Stories* selected and introduced by Germaine Brée, © 1960 by Germaine Brée, Dell Publishing Co., Inc.

Arnold Bennett, "The Sisters Qita," from *Tales of Five Towns*. Published by Chatto & Windus Ltd. By permission of A. P. Watt & Son and Mrs. Dorothy Cheston Bennett.

Ambrose Bierce, "A Psychological Shipwreck," from *Can Such Things Be*, The Cassell Publishing Co., New York, 1893.

Jorge Luis Borges, "The Secret Miracle," from *Labyrinths* by Jorge Luis Borges, translated by Harriet D. Onís. Copyright © 1962 by New Directions. Reprinted by permission of New Directions.

Elizabeth Bowen, "Her Table Spread," from *Look At All Those Roses* by Elizabeth Bowen. Copyright 1941 by Elizabeth Bowen. Reprinted by permission of Alfred A. Knopf, Inc.

Kay Boyle, "Astronomer's Wife," from *The White Horses of Vienna and Other Stories*. Copyright 1936, © 1964 by Kay Boyle. Reprinted by permission of Harcourt, Brace & World, Inc.

preface

Although a definitive literary history of the short story may never be written, The Realm of Fiction: Sixty-one Short Stories *suggests both by example and by arrangement the topography of this demanding yet elusive art form. By any reasonable definition the short story as a separate literary genre is now well over one hundred years old. From the mid-nineteenth century onward several generations of literary artists have contributed their best energies to short fiction; and in the post-war era the short story form continues to demonstrate new vitality, complexity, and charm. Every major artist to some extent alters the tradition and thus places new obligations on the responsible anthologist.*

The Realm of Fiction *brings together sixty-one representative stories from notable Russian, European, British, and American authors, including twenty-two nineteenth century masters, twenty-six great modern figures, and a final section by thirteen contemporary writers. The latter section, representing new dimensions of the short story—either experiments in craft or extremity of vision—has been arranged in a rough order of increasing difficulty and complexity. The main body of the text, however, has been arranged within the chronology of a national literary tradition. In most instances this tradition corresponds to the chronology of date of birth. Where the most interesting part of an author's work places him later (as is true of Conrad and James), I have not hesitated to ignore the date of birth. Above all, this arrangement stresses the continuity of the form. It encourages the student to recognize that excellence in the short story is not created in a vacuum; it develops within a tradition—which is to say that it is shaped by, and in turn shapes, our understanding of the past. The use of this book should help the student to become a practical critic of the short story, to learn what constitutes literary quality in the short story, and, by extension, in all literature.*

The resourceful teacher will not find the scheme of this book either overly formalized or easily exhausted. The number of selections is relatively large in order to give the instructor maximum latitude in selecting those stories best suited to the particular needs of his class and students. Similarly, to allow full freedom for individual teaching practices, the text omits pedagogical apparatus except for a general introduction and brief biographical notes on each author. Included with most of the biographical notes is a reference for further reading, in most cases to a short-story collection.

The main impulse behind The Realm of Fiction, *as with any anthology, is of course the pursuit of literary excellence—to provide a fresh collection of fiction of the highest merit. While there is no pursuit of the new merely for its own sake, the text includes the following five new translations, all commissioned specifically for this anthology and all but the last appearing in English for the first time:*

1. E. T. A. Hoffmann: *"Ritter Gluck" translated from the German by Peter Gontrum*
2. Karel Čapek: *"The Last Judgment" translated from the Czech by Norma Jeanne McFadden and Leopold Pospíšil*
3. Hermann Hesse: *"The Poet" translated from the German by Peter Gontrum*
4. Strates Myriveles: *"The Chronicle of an Old Rose-tree" translated from the modern Greek by Emmanuel Hatzantonis*
5. Fyodor Dostoevsky: *"A Christmas Tree and a Wedding" translated from the Russian by P. H. Porosky*

Along with memorable fiction by the major modern writers—Kafka and Mann, Joyce and Lawrence, Faulkner and Hemingway—other significant stories, such as those by Katayev, Vasconcelos, and Rosenfeld, appear for the first time in any known anthology-text. Established or new, these stories serve the same purpose: to quicken interest in all literature, past and present.

I am especially indebted to my wife, Elizabeth C. Hall, who is in fact a co-editor of this book, but who too modestly disclaims that title.

James B. Hall

contents

2. *the later accomplishment*

3. new dimensions

introduction

The short prose narrative is at once the oldest of literary forms and the newest to receive modern definition. In its primitive state the prose tale was orally realized—to entertain an audience, to chronicle history, or even to prophesy the future. Being functional, the prose tales survived; a few became the literary heritage of nations. Only about one hundred and fifty years ago, in widely separated countries, such literary artists as Turgenev, Mérimée, and Hawthorne began to transform the eighteenth century prose tale into an exacting, complex art form. Today the short story is still in the process of dynamic change.

Of all literary art forms the short story is the most deceptive. Its traditional focus on a single episode, its relative lack of mass—of density of character, variety of scene, and richness of detail—and its frequently casual tone all seem to suggest ease of composition, at least to the inexperienced reader. In contrast to the panorama of the novel, the short story must strike the unwary reader as an art of limited means, of modest resources. Actually, the apparent limitations of the short story are a measure of its strength—the control of all of its materials. Very possibly the deceptive nature of the short story was one reason for its wide appeal, for given conscious artists and new and more literate audiences, the form quickly became a worldwide institution. In the twentieth century the continued fecundity of short fiction is a striking fact of literary history.

The changes which came over the prose tale, on its way to becoming the modern short story, are not difficult to understand. The oldest known tale, *The Shipwrecked Sailor* (from Egyptian papyri, about 4000 B.C.), or the Book of Jonah (from the Old Testament, 350 to 750 B.C.), or tales from the *Decameron* (1353 A.D.) are not very different in literary quality from the eighteenth century tales that immediately preceded the short story. The latest ancestors of the short story in point of time are fictional essays, such as "The Vision of Mirza" by Addison in the *Spectator* (1711) or digressions within a novel, such as "The Tale of the Old Man of the Hill" in Fielding's *Tom Jones* (1748). Typically these short prose pieces lack restraint, or an economy of means; either the moral point is obtrusive and thus the artistic effect is thin, or they lack a meaningful plot structure, and thus are discursive and flat. Perhaps the greatest difference between the prose tale and the nineteenth century short story is the consciousness of technique on the part of the nineteenth century artist. It is precisely this consciousness, this commitment to short fiction as a demanding, distinctive art form that distinguishes Hawthorne and Poe as literary pioneers of great importance. Poe, in particular, felt that the crucial element in the short story was unity of effect—this effect coming from the artistic combination of "incident" and "tone." Poe was speaking of this necessary unity when he praised Hawthorne's stories by saying, "Every word *tells*, and there is not a word which does *not* tell . . ." Other American and European writers shared a similarly lofty concept of the short story as an art form of first importance, and thus they paved the way for the modern short story of the twentieth century.

Compressed statement—the embodiment of significance at several levels of meaning—distinguishes modern short stories of the highest quality. To convey multiple meanings, the artist frequently uses language which is metaphorical or figurative—a medium of expression which is both allusive and suggestive. The story which is resourceful in its exploitation of language will most gracefully support symbolic detail and symbolic actions; in fact, the use of symbolism, justified by an adequate language, is the most interesting and useful advance in narrative technique of modern times. Because of its heightened language the short story approaches poetry in intensity. Always, however, the writer's object remains complexity with control.

If the short story has become more complex and more intense, this does not imply that the modern writer ignores the older, established demands of the form. The modern short story—as a matter of course—comments on the quality and the nature of life; but where morality is a factor, the artist recognizes that the implied or the suggested is always more moving than the easy precept easily stated. Character, namely, imaginative characterizations, continues in importance, but now the focus of narration is on the mind or on the psychic states of the protagonists. Plot structure—a story's largest unit of composition—is recognized as an integral part of the meaning of the story; details are rigorously selected for their ability to "tell." If a story can be said to have literal, allegorical, symbolic, and even mythic levels of meaning, this does not imply that modern short fiction is only an intellectual exercise for the artists and a puzzle for the reader. Close reading, critical analysis, or the brutal fragmentation of a story may be a useful prelude to rendering critical judgment. Nevertheless, both the story's intention and the author's intention remain the same: to create a unified artistic statement which may give both knowledge and pleasure.

If the short story has moved towards complexity, there is little cause for regret. After all, the roots of our short fiction are in our scientific age, in a magnificently complex world initially described by Darwin, Marx, and Freud. That is the world in which we live, and if the literary artist is to render truthfully the altered circumstances of life and morality, he must of necessity impose new demands on his art form. This is true of all imaginative writing at the present time: the novel, poetry, and drama. The short story is no exception: the artists, the art form, and new multiple audiences respond complexly.

The stories in this book, each in its own way, describe a specific version of a complex world. In "The Last Judgment" (Part 2) by Karel Čapek, the conventional notion of an all-powerful God is contradicted. "Our Father Who Art in Heaven" by Valentin Katayev also concerns God, but the title is ironic: there is no earthly salvation for two innocent people who die in the terrible cold. "Ivy Day in the Committee Room" by James Joyce dramatizes a realm where neither God nor man offer salvation; the result is stasis, boredom, and the death of the Will. Taken together, these three stories dramatize the age-old relationship of man to God. Other stories in this book raise different questions about the nature of human experience, the conflicts of man and nature, or of man with one of his greatest antagonists, himself. Short stories, and all literature, are read in the faith that asking such questions is the first step to a better understanding not only of the world but of the self.

The thirteen stories in New Dimensions (Part 3) are examples of recent developments in short fiction both in America and abroad. They are arranged in a rough order of ascending difficulty to the end of extending the reader's capabilities with the modern short story. For example, "The Jewbird" by Bernard Malamud and "The Lottery" by Shirley Jackson are examples of the short story as modern fable. "Wedding Night" by Tommaso Landolfi and "Happy Marriage" by R. V. Cassill are significant studies, at the psychic level, of the complex realms of sex and marriage. "The Secret Room" by Alain Robbe-Grillet is an example of the French "new novel" technique; "Texts for Nothing" by Samuel Beckett is an example of short fiction that is virtually nonrepresentational—it represents "nothing"—and is a final statement of its kind.

If the stories in New Dimensions at first seem strange and if certain stories in the other sections of this book seem at first difficult, the rewards for close study are great. If education is the attainment not only of knowledge, but also of wisdom concerning the world and ourselves, then the short story form in all its manifestations can be a useful means to that ennobling end.

part 1

Russia: *Turgenev, Dostoevsky, Tolstoy, Chekhov*

Europe: *Hoffmann, Mérimée, Verga, de Maupassant*

England-Ireland: *Collins, Hardy, Bennett, Kipling, Wells, Wilde, Conrad*

United States: *Hawthorne, Poe, Harte, Bierce, Twain, Crane, Norris*

the

older

masters

a living relic

ivan turgenev

Ivan Turgenev (1818–1883), the son
of a wealthy landowner in Orel, was one
of the most influential writers in all of
Russian literature. Much of his adult life
was spent in France, where he absorbed
Western ideas and literary techniques. A
master of realism, Turgenev's novels
and short stories strongly influenced
the American writer Henry James. For
further reading: A Sportsman's
Sketches (1847–1852).

'O native land of long suffering,
Land of the Russian people.'
F. Tyutchev

A French proverb says that 'a dry fisherman and a
wet hunter are a sorry sight.' Never having had any taste for fishing, I
cannot decide what are the fisherman's feelings in fine bright weather,
and how far in bad weather the pleasure derived from the abundance of
fish compensates for the unpleasantness of being wet. But for the sportsman rain is a real calamity. It was to just this calamity that Yermolaï
and I were exposed on one of our expeditions after grouse in the Byel-
evsky district. The rain never ceased from early morning. What didn't
we do to escape it? We put macintosh capes almost right over our heads,
and stood under the trees to avoid the raindrops. . . . The waterproof
capes, to say nothing of their hindering our shooting, let the water
through in the most shameless fashion; and under the trees, though at
first, certainly, the rain did not reach us, afterwards the water collected
on the leaves suddenly rushed through, every branch dripped on us
like a waterspout, a chill stream made its way under our neck-ties, and
trickled down our spines. . . . This was 'quite unpleasant,' as Yermolaï
expressed it. 'No, Piotr Petrovitch,' he cried at last; 'we can't go on like

this. . . . There's no shooting to-day. The dogs' scent is drowned. The guns miss fire. . . . Pugh! What a mess!'

'What's to be done?' I queried.

'Well, let's go to Aleksyevka. You don't know it, perhaps—there's a settlement of that name belonging to your mother; it's seven miles from here. We'll stay the night there, and tomorrow. . . .'

'Come back here?'

'No, not here. . . . I know of some places beyond Aleksyevka . . . ever so much better than here for grouse!'

I did not proceed to question my faithful companion why he had not taken me to those parts before, and the same day we made our way to my mother's peasant settlement, the existence of which, I must confess, I had not even suspected up till then. At this settlement, it turned out, there was a little lodge. It was very old, but, as it had not been inhabited, it was clean; I passed a fairly tranquil night in it.

The next day I woke up very early. The sun had only just risen; there was not a single cloud in the sky; everything around shone with a double brilliance—the brightness of the fresh morning rays and of yesterday's downpour. While they were harnessing me a cart, I went for a stroll about a small orchard, now neglected and run wild, which enclosed the little lodge on all sides with its fragrant, sappy growth. Ah, how sweet it was in the open air, under the bright sky, where the larks were trilling, whence their bell-like notes rained down like silvery beads! On their wings, doubtless, they had carried off drops of dew, and their songs seemed steeped in dew. I took my cap off my head and drew a glad deep breath. . . . On the slope of a shallow ravine, close to the hedge, could be seen a beehive; a narrow path led to it, winding like a snake between dense walls of high grass and nettles, above which struggled up, God knows whence brought, the pointed stalks of dark-green hemp.

I turned along this path; I reached the beehive. Beside it stood a little wattled shanty, where they put the beehives for the winter. I peeped into the half-open door; it was dark, still, dry within; there was a scent of mint and balm. In the corner were some trestles fitted together, and on them, covered with a quilt, a little figure of some sort. . . . I was walking away.

'Master, master! Piotr Petrovitch!' I heard a voice, faint, slow, and hoarse, like the whispering of marsh rushes.

I stopped.

'Piotr Petrovitch! Come in, please!' the voice repeated. It came from the corner where were the trestles I had noticed.

I drew near, and was struck dumb with amazement. Before me lay a living human being; but what sort of a creature was it?

A head utterly withered, of a uniform coppery hue—like some very ancient holy picture, yellow with age; a sharp nose like a keen-edged knife; the lips could barely be seen—only the teeth flashed white and the eyes; and from under the kerchief some thin wisps of yellow hair straggled on to the forehead. At the chin, where the quilt was folded, two tiny hands of the same coppery hue were moving, the fingers slowly twitching like little sticks. I looked more intently; the face, far from being ugly, was positively beautiful, but strange and dreadful; and the face seemed the more dreadful to me that on it—on its metallic cheeks—I saw, struggling . . . struggling, and unable to form itself—a smile.

'You don't recognise me, master?' whispered the voice again: it seemed to be breathed from the almost unmoving lips. 'And, indeed, how should you? I'm Lukerya. . . . Do you remember, who used to lead the dance at your mother's, at Spasskoye? . . . Do you remember, I used to be leader of the choir too?'

'Lukerya!' I cried. 'Is it you? Can it be?'

'Yes, it's I, master—I, Lukerya.'

I did not know what to say, and gazed in stupefaction at the dark motionless face with the clear, death-like eyes fastened upon me. Was it possible? This mummy Lukerya—the greatest beauty in all our household —that tall, plump, pink-and-white, singing, laughing, dancing creature! Lukerya, our smart Lukerya, whom all our lads were courting, for whom I heaved some secret sighs—I, a boy of sixteen!

'Mercy, Lukerya!' I said at last; 'what is it has happened to you?'

'Oh, such a misfortune befel me! But don't mind me, sir; don't let my trouble revolt you; sit there on that little tub—a little nearer, or you won't be able to hear me. . . . I've not much of a voice now-a-days! . . . Well, I am glad to see you! What brought you to Aleksyevka?'

Lukerya spoke very softly and feebly, but without pausing.

'Yermolaï, the huntsman, brought me here. But you tell me . . .'

'Tell you about my trouble? Certainly, sir. It happened to me a long while ago now—six or seven years. I had only just been betrothed then to Vassily Polyakov—do you remember, such a fine-looking fellow he was, with curly hair?—he waited at table at your mother's. But you weren't in the country then; you had gone away to Moscow to your studies. We were very much in love, Vassily and me; I could never get him out of my head; and it was in the spring it all happened. Well, one night . . . not long before sunrise, it was . . . I couldn't sleep; a nightingale in the garden was singing so wonderfully sweet! . . . I could not help getting up and going out on to the steps to listen: It trilled and trilled . . . and all at once I fancied some one called me; it seemed like Vassya's voice, so softly, "Lusha!" . . . I looked round, and being half asleep, I suppose I missed my footing and fell straight down from the top-step, and flop on to the ground! And I thought I wasn't much hurt, for I got up directly and went back to my room. Only it seems something inside me—in my body—was broken. . . . Let me get my breath . . . half a minute . . . sir.'

Lukerya ceased, and I looked at her with surprise. What surprised me particularly was that she told her story almost cheerfully, without sighs and groans, not complaining nor asking for sympathy.

'Ever since that happened,' Lukerya went on, 'I began to pine away and get thin; my skin got dark; walking was difficult for me; and then— I lost the use of my legs altogether; I couldn't stand or sit; I had to lie down all the time. And I didn't care to eat or drink; I got worse and worse. Your mamma, in the kindness of her heart, made me see doctors, and sent me to a hospital. But there was no curing me. And not one doctor could even say what my illness was. What didn't they do to me? —they burnt my spine with hot irons, they put me in lumps of ice, and it was all no good. I got quite numb in the end. . . . So the gentle-men decided it was no use doctoring me any more, and there was no sense in keeping cripples up at the great house . . . well, and so they sent me here—because I've relations here. So here I live, as you see.'

Lukerya was silent again, and again she tried to smile.

'But this is awful—your position!' I cried . . . and not knowing how to go on, I asked: 'and what of Vassily Polyakov?' A most stupid question it was.

Lukerya turned her eyes a little away.

'What of Polyakov? He grieved—he grieved for a bit—and he is married to another, a girl from Glinnoe. Do you know Glinnoe? It's not far from us. Her name's Agrafena. He loved me dearly—but, you see, he's a young man; he couldn't stay a bachelor. And what sort of a helpmeet could I be? The wife he found for himself is a good, sweet woman—and they have children. He lives here; he's a clerk at a neighbour's; your mamma let him go off with a passport, and he's doing very well, praise God.'

'And so you go on lying here all the time?' I asked again.

'Yes, sir, I've been lying here seven years. In the summer-time I lie here in this shanty, and when it gets cold they move me out into the bathhouse: I lie there.'

'Who waits on you? Does any one look after you?'

'Oh, there are kind folks here as everywhere; they don't desert me. Yes, they see to me a little. As to food, I eat nothing to speak of; but water is here, in the pitcher; it's always kept full of pure spring water. I can reach to the pitcher myself: I've one arm still of use. There's a little girl here, an orphan; now and then she comes to see me, the kind child. She was here just now. . . . You didn't meet her? Such a pretty, fair little thing. She brings me flowers. We've some in the garden—there were some—but they've all disappeared. But, you know wild flowers too are nice; they smell even sweeter than garden flowers. Lilies of the valley, now . . . what could be sweeter?'

'And aren't you dull and miserable, my poor Lukerya?'

'Why, what is one to do? I wouldn't tell a lie about it. At first it was very wearisome; but later on I got used to it, I got more patient—it was nothing; there are others worse off still.'

'How do you mean?'

'Why, some haven't a roof to shelter them, and there are some blind or deaf; while I, thank God, have splendid sight, and hearing everything—everything. If a mole burrows in the ground—I hear even that. And I can smell every scent, even the faintest; When the buckwheat comes into flower in the meadow, or the lime-tree in the garden—I don't need to be told of it, even; I'm the first to know directly. Anyway, if there's the least bit of a wind blowing from that quarter. No, he who stirs God's wrath is far worse off than me. Look at this, again: anyone in health may easily fall into sin; but I'm cut off even from sin. The other day, father Aleksy, the priest, came to give me the sacrament, and he says: "There's no need," says he, "to confess you; you can't fall into sin in your condition, can you?" But I said to him; "How about sinning in thought, father?" "Ah, well," says he, and he laughed himself, "that's no great sin."

'But I fancy I'm no great sinner even in that way, in thought,' Lukerya went on, 'for I've trained myself not to think, and above all, not to remember. The time goes faster.'

I must own I was astonished. 'You're always alone, Lukerya: how can you prevent the thoughts from coming into your head? or are you constantly asleep?'

'Oh, no, sir! I can't always sleep. Though I've no great pain, still I've an ache, there, right inside, and in my bones too; it won't let me sleep as I ought. No . . . but there, I lie by myself; I lie here and lie here, and don't think: I feel that I'm alive, I breathe; and I put myself all into that. I look and listen. The bees buzz and hum in the hive; a dove sits on the roof and coos; a hen comes along with her chickens to peck up crumbs; or a sparrow flies in, or a butterfly—that's a great treat for me. Last year some swallows even built a nest over there in the corner, and brought up their little ones. Oh, how interesting it was! One would fly to the nest, press close, feed a young one, and off again. Look again: the other would be in her place already. Sometimes it wouldn't fly in, but only fly past the open door; and the little ones would begin to squeak, and open their beaks directly. . . . I was hoping for them back again the next year, but they say a sportsman here shot them with his gun. And what could he gain by it? It's hardly bigger, the swallow, than a beetle. . . . What wicked men you are, you sportsmen!'

'I don't shoot swallows,' I hastened to remark.

'And once,' Lukerya began again, 'it was comical, really. A hare ran in, it did really! The hounds, I suppose, were after it; anyway, it seemed to tumble straight in at the door! . . . It squatted quite near me, and sat so a long while; it kept sniffing with its nose, and twitching its whiskers —like a regular officer! and it looked at me. It understood, to be sure, that I was no danger to it. At last it got up, went hop-hop to the door, looked round in the doorway; and what did it look like? Such a funny fellow it was!'

Lukerya glanced at me, as much as to say, 'Wasn't it funny?' To satisfy her, I laughed. She moistened her parched lips.

'Well, in the winter, of course, I'm worse off, because it's dark: to burn a candle would be a pity, and what would be the use? I can read, to be sure, and was always fond of reading, but what could I read? There are no books of any kind, and even if there were, how could I hold a book? Father Aleksy brought me a calendar to entertain me, but he saw it was no good, so he took and carried it away again. But even though it's dark, there's always something to listen to: a cricket chirps, or a mouse begins scratching somewhere. That's when it's a good thing—not to think!'

'And I repeat the prayers too,' Lukerya went on, after taking breath a little; 'only I don't know many of them—the prayers, I mean. And besides, why should I weary the Lord God? What can I ask Him for? He knows better than I what I need. He has laid a cross upon me: that means that He loves me. So we are commanded to understand. I repeat the Lord's Prayer, the Hymn to the Virgin, the Supplication of all the Afflicted, and I lie still again, without any thought at all, and am all right!'

Two minutes passed by. I did not break the silence, and did not stir on the narrow tub which served me as a seat. The cruel stony stillness of the living, unlucky creature lying before me communicated itself to me; I too turned, as it were, numb.

'Listen, Lukerya,' I began at last; 'listen to the suggestion I'm going to make to you. Would you like me to arrange for them to take you to a hospital—a good hospital in the town? Who knows, perhaps you might yet be cured; anyway, you would not be alone' . . .

Lukerya's eyebrows fluttered faintly. 'Oh, no, sir,' she answered in a troubled whisper; 'don't move me into a hospital; don't touch me. I shall only have more agony to bear there! How could they cure me now? . . . Why, there was a doctor came here once; he wanted to examine me. I begged him, for Christ's sake, not to disturb me. It was no use. He began turning me over, pounding my hands and legs, and pulling me about. He said, "I'm doing this for Science; I'm a servant of Science—a scientific man! And you," he said, "really oughtn't to oppose me, because I've a medal given me for my labours, and it's for you simpletons I'm toiling." He mauled me about, told me the name of my disease—some wonderful long name—and with that he went away; and all my poor bones ached for a week after. You say "I'm all alone; always alone." Oh, no, I'm not always; they come to see me—I'm quiet—I don't bother them. The peasant girls come in and chat a bit; a pilgrim woman will wander in, and tell me tales of Jerusalem, of Kiev, of the holy towns. And I'm not afraid of being alone. Indeed, it's better—ay, ay! Master, don't touch me, don't take me to the hospital. . . . Thank you, you are kind; only don't touch me, there's a dear!'

'Well, as you like, as you like, Lukerya. You know, I only suggested it for your good.'

'I know, master, that it was for my good. But, master dear, who can help another? Who can enter into his soul? Every man must help himself! You won't believe me, perhaps. I lie here sometimes so alone . . . and it's as though there were no one else in the world but me. As if I alone were living! And it seems to me as though something were blessing me. . . . I'm carried away by dreams that are really marvellous!'

'What do you dream of, then, Lukerya?'

'That, too, master, I couldn't say; one can't explain. Besides, one forgets afterwards. It's like a cloud coming over and bursting, then it grows so fresh and sweet; but just what it was, there's no knowing! Only my idea is, if folks were near me, I should have nothing of that, and should feel nothing except my misfortune.'

Lukerya heaved a painful sigh. Her breathing, like her limbs, was not under her control.

'When I come to think, master, of you,' she began again, 'you are very sorry for me. But you mustn't be too sorry, really! I'll tell you one thing; for instance, I sometimes, even now. . . . Do you remember how merry I used to be in my time? A regular madcap! . . . So do you know what? I sing songs even now.'

'Sing? . . . You?'

'Yes; I sing the old songs, songs for choruses, for feasts, Christmas songs, all sorts! I know such a lot of them, you see, and I've not forgotten them. Only dance songs I don't sing. In my state now, it wouldn't suit me.'

'How do you sing them? . . . to yourself?'

'To myself, yes; and aloud too. I can't sing loud, but still one can understand it. I told you a little girl waits on me. A clever little orphan she is. So I have taught her; four songs she has learnt from me already. Don't you believe me? Wait a minute, I'll show you directly. . . .'

Lukerya took breath. . . . The thought that this half-dead creature was making ready to begin singing raised an involuntary feeling of dread in me. But before I could utter a word, a long-drawn-out, hardly audible, but pure and true note, was quivering in my ears . . . it was followed by a second and a third. 'In the meadows,' sang Lukerya. She sang, the expression of her stony face unchanged, even her eyes riveted on one spot. But how touchingly tinkled out that poor struggling little voice, that wavered like a thread of smoke: how she longed to pour out all her soul in it! . . . I felt no dread now; my heart throbbed with unutterable pity.

'Ah, I can't!' she said suddenly. 'I've not the strength. I'm so upset with joy at seeing you.'

She closed her eyes.

I laid my hand on her tiny, chill fingers. . . . She glanced at me, and her dark lids, fringed with golden eyelashes, closed again, and were still as an ancient statue's. An instant later they glistened in the half-darkness. . . . They were moistened by a tear.

As before, I did not stir.

'How silly I am!' said Lukerya suddenly, with unexpected force, and opened her eyes wide: she tried to wink the tears out of them. 'I ought to be ashamed! What am I doing? It's a long time since I have been like this . . . not since that day when Vassya-Polyakov was here last spring. While he sat with me and talked, I was all right; but when he had gone away, how I did cry in my loneliness! Where did I get the tears from? But, there! we girls get our tears for nothing. Master,' added Lukerya, 'perhaps you have a handkerchief. . . . If you won't mind, wipe my eyes.'

I made haste to carry out her desire, and left her the handkerchief. She refused it at first. . . . 'What good's such a gift to me?' she said. The handkerchief was plain enough, but clean and white. Afterwards she clutched it in her weak fingers, and did not loosen them again. As I got used to the darkness in which we both were, I could clearly make out her features, could even perceive the delicate flush that peeped out under the coppery hue of her face, could discover in the face, so at least it seemed to me, traces of its former beauty.

'You asked me, master,' Lukerya began again, 'whether I sleep. I sleep very little, but every time I fall asleep I've dreams—such splendid dreams! I'm never ill in my dreams; I'm always so well, and young. . . . There's one thing's sad: I wake up and long for a good stretch, and I'm all as if I were in chains. I once had such an exquisite dream! Shall I tell it to you? Well, listen. I dreamt I was standing in a meadow, and all round me was rye, so tall, and ripe as gold! . . . and I had a reddish dog with me—such a wicked dog; it kept trying to bite me. And I had a sickle in my hands; not a simple sickle; it seemed to be the moon itself—the moon as it is when it's the shape of a sickle. And with this same moon I had to cut the rye clean. Only I was very weary with the heat, and the moon blinded me, and I felt lazy; and cornflowers were growing all about, and such big ones! And they all turned their heads to me. And I thought in my dream I would pick them; Vassya had promised to come, so I'd pick myself a wreath first; I'd still time to plait it. I began picking cornflowers, but they kept melting away from between my fingers, do what I would. And I couldn't make myself a wreath. And meanwhile I heard someone coming up to me, so close, and calling, "Lusha! Lusha!". . . "Ah," I thought, "what a pity I hadn't time!" No matter, I put that moon on my head instead of cornflowers. I put it on like a tiara, and I was all brightness directly; I made the whole field light around me. And, behold! over the very top of the ears there came gliding very quickly towards me, not Vassya, but Christ Himself! And how I knew it was Christ I can't say; they don't paint Him like that—only it was He! No beard, tall, young, all in white, only His belt was golden; and He held out His hand to me. "Fear not," said He; "My bride adorned, follow Me; you shall lead the choral dance in the heavenly kingdom, and sing the songs of Paradise." And how I clung to His hand! My dog at once followed at my heels . . . but then we began to float upwards! He in front. . . . His wings spread wide over all the sky, long like a sea-gull's—and I after Him! And my dog had to stay behind. Then only I understood that that dog was my illness, and that in the heavenly kingdom there was no place for it.'

Lukerya paused a minute.

'And I had another dream, too,' she began again; 'but may be it was a vision. I really don't know. It seemed to me I was lying in this very shanty, and my dead parents, father and mother, come to me and bow low to me, but say nothing. And I asked them, "Why do you bow down to me, father and mother?" "Because," they said, "you suffer much in this world, so that you have not only set free your own soul, but have taken a great burden from off us too. And for us in the other world it is much easier. You have made an end of your own sins; now you are expiating our sins." And having said this, my parents bowed down to me again, and I could not see them; there was nothing but the walls to be seen. I was in great doubt afterwards what had happened with me. I even told the priest of it in confession. Only he thinks it was not a vision, because visions come only to the clerical gentry.'

'And I'll tell you another dream,' Lukerya went on. 'I dreamt I was sitting on the high-road, under a willow; I had a stick, had a wallet on my shoulders, and my head tied up in a kerchief, just like a pilgrim woman! And I had to go somewhere, a long, long way off, on a pilgrimage. And pilgrims kept coming past me; they came along slowly, all going one way; their faces were weary, and all very much like one another. And I dreamt that moving about among them was a woman, a head taller than the rest, and wearing a peculiar dress, not like ours—not Russian. And her face too was peculiar—a worn face and severe. And all the others moved away from her; but she suddenly turns, and comes straight to me. She stood still, and looked at me; and her eyes were yellow, large, and clear as a falcon's. And I ask her, "Who are you?" And she says to me, "I'm your death." Instead of being frightened, it was quite the other way. I was as pleased as could be; I crossed myself! And the woman, my death, says to me: "I'm sorry for you, Lukerya, but I can't take you with me. Farewell!" Good God; how sad I was then! . . . "Take me," said I, "good mother, take me, darling!" And my death turned to me, and began speaking to me. . . . I knew that she was appointing me my hour, but indistinctly, incomprehensibly. "After St. Peter's day," said she. . . . With that I awoke. . . . Yes, I have such wonderful dreams!'

Lukerya turned her eyes upwards . . . and sank into thought. . . .

'Only the sad thing is, sometimes a whole week will go by without my getting to sleep once. Last year a lady came to see me, and she gave me a little bottle of medicine against sleeplessness; she told me to take ten drops at a time. It did me so much good, and I used to sleep; only the bottle was all finished long ago. Do you know what medicine that was, and how to get it?'

The lady had obviously given Lukerya opium. I promised to get her another bottle like it, and could not refrain from again wondering aloud at her patience.

'Ah, master!' she answered, 'why do you say so? What do you mean by patience? There, Simeon Stylites now had patience certainly, great patience; for thirty years he stood on a pillar! And another saint had himself buried in the earth, right up to his breast, and the ants ate his face. . . . And I'll tell you what I was told by a good scholar: there was once a country, and the Ishmaelites made war on it, and they tortured and killed all the inhabitants; and do what they would the people could not get rid of them. And there appeared among these people a holy virgin; she took a great sword, put on armour weighing eighty pounds, went out against the Ishmaelites and drove them all beyond the sea. Only when she had driven them out, she said to them: "Now burn me, for that was my vow, that I would die a death by fire for my people." And the Ishmaelites took her and burnt her, and the people have been free ever since then! That was a noble deed, now! But what am I!'

I wondered to myself whence and in what shape the legend of Joan of Arc had reached her, and after a brief silence, I asked Lukerya how old she was.

'Twenty-eight . . . or nine. . . . It won't be thirty. But why count the years! I've something else to tell you. . . .'

Lukerya suddenly gave a sort of choked cough, and groaned. . . .

'You are talking a great deal,' I observed to her; 'it may be bad for you.'

'It's true,' she whispered, hardly audibly; 'it's time to end our talk; but what does it matter! Now, when you leave me, I can be silent as long as I like. Any way, I've opened my heart. . . .'

I began bidding her good-bye. I repeated my promise to send her the medicine, and asked her once more to think well and tell me—if there wasn't anything she wanted?'

'I want nothing; I am content with all, thank God!' she articulated with very great effort, but with emotion; 'God give good health to all! But there, master, you might speak a word to your mamma—the peasants here are poor—if she could take the least bit off their rent! They've not land enough, and no advantages. . . . They would pray to God for you. . . . But I want nothing; I'm quite contented with all.'

I gave Lukerya my word that I would carry out her request, and had already walked to the door. . . . She called me back again.

'Do you remember, master,' she said, and there was a gleam of something wonderful in her eyes and on her lips, 'what hair I used to have? Do you remember, right down to my knees! It was long before I could make up my mind to it. . . . Such hair as it was! But how could it be kept combed? In my state! . . . So I had it cut off. . . . Yes. . . . Well, good-bye, master! I can't talk any more.' . . .

That day, before setting off to shoot, I had a conversation with the village constable about Lukerya. I learnt from him that in the village they called Lukerya the 'Living Relic'; that she gave them no trouble, however; they never heard complaint or repining from her. 'She asks nothing, but, on the contrary, she's grateful for everything; a gentle soul, one must say, if any there be. Stricken of God,' so the constable concluded, 'for her sins, one must suppose; but we do not go into that. And as for judging her, no—no, we do not judge her. Let her be!'

A few weeks later I heard that Lukerya was dead. So her death had come for her . . . and 'after St. Peter's day.' They told me that on the day of her death she kept hearing the sound of bells, though it was reckoned over five miles from Aleksyevka to the church, and it was a week-day. Lukerya, however, had said that the sounds came not from the church, but from above! Probably she did not dare to say—from heaven.

a
christmas tree
and a
wedding

fyodor dostoevsky

Fyodor Dostoevsky (1821–1881) was a doctor's son who left military engineering to become a writer. Arrested in 1849 for alleged conspiracy, he was sentenced to Siberia. Later, in the midst of personal tragedy and poverty, he emerged as a major creative talent with such novels as Crime and Punishment (1866), The Idiot (1868–1869), The Possessed (1871), and The Brothers Karamazov (1879–1880). For further reading: White Nights, and Other Stories, translated by Constance Garnett (1918).

The other day I saw a wedding . . . but no! Better I tell you about the Christmas tree. The wedding was nice; I enjoyed it very much, but the other thing that happened was better. I do not know why, but while looking at the wedding, I thought about that Christmas tree. This was the way it happened.

On New Year's Eve, exactly five years ago, I was invited to a children's party. The host was a well-known businessman with many connections, friends and intrigues, so you might think the children's party was a pretext for the parents to meet each other and to talk things over in an innocent, casual and inadvertent manner.

I was an outsider. I did not have anything to contribute, and therefore I spent the evening on my own. There was another gentleman present who had no special family or position, but, like myself, had dropped in on this family happiness. He was the first to catch my eye. He was a tall, lean man, very serious and very properly dressed. Actually he was not enjoying this family-type party in the least. If he withdrew into a corner, he immediately stopped smiling and knit his thick bushy black eyebrows. Except for our host, the man had not a single acquaintance at the whole party. Obviously, he was terribly bored, but he was making a gallant effort to play the role of a perfectly happy, contented man. Afterwards I learned he was a gentleman from the provinces, with important, puzzling business in the capital; he had brought our host a letter of introduction, from a person our host did not patronize, so this man was invited to this children's party only out of courtesy. He didn't even play cards. They offered him no cigars; no one engaged him in conversation. Perhaps we recognized the bird by its feathers from a distance; that is why my gentleman was compelled to sit out the whole evening and stroke his whiskers merely to have something to do with his hands. His whiskers really were very fine, but he stroked them so diligently, you thought the whiskers came first, and were then fixed onto his face, the better to stroke them.

Besides this man—who had five well-fed boys—my attention was caught by a second gentleman. He was an important person. His name was Yulian Mastakovitch. With one glance, you saw he was a guest of honor. He looked down on the host much as the host looked down on the gentleman who stroked his whiskers. The host and hostess spoke to the important man from across a chasm of courtesy, waited on him, gave him drink, pampered him, and brought their guests to him for introductions. They did not take him to anyone.

When Yulian Mastakovitch commented, in regard to the evening, that he had seldom spent time in such a pleasant manner, I noticed tears sparkled in the host's eyes. In the presence of such a person, I was frightened, and, after admiring the children, I walked into a small deserted drawing-room and sat down beside an arbour of flowers which took up almost half of the room.

All the children were incredibly sweet. They absolutely refused to imitate their "elders," despite all the exhortations of their governesses and mothers. In an instant the children untwisted all the Christmas tree candy and broke half of the toys before they knew for whom they were intended. One small, black eyed, curly haired boy was especially nice. He kept wanting to shoot me with his wooden gun. But my attention was still more drawn to his sister, a girl of eleven, a quiet, pensive, pale little cupid with large thoughtful eyes. In some way, the children wounded her feelings, and so she came into the same room where I sat and busied herself in the corner—with her doll.

The guests respectfully pointed out one of the wealthy commissioned tax gatherers—her father. In a whisper someone said three hundred thousand roubles were already set aside for her dowry.

I swung around to look at those who were curious about such circumstances: my gaze fell on Yulian Mastakovitch. With his hands behind his back, with his head cocked a little to one side, he listened with extraordinary attention to the empty talk of the guests.

Later, I marveled at the wisdom of the host and hostess in the distribution of the children's gifts. The little girl—already the owner of three hundred thousand roubles—received the most expensive doll. Then followed presents lowering in value according to the class of the parents of these happy children. Finally, the last gift: a young boy, ten years-old, slender, small, freckled, red-haired, received only a book of stories about the marvels of nature and the tears of devotion—without pictures and even without engravings. He was the son of the governess of the hosts' children, a poor widow; he was a little boy, extremely oppressed and frightened. He wore a jacket made from a wretched nankeen. After he received his book, he walked around the other toys for a long time; he wanted to play with the other children, but he did not dare; he already felt and understood his position.

I love to watch children. They are extraordinarily fascinating in their first independent interests in life. I noticed the red-haired boy was so tempted by the costly toys of the other children, especially a theater in which he certainly wanted to take some kind of part, that he decided to act differently. He smiled and began playing with the other children. He gave away his apple to a puffy little boy, who had bound up a full handkerchief of sweets. He even went as far as to carry another boy on his back, so they would not turn him away from the theater. But a minute later, a kind of mischievous child gave him a considerable beating. The boy did not dare to cry. Here the governess, his mother, appeared and ordered him not to disturb the play of the other children. Then the boy went to the same room where the little girl was. She allowed him to join her. Very eagerly they both began to dress the expensive doll.

I had been already sitting in the ivy-covered arbour for a half an hour. I was almost asleep, yet listening to the little conversations of the red-haired boy and the little beauty with the dowry of three hundred thousand fussing over her doll.

Suddenly Yulian Mastakovitch walked into the room. Under cover of the quarreling children, he had noiselessly left the drawing-room. A minute before I noticed he was talking very fervently with the father of the future heiress, with whom he had just become acquainted. He discussed the advantages of one branch of the service over another. Now he stood deep in thought, as if he were calculating something on his fingers.

"Three hundred . . . three hundred," he whispered. "Eleven, twelve, thirteen," and so forth. "Sixteen—five years! Let us assume it is at four per cent—five times twelve is sixty, yes, to that sixty . . . now let us assume what it will be in five years—four hundred. Yes! Well . . . oh, but he won't hold to four per cent, the swindler. Maybe he can get eight or ten. Well, five hundred, let us assume five hundred thousand, the final measure, that's certain. Well, say a little extra for frills. H'm . . ."

He ended his reflection. He blew his nose, and intended to leave the room. Suddenly he glanced at the little girl and stopped short. He did not see me behind the pots of greenery. It seemed to me that he was really disturbed. Either his calculations had affected him, or something else. He rubbed his hands and could not stand in one place. This nervousness increased to the utmost limit. And then he stopped and threw another resolute glance at the future heiress. He was about to advance, but first he looked around. On tiptoe, as if he felt guilty, he approached the children. With a half-smile, he drew near, stooped, and kissed the little girl on the head. Not expecting the attack, she cried out, frightened.

"And what are you doing here, sweet child?" he asked in a whisper, looking around and patting the girl on the cheek.

"We are playing."

"Ah, With him?" Yulian Mastakovitch looked to one side at the boy. "And you, my dear, go into the drawing-room."

The boy kept silent and stared at him with open eyes.

Yulian Mastakovitch again looked around him and again stooped to the little girl.

"And what is this you have," he asked, "A dolly, sweet child?"

"A dolly," the little girl answered, wrinkling her face, a trifle shy.

"A dolly . . . and do you know, my sweet child, from what your dolly is made?"

"I don't know . . ." answered the little girl in a whisper, hanging her head.

"From rags, darling. You'd better go into the drawing-room to your companions, little boy," said Yulian Mastakovitch, staring severely at the child. The little girl and boy made a wry face and held onto each other's hand. They did not want to be separated.

"And do you know why they gave you that doll?" asked Yulian Mastakovitch, lowering his voice more and more.

"I don't know."

"Because you have been a sweet, well-behaved child all week."

Here Yulian Mastakovitch, emotional as could be, looked around and lowered his voice more and more, and finally asked, inaudibly, almost standing completely still from excitement and with an impatient voice:

"And will you love me, sweet little girl? When I come to visit your parents?"

Having said this, Yulian Mastakovitch tried once again to kiss the sweet girl. The red-haired boy, seeing that she wanted to cry, gripped her hand and began to whimper from sheer sympathy for her. Yulian Mastakovitch became angry, and not in jest.

"Go away. Go away from here, go away!" he said to the little boy. "Go into the drawing-room! Go in there to your companions!"

"No, he doesn't have to, doesn't have to! You go away," said the little girl, almost crying, "Leave him alone, leave him alone!"

Someone made a noise at the door.

Yulian Mastakovitch immediately raised his majestic body and became frightened. But the red-haired boy was even more startled than Yulian Mastakovitch. He left the little girl and quietly, guided by the wall, passed from the drawing-room into the dining-room. To avoid arousing suspicion, Yulian Mastakovitch also went into the dining-room. He was red as a lobster. He glanced into the mirror, as if he were disconcerted. He was perhaps annoyed with himself for his fervor and his impatience. At first perhaps he was so struck by the calculations on his fingers, so enticed and inspired that in spite of all his dignity and importance, he decided to act like a little boy, and directly pursue the object of his attentions even though she could not possibly be *his* object for at least five more years.

I followed the respectable gentleman into the dining-room. I beheld a strange sight. All red from vexation and anger, Yulian Mastakovitch frightened the red-haired boy, who was walking farther and farther, and in his fear did not know where to run.

"Go away. What are you doing here? Go away, you scamp, go away! You're stealing the fruits here, ah? You're stealing the fruits here? Go away, you reprobate. Go away. You snot-nosed boy, go away. Go to your companions!"

The frightened boy tried to get under the table. Then his persecutor, flushed as could be, took out his large batiste handkerchief and began to lash under the table at the child, who remained absolutely quiet.

It must be noted that Yulian Mastakovitch was a little stout. He was a man, well-filled out, red-faced, sleek, with a paunch, with thick legs; in short, what is called a fine figure of a man, round as a nut. He was sweating, puffing and turning terribly red. Finally, he was almost in a frenzy, so great was his feelings of indignation and perhaps (who knows?) jealousy.

I burst out laughing at the top of my voice. Yulian Mastakovitch turned around, and despite all his manners, he was confounded into dust. From the opposite door at that moment came the host. The little boy climbed out from under the table and wiped his elbows and knees. Yulian Mastakovitch hurriedly blew his nose on a handkerchief, which he held in his hand by a corner.

Meanwhile, the host gave the three of us a puzzled look. But as with a man who knows life and looks at it with dead seriousness, he immediately availed himself of the chance to catch his guest in private.

"Here's the little boy," he said pointing to the red-haired boy, "for whom I was intending to intercede, your honor . . ."

"Ah?" answered Yulian Mastakovitch, still not fully put in order.

"The son of my children's governess," the host continued with a pleading tone. "A poor woman, a widow, wife of an honest official; and therefore . . . Yulian Mastakovitch if it were possible . . ."

"Oh, no, no," hurriedly answered Yulian Mastakovitch, "no, excuse me, Filip Alexyevitch, it's no way possible. I've asked, there are no vacancies. If there were, there are already ten candidates—all better qualified than he . . . I'm very sorry. Very sorry . . ."

"I am sorry," repeated the host. "The little boy is modest, quiet . . ."

"A very mischievous boy, as I've noticed," answered Yulian Mastako-vitch, hysterically distorting his mouth. "Go away, little boy," he said addressing the child. "Why are you staying, go to your companions!"

It seemed he could not restrain himself. He glanced at me with one eye. In fun I could not restrain myself and burst out laughing directly in his face.

Yulian Mastakovitch immediately turned away, and clear enough for me to hear, he asked the host who was that strange young man. They whispered together and left the room. Afterwards, I saw Yulian Mastako-vitch listening to the host, mistrustfully shaking his head.

After laughing to my heart's content, I returned to the drawing-room. Surrounded by the fathers and mothers of the families and the host and hostess, the great man was uttering a mating call with warmth, towards a lady to whom he had just been introduced.

The lady was holding by the hand the girl, with whom ten minutes ago Yulian Mastakovitch had had the scene in the drawing-room. Now, he was showering praise and delight about the beauty, talent, grace and good manners of the sweet child. He was fawning, obviously, over the mamma; the mother listened to him almost in tears from delight. The father's lips made a smile; the host rejoiced because of the general satisfaction. All the guests were the same, and even the children stopped playing in order not to disturb the conversation. The whole atmosphere was saturated with reverence.

Later, as if touched to the depth of her heart, I heard the mother of the interesting child beg Yulian Mastakovitch to do her the special honor of presenting them his precious acquaintanceship; and I heard, with his kind of unaffected delight, Yulian Mastakovitch accepting the invitation. Afterwards, the guests all dispersed in different directions, as decency demanded; they spilled out to each other touching words of praise upon the commissioned tax gatherer who worked farmers, his wife, their daughter, and especially Yulian Mastakovitch.

"Is that gentleman married?" I asked, almost aloud, of one of my acquaintances, who was standing closest to Yulian Mastakovitch.

Yulian Mastakovitch threw at me a searching, malicious glance.

"No!" my friend answered me, chagrined to the bottom of his heart at my awkwardness, which I had displayed deliberately.

Recently, I walked by a certain church. The crowd, the congress of people startled me. All around they talked about the wedding. The day was cloudy, and it was starting to drizzle; I made my way through the crowd around the church and saw the bridegroom. He was a small, rotund, well-fed man with a slight paunch and highly dressed. He was running about, bustling, and giving orders. Finally, the voices of the crowd said that the bride was coming. I pushed my way through the crowd and saw a wonderful beauty, who had scarcely begun her first season. But the beauty was pale and sad. She looked distracted; it even seemed to me that her eyes were red from recent crying. The classical severity of every line of her face added a certain dignity and solemnity to her beauty. Through that severity and dignity, through that sadness, still appeared the first look of childish innocence—very naive, fluid, youthful, and yet neither asking nor entreating for mercy.

They were saying she was just sixteen years-old. Glancing carefully at the bridegroom, I suddenly recognized him as Yulian Mastakovitch, whom I had not seen for five years. I took a look at her. My God!

I began to push my way quickly out of the church. The voices of the crowd said the bride was rich: a dowry of five hundred thousand . . . and a trousseau with ever so much . . .

"It was a good calculation, though," I thought, and made my way out into the street.

the story of yemilyan and the empty drum

leo tolstoy

Leo Tolstoy (1828–1910) was born a nobleman, and after a carefree life in St. Petersburg and Moscow, he began to write fiction while on duty as an artillery officer in the Crimea. After marriage, he managed his estate and wrote some of the world's most remarkable novels, War and Peace *(1866) and* Anna Karenina *(1877). Before his death, Tolstoy renounced his work and his world, including his material possessions, in favor of the simple Christian existence of a Russian peasant. For further reading:* A Russian Proprietor, The Invaders, The Death of Ivan Ilytich, The Long Exile *(1899–1902).*

Yemilyan lived out as a day-laborer. Once upon a time he was on his way to the meadow where his work was, and lo and behold! a frog leaped out before him. He almost set his foot on it. But he stepped over it. Suddenly he heard some one calling to him from behind. He looked round and saw a beautiful girl standing there, and she said to him:—

"Yemilyan, why are you not married?"

"How could I be married, my pretty maid. Look at me; I have nothing at all. No one would take me."

"Well," said the girl, "take me for a wife."

The girl greatly pleased Yemilyan; said he:—

"I should like to; but where should we live?"

"That is something to think about," said the girl. "Hard work and little sleep is all that is required; but we can find clothes and food anywhere."

"Very good, I'm agreed; let us get married. Where shall we go?"

"Let us go to the city."

Yemilyan and the girl went to the city. The girl took him to a little cottage at the farther end of the city, and they were married and lived there.

One time the voyevode came to the city. He passed by Yemilyan's cottage, and Yemilyan's wife went out to look at him. When the voyevode saw her he was amazed.

"Where did such a beauty as that come from?"

He reined in his horse, and summoned Yemilyan's wife, and began to question her.

"Who are you?" he asked.

"The wife of the peasant Yemilyan," said she.

"How did it happen," said he, "that such a beautiful woman as you married a peasant? You ought to be a princess."

"Thank you," said she, "for your flattering remark, but I am satisfied with my husband."

The voyevode talked with her awhile, and then rode on his way. He reached his palace. But he could not help thinking of Yemilyan's wife. He lay awake all night long, planning how he might get her away from Yemilyan. He could not think of any way of doing it. He summoned his servants, and bade them devise some way. And the voyevode's servants said to him:—

"Take Yemilyan as your workman," said they. "We'll work him to death; his wife will be a widow, and then you can have her."

So the voyevode did; he sent for Yemilyan to come to him as a dvornik, and offered him a house for him and his wife.

The messengers came and told Yemilyan their story. But Yemilyan's wife said:—

"Very good," said she. "Go. Work there during the daytime, but at night return to me."

Yemilyan went. When he reached the palace, the voyevode's steward said to him:—

"Why have you come alone, without your wife?"

"Why should I bring her? Her place is at home."

In the voyevode's courtyard they give him so much work to do that two men could not have accomplished it. Yemilyan took hold of the work, but it seemed hopeless for him to finish it. But lo and behold! when evening came it was all done. The steward saw that he had finished it, and gave him four times as much for the next day. Yemilyan went home and found the house all neatly swept and in order; the fire was burning in the stove, the baking and boiling were under way. His wife was sitting at the table sewing and waiting for her husband. When he entered she met him, got supper ready, and, after he had had all he wanted to eat and drink, she began to ask him about his work.

"Well," said he, "it went badly. They gave me more than I had strength to do. They are going to kill me with work."

"Now, then," said she, "don't you worry about your work, and don't look back and don't look forward to see if much has been done and much remains to be done. Only work. All will come out right."

Yemilyan went to bed. The next morning he went to his work again. He took hold of it, and not once did he look round. And lo and behold! it was all done by four o'clock, and while it was still light he went home for the night. And though they kept adding to his tasks, still Yemilyan always managed to finish it up and go home for the night.

Thus passed a week. The voyevode's servants perceived that they could not overcome the muzhik by "black work." They began to impose handiwork upon him, but this also proved vain. Carpentry work and mason work and the art of thatching—whatever they imposed upon him, that Yemilyan got done in ample time for him to go home and spend the night with his wife. Thus passed a second week. The voyevode summoned his servants, and said:—

"I should like to know if I feed you for doing nothing? Here two weeks have passed and I can't see that you have done anything at all. You were going to put Yemilyan out of the way for me, but from the window I see him going home every afternoon, singing songs. I should like to know if you are scheming to turn me into ridicule?"

The servants began to justify themselves:—

"We tried with all our might," said they, "to kill him off by 'black work,' but we could not do anything with him. Everything we gave him to work at he worked out, and we could not tire him. Then we gave him handiwork to do, thinking he would not have wit enough to do it, but in this too we failed to get him. It is like magic. As soon as he touches anything it is done. It must be that either he or his wife practices some witchcraft. We are tired to death of him. And now we are trying to think of something that he can't do. We have decided to make him build a new cathedral in one day. So will you summon Yemilyan and command him to build a new cathedral opposite your palace in one day? And if he does not have it done, then we will have his head cut off as a punishment."

The voyevode sent for Yemilyan.

"Well," said he, "this is my command. Build me a new cathedral on the square opposite my palace, so that it shall be all done to-morrow evening. If you get it built, I will reward you; if you fail, I shall punish you."

Yemilyan heard the command, he turned round and went home.

"Well," said he to himself, "that's the end of me."

He went to his wife and said:—

"Get yourself ready, wife; we must make our escape somewhere or other, else we shall be ruined."

"Why," she said, "are you such a coward that you must run away?"

"How can I help being?" said he. "The voyevode has ordered me to come to-morrow and build a new cathedral all in one day. And if I don't get it built, he threatens to cut off my head. The only thing left to do is to escape while there is time."

But his wife would not hear to this.

"The voyevode has many servants. They will catch us anywhere. You can't escape from him. But since you have the power, you must obey him."

"Yes, but how can one obey him, if one has not the power?"

"Listen, batyushka. Don't you worry. Eat your supper and go to bed. In the morning get up a little earlier than usual; you'll have it all done."

Yemilyan went to bed; his wife wakened him.

"Go," said she, "build your cathedral as quickly as possible. Here are nails and a hammer; there'll be work enough for you for the day."

Yemilyan went to the city; when he got there the new cathedral was already standing in the midst of the square, almost finished. Yemilyan went to work to finish it; by evening it was all complete.

The voyevode woke up, he looked out of his palace window, and saw that the cathedral was already built. Yemilyan was walking up and down, here and there driving in nails. And the voyevode was not pleased to see the cathedral; he was vexed because he had nothing to punish Yemilyan for, and could not take away his wife. So he called his servants again.

"Yemilyan has accomplished his task; there is nothing to punish him for. This task," said he, "was too small for him. Something craftier must be thought up. Put your wits to work, or else I will punish you instead of him."

And the voyevode's servants suggested that he should command Yemilyan to make a river which should flow round the palace, and that ships should be sailing on it. The voyevode summoned Yemilyan, and laid before him the new task.

"If you are able," said he, "in one night to build a cathedral, then you will be able to do this also. See to it that to-morrow everything be as I have commanded. And if it is not ready, then I will cut off your head."

Yemilyan was more than ever discouraged, and he returned to his wife in a very gloomy frame of mind.

"Why," said his wife, "are you so discouraged? Have you some new task imposed on you?"

Yemilyan told her.

"We must make our escape," said he.

But his wife said:—

"You can't run away; they will catch you everywhere; you must obey."

"Yes, but how can I obey?"

"Well, batyushka, there is nothing to be discouraged about. Eat your supper and go to bed. But get up earlier than usual; everything will be in order."

Yemilyan went to bed and slept. Early in the morning his wife waked him.

"Go," said she, "go to the city, all is ready. You will find one mound only at the harbor. Take your spade and level it off."

Yemilyan started. He reached the city; round the palace was a river, ships were sailing on it. Yemilyan reached the harbor, he saw the uneven place, and began to level it.

The voyevode woke up, he saw a river where no river had been; ships were sailing on it and Yemilyan was leveling a mound with his spade. The voyevode was horror-struck and was not rejoiced at the sight of the river and the ships; but he was vexed because he could not punish Yemilyan. He said to himself:—

"There is no task that he cannot accomplish it. What shall we try now?"

He summoned his servants and proceeded to consult with them.

"Think up some task," said he, "that will be above Yemilyan's powers. For whatever you have so far devised for him, he has done at once, and it is impossible to take his wife from him."

The servants cudgeled their brains, and at last had a bright idea. They came to the voyevode and said:—

"You must summon Yemilyan and say to him:—

" 'Go somewhere, you know not where, and bring back something, you know not what.' He won't be able to escape from this. Wherever he goes you will say that he went to the wrong place, and whatever he brings back you will say that he brought back the wrong thing. Then you will be able to punish him and take away his wife."

This pleased the voyevode.

"This time," said he, "you have had a bright idea."

He sent for Yemilyan and said to him:—

"Go somewhere, you know not where, and bring back something, you know not what, and if you don't bring it, I will cut your head off."

Yemilyan went to his wife, and told her what the voyevode had said. His wife put on her thinking-cap.

"Well," said she, "they've been teaching the voyevode something to his own ruin. We must work now wisely."

She sat down, pondered for a while, and then said to her husband:—

"You will have to take a long journey—to our babushka, our grandmother—to the ancient peasant mother—and you must ask for her goodwill. And from her you will receive an object; then go straightway to the voyevode, and I shall be there. For now I shall not get out of their hands. They will take me by force, but not for long. If you do all the old babushka commands, you will speedily rescue me."

The wife got her husband ready; she gave him a wallet and gave him a spindle.

"Here, take this," said she, "and give it to her. By this she will know that you are my husband."

She showed him the way. Yemilyan started; he went beyond the city, and he saw some bowmen drilling. Yemilyan stopped and watched them. After the bowmen had practised, they sat down to rest. Yemilyan approached them and asked:—

"Do you know, my brethren, where I must go, not knowing where, to get something, not knowing what?"

The bowmen listened to what he had to say, and they were filled with wonder.

"Who sent you to find out?" they inquired.

"The voyevode," said he.

"No," said they, "we cannot help you."

After Yemilyan had sat a little while, he proceeded on his way.

He went and he went, and at last he came to a forest. In the forest lived the old babushka.

The old woman was sitting in a cottage—the ancient peasant mother—she was spinning flax—and she was weeping. When the old woman saw Yemilyan, she cried out to him:—

"What have you come for?"

Yemilyan gave her the distaff, and told her his wife had sent it to her. And Yemilyan began to tell her all about his life, how he had married the girl, how he had gone to the city to live, how he had been taken as a dvornik, how he had served the voyevode, how he had built the cathedral and made the river with the ships, and how now the voyevode had commanded him to go somewhere, not knowing where, to get something, he knew not what.

The old woman listened to him and ceased to weep. She began to mutter to herself.

"That is very good," said she, "but sit down, little son, and eat."

Yemilyan ate his fill, and the old woman began to talk with him.

"Here is a little ball," said she; "roll it before you and follow it, wherever it may roll. You will have to go far, even to the sea. When you reach the sea, you will find there a great city. When you enter the city, ask for a night's lodgings at the last house. There you will find what you need."

"But how shall I know it, babushka?"

"Well, when you see what men obey sooner than father and mother, that is what you want; seize on it and take it with you. You will take it to the voyevode, but he will say to you that you have not brought the thing that was required, and then do you say to him: 'Well, if it is not what is wanted it must be broken; then lift the thing a blow and take it down to the river, break it, and fling it into the water, and then you will recover your wife.'"

Yemilyan bade the old woman good-by, rolled the little ball ahead of him; it rolled and it rolled, and it took him to the sea, and by the sea was a great city. At the border of the city was a large house. Yemilyan there demanded hospitality for the night; it was granted, and he went to bed. He woke early in the morning and listened; the father was getting up, he called his son and sent him to split kindlings. But the son would not heed; "It is too early as yet," said he, "I shall have time enough." Yemilyan heard the mother get down from the oven and say:—

"Go little son, your father's bones pain him; would you make him go?"

"There's plenty of time."

The son made a smacking noise with his lips, and dropped off to sleep again. As soon as he had fallen asleep there was a noise like thunder, and a loud crash in the street. The son leaped down, put on his clothes, and ran down into the street. Yemilyan also jumped down and followed him to see what the son obeyed better than his parents. Yemilyan ran down and saw a man going along the street, carrying a round object and beating on it with sticks, and it rumbled, and the son listened to it. Yemilyan ran closer and examined the object, and saw that it was round like a small tub, and both ends were covered with skin. And he insisted on knowing what it was called.

"A drum," they told him.

Yemilyan was amazed, and asked them to give it to him. They refused to give it to him. So Yemilyan ceased to ask for it, but he walked along following it. He walked all that day, and when the man that had it lay down to sleep, Yemilyan seized his drum and ran off with it.

He ran and he ran, and at last came back to his own city. He expected to see his wife at home, but she was not there.

On the next day they had brought her to the voyevode. Yemilyan went to the voyevode's, and bade them announce him in these words:—

"Here! the man who went he knew not where, has come back, bringing he knows not what."

The voyevode bade Yemilyan to return the next day.

Yemilyan then ordered them to say to the voyevode:—

"I," said he, "have come to-day. I have brought what he bade me bring; let the voyevode come to me or I will come to him."

The voyevode replied:—

"Where did you go?" he asked.

"I don't know," said he.

"And what did you bring with you?"

Yemilyan was about to show it to him, but the voyevode refused to look at it:—

"It's nothing," said he.

"Yes, it's nothing," said Yemilyan; "but then one must beat on it, and the devil is in it."

Yemilyan came with the drum and beat on it.

As soon as he began to beat on it, all the voyevode's army came and joined Yemilyan. They saluted him and waited till he should give the word of command.

The voyevode began to shout to his bowmen from the window of his palace, forbidding them to follow Yemilyan. They refused to obey him, and followed Yemilyan. The voyevode perceived this, and ordered them to restore his wife to Yemilyan, and then asked him to give him the drum.

"I cannot," said Yemilyan. "I must beat it," said he, "and throw the scrapings into the river."

Yemilyan went with the drum to the river, and the bowmen followed him. Yemilyan beat the drum by the river, broke it into pieces, and flung them into the river. And all the bowmen scattered in all directions. But Yemilyan took his wife and brought her home. And from that time forth the voyevode ceased to bother him, and he lived long and happily ever after.

the

bet

anton chekhov

*Anton Pavlovich Chekhov (1860–1904)
was the son of an unsuccessful grocery store
owner in Taganrog on the Sea of Azov. While
earning a degree in medicine at the University
of Moscow, he began to write humorous sketches.
He died of tuberculosis at the age of forty-four,
but not before he had become one of the world's most
influential short-story writers. For further reading:* The
Tales of Chekhov, *translated by Constance Garnett
(1916–1922); specifically* The Chorus
Girl *(1886),* The Party
(1888), The Darling *(1898).*

It was a dark autumn night. The old banker was
pacing from corner to corner of his study, recalling to his mind the party
he gave in the autumn fifteen years ago. There were many clever people
at the party and much interesting conversation. They talked among other
things of capital punishment. The guests, among them not a few scholars
and journalists, for the most part disapproved of capital punishment.
They found it obsolete as a means of punishment, unfitted to a Christian
State and immoral. Some of them thought that capital punishment
should be replaced universally by life-imprisonment.

"I don't agree with you," said the host. "I myself have experienced
neither capital punishment nor life-imprisonment, but if one may judge
a priori, then in my opinion capital punishment is more moral and more
humane than imprisonment. Execution kills instantly, life-imprisonment
kills by degrees. Who is the more humane executioner, one who kills
you in a few seconds or one who draws the life out of you incessantly,
for years?"

"They're both equally immoral," remarked one of the guests, "because
their purpose is the same, to take away life. The State is not God. It
has no right to take away that which it cannot give back, if it should
so desire."

Among the company was a lawyer, a young man of about twenty-five.
On being asked his opinion, he said:

"Capital punishment and life-imprisonment are equally immoral; but
if I were offered the choice between them, I would certainly choose
the second. It's better to live somehow than not to live at all."

There ensued a lively discussion. The banker who was then younger
and more nervous suddenly lost his temper, banged his fist on the table,
and turning to the young lawyer, cried out:

"It's a lie. I bet you two millions you wouldn't stick in a cell even for five years."

"If you're serious," replied the lawyer, "then I bet I'll stay not five but fifteen."

"Fifteen! Done!" cried the banker. "Gentlemen, I stake two millions."

"Agreed. You stake two millions, I my freedom," said the lawyer.

So this wild, ridiculous bet came to pass. The banker, who at that time had too many millions to count, spoiled and capricious, was beside himself with rapture. During supper he said to the lawyer jokingly:

"Come to your senses, young man, before it's too late. Two millions are nothing to me, but you stand to lose three or four of the best years of your life. I say three or four, because you'll never stick it out any longer. Don't forget either, you unhappy man, that voluntary is much heavier than enforced imprisonment. The idea that you have the right to free yourself at any moment will poison the whole of your life in the cell. I pity you."

And now the banker, pacing from corner to corner, recalled all this and asked himself:

"Why did I make this bet? What's the good? The lawyer loses fifteen years of his life and I throw away two millions. Will it convince people that capital punishment is worse or better than imprisonment for life. No, No! all stuff and rubbish. On my part, it was the caprice of a well-fed man; on the lawyer's, pure greed of gold."

He recollected further what happened after the evening party. It was decided that the lawyer must undergo his imprisonment under the strictest observation, in a garden-wing of the banker's house. It was agreed that during the period he would be deprived of the right to cross the threshold, to see living people, to hear human voices, and to receive letters and newspapers. He was permitted to have a musical instrument, to read books, to write letters, to drink wine and smoke tobacco. By the agreement he could communicate, but only in silence, with the outside world through a little window specially constructed for this purpose. Everything necessary, books, music, wine, he could receive in any quantity by sending a note through the window. The agreement provided for all the minutest details, which made the confinement strictly solitary, and it obliged the lawyer to remain exactly fifteen years from twelve o'clock of November 14th, 1870, to twelve o'clock of November 14th, 1885. The least attempt on his part to violate the conditions, to escape if only for two minutes before the time freed the banker from the obligation to pay him the two millions.

During the first year of imprisonment, the lawyer, as far as it was possible to judge from his short notes, suffered terribly from loneliness and boredom. From his wing day and night came the sound of the piano.

He rejected wine and tobacco. "Wine," he wrote, "excites desires, and desires are the chief foes of a prisoner; besides, nothing is more boring than to drink good wine alone," and tobacco spoiled the air in his room. During the first year the lawyer was sent books of a light character; novels with a complicated love interest, stories of crime and fantasy, comedies, and so on.

In the second year the piano was heard no longer and the lawyer asked only for classics. In the fifth year, music was heard again, and the prisoner asked for wine. Those who watched him said that during the whole of that year he was only eating, drinking, and lying on his bed. He yawned often and talked angrily to himself. Books he did not read. Sometimes at nights he would sit down to write. He would write for a long time and tear it all up in the morning. More than once he was heard to weep.

In the second half of the sixth year, the prisoner began zealously to study languages, philosophy, and history. He fell on these subjects so hungrily that the banker hardly had time to get books enough for him. In the space of four years about six hundred volumes were bought at his request. It was while that passion lasted that the banker received the following letter from the prisoner: "My dear gaoler, I am writing these lines in six languages. Show them to experts. Let them read them. If they do not find one single mistake, I beg you to give orders to have a gun fired off in the garden. By the noise I shall know that my efforts have not been in vain. The geniuses of all ages and countries speak in different languages; but in them all burns the same flame. Oh, if you knew my heavenly happiness now that I can understand them!" The prisoner's desire was fulfilled. Two shots were fired in the garden by the banker's order.

Later on, after the tenth year, the lawyer sat immovable before his table and read only the New Testament. The banker found it strange that a man who in four years had mastered six hundred erudite volumes, should have spent nearly a year in reading one book, easy to understand and by no means thick. The New Testament was then replaced by the history of religions and theology.

During the last two years of his confinement the prisoner read an extraordinary amount, quite haphazardly. Now he would apply himself to the natural sciences, then would read Byron or Shakespeare. Notes used to come from him in which he asked to be sent at the same time a book on chemistry, a text-book of medicine, a novel, and some treatise on philosophy or theology. He read as though he were swimming in the sea among broken pieces of wreckage, and in his desire to save his life was eagerly grasping one piece after another.

II

The banker recalled all this, and thought:

"To-morrow at twelve o'clock he receives his freedom. Under the agreement, I shall have to pay him two millions. If I pay, it's all over with me. I am ruined for ever . . ."

Fifteen years before he had too many millions to count, but now he was afraid to ask himself which he had more of, money or debts. Gambling on the Stock-Exchange, risky speculation, and the recklessness of which he could not rid himself even in old age, had gradually brought his business to decay; and the fearless, self-confident, proud man of business had become an ordinary banker, trembling at every rise and fall in the market.

"That cursed bet," murmured the old man clutching his head in despair . . . "Why didn't the man die? He's only forty years old. He will take away my last penny, marry, enjoy life, gamble on the Exchange, and I will look on like an envious beggar and hear the same words from him every day: 'I'm obliged to you for the happiness of my life. Let me help you.' No, it's too much! The only escape from bankruptcy and disgrace—is that the man should die."

The clock had just struck three. The banker was listening. In the house everyone was asleep, and one could hear only the frozen trees whining outside the windows. Trying to make no sound, he took out of his safe the key of the door which had not been opened for fifteen years, put on his overcoat, and went out of the house. The garden was dark and cold. It was raining. A keen damp wind hovered howling over all the garden and gave the trees no rest. Though he strained his eyes, the banker could see neither the ground, nor the white statues, nor the garden-wing, nor the trees. Approaching the place where the garden-wing stood, he called the watchman twice. There was no answer. Evidently the watchman had taken shelter from the bad weather and was now asleep somewhere in the kitchen or the greenhouse.

"If I have the courage to fulfil my intention," thought the old man, "the suspicion will fall on the watchman first of all."

In the darkness he groped for the stairs and the door and entered the hall of the garden-wing, then poked his way into a narrow passage and struck a match. Not a soul was there. Someone's bed, with no bedclothes on it, stood there, and an iron stove was dark in the corner. The seals on the door that led into the prisoner's room were unbroken.

When the match went out, the old man, trembling from agitation, peeped into the little window.

In the prisoner's room a candle was burning dim. The prisoner himself sat by the table. Only his back, the hair on his head and his hands were visible. On the table, the two chairs, and on the carpet by the table, open books were strewn.

Five minutes passed and the prisoner never once stirred. Fifteen years' confinement had taught him to sit motionless. The banker tapped on the window with his finger, but the prisoner gave no movement in reply. Then the banker cautiously tore the seals from the door and put the key into the lock. The rusty lock gave a hoarse groan and the door creaked. The banker expected instantly to hear a cry of surprise and the sound of steps. Three minutes passed and it was as quiet behind the door as it had been before. He made up his mind to enter.

Before the table sat a man, unlike an ordinary human being. It was a skeleton, with tight-drawn skin, with a woman's long curly hair, and a shaggy beard. The colour of his face was yellow, of an earthy shade; the cheeks were sunken, the back long and narrow, and the hand upon which he leaned his hairy head was so lean and skinny that it was painful to look upon. His hair was already silvering with grey, and no one who glanced at the senile emaciation of the face would have believed that he was only forty years old. On the table, before his bended head, lay a sheet of paper on which something was written in a tiny hand.

"Poor devil," thought the banker, "he's asleep and probably seeing millions in his dreams. I have only to take and throw this half-dead thing on the bed, smother him a moment with the pillow, and the most careful examination will find no trace of unnatural death. But, first, let us read what he has written here."

The banker took the sheet from the table and read:

"To-morrow at twelve o'clock midnight, I shall obtain my freedom and the right to mix with people. But before I leave this room and see the sun I think it necessary to say a few words to you. On my own clear conscience and before God who sees me I declare to you that I despise freedom, life, health, and all that your books call the blessings of the world.

"For fifteen years I have diligently studied earthly life. True, I saw neither the earth nor the people, but in your books I drank fragrant wine, sang songs, hunted deer and wild boar in the forests, loved women . . . And beautiful women, like clouds ethereal, created by the magic of your poets' genius, visited me by night and whispered to me wonderful tales, which made my head drunken. In your books I climbed the summits of Elbruz and Mont Blanc and saw from there how the sun rose in the morning, and in the evening overflowed the sky, the ocean and the mountain ridges with a purple gold. From there I saw how above me lightnings glimmered, cleaving the clouds; I saw green forests, fields, rivers, lakes, cities; I heard sirens singing, and the playing of the pipes of Pan; I touched the wings of beautiful devils who came flying to me to speak of God . . . In your books I cast myself into bottomless abysses, worked miracles, burned cities to the ground, preached new religions, conquered whole countries . . .

"Your books gave me wisdom. All that unwearying human thought created in the centuries is compressed to a little lump in my skull. I know that I am more clever than you all.

"And I despise your books, despise all worldly blessings and wisdom. Everything is void, frail, visionary and delusive as a mirage. Though you be proud and wise and beautiful, yet will death wipe you from the face of the earth like the mice underground; and your posterity, your history, and the immortality of your men of genius will be as frozen slag, burnt down together with the terrestrial globe.

"You are mad, and gone the wrong way. You take lie for truth and ugliness for beauty. You would marvel if by certain conditions frogs and lizards should suddenly grow on apple and orange trees, instead of fruit, and if roses should begin to breathe the odour of a sweating horse. So do I marvel at you, who have bartered heaven for earth. I do not want to understand you.

"That I may show you in deed my contempt for that by which you live, I waive the two millions of which I once dreamed of as paradise, and which I now despise. That I may deprive myself of my right to them, I shall come out from here five minutes before the stipulated term, and thus shall violate the agreement."

When he had read, the banker put the sheet on the table, kissed the head of the strange man, and began to weep. He went out of the wing. Never at any other time, not even after his terrible losses on the Exchange, had he felt such contempt for himself as now. Coming home, he lay down on his bed, but agitation and tears kept him long from sleep . . .

The next morning the poor watchman came running to him and told him that they had seen the man who lived in the wing climbing through the window into the garden. He had gone to the gate and disappeared. With his servants the banker went instantly to the wing and established the escape of his prisoner. To avoid unnecessary rumours he took the paper with the renunciation from the table and, on his return, locked it in his safe.

ritter

gluck

e. t. a. hoffmann

*E. T. A. Hoffmann (1776–1822)
was born and educated in Germany. A virtuoso
talent, he was a painter and a composer as well
as a novelist and a short-story writer.
His total accomplishment and his position
as an early man of letters have made
Hoffmann an important figure in European
literature. For further reading:* Tales
by Hoffmann, *edited by*
Christopher Lazare (1946).

Late fall in Berlin usually has a few beautiful days.
The sun comes benignly out of the clouds and dries the moisture out
of the tepid air which blows through the streets. Then a long colorful
column of people comes into view, making their way through the linden
trees to the park: among them are dandies, townsmen with their wives
and their dear children in Sunday best, clergymen, Jewesses, young
lawyers, prostitutes, dancers, officers, and so on. Soon all the tables at
Klaus & Weber are occupied; the chicory coffee steams, the dandies are
lighting their cigars, there is conversation about war and about peace,
about the shoes of Madame Bethmann the actress (whether she re-
recently wore gray ones or green ones), about Fichte's treatise on high
tariff barriers, about counterfeit money, etc. Gradually everything blends
into an aria from the light opera *Fanchon,* with which an out of tune
harp, a few discordant violins, a consumptive flute, and a spasmodic
bassoon torture themselves and their audience. Close by the railing which
separates Weber's cafe from the Heerstrasse, there are several small
round tables and garden chairs; here one can breathe fresh air and can
observe people coming and going, but still be removed somewhat from
the cacophonous din of that confounded orchestra. I take a seat there
and give myself over to the light play of my phantasy, which provides
me with familiar figures with whom I can converse about knowledge,
about art, about everything which is supposed to be dearest to man.
The mass of strollers surges by me, becoming more and more colorful,
but nothing disturbs me, nothing can frighten away my imaginary company. Only the cursed trio from a completely worthless waltz tears me
out of my dream world. I am the only one to hear the shrill upper voice
of the violins and the jarring bass of the bassoon. They go up and down,
firmly clinging to each other in octaves which pierce the ear. Instinctively, like someone who is seized by a burning pain, I cry out,

"What crazy music! Those abominable octaves"—Next to me is a murmur:

"Cursed Fate! Another man who objects to octaves!"

I look up and only now become aware that, unnoticed by me, a man has taken a seat at the same table as mine. He fixes his eyes rigidly on me and my eyes cannot escape his stare.

I have never seen a head, never a figure which made such a deep impression on me so quickly. A softly curved nose was joined to a broad, open forehead, which had marked bulges above bushy, graying eyebrows, and under which the man's eyes flashed with an almost wild youthful fire. (The man was perhaps over fifty.) The delicately molded chin contrasted strangely with the tight shut mouth. A ludicrous smile, formed by the strange play of muscles in his sunken cheeks, seemed to protest against the expression of deep melancholy and seriousness lingering on his forehead. Only a few gray locks of hair lay behind the large ears which stood out from his head. A huge cloak enveloped this great lean figure. As I glanced at the man, he cast down his eyes and continued the activity which my outcry had probably interrupted. With evident pleasure he was shaking tobacco out of various small paper bags into a large snuff box which was standing before him, and wetting it with red wine from a pint-sized bottle. The music had stopped and I felt it necessary to speak to him.

"It is good that the music has stopped," I said, "I couldn't endure it."

The old man cast a fleeting glance at me and shook out the last paper bag.

"It would be better if they didn't play at all," I continued. "Do you agree with me?"

"I have no opinion," he said. "You are a musician and an expert . . ."

"You are mistaken; I am neither. Once I did learn to play the piano and the bass fiddle as part of my general education. At that time I was told that nothing creates a more unpleasant effect than having the bass move forward with the top melody in octaves. I accepted that then as authority, and have since found it valid."

"Really?" he interrupted me, got up, walked slowly and deliberately over to the musicians, all the while gazing off into space and striking his forehead with the flat part of his hand in the manner of one who wants to awaken some kind of memory. I saw him speaking with the musicians, whom he treated with authoritative dignity. He returned, and hardly had he seated himself when they began to play the overture of *Iphigenia in Aulis.*

His eyes half-closed, his folded arms resting on the table, he listened to the Andante. Softly moving his left foot, he indicated the entrance of the instruments: now he raised his head—glanced quickly around—his left hand rested with widespread fingers on the table, as if he were striking a chord on the piano, his right hand he lifted up into the air. He was a conductor indicating the entrance of another tempo to the orchestra—the right hand falls and the Allegro begins! A burning flush spreads over his pale cheeks: his eyebrows draw together over his wrinkled forehead, an inner fury inflames his wild expression gradually consuming the smile which was hovering about his half-opened mouth. Now he leans back, his eyebrows are raised, and the play of his muscles on his cheeks resumes; his eyes gleam, a deep inner pain resolves itself into a desire which grips all of his nerves. Shaken convulsively, he draws his breath from deep in his chest—beads of sweat stand out on his forehead. He indicates the entrance of the Tutti and other main passages. His right hand maintains the beat, with his left hand he takes out a cloth and runs it over his face.—In this way he gave flesh and color to the skeleton of the piece, as presented by the two violins in the overture. I heard the soft melting lament which the flute takes up after the storm of violins and basses has abated and the thunder of the drums is silent. I heard the gentle sounding tones of the violoncello and the bassoon, which filled my heart with inexpressible sadness. The Tutti returns; like a giant the Unison moves forward majestically, the somber lament dies among its crushing steps.

The overture was over; the man let both arms drop and he sat with closed eyes like someone exhausted by too great an exertion. His bottle was empty; I filled his glass with Burgundy, which I had ordered in the meantime. He sighed deeply and seemed to awaken from a dream. I urged him to drink, which he did without hesitation. While he gulped down the full glass without stopping, he cried out: "I am satisfied with the performance! The orchestra gave a good account of itself!"

"And yet," I began to speak, "yet they only gave us the weak outlines of a masterpiece."

"Do I judge correctly? You are not a Berliner."

"Quite right. I only stay here intermittently."

"The Burgundy is good; but it is getting cold out here."

"Then let's go into the room and empty the bottle there."

"A good suggestion. I don't know you; you don't know me. We don't want to ask each other's names; names at times are troublesome. I'm drinking Burgundy, we feel comfortable with one another, and so it is good."

He said all of this with good-natured cordiality. We had entered the room and when he sat down, he opened his cloak and I noticed with amazement that he wore an embroidered waistcoat with long tails, black velvet trousers, and a small silver sword. He buttoned the cloak carefully together.

"Why did you ask me whether I was a Berliner?" I began.

"Because it would have been necessary in that case to leave you."

"That sounds puzzling."

"Not in the least, as soon as I tell you that I—I am a composer."

"I still can't guess what you mean."

"Then forgive my outcry before, for I see that you are not at all an expert on Berlin and Berliners."

He stood up and walked back and forth a few times with great agitation. Then he stepped to the window and in a voice that was barely audible sang the Chorus of the Priestesses from *Iphigenia in Tauris*, now and then beating the entrance of the Tutti on the window panes. With astonishment I noticed that he introduced certain different turns of melody which were striking for their novelty and power. I didn't interfere with him. When he had finished he returned to his place. I was silent, quite taken by his unusual behavior and the fantastic expressions of a rare musical talent. After awhile he began to speak.

"Have you never composed?"

"Yes, I tried my hand at that art, but I found everything which I had written in moments of inspiration to be insipid and boring afterwards; so I left it alone."

"You have done wrong; for the fact that you rejected your early attempts is not an indication of lack of talent. One learns music as a boy because Papa and Mamma want it that way; from that time on there is fiddling and tinkling, but imperceptibly the senses become more receptive to melody. Perhaps it was the half-forgotten theme of a little song which one now decided to sing differently—the first real idea. So this embryo, nourished with difficulty by strange powers, grew to a giant which consumed everything around it and transformed it into its marrow and blood! Ha, how is it possible to indicate the thousands of ways one comes to compose! It is a wide highway, and there everyone is bustling around, cheering and screaming: We are the chosen people! We are at the goal!—Through the ivory gates there is a way into the realm of dreams; a few see the gate only once, still fewer go through it! The place has a mysterious aspect. Peculiar figures hover here and there, but they have distinction, some more than others. They can't be found on the highway,—only on the other side of the ivory gate. It is difficult to come out of this realm, because the monsters in front of Alcina's castle block the way—it's whirling—it's turning—many dream their dreams away in this dream world—they dissolve into a dream—they no longer even cast a shadow, otherwise they would perceive in that shadow the ray of light which shines through the land of dreams—they come to the truth,—the highest moment is the contact with the Eternal, the Inexpressible! Look at the Sun, it is a triad from which chords, like stars, shoot down and entangle you with fiery threads. You are changed into a chrysalis of fire, and you lie there until Psyche soars up to the sun."

With these last words, he sprang up, glanced at me, and threw his hands up in the air. Then he sat down again, quickly emptied the glass, which had been filled. There followed a silence, which I didn't want to interrupt, in order not to divert this extraordinary man. Finally he continued more calmly:

"When I was in the realm of dreams, thousands of pains and fears tormented me! It was night and the grinning faces of monsters rushed on me. One moment they plunged me into the abyss of the sea and the next moment lifted me into the heavens. Beams of light shot through the night, and these beams were tones which surrounded me with a lovely clarity. I awakened from my torments and saw a great, bright Eye, which looked into an organ. As it looked, tones came forth and shimmered and embraced each other in marvelous chords, as I had never thought of them before. Melodies streamed up and down. I swam in this stream and wanted to drown in it. Then the Eye stared at me and held me above the roaring waves. It became night again and two Colossi in shining armor approached me: Tonic Basic Tone, and of a Fifth Interval. They lifted me up but the Eye smiled and said: 'I know what fills your heart with yearning. It is the soft, gentle youth, Interval of a Third who will step among the Colossi. You will hear his sweet voice, see me again, and my melodies will become yours.'"

He paused.

"And you saw the Eye again?"

"Yes, I saw it again! For years I lived in the realm of dreams—there— yes there! I sat in a wonderful valley and listened to the flowers singing to each other. Only one sunflower was silent and sadly bowed its closed calyx to the ground. Invisible ties drew me to it—it raised its head—the calyx opened and out of it beamed the Eye at me. Now tones went from my head to the flowers which eagerly sucked them in. The leaves of the sunflower became larger and larger—waves of fire streamed out of them —they flowed around me—the Eye had disappeared and I had disappeared into the calyx."

With these last words, he had jumped up and hurried with rapid, youthful steps out of the room. I waited in vain for his return, and decided to leave and go into the city.

I was already in the area of the Brandenburg Gate when I saw a tall figure walking in the darkness and immediately recognized my peculiar friend. I addressed him:

"Why did you leave me so suddenly?"

"It was too hot and the Euphon began to ring."

"I don't understand you."

"So much the better."

"So much the worse, for I would like to understand you completely."

"You hear nothing?"

"No."

"—It has gone by! Let us go. Usually I don't like company,—but—you are not a composer—you are not a Berliner."

"I can't understand why you are so set against Berliners. Here, where art is held in high esteem and carried on in a high degree. It is my opinion that a man of your artistic temperament should be quite happy here."

"You are mistaken! To my despair I am damned to wander here in this desolate world like a departed spirit."

"A desolate world—Berlin?"

"Yes, it is desolate here, for no congenial spirit approaches me. I stand alone."

"But the artists! The composers!"

"Away with them! They carp and carp—refine everything to the finest degree; they stir up everything in order to find one miserable idea; with their chattering about art and the meaning of art, and whatever else, they can't approach the creation of a work of art. They begin to feel happy if they have been able to bring a few ideas to light; thus this frightful coldness here shows its great distance from the sun—it is like work done in Lapland."

"Your judgment seems much too hard to me. At least the wonderful performances in the theater must satisfy you."

"Once I brought myself to go again to the theater, in order to hear the opera of my young friend—what was it called? Ah, the whole world is in this opera! Through the colorful crowd of costumed people pass the spirits of the underworld, everything here is given voice and powerful sound—confound it, I mean *Don Giovanni*. But I couldn't endure the overture, which was hurried through prestissimo, without sense or understanding. So I had prepared myself through fasting and prayer, because I know that the Euphon is moved too much by these masses and it speaks then in an impure way!"

"If I am forced to admit that Mozart's works are neglected here for the most part (and it's hardly explainable), then Gluck's works on the other hand enjoy a worthy representation."

"Do you think so? Once I wanted to hear *Iphigenia in Tauris*. When I stepped into the theater, I hear that they are playing the overture to *Iphigenia in Aulis*. Hm, I think, an error. They are giving the other *Iphigenia*. I am astonished, when now the Andante from *Iphigenia in Tauris* began and the storm follows. Twenty years lie between these two operas. The whole effect, the whole well-calculated exposition of the tragedy is lost. A silent Sea—a Storm—the Greeks are cast on the shore, the opera comes to life! Do you think that the composer scribbled in the overture so that it could be played just as one pleases, like a little piece for the trumpet?"

"I admit my mistake. However, everything is being done to give Gluck's works more importance."

"Oh yes!" he said abruptly and smiled then more and more bitterly. Suddenly he got up and nothing could hold him back. In a flash he had disappeared. In vain I looked for him during the next few days in the park.

A few months had passed when I found myself quite late on a cold evening in a distant part of the city and was now hurrying to my home on the Friedrichstrasse. I had to go by the theatre; the surging music, the trumpets and drums reminded me that just then Gluck's *Armida* was being performed. I was on the verge of going in, when my attention was caught by a strange monologue close by the windows of the theatre where one could hear almost every note from the orchestra.

"Now the King is coming—they are playing the march—keep on beating. It is quite lively! Yes, yes, they have to do it eleven times today—the procession is otherwise not a procession. Ha ha—*maestoso*—move back, my children. Look, there is a character with his shoe strings dangling.—Right for the twelfth time! always ending up with the dominant key—Oh you eternal powers—that never ends! Now he bows—Armida thanks him graciously. Once more? correct, two soldiers are missing! Now they are stumbling into the recitative. What evil spirit holds me spellbound here?"

"The spell is broken," I cried. "Come!"

I took my strange acquaintance out of the park, for no one else would be talking to himself like that. I quickly grasped him by the arm and took him with me. He seemed surprised and followed me in silence. We were already in the Friedrichstrasse when he suddenly stood still. "I know you," he said. "You were in the park—we spoke about a lot of things—I drank some wine, became quite heated—afterwards the Euphon rang for two days—I have endured a great deal—but it is all past!"

"I am happy that chance has led me to you again. Let us get better acquainted. I don't live very far from here; how would it be if . . ."

"I cannot go to anyone's house."

"No, you are not going to escape me; I am going with you."

"Then you will have to walk with me a few hundred more steps. But didn't you want to go to the theatre?"

"I wanted to hear *Armida*, but now . . ."

"You shall now hear *Armida*. Come!"

We went up the Friedrichstrasse in silence; he turned quickly into a side street, and I was hardly able to follow him, so quickly did he walk up the street until he finally stopped before a plain-looking house. He knocked for a rather long time before the door was finally opened. Groping· in the darkness we reached the stairs and climbed to a room on an upper floor, where my guide carefully unlocked the door. I heard another door being opened; soon thereafter he appeared with a lighted lamp. The sight of the strangely furnished room surprised me not a little. Old fashioned richly decorated chairs, a wall clock with gilded casing, and a ponderous mirror gave the room a sad air of past grandeur. In the middle of the room stood a small piano on which was a large inkstand made of porcelain. Next to it lay a few pieces of ruled paper. A sharp glance at these preparations for composition convinced me, however, that nothing had been written for a long time, for the paper was quite yellowed and thick cobwebs covered the inkstand. The man stepped before a cabinet in the corner of the room, which I had not yet noticed, and when he drew away the curtain, I saw a row of finely bound books with golden inscriptions: *Orfeo, Armida, Alceste, Iphigenia,* etc., in short I saw all of Gluck's masterpieces standing together.

"You have Gluck's collected works?" I cried out.

He didn't answer, but his mouth was twisted into a convulsive smile and the twitching of the muscles in his sunken cheeks, momentarily distorted his face into a horrible mask. With his dismal glance rigidly fixed on me, he seized one of the books—it was *Armida*—and strode to the piano. I opened the piano quickly and set up the folded music stand; he seemed to like to see that. He opened up the book—who can describe my amazement!—I saw ruled pages, but not a note written on them."

"Now I will play the overture!" he said. "Please turn the pages at the appropriate times!" I promised him that I would and he proceeded to play magnificently and masterfully, with full harmonies, the majestic Tempo die Marcia with which the overture begins, almost entirely faithful to the original score. The Allegro, however, was only built on Gluck's main themes. He brought in so many new, ingenious expressions, that my amazement grew more and more. In particular his modulations were quite striking without being harsh and he knew how to add so many melodic variations to the main themes that they seemed to return in a new and rejuvenated form. His face glowed. One moment his eyebrows drew together and a long-suppressed anger struggled to break loose, the next moment his eyes were filled with tears of a deep sadness. At times he sang the theme with a pleasant tenor voice as both hands worked in careful variations; at times he knew how to imitate with his voice, in a quite special way, the hollow tone of the drums. Diligently I turned the pages while following his glances. The overture had ended and with closed eyes he fell back exhausted into his chair. However, he soon pulled himself together again and while he hastily turned several empty pages of the book, said with a somber voice:

"All of this, sir, I wrote when I came from the realm of dreams. But I betrayed the sacred world to the profane. An ice cold hand gripped my glowing heart! It didn't break but I was damned to wander in the profane world, like a departed spirit—without form, so that no one knew me, until the sunflower should lift me again to the Eternal. Ha—now let us sing Armida's scene!"

He now sang the final scene of *Armida* with an expression which penetrated my innermost being. Here too, he deviated noticeably from the original score, but his altered music was a greater intensification of Gluck's scene. Everything which can express hate, love, despair, and madness was powerfully united in tones. His voice seemed to be that of a young man, for it rose from deep sombreness to penetrating strength. All my nerves trembled—I was beside myself. When he had finished, I threw myself into his arms and cried in a choked voice:

"What is that? Who are you?"

He stood up and measured me with an earnest, piercing look. However, as I began to ask further questions, he escaped through a door with the lamp and left me in total darkness. Almost a quarter of an hour went by and I despaired of seeing him again. Oriented by the position of the piano, I was searching for the door when he suddenly entered with the lamp in his hand, dressed in an embroidered court costume of the 18th century, a rich waistcoat and sword at his side. I was paralyzed. Solemnly he approached me, took me by the hand and said with a strange smile: "I am the composer Gluck."

the taking of the redoubt

prosper mérimée

Prosper Mérimée (1803–1870), French short-story writer, novelist, and essayist, began to publish in 1829 and from the beginning of his career set a standard for short fiction unique in Europe. Perhaps his greatest contribution to the short-story form is in his use of the "simple" style of prose at a time when an ornate, excessive prose style was the fashion. For further reading: Little French Masterpieces (Mérimée volume), translated by George Burnham Ives (1903).

A military friend of mine, who died of fever in Greece some years ago, related to me one day the story of the first engagement in which he had taken part. His narrative was so striking that I wrote it down from memory as soon as I had an opportunity. It is as follows:—

On the evening of the 4th September I rejoined my regiment. I found the colonel in bivouac. At first he received me rather coolly, but, after having read General B——'s letter of recommendation, his manner changed, and he said a few kind words.

He introduced me to my captain, who had just returned from a reconnoitring expedition. This captain, whose acquaintance I had scarcely the time to make, was a tall, dark man, with a severe and forbidding expression. He had been a common soldier, and had won his commission and the cross on the battlefield. His voice was weak and hoarse, and contrasted strangely with his almost gigantic height. I was told that this strange voice was due to a ball which had pierced him through at the Battle of Jéna.

On hearing that I came from the school at Fontainebleau he shrugged his shoulders and said, "My lieutenant died yesterday." I understood that he meant to imply, "You are intended to take his place, and you are not up to it." A cutting reply rose to my lips, but I restrained myself.

Behind Fort Cheverino, which stood about two gunshots off our bivouac, rose the moon. It was large and red as it usually is when rising. But this evening it seemed to me to have an unusual splendour. For an instant the fort stood outlined in black against the shining orb, which looked like the cone of a volcano during eruption. An old soldier, near whom I was standing, remarked on the moon's colour.

"How very red it is!" he said; "it is a sign that it will cost much to take this precious fort."

I was always superstitious, and this omen, above all at such a moment, impressed me greatly. I laid myself down, but could not sleep. I got up and walked about for some time, watching the long lines of fire scattered over the heights beyond the village of Cheverino.

When I thought the fresh, sharp night air had sufficiently quickened my blood, I returned to the fire. I wrapped myself carefully in my cloak and closed my eyes, thinking not to open them before the morning. But sleep obstinately evaded me. Gradually my thoughts took a melancholy hue. I told myself I had not one friend amongst the hundred thousand men who covered that plain. If I were wounded I should go to the hospital, there to be treated without consideration by ignorant surgeons. All I had heard of surgical operations returned to my memory. My heart beat fast, and instinctively I arranged my handkerchief and pocket-book over my breast as a kind of cuirass. I was overcome with weariness, and I became more drowsy each moment, but at each moment some dark thought sprang up with greater force and woke me into a start.

Nevertheless weariness overcame me, and, when the reveille sounded, I was fast asleep. We fell into our ranks; the roll was called; then we piled arms again, and everything suggested that we were going to pass a quiet day.

About three o'clock an aide-de-camp arrived, bearing a despatch, and we were ordered to shoulder arms. Our skirmishers scattered themselves over the plain; we followed them slowly, and in about twenty minutes' time we saw all the outposts of the Russians fall back and re-enter the fort.

One battery of artillery was on our right, another on our left, but both were well in advance of us. They opened a sharp fire on the enemy, who answered briskly; and very soon the fort of Cheverino was hidden under thick clouds of smoke.

Our regiment was almost protected from the Russian fire by a ridge of earth. Since they aimed rather at our artillery than at us, their balls passed over our heads, or at the most cast earth and small stone at us.

The moment the order to advance was given us my captain looked at me so closely that I felt impelled to stroke my budding moustache two or three times with as nonchalant an air as possible. In fact, I had no fear; my only dread was that people might think me afraid. Furthermore, these inoffensive shots contributed to keep me in a calm state of mind. My vanity told me that I was really in danger, being at last under battery fire. I was delighted to find myself so cool, and I dreamed of the pleasure of relating in the drawing-room of Madame B——, Rue de Provence, the story of the taking of the fort of Cheverino. The colonel rode past our company and said to me, "Well, you are going to get it hot at your first battle."

I smiled with a truly military air, at the same time brushing from my sleeve some dust which a ball thirty paces off had thrown up.

It was evident that the Russians had noticed the miscarriage of their balls, for they replaced them by shells which could more easily reach us in the hollow where we were posted. One that burst near by knocked off my cap and killed a man close to me.

"I congratulate you," said the captain to me, as I picked up my cap. "Now you are safe for the day."

I was acquainted with the soldier's superstition that the axiom *non bis in idem* holds good as much on the battlefield as in the court of justice. I replaced my cap jauntily.

"That's a free and easy kind of greeting," I replied as jovially as possible. This poor joke seemed excellent under the circumstances.

"You are lucky," said the captain; "you need not fear anything more, and you will command a company to-night. I know very well that a bullet for me will find its billet to-day. Each time I have been wounded the officer next to me has been grazed by a spent bullet, and," he added in a lower and half-ashamed tone, "their names always began with a P."

I took courage; most people would have done the same; most people would have been equally struck with such prophetic words. Conscript as I was, I did not think I could confide my feelings to anybody. I thought I ought always to appear cool and brave.

About half an hour after, the fire of the Russians slackened considerably: then we sallied out of our cover to storm the fort.

Our regiment was composed of three battalions. The second was ordered to outflank the fort from the side of the gorge; the other two were to make the assault. I was in the third battalion.

Coming out from behind the buttress which had protected us, we were greeted by several rounds of fire, which did but little harm in our ranks. The whistling of the balls startled me: I kept looking round, thus bringing upon myself joking remarks from my more seasoned comrades.

"Upon the whole," I said, "a battle is not so very dreadful."

We advanced at the double, preceded by our sharpshooters; suddenly the Russians gave three cheers, three distinct hurrahs, then they stopped firing and became silent.

"I do not like that silence," said my captain; "it bodes no good to us."

I thought our men were a little too noisy, and I could not help inwardly contrasting their tumultuous clamour with the impressive silence of the enemy.

We quickly reached the outskirts of the fort, where the palisades had been broken and the earth thrown up by our balls. The soldiers leapt upon this newly broken ground with shouts of "Vive l'Empereur!" more loudly than one could have thought possible from men who had already shouted so much.

I raised my eyes, and never shall I forget the spectacle before me. Most of the smoke had risen, and was hanging like a canopy about twenty feet above the fort. Through the blue haze I could see the Russian Grenadiers, with arms fixed, like motionless statues, behind their half-destroyed parapet. I can see now each soldier, his left eye fixed on us, his right hidden by his raised gun. In an embrasure a few feet from us a man was holding a lighted fuse to a cannon.

I shuddered, and I thought my last hour had come.

"Now the fun begins," cried my captain. "Here goes!"

These were the last words I heard him speak.

A roll of drums sounded in the fort. I saw all the muskets levelled. I closed my eyes, and heard an appalling uproar, followed by shrieks and groans. I opened my eyes, surprised to find myself still alive. The fort was again wrapped in smoke. I was surrounded with wounded and dying. My captain lay stretched at my feet: his head had been smashed by a ball, and I was covered with his brains and blood. Out of all my company there were only six men and myself left standing.

A moment of stupor followed this carnage. The colonel, putting his hat on the end of his sword, was the first to climb the parapet, shouting "Vive l'Empereur!" He was soon followed by all the survivors. I can not remember clearly what followed. I do not know how we entered the fort. We fought hand to hand in such a dense smoke that we could not see. I suppose I hit, for I found my sabre covered with blood. At last I heard the shout "Victory!" and, the smoke clearing away, I saw the ground of the fort covered with blood and corpses. The guns especially were buried under heaps of dead. Scattered about in disorder stood about two hundred men in French uniform: some were loading their pieces, others wiping their bayonets. Eleven Russian prisoners were with them.

The colonel was lying covered with blood on a broken ammunition box near the gorge. Several soldiers crowded round him. joined them.

"Where is the senior captain?" he asked one of the sergeants.

The sergeant shrugged his shoulders in a significant way.

"And the senior lieutenant?"

"Here is the gentleman who came yesterday," said the sergeant in a perfectly calm voice.

The colonel smiled bitterly.

"Well, monsieur, you are commander-in-chief," said he to me. "Have the gorge of the fort fortified at once with these wagons. The enemy is in force, but General C—— is coming to support you."

"Colonel," I said to him, "you are badly wounded."

"A fig for that, my lad. We have taken the redoubt!"

Giovanni Verga (1840–1922) was born in Catania, Sicily. An early realist, he writes of suffering and poverty, but always with the sense of the continuity of life despite individual reversal and tragedy. One of the giants of Italian literature, his influence on twentieth-century imaginative writing is very great.

consolation

giovanni verga

One of his celebrated novels is The House by the Medlar Tree *(1881)*. For further reading: The She Wolf, and Other Stories, *translated by* Giovanni Cecchetti *(1958)*.

"You'll be happy, but first you'll have troubles," the fortuneteller had told Arlia.

Who would have imagined it when she married Manica, who had his fine barbershop on Fabbri Street, and she was a hairdresser too—both of them young and healthy? Only Father Calogero, her uncle, hadn't wanted to bless that marriage—had washed his hands of it like Pilate, as he said. He knew they were all consumptive in his own family, from father to son, and he had been able to put a little fat on himself by choosing the quiet life of a parish rector.

"The world is full of troubles," Father Calogero preached. "It's best to keep away from it."

The troubles had come, in fact, little by little. Arlia was always pregnant, year after year, so that her clients deserted her shop, because it was sad to see her come all out of breath and cursed with that big belly. Besides, she didn't have time to keep up to date with fashions. Her husband had dreamed of a big barbershop on the Avenue, with perfumes in the window, but in vain he could go on and on shaving beards at three *soldi* each. The children became consumptive one after the other, and before going to the cemetery gobbled up the small profit of the year.

Angiolino, who didn't want to die so young, complained during his fever:

"Mamma, why did you bring me into the world?" Just like his brothers who had died before him. The mother, thin and wan, standing before the little bed, didn't know what to answer. They had done the impossible; the children had eaten all kinds of things, cooked and raw: broths, medicines, pills as small as the head of a pin. Arlia had spent three *lire* for a Mass, and had gone to hear it on her knees in Saint Lawrence's, beating her breast for her sins. The Virgin in the picture seemed to be winking yes to her. But Manica, more sensible, would laugh with his crooked mouth, scratching his beard. Finally, the poor mother grabbed her veil like a crazy woman and ran to the fortuneteller. A countess, who had wanted to have her hair cut off out of desperation over her lover, had found consolation there.

"You'll be happy, but first you'll have troubles," answered the fortuneteller.

In vain her uncle, the priest, could say over and over again:

"It's all a fraud of Satan!"

You have to feel what it is like to have your heart black with bitterness as you wait for the verdict, while that old woman reads your whole destiny in the white of an egg. Afterward, it seemed to her that at home she would find her boy up, saying to her happily: "Mamma, I'm all better."

Instead, the boy was slowly wasting away, all skin and bones in his little bed, his eyes getting bigger and bigger. When Father Calogero, who knew about dead people, came to see his nephew, he called the mother aside and said:

"I'll take care of the funeral myself. Don't worry!"

But the unfortunate woman, beside the bed, went on hoping. Sometimes, when also Manica, with an eight-day beard and his back bent, came upstairs to see how his boy was doing, she pitied him because he didn't believe. How the poor man must have suffered! She, at least, had the words of the fortuneteller in her heart, like a burning lamp, till the moment when her uncle, the priest, sat at the foot of the bed with his stole on. Then when they carried her hope away inside her son's coffin, she felt a great darkness in her breast, and mumbled before the empty little bed:

"And what did the fortuneteller promise me?"

Because of all the heartache, her husband had taken to drinking. Finally, a great calm came slowly into her heart. Just like before. Now that all the troubles had fallen on her shoulders, happiness would come. That's the way it often is with the poor!

Fortunata, the last one of so many children, got up in the morning, pale and with rings the color of mother-of-pearl under her eyes, like her brothers who had died of consumption. The clients deserted Arlia one by one, the debts piled up, the shop became empty. Manica, her husband, waited for customers all day long, his nose against the clouded window.

Arlia asked her daughter:

"Does your heart tell you that what fate promised us will really come true?"

Fortunata didn't say anything, her eyes circled with black like her brothers', and fixed on a point that only she could see. One day her mother caught her on the stairs with a young man, who slipped away quickly when he saw somebody come, and the girl was left there all red in the face.

"Oh, poor me! . . . What are you doing here?"

Fortunata lowered her head.

"Who was that young man? What did he want?"

"Nothing."

"Tell your mother who's your own flesh and blood. If your father knew! . . ."

The girl's only answer was to raise her forehead and fix her blue eyes on her mother's face.

"Mamma, I don't want to die like the others!"

May was in flower, but the girl wore a different look on her face and had become uneasy under the anxious eyes of her mother. The neighbors warned:

"Arlia, watch your girl."

Even her husband, frowning, one day had taken her aside face to face, in the dark little shop, in order to repeat:

"Watch your daughter, understand? Let's at least not have our flesh and blood disgraced!"

The poor woman, seeing her daughter so wild-eyed, didn't dare question her. She only fixed her eyes on her with looks that went through to the heart. One night, in front of the open window, while the song of spring came up from the street, the girl buried her face in her mother's breast and confessed everything, crying bitter tears.

The poor mother fell into a chair, as if her legs had been cut off. And she kept stammering with her colorless lips:

"Ah, what'll we do now?"

She seemed to see Manica warmed by wine, his heart hardened by misfortune. But worst of all were the eyes of the girl when she answered: "See that window, Mamma? . . . See how high it is? . . ."

The young man, who was an honest fellow, had sent someone to see the uncle, the priest, to sound him out in order to know which way to turn. Father Calogero had purposely become a priest so that he wouldn't have to listen to the troubles of the world. It was no secret that Manica wasn't rich. The young man understood the refrain and sent word that he was sorry that he wasn't rich himself and wouldn't be able to do without a dowry.

Then Fortunata became really sick and began to cough as her brothers had done. Holding her arm around her mother, she often whispered, with her face red, and repeated:

"See how high that window is? . . ."

And her mother had to run here and there, to comb rich women's hair for the theater, the terror of that window always before her eyes if she couldn't find a dowry for her daughter, or if her husband learned about the blunder.

From time to time the fortuneteller's words came back into her mind, like a ray of light. One evening, passing before a lottery window as she was going back home tired and discouraged, the printed numbers fell under her eyes, and for the first time she got the idea of gambling. Then, with the little yellow slip in her pocket, it seemed to her as if she had her daughter healthy, her husband rich and her home peaceful. She also thought with tenderness of Angiolino and the other children who had long been underground in the Porta Magenta cemetery. It was a Friday, the day of the afflicted, and the spring twilight was serene.

And so it was every week. By going without food, she got together the few cents needed for the lottery ticket, so that she could live with the hope of that great happiness which was to come to her all at once. The blessed souls of her children would take care of it from up above. Manica, one day when the little yellow slips jumped out of the drawer as he was secretly looking for a few *lire* to drown his ill-humor at the tavern, flew into a terrible rage:

"So that's the way the money's been going! . . ."

His wife, trembling all over, didn't know what to answer.

"But listen, what if the Lord should send us the right numbers? . . . We have to leave the door open to luck."

And in her heart she was thinking of the words of the fortuneteller.

"If that's the only hope you've got . . . ," muttered Manica with a bitter smile.

"And what hope have you got?"

"Give me two *lire!*" he answered bluntly.

"Two *lire!* Holy Virgin! . . . What do you want them for?"

"Give me just one!" insisted Manica, his face distorted.

It was a dark day with snow everywhere and dampness that you felt in your bones. That night Manica came back home with his face shining and gay. Fortunata, instead kept saying:

"I'm the only one who can't find any consolation."

At times, she would have liked to have been under the grass in the cemetery, like her brothers. They, at least, weren't suffering any more, and even their parents, poor people, had become hardened.

"The Lord won't abandon us completely," stammered Arlia. "The fortuneteller told me so. And I've got an idea."

On Christmas Day they set the table with flowers and their best table-cloth, and this time they had invited her uncle, the priest, who was the only hope they had left. Manica rubbed his hands together and said:

"Today we've got to be happy and gay."

But the lamp hanging on the ceiling swayed sadly.

They had beef, roast turkey, and even a *panettone* that had a picture of the Cathedral of Milan. At dessert, the poor uncle, a good glass of *barbera* wine in his hand, seeing them lament on such a day, couldn't resist any more and had to promise the girl a dowry. The lover—Silvio Liotti, a clerk in a store, and well-informed—was heard from again: he was ready to make amends for the wrong he had done.

Manica, holding up a glass in his hand, said to Father Calogero:

"See this, sir? It cures many ills."

It was destiny, though, that where Arlia was, happiness didn't last. The son-in-law, a really fine fellow, ate up his wife's dowry, and after six months Fortunata, hungry and beaten, went back to her parents' home to tell her troubles and to show her bruises. Every year she too had a baby, just like her mother, and each one was bursting with health and ate like a horse. To the grandmother it seemed as if she were having babies again herself, because each one brought more trouble, even without dying of consumption. Having become old now, she had to run as far as Borgo Degli Ortolani and to Porta Garibaldi in order to earn four *lire* a month doing little jobs for the shopkeepers. Her husband, whose hands trembled, made hardly ten *lire* on Saturday, by cutting his customers and using spider webs to stop the blood. The rest of the week, he either sulked behind the dirty window or was at the tavern with his hat slanted over his ear.

And Arlia now spent the lottery money on brandy, drinking it secretly and hiding it under her apron; her consolation was to feel it warm her heart, as she sat before the window thinking of nothing, looking out at the wet, dripping roofs.

Guy de Maupassant (1850–1893) was born in Normandy and learned to write under a master novelist, Flaubert. A man of prodigious energy, de Maupassant wrote about sixteen volumes of short stories during his brief lifetime. Generally his work is marked by sensuality and a combination of both the comic and the tragic aspects of the human condition. For further reading: The House of Madam Tellier *(1881);* Madomoiselle Fifi *(1882);* Miss Harriet *(1884).*

the piece of string

guy de maupassant

It was market-day, and over all the roads round Goderville the peasants and their wives were coming towards the town. The men walked easily, lurching the whole body forward at every step. Their long legs were twisted and deformed by the slow, painful labors of the country:—by bending over to plough, which is what also makes their left shoulders too high and their figures crooked; and by reaping corn, which obliges them for steadiness' sake to spread their knees too wide. Their starched blue blouses, shining as though varnished, ornamented at collar and cuffs with little patterns of white stitch-work, and blown up big around their bony bodies, seemed exactly like balloons about to soar, but putting forth a head, two arms, and two feet.

Some of these fellows dragged a cow or a calf at the end of a rope. And just behind the animal, beating it over the back with a leaf-covered branch to hasten its pace, went their wives, carrying large baskets from which came forth the heads of chickens or the heads of ducks. These women walked with steps far shorter and quicker than the men; their figures, withered and upright, were adorned with scanty little shawls pinned over their flat bosoms; and they enveloped their heads each in a white cloth, close fastened round the hair and surmounted by a cap.

Now a char-à-banc passed by, drawn by a jerky-paced nag. It shook up strangely the two men on the seat. And the woman at the bottom of the cart held fast to its sides to lessen the hard joltings.

In the market-place at Goderville was a great crowd, a mingled multitude of men and beasts. The horns of cattle, the high and long-napped hats of wealthy peasants, the head-dresses of the women, came to the

surface of that sea. And voices clamorous, sharp, shrill, made a continuous and savage din. Above it a huge burst of laughter from the
sturdy lungs of a merry yokel would sometimes sound, and sometimes
a long bellow from a cow tied fast to the wall of a house.

It all smelled of the stable, of milk, of hay, and of perspiration, giving
off that half-human, half-animal odor which is peculiar to the men of
the fields.

Maître Hauchecorne, of Bréauté, had just arrived at Goderville, and
was taking his way towards the square, when he perceived on the ground
a little piece of string. Maître Hauchecorne, economical, like all true
Normans, reflected that everything was worth picking up which could
be of any use; and he stooped down—but painfully, because he suffered
from rheumatism. He took the bit of thin cord from the ground, and
was carefully preparing to roll it up when he saw Maître Malandain, the
harness-maker, on his door-step, looking at him. They had once had a
quarrel about a halter, and they had remained angry, bearing malice on
both sides. Maître Hauchecorne was overcome with a sort of shame at
being seen by his enemy looking in the dirt so for a bit of string. He
quickly hid his find beneath his blouse; then in the pocket of his
breeches; then pretended to be still looking for something on the ground
which he did not discover; and at last went off towards the market-place,
with his head bent forward, and a body almost doubled in two by
rheumatic pains.

He lost himself immediately in the crowd, which was clamorous, slow,
and agitated by interminable bargains. The peasants examined the cows,
went off, came back, always in great perplexity and fear of being cheated,
never quite daring to decide, spying at the eye of the seller, trying
ceaselessly to discover the tricks of the man and the defect in the beast.

The women, having placed their great baskets at their feet, had pulled
out the poultry, which lay upon the ground, tied by the legs, with eyes
scared, with combs scarlet.

They listened to propositions, maintaining the prices, with a dry
manner, with an impassible face; or, suddenly, perhaps, deciding to
take the lower price which was offered, they cried out to the customer,
who was departing slowly:

"All right, I'll let you have them, Mâit' Anthime."

Then, little by little, the square became empty, and when the *Angelus*
struck midday those who lived at a distance poured into the inns.

At Jourdain's the great room was filled with eaters, just as the vast
court was filled with vehicles of every sort—wagons, gigs, char-à-bancs,
tilburys, tilt-carts which have no name, yellow with mud, misshapen,
pieced together, raising their shafts to heaven like two arms, or it may
be with their nose in the dirt and their rear in the air.

Just opposite to where the diners were at table the huge fireplace, full of clear flame, threw a lively heat on the backs of those who sat along the right. Three spits were turning, loaded with chickens, with pigeons, and with joints of mutton; and a delectable odor of roast meat, and of gravy gushing over crisp brown skin, took wing from the hearth, kindled merriment, caused mouths to water.

All the aristocracy of the plough were eating there, at Maît' Jourdain's, the innkeeper's, a dealer in horses also, and a sharp fellow who had made a pretty penny in his day.

The dishes were passed round, were emptied, with jugs of yellow cider. Every one told of his affairs, of his purchases and his sales. They asked news about the crops. The weather was good for green stuffs, but a little wet for wheat.

All of a sudden the drum rolled in the court before the house. Every one, except some of the most indifferent, was on his feet at once, and ran to the door, to the windows, with his mouth still full and his napkin in his hand.

When the public crier had finished his tattoo he called forth in a jerky voice, making his pauses out of time:

"Be it known to the inhabitants of Goderville, and in general to all—persons present at the market, that there has been lost this morning, on the Beuzeville road between—nine and ten o'clock, a pocket-book of black leather, containing five hundred francs and business papers. You are requested to return it—to the mayor's office, at once, or to Maître Fortuné Houlbrèque, of Manneville. There will be twenty francs reward."

Then the man departed. They heard once more at a distance the dull beatings of the drum and the faint voice of the crier.

Then they began to talk of this event, reckoning up the chances which Maître Houlbrèque had of finding or of not finding his pocket-book again.

And the meal went on.

They were finishing their coffee when the corporal of gendarmes appeared on the threshold.

He asked:

"Is Maître Hauchecorne, of Bréauté, here?"

Maître Hauchecorne, seated at the other end of the table, answered: "Here I am."

And the corporal resumed:

"Maître Hauchecorne, will you have the kindness to come with me to the mayor's office? M. le Maire would like to speak to you."

The peasant, surprised and uneasy, gulped down his little glass of cognac, got up, and, even worse bent over than in the morning, since the first steps after a rest were always particularly difficult, started off, repeating:

"Here I am, here I am."

And he followed the corporal.

The mayor was waiting for him, seated in an arm-chair. He was the notary of the place, a tall, grave man of pompous speech.

"Maître Hauchecorne," said he, "this morning, on the Beuzeville road, you were seen to pick up the pocket-book lost by Maître Houlbréque, of Manneville."

The countryman, speechless, regarded the mayor, frightened already by this suspicion which rested on him he knew not why.

"I, I picked up that pocket-book?"

"Yes, you."

"I swear I didn't even know nothing about it at all."

"You were seen."

"They saw me, me? Who is that who saw me?"

"M. Malandain, the harness-maker."

Then the old man remembered, understood, and, reddening with anger:

"Ah, he saw me, did he, the rascal? He saw me picking up this string here, M'sieu' le Maire."

And, fumbling at the bottom of his pocket, he pulled out of it the little end of string.

But the mayor incredulously shook his head:

"You will not make me believe, Maître Hauchecorne, that M. Malandain, who is a man worthy of credit, has mistaken this string for a pocket-book."

The peasant, furious, raised his hand and spit as if to attest his good faith, repeating:

"For all that, it is the truth of the good God, the blessed truth, M'sieu' le Maire. There! on my soul and my salvation I repeat it."

The mayor continued:

"After having picked up the thing in question, you even looked for some time in the mud to see if a piece of money had not dropped out of it."

The good man was suffocated with indignation and with fear:

"If they can say!—if they can say . . . such lies as that to slander an honest man! If they can say!—"

He might protest, he was not believed.

He was confronted with M. Malandain, who repeated and sustained his testimony. They abused one another for an hour. At his own request Maître Hauchecorne was searched. Nothing was found upon him.

At last, the mayor, much perplexed, sent him away, warning him that he would inform the public prosecutor, and ask for orders.

The news had spread. When he left the mayor's office, the old man was surrounded, interrogated with a curiosity which was serious or mocking as the case might be, but into which no indignation entered. And he began to tell the story of the string. They did not believe him. They laughed.

He passed on, button-holed by every one, himself button-holing his acquaintances, beginning over and over again his tale and his protestations, showing his pockets turned inside out to prove that he had nothing.

They said to him:

"You old rogue, *va!*"

And he grew angry, exasperated, feverish, in despair at not being believed, and always telling his story.

The night came. It was time to go home. He set out with three of his neighbors, to whom he pointed out the place where he had picked up the end of string; and all the way he talked of his adventure.

That evening he made the round in the village of Bréauté, so as to tell every one. He met only unbelievers.

He was ill of it all night long.

The next day, about one in the afternoon, Marius Paumelle, a farm hand of Maître Breton, the market-gardener at Ymauville, returned the pocket-book and its contents to Maître Houlbrèque, of Manneville.

This man said, indeed, that he had found it on the road; but not knowing how to read, he had carried it home and given it to his master.

The news spread to the environs. Maître Hauchecorne was informed. He put himself at once upon the go, and began to relate his story as completed by the *dénouement*. He triumphed.

"What grieved me," said he, "was not the thing itself, do you understand; but it was the lies. There's nothing does you so much harm as being in disgrace for lying."

All day he talked of his adventure, he told it on the roads to the people who passed; at the cabaret to the people who drank; and the next Sunday, when they came out of church. He even stopped strangers to tell them about it. He was easy, now, and yet something worried him without his knowing exactly what it was. People had a joking manner while they listened. They did not seem convinced. He seemed to feel their tittle-tattle behind his back.

On Tuesday of the next week he went to market at Goderville, prompted entirely by the need of telling his story.

Malandain, standing on his door-step, began to laugh as he saw him pass. Why?

He accosted a farmer of Criquetot, who did not let him finish, and, giving him a punch in the pit of his stomach, cried in his face: "Oh you great rogue, *va!*" Then turned his heel upon him.

Maître Hauchecorne remained speechless, and grew more and more uneasy. Why had they called him "great rogue?"

When seated at table in Jourdain's tavern he began again to explain the whole affair.

A horse-dealer of Montivilliers shouted at him:

"Get out, get out you old scamp; I know all about your string!"

Hauchecorne stammered:

"But since they found it again, the pocket-book!"

But the other continued:

"Hold your tongue, daddy; there's one who finds it and there's another who returns it. And no one the wiser."

The peasant was choked. He understood at last. They accused him of having had the pocket-book brought back by an accomplice, by a confederate.

He tried to protest. The whole table began to laugh.

He could not finish his dinner, and went away amid a chorus of jeers.

He went home, ashamed and indignant, choked with rage, with confusion, the more cast-down since from his Norman cunning, he was, perhaps, capable of having done what they accused him of, and even of boasting of it as a good trick. His innocence dimly seemed to him impossible to prove, his craftiness being so well known. And he felt himself struck to the heart by the injustice of the suspicion.

Then he began anew to tell of his adventure, lengthening his recital every day, each time adding new proofs, more energetic protestations, and more solemn oaths which he thought of, which he prepared in his hours of solitude, his mind being entirely occupied by the story of the string. The more complicated his defence, the more artful his arguments, the less he was believed.

"Those are liars' proofs," they said behind his back.

He felt this; it preyed upon his heart. He exhausted himself in useless efforts.

He was visibly wasting away.

The jokers now made him tell the story of "The Piece of String" to amuse them, just as you make a soldier who has been on a campaign tell his story of the battle. His mind, struck at the root, grew weak.

About the end of December he took to his bed.

He died early in January, and, in the delirium of the death-agony, he protested his innocence, repeating:

"A little bit of string—a little bit of string—see, here it is, M'sieu' le Maire."

the traveler's story of a terribly strange bed

wilkie collins

Wilkie Collins (1824–1889) was the son of a painter, a lifelong resident of London, and a friend of Charles Dickens. Collins—whose personal life and his relationships with various women remain something of a mystery—turned to literature early and wrote novels, short stories, plays, and non-fiction. His most famous novel is The Woman in White *(1860).*
His short stories suggest the work of Poe, and it is said that Collins is a master of the story which hangs upon the well-kept secret.
For further reading: After Dark, *and Other Stories (1856).*

Shortly after my education at college was finished, I happened to be staying at Paris with an English friend. We were both young men then, and lived, I am afraid, rather a wild life, in the delightful city of our sojourn. One night we were idling about the neighborhood of the Palais Royal, doubtful to what amusement we should next betake ourselves. My friend proposed a visit to Frascati's; but his suggestion was not to my taste. I knew Frascati's, as the French saying is, by heart; had lost and won plenty of five-franc pieces there, merely for amusement's sake, until it was amusement no longer, and was thoroughly tired, in fact, of all the ghastly respectabilities of such a social anomaly as a respectable gambling-house. "For Heaven's sake," said I to my friend, "let us go somewhere where we can see a little genuine, blackguard, poverty-stricken gaming, with no false gingerbread glitter thrown over it at all. Let us get away from fashionable Frascati's, to a house where they don't mind letting in a man with a ragged coat, or a man with no coat, ragged or otherwise." "Very well," said my friend, "we needn't go out of the Palais Royal to find the sort of company you want. Here's the place just before us; as blackguard a place, by all report, as you could possibly wish to see." In another minute we arrived at the door, and entered the house.

When we got up stairs, and had left our hats and sticks with the door-keeper, we were admitted into the chief gambling-room. We did not find many people assembled there. But, few as the men were who looked up at us on our entrance, they were all types—lamentably true types—of their respective classes.

We had come to see blackguards; but these men were something worse. There is a comic side, more or less appreciable, in all black-guardism—here there was nothing but tragedy—mute, weird tragedy. The quiet in the room was horrible. The thin, haggard, long-haired young man, whose sunken eyes fiercely watched the turning up of the cards, never spoke; the flabby, fat-faced, pimply player, who pricked his piece of pasteboard perseveringly, to register how often black won, and how often red—never spoke; the dirty, wrinkled old man, with the vulture eyes and the darned great-coat, who had lost his last *sou*, and still looked on desperately, after he could play no longer—never spoke. Even the voice of the croupier sounded as if it were strangely dulled and thick-ened in the atmosphere of the room. I had entered the place to laugh, but the spectacle before me was something to weep over. I soon found it necessary to take refuge in excitement from the depression of spirits which was fast stealing on me. Unfortunately I sought the nearest excite-ment, by going to the table and beginning to play. Still more unfortu-nately, as the event will show, I won—won prodigiously; won incredibly; won at such a rate that the regular players at the table crowded round me; and staring at my stakes with hungry, superstitious eyes, whispered to one another that the English stranger was going to break the bank.

The game was *Rouge et Noir*. I had played at it in every city in Europe, without, however, the care or the wish to study the Theory of Chances—that philosopher's stone of all gamblers! And a gambler, in the strict sense of the word, I had never been. I was heartwhole from the corroding passion for play. My gaming was a mere idle amusement. I never resorted to it by necessity, because I never knew what it was to want money. I never practiced it so incessantly as to lose more than I could afford, or to gain more than I could coolly pocket without being thrown off my balance by my good luck. In short, I had hitherto frequented gambling-tables—just as I frequented ball-rooms and opera-houses—because they amused me, and because I had nothing better to do with my leisure hours.

But on this occasion it was very different—now, for the first time in my life, I felt what the passion for play really was. My success first bewildered, and then, in the most literal meaning of the word, intoxicated me. Incredible as it may appear, it is nevertheless true, that I only lost when I attempted to estimate chances, and played according to previous calculation. If I left every thing to luck, and staked without any care or consideration, I was sure to win—to win in the face of every recognized probability in favor of the bank. At first some of the men present ventured their money safely enough on my color; but I speedily increased my stakes to sums which they dared not risk. One after another they left off playing, and breathlessly looked on at my game.

Still, time after time, I staked higher and higher, and still won. The excitement in the room rose to fever pitch. The silence was interrupted by a deep-muttered chorus of oaths and exclamations in different languages, every time the gold was shoveled across to my side of the table —even the imperturbable croupier dashed his rake on the floor in a (French) fury of astonishment at my success. But one man present preserved his self-possession, and that man was my friend. He came to my side, and whispering in English, begged me to leave the place, satisfied with what I had already gained. I must do him the justice to say that he repeated his warnings and entreaties several times, and only left me and went away, after I had rejected his advice (I was to all intents and purposes gambling drunk) in terms which rendered it impossible for him to address me again that night.

Shortly after he had gone, a hoarse voice behind me cried, "Permit me, my dear sir—permit me to restore to their proper place two napoleons which you have dropped. Wonderful luck, sir! I pledge you my word of honor, as an old soldier, in the course of my long experience in this sort of thing, I never saw such luck as yours—never! Go on, sir— *Sacré mille bombes!* Go on boldly, and break the bank!"

I turned round and saw, nodding and smiling at me with inveterate civility, a tall man, dressed in a frogged and braided surtout.

If I had been in my senses, I should have considered him, personally, as being rather a suspicious specimen of an old soldier. He had goggling, blood-shot eyes, mangy mustaches, and a broken nose. His voice betrayed a barrack-room intonation of the worst order, and he had the dirtiest pair of hands I ever saw—even in France. These little personal peculiarities exercised, however, no repelling influence on me. In the mad excitement, the reckless triumph of that moment, I was ready to "fraternize" with any body who encouraged me in my game. I accepted the old soldier's offered pinch of snuff; clapped him on the back, and swore he was the honestest fellow in the world—the most glorious relic of the Grand Army that I had ever met with "Go on!" cried my military friend, snapping his fingers in ecstasy—"Go on, and win! Break the bank—*Mille tonnerres!* my gallant English comrade, break the bank!"

And I *did* go on—went on at such a rate, that in another quarter of an hour the croupier called out, "Gentlemen, the bank has discontinued for to-night." All the notes, and all the gold in that "bank," now lay in a heap under my hands; the whole floating capital of the gambling-house was waiting to pour into my pockets!

"Tie up the money in your pocket-handkerchief, my worthy sir," said the old soldier, as I wildly plunged my hands into my heap of gold. "Tie it up, as we used to tie up a bit of dinner in the Grand Army; your winnings are too heavy for any breeches-pockets that ever were sewed. There! that's it—shovel them in, notes and all! *Credié!* what luck! Stop! another napoleon on the floor! *Ah! sacré petit polisson de Napoleon!* have I found thee at last? Now then, sir—two tight double knots each way with your honorable permission, and the money's safe. Feel it! feel it, fortunate sir! hard and round as a cannon-ball— *Ah, bah!* if they had only fired such cannon-balls at us at Austerlitz—*nom d'une pipe!* if they only had! And now, as an ancient grenadier, as an ex-brave of the French army, what remains for me to do? I ask what? Simply this, to entreat my valued English friend to drink a bottle of Champagne with me, and toast the goddess Fortune in foaming goblets before we part!"

Excellent ex-brave! Convivial ancient grenadier! Champagne by all means! An English cheer for an old soldier! Hurra! hurra! Another English cheer for the goddess Fortune! Hurra! hurra! hurra!

"Bravo! the Englishman; the amiable, gracious Englishman, in whose veins circulates the vivacious blood of France! Another glass? *Ah, bah!*— the bottle is empty! Never mind! *Vive le vin!* I, the old soldier, order another bottle, and half a pound of *bonbons* with it!"

"No, no, ex-brave; never—ancient grenadier! *Your* bottle last time; *my* bottle this! Behold it! Toast away! The French Army! the great Napoleon! the present company! the croupier! the honest croupier's wife and daughters—if he has any! the Ladies generally! everybody in the world!"

By the time the second bottle of Champagne was emptied, I felt as if I had been drinking liquid fire—my brain seemed all aflame. No excess in wine had ever had this effect on me before in my life. Was it the result of a stimulant acting upon my system when I was in a highly excited state? Was my stomach in a particularly disordered condition? Or was the Champagne amazingly strong?

"Ex-brave of the French Army!" cried I, in a mad state of exhilaration, "*I* am on fire! how are *you?* You have set me on fire! Do you hear, my hero of Austerlitz? Let us have a third bottle of Champagne to put the flame out!"

The old soldier wagged his head, rolled his goggle-eyes, until I expected to see them slip out of their sockets; placed his dirty forefinger by the side of his broken nose; solemnly ejaculated "Coffee!" and immediately ran off into an inner room.

The word pronounced by the eccentric veteran seemed to have a magical effect on the rest of the company present. With one accord they all rose to depart. Probably they had expected to profit by my intoxication; but finding that my new friend was benevolently bent on preventing me from getting dead drunk, had now abandoned all hope of thriving pleasantly on my winnings. Whatever their motive might be, at any rate they went away in a body. When the old soldier returned, and sat down again opposite to me at the table, we had the room to ourselves. I could see the croupier, in a sort of vestibule which opened out of it, eating his supper in solitude. The silence was now deeper than ever.

A sudden change, too, had come over the "ex-brave." He assumed a portentously solemn look; and when he spoke to me again, his speech was ornamented by no oaths, enforced by no finger-snapping, enlivened by no apostrophes or exclamations.

"Listen, my dear sir," said he, in mysteriously confidential tones—"listen to an old soldier's advice. I have been to the mistress of the house (a very charming woman, with a genius for cookery!) to impress on her the necessity of making us some particularly strong and good coffee. You must drink this coffee in order to get rid of your little amiable exaltation of spirits before you think of going home—you *must,* my good and gracious friend! With all that money to take home to-night, it is a sacred duty to yourself to have your wits about you. You are known to be a winner to an enormous extent by several gentlemen present to-night, who, in a certain point of view, are very worthy and excellent fellows; but they are mortal men, my dear sir, and they have their amiable weaknesses! Need I say more? Ah, no, no! you understand me! Now, this is what you must do—send for a cabriolet when you feel quite well again—draw up all the windows when you get into it—and tell the driver to take you home only through the large and well-lighted thoroughfares. Do this; and you and your money will be safe. Do this; and to-morrow you will thank an old soldier for giving you a word of honest advice."

Just as the ex-brave ended his oration in very lachrymose tones, the coffee came in, ready poured out in two cups. My attentive friend handed me one of the cups with a bow. I was parched with thirst, and drank it off at a draught. Almost instantly afterward, I was seized with a fit of giddiness, and felt more completely intoxicated than ever. The room whirled round and round furiously; the old soldier seemed to be regularly bobbing up and down before me like the piston of a steam-engine. I was half deafened by a violent singing in my ears; a feeling of utter bewilderment, helplessness, idiocy, overcame me. I rose from my chair, holding on by the table to keep my balance; and stammered out that I felt dreadfully unwell—so unwell that I did not know how I was to get home.

"My dear friend," answered the old soldier—and even his voice seemed to be bobbing up and down as he spoke—"my dear friend, it would be madness to go home in *your* state; you would be sure to lose your money; you might be robbed and murdered with the greatest ease. *I* am going to sleep here: do *you* sleep here, too—they make up capital beds in this house—take one; sleep off the effects of the wine, and go home safely with your winnings to-morrow—to-morrow, in broad daylight."

I had but two ideas left: one, that I must never let go hold of my handkerchief full of money; the other, that I must lie down somewhere immediately, and fall off into a comfortable sleep. So I agreed to the proposal about the bed, and took the offered arm of the old soldier, carrying my money with my disengaged hand. Preceded by the croupier, we passed along some passages and up a flight of stairs into the bedroom which I was to occupy. The ex-brave shook me warmly by the hand, proposed that we should breakfast together, and then, followed by the croupier, left me for the night.

I ran to the wash-hand stand; drank some of the water in my jug; poured the rest out, and plunged my face into it; then sat down in a chair and tried to compose myself. I soon felt better. The change for my lungs, from the fetid atmosphere of the gambling-room to the cool air of the apartment I now occupied, the almost equally refreshing change for my eyes, from the glaring gas-lights of the "salon" to the dim, quiet flicker of one bedroom-candle, aided wonderfully the restorative effects of cold water. The giddiness left me, and I began to feel a little like a reasonable being again. My first thought was of the risk of sleeping all night in a gambling-house; my second, of the still greater risk of trying to get out after the house was closed, and of going home alone at night through the streets of Paris with a large sum of money about me. I had slept in worse places than this on my travels; so I determined to lock, bolt, and barricade my door, and take my chance till the next morning.

Accordingly, I secured myself against all intrusion; looked under the bed, and into the cupboard; tried the fastening of the window; and then, satisfied that I had taken every proper precaution, pulled off my upper clothing, put my light, which was a dim one, on the hearth among a feathery litter of wood-ashes, and got into bed, with the handkerchief full of money under my pillow.

I soon felt not only that I could not go to sleep, but that I could not even close my eyes. I was wide awake, and in a high fever. Every nerve in my body trembled—every one of my senses seemed to be preternaturally sharpened. I tossed and rolled, and tried every kind of position, and perseveringly sought out the cold corners of the bed, and all to no purpose. Now I thrust my arms over the clothes; now I poked them under the clothes; now I violently shot my legs straight out down to the bottom of the bed; now I convulsively coiled them up as near my chin as they would go; now I shook out my crumpled pillow, changed it to the cool side, patted it flat, and lay down quietly on my back; now I fiercely doubled it in two, set it up on end, thrust it against the board of the bed, and tried a sitting posture. Every effort was in vain; I groaned with vexation as I felt that I was in for a sleepless night.

What could I do? I had no book to read. And yet, unless I found out some method of diverting my mind, I felt certain that I was in the condition to imagine all sorts of horrors; to rack my brain with forebodings of every possible and impossible danger; in short, to pass the night in suffering all conceivable varieties of nervous terror.

I raised myself on my elbow, and looked about the room—which was brightened by a lovely moonlight pouring straight through the window—to see if it contained any pictures or ornaments that I could at all clearly distinguish. While my eyes wandered from wall to wall, a remembrance of Le Maistre's delightful little book, "Voyage autour de ma Chambre," occurred to me. I resolved to imitate the French author, and find occupation and amusement enough to relieve the tedium of my wakefulness, by making a mental inventory of every article of furniture I could see, and by following up to their sources the multitude of associations which even a chair, a table, or a wash-hand stand may be made to call forth.

In the nervous unsettled state of my mind at that moment, I found it much easier to make my inventory than to make my reflections, and thereupon soon gave up all hope of thinking in Le Maistre's fanciful track—or, indeed, of thinking at all. I looked about the room at the different articles of furniture, and did nothing more.

There was, first, the bed I was lying in; a four-post bed, of all things in the world to meet with in Paris—yes, a thorough clumsy British four-poster, with a regular top lined with chintz—the regular fringed valance all round—the regular stifling, unwholesome curtains, which I remembered having mechanically drawn back against the posts without particularly noticing the bed when I first got into the room. Then there was the marble-topped wash-hand stand, from which the water I had spilled, in my hurry to pour it out, was still dripping, slowly and more slowly, on to the brick floor. Then two small chairs, with my coat, waistcoat and trowsers flung on them. Then a large elbow-chair covered with dirty white dimity, with my cravat and shirt collar thrown over the back. Then a chest of drawers with two of the brass handles off, and a tawdry, broken china inkstand placed on it by way of ornament for the top. Then the dressing-table, adorned by a very small looking-glass, and a very large pincushion. Then the window—an unusually large window. Then a dark old picture, which the feeble candle dimly showed me. It was the picture of a fellow in a high Spanish hat, crowned with a plume of towering feathers. A swarthy, sinister ruffian, looking upward, shading his eyes with his hand, and looking intently upward—it might be at some tall gallows at which he was going to be hanged. At any rate, he had the appearance of thoroughly deserving it.

This picture put a kind of constraint upon me to look upward too—at the top of the bed. It was a gloomy and not an interesting object, and I looked back at the picture. I counted the feathers in the man's hat—they stood out in relief—three white, two green. I observed the crown of his hat, which was of a conical shape, according to the fashion supposed to have been favored by Guido Fawkes. I wondered what he was looking up at. It couldn't be at the stars; such a desperado was neither astrologer nor astronomer. It must be at the high gallows, and he was going to be hanged presently. Would the executioner come into possession of his conical crowned hat and plume of feathers? I counted the feathers again—three white, two green.

While I still lingered over this very improving and intellectual employment, my thoughts insensibly began to wander. The moonlight shining into the room reminded me of a certain moonlight night in England—the night after a picnic party in a Welsh valley. Every incident of the drive homeward, through lovely scenery, which the moonlight made lovelier than ever, came back to my remembrance; though I had never given the picnic a thought for years; though, if I had *tried* to recollect it, I could certainly have recalled little or nothing of that scene long past. Of all the wonderful faculties that help to tell us we are immortal, which speaks the sublime truth more eloquently than memory? Here was I, in a strange house of the most suspicious character, in a situation of uncertainty, and even of peril, which might seem to make the cool exercise of my recollection almost out of the question; nevertheless, remembering, quite involuntarily, places, people, conversations, minute circumstances of every kind, which I had thought forgotten forever; which I could not possibly have recalled at will, even under the most favorable auspices. And what cause had produced in a moment the whole of this strange, complicated, mysterious effect? Nothing but some rays of moonlight shining in at my bedroom window.

I was still thinking of the picnic—of our merriment on the drive home —of the sentimental young lady who *would* quote "Childe Harold" because it was moonlight. I was absorbed by these past scenes and past amusements, when, in an instant, the thread on which my memories hung snapped asunder; my attention immediately came back to present things more vividly than ever, and I found myself, I neither knew why nor wherefore, looking hard at the picture again.

Looking for what?

Good God! the man had pulled his hat down on his brows! No! the hat itself was gone! Where was the conical crown? Where the feathers— three white, two green? Not there! In place of the hat and feathers, what dusky object was it that now hid his forehead, his eyes, his shading hand?

Was the bed moving?

I turned on my back and looked up. Was I mad? drunk? dreaming? giddy again? or was the top of the bed really moving down—sinking slowly, regularly, silently, horribly, right down throughout the whole of its length and breadth—right down upon me, as I lay underneath?

My blood seemed to stand still. A deadly, paralyzing coldness stole all over me as I turned my head round on the pillow and determined to test whether the bed-top was really moving or not, by keeping my eye on the man in the picture.

The next look in that direction was enough. The dull, black, frowzy outline of the valance above me was within an inch of being parallel with his waist. I still looked breathlessly. And steadily and slowly—very slowly—I saw the figure, and the line of frame below the figure, vanish, as the valance moved down before it.

I am, constitutionally, any thing but timid. I have been on more than one occasion in peril of my life, and have not lost my self-possession for an instant; but when the conviction first settled on my mind that the bed-top was really moving, was steadily and continuously sinking down upon me, I looked up shuddering, helpless, panic-stricken, beneath the hideous machinery for murder, which was advancing closer and closer to suffocate me where I lay.

I looked up, motionless, speechless, breathless. The candle, fully spent, went out; but the moonlight still brightened the room. Down and down, without pausing and without sounding, came the bed-top, and still my panic terror seemed to bind me faster and faster to the mattress on which I lay—down and down it sank, till the dusty odor from the lining of the canopy came stealing into my nostrils.

At that final moment the instinct of self-preservation startled me out of my trance, and I moved at last. There was just room for me to roll myself sideways off the bed. As I dropped noiselessly to the floor, the edge of the murderous canopy touched me on the shoulder.

Without stopping to draw my breath, without wiping the cold sweat from my face, I rose instantly on my knees to watch the bed-top. I was literally spell-bound by it. If I had heard footsteps behind me, I could not have turned round; if a means of escape had been miraculously provided for me, I could not have moved to take advantage of it. The whole life in me was, at that moment, concentrated in my eyes.

It descended—the whole canopy, with the fringe round it, came down —down—close down; so close that there was not room now to squeeze my finger between the bed-top and the bed. I felt at the sides, and discovered that what had appeared to me from beneath to be the ordinary light canopy of a four-post bed was in reality a thick, broad mattress, the substance of which was concealed by the valance and its fringe. I looked up and saw the four posts rising hideously bare. In the middle of the bed-top was a huge wooden screw that had evidently worked it down through a hole in the ceiling, just as ordinary presses are worked down on the substance selected for compression. The frightful apparatus moved without making the faintest noise. There had been no creaking as it came down; there was now not the faintest sound from the room above. Amidst a dead and awful silence I beheld before me—in the nineteenth century, and in the civilized capital of France—such a machine for secret murder by suffocation as might have existed in the worst days of the Inquisition, in the lonely inns among the Hartz Mountains, in the mysterious tribunals of Westphalia! Still, as I looked on it, I could not move, I could hardly breathe, but I began to recover the power of thinking, and in a moment I discovered the murderous conspiracy framed against me in all its horror.

My cup of coffee had been drugged, and drugged too strongly. I had been saved from being smothered by having taken an overdose of some narcotic. How I had chafed and fretted at the fever fit which had preserved my life by keeping me awake! How recklessly I had confided myself to the two wretches who had led me into this room, determined, for the sake of my winnings, to kill me in my sleep by the surest and most horrible contrivance for secretly accomplishing my destruction! How many men, winners like me, had slept, as I had proposed to sleep, in that bed, and had never been seen or heard of more! I shuddered at the bare idea of it.

But ere long all thought was again suspended by the sight of the murderous canopy moving once more. After it had remained on the bed—as nearly as I could guess—about ten minutes, it began to move up again. The villains who worked it from above evidently believed that their purpose was now accomplished. Slowly and silently, as it had descended, that horrible bed-top rose toward its former place. When it reached the upper extremities of the four posts, it reached the ceiling too. Neither hole nor screw could be seen; the bed became in appearance an ordinary bed again—the canopy an ordinary canopy—even to the most suspicious eyes.

Now, for the first time, I was able to move—to rise from my knees—to dress myself in my upper clothing—and to consider of how I should escape. If I betrayed by the smallest noise that the attempt to suffocate me had failed, I was certain to be murdered. Had I made any noise already? I listened intently, looking toward the door.

No! no footsteps in the passage outside—no sound of a tread, light or heavy, in the room above—absolute silence everywhere. Besides locking and bolting my door, I had moved an old wooden chest against it, which I had found under the bed. To remove this chest (my blood ran cold as I thought of what its contents *might* be!) without making some disturbance was impossible; and, moreover, to think of escaping through the house, now barred up for the night, was sheer insanity. Only one chance was left me—the window. I stole to it on tiptoe.

My bedroom was on the first floor, above an *entresol,* and looked into the back street, which you have sketched in your view. I raised my hand to open the window, knowing that on that action hung, by the merest hair-breadth, my chance of safety. They keep vigilant watch in a House of Murder. If any part of the frame cracked, if the hinge creaked, I was a lost man! It must have occupied me at least five minutes, reckoning by time—five *hours,* reckoning by suspense—to open that window. I succeeded in doing it silently—in doing it with all the dexterity of a house-breaker—and then looked down into the street. To leap the distance beneath me would be almost certain destruction! Next, I looked round at the sides of the house. Down the left side ran the thick water-pipe; it passed close by the outer edge of the window. The moment I saw the pipe, I knew I was saved. My breath came and went freely for the first time since I had seen the canopy of the bed moving down upon me!

To some men the means of escape which I had discovered might have seemed difficult and dangerous enough—to *me* the prospect of slipping down the pipe into the street did not suggest even a thought of peril. I had always been accustomed, by the practice of gymnastics, to keep up my school-boy powers as a daring and expert climber; and knew that my head, hands, and feet would serve me faithfully in any hazards of ascent or descent. I had already got one leg over the window-sill, when I remembered the handkerchief filled with money under my pillow. I could well have afforded to leave it behind me, but I was revengefully determined that the miscreants of the gambling-house should miss their plunder as well as their victim. So I went back to the bed and tied the heavy handkerchief at my back by my cravat.

Just as I had made it tight and fixed it in a comfortable place, I thought I heard a sound of breathing outside the door. The chill feeling of horror ran through me again as I listened. No! dead silence still in the passage—I had only heard the night air blowing softly into the room. The next moment I was on the window-sill—and the next I had a firm grip on the water-pipe with my hands and knees.

I slid down into the street easily and quietly, as I thought I should, and immediately set off at the top of my speed to a branch "Prefecture" of Police, which I knew was situated in the immediate neighborhood. A "Sub-prefect," and several picked men among his subordinates, happened to be up, maturing, I believe, some scheme for discovering the perpetrator of a mysterious murder which all Paris was talking of just then. When I began my story, in a breathless hurry and in very bad French, I could see that the Sub-prefect suspected me of being a drunken Englishman who had robbed somebody; but he soon altered his opinion as I went on, and before I had any thing like concluded, he shoved all the papers before him into a drawer, put on his hat, supplied me with another (for I was bare-headed), ordered a file of soldiers, desired his expert followers to get ready all sorts of tools for breaking open doors and ripping up brick flooring, and took my arm, in the most friendly and familiar manner possible, to lead me with him out of the house. I will venture to say that when the Sub-prefect was a little boy, and was taken for the first time to the play, he was not half as much pleased as he was now at the job in prospect for him at the gambling-house!

Away we went through the streets, the Sub-prefect cross-examining and congratulating me in the same breath as we marched at the head of our formidable *posse comitatus*. Sentinels were placed at the back and front of the house the moment we got to it; a tremendous battery of knocks was directed against the door; a light appeared at a window; I was told to conceal myself behind the police—then came more knocks, and a cry of "Open in the name of the law!" At that terrible summons bolts and locks gave way before an invisible hand, and the moment after the Sub-prefect was in the passage, confronting a waiter half dressed and ghastly pale. This was the short dialogue which immediately took place:

"We want to see the Englishman who is sleeping in this house."

"He went away hours ago."

"He did no such thing. His friend went away; *he* remained. Show us to his bedroom!"

"I swear to you, Monsieur le Sous-prefect, he is not here! he—"

"I swear to you, Monsieur le Garçon, he is. He slept here—he didn't find your bed comfortable—he came to us to complain of it—here he is among my men—and here am I ready to look for a flea or two in his bedstead. Renaudin! (calling to one of the subordinates, and pointing to the waiter), collar that man, and tie his hands behind him. Now, then, gentlemen, let us walk up stairs!"

Every man and woman in the house was secured—the "Old Soldier" the first. Then I identified the bed in which I had slept, and then we went into the room above.

No object that was at all extraordinary appeared in any part of it. The Sub-prefect looked around the place, commanded everybody to be silent, stamped twice on the floor, called for a candle, looked attentively at the spot he had stamped on, and ordered the flooring there to be carefully taken up. This was done in no time. Lights were produced, and we saw a deep raftered cavity between the floor of this room and the ceiling of the room beneath. Through this cavity there ran perpendicularly a sort of case of iron thickly greased; and inside the case appeared the screw, which communicated with the bed-top below. Extra lengths of screw, freshly oiled; levers covered with felt; all the complete upper works of a heavy press—constructed with infernal ingenuity so as to join the fixtures below, and when taken to pieces again to go into the smallest possible compass—were next discovered and pulled out on the floor. After some little difficulty the Sub-prefect succeeded in putting the machinery together, and, leaving his men to work it, descended with me to the bedroom. The smothering canopy was then lowered, but not so noiselessly as I had seen it lowered. When I mentioned this to the Sub-prefect, his answer, simple as it was, had a terrible significance. "My men," said he, "are working down the bed-top for the first time—the men whose money you won were in better practice."

We left the house in the sole possession of two police agents—every one of the inmates being removed to prison on the spot. The Sub-prefect, after taking down my *"procès verbal"* in his office, returned with me to my hotel to get my passport. "Do you think," I asked, as I gave it to him, "that any men have really been smothered in that bed, as they tried to smother *me?"*

"I have seen dozens of drowned men laid out at the Morgue," answered the Sub-prefect, "in whose pocket-books were found letters stating that they had committed suicide in the Seine, because they had lost every thing at the gaming-table. Do I know how many of those men entered the same gambling-house that *you* entered ? won as *you won*? took that bed as *you* took it? slept in it? were smothered in it? and were privately thrown into the river, with a letter of explanation written by the murderers and placed in their pocket-books? No man can say how many or how few have suffered the fate from which you have escaped. The people of the gambling-house kept their bedstead machinery a secret from *us*—even from the police! The dead kept the rest of the secret for them. Good-night, or rather good-morning, Monsieur Faulkner! Be at my office again at nine o'clock—in the mean time, *au revoir!*"

The rest of my story is soon told. I was examined and re-examined; the gambling-house was strictly searched all through from top to bottom; the prisoners were separately interrogated; and two of the less guilty among them made a confession. I discovered that the Old Soldier was the master of the gambling-house—*justice* discovered that he had been drummed out of the army as a vagabond years ago; that he had been guilty of all sorts of villainies since; that he was in possession of stolen property, which the owners identified; and that he, the croupier, another accomplice, and the woman who had made my cup of coffee, were all in the secret of the bedstead. There appeared some reason to doubt whether the inferior persons attached to the house knew any thing of the suffocating machinery; and they received the benefit of that doubt, by being treated simply as thieves and vagabonds. As for the Old Soldier and his two head myrmidons, they went to the galleys; the woman who had drugged my coffee was imprisoned for I forget how many years; the regular attendants at the gambling-house were considered "suspicious," and placed under "surveillance;" and I became, for one whole week (which is a long time), the head "lion" in Parisian society. My adventure was dramatized by three illustrious play-makers, but never saw theatrical daylight; for the censorship forbade the introduction on the stage of a correct copy of the gambling-house bedstead.

One good result was produced by my adventure, which any censorship must have approved: it cured me of ever again trying *"Rouge et Noir"* as an amusement. The sight of a greencloth, with packs of cards and heaps of money on it, will henceforth be forever associated in my mind with the sight of a bed canopy descending to suffocate me in the silence and darkness of the night.

a tradition of 1804

thomas hardy

Thomas Hardy (1840–1928) left a career as an architect to become a poet, a novelist, and a writer of short stories. Hardy is much more than a regionalist writer, although the scenes from much of his work center on Wessex. As a novelist his work became increasingly pessimistic, as in his last novel Jude the Obscure *(1895). For further reading:* Wessex Tales *(1888);* Life's Little Ironies *(1894).*

The widely discussed possibility of an invasion of England through a Channel tunnel has more than once recalled old Solomon Selby's story to my mind.

The occasion on which I numbered myself among his audience was one evening when he was sitting in the yawning chimney-corner of the inn-kitchen, with some others who had gathered there, awaiting the cessation of the rain. Withdrawing the stem of his pipe from the dental notch in which it habitually rested, he leaned back in the recess behind him and smiled into the fire. The smile was neither mirthful nor sad, not precisely humorous nor altogether thoughtful. We who knew him recognized it in a moment: it was his narrative smile. Breaking off our few desultory remarks, we drew up closer, and thus began:

"My father, as you mid know, was a shepherd all his life, and lived out by the Cove, four miles yonder, where I was born and lived likewise, till I moved here shortly afore I wer married. The cottage that first knew me stood on the top of the down, near the sea; there was no house within a mile and a half of it; it was built o' purpose for the farm-shepherd, and had no other use. They tell me that it is now pulled down, but that you can see where it stood by the mounds of earth and a few broken bricks that are still lying about. It was a bleak and dreary place in winter-time, but in summer it was well enough, though the garden never came to much, because we could not get up a good shelter for the vegetables and currant bushes, and where there is much wind they don't thrive.

"Of all them years of my growing up the ones that bide clearest in my mind were eighteen hundred and three, four, and five. This was for two reasons: I had just then grown to an age when a child's eyes and ears take in and note down everything about him, and there was more at that date to bear in mind than there ever has been since with me. It was, as I need hardly tell ye, the time after the first peace, when Bonaparte was scheming his descent upon England. He had crossed the great Alp mountains, fought in Egypt, drubbed the Turks, the Austrians, and the Proossians, and now thought he'd have a slap at us. On the other side of the Channel, scarce out of sight and hail of a man standing on our English shore, the French army of a hundred and sixty thousand men and fifteen thousand horses had been brought together from all parts, and were drilling every day. Bonaparte had been three years a-making his preparations; and to ferry these soldiers and cannon and horses across he had contrived a couple of thousand flat-bottomed boats. These boats were small things, but wonderfully built. A good few of 'em were so made as to have a little stable on board each for the two horses that were to haul the cannon carried at the stern. To get in order all these, and other things required, he had assembled there five or six thousand fellows that worked at trades—carpenters, blacksmiths, wheelwrights, saddlers, and what not. Oh, 'twas a curious time!

"Every morning neighbor Boney would muster his multitude of soldiers on the beach, draw 'em up in line, practise 'em in the manœuvre of embarking, horses and all, till they could do it without a single hitch. My father drove a flock of ewes up into Sussex that year, and as he went along the drover's track over the high downs thereabout he could see this drilling actually going on—the accoutrements of the rank and file glittering in the sun like silver. It was thought and always said by my uncle Job, sergeant of foot (who used to know all about these matters), that Bonaparte meant to cross with oars on a calm night. The grand query with us was, Where would my gentleman land? Many of the common people thought it would be at Dover; others, who knew how unlikely it was that any skilful general would make a business of landing just where he was expected, said he'd go either east into the river Thames, or west'ard to some convenient place, most likely one of the little bays inside the Isle of Portland, between the Beal and St. Alban's Head—and for choice the three-quarter-round Cove, screened from every mortal eye, that seemed made o' purpose, out by where we lived, and which I've climmed up with two tubs of brandy across my shoulders on scores o' dark nights in my younger days. Some had heard that a part o' the French fleet would sail right round Scotland, and come up the Channel to a suitable haven. However, there was much doubt upon the matter; and no wonder, for after-years proved that Bonaparte himself could hardly make up his mind upon that great and very particular point—where to land. His uncertainty came about in this wise: that he could get no news as to where and how our troops lay in waiting, and that his knowledge of possible places where flat-bottomed boats might be quietly run ashore, and the men they brought marshalled in order, was dim to the last degree. Being flat-bottomed, they didn't require a harbor for unshipping their cargo of men, but a good shelving beach away from sight, and with a fair open road towards London. How the question posed that great Corsican tyrant (as we used to call him), what pains he took to settle it, and, above all, what a risk he ran on one particular night in trying to do so, were known only to one man here and there; and certainly to no maker of newspapers or printer of books, or my account o't would not have had so many heads shaken over it as it has by gentry who only believe what they see in printed lines.

"The flocks my father had charge of fed all about the downs near our house, overlooking the sea and shore each way for miles. In winter and early spring father was up a deal at nights, watching and tending the lambing. Often he'd go to bed early, and turn out at twelve or one; and on the other hand, he'd sometimes stay up till twelve or one, and then turn in to bed. As soon as I was old enough I used to help him, mostly in the way of keeping an eye upon the ewes while he was gone home to rest. This is what I was doing in a particular month in either the year four or five—I can't certainly fix which, but it was long before I was took away from the sheep-keeping to be bound prentice to a trade. Every night at that time I was at the fold, about half a mile, or it may be a little more, from our cottage, and no living thing at all with me but the ewes and young lambs. Afeard? No; I was never afeard of being alone at these times; for I had been reared in such an out-step place that the lack o' human beings at night made me less fearful than the sight of 'em. Directly I saw a man's shape after dark in a lonely place I was frightened out of my senses.

"One day in that month we were surprised by a visit from my uncle Job, the sergeant in the Sixty-first foot, then in camp on the downs above King George's watering-place, several miles to the west yonder. Uncle Job dropped in about dusk, and went up with my father to the fold for an hour or two. Then he came home, had a drop to drink from the tub of sperrits that the smugglers kept us in for housing their liquor when they'd made a run, and for burning 'em off when there was danger. After that he stretched himself out on the settle to sleep. I went to bed: at one o'clock father came home, and waking me to go and take his place, according to custom, went to bed himself. On my way out of the house I passed Uncle Job on the settle. He opened his eyes, and upon my telling him where I was going he said it was a shame that such a youngster as I should go up there all alone; and when he had fastened up his stock and waist-belt he set off along with me, taking a drop from the sperrit-tub in a little flat bottle that stood in the corner cupboard.

"By-and-by we drew up to the fold, saw that all was right, and then, to keep ourselves warm, curled up in a heap of straw that lay inside the thatched hurdles we had set up to break the stroke of the wind when there was any. To-night, however, there was none. It was one of those very still nights when, if you stand on the high hills anywhere within two or three miles of the sea, you can hear the rise and fall of the tide along the shore, coming and going every few moments like a sort of great snore of the sleeping world. Over the lower ground there was a bid of a mist, but on the hill where we lay the air was clear, and the moon, then in her last quarter, flung a fairly good light on the grass and scattered straw.

"While we lay there Uncle Job amused me by telling me strange stories of the wars he had served in and the wounds he had got. He had already fought the French in the Low Countries, and hoped to fight 'em again. His stories lasted so long that at last I was hardly sure that I was not a soldier myself, and had seen such service as he told of. The wonders of his tales quite bewildered my mind, till I fell asleep and dreamed of battle, smoke, and flying soldiers, all of a kind with the doings he had been bringing up to me.

"How long my nap lasted I am not prepared to say. But some faint sounds over and above the rustle of the ewes in the straw, the bleat of the lambs, and the tinkle of the sheep-bell brought me to my waking senses. Uncle Job was still beside me; but he too had fallen asleep. I looked out from the straw, and saw what it was that had aroused me. Two men, in boat cloaks, cocked hats, and swords, stood by the hurdles about twenty yards off.

"I turned my ear thitherward to catch what they were saying, but though I heard every word o't, not one did I understand. They spoke in a tongue that was not ours—in French, as I afterwards found. But if I could not gain the meaning of a word, I was shrewd boy enough to find out a deal of the talkers' business. By the light o' the moon I could see that one of 'em carried a roll of paper in his hand, while every moment he spoke quick to his comrade, and pointed right and left with the other hand to spots along the shore. There was no doubt that he was explaining to the second gentleman the shapes and features of the coast. What happened soon after made this still clearer to me.

"All this time I had not waked Uncle Job, but now I began to be afeard that they might light upon us, because uncle breathed so heavily through's nose. I put my mouth to his ear and whispered, 'Uncle Job.'

" 'What is it, my boy?' he said, just as if he hadn't been asleep at all.

" 'Hush!' says I. 'Two French generals—'

" 'French?' says he.

" 'Yes,' says I. Come to see where to land their army!'

"I pointed 'em out; but I could say no more, for the pair were coming at that moment much nearer to where we lay. As soon as they got as near as eight or ten yards, the officer with a roll in his hand stooped down to a slanting hurdle, unfastened his roll upon it, and spread it out. Then suddenly he sprung a dark-lantern open on the paper, and showed it to be a map.

" 'What be they looking at?' I whispered to Uncle Job.

" 'A chart of the Channel,' says the sergeant (knowing about such things).

"The other French officer now stooped likewise, and over the map they had a long consultation, as they pointed here and there on the paper, and then hither and thither at places along the shore beneath us. I noticed that the manner of one officer was very respectful towards the other, who seemed much his superior, the second in rank calling him by a sort of title that I did not know the sense of. The head one, on the other hand, was quite familiar with his friend, and more than once clapped him on the shoulder.

"Uncle Job had watched as well as I, but though the map had been in the lantern-light, their faces had always been in shade. But when they rose from stooping over the chart, the light flashed upward, and fell smart upon one of 'em's features. No sooner had this happened than Uncle Job gasped, and sank down as if he'd been in a fit.

" 'What is it—what is it, Uncle Job?' said I.

" 'O good God!' says he, under the straw.

" 'What?' says I.

" 'Boney!' he groaned out.

" 'Who?' says I.

" 'Bonaparty,' he said. 'The Corsican ogre. O that I had got but my new-flinted firelock, that there man should die! But I haven't got my new-flinted firelock, and that there man must live. So lie low, as you value your life!'

"I did lie low, as you mid suppose. But I couldn't help peeping. And then I too, lad as I was, knew that it was the face of Bonaparte. Not know Boney? I should think I did know Boney. I should have known him by half the light o' that lantern. If I had seen a picture of his features once, I had seen it a hundred times. There was his bullet head, his short neck, his round yaller cheeks and chin, his gloomy face, and his great, glowing eyes. He took off his hat to blow himself a bit, and there was the forelock in the middle of his forehead, as in all the draughts of him. In moving, his cloak fell a little open, and I could see for a moment his white-fronted jacket and one of his epaulets.

"But none of this lasted long. In a minute he and his general had rolled up the map, shut the lantern, and turned to go down towards the shore.

"Then Uncle Job came to himself a bit. 'Slipped across in the nighttime to see how to put his men ashore,' he said. 'The like o' that man's coolness eyes will never again see! Nephew, I must act in this, and immediate, or England's lost!'

"When they were over the brow, we crope out, and went some little way to look after them. Halfway down they were joined by two others, and six or seven minutes brought them to the shore. Then, from behind a rock, a boat came out into the weak moonlight of the Cove, and they jumped in; it put off instantly, and vanished in a few minutes between the two rocks that stand at the mouth of the Cove as we all know. We climmed back to where we had been before, and I could see, a little way out, a larger vessel, though still not very large. The little boat drew up alongside, was made fast at the stern as I suppose, for the largest sailed away, and we saw no more.

"My uncle Job told his officers as soon as he got back to camp; but what they thought of it I never heard—neither did he. Boney's army never came, and a good job for me; for the Cove below my father's house was where he meant to land, as this secret visit showed. We coastfolk should have been cut down one and all, and I should not have sat here to tell this tale."

We who listened to old Selby that night have been familiar with his simple gravestone for these ten years past. Thanks to the incredulity of the age, his tale has been seldom repeated. But if anything short of the direct testimony of his own eyes could persuade an auditor that Bonaparte had examined these shores for himself with a view to a practicable landing-place, it would have been Solomon Selby's manner of narrating the adventure which befell him on the down.

the
sisters
qita
arnold bennett

Arnold Bennett (1867–1931)
was born in Hanley, in the
center of England's Staffordshire pottery
industry. A thoroughly professional author,
Bennett turned his talents to journalism and
the theater as well as to novels and short stories. He
is best known for his novels Clayhanger (1910) and
The Old Wives' Tale (1908).
For further reading: Tales of
the Five Towns (1905).

The manuscript ran thus:

When I had finished my daily personal examination of the ropes and trapezes, I hesitated a moment, and then climbed up again, to the roof, where the red and the blue long ropes were fastened. I took my sharp scissors from my chatelaine, and gently fretted the blue rope with one blade of the scissors until only a single strand was left intact. I gazed down at the vast floor a hundred feet below. The afternoon varieties were over, and a phrenologist was talking to a small crowd of gapers in a corner. The rest of the floor was pretty empty save for the chairs and the fancy stalls, and the fatigued stall-girls in their black dresses. I too, had once almost been a stall-girl at the Aquarium! I descended. Few observed me in my severe street dress. Our secretary, Charles, attended me on the stage.

'Everything right, Miss Paquita?' he said, handing me my hat and gloves, which I had given him to hold.

I nodded. I could see that he thought I was in one of my stern, far-away moods.

'Miss Mariquita is waiting for you in the carriage,' he said.

We drove away in silence—I with my inborn melancholy too sad, Sally (Mariquita) too happy to speak. This daily afternoon drive was really part of our 'turn'! A team of four mules driven by a negro will make a sensation even in Regent Street. All London looked at us, and contrasted our impassive beauty—Mine mature (too mature!) and dark, Sally's so blonde and youthful, our simple costumes, and the fact that we stayed at an exclusive Mayfair hotel, with the stupendous flourish of our turnout. The renowned Sisters Qita—Paquita and Mariquita Qita—and the renowned mules of the Sisters Qita! Two hundred pounds a week at the Aquarium! Twenty-five thousand francs for one month at the Casino de Paris! Twelve thousand five hundred dollars for a tour of fifty performances in the States! Fifteen hundred pesos a night and a special train *de luxe* in Argentina and Brazil! I could see the loungers and the drivers talking and pointing as usual. The gilded loungers in Verrey's café got up and watched us through the windows as we passed. This was fame. For nearly twenty years I had been intimate with fame, and with the envy of women and the foolish homage of men.

We saw dozens of omnibuses bearing the legend 'Qita.' Then we met one which said: 'Empire Theatre. Valdès, the matchless juggler,' and Sally smiled with pleasure.

'He's coming to see our turn to-night, after his,' she remarked, blushing.

'Valdès? Why?' I asked, without turning my head.

'He wants us to sup with him, to celebrate our engagement.'

'When do you mean to get married?' I asked her shortly. I felt quite calm.

'I guess you're a Tartar to-day,' said the pretty thing, with a touch of her American sauciness. 'We haven't studied it out yet. It was only yesterday afternoon he kissed me for the first time.' Then she bent towards me with her characteristic plaintive, wistful appeal. 'Say! You aren't vexed, Selina, are you, because of this? Of course, he wants me to tour with him after we're married, and do a double act. He's got lots of dandy ideas for a double act. But I won't, I won't, Selina, unless you say the word. Now, don't you go and be cross, Selina.'

I let myself expand generously.

'My darling girl!' I said, glancing at her kindly. 'You ought to know me better. Of course I'm not cross. And of course you must tour with Valdès. I shall be all right. How do you suppose I managed before I invented you?' I smiled like an indulgent mother.

'Oh! I didn't mean that,' she said. 'I know you're frightfully clever. I'm nothing——'

'I hope you'll be awfully happy,' I whispered, squeezing her hand. 'And don't forget that I introduced him to you—I knew him years before you did. I'm the cause of this bliss—— Do you remember that cold morning in Berlin?'

'Oh! well, I should say!' she exclaimed in ecstasy.

When we reached our rooms in the hotel I kissed her warmly. Women do that sort of thing.

Then a card was brought to me. 'George Capey,' it said; and in pencil, 'Of the Five Towns.'

I shrugged my shoulders. Sally had gone to scribble a note to her Valdès. 'Show Mr. Capey in,' I said, and a natty young man entered, half nervousness, half audacity.

'How did you know I come from the Five Towns?' I questioned him.

'I am on the *Evening Mail*,' he said, 'where they know everything, madam.'

I was annoyed. 'Then they know, on the *Evening Mail* that Paquita Qita has never been interviewed, and never will be,' I said.

'Besides,' he went on, 'I come from the Five Towns myself.'

'Bursley?' I asked mechanically.

'Bursley,' he ejaculated; then added, 'you haven't been near old Bosley since——'

It was true.

'No,' I said hastily. 'It is many years since I have been in England, even. Do they know down there who Qita is?'

'Not they!' he replied.

I grew reflective. Stars such as I have no place of origin. We shoot up out of a void, and sink back into a void. I had forgotten Bursley and Bursley folk. Recollections rushed in upon me. . . . I felt beautifully sad. I drew off my gloves, and flung my hat on a chair with a movement that would have bewitched a man of the world, but Mr. George Capey was unimpressed. I laughed.

'What's the joke?' he inquired. I adored him for his Bursliness.

'I was just thinking of fat Mrs. Cartledge, who used to keep that fishmonger's shop in Oldcastle Street, opposite Bates's. I wonder if she's still there?'

'She is,' he said. 'And fatter than ever! She's getting on in years now.'

I broke the rule of a lifetime, and let him interview me.

'Tell them I'm thirty-seven,' I said. 'Yes, I mean it. Tell them.'

And then for another tit-bit I explained to him how I had discovered Sally at Koster and Bial's, in New York, five years ago, and made her my sister for stage purposes because I was lonely, and liked her American simplicity and twang. He departed full of tea and satisfaction.

It was our last night at the Aquarium. The place was crammed. The houses where I performed were always crammed. Our turn was in three parts, and lasted half an hour. The first part was a skirt dance in full afternoon dress (*danse de modernité*, I called it); the second was a double horizontal bar act; the third was the famous act of the red and blue ropes, in full evening dress. It was 10.45 when we climbed the silk ladders for the third part. High up in the roof, separated from each other by nearly the length of the great hall, Sally and I stood on two little platforms. I held the ends of the red and the blue ropes. I had to let the blue rope swing across the hall to her. She would seize it, and clutching it, sweep like the ball of an enormous pendulum from her platform to mine. (But would she?) I should then swing on the red rope to the platform she had left.

Then the band would stop for the thrilling moment, and the lights would be lowered. Each lighting and holding a powerful electric hand-light—one red, one blue—we should signal the drummer and plunge simultaneously into space, flash past each other in mid-flight, exchanging lights as we passed (this was the trick), and soar to opposite platforms again, amid frenzied applause. There were no nets.

That was what ought to occur.

I stood bowing to the floor of tiny upturned heads, and jerking the ropes a little. Then I let Sally's rope go with a push, and it dropped away from me, and in a few seconds she had it safe in her strong hand. She was taller than me, with a fuller figure, yet she looked quite small on her distant platform. All the evening I had been thinking of fat old Mrs. Cartledge messing and slopping among cod and halibut on white tiles. I could not get Bursley and my silly infancy out of my head. I followed my feverish career from the age of fifteen, when that strange Something in me, which makes an artist, had first driven me forth to conquer two continents. I thought of all the golden loves I had scorned, and my own love, which had been ignored, unnoticed, but which still obstinately burned. I glanced downwards and descried Valdès precisely where Sally had said he would be. Valdès, what a fool you were! And I hated a fool. I am one of those who can love and hate, who can love and despise, who can love and loathe the same object in the same moment. Then I signalled to Sally to plunge, and my eyes filled with tears. For, you see, somehow, in some senseless sentimental way, the thought of fat Mrs. Cartledge and my silly infancy had forced me to send Sally the red rope, not the blue one. We exchanged ropes on alternate nights, but this was her night for the blue one.

She swung over, alighting accurately at my side with that exquisite outward curve of the spine which had originally attracted me to her.

'You sent me the red one,' she said to me, after she had acknowledged the applause.

'Yes,' I said. 'Never mind; stick to it now you've got it. Here's the red light. Have you seen Valdès?'

She nodded.

I took the blue light and clutched the blue rope. Instead of murder—suicide, since it must be one or the other. And why not? Indeed, I censured myself in that second for having meant to kill Sally. Not because I was ashamed of the sin, but because the revenge would have been so pitiful and weak. If Valdès the matchless was capable of passing me over and kneeling to the pretty thing——

I stood ready. The world was to lose that fineness, that distinction, that originality, that disturbing subtlety, which constituted Paquita Qita. I plunged.

. . . I was on the other platform. The rope had held, then. I remembered nothing of the flight except that I had passed near the upturned, pleasant face of Valdès.

The band stopped. The lights of the hall were lowered. All was dark. I switched on my dazzling blue light; Sally switched on her red one. I stood ready. The rope could not possibly endure a second strain. I waved to Sally and signalled to the conductor. The world was to lose Paquita. The drum began its formidable roll. Whirrr! I plunged, and saw the red star rushing towards me. I snatched it and soared upwards. The blue rope seemed to tremble. As I came near the platform at decreasing speed, it seemed to stretch like elastic. It broke! The platform jumped up suddenly over my head, but I caught at the silk ladder. I was saved! There was a fearful silence, and then the appalling shock of hysterical applause from seven thousand throats. I slid down the ladder, ran across the stage into my dressing-room for a cloak, out again into the street. In two days I was in Buda-Pesth.

Rudyard Kipling (1865–1936) was born in Bombay, India, and educated in England. After working as a journalist in India, he returned to England to begin his meteoric rise to fame as a poet, novelist, and short-story writer. He was awarded the Nobel Prize for literature in 1907. For further reading: Plain Tales from the Hills *(1888);* Life's Handicap *(1891);* Under the Deodars *(1899).*

the story of muhammad din

rudyard kipling

> Who is the happy man? He that sees in his own house at home, little children crowned with dust, leaping and falling and crying.
>
> *Munichandra,* translated by Professor Peterson

The polo-ball was an old one, scarred, chipped, and dinted. It stood on the mantelpiece among the pipe-stems which Imam Din, *khitmatgar,* was cleaning for me.

"Does the Heaven-born want this ball?" said Imam Din, deferentially.

The Heaven-born set no particular store by it; but of what use was a polo-ball to a *khitmatgar?*

"By your Honor's favor, I have a little son. He has seen this ball, and desires it to play with. I do not want it for myself."

No one would for an instant accuse portly old Imam Din of wanting to play with polo-balls. He carried out the battered thing into the veranda; and there followed a hurricane of joyful squeaks, a patter of small feet, and the *thud-thud-thud* of the ball rolling along the ground. Evidently the little son had been waiting outside the door to secure his treasure. But how had he managed to see that polo-ball?

Next day, coming back from office half an hour earlier than usual, I was aware of a small figure in the dining-room—a tiny, plump figure in a ridiculously inadequate shirt which came, perhaps, half-way down the tubby stomach. It wandered round the room, thumb in mouth, crooning to itself as it took stock of the pictures. Undoubtedly this was the "little son."

He had no business in my room, of course; but was so deeply absorbed in his discoveries that he never noticed me in the doorway. I stepped into the room and startled him nearly into a fit. He sat down on the ground with a gasp. His eyes opened, and his mouth followed suit. I knew what was coming, and fled, followed by a long, dry howl which reached the servants' quarters far more quickly than any command of mine had ever done. In ten seconds Imam Din was in the dining-room. Then despairing sobs arose, and I returned to find Imam Din admonishing the small sinner who was using most of his shirt as a handkerchief.

"This boy," said Imam Din, judicially, "is a *budmash*—a big *budmash*. He will, without doubt, go to the *jail-khana* for his behavior." Renewed yells from the penitent, and an elaborate apology to myself from Imam Din.

"Tell the baby," said I, "that the *Sahib* is not angry, and take him away." Imam Din conveyed my forgiveness to the offender, who had now gathered all his shirt round his neck, stringwise, and the yell subsided into a sob. The two set off for the door. "His name," said Imam Din, as though the name were part of the crime, "is Muhammad Din, and he is a *budmash*." Freed from present danger, Muhammad Din turned round in his father's arms, and said gravely, "It is true that my name is Muhammad Din, *Tahib*, but I am not a *budmash*. I am a *man!*"

From that day dated my acquaintance with Muhammad Din. Never again did he come into my dining-room, but on the neutral ground of the garden, we greeted each other with much state, though our conversation was confined to "*Talaam, Tahib*" from his side, and "*Salaam, Muhammad Din*" from mine. Daily on my return from office, the little white shirt, and the fat little body used to rise from the shade of the creeper-covered trellis where they had been hid; and daily I checked my horse here, that my salutation might not be slurred over or given unseemly.

Muhammad Din never had any companions. He used to trot about the compound, in and out of the castor-oil bushes, on mysterious errands of his own. One day I stumbled upon some of his handiwork far down the grounds. He had half buried the polo-ball in dust, and stuck six shriveled old marigold flowers in a circle round it. Outside that circle again was a rude square, traced out in bits of red brick alternating with fragments of broken china; the whole bounded by a little bank of dust. The water-man from the well-curb put in a plea for the small architect, saying that it was only the play of a baby and did not much disfigure my garden.

Heaven knows that I had no intention of touching the child's work then or later; but, that evening, a stroll through the garden brought me unawares full on it; so that I trampled, before I knew, marigold-heads, dust-bank, and fragments of broken soap-dish into confusion past all hope of mending. Next morning, I came upon Muhammad Din crying softly to himself over the ruin I had wrought. Some one had cruelly told him that the *Sahib* was very angry with him for spoiling the garden, and had scattered his rubbish, using bad language the while. Muhammad Din labored for an hour at effacing every trace of the dust-bank and pottery fragments, and it was with a tearful and apologetic face that he said *"Talaam, Tahib,"* when I came home from office. A hasty inquiry resulted in Imam Din informing Muhammad Din that, by my singular favor, he was permitted to disport himself as he pleased. Whereat the child took heart and fell to tracing the ground-plan of an edifice which was to eclipse the marigold-polo-ball creation.

For some months, the chubby little eccentricity revolved in his humble orbit among the castor-oil bushes and in the dust; always fashioning magnificent palaces from the stale flowers thrown away by the bearer, smooth water-worn pebbles, bits of broken glass, and feathers pulled, I fancy, from my fowls—always alone, and always crooning to himself.

A gaily-spotted sea-shell was dropped one day close to the last of his little buildings; and I looked that Muhammad Din should build something more than ordinarily splendid on the strength of it. Nor was I disappointed. He meditated for the better part of an hour, and his crooning rose to a jubilant song. Then he began tracing in the dust. It would certainly be a wondrous palace, this one, for it was two yards long and a yard broad in ground-plan. But the palace was never completed.

Next day there was no Muhammad Din at the head of the carriage-drive, and no *"Talaam, Tahib"* to welcome my return. I had grown accustomed to the greeting, and its omission troubled me. Next day Imam Din told me that the child was suffering slightly from fever and needed quinine. He got the medicine, and an English Doctor.

"They have no stamina, these brats," said the Doctor, as he left Imam Din's quarters.

A week later, though I would have given much to have avoided it, I met on the road to the Mussulman burying-ground Imam Din, accompanied by one other friend, carrying in his arms, wrapped in a white cloth, all that was left of little Muhammad Din.

the lord of the dynamos

h. g. wells

Herbert George Wells (1866–1946) was born in Bromley and educated at the Royal College of Science, South Kensington. Wells became a teacher but soon turned to the writing of fiction. His novels often make use of his training and interest in science—for example, The Time Machine *and* The War of the Worlds. *His stories tend towards the fantastic, the extreme, and are often laid centuries in the future. For further reading:* Short Stories of H. G. Wells *(1927).*

The chief attendant of the three dynamos that buzzed and rattled at Camberwell, and kept the electric railway going, came out of Yorkshire, and his name was James Holroyd. He was a practical electrician, but fond of whiskey, a heavy red-haired brute with irregular teeth. He doubted the existence of the deity, but accepted Carnot's cycle, and he had read Shakespeare and found him weak in chemistry. His helper came out of the mysterious East, and his name was Azuma-zi. But Holroyd called him Pooh-bah. Holroyd liked a nigger help because he could stand kicking—a habit with Holroyd—and did not pry into the machinery and try to learn the ways of it. Certain odd possibilities of the negro mind brought into abrupt contact with the crown of our civilisation Holroyd never fully realised, though just at the end he got some inkling of them.

To define Azuma-zi was beyond ethnology. He was, perhaps, more negroid than anything else, though his hair was curly rather than frizzy, and his nose had a bridge. Moreover, his skin was brown rather than black, and the whites of his eyes were yellow. His broad cheek-bones and narrow chin gave his face something of the viperine V. His head, too, was broad behind, and low and narrow at the forehead, as if his brain had been twisted round in the reverse way to a European's. He was short of stature and still shorter of English. In conversation he made numerous odd noises of no known marketable value, and his infrequent words were carved and wrought into heraldic grotesqueness. Holroyd tried to elucidate his religious beliefs, and—especially after whiskey—

lectured to him against superstition and missionaries. Azuma-zi, however, shirked the discussion of his gods, even though he was kicked for it.

Azuma-zi had come, clad in white but insufficient raiment, out of the stoke-hole of the *Lord Clive*, from the Straits Settlements, and beyond, into London. He had heard even in his youth of the greatness and riches of London, where all the women are white and fair, and even the beggars in the streets are white; and he had arrived, with newly earned gold coins in his pocket, to worship at the shrine of civilisation. The day of his landing was a dismal one; the sky was dun, and a wind-worried drizzle filtered down to the greasy streets, but he plunged boldly into the delights of Shadwell, and was presently cast up, shattered in health, civilised in costume, penniless, and, except in matters of the direst necessity, practically a dumb animal, to toil for James Holroyd and to be bullied by him in the dynamo shed at Camberwell. And to James Holroyd bullying was a labour of love.

There were three dynamos with their engines at Camberwell. The two that have been there since the beginning are small machines; the larger one was new. The smaller machines made a reasonable noise; their straps hummed over the drums, every now and then the brushes buzzed and fizzled, and the air churned steadily, whoo! whoo! whoo! between their poles. One was loose in its foundations and kept the shed vibrating. But the big dynamo drowned these little noises altogether with the sustained drone of its iron core, which somehow set part of the iron-work humming. The place made the visitor's head reel with the throb, throb, throb of the engines, the rotation of the big wheels, the spinning ball-valves, the occasional spittings of the steam, and over all the deep, unceasing, surging note of the big dynamo. This last noise was from an engineering point of view a defect; but Azuma-zi accounted it unto the monster for mightiness and pride.

If it were possible we would have the noises of that shed always about the reader as he reads, we would tell all our story to such an accompaniment. It was a steady stream of din, from which the ear picked out first one threat and then another; there was the intermittent snorting, panting, and seething of the steam-engines, the suck and thud of their pistons, the dull beat on the air as the spokes of the great driving-wheels came round, a note the leather straps made as they ran tighter and looser, and a fretful tumult from the dynamos; and, over all, sometimes inaudible, as the ear tired of it, and then creeping back upon the senses again, was this trombone note of the big machine. The floor never felt steady and quiet beneath one's feet, but quivered and jarred. It was a confusing, unsteady place, and enough to send any one's thoughts jerking into odd zigzags. And for three months, while the big strike of the engineers was in progress, Holroyd, who was a blackleg, and Azuma-zi, who was a mere black, were never out of the stir and eddy of it, but slept and fed in the little wooden shanty between the shed and the gates.

Holroyd delivered a theological lecture on the text of his big machine soon after Azuma-zi came. He had to shout to be heard in the din. "Look at that," said Holroyd; "where's your 'eathen idol to match 'im?" And Azuma-zi looked. For a moment Holroyd was inaudible, and then Azuma-zi heard: "Kill a hundred men. Twelve per cent on the ordinary shares," said Holroyd, "and that's something like a Gord!"

Holroyd was proud of his big dynamo, and expatiated upon its size and power to Azuma-zi until heaven knows what odd currents of thought that, and the incessant whirling and shindy, set up within the curly, black cranium. He would explain in the most graphic manner the dozen or so ways in which a man might be killed by it, and once he gave Azuma-zi a shock as a sample of its quality. After that, in the breathing-times of his labour—it was heavy labour, being not only his own but most of Holroyd's—Azuma-zi would sit and watch the big machine. Now and then the brushes would sparkle and spit blue flashes, at which Holroyd would swear, but all the rest was as smooth and rhythmic as breathing. The band ran shouting over the shaft, and ever behind one as one watched was the complacent thud of the piston. So it lived all day in this big airy shed, with him and Holroyd to wait upon it; not prisoned up and slaving to drive a ship as the other engines he knew—mere captive devils of the British Solomon—had been, but a machine enthroned. Those two smaller dynamos, Azuma-zi by force of contrast despised; the large one he privately christened the Lord of the Dynamos. They were fretful and irregular, but the big dynamo was steady. How great it was! How serene and easy in its working! Greater and calmer even than the Buddahs he had seen at Rangoon, and yet not motionless, but living! The great black coils spun, spun, spun, the rings ran round under the brushes, and the deep note of its coil steadied the whole. It affected Azuma-zi queerly.

Azuma-zi was not fond of labour. He would sit about and watch the Lord of the Dynamos while Holroyd went away to persuade the yard porter to get whiskey, although his proper place was not in the dynamo shed but behind the engines, and, moreover, if Holroyd caught him skulking he got hit for it with a rod of stout copper wire. He would go and stand close to the colossus and look up at the great leather band running overhead. There was a black patch on the band that came round, and it pleased him somehow among all the clatter to watch this return again and again. Odd thoughts spun with the whirl of it. Scientific people tell us that savages give souls to rocks and trees—and a machine is a thousand times more alive than a rock or a tree. And Azuma-zi was practically a savage still; the veneer of civilisation lay no deeper than his slop suit, his bruises and the coal grime on his face and hands. His father before him had worshipped a meteoric stone, kindred blood, it may be, had splashed the broad wheels of Juggernaut.

He took every opportunity Holroyd gave him of touching and handling the great dynamo that was fascinating him. He polished and cleaned it until the metal parts were blinding in the sun. He felt a mysterious sense of service in doing this. He would go up to it and touch its spinning coils gently. The gods he had worshipped were all far away. The people in London hid their gods.

At last his dim feelings grew more distinct, and took shape in thoughts and acts. When he came into the roaring shed one morning he salaamed to the Lord of the Dynamos; and then, when Holroyd was away, he went and whispered to the thundering machine that he was its servant, and prayed it to have pity on him and save him from Holroyd. As he did so a rare gleam of light came in through the open archway of the throbbing machine-shed, and the Lord of the Dynamos, as he whirled and roared, was radiant with pale gold. Then Azuma-zi knew that his service was acceptable to his Lord. After that he did not feel so lonely as he had done, and he had indeed been very much alone in London. And even when his work time was over, which was rare, he loitered about the shed.

Then, the next time Holroyd maltreated him, Azuma-zi went presently to the Lord of the Dynamos and whispered, "Thou seest, O my Lord!" and the angry whirr of the machinery seemed to answer him. Thereafter it appeared to him that whenever Holroyd came into the shed a different note came into the sounds of the great dynamo. "My Lord bides his time," said Azuma-zi to himself. "The iniquity of the fool is not yet ripe." And he waited and watched for the day of reckoning. One day there was evidence of short circuiting, and Holroyd, making an unwary examination—it was in the afternoon—got a rather severe shock. Azuma-zi from behind the engine saw him jump off and curse at the peccant coil.

"He is warned," said Azuma-zi to himself. "Surely my Lord is very patient."

Holroyd had at first initiated his "nigger" into such elementary conceptions of the dynamo's working as would enable him to take temporary charge of the shed in his absence. But when he noticed the manner in which Azuma-zi hung about the monster, he became suspicious. He dimly perceived his assistant was "up to something," and connecting him with the anointing of the coils with oil that had rotted the varnish in one place, he issued an edict, shouted above the confusion of the machinery, "Don't 'ee go nigh that big dynamo any more, Pooh-bah, or a'll take thy skin off!" Besides, if it pleased Azuma-zi to be near the big machine, it was plain sense and decency to keep him away from it.

Azuma-zi obeyed at the time, but later he was caught bowing before the Lord of the Dynamos. At which Holroyd twisted his arm and kicked him as he turned to go away. As Azuma-zi presently stood behind the engine and glared at the back of the hated Holroyd, the noises of the machinery took a new rhythm, and sounded like four words in his native tongue.

It is hard to say exactly what madness is. I fancy Azuma-zi was mad. The incessant din and whirl of the dynamo shed may have churned up his little store of knowledge and big store of superstitious fancy, at last, into something akin to frenzy. At any rate, when the idea of making Holroyd a sacrifice to the Dynamo Fetich was thus suggested to him, it filled him with a strange tumult of exultant emotion.

That night the two men and their black shadows were alone in the shed together. The shed was lit with one big arc light that winked and flickered purple. The shadows lay black behind the dynamos, the ball governors of the engines whirled from light to darkness, and their pistons beat loud and steady. The world outside seen through the open end of the shed seemed incredibly dim and remote. It seemed absolutely silent, too, since the riot of the machinery drowned every external sound. Far away was the black fence of the yard with grey, shadowy houses behind, and above was the deep blue sky and the pale little stars. Azuma-zi suddenly walked across the centre of the shed above which the leather bands were running, and went into the shadow by the big dynamo. Holroyd heard a click, and the spin of the armature changed.

"What are you dewin' with that switch?" he bawled in surprise. "Ha'n't I told you—"

Then he saw the set expression of Azuma-zi's eyes as the Asiatic came out of the shadow towards him.

In another moment the two men were grappling fiercely in front of the great dynamo.

"You coffee-headed fool!" gasped Holroyd, with a brown hand at his throat. "Keep off those contact rings." In another moment he was tripped and reeling back upon the Lord of the Dynamos. He instinctively loosened his grip upon his antagonist to save himself from the machine.

The messenger, sent in furious haste from the station to find out what had happened in the dynamo shed, met Azuma-zi at the porter's lodge by the gate. Azuma-zi tried to explain something, but the messenger could make nothing of the black's incoherent English, and hurried on to the shed. The machines were all noisily at work, and nothing seemed to be disarranged. There was, however, a queer smell of singed hair. Then he saw an odd-looking, crumpled mass clinging to the front of the big dynamo, and, approaching, recognised the distorted remains of Holroyd.

The man stared and hesitated a moment. Then he saw the face and shut his eyes convulsively. He turned on his heel before he opened them, so that he should not see Holroyd again, and went out of the shed to get advice and help.

When Azuma-zi saw Holroyd die in the grip of the Great Dynamo he had been a little scared about the consequences of his act. Yet he felt strangely elated, and knew that the favour of the Lord Dynamo was upon him. His plan was already settled when he met the man coming from the station, and the scientific manager who speedily arrived on the scene jumped at the obvious conclusion of suicide. This expert scarcely noticed Azuma-zi except to ask a few questions. Did he see Holroyd kill himself? Azuma-zi explained he had been out of sight at the engine furnace until he heard a difference in the noise from the dynamo. It was not a difficult examination, being untinctured by suspicion.

The distorted remains of Holroyd, which the electrician removed from the machine, were hastily covered by the porter with a coffee-stained tablecloth. Somebody, by a happy inspiration, fetched a medical man. The expert was chiefly anxious to get the machine at work again, for seven or eight trains had stopped midway in the stuffy tunnels of the electric railway. Azuma-zi, answering or misunderstanding the questions of the people who had by authority or impudence come into the shed, was presently sent back to the stoke-hole by the scientific manager. Of course a crowd collected outside the gates of the yard,—a crowd, for no known reason, always hovers for a day or two near the scene of a sudden death in London; two or three reporters percolated somehow into the engine-shed, and one even got to Azuma-zi; but the scientific expert cleared them out again, being himself an amateur journalist.

Presently the body was carried away, and public interest departed with it. Azuma-zi remained very quietly at his furnace, seeing over and over again in the coals a figure that wriggled violently and became still. An hour after the murder, to any one coming into the shed it would have looked exactly as if nothing remarkable had ever happened there. Peeping presently from his engine-room the black saw the Lord Dynamo spin and whirl beside his little brothers, the driving wheels were beating round, and the steam in the pistons went thud, thud, exactly as it had been earlier in the evening. After all, from the mechanical point of view, it had been a most insignificant incident—the mere temporary deflection of a current. But now the slender form and slender shadow of the scientific manager replaced the sturdy outline of Holroyd travelling up and down the lane of light upon the vibrating floor under the straps between the engines and the dynamos.

"Have I not served my Lord?" said Azuma-zi, inaudibly, from his shadow, and the note of the great dynamo rang out full and clear. As he looked at the big, whirling mechanism the strange fascination of it that had been a little in abeyance since Holroyd's death resumed its sway.

Never had Azuma-zi seen a man killed so swiftly and pitilessly. The big, humming machine had slain its victim without wavering for a second from its steady beating. It was indeed a mighty god.

The unconscious scientific manager stood with his back to him, scribbling on a piece of paper. His shadow lay at the foot of the monster.

"Was the Lord Dynamo still hungry? His servant was ready."

Azuma-zi made a stealthy step forward, then stopped. The scientific manager suddenly stopped writing, and walked down the shed to the end-most of the dynamos, and began to examine the brushes.

Azuma-zi hesitated, and then slipped across noiselessly into the shadow by the switch. There he waited. Presently the manager's footsteps could be heard returning. He stopped in his old position, unconscious of the stoker crouching ten feet away from him. Then the big dynamo suddenly fizzled, and in another moment Azuma-zi had sprung out of the darkness upon him.

First, the scientific manager was gripped round the body and swung towards the big dynamo, then, kicking with his knee and forcing his antagonist's head down with his hands, he loosened the grip on his waist and swung round away from the machine. Then the black grasped him again, putting a curly head against his chest, and they swayed and panted as it seemed for an age or so. Then the scientific manager was impelled to catch a black ear in his teeth and bite furiously. The black yelled hideously.

They rolled over on the floor, and the black, who had apparently slipped from the vice of the teeth or parted with some ear—the scientific manager wondered which at the time—tried to throttle him. The scientific manager was making some ineffectual efforts to claw something with his hands and to kick, when the welcome sound of quick footsteps sounded on the floor. The next moment Azuma-zi had left him and darted towards the big dynamo. There was a splutter amid the roar.

The officer of the company, who had entered, stood staring as Azuma-zi caught the naked terminals in his hands, gave one horrible convulsion, and then hung motionless from the machine, his face violently distorted.

"I'm jolly glad you came in when you did," said the scientific manager, still sitting on the floor.

He looked at the still quivering figure. "It is not a nice death to die, apparently—but it is quick."

The official was still staring at the body. He was a man of slow apprehension.

There was a pause.

The scientific manager got up on his feet rather awkwardly. He ran his fingers along his collar thoughtfully, and moved his head to and fro several times.

"Poor Holroyd! I see now." Then almost mechanically he went towards the switch in the shadow and turned the current into the railway circuit again. As he did so the singed body loosened its grip upon the machine and fell forward on its face. The cone of the dynamo roared out loud and clear, and the armature beat the air.

So ended prematurely the Worship of the Dynamo Deity, perhaps the most short-lived of all religions. Yet withal it could boast a Martyrdom and a Human Sacrifice.

the remarkable rocket

oscar wilde

Oscar Wilde (1854–1900) was born in Dublin and educated at Trinity College, Dublin, and at Magdalen College, Oxford. A versatile genius, he wrote poems, fairy tales, plays, a novel (The Picture of Dorian Gray), and a number of short stories. His private life was London scandal; after a celebrated trial (1895) he was committed to prison for two years. For further reading: The Writings of Oscar Wilde (1931).

The King's son was going to be married, so there were general rejoicings. He had waited a whole year for his bride, and at last she had arrived. She was a Russian Princess, and had driven all the way from Finland in a sledge drawn by six reindeer. The sledge was shaped like a great golden swan, and between the swan's wings lay the little Princess herself. Her long ermine cloak reached right down to her feet, on her head was a tiny cap of silver tissue, and she was as pale as the Snow Palace in which she had always lived. So pale was she that as she drove through the streets all the people wondered. "She is like a white rose!" they cried, and they threw down flowers on her from the balconies.

At the gate of the Castle the Prince was waiting to receive her. He had dreamy violet eyes, and his hair was like fine gold. When he saw her he sank upon one knee, and kissed her hand.

"Your picture was beautiful," he murmured, "but you are more beautiful than your picture;" and the little Princess blushed.

"She was like a white rose before," said a young page to his neighbour, "but she is like a red rose now;" and the whole Court was delighted.

For the next three days everybody went about saying, "White rose, Red rose, Red rose, White rose," and the King gave orders that the Page's salary was to be doubled. As he received no salary at all this was not of much use to him, but it was considered a great honour and was duly published in the Court Gazette.

When the three days were over the marriage was celebrated. It was a magnificent ceremony, and the bride and bridegroom walked hand in hand under a canopy of purple velvet embroidered with little pearls. Then there was a State Banquet, which lasted for five hours. The Prince and Princess sat at the top of the Great Hall and drank out of a cup of clear crystal. Only true lovers could drink out of this cup, for if false lips touched it, it grew grey and dull and cloudy.

"It is quite clear that they love each other," said the little Page, "as clear as crystal!" and the King doubled his salary a second time.

"What an honour!" cried all the courtiers.

After the banquet there was to be a Ball. The bride and bridegroom were to dance the Rose-dance together, and the King had promised to play the flute. He played very badly, but no one had ever dared to tell him so, because he was the King. Indeed, he knew only two airs, and was never quite certain which one he was playing; but it made no matter, for, whatever he did, everybody cried out, "Charming! charming!"

The last item on the programme was a grand display of fireworks, to be let off exactly at midnight. The little Princess had never seen a firework in her life, so the King had given orders that the Royal Pyrotechnist should be in attendance on the day of her marriage.

"What are fireworks like?" she had asked the Prince, one morning, as she was walking on the terrace.

"They are like the Aurora Borealis," said the King, who always answered questions that were addressed to other people, "only much more natural. I prefer them to stars myself, as you always know when they are going to appear, and they are as delightful as my own flute-playing. You must certainly see them."

So at the end of the King's garden a great stand had been set up, and as soon as the Royal Pyrotechnist had put everything in its proper place, the fireworks began to talk to each other.

"The world is certainly very beautiful," cried a little Squib. "Just look at those yellow tulips. Why! if they were real crackers they could not be lovelier. I am very glad I have travelled. Travel improves the mind wonderfully, and does away with all one's prejudices."

"The King's garden is not the world, you foolish Squib," said a big Roman Candle; "the world is an enormous place, and it would take you three days to see it thoroughly."

"Any place you love is the world to you," exclaimed the pensive Catherine Wheel, who had been attached to an old deal box in early life, and prided herself on her broken heart; "but love is not fashionable any more, the poets have killed it. They wrote so much about it that nobody believed them, and I am not surprised. True love suffers, and is silent. I remember myself once—— But no matter now. Romance is a thing of the past."

"Nonsense!" said the Roman Candle, "Romance never dies. It is like the moon, and lives for ever. The bride and bridegroom, for instance, love each other very dearly. I heard all about them this morning from a brown-paper cartridge, who happened to be staying in the same drawer as myself, and he knew the latest Court news."

But the Catherine Wheel shook her head. "Romance is dead, Romance is dead, Romance is dead," she murmured. She was one of those people who think that, if you say the same thing over and over a great many times, it becomes true in the end.

Suddenly, a sharp, dry cough was heard, and they all looked round.

It came from a tall, supercilious-looking Rocket, who was tied to the end of a long stick. He always coughed before he made any observations, so as to attract attention.

"Ahem! ahem!" he said, and everybody listened except the poor Catherine Wheel, who was still shaking her head, and murmuring, "Romance is dead."

"Order! order!" cried out a Cracker. He was something of a politician, and had always taken a prominent part in the local elections, so he knew the proper Parliamentary expressions to use.

"Quite dead," whispered the Catherine Wheel, and she went off to sleep.

As soon as there was perfect silence, the Rocket coughed a third time and began. He spoke with a very slow, distinct voice, as if he were dictating his memoirs, and always looked over the shoulder of the person to whom he was talking. In fact, he had a most distinguished manner.

"How fortunate it is for the King's son," he remarked, "that he is to be married on the very day on which I am to be let off! Really, if it had not been arranged beforehand, it could not have turned out better for him; but Princes are always lucky."

"Dear me!" said the little Squib, "I thought it was quite the other way, and that we were to be let off in the Prince's honour."

"It may be so with you," he answered; "indeed, I have no doubt that it is, but with me it is different. I am a very remarkable Rocket, and come of remarkable parents. My mother was the most celebrated Catherine Wheel of her day, and was renowned for her graceful dancing. When she made her great public appearance she spun round nineteen times before she went out, and each time that she did so she threw into the air seven pink stars. She was three feet and a half in diameter, and made of the very best gunpowder. My father was a Rocket like myself, and of French extraction. He flew so high that the people were afraid that he would never come down again. He did, though, for he was of a kindly disposition, and he made a most brilliant descent in a shower of golden rain. The newspapers wrote about his performance in very flattering terms. Indeed, the Court Gazette called him a triumph of Pylotechnic art."

"Pyrotechnic, Pyrotechnic, you mean," said a Bengal Light; "I know it is Pyrotechnic, for I saw it written on my own canister."

"Well, I said Pylotechnic," answered the Rocket, in a severe tone of voice, and the Bengal Light felt so crushed that be began at once to bully the little squibs, in order to show that he was still a person of some importance.

"I was saying," continued the Rocket, "I was saying—— What was I saying?"

"You were talking about yourself," replied the Roman Candle.

"Of course; I knew I was discussing some interesting subject when I was so rudely interrupted. I hate rudeness and bad manners of every kind, for I am extremely sensitive. No one in the whole world is so sensitive as I am, I am quite sure of that."

"What is a sensitive person?" said the Cracker to the Roman Candle.

"A person who, because he has corns himself, always treads on other people's toes," answered the Roman Candle in a low whisper; and the Cracker nearly exploded with laughter.

"Pray, what are you laughing at?" inquired the Rocket; "I am not laughing."

"I am laughing because I am happy," replied the Cracker.

"That is a very selfish reason," said the Rocket angrily. "What right have you to be happy? You should be thinking about others. In fact, you should be thinking about me. I am always thinking about myself, and I expect everybody else to do the same. That is what is called sympathy. It is a beautiful virtue, and I possess it in a high degree. Suppose, for instance, anything happened to me to-night, what a misfortune that would be for every one! The Prince and Princess would never be happy again, their whole married life would be spoiled; and as for the King, I know he would not get over it. Really, when I begin to reflect on the importance of my position, I am almost moved to tears."

"If you want to give pleasure to others," cried the Roman Candle, "you had better keep yourself dry."

"Certainly," exclaimed the Bengal Light, who was now in better spirits; "that is only common sense."

"Common sense, indeed!" said the Rocket indignantly; "you forget that I am very uncommon, and very remarkable. Why, anybody can have common sense, provided that they have no imagination. But I have imagination, for I never think of things as they really are; I always think of them as being quite different. As for keeping myself dry, there is evidently no one here who can at all appreciate an emotional nature. Fortunately for myself, I don't care. The only thing that sustains one through life is the consciousness of the immense inferiority of everybody else, and this is a feeling I have always cultivated. But none of you have any hearts. Here you are laughing and making merry just as if the Prince and Princess had not just been married."

"Well, really," exclaimed a small Fire-balloon, "why not? It is a most joyful occasion, and when I soar up into the air I intend to tell the stars all about it. You will see them twinkle when I talk to them about the pretty bride."

"Ah, what a trivial view of life!" said the Rocket; "but it is only what I expected. There is nothing in you; you are hollow and empty. Why, perhaps the Prince and Princess may go to live in a country where there is a deep river, and perhaps they may have one only son, a little fairhaired boy with violet eyes like the Prince himself; and perhaps some day he may go out to walk with his nurse; and perhaps the nurse may go to sleep under a great elder-tree; and perhaps the little boy may fall into the deep river and be drowned. What a terrible misfortune! Poor people, to lose their only son! It is really too dreadful! I shall never get over it."

"But they have not lost their only son," said the Roman Candle; "no misfortune has happened to them at all."

"I never said that they had," replied the Rocket; "I said that they might. If they had lost their only son there would be no use in saying any more about the matter. I hate people who cry over spilt milk. But when I think that they might lose their only son, I certainly am very much affected."

"You certainly are!" cried the Bengal Light. "In fact, you are the most affected person I ever met."

"You are the rudest person I ever met," said the Rocket, "and you cannot understand my friendship for the Prince."

"Why, you don't even know him," growled the Roman Candle.

"I never said I knew him," answered the Rocket. "I dare say that if I knew him I should not be his friend at all. It is a very dangerous thing to know one's friends."

"You had really better keep yourself dry," said the Fire-balloon. "That is the important thing."

"Very important for you, I have no doubt," answered the Rocket, "but I shall weep if I choose;" and he actually burst into real tears, which flowed down his stick like raindrops, and nearly drowned two little beetles, who were just thinking of setting up house together, and were looking for a nice dry spot to live in.

"He must have a truly romantic nature," said the Catherine Wheel, "for he weeps when there is nothing at all to weep about;" and she heaved a deep sigh and thought about the deal box.

But the Roman Candle and the Bengal Light were quite indignant, and kept saying, "Humbug! humbug!" at the top of their voices. They were extremely practical, and whenever they objected to anything they called it humbug.

Then the moon rose like a wonderful silver shield; and the stars began to shine, and a sound of music came from the palace.

The Prince and Princess were leading the dance. They danced so beautifully that the tall white lilies peeped in at the window and watched them, and the great red poppies nodded their heads and beat time.

Then ten o'clock struck, and then eleven, and then twelve, and at the last stroke of midnight every one came out on the terrace, and the King sent for the Royal Pyrotechnist.

"Let the fireworks begin," said the King; and the Royal Pyrotechnist made a low bow, and marched down to the end of the garden. He had six attendants with him, each of whom carried a lighted torch at the end of a long pole.

It was certainly a magnificent display.

Whizz! Whizz! went the Catherine Wheel, as she spun round and round. Boom! Boom! went the Roman Candle. Then the Squibs danced all over the place, and the Bengal Lights made everything look scarlet. "Good-bye," cried the Fire-balloon, as he soared away, dropping tiny blue sparks. Bang! Bang! answered the Crackers, who were enjoying themselves immensely. Every one was a great success except the Remarkable Rocket. He was so damped with crying that he could not go off at all. The best thing in him was the gunpowder, and that was so wet with tears that it was of no use. All his poor relations, to whom he would never speak, except with a sneer, shot up into the sky like wonderful golden flowers with blossoms of fire. Huzza! Huzza! cried the Court; and the little Princess laughed with pleasure.

"I suppose they are reserving me for some grand occasion," said the Rocket; "no doubt that is what it means," and he looked more supercilious than ever.

The next day the workmen came to put everything tidy. "This is evidently, a deputation," said the Rocket; "I will receive them with becoming dignity:" so he put his nose in the air, and began to frown severely, as if he were thinking about some very important subject. But they took no notice of him at all till they were just going away. Then one of them caught sight of him. "Hallo!" he cried, "what a bad rocket!" and he threw him over the wall into the ditch.

"BAD ROCKET? BAD ROCKET?" he said, as he whirled through the air; "impossible! GRAND ROCKET, that is what the man said. BAD and GRAND sound very much the same, indeed they often are the same;" and he fell into the mud.

"It is not comfortable here," he remarked, "but no doubt it is some fashionable watering-place, and they have sent me away to recruit my health. My nerves are certainly very much shattered, and I require rest."

Then a little Frog, with bright jewelled eyes, and a green mottled coat, swam up to him.

"A new arrival, I see!" said the Frog. "Well, after all there is nothing like mud. Give me rainy weather and a ditch, and I am quite happy. Do you think it will be a wet afternoon? I am sure I hope so, but the sky is quite blue and cloudless. What a pity!"

"Ahem! ahem!" said the Rocket, and he began to cough.

"What a delightful voice you have!" cried the Frog. "Really it is quite like a croak, and croaking is, of course, the most musical sound in the world. You will hear our glee-club this evening. We sit in the old duck-pond close by the farmer's house, and as soon as the moon rises we begin. It is so entrancing that everybody lies awake to listen to us. In fact, it was only yesterday that I heard the farmer's wife say to her mother that she could not get a wink of sleep at night on account of us. It is most gratifying to find oneself so popular."

"Ahem! ahem!" said the Rocket angrily. He was very much annoyed that he could not get a word in.

"A delightful voice, certainly," continued the Frog; "I hope you will come over to the duck-pond. I am off to look for my daughters. I have six beautiful daughters, and I am so afraid the Pike may meet them. He is a perfect monster, and would have no hesitation in breakfasting off them. Well, good-bye; I have enjoyed our conversation very much, I assure you."

"Conversation, indeed!" said the Rocket. "You have talked the whole time yourself. That is not conversation."

"Somebody must listen," answered the Frog, "and I like to do all the talking myself. It saves time, and prevents arguments."

"But I like arguments," said the Rocket.

"I hope not," said the Frog complacently. "Arguments are extremely vulgar, for everybody in good society holds exactly the same opinions. Good-bye a second time; I see my daughters in the distance;" and the little Frog swam away.

"You are a very irritating person," said the Rocket, "and very ill-bred. I hate people who talk about themselves, as you do, when one wants to talk about oneself, as I do. It is what I call selfishness, and selfishness is a most detestable thing, especially to any one of my temperament, for I am well known for my sympathetic nature. In fact, you should take example by me; you could not possibly have a better model. Now that you have the chance you had better avail yourself of it, for I am going back to Court almost immediately. I am a great favourite at Court; in fact, the Prince and Princess were married yesterday in my honour. Of course, you know nothing of these matters, for you are a provincial."

"There is no good talking to him," said a Dragonfly, who was sitting on the top of a large brown bulrush; "no good at all, for he has gone away."

"Well, that is his loss, not mine," answered the Rocket. "I am not going to stop talking to him merely because he pays no attention. I like hearing myself talk. It is one of my greatest pleasures. I often have long conversations all by myself, and I am so clever that sometimes I don't understand a single word of what I am saying."

"Then you should certainly lecture on Philosophy," said the Dragonfly, and he spread a pair of lovely gauze wings and soared away into the sky.

"How very silly of him not to stay here!" said the Rocket. "I am sure that he has not often got such a chance of improving his mind. However, I don't care a bit. Genius like mine is sure to be appreciated some day;" and he sank down a little deeper into the mud.

After some time a large White Duck swam up to him. She had yellow legs, and webbed feet, and was considered a great beauty on account of her waddle.

"Quack, quack, quack," she said. "What a curious shape you are! May I ask were you born like that, or is it the result of an accident?"

"It is quite evident that you have always lived in the country," answered the Rocket, "otherwise you would know who I am. However, I excuse your ignorance. It would be unfair to expect other people to be as remarkable as oneself. You will no doubt be surprised to hear that I can fly up into the sky, and come down in a shower of golden rain."

"I don't think much of that," said the Duck, "as I cannot see what use it is to any one. Now, if you could plough the fields like the ox, or draw a cart like the horse, or look after the sheep like the collie-dog, that would be something."

"My good creature," cried the Rocket in a very haughty tone of voice, "I see that you belong to the lower orders. A person of my position is never useful. We have certain accomplishments, and that is more than sufficient. I have no sympathy myself with industry of any kind, least of all with such industries as you seem to recommend. Indeed, I have always been of opinion that hard work is simply the refuge of people who have nothing whatever to do."

"Well, well," said the Duck, who was of a very peaceful disposition, and never quarrelled with any one, "everybody has different tastes. I hope, at any rate, that you are going to take up your residence here."

"Oh! dear no," cried the Rocket. "I am merely a visitor, a distinguished visitor. The fact is that I find this place rather tedious. There is neither society here, nor solitude. In fact, it is essentially suburban. I shall probably go back to Court, for I know that I am destined to make a sensation in the world."

"I had thoughts of entering public life once myself," remarked the Duck; "there are so many things that need reforming. Indeed, I took the chair at a meeting some time ago, and we passed resolutions condemning everything that we did not like. However, they did not seem to have much effect. Now I go in for domesticity, and look after my family."

"I am made for public life," said the Rocket, "and so are all my relations, even the humblest of them. Whenever we appear we excite great attention. I have not actually appeared myself, but when I do so it will be a magnificent sight. As for domesticity, it ages one rapidly, and distracts one's mind from higher things."

"Ah! the higher things of life, how fine they are!" said the Duck; "and that reminds me how hungry I feel:" and she swam away down the stream, saying, "Quack, quack, quack."

"Come back! come back!" screamed the Rocket, "I have a great deal to say to you;" but the Duck paid no attention to him. "I am glad that she has gone," he said to himself, "she has a decidedly middle-class mind;" and he sank a little deeper still into the mud, and began to think about the loneliness of genius, when suddenly two little boys in white smocks came running down the bank, with a kettle and some faggots.

"This must be the deputation," said the Rocket, and he tried to look very dignified.

"Hallo!" cried one of the boys, "look at this old stick; I wonder how it came here:" and he picked the Rocket out of the ditch.

"OLD STICK!" said the Rocket, "impossible! GOLD STICK, that is what he said. Gold Stick is very complimentary. In fact, he mistakes me for one of the Court dignitaries!"

"Let us put it into the fire!" said the other boy, "it will help to boil the kettle."

So they piled the faggots together, and put the Rocket on top, and lit the fire.

"This is magnificent," cried the Rocket, "they are going to let me off in broad daylight, so that every one can see me."

"We will go to sleep now," they said, "and when we wake up the kettle will be boiled;" and they lay down on the grass, and shut their eyes.

The Rocket was very damp, so he took a long time to burn. At last, however, the fire caught him.

"Now I am going off!" he cried, and he made himself very stiff and straight. "I know I shall go much higher than the stars, much higher than the moon, much higher than the sun. In fact, I shall go so high that——"

Fizz! Fizz! Fizz! and he went straight up into the air.

"Delightful!" he cried, "I shall go on like this for ever. What a success I am!"

But nobody saw him.

Then he began to feel a curious tingling sensation all over him.

"Now I am going to explode," he cried. "I shall set the whole world on fire, and make such a noise that nobody will talk about anything else for a whole year." And he certainly did explode. Bang! Bang! Bang! went the gunpowder. There was no doubt about it.

But nobody heard him, not even the two little boys, for they were sound asleep.

Then all that was left of him was the stick, and this fell down on the back of a Goose who was taking a walk by the side of the ditch.

"Good heavens!" cried the Goose. "It is going to rain sticks;" and she rushed into the water.

"I knew I should create a great sensation," gasped the Rocket, and he went out.

an

outpost

of progress

joseph conrad

Joseph Conrad (1857–1924) was born in the Ukraine of Polish parents. He shipped as a sailor for twenty years before finally settling in England as a British citizen. Although he did not learn English until he was twenty-one, he is one of the great masters of English prose; and his novels, such as Lord Jim *(1900),* Nostromo *(1904), and* Victory *(1905), continue to engage our best literary minds. For further reading:* Tales of Unrest *(1898);* Youth, and Other Tales *(1902).*

I

There were two white men in charge of the trading station. Kayerts, the chief, was short and fat; Carlier, the assistant, was tall, with a large head and a very broad trunk perched upon a long pair of thin legs. The third man on the staff was a Sierra Leone nigger, who maintained that his name was Henry Price. However, for some reason or other, the natives down the river had given him the name of Makola, and it stuck to him through all his wanderings about the country. He spoke English and French with a warbling accent, wrote a beautiful hand, understood bookkeeping, and cherished in his innermost heart the worship of evil spirits. His wife was a negress from Loanda, very large and very noisy. Three children rolled about in sunshine before the door of his low, shed-like dwelling. Makola, taciturn and impenetrable, despised the two white men. He had charge of a small clay storehouse with a dried-grass roof, and pretended to keep a correct account of beads, cotton cloth, red kerchiefs, brass wire, and other trade goods it contained. Besides the storehouse and Makola's hut, there was only one large building in the cleared ground of the station. It was built neatly of reeds, with a verandah on all the four sides. There were three rooms in it. The one in the middle was the living-room, and had two rough tables and a few stools in it. The other two were the bedrooms for the white men. Each had a bedstead and a mosquito net for all furniture. The plank floor was littered with the belongings of the white men; open half-empty boxes, torn wearing apparel, old boots; all the things dirty, and all the things broken, that accumulate mysteriously round untidy men. There was also another dwelling-place some distance away from the buildings. In it, under a tall cross much out of the perpendicular, slept the man who had seen the beginning of all this; who had planned and had watched the construction of this outpost of progress. He had been, at home, an unsuccessful painter who, weary of pursuing fame on an empty stomach, had gone out there through high protections. He had been the first chief of that station. Makola had watched the energetic artist die of fever in the just finished house with his usual kind of "I told you so" indifference. Then, for a time, he dwelt alone with his family, his account books, and the Evil Spirit that rules the lands under the equator. He got on very well with his god. Perhaps he had propitiated him by a promise of more white men to play with, by and by. At any rate the director of the Great Trading Company, coming up in a steamer that resembled an enormous sardine box with a flat-roofed shed erected on it, found the station in good order, and Makola as usual quietly diligent. The director had the cross put up over the first agent's grave, and appointed Kayerts to the post. Carlier was told off as second in charge. The director was a man ruthless and efficient, who at times, but very imperceptibly, indulged in grim humour. He made a speech to Kayerts and Carlier, pointing out to them the promising aspect of this station. The nearest trading-post was about three hundred miles away. It was an exceptional opportunity for them to distinguish themselves and to earn percentages on the trade. This appointment was a favour done to beginners. Kayerts was moved almost to tears by his director's kindness. He would, he said, by doing his best, try to justify the flattering confidence, &c., &c. Kayerts had been in the Administration of the Telegraphs, and knew how to express himself correctly. Carlier, an ex-non-commissioned officer of cavalry in an army guaranteed from harm by several European Powers, was less impressed. If there were commissions to get, so much the better; and, trailing a sulky glance over the river, the forests, the impenetrable bush that seemed to cut off the station from the rest of the world, he muttered between his teeth, "We shall see, very soon."

Next day, some bales of cotton goods and a few cases of provisions having been thrown on shore, the sardine-box steamer went off, not to return for another six months. On the deck the director touched his cap to the two agents, who stood on the bank waving their hats, and turning to an old servant of the Company on his passage to headquarters, said, "Look at those two imbeciles. They must be mad at home to send me such specimens. I told those fellows to plant a vegetable garden, build new storehouses and fences, and construct a landing-stage. I bet nothing will be done! They won't know how to begin. I always thought the station on this river useless, and they just fit the station!"

"They will form themselves there," said the old stager with a quiet smile.

"At any rate, I am rid of them for six months," retorted the director.

The two men watched the steamer round the bend, then, ascending arm in arm the slope of the bank, returned to the station. They had been in this vast and dark country only a very short time, and as yet always in the midst of other white men, under the eye and guidance of their superiors. And now, dull as they were to the subtle influences of surroundings, they felt themselves very much alone, when suddenly left unassisted to face the wilderness; a wilderness rendered more strange, more incomprehensible by the mysterious glimpses of the vigorous life it contained. They were two perfectly insignificant and incapable individuals, whose existence is only rendered possible through the high organization of civilized crowds. Few men realize that their life, the very essence of their character, their capabilities and their audacities, are only the expression of their belief in the safety of their surroundings. The courage, the composure, the confidence; the emotions and principles; every great and every insignificant thought belongs not to the individual but to the crowd: to the crowd that believes blindly in the irresistible force of its institutions and of its morals, in the power of its police and of its opinion. But the contact with pure unmitigated savagery, with primitive nature and primitive man, brings sudden and profound trouble into the heart. To the sentiment of being alone of one's kind, to the clear perception of the loneliness of one's thoughts, of one's sensations—to the negation of the habitual, which is safe, there is added the affirmation of the unusual, which is dangerous; a suggestion of things vague, uncontrollable, and repulsive, whose discomposing intrusion excites the imagination and tries the civilized nerves of the foolish and the wise alike.

Kayerts and Carlier walked arm in arm, drawing close to one another as children do in the dark; and they had the same, not altogether unpleasant, sense of danger which one half suspects to be imaginary. They chatted persistently in familiar tones. "Our station is prettily situated," said one. The other assented with enthusiasm, enlarging volubly on the beauties of the situation. Then they passed near the grave. "Poor devil!" said Kayerts. "He died of fever, didn't he?" muttered Carlier, stopping short. "Why," retorted Kayerts, with indignation, "I've been told that the fellow exposed himself recklessly to the sun. The climate here, everybody says, is not all worse than at home, as long as you keep out of the sun. Do you hear that, Carlier? I am chief here, and my orders are that you should not expose yourself to the sun!" He assumed his superiority jocularly, but his meaning was serious. The idea that he would, perhaps, have to bury Carlier and remain alone, gave him an inward shiver. He felt suddenly that this Carlier was more precious to him here, in the centre of Africa, than a brother could be anywhere else. Carlier, entering into the spirit of the thing, made a military salute and answered in a brisk tone, "Your orders shall be attended to, chief!" Then he burst out laughing, slapped Kayerts on the back and shouted, "We shall let life run easily here! Just sit still and gather in the ivory those savages will bring. This country has its good points, after all!" They both laughed loudly while Carlier thought: "That poor Kayerts; he is so fat and unhealthy. It would be awful if I had to bury him here. He is a man I respect." . . . Before they reached the verandah of their house they called one another "my dear fellow."

The first day they were very active, pottering about with hammers and nails and red calico, to put up curtains, make their house habitable and pretty; resolved to settle down comfortably to their new life. For them an impossible task. To grapple effectually with even purely material problems requires more serenity of mind and more lofty courage than people generally imagine. No two beings could have been more unfitted for such a struggle. Society, not from any tenderness, but because of its strange needs, had taken care of those two men, forbidding them all independent thought, all initiative, all departure from routine; and forbidding it under pain of death. They could only live on condition of being machines. And now, released from the fostering care of men with pens behind the ears, or of men with gold lace on the sleeves, they were like those lifelong prisoners who, liberated after many years, do not know what use to make of their freedom. They did not know what use to make of their faculties, being both, through want of practice, incapable of independent thought.

At the end of two months Kayerts often would say, "If it was not for my Melie, you wouldn't catch me here." Melie was his daughter. He had thrown up his post in the Administration of the Telegraphs, though he had been for seventeen years perfectly happy there, to earn a dowry for his girl. His wife was dead, and the child was being brought up by his sisters. He regretted the streets, the pavements, the cafés, his friends of many years; all the things he used to see, day after day; all the thoughts suggested by familiar things—the thoughts effortless, monotonous, and soothing of a Government clerk; he regretted all the gossip, the small enmities, the mild venom, and the little jokes of Government offices. "If I had had a decent brother-in-law," Carlier would remark, "a fellow with a heart, I would not be here." He had left the army and had made himself so obnoxious to his family by his laziness and impudence, that an exasperated brother-in-law had made superhuman efforts to procure him an appointment in the Company as a second-class agent. Having not a penny in the world he was compelled to accept this means of livelihood as soon as it became quite clear to him that there was nothing more to squeeze out of his relations. He, like Kayerts, regretted his old life. He regretted the clink of sabre and spurs on a fine afternoon, the barrack-room witticisms, the girls of garrison towns; but, besides, he had also a sense of grievance. He was evidently a much ill-used man. This made him moody, at times. But the two men got on well together in the fellowship of their stupidity and laziness. Together they did nothing, absolutely nothing, and enjoyed the sense of the idleness for which they were paid. And in time they came to feel something resembling affection for one another.

They lived like blind men in a large room, aware only of what came in contact with them (and of that only imperfectly), but unable to see the general aspect of things. The river, the forest, all the great land throbbing with life, were like a great emptiness. Even the brilliant sunshine disclosed nothing intelligible. Things appeared and disappeared before their eyes in an unconnected and aimless kind of way. The river seemed to come from nowhere and flow nowhither. It flowed through a void. Out of that void, at times, came canoes, and men with spears in their hands would suddenly crowd the yard of the station. They were naked, glossy black, ornamented with snowy shells and glistening brass wire, perfect of limb. They made an uncouth babbling noise when they spoke, moved in a stately manner, and sent quick, wild glances out of their startled, never-resting eyes. Those warriors would squat in long rows, four or more deep, before the verandah, while their chiefs bargained for hours with Makola over an elephant tusk. Kayerts sat on his chair and looked down on the proceedings, understanding nothing. He stared at them with his round blue eyes, called out to Carlier, "Here, look! look at that fellow there—and that other one, to the left. Did you ever see such a face? Oh, the funny brute!"

Carlier, smoking native tobacco in a short wooden pipe, would swagger up twirling his moustaches, and surveying the warriors with haughty indulgence, would say—

"Fine animals. Brought any bone? Yes? It's not any too soon. Look at the muscles of that fellow—third from the end. I wouldn't care to get a punch on the nose from him. Fine arms, but legs no good below the knee. Couldn't make cavalry men of them." And after glancing down complacently at his own shanks, he always concluded: "Pah! Don't they stink! You, Makola! Take that herd over to the fetish" (the storehouse was in every station called the fetish, perhaps because of the spirit of civilization it contained) "and give them up some of the rubbish you keep there. I'd rather see it full of bone than full of rags."

Kayerts approved.

"Yes, yes! Go and finish that palaver over there, Mr. Makola. I will come round when you are ready, to weigh the tusk. We must be careful." Then turning to his companion: "This is the tribe that lives down the river; they are rather aromatic. I remember, they had been once before here. D'ye hear that row? What a fellow has got to put up with in this dog of a country! My head is split."

Such profitable visits were rare. For days the two pioneers of trade and progress would look on their empty courtyard in the vibrating brilliance of vertical sunshine. Below the high bank, the silent river flowed on glittering and steady. On the sands in the middle of the stream, hippos and alligators sunned themselves side by side. And stretching away in all directions, surrounding the insignificant cleared spot of the trading post, immense forests, hiding fateful complications of fantastic life, lay in the eloquent silence of mute greatness. The two men understood nothing, cared for nothing but for the passage of days that separated them from the steamer's return. Their predecessor had left some torn books. They took up these wrecks of novels, and, as they had never read anything of the kind before, they were surprised and amused. Then during long days there were interminable and silly discussions about plots and personages. In the centre of Africa they made acquaintance of Richelieu and of d'Artagnan, of Hawk's Eye and of Father Goriot, and of many other people. All these imaginary personages became subjects for gossip as if they had been living friends. They discounted their virtues, suspected their motives, decried their successes; were scandalized at their duplicity or were doubtful about their courage. The accounts of crimes filled them with indignation, while tender or pathetic passages moved them deeply. Carlier cleared his throat and said in a soldierly voice, "What nonsense!" Kayerts, his round eyes suffused with tears, his fat cheeks quivering, rubbed his bald head, and declared, "This is a splendid book. I had no idea there were such clever fellows in the world." They also found some old copies of a home paper. That print discussed what it was pleased to call "Our Colonial Expansion" in high-flown language. It spoke much of the rights and duties of civilization, of the sacredness of the civilizing work, and extolled the merits of those who went about bringing light, and faith and commerce to the dark places of the earth. Carlier and Kayerts read, wondered, and began to think better of themselves. Carlier said one evening, waving his hand about, "In a hundred years, there will be perhaps a town here. Quays, and warehouses, and barracks, and—and—billiard-rooms. Civilization, my boy, and virtue—and all. And then, chaps will read that two good fellows, Kayerts and Carlier, were the first civilized men to live in this very spot!" Kayerts nodded, "Yes, it is a consolation to think of that." They seemed to forget their dead predecessor; but, early one day, Carlier went out and replanted the cross firmly. "It used to make me squint whenever I walked that way," he explained to Kayerts over the morning coffee. "It made me squint, leaning over so much. So I planted it upright. And solid, I promise you! I suspended myself with both hands to the cross-piece. Not a move. Oh, I did that properly."

At times Gobila came to see them. Gobila was the chief of the neighboring villages. He was a gray-headed savage, thin and black, with a white cloth round his loins and a mangy panther skin hanging over his back. He came up with long strides of his skeleton legs, swinging a staff as tall as himself, and, entering the common room of the station, would squat on his heels to the left of the door. There he sat, watching Kayerts, and now and then making a speech which the other did not understand. Kayerts, without interrupting his occupation, would from time to time say in a friendly manner: "How goes it, you old image?" and they would smile at one another. The two whites had a liking for that old and incomprehensible creature, and called him Father Gobila. Gobila's manner was paternal, and he seemed really to love all white men. They all appeared to him very young, indistinguishably alike (except for stature), and he knew that they were all brothers, and also immortal. The death of the artist, who was the first white man whom he knew intimately, did not disturb this belief, because he was firmly convinced that the white stranger had pretended to die and got himself buried for some mysterious purpose of his own, into which it was useless to inquire. Perhaps it was his way of going home to his own country? At any rate, these were his brothers, and he transferred his absurd affection to them. They returned it in a way. Carlier slapped him on the back, and recklessly struck off matches for his amusement. Kayerts was always ready to let him have a sniff at the ammonia bottle. In short, they behaved just like that other white creature that had hidden itself in a hole in the ground. Gobila considered them attentively. Perhaps they were the same being with the other—or one of them was. He couldn't decide—clear up that mystery; but he remained always very friendly. In consequence of that friendship the women of Gobila's village walked in single file through the reedy grass, bringing every morning to the station, fowls, and sweet potatoes, and palm wine, and sometimes a goat. The Company never provisions the stations fully, and the agents required those local supplies to live. They had them through the good-will of Gobila, and lived well. Now and then one of them had a bout of fever, and the other nursed him with gentle devotion. They did not think much of it. It left them weaker, and their appearance changed for the worse. Carlier was hollow-eyed and irritable. Kayerts showed a drawn, flabby face above the rotundity of his stomach, which gave him a weird aspect. But being constantly together, they did not notice the change that took place gradually in their appearance, and also in their dispositions.

Five months passed in that way.

Then, one morning, as Kayerts and Carlier, lounging in their chairs under the verandah, talked about the approaching visit of the steamer, a knot of armed men came out of the forest and advanced towards the station. They were strangers to that part of the country. They were tall, slight, draped classically from neck to heel in blue fringed cloths, and carried percussion muskets over their bare right shoulders. Makola showed signs of excitement, and ran out of the storehouse (where he spent all his days) to meet these visitors. They came into the courtyard and looked about them with steady, scornful glances. Their leader, a powerful and determined-looking negro with bloodshot eyes, stood in front of the verandah and made a long speech. He gesticulated much, and ceased very suddenly.

There was something in his intonation, in the sounds of the long sentences he used, that startled the two whites. It was like a reminiscence of something not exactly familiar, and yet resembling the speech of civilized men. It sounded like one of those impossible languages which sometimes we hear in our dreams.

"What lingo is that?" said the amazed Carlier. "In the first moment I fancied the fellow was going to speak French. Anyway, it is a different kind of gibberish to what we ever heard."

"Yes," replied Kayerts. "Hey, Makola, what does he say? Where do they come from? Who are they?"

But Makola, who seemed to be standing on hot bricks, answered hurriedly, "I don't know. They come from very far. Perhaps Mrs. Price will understand. They are perhaps bad men."

The leader, after waiting for a while, said something sharply to Makola, who shook his head. Then the man, after looking round, noticed Makola's hut and walked over there. The next moment Mrs. Makola was heard speaking with great volubility. The other strangers—they were six in all—strolled about with an air of ease, put their heads through the door of the storeroom, congregated round the grave, pointed understandingly at the cross, and generally made themselves at home.

"I don't like those chaps—and, I say, Kayerts, they must be from the coast; they've got firearms," observed the sagacious Carlier.

Kayerts also did not like those chaps. They both, for the first time, became aware that they lived in conditions where the unusual may be dangerous, and that there was no power on earth outside of themselves to stand between them and the unusual. They became uneasy, went in and loaded their revolvers. Kayerts said, "We must order Makola to tell them to go away before dark."

The strangers left in the afternoon, after eating a meal prepared for them by Mrs. Makola. The immense woman was excited, and talked much with the visitors. She rattled away shrilly, pointing here and there at the forests and at the river. Makola sat apart and watched. At times he got up and whispered to his wife. He accompanied the strangers across the ravine at the back of the station-ground, and returned slowly looking very thoughtful. When questioned by the white men he was very strange, seemed not to understand, seemed to have forgotten French—seemed to have forgotten how to speak altogether. Kayerts and Carlier agreed that the nigger had had too much palm wine.

There was some talk about keeping a watch in turn, but in the evening everything seemed so quiet and peaceful that they retired as usual. All night they were disturbed by a lot of drumming in the villages. A deep, rapid roll near by would be followed by another far off—then all ceased. Soon short appeals would rattle out here and there, then all mingle together, increase, become vigorous and sustained, would spread out over the forest, roll through the night, unbroken and ceaseless, near and far, as if the whole land had been one immense drum booming out steadily an appeal to heaven. And through the deep and tremendous noise sudden yells that resembled snatches of songs from a madhouse darted shrill and high in discordant jets of sound which seemed to rush far above the earth and drive all peace from under the stars.

Carlier and Kayerts slept badly. They both thought they had heard shots fired during the night—but they could not agree as to the direction. In the morning Makola was gone somewhere. He returned about noon with one of yesterday's strangers, and eluded all Kayerts' attempts to close with him: had become deaf apparently. Kayerts wondered. Carlier, who had been fishing off the bank, came back and remarked while he showed his catch, "The niggers seem to be in a deuce of a stir; I wonder what's up. I saw about fifteen canoes cross the river during the two hours I was there fishing." Kayerts, worried, said, "Isn't this Makola very queer to-day?" Carlier advised, "Keep all our men together in case of some trouble."

II

There were ten station men who had been left by the Director. Those fellows, having engaged themselves to the Company for six months (without having any idea of a month in particular and only a very faint notion of time in general), had been serving the cause of progress for upwards of two years. Belonging to a tribe from a very distant part of the land of darkness and sorrow, they did not run away, naturally supposing that as wandering strangers they would be killed by the inhabitants of the country; in which they were right. They lived in straw huts on the slope of a ravine over-grown with reedy grass, just behind the station buildings. They were not happy, regretting the festive incantations, the sorceries, the human sacrifices of their own land; where they also had parents, brothers, sisters, admired chiefs, respected magicians, loved friends, and other ties supposed generally to be human. Besides, the rice rations served out by the Company did not agree with them, being a food unknown to their land, and to which they could not get used. Consequently they were unhealthy and miserable. Had they been of any other tribe they would have made up their minds to die—for nothing is easier to certain savages than suicide—and so have escaped from the puzzling difficulties of existence. But belonging, as they did, to a warlike tribe with filed teeth, they had more grit, and went on stupidly living through disease and sorrow. They did very little work, and had lost their splendid physique. Carlier and Kayerts doctored them assiduously without being able to bring them back into condition again. They were mustered every morning and told off to different tasks—grass-cutting, fence-building, tree-felling, &c., &c., which no power on earth could induce them to execute efficiently. The two whites had practically very little control over them.

In the afternoon Makola came over to the big house and found Kayerts watching three heavy columns of smoke rising above the forests. "What is that?" asked Kayerts. "Some villages burn," answered Makola, who seemed to have regained his wits. Then he said abruptly: "We have got very little ivory; bad six months' trading. Do you like get a little more ivory?"

"Yes," said Kayerts, eagerly. He thought of percentages which were low.

"Those men who came yesterday are traders from Loanda who have got more ivory than they can carry home. Shall I buy? I know their camp."

"Certainly," said Kayerts. "What are those traders?"

"Bad fellows," said Makola, indifferently. "They fight with people, and catch women and children. They are bad men, and got guns. There is a great disturbance in the country. Do you want ivory?"

"Yes," said Kayerts. Makola said nothing for a while. Then: "Those workmen of ours are no good at all," he muttered, looking round. "Station in very bad order, sir. Director will growl. Better get a fine lot of ivory, then he say nothing."

"I can't help it; the men won't work," said Kayerts. "When will you get that ivory?"

"Very soon," said Makola. "Perhaps to-night. You leave it to me, and keep indoors, sir. I think you had better give some palm wine to our men to make a dance this evening. Enjoy themselves. Work better to-morrow. There's plenty palm wine—gone a little sour."

Kayerts said "yes," and Makola, with his own hands carried big calabashes to the door of his hut. They stood there till the evening, and Mrs. Makola looked into every one. The men got them at sunset. When Kayerts and Carlier retired, a big bonfire was flaring before the men's huts. They could hear their shouts and drumming. Some men from Gobila's village had joined the station hands, and the entertainment was a great success.

In the middle of the night, Carlier waking suddenly, heard a man shout loudly; then a shot was fired. Only one. Carlier ran out and met Kayerts on the verandah. They were both startled. As they went across the yard to call Makola, they saw shadows moving in the night. One of them cried, "Don't shoot! It's me, Price." Then Makola appeared close to them. "Go back, go back, please," he urged, "you spoil all." "There are strange men about," said Carlier. "Never mind; I know," said Makola. Then he whispered, "All right. Bring ivory. Say nothing! I know my business." The two white men reluctantly went back to the house, but did not sleep. They heard footsteps, whispers, some groans. It seemed as if a lot of men came in, dumped heavy things on the ground, squabbled a long time, then went away. They lay on their hard beds and thought: "This Makola is invaluable." In the morning Carlier came out, very sleepy, and pulled at the cord of the big bell. The station hands mustered every morning to the sound of the bell. That morning nobody came. Kayerts turned out also, yawning. Across the yard they saw Makola come out of his hut, a tin basin of soapy water in his hand. Makola, a civilized nigger, was very neat in his person. He threw the soapsuds skillfully over a wretched little yellow cur he had, then turning his face to the agent's house, he shouted from the distance, "All the men gone last night!"

They heard him plainly, but in their surprise they both yelled out together: "What!" Then they stared at one another. "We are in a proper fix now," growled Carlier. "It's incredible!" muttered Kayerts. "I will go to the huts and see," said Carlier, striding off. Makola coming up found Kayerts standing alone.

"I can hardly believe it," said Kayerts, tearfully. "We took care of them as if they had been our children."

"They went with the coast people," said Makola after a moment of hesitation.

"What do I care with whom they went—the ungrateful brutes!" exclaimed the other. Then with sudden suspicion, and looking hard at Makola, he added: "What do you know about it?"

Makola moved his shoulders, looking down on the ground. "What do I know? I think only. Will you come and look at the ivory I've got there? It is a fine lot. You never saw such."

He moved towards the store. Kayerts followed him mechanically, thinking about the incredible desertion of the men. On the ground before the door of the fetish lay six splendid tusks.

"What did you give for it?" asked Kayerts, after surveying the lot with satisfaction.

"No regular trade," said Makola. "They brought the ivory and gave it to me. I told them to take what they most wanted in the station. It is a beautiful lot. No station can show such tusks. Those traders wanted carriers badly, and our men were no good here. No trade, no entry in books; all correct."

Kayerts nearly burst with indignation. "Why!" he shouted, "I believe you have sold our men for these tusks!" Makola stood impassive and silent. "I—I—will—I," stuttered Kayerts. "You fiend!" he yelled out.

"I did the best for you and the Company," said Makola, imperturbably. "Why you shout so much? Look at this tusk."

"I dismiss you! I will report you—I won't look at the tusk. I forbid you to touch them. I order you to throw them into the river. You—you!"

"You very red, Mr. Kayerts. If you are so irritable in the sun, you will get fever and die—like the first chief!" pronounced Makola impressively.

They stood still, contemplating one another with intense eyes, as if they had been looking with effort across immense distances. Kayerts shivered. Makola had meant no more than he said, but his words seemed to Kayerts full of ominous menace! He turned sharply and went away to the house. Makola retired into the bosom of his family; and the tusks, left lying before the store, looked very large and valuable in the sunshine.

Carlier came back on the verandah. "They're all gone, hey?" asked Kayerts from the far end of the common room in a muffled voice. "You did not find anybody?"

"Oh, yes," said Carlier, "I found one of Gobila's people lying dead before the huts—shot through the body. We heard that shot last night."

Kayerts came out quickly. He found his companion staring grimly over the yard at the tusks, away by the store. They both sat in silence for a while. Then Kayerts related his conversation with Makola. Carlier said nothing. At the midday meal they ate very little. They hardly exchanged a word that day. A great silence seemed to lie heavily over the station and press on their lips. Makola did not open the store; he spent the day playing with his children. He lay full-length on a mat outside his door, and the youngsters sat on his chest and clambered all over him. It was a touching picture. Mrs. Makola was busy cooking all day as usual. The white men made a somewhat better meal in the evening. Afterwards, Carlier smoking his pipe strolled over to the store; he stood for a long time over the tusks, touched one or two with his foot, even tried to lift the largest one by its small end. He came back to his chief, who had not stirred from the verandah, threw himself in the chair and said—

"I can see it! They were pounced upon while they slept heavily after drinking all that palm wine you've allowed Makola to give them. A put-up job! See? The worst is, some of Gobila's people were there, and got carried off too, no doubt. The least drunk woke up, and got shot for his sobriety. This is a funny country. What will you do now?"

"We can't touch it, of course," said Kayerts.

"Of course not," assented Carlier.

"Slavery is an awful thing," stammered out Kayerts in an unsteady voice.

"Frightful—the sufferings," grunted Carlier with conviction.

They believed their words. Everybody shows a respectful deference to certain sounds that he and his fellows can make. But about feelings people really know nothing. We talk with indignation or enthusiasm; we talk about oppression, cruelty, crime, devotion, self-sacrifice, virtue, and we know nothing real beyond the words. Nobody knows what suffering or sacrifice mean—except, perhaps the victims of the mysterious purpose of these illusions.

Next morning they saw Makola very busy setting up in the yard the big scales used for weighing ivory. By and by Carlier said: "What's that filthy scoundrel up to?" and lounged out into the yard. Kayerts followed. They stood watching. Makola took no notice. When the balance was swung true, he tried to lift a tusk into the scale. It was too heavy. He looked up helplessly without a word, and for a minute they stood round that balance as mute and still as three statues. Suddenly Carlier said: "Catch hold of the other end, Makola—you beast!" and together they swung the tusk up. Kayerts trembled in every limb. He muttered, "I say! O! I say!" and putting his hand in his pocket found there a dirty bit of paper and the stump of a pencil. He turned his back on the others, as if about to do something tricky, and noted stealthily the weights which Carlier shouted out to him with unnecessary loudness. When all was over Makola whispered to himself: "The sun's very strong here for the tusks." Carlier said to Kayerts in a careless tone: "I say, chief, I might just as well give him a lift with this lot into the store."

As they were going back to the house Kayerts observed with a sigh: "It had to be done." And Carlier said: "It's deplorable, but, the men being Company's men the ivory is Company's ivory. We must look after it." "I will report to the Director, of course," said Kayerts. "Of course; let him decide," approved Carlier.

At midday they made a hearty meal. Kayerts sighed from time to time. Whenever they mentioned Makola's name they always added to it an opprobrious epithet. It eased their conscience. Makola gave himself a half-holiday, and bathed his children in the river. No one from Gobila's villages came near the station that day. No one came the next day, and the next, nor for a whole week. Gobila's people might have been dead and buried for any sign of life they gave. But they were only mourning for those they had lost by the witchcraft of white men, who had brought wicked people into their country. The wicked people were gone, but fear remained. Fear always remains. A man may destroy everything within himself, love and hate and belief, and even doubt; but as long as he clings to life he cannot destroy fear: the fear, subtle, indestructible, and terrible, that pervades his being; that tinges his thoughts; that lurks in his heart; that watches on his lips the struggle of his last breath. In his fear, the mild old Gobila offered extra human sacrifices to all the Evil Spirits that had taken possession of his white friends. His heart was heavy. Some warriors spoke about burning and killing, but the cautious old savage dissuaded them. Who could foresee the woe those mysterious creatures, if irritated, might bring? They should be left alone. Perhaps in time they would disappear into the earth as the first one had disappeared. His people must keep away from them, and hope for the best.

Kayerts and Carlier did not disappear, but remained above on this earth, that, somehow, they fancied had become bigger and very empty. It was not the absolute and dumb solitude of the post that impressed them so much as an inarticulate feeling that something from within them was gone, something that worked for their safety, and had kept the wilderness from interfering with their hearts. The images of home; the memory of people like them, of men that thought and felt as they used to think and feel, receded into distances made indistinct by the glare of unclouded sunshine. And out of the great silence of the surrounding wilderness, its very hopelessness and savagery seemed to approach them nearer, to draw them gently, to look upon them, to envelop them with a solicitude irresistible, familiar, and disgusting.

Days lengthened into weeks, then into months. Gobila's people drummed and yelled to every new moon, as of yore, but kept away from the station. Makola and Carlier tried once in a canoe to open communications, but were received with a shower of arrows, and had to fly back to the station for dear life. That attempt set the country up and down the river into an uproar that could be very distinctly heard for days. The steamer was late. At first they spoke of delay jauntily, then anxiously, then gloomily. The matter was becoming serious. Stores were running short. Carlier cast his lines off the bank, but the river was low, and the fish kept out in the stream. They dared not stroll far way from the station to shoot. Moreover, there was no game in the impenetrable forest. Once

Carlier shot a hippo in the river. They had no boat to secure it, and it sank. When it floated up it drifted away, and Gobila's people secured the carcase. It was the occasion for a national holiday, but Carlier had a fit of rage over it and talked about the necessity of exterminating all the niggers before the country could be made habitable. Kayerts mooned about silently; spent hours looking at the portrait of his Melie. It represented a little girl with long bleached tresses and a rather sour face. His legs were much swollen, and he could hardly walk. Carlier, undermined by fever, could not swagger any more, but kept tottering about, still with a devil-may-care air, as became a man who remembered his crack regiment. He had become hoarse, sarcastic, and inclined to say unpleasant things. He called it "being frank with you." They had long ago reckoned their percentages on trade, including in them that last deal of "this infamous Makola." They had also concluded not to say anything about it. Kayerts hesitated at first—was afraid of the Director.

"He has seen worse things done on the quiet," maintained Carlier, with a hoarse laugh. "Trust him! He won't thank you if you blab. He is no better than you or me. Who will talk if we hold our tongues? There is nobody here."

That was the root of the trouble! There was nobody there; and being left there alone with their weakness, they became daily more like a pair of accomplices than like a couple of devoted friends. They had heard nothing from home for eight months. Every evening they said, "Tomorrow we shall see the steamer." But one of the Company's steamers had been wrecked, and the Director was busy with the other, relieving very distant and important stations on the main river. He thought that the useless station, and the useless men, could wait. Meantime Kayerts and Carlier lived on rice boiled without salt, and cursed the Company, all Africa, and the day they were born. One must have lived on such diet to discover what ghastly trouble the necessity of swallowing one's food may become. There was literally nothing else in the station but rice and coffee; they drank the coffee without sugar. The last fifteen lumps Kayerts had solemnly locked away in his box, together with a half-bottle of Cognâc, "in case of sickness," he explained. Carlier approved. "When one is sick," he said, "any little extra like that is cheering."

They waited. Rank grass began to sprout over the courtyard. The bell never rang now. Days passed, silent, exasperating, and slow. When the two men spoke, they snarled; and their silences were bitter, as if tinged by the bitterness of their thoughts.

One day after a lunch of boiled rice, Carlier put down his cup untasted, and said: "Hang it all! Let's have a decent cup of coffee for once. Bring out that sugar, Kayerts!"

"For the sick," muttered Kayerts, without looking up.

"For the sick," mocked Carlier. "Bosh! . . . Well! I am sick."

"You are no more sick than I am, and I go without," said Kayerts in a peaceful tone.

"Come! out with that sugar, you stingy old slave-dealer."

Kayerts looked up quickly. Carlier was smiling with marked insolence. And suddenly it seemed to Kayerts that he had never seen that man before. Who was he? He knew nothing about him. What was he capable of? There was a surprising flash of violent emotion within him, as if in the presence of something undreamt-of, dangerous, and final. But he managed to pronounce with composure—

"That joke is in very bad taste. Don't repeat it."

"Joke!" said Carlier, hitching himself forward on his seat. "I am hungry—I am sick—I don't joke! I hate hypocrites. You are a hypocrite. You are a slave-dealer. I am a slave-dealer. There's nothing but slave-dealers in this cursed country. I mean to have sugar in my coffee to-day, anyhow!"

"I forbid you to speak to me in that way," said Kayerts with a fair show of resolution.

"You!—What?" shouted Carlier, jumping up.

Kayerts stood up also. "I am your chief," he began, trying to master the shakiness of his voice.

"What?" yelled the other. "Who's chief? There's no chief here. There's nothing here: there's nothing but you and I. Fetch the sugar—you pot-bellied ass."

"Hold your tongue. Go out of this room," screamed Kayerts. "I dismiss you—you scoundrel!"

Carlier swung a stool. All at once he looked dangerously in earnest. "You flabby, good-for-nothing civilian—take that!" he howled.

Kayerts dropped under the table, and the stool struck the grass inner wall of the room. Then, as Carlier was trying to upset the table, Kayerts in desperation made a blind rush, head low, like a cornered pig would do, and over-turning his friend, bolted along the verandah, and into his room. He locked the door, snatched his revolver, and stood panting. In less than a minute Carlier was kicking at the door furiously, howling, "If you don't bring out that sugar, I will shoot you at sight, like a dog. Now then—one—two—three. You won't? I will show you who's the master."

Kayerts thought the door would fall in, and scrambled through the square hole that served for a window in his room. There was then the whole breadth of the house between them. But the other was apparently not strong enough to break in the door, and Kayerts heard him running round. Then he also began to run laboriously on his swollen legs. He ran as quickly as he could, grasping the revolver, and unable yet to understand what was happening to him. He saw in succession Makola's house, the store, the river, the ravine, and the low bushes; and he saw all those things again as he ran for the second time round the house. Then again they flashed past him. That morning he could not have walked a yard without a groan.

And now he ran. He ran fast enough to keep out of sight of the other man.

Then as, weak and desperate, he thought, "Before I finish the next round I shall die," he heard the other man stumble heavily, then stop. He stopped also. He had the back and Carlier the front of the house, as before. He heard him drop into a chair cursing, and suddenly his own legs gave way, and he slid down into a sitting posture with his back to the wall. His mouth was as dry as a cinder, and his face was wet with perspiration—and tears. What was it all about? He thought it must be a horrible illusion; he thought he was dreaming; he thought he was going mad! After a while he collected his senses. What did they quarrel about? That sugar! How absurd! He would give it to him—didn't want it himself. And he began scrambling to his feet with a sudden feeling of security. But before he had fairly stood upright, a common-sense reflection occurred to him and drove him back into despair. He thought: "If I give way now to that brute of a soldier, he will begin this horror again tomorrow—and the day after—every day—raise other pretensions, trample on me, torture me, make me his slave—and I will be lost! Lost! The steamer may not come for days—may never come." He shook so that he had to sit down on the floor again. He shivered forlornly. He felt he could not, would not move any more. He was completely distracted by the sudden perception that the position was without issue—that death and life had in a moment become equally difficult and terrible.

All at once he heard the other push his chair back; and he leaped to his feet with extreme facility. He listened and got confused. Must run again! Right or left? He heard footsteps. He darted to the left, grasping his revolver, and at the very same instant, as it seemed to him, they came into violent collision. Both shouted with surprise. A loud explosion took place between them; a roar of red fire, thick smoke; and Kayerts, deafened and blinded, rushed back thinking: "I am hit—it's all over." He expected the other to come round—to gloat over his agony. He caught hold of an upright of the roof—"All over!" Then he heard a crashing fall on the other side of the house, as if somebody had tumbled headlong over a chair—then silence. Nothing more happened. He did not die. Only his shoulder felt as if it had been badly wrenched, and he had lost his revolver. He was disarmed and helpless! He waited for his fate. The other man made no sound. It was a stratagem. He was stalking him now! Along what side? Perhaps he was taking aim this very minute! After a few moments of an agony frightful and absurd, he decided to go and meet his doom. He was prepared for every surrender. He turned the corner, steadying himself with one hand on the wall; made a few paces, and nearly swooned. He had seen on the floor, protruding past the other corner, a pair of turned-up feet. A pair of white naked feet in red slippers. He felt deadly sick, and stood for a time in profound darkness. Then Makola appeared before him, saying quietly: "Come along, Mr. Kayerts. He is dead." He burst into tears of gratitude; a loud, sobbing fit of crying. After a time he found himself sitting in a chair and looking at Carlier, who lay stretched on his back. Makola was kneeling over the body.

"Is this your revolver?" asked Makola, getting up.

"Yes," said Kayerts; then he added very quickly, "He ran after me to shoot me—you saw!"

"Yes, I saw," said Makola. "There is only one revolver; where's his?"

"Don't know," whispered Kayerts in a voice that had become suddenly very faint.

"I will go and look for it," said the other, gently. He made the round along the verandah, while Kayerts sat still and looked at the corpse. Makola came back empty-handed, stood in deep thought, then stepped quietly into the dead man's room, and came out directly with a revolver, which he held up before Kayerts. Kayerts shut his eyes. Everything was going round. He found life more terrible and difficult than death. He had shot an unarmed man.

After meditating for a while, Makola said softly, pointing at the dead man who lay there with his right eye blown out—

"He died of fever." Kayerts looked at him with a stony stare. "Yes," repeated Makola, thoughtfully, stepping over the corpse, "I think he died of fever. Bury him to-morrow."

And he went away slowly to his expectant wife, leaving the two white men alone on the verandah.

Night came, and Kayerts sat unmoving on his chair. He sat quiet as if he had taken a dose of opium. The violence of the emotions he had passed through produced a feeling of exhausted serenity. He had plumbed in one short afternoon the depths of horror and despair, and now found repose in the conviction that life had no more secrets for him: neither had death! He sat by the corpse thinking; thinking very actively, thinking very new thoughts. He seemed to have broken loose from himself altogether. His old thoughts, convictions, likes and dislikes, things he respected and things he abhorred, appeared in their true light at last! Appeared contemptible and childish, false and ridiculous. He revelled in his new wisdom while he sat by the man he had killed. He argued with himself about all things under heaven with that kind of wrong-headed lucidity which may be observed in some lunatics. Incidentally he reflected that the fellow dead there had been a noxious beast anyway; that men died every day in thousands; perhaps in hundreds of thousands—who could tell?—and that in the number, that one death could not possibly make any difference; couldn't have any importance, at least to a thinking creature. He, Kayerts, was a thinking creature. He had been all his life, till that moment, a believer in a lot of nonsense like the rest of mankind—who are fools; but now he thought! He knew! He was at peace; he was familiar with the highest wisdom! Then he tried to imagine himself dead, and Carlier sitting in his chair watching him; and his attempt met with such unexpected success, that in a very few moments he became not at all sure who was dead and who was alive. This extraordinary achievement of his fancy startled him, however, and by a clever and timely effort of mind he saved himself just in time from becoming Carlier. His heart thumped, and he felt hot all over at the thought of that danger. Carlier! What a beastly thing! To compose his now disturbed nerves—and no wonder!—he tried to whistle a little. Then, suddenly, he fell asleep, or thought he had slept; but at any rate there was a fog, and somebody had whistled in the fog.

He stood up. The day had come, and a heavy mist had descended upon the land: the mist penetrating, enveloping, and silent; the morning mist of tropical lands; the mist that clings and kills; the mist white and deadly, immaculate and poisonous. He stood up, saw the body, and threw his arms above his head with a cry like that of a man who, waking from a trance, finds himself immured forever in a tomb. "*Help! . . . . My God!*"

A shriek inhuman, vibrating and sudden, pierced like a sharp dart the white shroud of that land of sorrow. Three short, impatient screeches followed, and then, for a time, the fog-wreaths rolled on, undisturbed, through a formidable silence. Then many more shrieks, rapid and piercing, like the yells of some exasperated and ruthless creature, rent the air. Progress was calling to Kayerts from the river. Progress and civilization and all the virtues. Society was calling to its accomplished child to come, to be taken care of, to be instructed, to be judged, to be condemned; it called him to return to that rubbish heap from which he had wandered away, so that justice could be done.

Kayerts heard and understood. He stumbled out of the verandah, leaving the other man quite alone for the first time since they had been thrown there together. He groped his way through the fog, calling in his ignorance upon the invisible heaven to undo its work. Makola flitted by in the mist, shouting as he ran—

"Steamer! Steamer! They can't see. They whistle for the station. I go ring the bell. Go down to the landing, sir. I ring."

He disappeared. Kayerts stood still. He looked upwards; the fog rolled low over his head. He looked round like a man who has lost his way; and he saw a dark smudge, a cross-shaped stain, upon the shifting purity of the mist. As he began to stumble toward it, the station bell rang in a tumultuous peal its answer to the impatient clamour of the steamer.

The Managing Director of the Great Civilizing Company (since we know that civilization follows trade) landed first, and incontinently lost sight of the steamer. The fog down by the river was exceedingly dense; above, at the station, the bell rang unceasing and brazen.

The Director shouted loudly to the steamer:

"There is nobody down to meet us; there may be something wrong, though they are ringing. You had better come, too!"

And he began to toil up the steep bank. The captain and the engine-driver of the boat followed behind. As they scrambled up the fog thinned, and they could see their Director a good way ahead. Suddenly they saw him start forward, calling to them over his shoulder:—"Run! Run to the house! I've found one of them. Run, look for the other!"

He had found one of them! And even he, the man of varied and startling experience, was somewhat discomposed by the manner of this finding. He stood and fumbled in his pockets (for a knife) while he faced Kayerts, who was hanging by a leather strap from the cross. He had evidently climbed the grave, which was high and narrow, and after tying the end of the strap to the arm, had swung himself off. His toes were only a couple of inches above the ground; his arms hung stiffly down; he seemed to be standing rigidly at attention, but with one purple cheek playfully posed on the shoulder. And, irreverently, he was putting out a swollen tongue at his Managing Director.

young

goodman

brown

nathaniel hawthorne

Nathaniel Hawthorne (1804–1864) was born in Salem, Massachusetts. After college he spent a dozen years in relative obscurity before gaining recognition with his first collection of tales. His work, characteristically, blends realism, melodrama, the Gothic conventions; his themes center on the mysteries of the human heart, the nature of sin, and the meaning of "darkness." For further reading: Twice-Told Tales *(1837 and 1842);* The Snow Image and Other Twice-Told Tales *(1852);* Tales by Hawthorne, *edited by Carl Van Doren (1921).*

Young Goodman Brown came forth at sunset into the street at Salem village; but put his head back, after crossing the threshold, to exchange a parting kiss with his young wife. And Faith, as the wife was aptly named, thrust her own pretty head into the street, letting the wind play with the pink ribbons of her cap while she called to Goodman Brown.

"Dearest heart," whispered she, softly and rather sadly, when her lips were close to his ear, "prithee put off your journey until sunrise and sleep in your own bed to-night. A lone woman is troubled with such dreams and such thoughts that she's afeard of herself sometimes. Pray tarry with me this night, dear husband, of all nights in the year."

"My love and my Faith," replied young Goodman Brown, "of all nights in the year, this one night must I tarry away from thee. My journey, as thou callest it, forth and back again, must needs be done 'twixt now and sunrise. What, my sweet, pretty wife, dost thou doubt me already, and we but three months married?"

"Then God bless you!" said Faith, with the pink ribbons; "and may you find all well when you come back."

"Amen!" cried Goodman Brown. "Say thy prayers, dear Faith, and go to bed at dusk, and no harm will come to thee."

So they parted; and the young man pursued his way until, being about to turn the corner by the meeting-house, he looked back and saw

124

the head of Faith still peeping after him with a melancholy air, in spite of her pink ribbons.

"Poor little Faith!" thought he, for his heart smote him. "What a wretch am I to leave her on such an errand! She talks of dreams, too. Methought as she spoke there was trouble in her face, as if a dream had warned her what work is to be done to-night. But no, no; 't would kill her to think it. Well, she's a blessed angel on earth; and after this one night I'll cling to her skirts and follow her to heaven."

With this excellent resolve for the future, Goodman Brown felt himself justified in making more haste on his present evil purpose. He had taken a dreary road, darkened by all the gloomiest trees of the forest, which barely stood aside to let the narrow path creep through, and closed immediately behind. It was all as lonely as could be; and there is this peculiarity in such a solitude, that the traveller knows not who may be concealed by the innumerable trunks and the thick boughs overhead; so that with lonely footsteps he may yet be passing through an unseen multitude.

"There may be a devilish Indian behind every tree," said Goodman Brown to himself; and he glanced fearfully behind him as he added, "What if the devil himself should be at my very elbow!"

His head being turned back, he passed a crook of the road, and, looking forward again, beheld the figure of a man, in grave and decent attire, seated at the foot of an old tree. He arose at Goodman Brown's approach and walked onward side by side with him.

"You are late, Goodman Brown," said he. "The clock of the Old South was striking as I came through Boston, and that is full fifteen minutes agone."

"Faith kept me back a while," replied the young man, with a tremor in his voice, caused by the sudden appearance of his companion, though not wholly unexpected.

It was now deep dusk in the forest, and deepest in that part of it where these two were journeying. As nearly as could be discerned, the second traveller was about fifty years old, apparently in the same rank of life as Goodman Brown, and bearing a considerable resemblance to him, though perhaps more in expression than features. Still they might have been taken for father and son. And yet, though the elder person was as simply clad as the younger, and as simple in manner too, he had an indescribable air of one who knew the world, and who would not have felt abashed at the governor's dinner table or in King William's court, were it possible that his affairs should call him thither. But the only thing about him that could be fixed upon as remarkable was his staff, which bore the likeness of a great black snake, so curiously wrought that it might almost be seen to twist and wriggle itself like a living serpent.

This, of course, must have been an ocular deception, assisted by the uncertain light.

"Come, Goodman Brown," cried his fellow-traveller, "this is a dull pace for the beginning of a journey. Take my staff, if you are so soon weary."

"Friend," said the other, exchanging his slow pace for a full stop, "having kept covenant by meeting thee here, it is my purpose now to return whence I came. I have scruples touching the matter thou wot'st of."

"Sayest thou so?" replied he of the serpent, smiling apart. "Let us walk on, nevertheless, reasoning as we go; and if I convince thee not thou shalt turn back. We are but a little way in the forest yet."

"Too far! too far!" exclaimed the goodman, unconsciously resuming his walk. "My father never went into the woods on such an errand, nor his father before him. We have been a race of honest men and good Christians since the days of the martyrs; and shall I be the first of the name of Brown that ever took this path and kept"—

"Such company, thou wouldst say," observed the elder person, interpreting his pause. "Well said, Goodman Brown! I have been as well acquainted with your family as with ever a one among the Puritans; and that's no trifle to say. I helped your grandfather, the constable, when he lashed the Quaker woman so smartly through the streets of Salem; and it was I that brought your father a pitch-pine knot, kindled at my own hearth, to set fire to an Indian village, in King Philip's war. They were my good friends, both; and many a pleasant walk have we had along this path, and returned merrily after midnight. I would fain be friends with you for their sake."

"If it be as thou sayest," replied Goodman Brown, "I marvel they never spoke of these matters; or, verily, I marvel not, seeing that the least rumor of the sort would have driven them from New England. We are a people of prayer, and good works to boot, and abide no such wickedness."

"Wickedness or not," said the traveller with the twisted staff, "I have a very general acquaintance here in New England. The deacons of many a church have drunk the communion wine with me; the selectmen of divers towns make me their chairman; and a majority of the Great and General Court are firm supporters of my interest. The governor and I, too—But these are state secrets."

"Can this be so?" cried Goodman Brown, with a stare of amazement at his undisturbed companion. "Howbeit, I have nothing to do with the governor and council; they have their own ways, and are no rule for a simple husbandman like me. But, were I to go on with thee, how should I meet the eye of that good old man, our minister, at Salem village? Oh, his voice would make me tremble both Sabbath day and lecture day."

Thus far the elder traveller had listened with due gravity; but now burst into a fit of irrepressible mirth, shaking himself so violently that his snake-like staff actually seemed to wriggle in sympathy.

"Ha! ha! ha!" shouted he again and again; then composing himself, "Well, go on, Goodman Brown, go on; but, prithee, don't kill me with laughing."

"Well, then, to end the matter at once," said Goodman Brown, considerably nettled, "there is my wife, Faith. It would break her dear little heart; and I'd rather break my own."

"Nay, if that be the case," answered the other, "e'en go thy ways, Goodman Brown. I would not for twenty old women like the one hobbling before us that Faith should come to any harm."

As he spoke he pointed his staff at a female figure on the path, in whom Goodman Brown recognized a very pious and exemplary dame, who had taught him his catechism in youth, and was still his moral and spiritual adviser, jointly with the minister and Deacon Gookin.

"A marvel, truly, that Goody Cloyse should be so far in the wilderness at nightfall," said he. "But with your leave, friend, I shall take a cut through the woods until we have left this Christian woman behind. Being a stranger to you, she might ask whom I was consorting with and whither I was going."

"Be it so," said his fellow-traveller. "Betake you to the woods, and let me keep the path."

Accordingly the young man turned aside, but took care to watch his companion, who advanced softly along the road until he had come within a staff's length of the old dame. She, meanwhile, was making the best of her way, with singular speed for so aged a woman, and mumbling some indistinct words—a prayer, doubtless—as she went. The traveller put forth his staff and touched her withered neck with what seemed the serpent's tail.

"The devil!" screamed the pious old lady.

"Then Goody Cloyse knows her old friend?" observed the traveller, confronting her and leaning on his writhing stick.

"Ah, forsooth, and is it your worship indeed?" cried the good dame. "Yea, truly is it, and in the very image of my old gossip, Goodman Brown, the grandfather of the silly fellow that now is. But—would your worship believe it?—my broomstick hath strangely disappeared, stolen, as I suspect, by that unhanged witch, Goody Cory, and that, too, when I was all anointed with the juice of smallage, and cinquefoil, and wolf's bane"—

"Mingled with fine wheat and the fat of a new-born babe," said the shape of old Goodman Brown.

"Ah, your worship knows the recipe," cried the old lady, cackling aloud. "So, as I was saying, being all ready for the meeting, and no horse to ride on, I made up my mind to foot it; for they tell me there is a nice young man to be taken into communion to-night. But now your good worship will lend me your arm, and we shall be there in a twinkling."

"That can hardly be," answered her friend. "I may not spare you my arm, Goody Cloyse; but here is my staff, if you will."

So saying, he threw it down at her feet, where, perhaps, it assumed life, being one of the rods which its owner had formerly lent to the Egyptian magi. Of this fact, however, Goodman Brown could not take cognizance. He had cast up his eyes in astonishment, and, looking down again, beheld neither Goody Cloyse nor the serpentine staff, but his fellow-traveller alone, who waited for him as calmly as if nothing had happened.

"That old woman taught me my catechism," said the young man; and there was a world of meaning in this simple comment.

They continued to walk onward, while the elder traveller exhorted his companion to make good speed and persevere in the path, discoursing so aptly that his arguments seemed rather to spring up in the bosom of his auditor than to be suggested by himself. As they went, he plucked a branch of maple to serve for a walking stick, and began to strip it of the twigs and little boughs, which were wet with evening dew. The moment his fingers touched them they became strangely withered and dried up as with a week's sunshine. Thus the pair proceeded, at a good free pace, until suddenly, in a gloomy hollow of the road, Goodman Brown sat himself down on the stump of a tree and refused to go any farther.

"Friend," said he, stubbornly, "my mind is made up. Not another step will I budge on this errand. What if a wretched old woman do choose to go to the devil when I thought she was going to heaven: is that any reason why I should quit my dear Faith and go after her?"

"You will think better of this by and by," said his acquaintance, composedly. "Sit here and rest yourself a while; and when you feel like moving again, there is my staff to help you along."

Without more words, he threw his companion the maple stick, and was as speedily out of sight as if he had vanished into the deepening gloom. The young man sat a few moments by the roadside, applauding himself greatly, and thinking with how clear a conscience he should meet the minister in his morning walk, nor shrink from the eye of good old Deacon Gookin. And what calm sleep would be his that very night, which was to have been spent so wickedly, but so purely and sweetly now, in the arms of Faith! Amidst these pleasant and praiseworthy meditations, Goodman Brown heard the tramp of horses along the road, and deemed it advisable to conceal himself within the verge of the forest, conscious of the guilty purpose that had brought him thither, though now so happily turned from it.

On came the hoof tramps and the voices of the riders, two grave old voices, conversing soberly as they drew near. These mingled sounds appeared to pass along the road, within a few yards of the young man's hiding-place; but, owing doubtless to the depth of the gloom at that particular spot, neither the travellers nor their steeds were visible. Though their figures brushed the small boughs by the wayside, it could not be seen that they intercepted, even for a moment, the faint gleam from the strip of bright sky athwart which they must have passed. Goodman Brown alternately crouched and stood on tiptoe, pulling aside the branches and thrusting forth his head as far as he durst without discerning so much as a shadow. It vexed him the more, because he could have sworn, were such a thing possible, that he recognized the voices of the minister and Deacon Gookin, jogging along quietly, as they were wont to do, when bound to some ordination or ecclesiastical council. While yet within hearing, one of the riders stopped to pluck a switch.

"Of the two, reverend sir," said the voice like the deacon's, "I had rather miss an ordination dinner than to-night's meeting. They tell me that some of our community are to be here from Falmouth and beyond, and others from Connecticut and Rhode Island, besides several of the Indian powwows, who, after their fashion, know almost as much deviltry as the best of us. Moreover, there is a goodly young woman to be taken into communion."

"Mighty well, Deacon Gookin!" replied the solemn old tones of the minister. "Spur up, or we shall be late. Nothing can be done, you know, until I get on the ground."

The hoofs clattered again; and the voices, talking so strangely in the empty air, passed on through the forest, where no church had ever been gathered or solitary Christian prayed. Whither, then, could these holy men be journeying so deep into the heathen wilderness? Young Goodman Brown caught hold of a tree for support, being ready to sink down on the ground, faint and overburdened with the heavy sickness of his heart. He looked up to the sky, doubting whether there really was a heaven above him. Yet there was the blue arch, and the stars brightening in it.

"With heaven above and Faith below, I will yet stand firm against the devil!" cried Goodman Brown.

While he still gazed upward into the deep arch of the firmament and had lifted his hands to pray, a cloud, though no wind was stirring, hurried across the zenith and hid the brightening stars. The blue sky was still visible, except directly overhead, where this black mass of cloud was sweeping swiftly northward. Aloft in the air, as if from the depths of the cloud, came a confused and doubtful sound of voices. Once the listener fancied that he could distinguish the accents of towns-people of his own, men and women, both pious and ungodly, many of whom he had met at the communion table, and had seen others rioting at the tavern. The next moment, so indistinct were the sounds, he doubted whether he had heard aught but the murmur of the old forest, whispering without a wind. Then came a stronger swell of those familiar tones, heard daily in the sunshine at Salem village, but never until now from a cloud of night. There was one voice, of a young woman, uttering lamentations, yet with an uncertain sorrow, and entreating for some favor, which, perhaps, it would grieve her to obtain; and all the unseen multitude, both saints and sinners, seemed to encourage her onward.

"Faith!" shouted Goodman Brown, in a voice of agony and desperation; and the echoes of the forest mocked him, crying, "Faith! Faith!" as if bewildered wretches were seeking her all through the wilderness.

The cry of grief, rage, and terror was yet piercing the night, when the unhappy husband held his breath for a response. There was a scream, drowned immediately in a louder murmur of voices, fading into far-off laughter, as the dark cloud swept away, leaving the clear and silent sky above Goodman Brown. But something fluttered lightly down through the air and caught on the branch of a tree. The young man seized it, and beheld a pink ribbon.

"My Faith is gone!" cried he, after one stupefied moment. "There is no good on earth; and sin is but a name. Come, devil; for to thee is this world given."

And, maddened with despair, so that he laughed loud and long, did Goodman Brown grasp his staff and set forth again, at such a rate that he seemed to fly along the forest path rather than to walk or run. The road grew wilder and drearier and more faintly traced, and vanished at length, leaving him in the heart of the dark wilderness, still rushing onward with the instinct that guides mortal man to evil. The whole forest was peopled with frightful sounds—the creaking of the trees, the howling of wild beasts, and the yell of Indians; while sometimes the wind tolled like a distant church bell, and sometimes gave a broad roar around the traveller, as if all Nature were laughing him to scorn. But he was himself the chief horror of the scene, and shrank not from its other horrors.

"Ha! ha! ha!" roared Goodman Brown when the wind laughed at him. "Let us hear which will laugh loudest. Think not to frighten me with your deviltry. Come witch, come wizard, come Indian powwow, come devil himself, and here comes Goodman Brown. You may as well fear him as he fear you."

In truth, all through the haunted forest there could be nothing more frightful than the figure of Goodman Brown. On he flew among the black pines, brandishing his staff with frenzied gestures, now giving vent to an inspiration of horrid blasphemy, and now shouting forth such laughter as set all the echoes of the forest laughing like demons around him. The fiend in his own shape is less hideous than when he rages in the breast of man. Thus sped the demoniac on his course, until, quivering among the trees, he saw a red light before him, as when the felled trunks and branches of a clearing have been set on fire, and throw up their lurid blaze against the sky, at the hour of midnight. He paused, in a lull of the tempest that had driven him onward, and heard the swell of what seemed a hymn, rolling solemnly from a distance with the weight of many voices. He knew the tune; it was a familiar one in the choir of the village meeting-house. The verse died heavily away, and was lengthened by a chorus, not of human voices, but of all the sounds of the benighted wilderness pealing in awful harmony together. Goodman Brown cried out, and his cry was lost to his own ear by its unison with the cry of the desert.

In the interval of silence he stole forward until the light glared full upon his eyes. At one extremity of an open space, hemmed in by the dark wall of the forest, arose a rock, bearing some rude, natural resemblance either to an altar or a pulpit, and surrounded by four blazing pines, their tops aflame, their stems untouched, like candles at an evening meeting. The mass of foliage that had overgrown the summit of the rock was all on fire, blazing high into the night and fitfully illuminating the whole field. Each pendent twig and leafy festoon was in a blaze. As the red light arose and fell, a numerous congregation alternately shone forth, then disappeared in shadow, and again grew, as it were, out of the darkness, peopling the heart of the solitary woods at once.

"A grave and dark-clad company," quoth Goodman Brown.

In truth they were such. Among them, quivering to and fro between gloom and splendor, appeared faces that would be seen next day at the council board of the province, and others which, Sabbath after Sabbath, looked devoutly heavenward, and benignantly over the crowded pews, from the holiest pulpits in the land. Some affirm that the lady of the governor was there. At least there were high dames well known to her, and wives of honored husbands, and widows, a great multitude, and ancient maidens, all of excellent repute, and fair young girls, who trembled lest their mothers should espy them. Either the sudden gleams of light flashing over the obscure field bedazzled Goodman Brown, or he recognized a score of the church members of Salem village famous for their especial sanctity. Good old Deacon Gookin had arrived, and waited at the skirts of that venerable saint, his revered pastor. But, irreverently consorting with these grave, reputable, and pious people, these elders of the church, these chaste dames and dewy virgins, there were men of dissolute lives and women of spotted fame, wretches given over to all mean and filthy vice, and suspected even of horrid crimes. It was strange to see that the good shrank not from the wicked, nor were the sinners abashed by the saints. Scattered also among their pale-faced enemies were the Indian priests, or powwows, who had often scared their native forest with more hideous incantations than any known to English witchcraft.

"But where is Faith?" thought Goodman Brown, and, as hope came into his heart, he trembled.

Another verse of the hymn arose, a slow and mournful strain, such as the pious love, but joined to words which expressed all that our nature can conceive of sin, and darkly hinted at far more. Unfathomable to mere mortals is the lore of fiends. Verse after verse was sung; and still the chorus of the desert swelled between like the deepest tone of a mighty organ; and with the final peal of that dreadful anthem there came a sound, as if the roaring wind, the rushing streams, the howling beasts, and every other voice of the unconcerted wilderness were mingling and according with the voice of guilty man in homage to the prince of all. The four blazing pines threw up a loftier flame, and obscurely discovered shapes and visages of horror on the smoke wreaths above the impious assembly. At the same moment the fire on the rock shot redly forth and formed a glowing arch above its base, where now appeared a figure. With reverence be it spoken, the figure bore no slight similitude, both in garb and manner, to some grave divine of the New England churches.

"Bring forth the converts!" cried a voice that echoed through the field and rolled into the forest.

At the word, Goodman Brown stepped forth from the shadow of the trees and approached the congregation, with whom he felt a loathful brotherhood by the sympathy of all that was wicked in his heart. He could have well-nigh sworn that the shape of his own dead father beckoned him to advance, looking downward from a smoke wreath, while a woman, with dim features of despair, threw out her hand to warn him back. Was it his mother? But he had no power to retreat one step, nor to resist, even in thought, when the minister and good old Deacon Gookin seized his arms and led him to the blazing rock. Thither came also the slender form of a veiled female, led between Goody Cloyse, that pious teacher of the catechism, and Martha Carrier, who had received the devil's promise to be queen of hell. A rampant hag was she. And there stood the proselytes beneath the canopy of fire.

"Welcome, my children," said the dark figure, "to the communion of your race. Ye have found thus young your nature and your destiny. My children, look behind you!"

They turned; and flashing forth, as it were, in a sheet of flame, the fiend worshippers were seen; the smile of welcome gleamed darkly on every visage.

"There," resumed the sable form, "are all whom ye have reverenced from youth. Ye deemed them holier than yourselves, and shrank from your own sin, contrasting it with their lives of righteousness and prayerful aspirations heavenward. Yet here are they all in my worshipping assembly. This night it shall be granted you to know their secret deeds: how hoary-bearded elders of the church have whispered wanton words to the young maids of their households; how many a woman, eager for widows' weeds, has given her husband a drink at bedtime and let him sleep his last sleep in her bosom; how beardless youths have made haste to inherit their fathers' wealth; and how fair damsels—blush not, sweet ones—have dug little graves in the garden, and bidden me, the sole guest, to an infant's funeral. By the sympathy of your human hearts for sin ye shall scent out all the places—whether in church, bed-chamber, street, field, or forest—where crime has been committed, and shall exult to behold the whole earth one stain of guilt, one mighty blood spot. Far more than this. It shall be yours to penetrate, in every bosom, the deep mystery of sin, the fountain of all wicked arts, and which inexhaustibly supplies more evil impulses than human power—than my power at its utmost—can make manifest in deeds. And now, my children, look upon each other."

They did so; and, by the blaze of the hell-kindled torches, the wretched man beheld his Faith, and the wife her husband, trembling before that unhallowed altar.

"Lo, there ye stand, my children," said the figure, in a deep and solemn tone, almost sad with its despairing awfulness, as if his once angelic nature could yet mourn for our miserable race. "Depending upon one another's hearts, ye had still hoped that virtue were not all a dream. Now are ye undeceived. Evil is the nature of mankind. Evil must be your only happiness. Welcome again, my children, to the communion of your race."

"Welcome," repeated the fiend worshippers, in one cry of despair and triumph.

And there they stood, the only pair, as it seemed, who were yet hesitating on the verge of wickedness in this dark world. A basin was hollowed, naturally, in the rock. Did it contain water, reddened by the lurid light? or was it blood? or, perchance, a liquid flame? Herein did the shape of evil dip his hand and prepare to lay the mark of baptism upon their foreheads, that they might be partakers of the mystery of sin, more conscious of the secret guilt of others, both in deed and thought, than they could now be of their own. The husband cast one look at his pale wife, and Faith at him. What polluted wretches would the next glance show them to each other, shuddering alike at what they disclosed and what they saw!

"Faith! Faith!" cried the husband, "look up to heaven, and resist the wicked one."

Whether Faith obeyed he knew not. Hardly had he spoken when he found himself amid calm night and solitude, listening to a roar of the wind which died heavily away through the forest. He staggered against the rock, and felt it chill and damp; while a hanging twig, that had been all on fire, besprinkled his cheek with the coldest dew.

The next morning young Goodman Brown came slowly into the street of Salem village, staring around him like a bewildered man. The good old minister was taking a walk along the graveyard to get an appetite for breakfast and meditate his sermon, and bestowed a blessing, as he passed, on Goodman Brown. He shrank from the venerable saint as if to avoid an anathema. Old Deacon Gookin was at domestic worship, and the holy words of his prayer were heard through the open window. "What God doth the wizard pray to?" quoth Goodman Brown. Goody Cloyse, that excellent old Christian, stood in the early sunshine at her own lattice, catechizing a little girl who had brought her a pint of morning's milk. Goodman Brown snatched away the child as from the grasp of the fiend himself. Turning the corner by the meeting-house, he spied the head of Faith, with the pink ribbons, gazing anxiously forth, and bursting into such joy at sight of him that she skipped along the street and almost kissed her husband before the whole village. But Goodman Brown looked sternly and sadly into her face, and passed on without a greeting.

Had Goodman Brown fallen asleep in the forest and only dreamed a wild dream of a witch-meeting?

Be it so if you will; but, alas! it was a dream of evil omen for young Goodman Brown. A stern, a sad, a darkly meditative, a distrustful, if not a desperate man did he become from the night of that fearful dream. On the Sabbath day, when the congregation were singing a holy psalm, he could not listen because an anthem of sin rushed loudly upon his ear and drowned all the blessed strain. When the minister spoke from the pulpit with power and fervid eloquence, and, with his hand on the open Bible, of the sacred truths of our religion, and of saint-like lives and triumphant deaths, and of future bliss or misery unutterable, then did Goodman Brown turn pale, dreading lest the roof should thunder down upon the gray blasphemer and his hearers. Often, awaking suddenly at midnight, he shrank from the bosom of Faith; and at morning or eventide, when the family knelt down at prayer, he scowled and muttered to himself, and gazed sternly at his wife, and turned away. And when he had lived long, and was borne to his grave a hoary corpse, followed by Faith, an aged woman, and children and grandchildren, a goodly procession, besides neighbors not a few, they carved no hopeful verse upon his tombstone, for his dying hour was gloom.

the
black
cat
edgar allan poe

Edgar Allan Poe (1809–1849) was the son of an actor and an actress, both of whom died when he was a child; he later lived with John Allan, a wealthy businessman from Virginia. Poe left the Military Academy at West Point without a commission and became a poet, a critic, and a celebrated—if unstable—writer of short stories. He died in Baltimore— under somewhat mysterious circumstances— probably by violence. For further reading: Tales of the Grotesque and Arabesque *(1840);* Poe's Short Stories, *edited by Killis Campbell (1927).*

For the most wild, yet most homely narrative which I am about to pen, I neither expect nor solicit belief. Mad indeed would I be to expect it, in a case where my very senses reject their own evidence. Yet, mad am I not—and very surely do I not dream. But tomorrow I die, and to-day I would unburthen my soul. My immediate purpose is to place before the world, plainly, succinctly, and without comment, a series of mere household events. In their consequences, these events have terrified—have tortured—have destroyed me. Yet I will not attempt to expound them. To me, they have presented little but Horror—

to many they will seem less terrible than *baroques*. Hereafter, perhaps, some intellect may be found which will reduce my phantasm to the common-place—some intellect more calm, more logical and far less excitable than my own, which will perceive, in the circumstances I detail with awe, nothing more than an ordinary succession of very natural causes and effects.

From my infancy I was noted for the docility and humanity of my disposition. My tenderness of heart was even so conspicuous as to make me the jest of my companions. I was especially fond of animals, and was indulged by my parents with a great variety of pets. With these I spent most of my time, and never was so happy as when feeding and caressing them. This peculiarity of character grew with my growth, and, in my manhood, I derived from it one of my principal sources of pleasure. To those who have cherished an affection for a faithful and sagacious dog, I need hardly be at the trouble of explaining the nature or the intensity of the gratification thus derivable. There is something in the unselfish and self-sacrificing love of a brute, which goes directly to the heart of him who has had frequent occasion to test the paltry friendship and gossamer fidelity of mere *Man*.

I married early, and was happy to find in my wife a disposition not uncongenial with my own. Observing my partiality for domestic pets, she lost no opportunity of procuring those of the most agreeable kind. We had birds, gold fish, a fine dog, rabbits, a small monkey, and *a cat*.

This latter was a remarkably large and beautiful animal, entirely black, and sagacious to an astonishing degree. In speaking of his intelligence, my wife, who at heart was not a little tinctured with superstition, made frequent allusion to the ancient popular notion, which regarded all black cats as witches in disguise. Not that she was ever *serious* upon this point—and I mention the matter at all for no better reason than that it happens, just now, to be remembered.

Pluto—this was the cat's name—was my favorite pet and playmate. I alone fed him, and he attended me wherever I went about the house. It was even with difficulty that I could prevent him from following me through the streets.

Our friendship lasted, in this manner, for several years, during which my general temperament and character—through the instrumentality of the Fiend Intemperance—had (I blush to confess it) experienced a radical alteration for the worse. I grew, day by day, more moody, more irritable, more regardless of the feelings of others. I suffered myself to use intemperate language to my wife. At length, I even offered her personal violence. My pets, of course, were made to feel the change in my disposition. I not only neglected, but ill-used them. For Pluto, however, I still retained sufficient regard to restrain me from maltreating him, as I made no scruple of maltreating the rabbits, the monkey, or even the dog, when by accident, or through affection, they came in my way. But my disease grew upon me—for what disease is like Alcohol!—and at length even Pluto, who was now becoming old, and consequently somewhat peevish—even Pluto began to experience the effects of my ill temper.

One night, returning home, much intoxicated, from one of my haunts about town, I fancied that the cat avoided my presence. I seized him; when, in his fright at my violence, he inflicted a slight wound upon my hand with his teeth. The fury of a demon instantly possessed me. I knew myself no longer. My original soul seemed, at once, to take its flight from my body; and a more than fiendish malevolence, gin-nurtured, thrilled every fibre of my frame. I took from my waistcoat-pocket a pen-knife, opened it, grasped the poor beast by the throat, and deliberately cut one of its eyes from the socket! I blush, I burn, I shudder, while I pen the damnable atrocity.

When reason returned with the morning—when I had slept off the fumes of the night's debauch—I experienced a sentiment half of horror, half of remorse, for the crime of which I had been guilty; but it was, at best, a feeble and equivocal feeling, and the soul remained untouched. I again plunged into excess, and soon drowned in wine all memory of the deed.

In the meantime the cat slowly recovered. The socket of the lost eye presented, it is true, a frightful appearance, but he no longer appeared to suffer any pain. He went about the house as usual, but, as might be expected, fled in extreme terror at my approach. I had so much of my old heart left, as to be at first grieved by this evident dislike on the part of a creature which had once so loved me. But this feeling soon gave place to irritation. And then came, as if to my final and irrevocable overthrow, the spirit of PERVERSENESS. Of this spirit philosophy takes no account. Yet I am not more sure that my soul lives, than I am that perverseness is one of the primitive impulses of the human heart—one of the indivisible primary faculties, or sentiments, which give direction to the character of Man. Who has not, a hundred times, found himself committing a vile or a silly action, for no other reason that because he knows he should *not?* Have we not a perpetual inclination, in the teeth of our best judgment, to violate that which is *Law,* merely because we understand it to be such? This spirit of perverseness, I say, came to my final overthrow. It was this unfathomable longing of the soul *to vex itself* —to offer violence to its own nature—to do wrong for the wrong's sake only—that urged me to continue and finally to consummate the injury I had inflicted upon the unoffending brute. One morning, in cold blood, I slipped a noose about his neck and hung it to the limb of a tree;—hung

it with the tears streaming from my eyes, and with the bitterest remorse
at my heart;—hung it *because* I knew that it had loved me, and *because*
I felt it had given me no reason of offense;—hung it *because* I knew that
in so doing I was committing a sin—a deadly sin that would so jeopardize
my immortal soul as to place it—if such a thing were possible—even
beyond the reach of the infinite mercy of the Most Merciful and Most
Terrible God.

On the night of the day on which this cruel deed was done, I was
aroused from sleep by the cry of fire. The curtains of my bed were in
flames. The whole house was blazing. It was with great difficulty that my
wife, a servant, and myself, made our escape from the conflagration.
The destruction was complete. My entire worldly wealth was swallowed
up, and I resigned myself thenceforward to despair.

I am above the weakness of seeking to establish a sequence of cause
and effect, between the disaster and the atrocity. But I am detailing a
chain of facts—and wish not to leave even a possible link imperfect. On
the day succeeding the fire, I visited the ruins. The walls, with one
exception, had fallen in. This exception was found in a compartment
wall, not very thick, which stood about the middle of the house, and
against which had rested the head of my bed. The plastering had here,
in great measure, resisted the action of the fire—a fact which I attributed
to its having been recently spread. About this wall a dense crowd were
collected, and many persons seemed to be examining a particular portion
of it with very minute and eager attention. The words "strange!" "singular!" and other similar expressions, excited my curiosity. I approached
and saw, as if graven in *bas relief* upon the white surface, the figure of
a gigantic *cat*. The impression was given with an accuracy truly marvellous. There was a rope about the animal's neck.

When I first beheld this apparition—for I could scarcely regard it as
less—my wonder and my terror were extreme. But at length reflection
came to my aid. The cat, I remembered, had been hung in a garden
adjacent to the house. Upon the alarm of fire, this garden had been
immediately filled by the crowd—by some one of whom the animal must
have been cut from the tree and thrown, through an open window, into
my chamber. This had probably been done with the view of arousing me
from sleep. The falling of other walls had compressed the victim of my
cruelty into the substance of the freshly-spread plaster; the lime of which,
with the flames, and the *ammonia* from the carcass, had then accomplished the portraiture as I saw it.

Although I thus readily accounted to my reason, if not altogether to
my conscience, for the startling fact just detailed, it did not the less fail
to make a deep impression upon my fancy. For months I could not rid
myself of the phantasm of the cat; and, during this period, there came

back into my spirit a half-sentiment that seemed, but was not, remorse. I went so far as to regret the loss of the animal, and to look about me, among the vile haunts which I now habitually frequented, for another pet of the same species, and of somewhat similar appearance, with which to supply its place.

One night as I sat, half stupified, in a den of more than infamy, my attention was suddenly drawn to some black object, reposing upon the head of one of the immense hogheads of Gin, or of Rum, which constituted the chief furniture of the apartment. I had been looking steadily at the top of this hogshead for some minutes, and what now caused me surprise was the fact that I had not sooner perceived the object thereupon. I approached it, and touched it with my hand. It was a black cat —a very large one—fully as large as Pluto, and closely resembling him in every respect but one. Pluto had not a white hair upon any portion of his body; but this cat had a large, although indefinite splotch of white, covering nearly the whole region of the breast.

Upon my touching him, he immediately arose, purred loudly, rubbed against my hand, and appeared delighted with my notice. This, then, was the very creature of which I was in search. I at once offered to purchase it of the landlord; but this person made no claim to it—knew nothing of it—had never seen it before.

I continued my caresses, and, when I prepared to go home, the animal evinced a disposition to accompany me. I permitted it to do so; occasionally stooping and patting it as I proceeded. When it reached the house it domesticated itself at once, and became immediately a great favorite with my wife.

For my own part, I soon found a dislike to it arising within me. This was just the reverse of what I had anticipated; but I know not how or why it was—its evident fondness for myself rather disgusted and annoyed. By slow degrees, these feelings of disgust and annoyance rose into the bitterness of hatred. I avoided the creature; a certain sense of shame, and the remembrance of my former deed of cruelty, preventing me from physically abusing it. I did not, for some weeks, strike, or otherwise violently ill use it; but gradually—very gradually—I came to look upon it with unutterable loathing, and to flee silently from its odious presence, as from the breath of a pestilence.

What added, no doubt, to my hatred of the beast, was the discovery, on the morning after I brought it home, that, like Pluto, it also had been deprived of one of its eyes. This circumstance, however, only endeared it to my wife, who, as I have already said, possessed, in a high degree, that humanity of feeling which had once been my distinguishing trait, and the source of many of my simplest and purest pleasures.

With my aversion to this cat, however, its partiality for myself seemed to increase. It followed my footsteps with a pertinacity which it would be difficult to make the reader comprehend. Whenever I sat, it would crouch beneath my chair, or spring upon my knees, covering me with its loathsome caresses. If I arose to walk it would get between my feet and thus nearly throw me down, or, fastening its long and sharp claws in my dress, clamber, in this manner, to my breast. At such times, although I longed to destroy it with a blow, I was yet withheld from so doing, partly by a memory of my former crime, but chiefly—let me confess it at once—by absolute *dread* of the beast.

This dread was not exactly a dread of physical evil—and yet I should be at a loss how otherwise to define it. I am almost ashamed to own— yes, even in this felon's cell, I am almost ashamed to own—that the terror and horror with which the animal inspired me, had been heightened by one of the merest chimæras it would be possible to conceive. My wife had called my attention, more than once, to the character of the mark of white hair, of which I have spoken, and which constituted the sole visible difference between the strange beast and the one I had destroyed. The reader will remember that this mark, although large, had been originally very indefinite; but, by slow degrees—degrees nearly imperceptible, and which for a long time my Reason struggled to reject as fanciful—it had, at length, assumed a rigorous distinctness of outline. It was now the representation of an object that I shudder to name—and for this, above all, I loathed, and dreaded, and would have rid myself of the monster *had I dared*—it was now, I say, the image of a hideous—ghastly thing—of the GALLOWS!—oh, mournful and terrible engine of Horror and of Crime—of Agony and of Death!

And now was I indeed wretched beyond the wretchedness of mere Humanity. And *a brute beast*—whose fellow I had contemptuously destroyed—*a brute beast* to work out for *me*—for me a man, fashioned in the image of the High God—so much of insufferable wo! Alas! neither by day nor by night knew I the blessing of Rest any more! During the former the creature left me no moment alone; and, in the latter, I started, hourly, from dreams of unutterable fear, to find the hot breath of *the thing* upon my face, and its vast weight—an incarnate Night-Mare that I had no power to shake off—incumbent eternally upon my *heart!*

Beneath the pressure of torments such as these, the feeble remnant of the good within me succumbed. Evil thoughts became my sole intimates—the darkest and most evil of thoughts. The moodiness of my usual temper increased to hatred of all things and of all mankind; while, from the sudden, frequent, and ungovernable outbursts of a fury to which I now blindly abandoned myself, my uncomplaining wife, alas! was the most usual and the most patient of sufferers.

One day she accompanied me, upon some household errand, into the cellar of the old building which our poverty compelled us to inhabit. The cat followed me down the steep stairs, and, nearly throwing me headlong, exasperated me to madness. Uplifting an axe, and forgetting, in my wrath, the childish dread which had hitherto stayed my hand, I aimed a blow at the animal which, of course, would have proved instantly fatal had it descended as I wished. But this blow was arrested by the hand of my wife. Goaded, by the interference, into a rage more than demoniacal, I withdrew my arm from her grasp and buried the axe in her brain. She fell dead upon the spot, without a groan.

This hideous murder accomplished, I sat myself forthwith, and with entire deliberation, to the task of concealing the body. I knew that I could not remove it from the house, either by day or by night, without the risk of being observed by the neighbors. Many projects entered my mind. At one period I thought of cutting the corpse into minute fragments, and destroying them by fire. At another, I resolved to dig a grave for it in the floor of the cellar. Again, I deliberated about casting it in the well in the yard—about packing it in a box, as if merchandize, with the usual arrangements, and so getting a porter to take it from the house. Finally I hit upon what I considered a far better expedient than either of these. I determined to wall it up in the cellar—as the monks of the middle ages are recorded to have walled up their victims.

For a purpose such as this the cellar was well adapted. Its walls were loosely constructed, and had lately been plastered throughout with a rough plaster, which the dampness of the atmosphere had prevented from hardening. Moreover, in one of the walls was a projection, caused by a false chimney, or fireplace, that had been filled up, and made to resemble the rest of the cellar. I made no doubt that I could readily displace the bricks at this point, insert the corpse, and wall the whole up as before, so that no eye could detect anything suspicious.

And in this calculation I was not deceived. By means of a crow-bar I easily dislodged the bricks, and, having carefully deposited the body against the inner wall, I propped it in that position, while, with little trouble, I re-laid the whole structure as it orginally stood. Having procured mortar, sand, and hair, with every possible precaution, I prepared a plaster which could not be distinguished from the old, and with this I very carefully went over the new brick-work. When I had finished, I felt satisfied that all was right. The wall did not present the slightest appearance of having been disturbed. The rubbish on the floor was picked up with the minutest care. I looked around triumphantly, and said to myself—"Here at least, then, my labor has not been in vain."

My next step was to look for the beast which had been the cause of so much wretchedness; for I had, at length, firmly resolved to put it to death. Had I been able to meet with it, at the moment, there could have been no doubt of its fate; but it appeared that the crafty animal had been alarmed at the violence of my previous anger, and forebore to present itself in my present mood. It is impossible to describe, or to imagine, the deep, the blissful sense of relief which the absence of the detested creature occasioned in my bosom. It did not make its appearance during the night—and thus for one night at least, since its introduction into the house, I soundly and tranquilly slept; aye, *slept* even with the burden of murder upon my soul!

The second and the third day passed, and still my tormentor came not. Once again I breathed as a freeman. The monster, in terror, had fled the premises forever! I should behold it no more! My happiness was supreme! The guilt of my dark deed disturbed me but little. Some few inquiries had been made, but these had been readily answered. Even a search had been instituted—but of course nothing was to be discovered. I looked upon my future felicity as secured.

Upon the fourth day of the assassination, a party of the police came, very unexpectedly, into the house, and proceeded again to make rigorous investigation of the premises. Secure, however, in the inscrutability of my place of concealment, I felt no embarrassment whatever. The officers bade me accompany them in their search. They left no nook or corner unexplored. At length, for the third or fourth time, they descended into the cellar. I quivered not in a muscle. My heart beat calmly as that of one who slumbers in innocence. I walked the cellar from end to end. I folded my arms upon my bosom, and roamed easily to and fro. The police were thoroughly satisfied and prepared to depart. The glee at my heart was too strong to be restrained. I burned to say if but one word, by way of triumph, and to render doubly sure their assurance of my guiltlessness.

"Gentlemen," I said at last, as the party ascended the steps, "I delight to have allayed your suspicions. I wish you all health, and a little more courtesy. By the bye, gentlemen, this—this is a very well constructed house." [In the rabid desire to say something easily, I scarcely knew what I uttered at all.]—"I may say an *excellently* well constructed house. These walls—are you going, gentlemen—these walls are solidly put together;" and here, through the mere phrenzy of bravado, I rapped heavily, with a cane which I held in my hand, upon that very portion of the brick-work behind which stood the corpse of the wife of my bosom.

But may God shield and deliver me from the fangs of the Arch-Fiend! No sooner had the reverberation of my blows sunk into silence, than I was answered by a voice from within the tomb!—by a cry, at first muffled and broken, like the sobbing of a child, and then quickly swelling into one long, loud, and continuous scream, utterly anomalous and inhuman—a howl—a wailing shriek, half of horror and half of triumph, such as might have arisen only out of hell, conjointly from the throats of the damned in their agony and of the demons that exult in the damnation.

Of my own thoughts it is folly to speak. Swooning, I staggered to the opposite wall. For one instant the party upon the stairs remained motionless, through extremity of terror and of awe. In the next, a dozen stout arms were toiling at the wall. It fell bodily. The corpse, already greatly decayed and clotted with gore, stood erect before the eyes of the spectators. Upon its head, with red extended mouth and solitary eye of fire, sat the hideous beast whose craft had seduced me into murder, and whose informing voice had consigned me to the hangman. I had walled the monster up within the tomb!

Francis Bret Harte (1836–1902) was born in Albany, New York. He moved to California at the age of fifteen and there saw the last of the gold rush of '49. After gaining fame for his highly stylized stories in the Overland Monthly—*of which he was the first editor*—Harte *left the West and became the American consul in Crefeld, Germany, and later in Glasgow. For further reading:* The Luck of Roaring Camp and Other Sketches *(1870);* Tales of the Argonauts *(1875).*

tennessee's partner

bret harte

I do not think that we ever knew his real name. Our ignorance of it certainly never gave us any social inconvenience, for at Sandy Bar in 1854 most men were christened anew. Sometimes these appellatives were derived from some distinctiveness of dress, as in the case of "Dungaree Jack"; or from some peculiarity of habit, as shown in "Saleratus Bill," so called from an undue proportion of that chemical in his daily bread; or from some unlucky slip, as exhibited in "The Iron Pirate," a mild, inoffensive man, who earned that baleful title by his unfortunate mispronunciation of the term "iron pyrites." Perhaps this may have been the beginning of a rude heraldry; but I am constrained to think that it was because a man's real name in that day rested solely upon his own unsupported statement. "Call yourself Clifford, do you?" said Boston, addressing a timid new-comer with infinite scorn; "hell is full of such Cliffords!" He then introduced the unfortunate man, whose name happened to be really Clifford, as "Jay-bird Charley,"—an unhallowed inspiration of the moment, that clung to him ever after.

But to return to Tennessee's Partner, whom we never knew by any other than this relative title; that he had ever existed as a separate and distinct individuality we only learned later. It seems that in 1853 he left Poker Flat to go to San Francisco, ostensibly to procure a wife. He never got any farther than Stockton. At that place he was attracted by a young person who waited upon the table at the hotel where he took his meals. One morning he said something to her which caused her to smile not unkindly, to somewhat coquettishly break a plate of toast over his upturned, serious, simple face, and to retreat to the kitchen. He followed her, and emerged a few moments later, covered with more toast and victory. That day week they were married by a Justice of the Peace, and returned to Poker Flat. I am aware that something more might be made of this episode, but I prefer to tell it as it was current at Sandy Bar,—in the gulches and bar-rooms,—where all sentiment was modified by a strong sense of humor.

Of their married felicity but little is known, perhaps for the reason that Tennessee, then living with his partner, one day took occasion to say something to the bride on his own account, at which, it is said, she smiled not unkindly and chastely retreated,—this time as far as Marysville, where Tennessee followed her, and where they went to housekeeping without the aid of a Justice of the Peace. Tennessee's Partner took the loss of his wife simply and seriously, as was his fashion. But to everybody's surprise, when Tennessee one day returned from Marysville, without his partner's wife,—she having smiled and retreated with somebody else,—Tennessee's Partner was the first man to shake his hand and greet him with affection. The boys who had gathered in the cañon to see the shooting were naturally indignant. Their indignation might have found vent in sarcasm but for a certain look in Tennessee's Partner's eye that indicated a lack of humorous appreciation. In fact, he was a grave man, with a steady application to practical detail which was unpleasant in a difficulty.

Meanwhile a popular feeling against Tennessee had grown up on the Bar. He was known to be a gambler; he was suspected to be a thief. In these suspicions Tennessee's Partner was equally compromised; his continued intimacy with Tennessee after the affair above quoted could only be accounted for on the hypothesis of a copartnership of crime. At last Tennessee's guilt became flagrant. One day he overtook a stranger on his way to Red Dog. The stranger afterward related that Tennessee beguiled the time with interesting anecdote and reminiscence, but illogically concluded the interview in the following words: "And now, young man, I'll trouble you for your knife, your pistols, and your money. You see your weppings might get you into trouble at Red Dog, and your money's a temptation to the evilly disposed. I think you said your address was San Francisco. I shall endeavor to call." It may be stated here that Tennessee had a fine flow of humor, which no business preoccupation could wholly subdue.

This exploit was his last. Red Dog and Sandy Bar made common cause against the highwayman. Tennessee was hunted in very much the same fashion as his prototype, the grizzly. As the toils closed around him, he made a desperate dash through the Bar, emptying his revolver at the crowd before the Arcade Saloon, and so on up Grizzly Cañon; but at its farther extremity he was stopped by a small man on a gray horse. The men looked at each other a moment in silence. Both were fearless, both self-possessed and independent; and both types of a civilization that in the seventeenth century would have been called heroic, but, in the nineteenth, simply "reckless." "What have you got there?— I call," said Tennessee, quietly. "Two bowers and an ace," said the stranger, as quietly, showing two revolvers and a bowie-knife. "That takes me," returned Tennessee; and with this gamblers' epigram, he threw away his useless pistol, and rode back with his captor.

It was a warm night. The cool breeze which usually sprang up with the going down of the sun behind the *chaparrel*-crested mountain was that evening withheld from Sandy Bar. The little cañon was stifling with heated resinous odors, and the decaying drift-wood on the Bar sent forth faint, sickening exhalations. The feverishness of day, and its fierce passions, still filled the camp. Lights moved restlessly along the bank of the river, striking no answering reflection from its tawny current. Against the blackness of the pines the windows of the old loft above the express-office stood out staringly bright; and through their curtainless panes the loungers below could see the forms of those who were even then deciding the fate of Tennessee. And above all this, etched on the dark firmament, rose the Sierra, remote and passionless, crowned with remoter passionless stars.

The trial of Tennessee was conducted as fairly as was consistent with a judge and jury who felt themselves to some extent obliged to justify, in their verdict, the previous irregularities of arrest and indictment. The law of Sandy Bar was implacable, but not vengeful. The excitement and personal feeling of the chase were over; with Tennessee safe in their hands they were ready to listen patiently to any defence, which they were already satisfied was insufficient. There being no doubt in their own minds, they were willing to give the prisoner the benefit of any that might exist. Secure in the hypothesis that he ought to be hanged, on general principles, they indulged him with more latitude of defence than his reckless hardihood seemed to ask. The Judge appeared to be more anxious than the prisoner, who, otherwise unconcerned, evidently took a grim pleasure in the responsibility he had created. "I don't take any hand in this yer game," had been his invariable, but good-humored reply to all questions. The Judge—who was also his captor—for a moment vaguely regretted that he had not shot him "on sight," that morning, but presently dismissed this human weakness as unworthy of the judicial mind. Nevertheless, when there was a tap at the door, and it was said that Tennessee's Partner was there on behalf of the prisoner, he was admitted at once without question. Perhaps the younger members of the jury, to whom the proceedings were becoming irksomely thoughtful, hailed him as a relief.

For he was not, certainly, an imposing figure. Short and stout, with a square face, sunburned into a preternatural redness, clad in a loose duck "jumper," and trousers streaked and splashed with red soil, his aspect under any circumstances would have been quaint, and was now even ridiculous. As he stooped to deposit at his feet a heavy carpet-bag he was carrying, it became obvious, from partially developed legends and inscriptions, that the material with which his trousers had been patched had been originally intended for a less ambitious covering. Yet he advanced with great gravity, and after having shaken the hand of each person in the room with labored cordiality, he wiped his serious, perplexed face on a red bandanna handkerchief, a shade lighter than his complexion, laid his powerful hand upon the table to steady himself, and thus addressed the Judge:—

"I was passin' by," he began, by way of apology, "and I thought I'd just step in and see how things was gittin' on with Tennessee thar,—my pardner. It's a hot night. I disremember any sich weather before on the Bar."

He paused a moment, but nobody volunteering any other meteorological recollection, he again had recourse to his pocket-handkerchief, and for some moments mopped his face diligently.

"Have you anything to say in behalf of the prisoner?" said the Judge, finally.

"Thet's it," said Tennessee's Partner, in a tone of relief. "I come yar as Tennessee's pardner,—knowing him nigh on four year, off and on, wet and dry, in luck and out o' luck. His ways ain't allers my ways, but thar ain't any p'ints in that young man, thar ain't any liveliness as he's been up to, as I don't know. And you sez to me, sez you,—confidential-like, and between man and man,—sez you, 'Do you know anything in his behalf?' and I sez to you, sez I,—confidential-like, as between man and man,—'What should a man know of his pardner?'"

"Is this all you have to say?" asked the Judge, impatiently, feeling, perhaps, that a dangerous sympathy of humor was beginning to humanize the Court.

"That's so," continued Tennessee's Partner. "It ain't for me to say anything agin' him. And now, what's the case? Here's Tennessee wants money, wants it bad, and doesn't like to ask it of his old pardner. Well, what does Tennessee do? He lays for a stranger, and he fetches that stranger. And you lays for *him,* and you fetches *him;* and the honors is easy. And I put it to you, bein' a far-minded man, and to you, gentlemen, all, as far-minded men, ef this is n't so."

"Prisoner," said the Judge, interrupting, "have you any questions to ask this man?"

"No! no!" continued Tennessee's Partner, hastily. "I play this yer hand alone. To come down to the bed-rock, it's just this: Tennessee, thar, has played it pretty rough and expensive-like on a stranger, and on this yer camp. And now, what's the fair thing? Some would say more; some would say less. Here's seventeen hundred dollars in coarse gold and a watch,—it's about all my pile,—and call it square!" And before a hand could be raised to prevent him, he had emptied the contents of the carpet-bag upon the table.

For a moment his life was in jeopardy. One or two men sprang to their feet, several hands groped for hidden weapons, and a suggestion to "throw him from the window" was only overridden by a gesture from the Judge. Tennessee laughed. And apparently oblivious of the excitement, Tennessee's Partner improved the opportunity to mop his face again with his handkerchief.

When order was restored, and the man was made to understand, by the use of forcible figures and rhetoric, that Tennessee's offence could not be condoned by money, his face took a more serious and sanguinary hue, and those who were nearest to him noticed that his rough hand trembled slightly on the table. He hesitated a moment as he slowly returned the gold to the carpet-bag, as if he had not yet entirely caught the elevated sense of justice which swayed the tribunal, and was perplexed with the belief that he had not offered enough. Then he turned to the Judge, and saying, "This yer is a lone hand, played alone, and without my pardner," he bowed to the jury and was about to withdraw, when the Judge called him back. "If you have anything to say to Tennessee, you had better say it now." For the first time that evening the eyes of the prisoner and his strange advocate met. Tennessee smiled, showed his white teeth, and, saying, "Euchred, old man!" held out his hand. Tennessee's Partner took it in his own, and saying, "I just dropped in as I was passin' to see how things was gettin' on," let the hand passively fall, and adding that "it was a warm night," again mopped his face with his handkerchief, and without another word withdrew.

The two men never again met each other alive. For the unparalleled insult of a bribe offered to Judge Lynch—who, whether bigoted, weak, or narrow, was at least incorruptible—firmly fixed in the mind of that mythical personage any wavering determination of Tennessee's fate; and at the break of day he was marched, closely guarded, to meet it at the top of Marley's Hill.

How he met it, how cool he was, how he refused to say anything, how perfect were the arrangements of the committee, were all duly reported, with the addition of a warning moral and example to all future evil-doers, in the Red Dog Clarion, by its editor, who was present, and to whose vigorous English I cheerfully refer the reader. But the beauty of that midsummer morning, the blessed amity of earth and air and sky, the awakened life of the free woods and hills, the joyous renewal and promise of Nature, and above all, the infinite Serenity that thrilled through each, was not reported, as not being a part of the social lesson. And yet, when the weak and foolish deed was done, and a life, with its possibilities and responsibilities, had passed out of the misshapen thing that dangled between earth and sky, the birds sang, the flowers bloomed, the sun shone, as cheerily as before; and possibly the Red Dog Clarion was right.

Tennessee's Partner was not in the group that surrounded the ominous tree. But as they turned to disperse attention was drawn to the singular appearance of a motionless donkey-cart halted at the side of the road. As they approached, they at once recognized the venerable "Jenny" and the two-wheeled cart as the property of Tennessee's Partner,—used by him in carrying dirt from his claim; and a few paces distant the owner of the equipage himself, sitting under a buckeye-tree, wiping the perspiration from his glowing face. In answer to an inquiry, he said he had come for the body of the "diseased," "if it was all the same to the committee." He did n't wish to "hurry anything"; he could "wait." He was not working that day; and when the gentlemen were done with the "diseased," he would take him. "Ef thar is any present," he added, in his simple, serious way, "as would care to jine in the fun'l, they kin come." Perhaps it was from a sense of humor, which I have already intimated was a feature of Sandy Bar,—perhaps it was from something even better than that; but two thirds of the loungers accepted the invitation at once.

It was noon when the body of Tennessee was delivered into the hands of his partner. As the cart drew up to the fatal tree, we noticed that it contained a rough, oblong box,—apparently made from a section of sluicing,—and half filled with bark and the tassels of pine. The cart was further decorated with slips of willow, and made fragrant with buckeye-blossoms. When the body was deposited in the box, Tennessee's Partner drew over it a piece of tarred canvas, and gravely mounting the narrow seat in front, with his feet upon the shafts, urged the little donkey forward. The equipage moved slowly on, at that decorous pace which was habitual with "Jenny" even under less solemn circumstances. The men—half curiously, half jestingly, but all good-humoredly—strolled along beside the cart; some in advance, some a little in the rear of the homely catafalque. But, whether from the narrowing of the road or some present sense of decorum, as the cart passed on, the company fell to the rear in couples, keeping step, and otherwise assuming the external show of a formal procession. Jack Folinsbee, who had at the outset played a funeral march in dumb show upon an imaginary trombone, desisted, from a lack of sympathy and appreciation,—not having, perhaps, your true humorist's capacity to be content with the enjoyment of his own fun.

The way led through Grizzly Cañon,—by this time clothed in funereal drapery and shadows. The redwoods, burying their moccasined feet in the red soil, stood in Indian-file along the track, trailing an uncouth benediction from their bending boughs upon the passing bier. A hare, surprised into helpless inactivity, sat upright and pulsating in the ferns by the roadside, as the *cortége* went by. Squirrels hastened to gain a secure outlook from higher boughs; and the blue-jays, spreading their wings, fluttered before them like outriders, until the outskirts of Sandy Bar were reached, and the solitary cabin of Tennessee's Partner.

Viewed under more favorable circumstances, it would not have been a cheerful place. The unpicturesque site, the rude and unlovely outlines, the unsavory details, which distinguish the nest-building of the California miner, were all here, with the dreariness of decay superadded. A few paces from the cabin there was a rough enclosure, which, in the brief days of Tennessee's Partner's matrimonial felicity, had been used as a garden, but was now overgrown with fern. As we approached it we were surprised to find that what we had taken for a recent attempt at cultivation was the broken soil about an open grave.

The cart was halted before the enclosure; and rejecting the offers of assistance with the same air of simple self-reliance he had displayed throughout, Tennessee's Partner lifted the rough coffin on his back, and deposited it, unaided, within the shallow grave. He then nailed down the board which served as a lid; and mounting the little mound of earth beside it, took off his hat, and slowly mopped his face with his handkerchief. This the crowd felt was a preliminary to speech; and they disposed themselves variously on stumps and boulders, and sat expectant.

"When a man," began Tennessee's Partner, slowly, "has been running free all day, what's the natural thing for him to do? Why, to come home. And if he ain't in a condition to go home, what can his best friend do? Why, bring him home! And here's Tennessee has been running free, and we brings him home from his wandering." He paused, and picked up a fragment of quartz, rubbed it thoughtfully on his sleeve, and went on: "It ain't the first time that I've packed him on my back, as you see'd me now. It ain't the first time that I brought him to this yer cabin when he could n't help himself; it ain't the first time that I and 'Jinny' have waited for him on yon hill, and picked him up and so fetched him home, when he could n't speak, and did n't know me. And now that it's the last time, why—" he paused, and rubbed the quartz gently on his sleeve—"you see it's sort of rough on his pardner. And now, gentlemen," he added, abruptly, picking up his long-handled shovel, "the fun'l 's over; and my thanks, and Tennessee's thanks, to you for your trouble."

Resisting any proffers of assistance, he began to fill in the grave, turning his back upon the crowd, that after a few moments' hesitation gradually withdrew. As they crossed the little ridge that hid Sandy Bar from view, some, looking back, thought they could see Tennessee's Partner, his work done, sitting upon the grave, his shovel between his knees, and his face buried in his red bandanna handkerchief. But it was argued by others that you could n't tell his face from his handkerchief at that distance; and this point remained undecided.

In the reaction that followed the feverish excitement of that day, Tennessee's Partner was not forgotten. A secret investigation had cleared him of any complicity in Tennessee's guilt, and left only a suspicion of his general sanity. Sandy Bar made a point of calling on him, and proffering various uncouth, but well-meant kindnesses. But from that day his rude health and great strength seemed visibly to decline; and when the rainy season fairly set in, and the tiny grass-blades were beginning to peep from the rocky mound above Tennessee's grave, he took to his bed.

One night, when the pines beside the cabin were swaying in the storm, and trailing their slender fingers over the roof, and the roar and rush of the swollen river were heard below, Tennessee's Partner lifted his head from the pillow, saying, "It is time to go for Tennessee; I must put 'Jinny' in the cart"; and would have risen from his bed but for the restraint of his attendant. Struggling, he still pursued his singular fancy: "There, now, steady, 'Jinny,'—steady, old girl. How dark it is! Look out for the ruts,—and look out for him, too, old gal. Sometimes, you know, when he's blind drunk, he drops down right in the trail. Keep on straight up to the pine on the top of the hill. Thar—I told you so!—thar he is,— coming this way, too,—all by himself, sober, and his face a-shining. Tennessee! Pardner!"

And so they met.

a psychological shipwreck

ambrose bierce

Ambrose Bierce (1842–1914) was born in Ohio and served as a staff officer in the Civil War. Later, in San Francisco, he became an editor, a journalist, and a writer of polemics and short fiction. His work deals with the macabre, the supernatural, the malevolent; his heroes are victims— often lonely men, the doomed. Bierce went to Mexico and was probably shot by one or another revolutionary faction. For further reading: Tales of Soldiers and Civilians *(1891); also published as* In the Midst of Life *(1898).*

In the summer of 1874 I was in Liverpool, whither I had gone on business for the mercantile house of Bronson & Jarrett, New York. I am William Jarrett; my partner was Zenas Bronson. The firm failed last year, and unable to endure the fall from affluence to poverty he died.

Having finished my business, and feeling the lassitude and exhaustion incident to its dispatch, I felt that a protracted sea voyage would be both agreeable and beneficial, so instead of embarking for my return on one of the many fine passenger steamers I booked for New York on the sailing vessel *Morrow*, upon which I had shipped a large and valuable invoice of the goods I had bought. The *Morrow* was an English ship with, of course, but little accommodation for passengers, of whom there were only myself, a young woman and her servant, who was a middle-aged negress. I thought it singular that a traveling English girl should be so attended, but she afterward explained to me that the woman had been left with her family by a man and his wife from South Carolina, both of whom had died on the same day at the house of the young lady's father in Devonshire—a circumstance in itself sufficiently uncommon to remain rather distinctly in my memory, even had it not afterward transpired in conversation with the young lady that the name of the man was William Jarrett, the same as my own. I knew that a branch of my family had settled in South Carolina, but of them and their history I was ignorant.

The *Morrow* sailed from the mouth of the Mersey on the 15th of June and for several weeks we had fair breezes and unclouded skies. The skipper, an admirable seaman but nothing more, favored us with very little of his society, except at his table; and the young woman, Miss Janette Harford, and I became very well acquainted. We were, in truth, nearly always together, and being of an introspective turn of mind I often endeavored to analyze and define the novel feeling with which she inspired me—a secret, subtle, but powerful attraction which constantly impelled me to seek her; but the attempt was hopeless. I could only be sure that at least it was not love. Having assured myself of this and being certain that she was quite as whole-hearted, I ventured one evening (I remember it was on the 3d of July) as we sat on deck to ask her, laughingly, if she could assist me to resolve my psychological doubt.

For a moment she was silent, with averted face, and I began to fear I had been extremely rude and indelicate; then she fixed her eyes gravely on my own. In an instant my mind was dominated by as strange a fancy as ever entered human consciousness. It seemed as if she were looking at me, not *with*, but *through*, those eyes—from an immeasurable distance behind them—and that a number of other persons, men, women and children, upon whose faces I caught strangely familiar evanescent expressions, clustered about her, struggling with gentle eagerness to look at me through the same orbs. Ship, ocean, sky—all had vanished. I was conscious of nothing but the figures in this extraordinary and fantastic scene. Then all at once darkness fell upon me, and anon from out of it, as to one who grows accustomed by degrees to a dimmer light, my former surroundings of deck and mast and cordage slowly resolved themselves. Miss Harford had closed her eyes and was leaning back in her chair, apparently asleep, the book she had been reading open in her lap. Impelled by surely I cannot say what motive, I glanced at the top of the page; it was a copy of that rare and curious work, "Denneker's Meditations," and the lady's index finger rested on this passage:

"To sundry it is given to be drawn away, and to be apart from the body for a season; for, as concerning rills which would flow across each other the weaker is borne along by the stronger, so there be certain of kin whose paths intersecting, their souls do bear company, the while their bodies go fore-appointed ways, unknowing."

Miss Harford arose, shuddering; the sun had sunk below the horizon, but it was not cold. There was not a breath of wind; there were no clouds in the sky, yet not a star was visible. A hurried tramping sounded on the deck; the captain, summoned from below, joined the first officer, who stood looking at the barometer. "Good God!" I heard him exclaim.

An hour later the form of Janette Harford, invisible in the darkness and spray, was torn from my grasp by the cruel vortex of the sinking ship, and I fainted in the cordage of the floating mast to which I had lashed myself.

It was by lamplight that I awoke. I lay in a berth amid the familiar surroundings of the stateroom of a steamer. On a couch opposite sat a man, half undressed for bed, reading a book. I recognized the face of my friend Gordon Doyle, whom I had met in Liverpool on the day of my embarkation, when he was himself about to sail on the steamer *City of Prague*, on which he had urged me to accompany him.

After some moments I now spoke his name. He simply said, "Well," and turned a leaf in his book without removing his eyes from the page.

"Doyle," I repeated, "did they save *her?*"

He now deigned to look at me and smiled as if amused. He evidently thought me but half awake.

"Her? Whom do you mean?"

"Janette Harford."

His amusement turned to amazement; he stared at me fixedly, saying nothing.

"You will tell me after a while," I continued; "I suppose you will tell me after a while."

A moment later I asked: "What ship is this?"

Doyle stared again. "The steamer *City of Prague*, bound from Liverpool to New York, three weeks out with a broken shaft. Principal passenger, Mr. Gordon Doyle; ditto lunatic, Mr. William Jarrett. These two distinguished travelers embarked together, but they are about to part, it being the resolute intention of the former to pitch the latter overboard."

I sat bolt upright. "Do you mean to say that I have been for three weeks a passenger on this steamer?"

"Yes, pretty nearly; this is the 3d of July."

"Have I been ill?"

"Right as a trivet all the time, and punctual at your meals."

"My God! Doyle, there is some mystery here; do have the goodness to be serious. Was I not rescued from the wreck of the ship *Morrow?*"

Doyle changed color, and approaching me, laid his fingers on my wrist. A moment later, "What do you know of Janette Harford?" he asked very calmly.

"First tell me what *you* know of her?"

Mr. Doyle gazed at me for some moments as if thinking what to do, then seating himself again on the couch, said:

"Why should I not? I am engaged to marry Janette Harford, whom I met a year ago in London. Her family, one of the wealthiest in Devonshire, cut up rough about it, and we eloped—are eloping rather, for on the day that you and I walked to the landing stage to go aboard this steamer she and her faithful servant, a negress, passed us, driving to the ship *Morrow*. She would not consent to go in the same vessel with me, and it had been deemed best that she take a sailing vessel in order to avoid observation and lessen the risk of detection. I am now alarmed lest this cursed breaking of our machinery may detain us so long that the *Morrow* will get to New York before us, and the poor girl will not know where to go."

I lay still in my berth—so still I hardly breathed. But the subject was evidently not displeasing to Doyle, and after a short pause he resumed:

"By the way, she is only an adopted daughter of the Harfords. Her mother was killed at their place by being thrown from a horse while hunting, and her father, mad with grief, made away with himself the same day. No one ever claimed the child, and after a reasonable time they adopted her. She has grown up in the belief that she is their daughter."

"Doyle, what book are you reading?"

"Oh, it's called 'Denneker's Meditations.' It's a rum lot, Janette gave it to me; she happened to have two copies. Want to see it?"

He tossed me the volume, which opened as it fell. On one of the exposed pages was a marked passage:

"To sundry it is given to be drawn away, and to be apart from the body for a season; for, as concerning rills which would flow across each other the weaker is borne along by the stronger, so there be certain of kin whose paths intersecting, their souls do bear company, the while their bodies go fore-appointed ways, unknowing."

"She had—she has—a singular taste in reading," I managed to say, mastering my agitation.

"Yes. And now perhaps you will have the kindness to explain how you knew her name and that of the ship she sailed in."

"You talked of her in your sleep," I said.

A week later we were towed into the port of New York. But the *Morrow* was never heard from.

jim baker's blue-jay yarn

mark twain

Samuel Langhorne Clemens (1835–1910) grew up in Hannibal, Missouri. He became a steamboat pilot, but left for the West when river traffic was disrupted by the Civil War. He achieved fame as a journalist, lecturer, and humorist. His novels are landmarks in American literature; his sketches and stories frequently exploit folk materials—the tall story, the practical joke. For further reading: A Tramp Abroad *(1880);* The Celebrated Jumping Frog of Calaveras County *(1867).*

Animals talk to each other, of course. There can be no question about that; but I suppose there are very few people who can understand them. I never knew but one man who could. I knew he could, however, because he told me so himself. He was a middle-aged, simple-hearted miner who had lived in a lonely corner of California, among the woods and mountains, a good many years, and had studied the ways of his only neighbors, the beasts and the birds, until he believed he could accurately translate any remark which they made. This was Jim Baker. According to Jim Baker, some animals have only a limited education, and use only very simple words, and scarcely ever a comparison or a flowery figure; whereas, certain other animals have a large vocabulary, a fine command of language and a ready and fluent delivery; consequently these latter talk a great deal; they like it; they are conscious of their talent, and they enjoy "showing off." Baker said, that after long and careful observation, he had come to the conclusion that the blue-jays were the best talkers he had found among birds and beasts. Said he:—

"There's more *to* a blue-jay than any other creature. He has got more moods, and more different kinds of feelings than other creature; and mind you, whatever a blue-jay feels, he can put into language. And no mere common-place language, either, but rattling, out-and-out book talk—and bristling with metaphor, too—just bristling! And as for command of language—why *you* never see a blue-jay get stuck for a word. No man ever did. They just boil out of him! And another thing: I've noticed a good deal, and there's no bird, or cow, or anything that uses as good grammar as a blue-jay. You may say a cat uses good grammar. Well, a cat does—but you let a cat get excited, once; you let a cat get to pulling fur with another cat on a shed, nights, and you'll hear grammar that will give you the lockjaw. Ignorant people think it's the *noise* which fighting cats make that is so aggravating, but it ain't so; it's the sickening grammar they use. Now I've never heard a jay use bad grammar but very seldom; and when they do, they are as ashamed as a human; they shut right down and leave.

"You may call a jay a bird. Well, so he is, in a measure—because he's got feathers on him, and don't belong to no church, perhaps; but otherwise he is just as much a human as you be. And I'll tell you for why. A jay's gifts, and instincts, and feelings, and interests, cover the whole ground. A jay hasn't got any more principle than a Congressman. A jay will lie, a jay will steal, a jay will deceive, a jay will betray; and four times out of five, a jay will go back on his solemnest promise. The sacredness of an obligation is a thing which you can't cram into no blue-jay's head. Now on top of all this, there's another thing: a jay can out-swear any gentleman in the mines. You think a cat can swear. Well, a cat can; but you give a blue-jay a subject that calls for his reserve-powers, and where is your cat? Don't talk to *me*—I know too much about this thing. And there's yet another thing: in the one little particular of scolding—just good, clean, out-and-out scolding—a blue-jay can lay over anything, human or divine. Yes, sir, a jay is everything that a man is. A jay can cry, a jay can laugh, a jay can feel shame, a jay can reason and plan and discuss, a jay likes gossip and scandal, a jay has got a sense of humor, a jay knows when he is an ass just as well as you do—maybe better. If a jay ain't human, he better take in his sign, that's all. Now I'm going to tell you a perfectly true fact about some blue-jays."

"When I first begun to understand jay language correctly, there was a little incident happened here. Seven years ago, the last man in this region but me, moved away. There stands his house,—been empty ever since; a log house, with a plank roof—just one big room, and no more; no ceiling—nothing between the rafters and the floor. Well, one Sunday morning I was sitting out here in front of my cabin, with my cat, taking the sun, and looking at the blue hills, and listening to the leaves rustling; so lonely in the trees, and thinking of the home away yonder in the States, that I hadn't heard from in thirteen years, when a blue jay lit on that house, with an acorn in his mouth, and says, 'Hello, I reckon I've struck something.' When he spoke, the acorn dropped out of his mouth and rolled down the roof, of course, but he didn't care; his mind was all on the thing he had struck. It was a knot-hole in the roof. He cocked his head to one side, shut one eye and put the other one to the hole, like a 'possum looking down a jug; then he glanced up with his bright eyes, gave a wink or two with his wings—which signifies gratification, you understand,—and says, 'It looks like a hole, it's located like a hole,—blamed if I don't believe it *is* a hole!'

"Then he cocked his head down and took another look; he glances up perfectly joyful, this time; winks his wings and his tail both, and says, 'O, no, this ain't no fat thing, I reckon! If I ain't in luck!—why it's a perfectly elegant hole!' So he flew down and got that acorn, and fetched it up and dropped it in, and was just tilting his head back, with the heavenliest smile on his face, when all of a sudden he was paralyzed into a listening attitude and that smile faded gradually out of his countenance like breath off'n a razor, and the queerest look of surprise took its place. Then he says, 'Why I didn't hear it fall!' He cocked his eye at the hole again, and took a long look; raised up and shook his head; stepped around to the other side of the hole and took another look from that side; shook his head again. He studied a while, then he just went into the *de*tails—walked round and round the hole and spied into it from every point of the compass. No use. Now he took a thinking attitude on the comb of the roof and scratched the back of his head with his right foot a minute, and finally says, 'Well, it's too many for *me*, that's certain; must be a mighty long hole; however, I ain't got no time to fool around here, I got to 'tend to business; I reckon it's all right—chance it, anyway.'

"So he flew off and fetched another acorn and dropped it in, and tried to flirt his eye to the hole quick enough to see what become of it, but he was too late. He held his eye there as much as a minute; then he raised up and sighed, and says, 'Consound it, I don't seem to understand this thing, no way; however, I'll tackle her again.' He fetched another acorn, and done his level best to see what become of it, but he couldn't. He says, 'Well, I never struck no such a hole as this, before; I'm of the opinion it's a totally new kind of a hole.' Then he begun to get mad. He held in for a spell, walking up and down the comb of the roof and shaking his head and muttering to himself; but his feelings got the upper hand of him, presently, and he broke loose and cussed himself black in the face. I never see a bird take on so about a little thing. When he got through he walks to the hole and looks in again for half a minute; then he says, 'Well, you're a long hole, and a deep hole, and a mighty singular hole altogether—but I've started in to fill you, and I'm d—d if I *don't* fill you, if it takes a hundred years!'

"And with that, away he went. You never see a bird work so since you was born. He laid into his work like a nigger, and the way he hove acorns into that hole for about two hours and a half was one of the most exciting and astonishing spectacles I ever struck. He never stopped to take a look any more—he just hove 'em in and went for more. Well at last he could hardly flop his wings, he was so tuckered out. He comes a-drooping down, once more, sweating like an ice-pitcher, drops his acorn in and says, '*Now* I guess I've got the bulge on you by this time!' So he bent down for a look. If you'll believe me, when his head come up again he was just pale with rage. He says, 'I've shoveled acorns enough in there to keep the family thirty years, and if I can see a sign of one of 'em I wish I may land in a museum with a belly full of sawdust in two minutes!'

"He just had strength enough to crawl up on to the comb and lean his back agin the chimbly, and then he collected his impressions and begun to free his mind. I see in a second that what I had mistook for profanity in the mines was only just the rudiments, as you may say.

"Another jay was going by, and heard him doing his devotions, and stops to inquire what was up. The sufferer told him the whole circumstance, and says, 'Now yonder's the hole, and if you don't believe me, go and look for yourself.' So this fellow went and looked, and comes back and says, 'How many did you say you put in there?' 'Not any less than two tons,' says the sufferer. The other jay went and looked again. He couldn't seem to make it out, so he raised a yell, and three more jays come. They all examined the hole, they all made the sufferer tell it over again, then they all discussed it, and got off as many leather-headed opinions about it as an average crowd of humans could have done.

"They called in more jays; then more and more, till pretty soon this whole region 'peared to have a blue flush about it. There must have been five thousand of them; and such another jawing and disputing and ripping and cussing, you never heard. Every jay in the whole lot put his eye to the hole and delivered a more chuckle-headed opinion about the mystery than the jay that went there before him. They examined the house all over, too. The door was standing half open, and at last one old jay happened to go and light on it and look in. Of course that knocked the mystery galley-west in a second. There lay the acorns, scattered all over the floor. He flopped his wings and raised a whoop. 'Come here!' he says, 'Come here, everybody; hang'd if this fool hasn't been trying to fill up a house with acorns!' They all came a-swooping down like a blue cloud, and as each fellow lit on the door and took a glance, the whole absurdity of the contract that that first jay had tackled hit him home and he fell over backwards suffocating with laughter, and the next jay took his place and done the same.

"Well, sir, they roosted around here on the house-top and the trees for an hour, and guffawed over that thing like human beings. It ain't any use to tell me a blue-jay hasn't got a sense of humor, because I know better. And memory, too. They brought jays here from all over the United States to look down that hole, every summer for three years. Other birds too. And they could all see the point, except an owl that come from Nova Scotia to visit the Yo Semite, and he took this thing in on his way back. He said the couldn't see anything funny in it. But then he was a good deal disappointed about Yo Semite, too."

the bride comes to yellow sky

stephen crane

Stephen Crane (1871–1900) was born in New Jersey. After leaving college he became a reporter and a war correspondent. In addition to reportage, he began to write poetry, novels, and short fiction. In general his work exploits realistic detail selected for symbolic values. His literary method has been called "impressionistic," but this scarcely does justice to the intensity of his best work. For further reading: The Monster and Other Stories (1899).

I

The great Pullman was whirling onward with such dignity of motion that a glance from the window seemed simply to prove that the plains of Texas were pouring eastward. Vast flats of green grass, dull-hued spaces of mesquit and cactus, little groups of frame houses, woods of light and tender trees, all were sweeping into the east, sweeping over the horizon, a precipice.

A newly married pair had boarded this coach at San Antonio. The man's face was reddened from many days in the wind and sun, and a direct result of his new black clothes was that his brick-colored hands were constantly performing in a most conscious fashion. From time to time he looked down respectfully at his attire. He sat with a hand on each knee, like a man waiting in a barber's shop. The glances he devoted to other passengers were furtive and shy.

The bride was not pretty, nor was she very young. She wore a dress of blue cashmere, with small reservations of velvet here and there, and with steel buttons abounding. She continually twisted her head to regard her puff sleeves, very stiff, straight, and high. They embarrassed her. It was quite apparent that she had cooked, and that she expected to cook, dutifully. The blushes caused by the careless scrutiny of some passengers as she had entered the car were strange to see upon this plain, under-class countenance, which was drawn in placid, almost emotionless lines.

They were evidently very happy. "Ever been in a parlor-car before?" he asked, smiling with delight.

"No," she answered; "I never was. It's fine, ain't it?"

"Great! And then after a while we'll go forward to the diner, and get a big lay-out. Finest meal in the world. Charge a dollar."

"Oh, do they?" cried the bride. "Charge a dollar? Why, that's too much—for us—ain't it, Jack?"

"Not this trip, anyhow," he answered bravely. "We're going to go the whole thing."

Later he explained to her about the trains. "You see, it's a thousand miles from one end of Texas to the other; and this train runs right across it, and never stops but four times." He had the pride of an owner. He pointed out to her the dazzling fittings of the coach; and in truth her eyes opened wider as she contemplated the sea-green figured velvet, the shining brass, silver, and glass, the wood that gleamed as darkly brilliant as the surface of a pool of oil. At one end a bronze figure sturdily held a support for a separated chamber, and at convenient places on the ceiling were frescos in olive and silver.

To the minds of the pair, their surroundings reflected the glory of their marriage that morning in San Antonio; this was the environment of their new estate; and the man's face in particular beamed with an elation that made him appear ridiculous to the negro porter. This individual at times surveyed them from afar with an amused and superior grin. On other occasions he bullied them with skill in ways that did not make it exactly plain to them that they were being bullied. He subtly used all the manners of the most unconquerable kind of snobbery. He oppressed them; but of this oppression they had small knowledge, and they speedily forgot that infrequently a number of travelers covered them with stares of derisive enjoyment. Historically there was supposed to be something infinitely humorous in their situation.

"We are due in Yellow Sky at 3:42," he said, looking tenderly into her eyes.

"Oh, are we?" she said, as if she had not been aware of it. To evince surprise at her husband's statement was part of her wifely amiability. She took from a pocket a little silver watch; and as she held it before her, and stared at it with a frown of attention, the new husband's face shone.

"I bought it in San Anton' from a friend of mine," he told her gleefully.

"It's seventeen minutes past twelve," she said, looking up at him with a kind of shy and clumsy coquetry. A passenger, noting this play, grew excessively sardonic, and winked at himself in one of the numerous mirrors.

At last they went to the dining-car. Two rows of negro waiters, in glowing white suits, surveyed their entrance with the interest, and also the equanimity, of men who had been forewarned. The pair fell to the lot of a waiter who happened to feel pleasure in steering them through their meal. He viewed them with the manner of a fatherly pilot, his countenance radiant with benevolence. The patronage, entwined with the ordinary deference, was not plain to them. And yet, as they returned to their coach, they showed in their faces a sense of escape.

To the left, miles down a long purple slope, was a little ribbon of mist where moved the keening Rio Grande. The train was approaching it at an angle, and the apex was Yellow Sky. Presently it was apparent that, as the distance from Yellow Sky grew shorter, the husband became commensurately restless. His brick-red hands were more insistent in their prominence. Occasionally he was even rather absent-minded and far-away when the bride leaned forward and addressed him.

As a matter of truth, Jack Potter was beginning to find the shadow of a deed weigh upon him like a leaden slab. He, the town marshal of Yellow Sky, a man known, liked, and feared in his corner, a prominent person, had gone to San Antonio to meet a girl he believed he loved, and there, after the usual prayers, had actually induced her to marry him, without consulting Yellow Sky for any part of the transaction. He was now bringing his bride before an innocent and unsuspecting community.

Of course people in Yellow Sky married as it pleased them, in accordance with a general custom; but such was Potter's thought of his duty to his friends, or of their idea of his duty, or of an unspoken form which does not control men in these matters, that he felt he was heinous. He had committed an extraordinary crime. Face to face with this girl in San Antonio, and spurred by his sharp impulse, he had gone headlong over all the social hedges. At San Antonio he was like a man hidden in the dark. A knife to sever any friendly duty, any form, was easy to his hand in that remote city. But the hour of Yellow Sky— the hour of daylight—was approaching.

He knew full well that his marriage was an important thing to his town. It could only be exceeded by the burning of the new hotel. His friends could not forgive him. Frequently he had reflected on the advisability of telling them by telegraph, but a new cowardice had been upon him. He feared to do it. And now the train was hurrying him toward a scene of amazement, glee, and reproach. He glanced out of the window at the line of haze swinging slowly in toward the train.

Yellow Sky had a kind of brass band, which played painfully, to the delight of the populace. He laughed without heart as he thought of it. If the citizens could dream of his prospective arrival with his bride, they would parade the band at the station and escort them, amid cheers and laughing congratulations, to his adobe home.

He resolved that he would use all the devices of speed and plainscraft in making the journey from the station to his house. Once within that safe citadel, he could issue some sort of a vocal bulletin, and then not go among the citizens until they had time to wear off a little of their enthusiasm.

The bride looked anxiously at him. "What's worrying you, Jack?"

He laughed again. "I'm not worrying, girl; I'm only thinking of Yellow Sky."

She flushed in comprehension.

A sense of mutual guilt invaded their minds and developed a finer tenderness. They looked at each other with eyes softly aglow. But Potter often laughed the same nervous laugh; the flush upon the bride's face seemed quite permanent.

The traitor to the feelings of Yellow Sky narrowly watched the speeding landscape. "We're nearly there," he said.

Presently the porter came and announced the proximity of Potter's home. He held a brush in his hand, and, with all his airy superiority gone, he brushed Potter's new clothes as the latter slowly turned this way and that way. Potter fumbled out a coin and gave it to the porter, as he had seen others do. It was a heavy and muscle-bound business, as that of a man shoeing his first horse.

The porter took their bag, and as the train began to slow they moved forward to the hooded platform of the car. Presently the two engines and their long string of coaches rushed into the station of Yellow Sky.

"They have to take water here," said Potter, from a constricted throat and in mournful cadence, as one announcing death. Before the train stopped his eye had swept the length of the platform, and he was glad and astonished to see there was none upon it but the station-agent, who, with a slightly hurried and anxious air, was walking toward the water-tanks. When the train had halted, the porter alighted first, and placed in position a little temporary step.

"Come on, girl," said Potter, hoarsely. As he helped her down they each laughed on a false note. He took the bag from the negro, and bade his wife cling to his arm. As they slunk rapidly away, his hang-dog glance perceived that they were unloading the two trunks, and also that the station-agent, far ahead near the baggage-car, had turned and was running toward him, making gestures. He laughed, and groaned as he laughed, when he noted the first effect of his marital bliss upon Yellow Sky. He gripped his wife's arm firmly to his side, and they fled. Behind them the porter stood, chuckling fatuously.

II

The California express on the Southern Railway was due at Yellow Sky in twenty-one minutes. There were six men at the bar of the Weary Gentleman Saloon. One was a drummer, who talked a great deal and rapidly; three were Texans, who did not care to talk at that time; and two were Mexican sheep-herders, who did not talk as a general practice in the Weary Gentleman Saloon. The barkeeper's dog lay on the board walk that crossed in front of the door. His head was on his paws, and he glanced drowsily here and there with the constant vigilance of a dog that is kicked on occasion. Across the sandy street were some vivid green grass-plots, so wonderful in appearance, amid the sands that burned near them in a blazing sun, that they caused a doubt in the mind. They exactly resembled the grass mats used to represent lawns on the stage. At the cooler end of the railway station, a man without a coat sat in a tilted chair and smoked his pipe. The fresh-cut bank of the Rio Grande circled near the town, and there could be seen beyond it a great plum-colored plain of mesquit.

Save for the busy drummer and his companions in the saloon, Yellow Sky was dozing. The new-comer leaned gracefully upon the bar, and recited many tales with the confidence of a bard who has come upon a new field.

"—and at the moment that the old man fell down-stairs with the bureau in his arms, the old woman was coming up with two scuttles of coal, and of course—"

The drummer's tale was interrupted by a young man who suddenly appeared in the open door. He cried: "Scratchy Wilson's drunk, and has turned loose with both hands." The two Mexicans at once set down their glasses and faded out of the rear entrance of the saloon.

The drummer, innocent and jocular, answered: "All right, old man. S'pose he has? Come in and have a drink, anyhow."

But the information had made such an obvious cleft in every skull in the room that the drummer was obliged to see its importance. All had become instantly solemn. "Say," said he, mystified, "what is this?" His three companions made the introductory gesture of eloquent speech; but the young man at the door forestalled them.

"It means, my friend," he answered, as he came into the saloon, "that for the next two hours this town won't be a health resort."

The barkeeper went to the door, and locked and barred it; reaching out of the window, he pulled in heavy wooden shutters, and barred them. Immediately a solemn, chapel-like gloom was upon the place. The drummer was looking from one to another.

"But say," he cried, "what is this, anyhow? You don't mean there is going to be a gun-fight?"

"Don't know whether there'll be a fight or not," answered one man, grimly; "but there'll be some shootin'—some good shootin'."

The young man who had warned them waved his hand. "Oh, there'll be a fight fast enough, if any one wants it. Anybody can get a fight out there in the street. There's a fight just waiting."

The drummer seemed to be swayed between the interest of a foreigner and a perception of personal danger.

"What did you say his name was?" he asked.

"Scratchy Wilson," they answered in chorus.

"And will he kill anybody? What are you going to do? Does this happen often? Does he rampage around like this once a week or so? Can he break in that door?"

"No; he can't break down that door," replied the barkeeper. "He's tried it three times. But when he comes you'd better lay down on the floor, stranger. He's dead sure to shoot at it, and a bullet may come through."

Thereafter the drummer kept a strict eye upon the door. The time had not yet been called for him to hug the floor, but, as a minor precaution, he sidled near to the wall. "Will he kill anybody?" he said again.

The men laughed low and scornfully at the question.

"He's out to shoot, and he's out for trouble. Don't see any good in experimentin' with him."

"But what do you do in a case like this? What do you do?"

A man responded: "Why, he and Jack Potter—"

"But," in chorus the other men interrupted, "Jack Potter's in San Anton'."

"Well, who is he? What's he got to do with it?"

"Oh, he's the town marshal. He goes out and fights Scratchy when he gets on one of these tears."

"Wow!" said the drummer, mopping his brow. "Nice job he's got."

The voices had toned away to mere whisperings. The drummer wished to ask further questions, which were born of an increasing anxiety and bewilderment; but when he attempted them, the men merely looked at him in irritation and motioned him to remain silent. A tense waiting hush was upon them. In the deep shadows of the room their eyes shone as they listened for sounds from the street. One man made three gestures at the barkeeper; and the latter, moving like a ghost, handed him a glass and a bottle. The man poured a full glass of whisky, and set down the bottle noiselessly. He gulped the whisky in a swallow, and turned again toward the door in immovable silence. The drummer saw that the barkeeper, without a sound, had taken a Winchester from beneath the bar. Later he saw this individual beckoning to him, so he tiptoed across the room.

"You better come with me back of the bar."

"No, thanks," said the drummer, perspiring; "I'd rather be where I can make a break for the back door."

Whereupon the man of bottles made a kindly but peremptory gesture. The drummer obeyed it, and, finding himself seated on a box with his head below the level of the bar, balm was laid upon his soul at sight of various zinc and copper fittings that bore a resemblance to armor-plate. The barkeeper took a seat comfortably upon an adjacent box.

"You see," he whispered, "this here Scratchy Wilson is a wonder with a gun—a perfect wonder; and when he goes on the war-trail, we hunt our holes—naturally. He's about the last one of the old gang that used to hang out along the river here. He's a terror when he's drunk. When he's sober he's all right—kind of simple—would n't hurt a fly—nicest fellow in town. But when he's drunk—whoo!"

There were periods of stillness. "I wish Jack Potter was back from San Anton'," said the barkeeper. "He shot Wilson up once,—in the leg,—and he would sail in and pull out the kinks in this thing."

Presently they heard from a distance the sound of a shot, followed by three wild yowls. It instantly removed a bond from the men in the darkened saloon. There was a shuffling of feet. They looked at each other. "Here he comes," they said.

III

A man in a maroon-colored flannel shirt, which had been purchased for purposes of decoration, and made principally by some Jewish women on the East Side of New York, rounded a corner and walked into the middle of the main street of Yellow Sky. In either hand the man held a long, heavy, blue-black revolver. Often he yelled, and these cries rang through a semblance of a deserted village, shrilly flying over the roofs in a volume that seemed to have no relation to the ordinary vocal strength of a man. It was as if the surrounding stillness formed the arch of a tomb over him. These cries of ferocious challenge rang against walls of silence. And his boots had red tops with gilded imprints, of the kind beloved in winter by little sledding boys on the hillsides of New England.

The man's face flamed in a rage begot of whisky. His eyes, rolling, and yet keen for ambush, hunted the still doorways and windows. He walked with the creeping movement of the midnight cat. As it occurred to him, he roared menacing information. The long revolvers in his hands were as easy as straws; they were moved with an electric swiftness. The little fingers of each hand played sometimes in a musician's way. Plain from the low collar of the shirt, the cords of his neck straightened and sank, straightened and sank, as passion moved him. The only sounds were his terrible invitations. The calm adobes preserved their demeanor at the passing of this small thing in the middle of the street.

There was no offer of fight—no offer of fight. The man called to the sky. There were no attractions. He bellowed and fumed and swayed his revolvers here and everywhere.

The dog of the barkeeper of the Weary Gentleman Saloon had not appreciated the advance of events. He yet lay dozing in front of his master's door. At sight of the dog, the man paused and raised his revolver humorously. At sight of the man, the dog sprang up and walked diagonally away, with a sullen head, and growling. The man yelled, and the dog broke into a gallop. As it was about to enter an alley, there was a loud noise, a whistling, and something spat the ground directly before it. The dog screamed, and, wheeling in terror, galloped headlong in a new direction. Again there was a noise, a whistling, and sand was kicked viciously before it. Fear-stricken, the dog turned and flurried like an animal in a pen. The man stood laughing, his weapons at his hips.

Ultimately the man was attracted by the closed door of the Weary Gentleman Saloon. He went to it, and, hammering with a revolver, demanded drink.

The door remaining imperturbable, he picked a bit of paper from the walk, and nailed it to the framework with a knife. He then turned his back contemptuously upon this popular resort, and, walking to the opposite side of the street, and spinning there on his heel quickly and lithely, fired at the bit of paper. He missed it by a half-inch. He swore at himself, and went away. Later he comfortably fusilladed the windows of his most intimate friend. The man was playing with this town; it was a toy for him.

But still there was no offer of fight. The name of Jack Potter, his ancient antagonist, entered his mind, and he concluded that it would be a glad thing if he should go to Potter's house, and by bombardment induce him to come out and fight. He moved in the direction of his desire, chanting Apache scalp-music.

When he arrived at it, Potter's house presented the same still front as had the other adobes. Taking up a strategic position, the man howled a challenge. But this house regarded him as might a great stone god. It gave no sign. After a decent wait, the man howled further challenges, mingling with them wonderful epithets.

Presently there came the spectacle of a man churning himself into deepest rage over the immobility of a house. He fumed at it as the winter wind attacks a prairie cabin in the North. To the distance there should have gone the sound of a tumult like the fighting of two hundred Mexicans. As necessity bade him, he paused for breath or to reload his revolvers.

IV

Potter and his bride walked sheepishly and with speed. Sometimes they laughed together shamefacedly and low.

"Next corner, dear," he said finally.

They put forth the efforts of a pair walking bowed against a strong wind. Potter was about to raise a finger to point the first appearance of the new home when, as they circled the corner, they came face to face with a man in a maroon-colored shirt, who was feverishly pushing cartridges into a large revolver. Upon the instant the man dropped his revolver to the ground, and, like lightning, whipped another from its holster. The second weapon was aimed at the bridegroom's chest.

There was a silence. Potter's mouth seemed to be merely a grave for his tongue. He exhibited an instinct to at once loosen his arm from the woman's grip, and he dropped the bag to the sand. As for the bride, her face had gone as yellow as old cloth. She was a slave to hideous rites, gazing at the apparitional snake.

The two men faced each other at a distance of three paces. He of the revolver smiled with a new and quiet ferocity.

"Tried to sneak up on me," he said. "Tried to sneak up on me!" His eyes grew more baleful. As Potter made a slight movement, the man thrust his revolver venomously forward. "No; don't you do it, Jack Potter. Don't you move a finger toward a gun just yet. Don't you move an eyelash. The time has come for me to settle with you, and I'm goin' to do it my own way, and loaf along with no interferin'. So if you don't want a gun bent on you, just mind what I tell you."

Potter looked at his enemy. "I ain't got a gun on me, Scratchy," he

said. "Honest, I ain't." He was stiffening and steadying, but yet somewhere at the back of his mind a vision of the Pullman floated: the sea-
green figured velvet, the shining brass, silver, and glass, the wood that
gleamed as darkly brilliant as the surface of a pool of oil—all the glory
of the marriage, the environment of the new estate. "You know I fight
when it comes to fighting, Scratchy Wilson; but I ain't got a gun on me.
You'll have to do all the shootin' yourself."

His enemy's face went livid. He stepped forward, and lashed his
weapon to and fro before Potter's chest. "Don't you tell me you ain't
got no gun on you, you whelp. Don't tell me no lie like that. There
ain't a man in Texas ever seen you without no gun. Don't take me for
no kid." His eyes blazed with light, and his throat worked like a
pump.

"I ain't takin' you for no kid," answered Potter. His heels had not
moved an inch backward. "I'm takin' you for a —— fool. I tell you I
ain't got a gun, and I ain't. If you're goin' to shoot me up, you better
begin now; you'll never get a chance like this again."

So much enforced reasoning had told on Wilson's rage; he was
calmer. "If you ain't got a gun, why ain't you got a gun?" he sneered.
"Been to Sunday-school?"

"I ain't got a gun because I've just come from San Anton' with my
wife. I'm married," said Potter. "And if I'd thought there was going to
be any galoots like you prowling around when I brought my wife home,
I'd had a gun, and don't you forget it."

"Married!" said Scratchy, not at all comprehending.

"Yes, married. I'm married," said Potter, distinctly.

"Married?" said Scratchy. Seemingly for the first time, he saw the
drooping, drowning woman at the other man's side. "No!" he said. He
was like a creature allowed a glimpse of another world. He moved a
pace backward, and his arm, with the revolver, dropped to his side.
"Is this the lady?" he asked.

"Yes; this is the lady," answered Potter.

There was another period of silence.

"Well," said Wilson at last, slowly, "I s'pose it's all off now."

"It's all off if you say so, Scratchy. You know I did n't make the
trouble." Potter lifted his valise.

"Well, I 'low it's off, Jack," said Wilson. He was looking at the ground.
"Married!" He was not a student of chivalry; it was merely that in the
presence of this foreign condition he was a simple child of the earlier
plains. He picked up his starboard revolver, and, placing both weapons
in their holsters, he went away. His feet made funnel-shaped tracks in
the heavy sand.

Frank Norris (1870–1902) left Chicago to become an
art student in Paris. He returned to America
to study and later worked as a
magazine editor and journalist, most
notably as a foreign correspondent
in Cuba during the Spanish-
American War. Widely recognized
for his novels of social problems
and corruption in business, his most
famous works are The Octopus
(1901) and The Pit (1903).
For further reading: A Deal in
Wheat and Other Stories (1903).

a deal
in wheat
frank norris

I

The Bear—Wheat at Sixty-two

As Sam Lewiston backed the horse into the shafts
of his buckboard and began hitching the tugs to the whiffletree, his wife
came out from the kitchen door of the house and drew near, and stood
for some time at the horse's head, her arms folded and her apron rolled
around them. For a long moment neither spoke. They had talked over
the situation so long and so comprehensively the night before that there
seemed to be nothing more to say.

The time was late in the summer, the place a ranch in southwestern
Kansas, and Lewiston and his wife were two of a vast population of
farmers, wheat growers, who at that moment were passing through a
crisis—a crisis that at any moment might culminate in tragedy. Wheat
was down to sixty-six.

At length Emma Lewiston spoke.

"Well," she hazarded, looking vaguely out across the ranch toward
the horizon, leagues distant; "well, Sam, there's always that offer of
brother Joe's. We can quit—and go to Chicago—if the worst comes."

"And give up!" exclaimed Lewiston, running the lines through the
torets. "Leave the ranch! Give up! After all these years!"

His wife made no reply for the moment. Lewiston climbed into the
buckboard and gathered up the lines. "Well, here goes for the last try,
Emmie," he said. "Good-by, girl. Maybe things will look better in town
to-day."

"Maybe," she said gravely. She kissed her husband good-by and stood for some time looking after the buckboard traveling toward the town in a moving pillar of dust.

"I don't know," she murmured at length; "I don't know just how we're going to make out."

When he reached town, Lewiston tied the horse to the iron railing in front of the Odd Fellows' Hall, the ground floor of which was occupied by the post-office, and went across the street and up the stairway of a building of brick and granite—quite the most pretentious structure of the town—and knocked at a door upon the first landing. The door was furnished with a pane of frosted glass, on which, in gold letters, was inscribed, "Bridges & Co., Grain Dealers."

Bridges himself, a middle-aged man who wore a velvet skull-cap and who was smoking a Pittsburg stogie, met the farmer at the counter and the two exchanged perfunctory greetings.

"Well," said Lewiston, tentatively, after awhile.

"Well, Lewiston," said the other, "I can't take that wheat of yours at any better than sixty-two."

"Sixty-*two*."

"It's the Chicago price that does it, Lewiston. Truslow is bearing the stuff for all he's worth. It's Truslow and the bear clique that stick the knife into us. The price broke again this morning. We've just got a wire."

"Good heavens," murmured Lewiston, looking vaguely from side to side. "That—that ruins me. I *can't* carry my grain any longer—what with storage charges and—and——Bridges, I don't see just how I'm going to make out. Sixty-two cents a bushel! Why, man, what with this and with that it's cost me nearly a dollar a bushel to raise that wheat, and now Truslow——"

He turned away abruptly with a quick gesture of infinite discouragement.

He went down the stairs, and making his way to where his buckboard was hitched, got in, and, with eyes vacant, the reins slipping and sliding in his limp, half-open hands, drove slowly back to the ranch. His wife had seen him coming, and met him as he drew up before the barn.

"Well?" she demanded.

"Emmie," he said as he got out of the buckboard, laying his arm across her shoulder, "Emmie, I guess we'll take up with Joe's offer. We'll go to Chicago. We're cleaned out!"

II

The Bull—Wheat at a Dollar-ten

. . . —— *and said Party of the Second Part further covenants and agrees to merchandise such wheat in foreign ports, it being understood and agreed between the Party of the First Part and the Party of the Second Part that the wheat hereinbefore mentioned is released and sold to the Party of the Second Part for export purposes only, and not for consumption or distribution within the boundaries of the United States of America or of Canada.*

"Now, Mr. Gates, if you will sign for Mr. Truslow I guess that'll be all," remarked Hornung when he had finished reading.

Hornung affixed his signature to the two documents and passed them over to Gates, who signed for his principal and client, Truslow—or, as he had been called ever since he had gone into the fight against Hornung's corner—the Great Bear. Hornung's secretary was called in and witnessed the signatures, and Gates thrust the contract into his Gladstone bag and stood up, smoothing his hat.

"You will deliver the warehouse receipts for the grain," began Gates.

"I'll send a messenger to Truslow's office before noon," interrupted Hornung. "You can pay by certified check through the Illinois Trust people."

When the other had taken himself off, Hornung sat for some moments gazing abstractedly toward his office windows, thinking over the whole matter. He had just agreed to release to Truslow, at the rate of one dollar and ten cents per bushel, one hundred thousand out of the two million and odd bushels of wheat that he, Hornung, controlled, or actually owned. And for the moment he was wondering if, after all, he had done wisely in not goring the Great Bear to actual financial death. He had made him pay one hundred thousand dollars. Truslow was good for this amount. Would it not have been better to have put a prohibitive figure on the grain and forced the Bear into bankruptcy? True, Hornung would then be without his enemy's money, but Truslow would have been eliminated from the situation, and that—so Hornung told himself—was always a consummation most devoutly, strenuously and diligently to be striven for. Truslow once dead was dead, but the Bear was never more dangerous than when desperate.

"But so long as he can't get *wheat,*" muttered Hornung at the end of his reflections, "he can't hurt me. And he can't get it. That I *know.*"

For Hornung controlled the situation. So far back as the February of that year an "unknown bull" had been making his presence felt on the floor of the Board of Trade. By the middle of March the commercial reports of the daily press had begun to speak of "the powerful bull clique"; a few weeks later that legendary condition of affairs implied and epitomized in the magic words "Dollar Wheat" had been attained, and by the first of April, when the price had been boosted to one dollar and ten cents a bushel, Hornung had disclosed his hand, and in place of mere rumours, the definite and authoritative news that May wheat had been cornered in the Chicago pit went flashing around the world from Liverpool to Odessa and from Duluth to Buenos Ayres.

It was—so the veteran operators were persuaded—Truslow himself who had made Hornung's corner possible. The Great Bear had for once over-reached himself, and, believing himself all-powerful, had hammered the price just the fatal fraction too far down. Wheat had gone to sixty-two—for the time, and under the circumstances, an abnormal price. When the reaction came it was tremendous. Hornung saw his chance, seized it, and in a few months had turned the tables, had cornered the product, and virtually driven the bear clique out of the pit.

On the same day that the delivery of the hundred thousand bushels was made to Truslow, Hornung met his broker at his lunch club.

"Well," said the latter, "I see you let go that line of stuff to Truslow." Hornung nodded; but the broker added:

"Remember, I was against it from the very beginning. I know we've cleared up over a hundred thou'. I would have fifty times preferred to have lost twice that and *smashed Truslow dead*. Bet you what you like he makes us pay for it somehow."

"Huh!" grunted his principal. "How about insurance, and warehouse charges, and carrying expenses on that lot? Guess we'd have had to pay those, too, if we'd held on."

But the other put up his chin, unwilling to be persuaded. "I won't sleep easy," he declared, "till Truslow is busted."

III

The Pit

Just as Going mounted the steps on the edge of the pit the great gong struck, a roar of a hundred voices developed with the swiftness of successive explosions, the rush of a hundred men surging downward to the centre of the pit filled the air with the stamp and grind of feet, a hundred hands in eager strenuous gestures tossed upward from out the brown of the crowd, the official reporter in his cage on the margin of the pit leaned far forward with straining ear to catch the opening bid, and another day of battle was begun.

Since the sale of the hundred thousand bushels of wheat to Truslow the "Hornung crowd" had steadily shouldered the price higher until on this particular morning it stood at one dollar and a half. That was Hornung's price. No one else had any grain to sell.

But not ten minutes after the opening, Going was surprised out of all countenance to hear shouted from the other side of the pit these words:

"Sell May at one-fifty."

Going was for the moment touching elbows with Kimbark on one side and with Merriam on the other, all three belonging to the "Hornung crowd." Their answering challenge of *"Sold"* was as the voice of one man. They did not pause to reflect upon the strangeness of the circumstance. (That was for afterward.) Their response to the offer was as unconscious as reflex action and almost as rapid, and before the pit was well aware of what had happened the transaction of one thousand bushels was down upon Going's trading-card and fifteen hundred dollars had changed hands. But here was a marvel—the whole available supply of wheat cornered, Hornung master of the situation, invincible, unassailable; yet behold a man willing to sell, a Bear bold enough to raise his head.

"That was Kennedy, wasn't it, who made that offer?" asked Kimbark, as Going noted down the trade—"Kennedy, that new man?"

"Yes; who do you suppose he's selling for; who's willing to go short at this stage of the game?"

"Maybe he ain't short."

"Short! Great heavens, man; where'd he get the stuff?"

"Blamed if I know. We can account for every handful of May. Steady! Oh, there he goes again."

"Sell a thousand May at one-fifty," vociferated the bear-broker, throwing out his hand, one finger raised to indicate the number of "contracts" offered. This time it was evident that he was attacking the Hornung crowd deliberately, for, ignoring the jam of traders that swept toward him, he looked across the pit to where Going and Kimbark were shouting "*Sold! Sold!*" and nodded his head.

A second time Going made memoranda of the trade, and either the Hornung holdings were increased by two thousand bushels of May wheat or the Hornung bank account swelled by at least three thousand dollars of some unknown short's money.

Of late—so sure was the bull crowd of its position—no one had even thought of glancing at the inspection sheet on the bulletin board. But now one of Going's messengers hurried up to him with the announcement that this sheet showed receipts at Chicago for that morning of twenty-five thousand bushels, and not credited to Hornung. Some one had got hold of a line of wheat overlooked by the "clique" and was dumping it upon them.

"Wire the Chief," said Going over his shoulder to Merriam. This one struggled out of the crowd, and on a telegraph blank scribbled:

"Strong bear movement—New man—Kennedy—Selling in lots of five contracts—Chicago receipts twenty-five thousand."

The message was despatched, and in a few moments the answer came back, laconic, of military terseness:

"Support the market."

And Going obeyed, Merriam and Kimbark following, the new broker fairly throwing the wheat at them in thousand-bushel lots.

"Sell May at 'fifty; sell May; sell May." A moment's indecision, an instant's hesitation, the first faint suggestion of weakness, and the market would have broken under them. But for the better part of four hours they stood their ground, taking all that was offered, in constant communication with the Chief, and from time to time stimulated and steadied by his brief, unvarying command:

"Support the market."

At the close of the session they had bought in the twenty-five thousand bushels of May. Hornung's position was as stable as a rock, and the price closed even with the opening figure—one dollar and a half.

But the morning's work was the talk of all La Salle Street. Who was back of the raid? What was the meaning of this unexpected selling? For weeks the pit trading had been merely nominal. Truslow, the Great Bear, from whom the most serious attack might have been expected, had gone to his country seat at Geneva Lake, in Wisconsin, declaring himself to be out of the market entirely. He went bass-fishing every day.

IV

The Belt Line

On a certain day toward the middle of the month, at a time when the mysterious Bear had unloaded some eighty thousand bushels upon Hornung, a conference was held in the library of Hornung's home. His broker attended it, and also a clean-faced, bright-eyed individual whose name of Cyrus Ryder might have been found upon the pay-roll of a rather well-known detective agency. For upward of half an hour after the conference began the detective spoke, the other two listening attentively, gravely.

"Then, last of all," concluded Ryder, "I made out I was a hobo, and began stealing rides on the Belt Line Railroad. Know the road? It just circles Chicago. Truslow owns it. Yes? Well, then I began to catch on. I noticed that cars of certain numbers—thirty-one nought thirty-four, thirty-two one ninety—well, the numbers don't matter, but anyhow, these cars were always switched onto the sidings by Mr. Truslow's main elevator D soon as they came in. The wheat was shunted in, and they were pulled out again. Well, I spotted one car and stole a ride on her. Say, look here, *that car went right around the city on the Belt, and came back to D again, and the same wheat in her all the time.* The grain was reinspected—it was raw, I tell you—and the warehouse receipts made out just as though the stuff had come in from Kansas or Iowa."

"The same wheat all the time!" interrupted Hornung.

"The same wheat—your wheat, that you sold to Truslow."

"Great snakes!" ejaculated Hornung's broker. "Truslow never took it abroad at all."

"Took it abroad! Say, he's just been running it around Chicago, like the supers in 'Shenandoah,' round an' round, so you'd think it was a new lot, an' selling it back to you again."

"No wonder we couldn't account for so much wheat."

"Bought it from us at one-ten, and made us buy it back—our own wheat—at one-fifty."

Hornung and his broker looked at each other in silence for a moment. Then all at once Hornung struck the arm of his chair with his fist and exploded in a roar of laughter. The broker stared for one bewildered moment, then followed his example.

"Sold! Sold!" shouted Hornung almost gleefully. "Upon my soul it's as good as a Gilbert and Sullivan show. And we—— Oh, Lord! Billy, shake on it, and hats off to my distinguished friend, Truslow. He'll be President some day. Hey! What? Prosecute him? Not I."

"He's done us out of a neat hatful of dollars for all that," observed the broker, suddenly grave.

"Billy, it's worth the price."

"We've got to make it up somehow."

"Well, tell you what. We were going to boost the price to one seventy-five next week, and make that our settlement figure."

"Can't do it now. Can't afford it."

"No. Here; we'll let out a big link; we'll put wheat at two dollars, and let it go at that."

"Two it is, then," said the broker.

V

The Bread Line

The street was very dark and absolutely deserted. It was a district on the "South Side," not far from the Chicago River, given up largely to wholesale stores, and after nightfall was empty of all life. The echoes slept but lightly hereabouts, and the slightest footfall, the faintest noise, woke them upon the instant and sent them clamouring up and down the length of the pavement between the iron shuttered fronts. The only light visible came from the side door of a certain "Vienna" bakery, where at one o'clock in the morning loaves of bread were given away to any who should ask. Every evening about nine o'clock the outcasts began to gather about the side door. The stragglers came in rapidly, and the line—the "bread line," as it was called—began to form. By midnight it was usually some hundred yards in length, stretching almost the entire length of the block.

Toward ten in the evening, his coat collar turned up against the fine drizzle that pervaded the air, his hands in his pockets, his elbows gripping his sides, Sam Lewiston came up and silently took his place at the end of the line.

Unable to conduct his farm upon a paying basis at the time when Truslow, the "Great Bear," had sent the price of grain down to sixty-two cents a bushel, Lewiston had turned over his entire property to his creditors, and, leaving Kansas for good, had abandoned farming, and had left his wife at her sister's boarding-house in Topeka with the understanding that she was to join him in Chicago so soon as he had found a steady job. Then he had come to Chicago and had turned workman. His brother Joe conducted a small hat factory on Archer Avenue, and for a time he found there a meager employment. But difficulties had occurred, times were bad, the hat factory was involved in debts, the repealing of a certain import duty on manufactured felt overcrowded the home market with cheap Belgian and French products, and in the end his brother had assigned and gone to Milwaukee.

Thrown out of work, Lewiston drifted aimlessly about Chicago, from pillar to post, working a little, earning here a dollar, there a dime, but always sinking, sinking, till at last the ooze of the lowest bottom dragged at his feet and the rush of the great ebb went over him and engulfed him and shut him out from the light, and a park bench became his home and the "bread line" his chief makeshift of subsistence.

He stood now in the enfolding drizzle, sodden, stupefied with fatigue. Before and behind stretched the line. There was no talking. There was no sound. The street was empty. It was so still that the passing of a cable-car in the adjoining thoroughfare grated like prolonged rolling explosions, beginning and ending at immeasurable distances. The drizzle descended incessantly. After a long time midnight struck.

There was something ominous and gravely impressive in this interminable line of dark figures, close-pressed, soundless; a crowd, yet absolutely still; a close-packed, silent file, waiting, waiting in the vast deserted night-ridden street; waiting without a word, without a movement, there under the night and under the slow-moving mists of rain.

Few in the crowd were professional beggars. Most of them were workmen, long since out of work, forced into idleness by long-continued "hard times," by ill luck, by sickness. To them the "bread line" was a godsend. At least they could not starve. Between jobs here in the end was something to hold them up—a small platform, as it were, above the sweep of black water, where for a moment they might pause and take breath before the plunge.

The period of waiting on this night of rain seemed endless to those silent, hungry men; but at length there was a stir. The line moved. The side door opened. Ah, at last! They were going to hand out the bread.

But instead of the usual white-aproned undercook with his crowded hampers there now appeared in the doorway a new man—a young fellow who looked like a bookkeeper's assistant. He bore in his hand a placard, which he tacked to the outside of the door. Then he disappeared within the bakery, locking the door after him.

A shudder of poignant despair, an unformed, inarticulate sense of calamity, seemed to run from end to end of the line. What had happened? Those in the rear, unable to read the placard, surged forward, a sense of bitter disappointment clutching at their hearts.

The line broke up, disintegrated into a shapeless throng—a throng that crowded forward and collected in front of the shut door whereon the placard was affixed. Lewiston, with the others, pushed forward. On the placard he read these words:

"Owing to the fact that the price of grain has been increased to two dollars a bushel, there will be no distribution of bread from this bakery until further notice."

Lewiston turned away, dumb, bewildered. Till morning he walked the streets, going on without purpose, without direction. But now at last his luck had turned. Overnight the wheel of his fortunes had creaked and swung upon its axis, and before noon he had found a job in the street-cleaning brigade. In the course of time he rose to be first shift-boss, then deputy inspector, then inspector, promoted to the dignity of driving in a red wagon with rubber tires and drawing a salary instead of mere wages. The wife was sent for and a new start made.

But Lewiston never forgot. Dimly he began to see the significance of things. Caught once in the cogs and wheels of a great and terrible engine, he had seen—none better—its workings. Of all the men who had vainly stood in the "bread line" on that rainy night in early summer, he, perhaps, had been the only one who had struggled up to the surface again. How many others had gone down in the great ebb? Grim question; he dared not think how many.

He had seen the two ends of a great wheat operation—a battle between Bear and Bull. The stories (subsequently published in the city's press) of Truslow's countermove in selling Hornung his own wheat, supplied the unseen section. The farmer—he who raised the wheat—was ruined upon one hand; the working-man—he who consumed it—was ruined upon the other. But between the two, the great operators, who never saw the wheat they traded in, bought and sold the world's food, gambled in the nourishment of entire nations, practised their tricks, their chicanery and oblique shifty "deals," were reconciled in their differences, and went on through their appointed way, jovial, contented, enthroned, and unassailable.

part 2

Russia: *Averchenko, Babel, Katayev*

Europe: *Mann, Hesse, Kafka, Čapek, Myriveles, Sartre*

England-Ireland: *Joyce, Lawrence, Mansfield, Forster,*
Woolf, Bowen, Greene, O'Connor

United States: *James, O. Henry, Anderson,*
Fitzgerald, Hemingway,
Faulkner, Porter, Farrell,
Boyle

the

later

accomplishment

the young man who flew past

arcadii averchenko

Arcadii Timotheich
Averchenko (1881–1925) was a
skit writer, a dramatist,
and a humorist.
His fantastic
skits were played in
such theatre-cabarets
as the Crooked
Mirror in St. Petersburg.
He left Russia in 1917
and died in Constantinople.
Few of his stories are
available in English.

This sad and tragic occurrence began thus:

Three persons, in three different poses, were carrying on an animated conversation on the sixth floor of a large apartment building.

The woman, with plump beautiful arms, was clutching a bed sheet to her breast, forgetting that a bed sheet could not do double duty and cover her shapely bare knees at the same time. The woman was crying, and in the intervals between sobs she was saying:

"Oh, John! I swear to you I'm not guilty! He set my head in a whirl, he seduced me—and, I assure you, all against my will! I resisted—"

One of the men, still in his hat and overcoat, was gesticulating wildly and upbraiding the third person in the room:

"Scoundrel! I'm going to show you right now that you will perish like a cur and the law will be on my side! You shall pay for this meek victim! You reptile! You base seducer!"

The third in this room was a young man who, although not dressed with the greatest meticulousness at the present moment, bore himself, nevertheless, with great dignity.

"I? Why, I haven't done anything! I——" he protested, gazing sadly into an empty corner of the room.

"You haven't? Take this, then, you scoundrel!"

The powerful man in the overcoat flung open the window giving out upon the street, gathered the young man who was none too meticulously dressed in his arms, and heaved him out.

181

Finding himself flying through the air the young man bashfully buttoned his vest, and whispered to himself in consolation:

"Never mind! Our failures merely serve to harden us!"

And he kept on flying downward.

He had not yet had time to reach the next floor (the fifth) in his flight, when a deep sigh issued from his breast.

A recollection of the woman whom he had just left poisoned with its bitterness all the delight in the sensation of flying.

"My God!" thought the young man. "Why, I loved her! And she could not find the courage even to confess everything to her husband! God be with her! Now I can feel that she is distant, and indifferent to me."

With this last thought he had already reached the fifth floor and, as he flew past a window he peeked in, prompted by curiosity.

A young student was sitting reading a book at a lopsided table, his head propped up in his hands.

Seeing him, the young man who was flying past recalled his life; recalled that heretofore he had passed all his days in worldly distractions, forgetful of learning and books; and he felt drawn to the light of knowledge, to the discovery of nature's mysteries with a searching mind, drawn to admiration before the genius of the great masters of words.

"Dear, beloved student!" he wanted to cry out to the man reading, "you have awakened within me all my dormant aspirations and cured me of the empty infatuation with the vanities of life, which have led me to such grievous disenchantment on the sixth floor—"

But, not wishing to distract the student from his studies, the young man refrained from calling out, flying down to the fourth floor instead, and here his thoughts took a different turn.

His heart contracted with a strange sweet pain, while his head grew dizzy—from delight and admiration.

A young woman was sitting at the window of the fourth floor and, with a sewing machine before her, was at work upon something.

But her beautiful white hands had forgotten about work at that moment, and her eyes—blue as cornflowers—were looking into the distance, pensive and dreamy.

The young man could not take his eyes off this vision, and some new feeling, great and mighty, spread and grew within his heart.

And he understood that all his former encounters with women had been no more than empty infatuations, and that only now he understood that strange mysterious word—Love.

And he was attracted to the quiet domestic life; to the endearments of a being beloved beyond words; to a smiling existence, joyous and peaceful.

The next story, past which he was flying just then, confirmed him still more in his inclination.

In the window of the third floor he saw a mother who, singing a soft lullaby and laughing, was bouncing a plump smiling baby; love, and a kind maternal pride were sparkling in her eyes.

"I, too, want to marry the girl on the fourth floor, and have just such rosy plump children as the one on the third floor," mused the young man, "and I would devote myself entirely to my family and find my happiness in this self-sacrifice."

But the second floor was now approaching. And the picture which the young man saw in a window of this floor forced his heart to contract again.

A man with disheveled hair and wandering gaze was seated at a luxurious writing table. He was gazing at a framed photograph before him; at the same time he was writing with his right hand and, holding a revolver in his left, was pressing its muzzle to his temple.

"Stop, madman!" the young man wanted to call out. "Life is so beautiful!" But some instinctive feeling restrained him.

The luxurious appointments of the room, its richness and comfort, led the young man to reflect that there was something else in life which could disrupt even all this comfort and contentment, as well as a whole family; something of the utmost force—mighty, terrific. . . .

"What can it be?" he wondered with a heavy heart. And, as if on purpose, Life gave him a harsh unceremonious answer in a window of the first floor, which he had reached by now.

Nearly concealed by the draperies, a young man was sitting at the window, sans coat and vest; a half-dressed woman was sitting on his knees, lovingly entwining the head of her beloved with her round rosy arms and passionately hugging him to her magnificent bosom. . . .

The young man who was flying past recalled that he had seen this woman (well-dressed) out walking with her husband—but this man was decidedly not her husband. Her husband was older, with curly black hair, half-gray, while this man had beautiful fair hair.

And the young man recalled his former plans: of studying, after the student's example; of marrying the girl on the fourth floor; of a peaceful, domestic life, à la the third—and once more his heart was heavily oppressed.

He perceived all the ephemerality, all the uncertainty of the happiness of which he had dreamed; beheld, in the near future, a whole procession of young men with beautiful fair hair about his wife and himself; remembered the torments of the man on the second floor and the measures which that man was taking to free himself from these torments —and he understood.

"After all I have witnessed living is not worth while! It is both foolish and tormenting," thought the young man, with a sickly, sardonic smile; and, contracting his eyebrows, he determinedly finished his flight to the very sidewalk.

Nor did his heart tremble when he touched the flagstones of the pavement with his hands and, breaking those now useless members, he dashed out his brains against the hard indifferent stone.

And, when the curious gathered around his motionless body, it never occurred to any of them what a complex drama the young man had lived through just a few moments before.

the awakening

isaac babel

Isaac Babel (1894–1941) was born in Odessa, the son of a Jewish shopkeeper. He graduated from Nicholas I Commercial School and at fifteen began to write stories in French; in the civil war Babel was assigned to Budyonny's cavalry as a correspondent for ROSTA (later TASS). Arrested in 1939, his certificate of death is dated 1941. Fifteen years later the sentence was "revoked." For further reading: Red Cavalry *(1926);* Odessa Stories *(1923);* Collected Stories *(1955).*

All the people in our circle—small-time middlemen, shop-keepers, clerks in banks and steamship offices—were teaching their children music. Our fathers, seeing no way out for themselves, had struck on the notion of a lottery. This lottery they founded on the bones of the little ones. Odessa was possessed by this madness more than other towns were and, true enough, for several decades running our town supplied the Wunderkinder for the concert platforms of the world. Mischa Elman, Zimbalist, Gabrilovitch—they all came from Odessa! Jascha Heifetz got his start among us.

When a boy turned four or five his mother would lead the tiny and puny creature to Mr. Zagursky. Zagursky ran a factory of Wunderkinder, a factory that turned out Jewish dwarfs in little lace collars and little pumps of patent leather. He sought them out in the lairs of Moldavanka, in the malodorous courtyards of the Old Market. Zagursky gave them the first impetus; later on the children were sent off to Professor Auer in St. Petersburg. Mighty harmony dwelt within the souls of these starvelings with their bloated livid heads. They became celebrated virtuosi. And so my father decided to catch up with them, even though I was overage for a Wunderkind—I was going on fourteen; in height and puniness, however, I might have passed for an eight-year-old. Which constituted the last hope.

I was led off to Zagursky. Because of his high regard for my grandfather he consented to take only one rouble for each lesson—a cheap enough rate. My grandfather, Leivi Itzok, was the laughingstock of the town and, at the same time, its ornament. He walked about the streets in an opera hat and foot clouts and resolved points of doubt in the most obscure matters. They would ask him what a Gobelin was, why the Jacobins had betrayed Robespierre, how synthetic silk was prepared, what the Caesarian section was. My grandfather was able to answer all these questions. So, out of high regard for his learning and madness Zagursky took only one rouble a lesson from us. And it was also because he was afraid of Grandfather that he went to a lot of bother with me, since there was really nothing to bother with. The sounds slithered off my violin like metal shavings. These sounds grated on my own heart, yet my father would not give up. The talk at home was about nothing but Mischa Elman, who had been exempted from military service by the Czar himself. Zimbalist, according to information gathered by my father, had been presented to the King of England and had played at Buckingham Palace; the parents of Gabrilovitch had bought two mansions in St. Petersburg. These Wunderkinder had brought riches to their parents. My father might have reconciled himself to poverty, but fame was something he had to have.

"It is impossible," people who dined at his expense used to murmur in his ear, "it is impossible that the grandson of such a grandfather should fail—" However, my mind was on other things. During my violin exercises I would put the books of Turgenev or Dumas on the music stand and, as I scraped away, kept devouring page after page. In the daytime I told all sorts of cock-and-bull stories to the little boys in the neighborhood; at night I transferred these stories to paper. Writing was a hereditary compulsion in the family. Leivi Itzok, who had become touched in his old age, had been writing a novel all his life under the title of *The Man Without a Head*. I took after him.

Three times a week, loaded down with violin case and music, I used to plod to Witte Street (at one time called Gentry Street), to Zagursky's studio. There, lined along the wall awaiting their turns, hysterically fervent Jewish women sat hugging against their weak knees violins the dimensions of which exceeded those of the beings who were slated to play them in Buckingham Palace.

The door to the sanctum would open. Big-headed, freckled children with necks as slender as flower stalks and a hectic flush on their cheeks would come staggering out of Zagursky's study. The door would slam to after swallowing up the next dwarf. On the other side of the wall the teacher, sporting a Windsor tie, and curly red hair and legs more fluid than solid, was straining himself, chanting the notes and conducting. The director of this monstrous lottery was populating Moldavanka and the stygian dead ends of the Old Market with the specters of pizzicato and cantilena. Later on Professor Auer brought this sing-song to a diabolical brilliance.

I had no business among these sectarians. Much the same sort of dwarf as all of them, I nevertheless discerned a different admonition in the voice of my ancestors.

The first step came hard to me. One day I left the house laden like a beast of burden with violin case, violin, notes and twelve roubles— payment for a month's tuition. I was walking along Nezhinskaya Street and should have turned into Gentry Street to get to Zagursky's house; instead I went up Tiraspolskaya and found myself in the port. The hours supposed to be spent in learning the violin flew by in Practical Harbor. Thus did my liberation begin. Zagursky's reception room never saw me again. Matters of greater importance took up all my thoughts. Together with Nemanov, a classmate of mine, I took to haunting the steamer *Kensington*, visiting a certain old sailor by the name of Mr. Trottybairn. Nemanov was a year younger than I, but from the age of eight he had been carrying on the most intricate trading in the world. He was a genius in business and carried out whatever he promised to do. He is now a millionaire in New York, a director of the General Motors company, a firm which is just as tremendous as Ford. Nemanov dragged me along everywhere because I submitted to him in all things without offering a word of objection. He used to buy tobacco pipes from Mr. Trottybairn which were smuggled in. These pipes were turned out at Lincoln by a brother of the old sailor.

"Gentlemen," Mr. Trottybairn used to say to us, "mark my word: children must be made with one's own hands. Smoking a factory-made pipe is the same as putting an enema tube into your mouth. Do you know who Benvenuto Cellini was? There was a master! My brother in Lincoln could tell you about him. My brother doesn't stand in anybody's way. He is simply convinced that children must be made with one's own hands and not the hands of others. We cannot do otherwise than agree with him, gentlemen."

Nemanov sold Trottybairn's pipes to bank directors, foreign consuls, wealthy Greeks. He made 100 percent profit on them.

The pipes of the Lincoln master breathed poesy. A thought, a drop of eternity had been set within each one of them. A small yellow eye glinted in the mouthpiece of each; their cases were lined with satin. I tried to picture to myself how Matthew Trottybairn, the last of the master pipe makers, was living in old England as he resisted the course of things.

"We cannot do otherwise than agree, gentlemen, that children must be made with one's own hands."

The heavy waves near the sea wall removed me further and further from our house, permeated with the smell of onions and Jewish destiny. From Practical Harbor I migrated to the other side of the breakwater, where a small patch of sandy shoal was inhabited by urchins from Seafront Street. They did not bother putting on their pants from morning till night, diving under the wherries, stealing coconuts for their dinner, and biding their time till the watermelon-laden barges would come trailing one another from Kherson and Kamenka and they would have a chance to split some of these watermelons against the stanchions in the port.

To be able to swim became a dream of mine. It was shameful to confess to these bronzed urchins that I, who had been born in Odessa, had not seen the sea until I was ten and that at fourteen I still did not know how to swim.

How late it befell me to learn the things one had to know! In my childhood, nailed down to the Gemara, I had led the life of a sage; when I grew up I took to climbing trees.

The ability to swim proved beyond me. The hydrophobia of all my ancestors—Spanish rabbis and Frankford money-changers—kept dragging me to the bottom. The water would not bear me up. Covered with welts, bloated with briny water, I would return to shore, to my violin and notes. I was bound to the instruments of my crime and was dragging them with me. The struggle of the rabbis against the sea continued until such time as the water god of those places—Ephim Nikitich Smolich, a proofreader on the Odessa *News*—took pity on me. Pity for little Jewish boys dwelt within the athletic bosom of this man. He was supreme ruler over hordes of rachitic starvelings. Nikitich used to collect them from the bedbug-ridden hovels of Moldavanka, lead them to the sea, bury them in the sand, do gymnastics with them, dive with them, teach them songs and, as he broiled himself under the direct rays of the sun, would tell them stories about fishermen and animals. To grownups Nikitich explained that he was a natural philosopher. The Jewish children laughed so hard at Nikitich's stories that they rolled on the ground; they fawned and squealed like puppies. The sun spattered them with crawling freckles that were the color of lizards.

This old man watched my monomachy against the sea as a silent bystander. Perceiving that the fight was hopeless and that I would never learn how to swim, he included me among the number of the lodgers in his heart. All of it was here with us, that gay heart of his; it never put on airs, it was not tainted with greed and was not disquieted. With his coppery shoulders, the head of an aged gladiator and bronzed legs that were just the least bid bandy, he would lie in our midst beyond the breakwater as if he were the sovereign of those waters abounding in watermelon rinds and reeking of kerosene. I came to love this man as only a boy afflicted with hysteria and headaches can come to love an athlete. I would not leave his side and tried to be of service to him.

"Don't go at it so hard," he told me. "Strengthen your nerves. Swimming will come of itself. How can it be that the water won't bear you up—why shouldn't it?"

Noticing how I was drawn to him, Nikitich made an exception of me among all his disciples, inviting me to visit him in his clean, roomy garret carpeted with matting, showed me his dogs, his hedgehog, turtle and pigeons. In exchange for this largess I brought him a tragedy I had written recently.

"I just knew that you wrote a bit," said Nikitich. "You even have that look about you. More and more often your eyes don't watch anything in particular—"

He read my writings, shrugged, passed his hand over his short gray curls, paced about his garret a little.

"I would guess," he pronounced drawlingly, pausing after each word, "that the divine spark is in you—"

We went out into the street. The old man stopped, tapped his stick hard against the sidewalk and fixed me with his eyes.

"What do you lack? The fact that you're young is no calamity—that will pass with the years. . . . What you lack is a feeling for nature."

With his stick he pointed out a tree to me; it had a brownish trunk and a low crown.

"What tree is that?"

I did not know.

"What's growing on that bush?"

I did not know that either. We were walking through a small square on the Alexandrovsky Prospect. The old man kept pointing his stick at all the trees; he clutched my shoulder whenever birds happened to fly past and compelled me to listen to the individual voice of each.

"What bird is singing now?"

I could not tell him anything in answer. The names of trees and birds, their division into genera, where the birds were flying to, what direction the sun rose in, when the dew was heaviest—all these things were beyond my ken.

"And you have the audacity to write? A man who does not live in the midst of nature the way a stone or an animal lives won't write two worth-while lines in his whole lifetime. Your landscapes resemble descriptions of stage sets. What were your parents thinking about for fourteen years, may the Devil take me?"

What had my parents been thinking about? About protested promissory notes, about Mischa Elman's mansions. I did not say anything about this to Nikitich; I kept my mouth shut.

At home, during dinner, I did not touch my food. It stuck in my throat.

"A feeling for nature!" I kept thinking. "My God, why had no conception of that ever entered my head? Where can I find a man who will explain everything to me about the ways of birds and the names of trees? What do I know about them? I might be able to recognize lilacs—and even then only when they're in bloom. Lilacs—and acacias. De Ribas and Greek streets are lined with acacias—"

At dinner Father told a new story about Jascha Heifetz. Just before reaching Robinat's, Father had run into Mendelson, Jascha's uncle. The boy, it turned out, was getting eight hundred roubles for each appearance. Count that up—see how much that comes to if one gives fifteen concerts a month!

I did count it up: the result was twelve thousand a month. As I was doing the multiplication and carrying four, I happened to look out the window. In a gently billowing cape, with his tightly coiled, rusty-colored curls struggling out from under his soft hat, leaning upon a cane, Mr. Zagursky, my music teacher, was making stately progress through our small, concrete-paved courtyard. One could hardly say that he had been very prompt in discovering my truancy. By now more than three months had passed since my violin had foundered on the sands near the breakwater.

Zagursky was approaching our front door. I made a dash for the back entrance—and remembered it had been nailed up the evening before to keep burglars out. Whereupon I locked myself in the washroom. Within half an hour the whole family had gathered around my door. The women were weeping. One of my grandmothers was rubbing her fat shoulder against the door and going off into hysterical peals of sobbing. My father was silent. When he did break into speech he was quieter and more articulate than he had ever been in his whole life.

"I am an officer in the army," said my father. "I have an estate. I go hunting. The mouzhiks pay me rent. I have placed my son in the Cadet Corps. There is no need for me to worry about my son—"

He fell silent. The women were breathing hard. Then a terrific blow crashed against the washroom door. My father was pounding against it with his whole body; he persisted in running full tilt against it.

"I am an officer in the army!" he was screaming. "I go hunting! I'll kill him—this is the end!"

The hook flew off the door; there was a bolt on the door—it was still holding my a single nail. The women were rolling on the floor, they were catching my father's legs; out of his mind by now, he was struggling to get free. An old woman—my father's mother—came hurrying to find out what the hubbub was about.

"My child," she said to her son in Yiddish, "great is our grief. It has no bounds. The only thing lacking in our house is bloodshed. I do not want to see bloodshed in our house—"

My father broke into moans. I heard his steps receding. The bolt was hanging by its single nail.

I sat in my fortress till nightfall. When everybody had gone to bed my Aunt Bobka led me off to my grandmother's. The way there was a long one. The moonlight lay in a catalepsy upon unknown bushes, upon trees for which there were no names. . . . Some unseen bird in the distance emitted a whistle and became extinguished: it may have gone to sleep. . . . What bird was it? What did they call it? Is there any dewfall of evenings? Where is the constellation of Ursa Major located? Where does the sun rise? . . .

We were walking along Post Office Street. Aunt Bobka had a firm hold of my hand, so that I would not run away. She was right. Flight was what I had in mind.

"our father who art in heaven"

valentin katayev

Valentin Petrovich Katayev (1897–) volunteered for military service in World War I, was wounded, and gassed. In the 1920s he wrote satiric stories and plays; by the 1930s his fiction-criticism supported the Soviet regime. Katayev's works (in five volumes) appeared in Russia in 1956.

"I want to sleep. I'm cold."

"Lord! I want to sleep too. Get dressed. And that's enough nonsense. Put on your scarf. Put on your cap. Put on your boots. Where are your mittens? Stand still. Stop squirming."

When the little boy was dressed, she took him by the hand and they left the house. The boy was not yet fully awake. He was four years old. He shivered from the cold and stumbled along. It was just beginning to get light. There was a frosty blue fog outside. The mother tightened the scarf on the boy's neck, straightened his collar, and kissed his sleepy, mischievous face.

The dry wild grape vines, hanging from the broken-down wooden arcades, seemed sugary from the hoarfrost. It was twenty-five degrees below zero. Thick steam poured out of their mouths. The courtyard was littered with ice-covered garbage.

"Mama, where are we going?"

"I told you—for a walk."

"Then why did you take a suitcase?"

"Just because. Now be quiet. Don't chatter. Keep your mouth closed or you'll catch cold. You see how cold it is. Better look where you're going or you'll slip."

A doorman dressed in a sheepskin coat and a white apron with a nameplate on his chest stood at the gate. She walked past him without looking. He closed the door silently behind them and fastened it with a great iron hook. They set out along the street. There was no snow—everything was covered with ice and frost. And wherever there was neither ice nor frost there was smooth stone or earth as smooth and hard as stone. They walked under the bare, black acacia trees which were shaking resiliently in the cold.

The mother and son were dressed almost identically. They wore quite good coats made of artificial monkey-fur, soft leather boots and gaily colored wool mittens. The mother wore a checked kerchief on her head and the son wore a round monkey-fur cap with ear-flaps. The street was deserted. When they reached the crossing, the loudspeaker of the public address system gave such a loud crackle that the woman started. But she realized at once that the morning broadcast was beginning. As usual, it began with the crowing of a rooster. The exceedingly loud voice of the rooster shouted musically along the length of the street, heralding the beginning of a new day. The boy looked up at the loudspeaker.

"Mama, is that a rooster?"

"Yes, darling."

"Isn't he cold up there?"

"No, he's not cold up there. Now don't squirm. And watch where you're going."

Then the loudspeaker crackled again, and a gentle, childish voice repeated with angelic tones:

"Good morning! Good morning! Good morning!"

Then the same voice, slowly, with great feeling, recited the prayer:

"Our Father Who art in heaven, hallowed be Thy name, Thy kingdom come, Thy will be done. . . ."

On the corner the woman turned away from the wind and almost ran up the alley, dragging the boy behind her, as if this too loud and too gentle voice were pursuing her. Soon the voice stopped. The prayer was finished. The wind blew from the sea across the icy passages of the streets. Ahead of them a bonfire was blazing, surrounded by a crimson fog, with a German guard warming himself beside it. The woman turned and crossed to the other side. The boy ran beside her, stamping his little leather boots. His cheeks were as red as cranberries. A frozen drop hung beneath his nose.

"Mama, are we taking a walk now?" the little boy asked.

"Yes, we are."

"I don't like to walk so fast."

"Be patient."

They walked through a courtyard and came out on another street. It was already light. The pink dawn shone brittlely through light and dark blue clouds of steam and hoarfrost. It was so cold that one's jaws shut and puckered just from its rosy color as from something sour. Several people appeared on the street. They walked in one direction. Almost all of them carried bundles. Some pushed their bundles before them on carts, or dragged along loaded sleds that scratched the bare pavement with their runners.

From all ends of the city, on this morning, people with heavy loads trudged slowly in one direction, like ants. These were Jews on their way to the ghetto. The ghetto was set up in the Peresip district, in that dull, depressed part of the city where scorched oil tanks stood at sea level, looking like traveling circus tents. The Fascists had surrounded a few dirty blocks with two rows of rusty barbed wire and left only one entrance, as in a mousetrap. The Jews made their way under the railroad bridges. They slipped on the icy sidewalks. There were old people among them who couldn't walk and some people sick with typhus. These were carried on stretchers. Some would fall down and remain lying there, leaning back against a lamp post or hugging an iron hitching post. Nobody was escorting them to the ghetto. They were going there by themselves, without any convoy. They knew that whoever stayed home would be shot. Therefore they were going by themselves. Anyone who gave shelter to a Jew would also be shot. For one hidden Jew everyone living in the apartment would be shot, without exception. From all parts of the city, along steep slopes, under railroad bridges, the Jews made their way to the ghetto, pushing their wheelbarrows before them, leading their bundled children by the hand. They walked one behind the other, like ants, passing houses and frost-covered trees. They walked past locked doors and gates, past smoky bonfires where German and Rumanian soldiers warmed themselves. The soldiers paid no attention to the Jews and went on warming themselves, stamping their boots and rubbing their ears with their mittens.

It was horribly cold. It was unusually cold even for a northern city. But for Odessa it was simply monstrous. Such cold hits Odessa once in thirty years. A tiny circle of sun shone weakly through clouds of thick blue and green steam. Hardened sparrows lay on the highways, killed in mid-flight by the cold. The sea was frozen to the very horizon. It was white. The wind blew in from it.

The woman looked like a Russian. The boy also looked Russian. The boy's father was a Russian. But this meant nothing: the mother was a Jew. They were required to go to the ghetto. The boy's father was an officer in the Red Army. The woman had torn up her passport and had thrown it into the ice-covered toilet that morning. She had gone out of the house with her son, counting on walking about the city until everything calmed down. She thought she'd manage it somehow. It was insane to go to the ghetto. That meant certain death. And so she had begun to walk about the city with her son, trying to avoid the most crowded streets. At first, thinking that they were taking a walk, the boy was quiet. But soon he began to misbehave.

"Mama, why are we walking all the time?"

"We're taking a walk."

"We never walk so fast. I'm tired."

"Be patient, darling. I'm also tired. But you see I'm not misbehaving."

She noticed that she really was walking too fast, almost running, as if someone were chasing her. She made herself slow down. The boy looked up at her and hardly recognized her. He saw with horror her swollen, bitten lips, the lock of hair, gray with frost, hanging untidily out of her kerchief, and her fixed, harsh, glassy eyes. That kind of eyes he had seen before only on his toy animals. She was looking at her watch and didn't see him. Squeezing his little hand, she dragged the boy behind her. He grew frightened. He began to cry.

"I want to go home. I want to go peepee."

Hastily she led him behind a billboard covered with German notices. While she unbuttoned and then buttoned him, shielding him from the wind, the boy continued to cry and shake from the cold. When they began to walk again he cried that he was hungry. She took him to a milk-bar, but two Rumanian policemen in heavy fur coats and dog-skin collars were eating there; because she had no documents and was afraid they'd be arrested and sent to the ghetto, she pretended she had walked into the wrong store by mistake. She excused herself and quickly slammed the door. The boy ran after her, understanding nothing and crying. The next milk-bar was empty. Relieved, they crossed the doorstep with a horseshoe nailed to it. There the woman bought a bottle of fermented milk and a thick roll for the boy. The bundled little boy, sitting on a tall chair, drank the fermented milk, which he loved, and chewed on the roll and she thought feverishly about what to do next. She could think of nothing. But there was an iron stove burning in the milk-bar and at least they could warm up. It seemed to the woman that the proprietress of the milk-bar was looking at her too carefully. She quickly began to pay the bill. The proprietress looked out of the window uneasily and invited the woman to sit by the stove a while longer. The stove was red-hot. It was almost cherry-colored, a little darker. Sparks flew about from it. The heat made the boy sleepy. He could hardly keep his eyes open. But the woman began to fidget. She thanked the proprietress and told her she was in a hurry. But still they sat there for nearly an hour. The sleepy, full little boy could hardly stand on his feet. She shook him by the shoulders, straightened his collar and pushed him lightly toward the door. He stumbled over the horseshoe. The woman took the boy's hand and again led him along the street. The street was lined with old plane trees. They walked by the dappled plane trees with their soft, frost-covered bark.

"I want to go to sleep," said the little boy, screwing up his face from the icy wind.

She pretended she didn't hear him. She knew that their situation was desperate. She had almost no friends in the city. She had come here two months before the war began and then found herself stranded. She was completely alone.

"My knees are frozen," the little boy whimpered.

She took him to one side and rubbed his knees. He quieted down. Suddenly she remembered that there was, after all, one family in the city whom she knew. They had met on the steamer *Georgia* on the way from Novorossiisk to Odessa and then several times afterward. This was the young Pavlovskys: he was an instructor at the University, and she had just finished the building trades' school. Her name was Vera. The women had taken a liking to each other and had managed to become friends while the steamer was going from Novorossiisk to Odessa. They had visited each other a few times afterward. The men too had become friends—once they had even gotten drunk together. Another time they had all gone together to a soccer game—Kharkov vs. Odessa. The Pavlovskys had rooted for Odessa; she and her husband had rooted for Kharkov. Odessa won. God, what went on then in that huge new stadium overlooking the sea! Screams, howls, columns of dust. . . . They almost came to blows. But now it was only pleasant to think about. Pavlovsky was out of town, in the Red Army. But Vera was stranded too, hadn't managed to get evacuated. Recently she had seen Vera in the Alexandrovsky market, and they had even chatted for a while. But it wasn't safe to stop too long at the market place. The Germans started round-ups almost every day. The women spoke for hardly five minutes. They hadn't met since then. But probably Vera was in the city. Where else could she go? The Pavlovskys were Russians. She might try to sit it out at Vera's. In any case, she could leave the boy there. The Pavlovskys lived quite far away, on Pirogovskaya and the corner of Frantsuzky Boulevard. The woman turned around.

"Where are we going, Mama? Home?"

"No, darling, we're going visiting."

"Where?"

"Do you remember Aunt Vera Pavlovsky? We're going to visit Aunt Vera Pavlovsky."

"Good," said the boy, reassured. He loved to go visiting. He became more cheerful.

They walked across the Stroganovsky Bridge over the street leading to the harbor. The street was called Karantinny Hill. Below stood a group of rectangular sandstone houses. Some of them had been reduced to piles

of rubble. Some had been burned down. The round arches of another
bridge could be made out at the bottom of the hill and beyond the arches
the angular ruins of the harbor came into view. Farther still, above the
burned-out, fallen roof-tops lay the white sea, frozen to the horizon. On
the horizon itself a band of unfrozen water shone deep blue. Several
Rumanian troop-ships painted lead gray stood in the ice near the ruins
of the famous Odessa lighthouse. Above the city on the mountain, far
off to the left, the dome of the municipal theater shone like a sea shell
through clouds of pink and delicate light-blue steam. The fencing of the
Stroganovsky Bridge was made up of a long row of high, iron spikes.
The spikes were a severe black. Below, people were climbing up Karantinny Hill with buckets. The water splashed out of the buckets and froze
on the pavement, glistening like glass in the opaque light of the pink
sun. All this was very beautiful. If worse came to worse, they could
stay for a while at the Pavlovskys' and figure out what to do next.

They walked a very long time. The boy was tired but did not misbehave. He tramped on quickly in his little leather boots, just managing
to keep up with his mother. He wanted to get to Aunt Vera's as fast as
possible. He loved to go visiting. His mother wiped his whitened cheeks
several times on the way. A bonfire was burning on the sidewalk next
to the house where the Pavlovskys lived and some soldiers were warming
themselves around it. The house was large, divided into several sections.
The gate was locked with a chain. A round-up was going on. The documents of everyone going in and out were being checked. Pretending she
was in a hurry, the woman walked past the gate. No one paid any attention to her. The boy began to misbehave again. Then she took him
in her arms and began to run, stamping her feet on the dark-blue lava-
stone sidewalk. The boy calmed down. Again she began to roam about
the city. It seemed to her that she was appearing in the same places too
often and that people were beginning to notice her. Then she had the
idea of spending a few hours at the movies. The showing started early
since to be on the street after eight was forbidden on pain of death.

She felt nauseated and dizzy in the close, smelly hall, packed with
soldiers and prostitutes driven in there, like herself, by the cold. But
at least it was warm and they could sit down. She undid the scarf
on the boy's neck and he fell right asleep, clutching her arm with
both hands. She sat through two shows without leaving the hall,
barely following what was happening on the screen. It seemed to
be a war newsreel and then a comedy or something like that: she
couldn't catch the thread of it. Everything was muddled. Sometimes the
screen was filled with the head of a pretty girl and blond ringlets
snuggling her cheek against the flat chest of a tall headless man, then
they would sing a duet, then the girl would get into a sleek sports car,

then sometimes there were black fountains of explosions, one, two, three, four in a row—with a tinny roar as if someone were tearing roofing iron into long strips—one, two, three, four strips in one stroke while black hunks of earth came down like hail, striking the tin drum, and tanks crawled along the shell-scarred earth with funeral crosses, grinding and plunging and shooting still longer tongues of flame and whirling streams of white smoke.

A German soldier wearing embroidered felt boots and a Russian fur cap with ear-flaps was leaning heavily against the woman's shoulder and tickling the boy's cheek with a big, dirty finger, trying to wake him up. He smelled strongly of garlic and raw alcohol. He laughed good-naturedly all the while, repeating idiotically, "Don't sleep, bube. Don't sleep, bube."

"Bube" means "little boy" in German. The boy didn't wake up, but only moved his head slightly and whimpered in his sleep. Then the German dropped his heavy head on the woman's shoulder, putting one arm around her, and began to knead the little boy's face with the other hand. The woman kept quiet, afraid of making the soldier angry. She was afraid he'd ask to see her documents. The German smelled of smoked fish. She was nauseated but made a terrific effort not to flare up. She kept persuading herself to stay calm. After all, the German wasn't doing anything especially awful. He was simply a boor. An altogether decent Fritz. Bearable. Moreover, the German soon fell asleep on her shoulder. She sat without moving. The German was very heavy. But she was glad he was asleep.

The girl with the blond ringlets moved across the screen again, and long shafts of black and white rays moved through the whole theater with her. And with an iron roar the black fountains flew up, and tanks crawled on, and German battalions marched across the desert sands, and an enormous German flag was mounted on the top of the Eiffel Tower, and Hitler with a little sharp nose and a lady's chin barked out from the screen, sticking out his womanish rear end, rolling his eyes and opening and closing his mouth very quickly. He opened and closed his mouth so quickly that the sound came a little behind: arf, arf, arf, arf. . . .

Soldiers were pinching girls in the dark and the girls were squealing. The hall was terribly hot and stuffy and smelled of garlic, smoked fish, raw alcohol, aspirin and the Rumanian perfume "Chat-Noir." Still and all, it was better here than out in the cold. The woman had rested a bit. The boy had had enough sleep. But the last show was over and they had to go out again. She took the boy by the hand and they set out. The city was completely dark. Only the dense, frosty steam curled in among the darkened houses. It made one's eyelashes stick together. Smoking bonfires, almost smothered by the cold, were burning in the streets. Somewhere, from time to time, solitary shots rang out. Patrols walked up and down the streets. It was after eight. She picked up the sleepy child and began to run, almost out of her mind from the one thought that a patrol might stop them. She chose the most deserted alleys. Plane trees and acacias, covered with frost, lined the streets like ghosts. The city was empty and dark. From time to time a door would open in that blackness, and along with the bright band of light suddenly lighting up the frozen cars by the entrance, the passionate, piercing squeak of a violin rushed out for a moment. The woman ran safely to the Shevchenko Park of Culture and Rest. The enormous park lay along the sea. Here all was quiet, forsaken. It was especially quiet down below, at the bottom of the precipice by the sea frozen to the horizon. Silence as thick as a wall lay over the sea. A few big stars twinkled above the white branches of the trees. The light blue beam of a searchlight slid among the stars.

She walked along the broad asphalt pathway. On the left was the very same stadium where they had all gone together for the Odessa-Kharkov match. Beyond the wreckage of the stadium was the sea. It wasn't visible in the dark, but one could sense it right away from the silence. The park stretched out to the right. The broad asphalt pathway glittered like emery paper in the starlight. As the woman walked along she noted the different species of trees. Here were catalpas with their long pods hanging almost to the ground like strings. And here were pyramidal acacias, plane trees, thuyas, vinegar trees. Covered with heavy frost, they melted together and bent down to the ground like clouds. She took a deep breath and walked more slowly along the endlessly long row of empty benches. But on one of the benches someone was sitting! She walked by with a pounding heart. The black figure, its head leaning on the back of the bench, didn't move. The woman noticed then that the person was half covered with frost, like a tree. Above the black cupola of the observatory which rose up among the white clouds of the park twinkled the cut-glass stars of the Big Dipper. It was very quiet and not at all frightening here. Maybe it wasn't frightening because the woman was so tired.

And the next morning, before it was completely light, trucks drove through the city picking up the bodies of people who had frozen during the night. One truck drove slowly along the broad asphalt pathway in the Shevchenko Park of Culture and Rest.

The truck stopped twice. It stopped first at the bench where a frozen old man was sitting. It stopped a second time by the bench where a woman and a little boy were sitting. She was holding the boy by the hand. They were sitting side by side. They were dressed almost identically. They wore quite good coats made of artificial monkey-fur, soft leather boots and gaily colored wool mittens. They were sitting as if alive, only their faces, covered with frost during the night, were completely white and fluffy, and a fringe of ice hung from their eyelashes. When the soldiers picked them up they didn't straighten out. The soldiers swung around and threw the woman, her legs still in a sitting position, into the truck. She knocked against the old man like a piece of wood. Then the soldiers swung around and lightly threw in the boy, his legs still in a sitting position. He knocked against the woman like a piece of wood and bounced back a little.

As the truck was rolling away, a rooster began to crow from the loudspeaker of the public address system, heralding the beginning of a new day. Then a gentle childish voice repeated with angelic tones:

"Good morning! Good morning! Good morning!"

Then the same voice, slowly, with great feeling, recited the Lord's Prayer:

"Our Father, Who art in heaven, hallowed be Thy name, Thy kingdom come. . . ."

tobias mindernickel

thomas mann

Thomas Mann (1875–1955) was born in Lubeck, Germany, but after the advent of Hitler he lived mostly in the United States. A Nobel Prize winner, his early reputation was established by Buddenbrooks *(1901); his best-known novel is* The Magic Mountain *(1924). For further reading:* Stories of Three Decades, *translated by H. T. Lowe-Porter (1936).*

One of the streets running steeply up from the docks to the middle town was named Gray's Road. At about the middle of it, on the right, stood Number 47, a narrow, dingy-looking building no different from its neighbours. On the ground floor was a chandler's shop where you could buy overshoes and castor oil. Crossing the entry along a courtyard full of cats and mounting the mean and shabby, musty-smelling stair, you arrived at the upper storeys. In the first, on the left, lived a cabinet-maker; on the right a midwife. In the second, on the left a cobbler, on the right a lady who began to sing loudly whenever she heard steps on the stair. In the third on the left, nobody; but on the right a man named Mindernickel—and Tobias to boot. There was a story about this man; I tell it, because it is both puzzling and sinister, to an extraordinary degree.

Mindernickel's exterior was odd, striking, and provoking to laughter. When he took a walk, his meagre form moving up the street supported by a cane, he would be dressed in black from head to heels. He wore a shabby old-fashioned top hat with a curved brim, a frock-coat shining with age, and equally shabby trousers, fringed round the bottoms and so short that you could see the elastic sides to his boots. True, these garments were all most carefully brushed. His scrawny neck seemed longer because it rose out of a low turn-down collar. His hair had gone grey and he wore it brushed down smooth on the temples. His wide hat-brim shaded a smooth-shaven sallow face with sunken cheeks, red-rimmed eyes which were usually directed at the floor, and two deep, fretful furrows running from the nose to the drooping corners of the mouth.

Mindernickel seldom left his house—and this for a very good reason. For whenever he appeared in the street a mob of children would collect and sally behind him, laughing, mocking, singing—"Ho, ho, Tobias!" they would cry, tugging at his coat-tails, while people came to their doors to laugh. He made no defence; glancing timidly round, with shoulders drawn up and head stuck out, he continued on his way, like a man hurrying through a driving rain without an umbrella. Even while they were laughing in his face he would bow politely and humbly to people as he passed. Further on, when the children had stopped behind and he was not known, and scarcely noted, his manner did not change. He still hurried on, still stooped, as though a thousand mocking eyes were on him. If it chanced that he lifted his timid, irresolute gaze from the ground, you would see that, strangely enough, he was not able to fix it steadily upon anyone or anything. It may sound strange, but there seemed to be missing in him the natural superiority with which the normal, perceptive individual looks out upon the phenomenal world. He seemed to measure himself against each phenomenon, and find himself wanting; his gaze shifted and fell, it grovelled before men and things.

What was the matter with this man, who was always alone and unhappy even beyond the common lot? His clothing belonged to the middle class; a certain slow gesture he had, of his hand across his chin, betrayed that he was not of the common people among whom he lived. How had fate been playing with him? God only knows. His face looked as though life had hit him between the eyes, with a scornful laugh. On the other hand, perhaps it was a question of no cruel blow but simply that he was not up to it. The painful shrinking and humility expressed in his whole figure did indeed suggest that nature had denied him the measure of strength, equilibrium, and backbone which a man requires if he is to live with his head erect.

When he had taken a turn up into the town and come back to Grey's Road, where the children welcomed him with lusty bawlings, he went into the house and up the stuffy stair into his own bare room. It had but one piece of furniture worthy the name, a solid Empire chest of drawers with brass handles, a thing of dignity and beauty. The view from the window was hopelessly cut off by the heavy side wall of the next house; a flower-pot full of earth stood on the ledge, but there was nothing growing in it. Tobias Mindernickel went up to it sometimes and smelled at the earth. Next to this room was a dark little bedchamber. Tobias on coming in would lay hat and stick on the table, sit down on the dusty green-covered sofa, prop his chin with his hand, and stare at the floor with his eyebrows raised. He seemed to have nothing else to do.

As for Tobias Mindernickel's character, it is hard to judge of that. Some favourable light seems to be cast by the following episode. One day this strange man left his house and was pounced upon by a troop of children who followed him with laughter and jeers. One of them, a lad of ten years, tripped over another child's foot and fell so heavily to the pavement that blood burst from his nose and ran from his forehead. He lay there and wept. Tobias turned at once, went up to the lad, and began to console him in a mild and quavering voice. "You poor child," said he, "have you hurt yourself? You are bleeding—look how the blood is running down from his forehead. Yes, yes, you do look miserable, you weep because it hurts you so. I pity you. Of course, you did it yourself, but I will tie my handkerchief round your head. There, there! Now pull yourself together and get up." And actually with the words he bound his own handkerchief round the bruise and helped the lad to his feet. Then he went away. But he looked a different man. He held himself erect and stepped out firmly, drawing longer breaths under his narrow coat. His eyes looked larger and brighter, he looked squarely at people and things, while an expression of joy so strong as to be almost painful tightened the corners of his mouth.

After this for a while there was less tendency to jeer at him among the denizens of Grey's Road. But they forgot his astonishing behavior with the lapse of time, and once more the cruel cries resounded from dozens of lusty throats behind the bent and infirm man: "Ho, ho, Tobias!"

One sunny morning at eleven o'clock Mindernickel left the house and betook himself through the town to the Lerchenberg, a long ridge which constitutes the afternoon walk of good society. Today the spring weather was so fine that even in the forenoon there were some carriages as well as pedestrians moving about. On the main road, under a tree, stood a man with a young hound on a leash, exhibiting it for sale. It was a muscular little animal about four months old, with black ears and black rings round its eyes.

Tobias at a distance of ten paces noticed this; he stood still, rubbed his chin with his hand, and considered the man, and the hound alertly wagging its tail. He went forward, circling three times round the tree, with the crook of his stick pressed against his lips. Then he stepped up to the man, and keeping his eye fixed on the dog, he said in a low, hurried tone: "What are you asking for the dog?"

"Ten marks," answered the man.

Tobias kept still a moment, then he said with some hesitation: "Ten marks?"

"Yes," said the man.

Tobias drew a black leather purse from his pocket, took out a note for five marks, one three-mark and one two-mark piece, and quickly handed them to the man. Then he seized the leash, and two or three people who had been watching the bargain laughed to see him as he gave a quick, frightened look about him and, with his shoulders stooped, dragged away the whimpering and protesting beast. It struggled the whole of the way, bracing its forefeet and looking up pathetically in its new master's face. But Tobias pulled, in silence, with energy and succeeded in getting through the town.

An outcry arose among the urchins of Grey's Road when Tobias appeared with the dog. He lifted it in his arms, while they danced round, pulling at his coat and jeering; carried it up the stair and bore it into his own room, where he set it on the floor, still whimpering. Stooping over and patting it with kindly condescension he told it:

"There, there, little man, you need not be afraid of me; that is quite unnecessary."

He took a plate of cooked meat and potatoes out of a drawer and tossed the dog a part of it, whereat it ceased to whine and ate the food with loud relish, wagging its tail.

"And I will call you Esau," said Tobias. "Do you understand? That will be easy for you to remember." Pointing to the floor in front of him he said, in a tone of command:

"Esau!"

And the dog, probably in the hope of getting more to eat, did come up to him. Tobias clapped him gently on the flank and said:

"That's right, good doggy, good doggy!"

He stepped back a few paces, pointed to the floor again, and commanded:

"Esau!"

And the dog sprang to him quite blithely, wagging its tail, and licked its master's boots.

Tobias repeated the performance with unflagging zest, some twelve or fourteen times. Then the dog got tired, it wanted to rest and digest its meal. It lay down, in the sagacious and charming attitude of a hunting dog, with both long, slender forelegs stretched before it, close together.

"Once more," said Tobias. "Esau!"

But Esau turned his head aside and stopped where he was.

"Esau!" Tobias's voice was raised, his tone more dictatorial still. "You've got to come, even if you are tired."

But Esau laid his head on his paws and came not at all.

"Listen to me," said Tobias, and his voice was now low and threatening; "you'd best obey or you will find out what I do when I am angry."

But the dog hardly moved his tail.

Then Mindernickel was seized by a mad and extravagant fit of anger. He clutched his black stick, lifted up Esau by the nape of the neck, and in a frenzy of rage he beat the yelping animal, repeating over and over in a horrible, hissing voice:

"What, you do not obey me? You dare to disobey me?"

At last he flung the stick from him, set down the crying animal, and with his hands upon his back began to pace the room, his breast heaving, and flinging upon Esau an occasional proud and angry look. When this had gone on for some time, he stopped in front of the dog as it lay on its back, moving its fore-paws imploringly. He crossed his arms on his chest and spoke with a frightful hardness and coldness of look and tone —like Napoleon, when he stood before a company that had lost its standard in battle:

"May I ask you what you think of your conduct?"

And the dog, delighted at this condescension, crawled closer, nestled against its master's leg, and looked up at him bright-eyed.

For a while Tobias gazed at the humble creature with silent contempt. Then as the touching warmth of Esau's body communicated itself to his leg he lifted Esau up.

"Well, I will have pity on you," he said. But when the good beast essayed to lick his face his voice suddenly broke with melancholy emotion. He pressed the dog passionately to his breast, his eyes filling with tears, unable to go on. Chokingly he said:

"You see, you are my only . . . my only . . ." He put Esau to bed, with great care, on the sofa, supported his own chin with his hand, and gazed at him with mild eyes, speechlessly.

Tobias Mindernickel left his room now even less often than before; he had no wish to show himself with Esau in public. He gave his whole time to the dog, from morning to night; feeding him, washing his eyes, teaching him commands, scolding him, and talking to him as though he were human. Esau, alas, did not always behave to his master's satisfaction. When he lay beside Tobias on the sofa, dull with lack of air and exercise, and gazed at him with soft, melancholy eyes, Tobias was pleased. He sat content and quiet, tenderly stroking Esau's back as he said: "Poor fellow, how sadly you look at me! Yes, yes, life is sad, that you will learn before you are much older."

But sometimes Esau was wild, beside himself with the urge to exercise his hunting instincts; he would dash about the room, worry a slipper, leap on the chairs, or roll over and over with sheer excess of spirits. Then Tobias followed his motions from afar with a helpless, disapproving, wandering air and a hateful, peevish smile. At last he would brusquely call Esau to him and say:

"That's enough now, stop dashing about like that—there is no reason for such high spirits."

Once it even happened that Esau got out of the room and bounced down the stairs to the street, where he at once began to chase a cat, to eat dung in the road, and jump up at the children frantic with joy. But when the distressed Tobias appeared with his wry face, half the street roared with laughter to see him, and it was painful to behold the dog bounding away in the other direction from his master. That day Tobias in his anger beat him for a long time.

One day, when he had had the dog for some weeks, Tobias took a loaf of bread out of the chest of drawers and began stooping over to cut off little pieces with his big bone-handled knife and let them drop on the floor for Esau to eat. The dog was frantic with hunger and playfulness; it jumped up at the bread, and the long-handled knife in the clumsy hands of Tobias ran into its right shoulder-blade. It fell bleeding to the ground.

In great alarm Tobias flung bread and knife aside and bent over the injured animal. Then the expression of his face changed, actually a gleam of relief and happiness passed over it. With the greatest care he lifted the wounded animal to the sofa—and then with what inexhaustible care and devotion he began to tend the invalid. He did not stir all day from its side, he took it to sleep on his own bed, he washed and bandaged, stroked and caressed and consoled it with unwearying solicitude.

"Does it hurt so much?" he asked. "Yes, you are suffering a good deal, my poor friend. But we must be quiet, we must try to bear it." And the look on his face was one of gentle and melancholy happiness. But as Esau got better and the wound healed, so the spirits of Tobias sank again. He paid no more attention to the wound, confining his sympathy to words and caresses. But it had gone on well, Esau's constitution was sound; he began to move about once more. One day after he had finished off a whole plate of milk and white bread he seemed quite right again; jumped down from the sofa to rush about the room, barking joyously, with all his former lack of restraint. He tugged at the bed-covers, chased a potato round the room, and rolled over and over in his excitement.

Tobias stood by the flower-pot in the window. His arms stuck out long and lean from the ragged sleeves and he mechanically twisted the hair that hung down from his temples. His figure stood out black and uncanny against the grey wall of the next building. His face was pale and drawn with suffering and he followed Esau's pranks unmoving, with a sidelong, jealous, wicked look. But suddenly he pulled himself together, approached the dog, and made it stop jumping about; he took it slowly in his arms.

"Now, poor creature," he began, in a lachrymose tone—but Esau was not minded to be pitied, his spirits were too high. He gave a brisk snap at the hand which would have stroked him; he escaped from the arms to the floor, where he jumped mockingly aside and ran off, with a joyous bark.

That which now happened was so shocking, so inconceivable, that I simply cannot tell it in any detail. Tobias Mindernickel stood leaning a little forward, his arms hanging down; his lips were compressed, the balls of his eyes vibrated uncannily in their sockets. Suddenly with a sort of frantic leap, he seized the animal, a large bright object gleamed in his hand—and then he flung Esau to the ground with a cut which ran from the right shoulder deep into the chest. The dog made no sound, he simply fell on his side, bleeding and quivering.

The next minute he was on the sofa with Tobias kneeling before him, pressing a cloth on the wound and stammering:

"My poor brute, my poor dog! How sad everything is! How sad it is for both of us! You suffer—yes, yes, I know. You lie there so pathetic—but I am with you, I will console you—here is my best handkerchief—"

But Esau lay there and rattled in his throat. His clouded, questioning eyes were directed upon his master, with a look of complaining, innocence, and incomprehension—and then he stretched out his legs a little and died.

But Tobias stood there motionless, as he was. He had laid his face against Esau's body and he wept bitter tears.

the
poet

hermann hesse

Hermann Hesse (1877–1962)
was born in Wuttemberg, and
after several jobs—none satisfactory—
he began to publish novels after the turn of the
century. A major theme in his work is the quest for
peace in a world that somewhat resembles a jungle.
His most celebrated novel is Magister
Ludi (1943); he was awarded
the Nobel Prize in 1946.

There is a story told that the Chinese poet, Han Fook, while yet a young man had a strange and compelling wish to learn all there was to learn about the art of poetry, and to strive for perfection in the writing of it. In those days, he was still living in his home on the Yellow River, and with the help of his family who loved him dearly, he had just become engaged to a young lady of good family. The marriage was to be set for a day which promised good fortune. Han Fook was then twenty years old, a handsome youth, modest, well mannered, schooled in the sciences, and despite his youth, was already recognized among men of letters of his homeland for some excellent verse. Without being exactly rich, he had the prospect of an adequate fortune which would be augmented by the dowry of his bride. Since this bride was, moreover, very beautiful and virtuous, nothing seemed to be lacking for the young man's happiness. Nevertheless, he was not satisfied, for his heart was filled with the ambition to become a perfect poet.

One evening, as a festival of lanterns was being celebrated on the river, it so happened that Han Fook was wandering alone on the far bank of the river. He leaned against the trunk of a tree which grew over the water, and saw reflected in the river thousands of lights swimming and shimmering. He saw men and women and young girls greeting each other on the boats and floats, all glowing like beautiful flowers in their festive dress. He heard the soft murmur of the shining water, the songs of the girls, the humming of the zithers, the sweet tones of the flutes, and over the whole scene the blue night hovered like the vaulting of a temple. His heart beat faster as he gave in to the mood rising within him. He was the only witness to all this beauty! Even though he longed to cross the river and to enjoy the festival in the company of his bride and his friends, he wanted even more ardently to remain an observer, to drink in his own impressions of the scene, and then to transform them into a perfect poem. The poem would reflect the deep blue of the night, the play of light on the water, the joy of the festival guests, and also the yearning of the silent onlooker who leans on the trunk of the tree over the river. He sensed that if even he were to experience all the festivals and all the pleasures of the earth, they would not make him completely happy, for he knew that he would remain an onlooker, a stranger, as it were, isolated in the midst of life. He sensed the unique quality of his soul, which at once compelled him to feel deeply the beauty of the earth, and also to know the secret longings of an outsider. The thought made him sad, but as he pursued it further, he realized that true happiness and satisfaction could only be his if he could once succeed in creating with his poetry a perfect mirror image of the world. In this way he would possess the world itself, refined and immortalized in reflected images.

Han Fook scarcely knew whether he was still awake or had fallen asleep when he heard a slight sound and saw a stranger standing next to the tree trunk. It was an old man with a venerable air, clad in violet-colored robes. Han Fook rose and spoke to the stranger with the usual words of greeting for old men and eminent people. The stranger, however, smiled, and spoke a few lines of poetry. The young man's heart stood still in wonder, for in these lines was all the beauty and perfection which he had just experienced, expressed according to all the rules of the great poets. "Oh, who are you," he asked, bowing deeply, "you who can see into my soul and who speak more beautiful verses than I have ever heard from my teachers?"

The stranger smiled the smile of one who has attained perfection, and said, "If you wish to become a poet, then come with me. You will find my hut by the source of the great river in the northwest mountains. I am called the Master of the Perfect Word."

With that the old man stepped into the narrow shadow cast by the tree and disappeared immediately. Han Fook, after searching for him in vain and finding not even a trace, now firmly believed that everything had been a dream brought on by fatigue. He hurried over to the boats across the river and took part in the festival, but between conversations and the sound of the flutes, he continued to hear the voice of the stranger. Han Fook's very soul seemed to have gone away with the man, for he sat apart with dreaming eyes among the merrymakers who teased him for his lovesickness.

A few days later, Han Fook's father wanted to call his friends and relatives together in order to set the day of the wedding. But the bridegroom opposed his father, saying: "Forgive me if I seem to violate the obedience which a son owes his father. But you know how great is my longing to distinguish myself in the art of poetry. Even though a few of my friends praise my poems, I well know that I am still a beginner and still have a long way to go. Therefore I ask you to let me go for awhile into isolation in order to pursue my studies of poetry, because once I have a wife and a house to take care of, I will be held back from those things. Now, while I am still young and free from other duties, I would like to live for some time for my poetry alone—and my poetry will, I hope, bring me joy and fame."

The father was amazed at this speech, and he said, "You must love this art above everything else, since you even want to postpone your wedding because of it. Or, if something has come between you and your bride, then tell me so that I can help you bring about a reconciliation or provide you with another bride."

But the son swore that he loved his bride no less than before, and that not even the shadow of a disagreement had fallen between them. At the same time he told his father that a great master had revealed himself to him in a dream on the day of the lantern festival, and that it was his greatest wish in the world to become the pupil of this master.

"Well and good," said the father, "then I will give you a year. In this time you may pursue this dream of yours which may have been sent to you by a god."

"It may be two years," said Han Fook hesitantly, "who can tell?"

The father let him go and was grieved. The young man wrote a letter to his bride, took leave of his family, and went his way.

When he had traveled for a very long time, he reached the source of the river and found a bamboo hut standing by itself in the wilderness. On a braided mat in front of the hut sat the old man whom Han Fook had seen on the bank by the tree trunk. The old man sat and played his lute, and when he saw the guest approach respectfully, he did not get up, nor did he greet him. He only smiled and let his sensitive fingers play over the strings. A magic music flowed like a silver cloud through the valley, so that the young man stood in wondering astonishment and forgot everything else until the Master of the Perfect Word put aside his small lute and stepped into his hut. So Han Fook followed him with awe and remained with him as his servant and pupil.

A month passed, and Han Fook had learned to despise all poems which he had written before. He erased them from his memory. And after a few more months he erased even those poems from his memory which he had learned from his teachers at home. The Master spoke hardly a word with him. Silently, he taught Han Fook the art of lute playing until the very being of the pupil was filled with music. Once Han Fook composed a small poem, in which he described the flight of two birds across the autumnal sky, a poem which pleased him quite well. He didn't dare show it to the Master, but one evening he sang it near the hut. The Master heard it well but said not a word. He only played softly on his lute. Immediately the air became cool and the darkness increased; a sharp wind arose even though it was the middle of summer. Across the sky, which had now become gray, flew two lines of birds in their mighty yearning for new lands. All of this was so much more beautiful and more perfect than the verses of the pupil, that Han Fook became sad and silent, and felt himself worthless. The old man made this come to pass each time. When a year had gone by, Han Fook had learned lute playing almost to perfection, but the art of poetry appeared ever more difficult and more sublime.

When two years had gone by, the young man became overwhelmingly homesick for his family, for his homeland, and for his bride. So he asked the Master to let him travel.

The Master smiled and nodded. "You are free," he said, "and may go wherever you want. You may come again, you may stay away, just as you like."

So the pupil started on his journey and travelled without stopping until one morning in the dawn he stood on his native shore and looked over the vaulted bridge to his home town. He crept furtively into his father's garden, and heard through the bedroom window the breathing of his father who was still asleep. Stealing among the trees next to the house of his bride, he climbed to the top of a pear tree and saw his bride standing in her room, combing her hair. When he compared the sight before his eyes with the vision that he had painted of it in his homesick imaginings, it became clear to him that he was indeed destined to be a poet: that in the dreams of poets there is a beauty and grace which one searches for in vain in everyday reality. So he climbed down from the tree, fled from the garden, fled over the bridge out of his native town, and returned to the high valley in the mountains. There as before sat the Master in front of his hut on his simple mat, plucking the lute with his fingers. Instead of a greeting, he spoke two verses about the blessings of art. Upon hearing these deep and harmonious sounds, Han Fook's eyes became filled with tears.

Again Han Fook remained with the Master of the Perfect Word, who now gave him lessons on the zither since he had mastered the lute. The months vanished like snow in the west wind. Twice more it happened that homesickness overcame him. The first time he ran away secretly into the night, but before he had reached the last curve in the valley, the night wind blew over the zither which hung in the door of the hut and the sounds flowed after Han Fook and called him to return in such a way that he could not resist. The other time, however, he dreamed that he was planting a young tree in his garden and that his wife was standing by him and that his children were sprinkling the tree with wine and milk. When he awoke, the moon shone into his room. He got up, bewildered, and saw the Master lying asleep next to him, his gray beard trembling gently. Suddenly a feeling of bitter hatred towards this man came over him—this person who, it seemed to him, had destroyed his life and deceived him about his future. He wanted to fall upon him and murder him, when the old man opened his eyes and began immediately to smile with a fine, sad gentleness which disarmed the pupil. "Remember, Han Fook," said the old man quietly, "you are free to do whatever you wish. You may go into your home country and plant trees, you may hate me, or strike me dead,—it is of little importance."

"Oh, how could I hate you?" cried the poet deeply moved. "That would be like hating heaven itself."

So he remained, and learned to play the zither, and after that the flute. Later he began to write poems under the Master's direction. Slowly he learned the mysterious art of saying only that which is simple and straight-forward, but in such a way as to stir up the listener's soul as the wind stirs up the surface of the water. He described the coming of the sun as it hesitates on the edge of the mountains, and the soundless slipping away of fish when they flee like shadows under the water, and the gentle rocking of a young willow in the spring winds. To hear it was not just to hear about the sun, the play of the fish, or the murmuring of the willow; rather it seemed that heaven and earth harmonized each time for a moment of perfect music. Each listener thought with joy or sorrow on whatever he loved or hated: a boy's thoughts would turn to games, a young man's to his beloved, and the old man's to death.

Han Fook no longer knew how many years he spent with the Master at the source of the great river. Often it seemed to him that he had entered the valley only yesterday and been welcomed by the old man's string music. Often he felt as if all the ages of Man and Time itself had fallen away and become insubstantial.

One morning he awoke alone in the hut and though he looked and called everywhere, the Master had disappeared. Overnight fall seemed to have come. A raw wind shook the old hut and large flocks of migrating birds flew over the ridge of the mountain range, although it was not yet time for them to do so.

Then Han Fook took his little lute and descended into his native country. Wherever he encountered people, they greeted him with the sign of greeting which is due old men and eminent people. When he came to his native town, his father, his bride, and his relatives had died. Other people lived in their houses. That evening, a lantern festival was celebrated on the river. The poet Han Fook stood on the far side of the river, on the darker side of the river, leaning against the trunk of an old tree. When he began to play his little lute, then the women sighed and glanced, delighted and disturbed, into the night. The young men called to the lute player, but they could not find him. They called loudly, because not one of them had ever heard such sounds from a lute before. But Han Fook smiled. He looked into the river, where the reflected images of a thousand lanterns were swimming. Just as he no longer knew how to distinguish the reflected images from the real ones, so he found no difference in his soul between this festival and the first one, when he had stood here as a young man and heard the words of the strange Master.

jackals and arabs

franz kafka

Franz Kafka (1883–1924) studied law and was later employed in the workmen's compensation bureau of the Austrian government. His work presents dreamlike situations which are at once realistic in detail and symbolic by implication. Most of his books were published posthumously, including his three novels: The Trial *(1925);* The Castle *(1926);* Amerika *(1927). For further reading:* The Penal Colony, *translated by Willa and Edwin Muir (1948).*

We were camping in the oasis. My companions were asleep. The tall, white figure of an Arab passed by; he had been seeing to the camels and was on his way to his own sleeping place.

I threw myself on my back in the grass; I tried to fall asleep; I could not; a jackal howled in the distance; I sat up again. And what had been so far away was all at once quite near. Jackals were swarming round me, eyes gleaming dull gold and vanishing again, lithe bodies moving nimbly and rhythmically, as if at the crack of a whip.

One jackal came from behind me, nudging right under my arm, pressing against me, as if he needed my warmth, and then stood before me and spoke to me almost eye to eye.

"I am the oldest jackal far and wide. I am delighted to have met you here at last. I had almost given up hope, since we have been waiting endless years for you; my mother waited for you, and her mother, and all our fore-mothers right back to the first mother of all the jackals. It is true, believe me!"

"That is surprising," said I, forgetting to kindle the pile of firewood which lay ready to smoke away jackals, "that is very surprising for me to hear. It is by pure chance that I have come here from the far North, and I am making only a short tour of your country. What do you jackals want, then?"

As if emboldened by this perhaps too friendly inquiry the ring of jackals closed in on me; all were panting and openmouthed.

"We know," began the eldest, "that you have come from the North; that is just what we base our hopes on. You Northerners have the kind of intelligence that is not to be found among Arabs. Not a spark of intelligence, let me tell you, can be struck from their cold arrogance. They kill animals for food, and carrion they despise."

"Not so loud," said I, "there are Arabs sleeping near by."

"You are indeed a stranger here," said the jackal, "or you would know that never in the history of the world has any jackal been afraid of an Arab. Why should we fear them? Is it not misfortune enough for us to be exiled among such creatures?"

"Maybe, maybe," said I, "matters so far outside my province I am not competent to judge; it seems to me a very old quarrel; I suppose it's in the blood, and perhaps will only end with it."

"You are very clever," said the old jackal; and they all began to pant more quickly; the air pumped out of their lungs although they were standing still; a rank smell which at times I had to set my teeth to endure streamed from their open jaws, "you are very clever; what you have just said agrees with our old tradition. So we shall draw blood from them and the quarrel will be over."

"Oh!" said I, more vehemently than I intended, "they'll defend themselves; they'll shoot you down in dozens with their muskets."

"You misunderstand us," said he, "a human failing which persists apparently even in the far North. We're not proposing to kill them. All the water in the Nile couldn't cleanse us of that. Why, the mere sight of their living flesh makes us turn tail and flee into cleaner air, into the desert, which for that very reason is our home."

And all the jackals around, including many new-comers from farther away, dropped their muzzles between their forelegs and wiped them with their paws; it was as if they were trying to conceal a disgust so overpowering that I felt like leaping over their heads to get away.

"Then what are you proposing to do?" I asked, trying to rise to my feet; but I could not get up; two young beasts behind me had locked their teeth through my coat and shirt; I had to go on sitting. "These are your trainbearers," explained the old jackal, quite seriously, "a mark of honor." "They must let go!" I cried, turning now to the old jackal, now to the youngsters. "They will, of course," said the old one, "if that is your wish. But it will take a little time, for they have got their teeth well in, as is our custom, and must first loosen their jaws bit by bit. Meanwhile, give ear to our petition." "Your conduct hasn't exactly inclined me to grant it," said I. "Don't hold it against us that we are clumsy," said he, and now for the first time had recourse to the natural plaintiveness of his voice, "we are poor creatures, we have nothing but our teeth; whatever we want to do, good or bad, we can tackle it only with our teeth." "Well, what do you want?" I asked, not much mollified.

"Sir," he cried, and all the jackals howled together; very remotely it seemed to resemble a melody. "Sir, we want you to end this quarrel that divides the world. You are exactly the man whom our ancestors foretold as born to do it. We want to be troubled no more by Arabs; room to breathe; a skyline cleansed of them; no more bleating of sheep knifed by an Arab; every beast to die a natural death; no interference till we have drained the carcass empty and picked its bones clean. Cleanliness, nothing but cleanliness is what we want"—and now they were all lamenting and sobbing—"how can you bear to live in such a world, O noble heart and kindly bowels? Filth is their white; filth is their black; their beards are a horror; the very sight of their eye sockets makes one want to spit; and when they lift an arm, the murk of hell yawns in the armpit. And so, sir, and so, dear sir, by means of your all-powerful hands slit their throats through with these scissors!" And in answer to a jerk of his head a jackal came trotting up with a small pair of sewing scissors, covered with ancient rust, dangling from an eyetooth.

"Well, here's the scissors at last, and high time to stop!" cried the Arab leader of our caravan who had crept upwind towards us and now cracked his great whip.

The jackals fled in haste, but at some little distance rallied in a close huddle, all the brutes so tightly packed and rigid that they looked as if penned in a small fold girt by flickering will-o'-the-wisps.

"So you've been treated to their entertainment too, sir," said the Arab, laughing as gaily as the reserve of his race permitted. "You know, then, what the brutes are after?" I asked. "Of course," said he, "it's common knowledge; so long as Arabs exist, that pair of scissors goes wandering through the desert and will wander with us to the end of our days. Every European is offered it for the great work; every European is just the man that Fate has chosen for them. They have the most lunatic hopes, these beasts; they're just fools, utter fools. That's why we like them; they are our dogs; finer dogs than any of yours. Watch this, now, a camel died last night and I have had it brought here."

Four men came up with the heavy carcass and threw it down before us. It had hardly touched the ground before the jackals lifted up their voices. As if irresistibly drawn by cords each of them began to waver forward, crawling on his belly. They had forgotten the Arabs, forgotten their hatred, the all-obliterating immediate presence of the stinking carrion bewitched them. One was already at the camel's throat, sinking his teeth straight into an artery. Like a vehement small pump endeavoring with as much determination as hopefulness to extinguish some raging fire, every muscle in his body twitched and labored at the task. In a trice they were all on top of the carcass, laboring in common, piled mountain-high.

And now the caravan leader lashed his cutting whip crisscross over their backs. They lifted their heads; half swooning in ectasy; saw the Arabs standing before them; felt the sting of the whip on their muzzles; leaped and ran backwards a stretch. But the camel's blood was already lying in pools, reeking to heaven, the carcass was torn wide open in many places. They could not resist it; they were back again; once more the leader lifted his whip; I stayed his arm.

"You are right, sir," said he, "we'll leave them to their business; besides, it's time to break camp. Well, you've seen them. Marvelous creatures, aren't they? And how they hate us!"

the
last
judgment
karel čapek

Karel Čapek
(1890–1938) was a Czech novelist,
playwright, and short-story
writer of great genius. His best novel,
The War with the Newts, *anticipates
the Fascist domination of Europe; his
plays are "futuristic" and often comic.
He invented the word "robot."
Čapek supposedly died of a heart
attack as parts of the German
army entered Prague during
World War II. For further reading:*
Tales from Two Pockets (1943).

The notorious multiple-killer Kugler, pursued by several warrants and a whole army of policemen and detectives, swore that he'd never be taken. He wasn't, either—at least not alive. The last of his nine murderous deeds was shooting a policeman who tried to arrest him. The policeman indeed died, but not before putting a total of seven bullets into Kugler. Of these seven, three were fatal. Kugler's death came so quickly that he felt no pain. And so it seemed Kugler had escaped earthly justice.

When his soul left his body, it should have been surprised at the sight of the next world—a world beyond space, grey, and infinitely desolate—but it wasn't. A man who has been jailed on two continents looks upon the next life merely as new surroundings. Kugler expected to struggle through, equipped only with a bit of courage, as he had in the last world.

At length the inevitable Last Judgment got around to Kugler.

Heaven being eternally in a state of emergency, Kugler was brought before a special court of three judges and not, as his previous conduct would ordinarily merit, before a jury. The courtroom was furnished simply, almost like courtrooms on earth, with this one exception: there was no provision for swearing in witnesses. In time, however, the reason for this will become apparent.

The judges were old and worthy councillors with austere, bored faces. Kugler complied with the usual tedious formalities: Ferdinand Kugler, unemployed, born on such and such a date, died . . . at this point it was shown Kugler didn't know the date of his own death. Immediately he realized this was a damaging omission in the eyes of the judges; his spirit of helpfulness faded.

"Do you plead guilty or not guilty?" asked the presiding judge.

"Not guilty," said Kugler obdurately.

"Bring in the first witness," the judge sighed.

Opposite Kugler appeared an extraordinary gentleman, stately, bearded, and clothed in a blue robe strewn with golden stars.

At his entrance the judges arose. Even Kugler stood up, reluctant but fascinated. Only when the old gentleman took a seat did the judges again sit down.

"Witness," began the presiding judge, "Omniscient God, this court has summoned You in order to hear Your testimony in the case against Kugler, Ferdinand. As You are the Supreme Truth, You need not take the oath. In the interest of the proceedings, however, we ask You to keep to the subject at hand rather than branch out into particulars—unless they have a bearing on this case.

"And you, Kugler, don't interrupt the Witness. He knows everything, so there's no use denying anything.

"And now, Witness, if You would please begin."

That said, the presiding judge took off his spectacles and leaned comfortably on the bench before him, evidently in preparation for a long speech by the Witness. The oldest of the three judges nestled down in sleep. The recording angel opened the Book of Life.

God, the Witness, coughed lightly and began:

"Yes. Kugler, Ferdinand. Ferdinand Kugler, son of a factory worker, was a bad, unmanageable child from his earliest days. He loved his mother dearly, but was unable to show it; this made him unruly and defiant. Young man, you irked everyone! Do you remember how you bit your father on the thumb when he tried to spank you? You had stolen a rose from the notary's garden."

"The rose was for Irma, the tax collector's daughter," Kugler said.

"I know," said God. "Irma was seven years old at that time. Did you ever hear what happened to her?"

"No, I didn't."

"She married Oscar, the son of the factory owner. But she contracted a venereal disease from him and died of a miscarriage. You remember Rudy Zaruba?"

"What happened to him?"

"Why, he joined the navy and died accidentally in Bombay. You two were the worst boys in the whole town. Kugler, Ferdinand, was a thief before his tenth year and an inveterate liar. He kept bad company, too: old Gribble, for instance, a drunkard and an idler, living on handouts. Nevertheless, Kugler shared many of his own meals with Gribble."

The presiding judge motioned with his hand, as if much of this was perhaps unnecessary, but Kugler himself asked hesitantly, "And . . . what happened to his daughter?"

"Mary?" asked God. "She lowered herself considerably. In her fourteenth year she married. In her twentieth year she died, remembering you in the agony of her death. By your fourteenth year you were nearly a drunkard yourself, and you often ran away from home. Your father's death came about from grief and worry; your mother's eyes faded from crying. You brought dishonor to your home, and your sister, your pretty sister Martha, never married. No young man would come calling at the home of a thief. She's still living alone and in poverty, sewing until late each night. Scrimping has exhausted her, and patronizing customers hurt her pride."

"What's she doing right now?"

"This very minute she's buying thread at Wolfe's. Do you remember that shop? Once, when you were six years old, you bought a colored glass marble there. On that very same day you lost it and never, never found it. Do you remember how you cried with rage?"

"Whatever happened to it?" Kugler asked eagerly.

"Well, it rolled into the drain and under the gutterspout. As a matter of fact, it's still there, after thirty years. Right now it's raining on earth and your marble is shivering in the gush of cold water."

Kugler bent his head, overcome by this revelation.

But the presiding judge fitted his spectacles back on his nose and said mildly, "Witness, we are obliged to get on with the case. Has the accused committed murder?"

Here the Witness nodded his head.

"He murdered nine people. The first one he killed in a brawl, and it was during his prison term for this crime that he became completely corrupted. The second victim was his unfaithful sweetheart. For that he was sentenced to death, but he escaped. The third was an old man whom he robbed. The fourth was a night watchman."

"Then he died?" Kugler asked.

"He died after three days in terrible pain," God said. "And he left six children behind him. The fifth and sixth victims were an old married couple. He killed them with an axe and found only sixteen dollars, although they had twenty thousand hidden away."

Kugler jumped up.

"Where?"

"In the straw mattress," God said. "In a linen sack inside the mattress. That's where they hid all the money they acquired from greed and penny-pinching. The seventh man he killed in America; a countryman of his, a bewildered, friendless immigrant."

"So it was in the mattress," whispered Kugler in amazement.

"Yes," continued God. "The eighth man was merely a passerby who happened to be in Kugler's way when Kugler was trying to outrun the police. At that time Kugler had periostitis and was delirious from the pain. Young man, you were suffering terribly. The ninth and last was the policeman who killed Kugler exactly when Kugler shot him."

"And why did the accused commit murder?" asked the presiding judge.

"For the same reasons others have," answered God. "Out of anger or desire for money; both deliberately and accidentally—some with pleasure, others from necessity. However, he was generous and often helpful. He was kind to women, gentle with animals, and he kept his word. Am I to mention his good deeds?"

"Thank You," said the presiding judge, "but it isn't necessary. Does the accused have anything to say in his own defense?"

"No," Kugler replied with honest indifference.

"The judges of this court will now take this matter under advisement," declared the presiding judge, and the three of them withdrew.

Only God and Kugler remained in the courtroom.

"Who are they?" asked Kugler, indicating with his head the men who had just left.

"People like you," answered God. "They were judges on earth, so they're judges here as well."

Kugler nibbled his fingertips. "I expected . . . I mean, I never really thought about it. But I figured You would judge, since—"

"Since I'm God," finished the Stately Gentleman. "But that's just it, don't you see? Because I know everything, I can't possibly judge. That wouldn't do at all. By the way, do you know who turned you in this time?"

"No, I don't," said Kugler, surprised.

"Lucky, the waitress. She did it out of jealousy."

"Excuse me," Kugler ventured, "but You forgot about that good-for-nothing Teddy I shot in Chicago."

"Not at all," God said. "He recovered and is alive this very minute. I know he's an informer, but otherwise he's a very good man and terribly fond of children. You shouldn't think of any person as being completely worthless."

"But I still don't understand why You aren't the judge," Kugler said thoughtfully.

"Because my knowledge is infinite. If judges knew everything, absolutely everything, then they would also understand everything. Their hearts would ache. They couldn't sit in judgment—and neither can I. As it is, they know only about your crimes. I know all about you. The entire Kugler. And that's why I cannot judge."

"But why are they judging . . . the same people who were judges on earth?"

"Because man belongs to man. As you see, I'm only the witness. But the verdict is determined by man, even in heaven. Believe me, Kugler, this is the way it should be. Man isn't worthy of divine judgment. He deserves to be judged only by other men."

At that moment the three returned from their deliberation.

In heavy tones the presiding judge announced, "For repeated crimes of first degree murder, manslaughter, robbery, disrespect for the law, illegally carrying weapons, and for the theft of a rose: Kugler, Ferdinand, is sentenced to lifelong punishment in hell. The sentence is to begin immediately.

"Next case, please: Torrance, Frank.

"Is the accused present in court?"

the chronicle of an old rose-tree

strates myriveles

Strates Myriveles (1892–) is one of the foremost men of letters in modern Greece. A novelist and short-story writer, his work is notable for its emotional tone and its exploitation of materials which are "patriotic" by implication or by overt statement. The short fiction of Myriveles is far too little known in the English-speaking world.

I want to write the story of a rose-tree. We lived together for sixteen long years, sixteen of the most significant years of my life, replete with harrowing events. I loved that rose-tree, for she was an old rose-tree with many branches and many roses. I feel she was fond of me, too. Such a feeling can blossom between a man and a tree.

I know a true, strange story, told to me at Mytilini, a long time ago by some old convicts who were serving life-sentences at Castro. One of them had committed an appalling murder. He set fire to his house and burned up his wife and children—thinking the children weren't his. He was the one who told me what happened, his eyes scalding in tears. Such a mystery is man.

During his long years behind bars, he was once acquainted with another convict, a lad who had come to prison fresh as a daisy, and had left as a man with gray hair. In the prison yard, the lad planted a walnut; it sprouted. All his thoughts and cares from that time on were for tending this plant. For fear that it might get hurt before it became strong he surrounded it with wire; he watered it with his ration of drinking water. Years passed, and the lad became a man; the walnut tree grew up, sturdy and joyful.

One day the warden called the man into his office. He had been granted a pardon, and he could get his stuff and go. The prisoner stood speechless, amazed.

"And the walnut tree?" he stammered.

"What do you mean, the walnut tree?"

"I have no one in the world but that walnut tree," said the stunned prisoner.

The warden laughed.

"Well, what can we do? The walnut tree has to stay in its place."

The prisoner lowered his head; he could speak no more. He made a bundle of his rags. He sat on the horse-block facing the tree, and looked at it and shed bitter tears. Then a miracle happened, witnessed by all the prisoners who still tell of it. In the spring time of its life, all green with fresh, cool foliage, the tree began to wither. The leaves turned ragged and yellow; they crumpled completely, and fell. The trunk, too, dried down to its roots.

The old man's eyes were big with burning tears while he told me this story.

But my rose-tree did not commit suicide because of grief. A knife cut off her life.

But let me tell her story from the beginning.

When the Germans entered Athens, I received a telegram from my uncle who owned a house there. He was stranded on Lesbos, where he died a year later, at eighty-five. His telegram told me to move my wife and children immediately into his vacant home—before the Germans requisitioned it.

It was an old Athenian mansion, two stories, with eight large rooms, and a small garden in front. A beautiful trellis overarched the garden gate; each spring the fragrance of leaves and flowers filled all of Eresso

Street. In the middle of the yard, in the middle of a white and gray marble patio, there stood the rose-tree: a grand rose-tree. How old was she? I seem to remember her from my student years when I went sometimes to visit my uncle. Three trunks grew upward for more than six feet, each trunk big as my arm. Higher, a multitude of branches were always loaded with roses, and gave off a strong scent, winter and summer, for the blossoms appeared the year round. Around the courtyard was an iron fence, and the rose-tree hung over the spiked top, enticing the passers-by with her roses.

My uncle, the owner, was a strange old bachelor who spent most of his life in this house. As a student he came from the island, and he had rented one of its rooms from the first owner, an old French countess. Finally he bought the house and let her stay until she died of old age. She was a childless woman, alone, without anyone in the world. Alone, she idled her time reading old Parisian magazines, or she sometimes hummed Parisian songs of times past. She hummed them softly and heard them all alone. My uncle was like a parched reed; he lived alone there during and after his student years, an engineer by profession. He was slender, tall, austere, and always an elegant, meticulous dresser. He wore a fuzzed gray top hat, dangled a slim cane, and wrote in an impeccable *katharevousa*. He lived all alone beneath the gilded ceilings in those eight large rooms.

My uncle, it seemed, was also in love with the rose-tree; and she must have been the one and only love in his life, a life never adorned by a woman's grace. I say he must have been in love, for when the rose-tree grew tall above the iron spikes, the street urchins climbed the fence to gather the flowers. One day my uncle seized his pistol and chased them away—like a jealous lover. That day he called in workers to double the height of the iron fence so that no young rival could molest his tree.

In the sixteen years I lived there the rose-tree grew taller and taller, and put new branches over the second iron spikes.

My study was on the ground floor. It looked out a large window and into the yard. There the flowers of the rose-tree were abundant and rich in fragrance, for they were mayroses. To be sure the tree bloomed best in spring, but miraculously there were also blossoms in winter, in the fall, and all the year round. Even when Athens was covered with snow, she kept giving roses. If I opened my window, she spilled her branches into my room, soothing the bitter years of the occupation and the Communist reign of terror. She gave me great comfort. She was a symbol of hope. We were cold and hungry. We listened to the bullets ricocheting off the iron fence, but the rose-tree moved her blooming branches near us. No matter, we used to say. The sun will rise again, the grapes and peaches will bear fruit again, and love will come again to men who have become wild beasts, driven by a stupid, incomprehensible hate.

The streets had become deserted; no one dared show his face. One day a young woman passed by Exarcheia, hugging the walls. She held a bottle of milk. A rascal, on a rooftop, saw her, took aim and fired, killing her. Two or three neighbors rushed out to the rescue. Holding the bottle tight to her chest, she lived long enough to say:

"Give the milk to my child, neighbors . . ."

Then she died.

I cut a rose, put it in a vase on my desk, in memory of the unknown mother. Later, peace gradually came and Greek ceased to fear Greek. Spring came, and our rose-tree reddened from top to bottom. It was so old, and yet so brimming with youth. Passers-by walked outside and stopped on the sidewalk to look at it, as one looks at a beautiful woman. They smiled at her and inhaled her strong fragrance. Couples in love stopped and asked for a rose. My jealous uncle was no longer alive, and those of us in the courtyard offered the blossoms. When we were not at home, a young gallant clambered up the fence, and holding to an iron spike, reached out to steal a rose for his young, fair Juliana.

Once I watched him from my desk, scampering down, jumping back red of face, redder than his rose, looking all around for fear that he might have been seen. The man behind the window saw him and smiled, for he too had stolen roses and even now, on occasion, cannot leave them alone. But the lad was not aware of that. The young man was of heroic countenance, as if he had plucked an edelweiss from the steepest peak of the Alps. For that, the man inside smiles at the rose-tree whose pillaged branch is still moving. The two exchange an understanding glance, so intended.

Then the good old days returned. Holy week came, churches opened their doors, and the Athenians swallowed their tears and waited for Easter. Then the maidens of the neighborhood came—and Neapolis has many lovely maidens—knocked at our door and asked that the rose-tree contribute to the decoration of the Epitaph. The young myrrh-bearers left with their baskets full.

All this, and much more, belongs to the Annals of the Rose-tree. I wonder how much more interesting the old rose-tree's own diary would be, starting with the time when the hands of the young French aristocrat first planted and watered the bush every evening from the well of the yard. Those hands which aged year by year within the eight empty rooms, withered, disfigured, died, and disintegrated many years ago.

And so did that young islander, the student of the Polytechnic, for forty years the only occupant of the house, who lived, grew, and grayed near the rose-tree. That jealous lover of hers who once when he saw a flock of urchins plundering its roses, chased them, waving his pistol. At that time he was a high state official, with a white mustache and a thin cane with a silver handle. He remained faithful to our rose-tree till he died.

Our old rose-tree also had its heroic and tragic days. Every March 25 of our four-year occupation by the Germans, every October 28 of our cruel occupation, my children and all young school children, cut all the roses to take to the tomb of the Unknown Soldier. Schoolboys and girls marched in procession with bouquets held high, and with the National Anthem on their lips. All around, bullets from the machine guns hissed; the armored car tracks chewed Athen's asphalt. But our children advanced in formation, still singing. They looked hungry and gaunt, their legs emaciated, the bloom of youth gone from their faces.

But high in their hands, above their heads, the roses shone red. The conquerors grabbed the flowers, trampled them furiously. The children returned dusty, dirty, ragged, bruised, beaten by rifle butts. But their great eyes shone with the Greek flame that burned inside them day and night.

Then came the blackest December that ever hovered over Athens. For forty days mortars boomed and burst, shattering the branches of the rose-tree. Neapolis was stunned, silent in fear and horror. One day the old rose-tree stooped: below her branches the sidewalk by our gate was red. It was not the red paint with which the maniacs splashed walls with their slogans of fratricide. It was blood. Real, warm, oozing blood gushing from large wounds from a street that had known only the joyful shouts of children. Now the street echoed the moans of murdered men, six or seven innocent persons dying there.

After their homes had been blown up by the maniacs, these men had started from a corner of Athens, roving the streets, seeking shelter. A little bell hung from the top of our yard gate. My wife heard the bell ringing, ringing furiously. Germans, she thought, and was afraid to open the gate. When the row ceased, she found in front of our gate a heap of wretched, bloody corpses. These men had been ringing the little bell, seeking refuge.

But our old rose-tree was still there. Her roses spread and heartened us. Roses are everywhere, she said to us. It is enough to push aside the leaves and thorns, she kept telling us. Always there is a cool spring, delicate and pure, waiting, its hands filled with flowers. Even in the heartaches of men there is green in the heart of winter. Heave open your soul's windows, and they will find a way of placing their bouquets inside. Deep inside.

When I first occupied the house, the rose-tree filled the whole square of the yard, in the plot of ground at the center of the flagstone patio.

Then two significant events occurred in that space. First, a new little plant sprung from the soil; no one knew what it was. Partaking of the water we gave the rose-tree, it kept growing under the rose's shade. When the new plant was about knee-high, a friend who knew about trees told us that by its leaves it looked like a plum-tree. Each year it grew fast, taking its water and nourishment from the same soil that fed the thick roots of the rose-tree. With the years, its slender trunk made its way through the branches that shaded it and popped out in full view of the sun it had been reaching for. It had become a grown tree, a strong, powerful tree that selfishly overwhelmed our rose-tree.

One spring, for the first time, its foliage filled with white blossoms, and then its branches bowed with red plums. It was bedecked with fruit like a Christmas tree. It covered the rose-tree, spread its branches triumphantly above the yard, and hung its plums invitingly over the iron fence. The street urchins no longer climbed the fence for roses. Suspended from the fence, they reached the tips of the plum branches and filled their pockets with unripe plums. The shady branches of the plum had shrouded the rose-tree which had accorded it hospitality for so many years, and the rose-tree began to wither. The other was a new life, rampant, straining for light and juices; under the earth its roots swelled strong and avid, clutched the roots of the rose-tree, hugging them, twining around them, and sucking their soil. I watched this drama day after day. Now the plum tree soared in full beauty and untrammeled youth, spread its branches everywhere, conquered air, and light, and also conquered the soil.

Our rose-tree began to wither. Most of the trunks began to rot, and I cut them to rid the space of dried up branches. Each spring a few new shoots sprang from the roots, but they made little progress. They were sickly and feeble. They grew a little, then they wilted and withered. The remaining stalk produced only a few flowers. There was no longer the abundance of past years. But the rose-tree persisted in giving forth some flowers, in revealing her presence even in this desperate battle. Finally she made the great decision. She imitated her adversary. From a large, thick bush, she became a climbing rose. She gathered all her remaining forces into upward growth and began to climb the plum tree, in two twining tresses, like two green snakes that twirled upward in search of the sun. To succeed in this, she used as support the very stout trunk of the plum tree. She clung to it and began to climb among its limbs. It was a relentless struggle to the end. Each time the two stalks gained growth, they stopped to rest at that step, on some node of the tree, and then sprang upward again.

We saw this metamorphosis and thought that that was the end, that we would no longer see roses. Then we stopped paying attention to what was happening. By now the rose was so entwined with the plum tree that we could no longer tell them apart.

Meanwhile, the plum tree grew taller, as high as our two-story house. On the second floor, above my study, was my son's study. I rarely went up there because I did not want to intrude while he worked. But one day, when he was away in the country, I entered the room and stood at the window. When I opened the outside shutters, suddenly a branch whisked in and a fragrance caressed my face. It was a large cluster of roses. They had bloomed in the crown of the plum tree, in the splendid sun, a trophy, and a shout of victory.

It was something thrilling.

From then on, high up in the branches of the plum tree, we saw more roses. The last roses kept blooming.

The plum tree was the first, most significant event in the life of the old rose-tree. The second event was something more modest, but quite pleasing.

In the enclosed square where the two trees stood, from the year that we moved into the house, there grew two night-blooming plants. They sprang up each year, on opposite sides of the square, one to the left, one to the right. Who knows where the seeds came from? Each year the two stems emerged. They were fragile, succulent, full of sap and vigor. When fall came, they put out red buds which opened at dusk and gave forth a strong aroma all through the night. It was a sweet aroma that one could almost taste. In bloom they stood on each side of the rose and the plum tree like two large lighted candlesticks. They withered with winter, and we raked them away with the leaves. In time the soil was trampled on, and the earth became hard as concrete. The plants poked up again, nevertheless, each late spring, all freshness anew, growing within a few days and becoming loaded with buds. We had these annuals all sixteen years that we had the house.

Now the old mansion has been torn down in order to raise a new building. Down came the double iron fence that protected the rose-tree from her passing lovers. And down came the plum tree, chopped down, falling with the rose-tree in its embrace. So were the two luminous night-blooming plants extinguished forever. And with them died the romantic memory of the old French countess, whose spirit till then only the flowers of the rose-tree evoked. And so remembrance of the tall, slender old bachelor died, too, he who guarded the roses with his loaded revolver.

In this short story I wanted to save some vestiges from the life of sixteen years, a life filled with fears and griefs, and with the joys and anguish of children and trees.

the wall

jean-paul sartre

Jean-Paul Sartre (1905–   ), novelist, short-story writer, critic, and literary theorist, is a professor of philosophy in Paris. Nausea (1938) is considered his most interesting novel. Sartre's contribution to the intellectual history of the age is in the area of existential thought. For further reading: Intimacy, translated by Lloyd Alexander (1949).

They pushed us into a big white room and I began to blink because the light hurt my eyes. Then I saw a table and four men behind the table, civilians, looking over the papers. They had bunched another group of prisoners in the back and we had to cross the whole room to join them. There were several I knew and some others who must have been foreigners. The two in front of me were blond with round skulls; they looked alike. I suppose they were French. The smaller one kept hitching up his pants; nerves.

It lasted about three hours; I was dizzy and my head was empty; but the room was well heated and I found that pleasant enough: for the past 24 hours we hadn't stopped shivering. The guards brought the prisoners up to the table, one after the other. The four men asked each one his name and occupation. Most of the time they didn't go any further —or they would simply ask a question here and there: "Did you have anything to do with the sabotage of munitions?" Or "Where were you the morning of the 9th and what were you doing?" They didn't listen to the answers or at least didn't seem to. They were quiet for a moment and then looking straight in front of them began to write. They asked Tom if it were true he was in the International Brigade; Tom couldn't tell them otherwise because of the papers they found in his coat. They didn't ask Juan anything but they wrote for a long time after he told them his name.

"My brother José is the anarchist," Juan said, "you know he isn't here any more. I don't belong to any party, I never had anything to do with politics."

They didn't answer. Juan went on, "I haven't done anything. I don't want to pay for somebody else."

His lips trembled. A guard shut him up and took him away. It was my turn.

"Your name is Pablo Ibbieta?"

"Yes."

The man looked at the papers and asked me, "Where's Ramon Gris?"

"I don't know."

"You hid him in your house from the 6th to the 19th."

"No."

They wrote for a minute and then the guards took me out. In the corridor Tom and Juan were waiting between two guards. We started walking. Tom asked one of the guards, "So?"

"So what?" the guard said.

"Was that the cross-examination or the sentence?"

"Sentence," the guard said.

"What are they going to do with us?"

The guard answered dryly, "Sentence will be read in your cell."

As a matter of fact, our cell was one of the hospital cellars. It was terrifically cold there because of the drafts. We shivered all night and it wasn't much better during the day. I had spent the previous five days in a cell in a monastery, a sort of hole in the wall that must have dated from the middle ages: since there were a lot of prisoners and not much room, they locked us up anywhere. I didn't miss my cell; I hadn't suffered too much from the cold but I was alone; after a long time it gets irritating. In the cellar I had company. Juan hardly ever spoke: he was afraid and he was too young to have anything to say. But Tom was a good talker and he knew Spanish well.

There was a bench in the cellar and four mats. When they took us back we sat and waited in silence. After a long moment, Tom said, "We're screwed."

"I think so too," I said, "but I don't think they'll do anything to the kid."

"They don't have a thing against him," said Tom. "He's the brother of a militiaman and that's all."

I looked at Juan: he didn't seem to hear. Tom went on, "You know what they do in Saragossa? They lay the men down on the road and run over them with trucks. A Moroccan deserter told us that. They said it was to save ammunition."

"It doesn't save gas," I said.

I was annoyed at Tom: he shouldn't have said that.

"Then there's officers walking along the road," he went on, "supervising it all. They stick their hands in their pockets and smoke cigarettes. You think they finish off the guys? Hell no. They let them scream. Sometimes for an hour. The Moroccan said he damned near puked the first time."

"I don't believe they'll do that here," I said. "Unless they're really short on ammunition."

Day was coming in through four airholes and a round opening they had made in the ceiling on the left, and you could see the sky through it. Through this hole, usually closed by a trap, they unloaded coal into the cellar. Just below the hole there was a big pile of coal dust; it had been used to heat the hospital but since the beginning of the war the patients were evacuated and the coal stayed there, unused; sometimes it even got rained on because they had forgotten to close the trap.

Tom began to shiver. "Good Jesus Christ I'm cold," he said. "Here it goes again."

He got up and began to do exercises. At each movement his shirt opened on his chest, white and hairy. He lay on his back, raised his legs in the air and bicycled. I saw his great rump trembling. Tom was husky but he had too much fat. I thought how rifle bullets or the sharp points of bayonets would soon be sunk into this mass of tender flesh as in a lump of butter. It wouldn't have made me feel like that if he'd been thin.

I wasn't exactly cold, but I couldn't feel my arms and shoulders any more. Sometimes I had the impression I was missing something and began to look around for my coat and then suddenly remembered they hadn't given me a coat. It was rather uncomfortable. They took our clothes and gave them to their soldiers, leaving us only our shirts—and those canvas pants that hospital patients wear in the middle of summer. After a while Tom got up and sat next to me, breathing heavily.

"Warmer?"

"Good Christ, no. But I'm out of wind."

Around eight o'clock in the evening a major came in with two *falangistas*. He had a sheet of paper in his hand. He asked the guard, "What are the names of those three?"

"Steinbock, Ibbieta and Mirbal," the guard said.

The major put on his eyeglasses and scanned the list: "Steinbock . . . Steinbock . . . Oh yes . . . You are sentenced to death. You will be shot tomorrow morning." He went on looking. "The other two as well."

"That's not possible," Juan said. "Not me."

The major looked at him amazed. "What's your name?"

"Juan Mirbal," he said.

"Well, your name is there," said the major. "You're sentenced."

"I didn't do anything," Juan said.

The major shrugged his shoulders and turned to Tom and me.

"You're Basque?"

"Nobody is Basque."

He looked annoyed. "They told me there were three Basques. I'm not going to waste my time running after them. Then naturally you don't want a priest?"

We didn't even answer.

He said, "A Belgian doctor is coming shortly. He is authorized to spend the night with you." He made a military salute and left.

"What did I tell you," Tom said. "We get it."

"Yes," I said, "it's a rotten deal for the kid."

I said that to be decent but I didn't like the kid. His face was too thin and fear and suffering had disfigured it, twisting all his features. Three days before he was a smart sort of kid, not too bad; but now he looked like an old fairy and I thought how he'd never be young again, even if they were to let him go. It wouldn't have been too hard to have a little pity for him but pity disgusts me, or rather it horrifies me. He hadn't said anything more but he had turned grey; his face and hands were both grey. He sat down again and looked at the ground with round eyes. Tom was good hearted, he wanted to take his arm, but the kid tore himself away violently and made a face.

"Let him alone," I said in a low voice, "you can see he's going to blubber."

Tom obeyed regretfully; he would have liked to comfort the kid, it would have passed his time and he wouldn't have been tempted to think about himself. But it annoyed me: I'd never thought about death because I never had any reason to, but now the reason was here and there was nothing to do but think about it.

Tom began to talk. "So you think you've knocked guys off, do you?" he asked me. I didn't answer. He began explaining to me that he had knocked off six since the beginning of August; he didn't realize the situation and I could tell he didn't *want* to realize it. I hadn't quite realized it myself, I wondered if it hurt much, I thought of bullets, I imagined their burning hail through my body. All that was beside the real question; but I was calm: we had all night to understand. After a while Tom stopped talking and I watched him out of the corner of my eye; I saw he too had turned grey and he looked rotten; I told myself "Now it starts." It was almost dark, a dim glow filtered through the airholes and the pile of coal and made a big stain beneath the spot of sky; I could already see a star through the hole in the ceiling: the night would be pure and icy.

The door opened and two guards came in, followed by a blonde man in a tan uniform. He saluted us. "I am the doctor," he said. "I have authorization to help you in these trying hours."

He had an agreeable and distinguished voice. I said, "What do you want here?"

"I am at your disposal. I shall do all I can to make your last moments less difficult."

"What did you come here for? There are others, the hospital's full of them."

"I was sent here," he answered with a vague look. "Ah! Would you like to smoke?" he added hurriedly, "I have cigarettes and even cigars."

He offered us English cigarettes and *puros,* but we refused. I looked him in the eyes and he seemed irritated. I said to him, "You aren't here on an errand of mercy. Besides, I know you. I saw you with the fascists in the barracks yard the day I was arrested."

I was going to continue, but something surprising suddenly happened to me; the presence of this doctor no longer interested me. Generally when I'm on somebody I don't let go. But the desire to talk left me completely; I shrugged and turned my eyes away. A little later I raised my head; he was watching me curiously. The guards were sitting on a mat. Pedro, the tall thin one, was twiddling his thumbs, the other shook his head from time to time to keep from falling asleep.

"Do you want a light?" Pedro suddenly asked the doctor. The other nodded "Yes": I think he was about as smart as a log, but he surely wasn't bad. Looking in his cold blue eyes it seemed to me that his only sin was lack of imagination. Pedro went out and came back with an oil lamp which he set on the corner of the bench. It gave a bad light but it was better than nothing: they had left us in the dark the night before. For a long time I watched the circle of light the lamp made on the ceiling. I was fascinated. Then suddenly I woke up, the circle of light disappeared and I felt myself crushed under an enormous weight. It was not the thought of death or fear; it was nameless. My cheeks burned and my head ached.

I shook myself and looked at my two friends. Tom had hidden his face in his hands. I could only see the fat white nape of his neck. Little Juan was the worst; his mouth was open and his nostrils trembled. The doctor went to him and put his hand on his shoulder to comfort him, but his eyes stayed cold. Then I saw the Belgian's hand drop stealthily along Juan's arm, down to the wrist. Juan paid no attention. The Belgian took his wrist between three fingers, distractedly, the same time drawing back a little and turning his back to me. But I leaned backward and saw him take a watch from his pocket and look at it for a moment, never letting go of the wrist. After a minute he let the hand fall inert and went and leaned his back against the wall, then, as if he suddenly remembered something very important which had to be jotted down on the spot, he took a notebook from his pocket and wrote a few lines. "Bastard," I thought angrily, "let him come and take my pulse. I'll shove my fist in his rotten face."

He didn't come but I felt him watching me. I raised my head and returned his look. Impersonally, he said to me, "Doesn't it seem cold to you here?" He looked cold, he was blue.

"I'm not cold," I told him.

He never took his hard eyes off me. Suddenly I understood and my hands went to my face: I was drenched in sweat. In this cellar, in the midst of winter, in the midst of drafts, I was sweating. I ran my hands through my hair, gummed together with perspiration; at the same time I saw my shirt was damp and sticking to my skin: I had been dripping for an hour and hadn't felt it. But that swine of a Belgian hadn't missed a thing; he had seen the drops rolling down my cheeks and thought: this is the manifestation of an almost pathological state of terror; and he had felt normal and proud of being alive because he was cold. I wanted to stand up and smash his face but no sooner had I made the slightest gesture than my rage and shame were wiped out; I fell back on the bench with indifference.

I satisfied myself by rubbing my neck with my handkerchief because now I felt the sweat dropping from my hair onto my neck and it was unpleasant. I soon gave up rubbing, it was useless; my handkerchief was already soaked and I was still sweating. My buttocks were sweating too and my damp trousers were glued to the bench.

Suddenly Juan spoke. "You're a doctor?"

"Yes," the Belgian said.

"Does it hurt . . . very long?"

"Huh? When . . . ? Oh, no," the Belgian said paternally. "Not at all. It's over quickly." He acted as though he were calming a cash customer.

"But I . . . they told me . . . sometimes they have to fire twice."

"Sometimes," the Belgian said, nodding. "It may happen that the first volley reaches no vital organs."

"Then they have to reload their rifles and aim all over again?" He thought for a moment and then added hoarsely, "That takes time!"

He had a terrible fear of suffering, it was all he thought about: it was his age. I never thought much about it and it wasn't fear of suffering that made me sweat.

I got up and walked to the pile of coal dust. Tom jumped up and threw me a hateful look: I had annoyed him because my shoes squeaked. I wondered if my face looked as frightened as his: I saw he was sweating too. The sky was superb, no light filtered into the dark corner and I had only to raise my head to see the Big Dipper. But it wasn't like it had been: the night before I could see a great piece of sky from my monastery cell and each hour of the day brought me a different memory. Morning, when the sky was a hard, light blue, I thought of beaches on the Atlantic; at noon I saw the sun and I remembered a bar in Seville where I drank *manzanilla* and ate olives and anchovies; afternoons I was in the shade and I thought of the deep shadow which spreads over half a bull-ring leaving the other half shimmering in sunlight; it was really hard to see the whole world reflected in the sky like that. But now

I could watch the sky as much as I pleased, it no longer evoked anything in me. I liked that better. I came back and sat near Tom. A long moment passed.

Tom began speaking in a low voice. He had to talk, without that he wouldn't have been able to recognize himself in his own mind. I thought he was talking to me but he wasn't looking at me. He was undoubtedly afraid to see me as I was, grey and sweating: we were alike and worse than mirrors of each other. He watched the Belgian, the living.

"Do you understand?" he said. "I don't understand."

I began to speak in a low voice too. I watched the Belgian.

"Why? What's the matter?"

"Something is going to happen to us that I can't understand."

There was a strange smell about Tom. It seemed to me I was more sensitive than usual to odors. I grinned. "You'll understand in a while."

"It isn't clear," he said obstinately. "I want to be brave but first I have to know . . . Listen, they're going to take us into the courtyard. Good. They're going to stand up in front of us. How many?"

"I don't know. Five or eight. Not more."

"All right. There'll be eight. Someone'll holler 'aim!' and I'll see eight rifles looking at me. I'll think how I'd like to get inside the wall, I'll push against it with my back . . . with every ounce of strength I have, but the wall will stay, like in a nightmare. I can imagine all that. If you only knew how well I can imagine it."

"All right, all right!" I said, "I can imagine it too."

"It must hurt like hell. You know, they aim at the eyes and the mouth to disfigure you," he added mechanically. "I can feel the wounds already; I've had pains in my head and in my neck for the past hour. Not real pains. Worse. This is what I'm going to feel tomorrow morning. And then what?"

I well understood what he meant but I didn't want to act as if I did. I had pains too, pains in my body like a crowd of tiny scars. I couldn't get used to it. But I was like him, I attached no importance to it. "After," I said, "you'll be pushing up daisies."

He began to talk to himself: he never stopped watching the Belgian. The Belgian didn't seem to be listening. I knew what he had come to do; he wasn't interested in what we thought; he came to watch our bodies, bodies dying in agony while yet alive.

"It's like a nightmare," Tom was saying. "You want to think of something, you always have the impression that it's all right, that you're going to understand and then it slips, it escapes you and fades away. I tell myself there will be nothing afterwards. But I don't understand what it means. Sometimes I almost can . . . and then it fades away and

I start thinking about the pains again, bullets, explosions. I'm a materialist, I swear it to you; I'm not going crazy. But something's the matter. I see my corpse; that's not hard but *I'm* the one who sees it, with *my* eyes. I've got to think . . . think that I won't see anything anymore and the world will go on for the others. We aren't made to think that, Pablo. Believe me: I've already stayed up a whole night waiting for something. But this isn't the same: this will creep up behind us, Pablo, and we won't be able to prepare for it."

"Shut up," I said, "Do you want me to call a priest?"

He didn't answer. I had already noticed he had the tendency to act like a prophet and call me Pablo, speaking in a toneless voice. I didn't like that: but it seems all the Irish are that way. I had the vague impression he smelled of urine. Fundamentally, I hadn't much sympathy for Tom and I didn't see why, under the pretext of dying together, I should have any more. It would have been different with some others. With Ramon Gris, for example. But I felt alone between Tom and Juan. I liked that better, anyhow: with Ramon I might have been more deeply moved. But I was terribly hard just then and I wanted to stay hard.

He kept on chewing his words, with something like distraction. He certainly talked to keep himself from thinking. He smelled of urine like an old prostate case. Naturally, I agreed with him, I could have said everything he said: it isn't *natural* to die. And since I was going to die, nothing seemed natural to me, not this pile of coal dust, or the bench, or Pedro's ugly face. Only it didn't please me to think the same things as Tom. And I knew that, all through the night, every five minutes, we would keep on thinking things at the same time. I looked at him sideways and for the first time he seemed strange to me: he wore death on his face. My pride was wounded: for the past twenty-four hours I had lived next to Tom, I had listened to him, I had spoken to him and I knew we had nothing in common. And now we looked as much alike as twin brothers, simply because we were going to die together. Tom took my hand without looking at me.

"Pablo, I wonder . . . I wonder if it's really true that everything ends."

I took my hand away and said, "Look between your feet, you pig."

There was a big puddle between his feet and drops fell from his pants-leg.

"What is it?" he asked frightened.

"You're pissing in your pants," I told him.

"It isn't true," he said furiously. "I'm not pissing. I don't feel anything."

The Belgian approached us. He asked with false solicitude, "Do you feel ill?"

Tom did not answer. The Belgian looked at the puddle and said nothing.

"I don't know what it is," Tom said ferociously. "But I'm not afraid. I swear I'm not afraid."

The Belgian did not answer. Tom got up and went to piss in a corner. He came back buttoning his fly, and sat down without a word. The Belgian was taking notes.

All three of us watched him because he was alive. He had the motions of a living human being, the cares of a living human being; he shivered in the cellar the way the living are supposed to shiver; he had an obedient, well-fed body. The rest of us hardly felt ours—not in the same way anyhow. I wanted to feel my pants between my legs but I didn't dare; I watched the Belgian, balancing on his legs, master of his muscles, someone who could think about tomorrow. There we were, three blood-less shadows; we watched him and we sucked his life like vampires.

Finally he went over to little Juan. Did he want to feel his neck for some professional motive or was he obeying an impulse of charity? If he was acting by charity it was the only time during the whole night.

He caressed Juan's head and neck. The kid let himself be handled, his eyes never leaving him, then suddenly, he seized the hand and looked at it strangely. He held the Belgian's hand between his own two hands and there was nothing pleasant about them, two grey pincers gripping his fat and reddish hand. I suspected what was going to happen and Tom must have suspected it too: but the Belgian didn't see a thing, he smiled paternally. After a moment the kid brought the fat red hand to his mouth and tried to bite it. The Belgian pulled away quickly and stumbled back against the wall. For a second he looked at us with horror, he must have suddenly understood that we were not men like him. I began to laugh and one of the guards jumped up. The other was asleep, his wide open eyes were blank.

I felt relaxed and over-excited at the same time. I didn't want to think any more about what would happen at dawn, at death. It made no sense. I only found words or emptiness. But as soon as I tried to think of anything else I saw rifle barrels pointing at me. Perhaps I lived through my execution twenty times; once I even thought it was for good: I must have slept a minute. They were dragging me to the wall and I was struggling; I was asking for mercy. I woke up with a start and looked at the Belgian: I was afraid I might have cried out in my sleep. But he was stroking his moustache, he hadn't noticed anything. If I had wanted to, I think I could have slept a while; I had been awake for forty-eight hours. I was at the end of my rope. But I didn't want to lose two hours of life: they would come to wake me up at dawn, I would follow them, stupefied with sleep and I would have croaked without so much as an "Oof!"; I didn't want that, I didn't want to die like an ani-mal, I wanted to understand. Then I was afraid of having nightmares.

I got up, walked back and forth, and, to change my ideas, I began to think about my past life. A crowd of memories came back to me pell-mell. There were good and bad ones—or at least I called them that *before*. There were faces and incidents. I saw the face of a little *novillero* who was gored in Valencia during the *Feria*, the face of one of my uncles, the face of Ramon Gris. I remembered my whole life: how I was out of work for three months in 1926, how I almost starved to death. I remembered a night I spent on a bench in Grenada: I hadn't eaten for three days. I was angry, I didn't want to die. That made me smile. How madly I ran after happiness, after women, after liberty. Why? I wanted to free Spain, I admired Pi y Margall, I joined the anarchist movement, I spoke in public meetings: I took everything as seriously as if I were immortal.

At that moment I felt that I had my whole life in front of me, and I thought, "It's a damned lie." It was worth nothing because it was finished. I wondered how I'd been able to walk, to laugh with the girls: I wouldn't have moved so much as my little finger if I had only imagined I would die like this. My life was in front of me, shut, closed, like a bag and yet everything inside of it was unfinished. For an instant I tried to judge it. I wanted to tell myself, this is a beautiful life. But I couldn't pass judgment on it; it was only a sketch; I had spent my time counterfeiting eternity, I had understood nothing. I missed nothing: there were so many things I could have missed, the taste of *manzanilla* or the baths I took in summer in a little creek near Cadiz; but death had disenchanted everything.

The Belgian suddenly had a bright idea. "My friends," he told us, "I will undertake—if the military administration will allow it—to send a message for you, a souvenir to those who love you . . ."

Tom mumbled, "I don't have anybody."

I said nothing. Tom waited an instant then looked at me with curiosity. "You don't have anything to say to Concha?"

"No."

I hated this tender complicity: it was my own fault, I had talked about Concha the night before, I should have controlled myself. I was with her for a year. Last night I would have given an arm to see her again for five minutes. That was why I talked about her, it was stronger than I was. Now I had no more desire to see her, I had nothing more to say to her. I would not even have wanted to hold her in my arms: my body filled me with horror because it was grey and sweating—and I wasn't sure that her body didn't fill me with horror. Concha would cry when she found out I was dead, she would have no taste for life for months afterwards. But I was still the one who was going to die. I thought of her soft, beautiful eyes. When she looked at me something passed from her to me. But I knew it was over: if she looked at me *now* the look would stay in her eyes, it wouldn't reach me. I was alone.

Tom was alone too but not in the same way. Sitting cross-legged, he had begun to stare at the bench with a sort of smile, he looked amazed. He put out his hand and touched the wood cautiously as if he were afraid of breaking something, then drew back his hand quickly and shuddered. If I had been Tom I wouldn't have amused myself by touching the bench; this was some more Irish nonsense, but I too found that objects had a funny look: they were more obliterated, less dense than usual. It was enough for me to look at the bench, the lamp, the pile of coal dust, to feel that I was going to die. Naturally I couldn't think clearly about my death but I saw it everywhere, on things, in the way things fell back and kept their distance, discreetly, as people who speak quietly at the bedside of a dying man. It was *his* death which Tom had just touched on the bench.

In the state I was in, if someone had come and told me I could go home quietly, that they would leave me my life whole, it would have left me cold: several hours or several years of waiting is all the same when you have lost the illusion of being eternal. I clung to nothing, in a way I was calm. But it was a horrible calm—because of my body; my body, I saw with its eyes, I heard with its ears, but it was no longer me; it sweated and trembled by itself and I didn't recognize it any more. I had to touch it and look at it to find out what was happening, as if it were the body of someone else. At times I could still feel it, I felt sinkings, and fallings, as when you're in a plane taking a nosedive, or I felt my heart beating. But that didn't reassure me. Everything that came from my body was all cock-eyed. Most of the time it was quiet and I felt no more than a sort of weight, a filthy presence against me; I had the impression of being tied to an enormous vermin. Once I felt my pants and I felt they were damp; I didn't know whether it was sweat or urine, but I went to piss on the coal pile as a precaution.

The Belgian took out his watch, looked at it. He said, "It's three-thirty."

Bastard! He must have done it on purpose. Tom jumped; we hadn't noticed time was running out; night surrounded us like a shapeless, somber mass, I couldn't even remember that it had begun.

Little Juan began to cry. He wrung his hands, pleaded, "I don't want to die. I don't want to die."

He ran across the whole cellar waving his arms in the air, then fell sobbing on one of the mats. Tom watched him with mournful eyes, without the slightest desire to console him. Because it wasn't worth the trouble: the kid made more noise than we did, but he was less touched: he was like a sick man who defends himself against his illness by fever. It's much more serious when there isn't any fever.

He wept: I could clearly see he was pitying himself; he wasn't thinking about death. For one second, one single second, I wanted to weep myself, to weep with pity for myself. But the opposite happened: I glanced at the kid, I saw his thin sobbing shoulders and I felt inhuman: I could pity neither the others nor myself. I said to myself, "I want to die cleanly."

Tom had gotten up, he placed himself just under the round opening and began to watch for daylight. I was determined to die cleanly and I only thought of that. But ever since the doctor told us the time, I felt time flying, flowing away drop by drop.

It was still dark when I heard Tom's voice: "Do you hear them?"

Men were marching in the courtyard.

"Yes."

"What the hell are they doing? They can't shoot in the dark."

After a while we heard no more. I said to Tom, "It's day."

Pedro got up, yawning, and came to blow out the lamp. He said to his buddy, "Cold as hell."

The cellar was all grey. We heard shots in the distance.

"It's starting," I told Tom. "They must do it in the court in the rear."

Tom asked the doctor for a cigarette. I didn't want one; I didn't want cigarettes or alcohol. From that moment on they didn't stop firing.

"Do you realize what's happening?" Tom said.

He wanted to add something but kept quiet, watching the door. The door opened and a lieutenant came in with four soldiers. Tom dropped his cigarette.

"Steinbock?"

Tom didn't answer. Pedro pointed him out.

"Juan Mirbal?"

"On the mat."

"Get up," the lieutenant said.

Juan did not move. Two soldiers took him under the arms and set him on his feet. But he fell as soon as they released him.

The soldiers hesitated.

"He's not the first sick one," said the lieutenant. "You two carry him; they'll fix it up down there."

He turned to Tom. "Let's go."

Tom went out between two soldiers. Two others followed, carrying the kid by the armpits. He hadn't fainted; his eyes were wide open and tears ran down his cheeks. When I wanted to go out the lieutenant stopped me.

"You Ibbieta?"

"Yes."

"You wait here; they'll come for you later."

They left. The Belgian and the two jailers left too, I was alone. I did not understand what was happening to me but I would have liked it better if they had gotten it over with right away. I heard shots at almost regular intervals; I shook with each one of them. I wanted to scream and tear out my hair. But I gritted my teeth and pushed my hands in my pockets because I wanted to stay clean.

After an hour they came to get me and led me to the first floor, to a small room that smelt of cigars and where the heat was stifling. There were two officers sitting smoking in the armchairs, papers on their knees.

"You're Ibbieta?"

"Yes."

"Where is Ramon Gris?"

"I don't know."

The one questioning me was short and fat. His eyes were hard behind his glasses. He said to me, "Come here."

I went to him. He got up and took my arms, staring at me with a look that should have pushed me into the earth. At the same time he pinched my biceps with all his might. It wasn't to hurt me, it was only a game: he wanted to dominate me. He also thought he had to blow his stinking breath square in my face. We stayed for a moment like that, and I almost felt like laughing. It takes a lot to intimidate a man who is going to die; it didn't work. He pushed me back violently and sat down again. He said, "It's his life against yours. You can have yours if you tell us where he is."

These men dolled up with their riding crops and boots were still going to die. A little later than I, but not too much. They busied themselves looking for names in their crumpled papers, they ran after other men to imprison or suppress them; they had opinions on the future of Spain and on other subjects. Their little activities seemed shocking and burlesqued to me; I couldn't put myself in their place, I thought they were insane. The little man was still looking at me, whipping his boots with the riding crop. All his gestures were calculated to give him the look of a live and ferocious beast.

"So? You understand?"

"I don't know where Gris is," I answered. "I thought he was in Madrid."

The other officer raised his pale hand indolently. This indolence was also calculated. I saw through all their little schemes and I was stupefied to find there were men who amused themselves that way.

"You have a quarter of an hour to think it over," he said slowly. "Take him to the laundry, bring him back in fifteen minutes. If he still refuses he will be executed on the spot."

They knew what they were doing: I had passed the night in waiting; then they had made me wait an hour in the cellar while they shot Tom and Juan and now they were locking me up in the laundry; they must have prepared their game the night before. They told themselves that nerves eventually wear out and they hoped to get me that way.

They were badly mistaken. In the laundry I sat on a stool because I felt very weak and I began to think. But not about their proposition. Of course I knew where Gris was; he was hiding with his cousins, four kilometers from the city. I also knew that I would not reveal his hiding place unless they tortured me (but they didn't seem to be thinking about that). All that was perfectly regulated, definite and in no way interested me. Only I would have liked to understand the reasons for my conduct. I would rather die than give up Gris. Why? I didn't like Ramon Gris any more. My friendship for him had died a little while before dawn at the same time as my love for Concha, at the same time as my desire to live. Undoubtedly I thought highly of him: he was tough. But it was not for this reason that I consented to die in his place; his life had no more value than mine; no life had value. They were going to slap a man up against a wall and shoot at him until he died, whether it was I or Gris or somebody else made no difference. I knew he was more useful than I to the cause of Spain but I thought to hell with Spain and anarchy; nothing was important. Yet I was there, I could save my skin and give up Gris and I refused to do it. I found that somehow comic; it was obstinacy. I thought, "I must be stubborn!" And a droll sort of gaiety spread over me.

They came for me and brought me back to the two officers. A rat ran out from under my feet and that amused me. I turned to one of the *falangistas* and said, "Did you see the rat?"

He didn't answer. He was very sober, he took himself seriously. I wanted to laugh but I held myself back because I was afraid that once I got started I wouldn't be able to stop. The *falangista* had a moustache. I said to him again, "You ought to shave off your moustache, idiot." I thought it funny that he would let the hairs of his living being invade his face. He kicked me without great conviction and I kept quiet.

"Well," said the fat officer, "have you thought about it?"

I looked at them with curiosity, as insects of a very rare species. I told them, "I know where he is. He is hidden in the cemetery. In a vault or in the gravediggers' shack."

It was a farce. I wanted to see them stand up, buckle their belts and give orders busily.

They jumped to their feet. "Let's go. Molés, go get fifteen men from Lieutenant Lopez. You," the fat man said, "I'll let you off if you're telling the truth, but it'll cost you plenty if you're making monkeys out of us."

They left in a great clatter and I waited peacefully under the guard of *falangistas*. From time to time I smiled, thinking about the spectacle they would make. I felt stunned and malicious. I imagined them lifting up tombstones, opening the doors of the vaults one by one. I represented this situation to myself as if I had been someone else: this prisoner obstinately playing the hero, these grim *falangistas* with their moustaches and their men in uniform running among the graves; it was irresistibly funny. After half an hour the little fat man came back alone. I thought he had come to give the orders to execute me. The others must have stayed in the cemetery.

The officer looked at me. He didn't look at all sheepish. "Take him into the big courtyard with the others," he said. "After the military operations a regular court will decide what happens to him."

"Then they're not . . . not going to shoot me? . . ."

"Not now, anyway. What happens afterwards is none of my business."

I still didn't understand. I asked, "But why?"

He shrugged his shoulders without answering and the soldiers took me away. In the big courtyard there were about a hundred prisoners, women, children and a few old men. I began walking around the central grass-plot, I was stupefied. At noon they let us eat in the mess hall. Two or three people questioned me. I must have known them, but I didn't answer: I didn't even know where I was.

Around evening they pushed about ten new prisoners into the court. I recognized Garcia, the baker. He said, "What damned luck you have! I didn't think I'd see you alive."

"They sentenced me to death," I said, "and then they changed their minds, I don't know why."

"They arrested me at two o'clock," Garcia said.

"Why?" Garcia had nothing to do with politics.

"I don't know," he said. "They arrest everybody who doesn't think the way they do." He lowered his voice. "They got Gris."

I began to tremble. "When?"

"This morning. He messed it up. He left his cousin's on Tuesday because they had an argument. There were plenty of people to hide him but he didn't want to owe anything to anybody. He said, 'I'd go hide in Ibbieta's place, but they got him, so I'll go hide in the cemetery.' "

"In the cemetery?"

"Yes. What a fool. Of course they went by there this morning, that was sure to happen. They found him in the gravediggers' shack. He shot at them and they got him."

"In the cemetery!"

Everything began to spin and I found myself sitting on the ground: I laughed so hard I cried.

ivy day in the committee room

james joyce

James Joyce (1882–1941), a poet, short-story writer, and novelist, was born in Ireland. However, for most of his adult life, Joyce lived in self-imposed exile, mostly in Italy and France. Partially blind, impoverished, his works banned by the censors and pirated by publishers, Joyce nevertheless forged one of the greatest literary careers in the twentieth century. His major novel Ulysses (1922), on which he worked seven years, was banned in Ireland and did not become legally available in the United States until 1933. For further reading: Dubliners (1914).

Old Jack raked the cinders together with a piece of cardboard and spread them judiciously over the whitening dome of coals. When the dome was thinly covered his face lapsed into darkness but, as he set himself to fan the fire again, his crouching shadow ascended the opposite wall and his face slowly re-emerged into light. It was an old man's face, very bony and hairy. The moist blue eyes blinked at the fire and the moist mouth fell open at times, munching once or twice mechanically when it closed. When the cinders had caught he laid the piece of cardboard against the wall, sighed and said:

"That's better now, Mr. O'Connor."

Mr. O'Connor, a grey-haired young man, whose face was disfigured by many blotches and pimples, had just brought the tobacco for a cigarette into a shapely cylinder but when spoken to he undid his handiwork meditatively. Then he began to roll the tobacco again meditatively and after a moment's thought decided to lick the paper.

"Did Mr. Tierney say when he'd be back?" he asked in a husky falsetto.

"He didn't say."

Mr. O'Connor put his cigarette into his mouth and began to search his pockets. He took out a pack of thin pasteboard cards.

"I'll get you a match," said the old man.

"Never mind, this'll do," said Mr. O'Connor.

He selected one of the cards and read what was printed on it:

MUNICIPAL ELECTIONS

ROYAL EXCHANGE WARD

Mr. Richard J. Tierney, P.L.G., respectfully solicits the favour of your vote and influence at the coming election in the Royal Exchange Ward.

Mr. O'Connor had been engaged by Tierney's agent to canvass one part of the ward but, as the weather was inclement and his boots let in the wet, he spent a great part of the day sitting by the fire in the Committee Room in Wicklow Street with Jack, the old caretaker. They had been sitting thus since the short day had grown dark. It was the sixth of October, dismal and cold out of doors.

Mr. O'Connor tore a strip off the card and, lighting it, lit his cigarette. As he did so the flame lit up a leaf of dark glossy ivy in the lapel of his coat. The old man watched him attentively and then, taking up the piece of cardboard again, began to fan the fire slowly while his companion smoked.

"Ah, yes," he said, continuing, "it's hard to know what way to bring up children. Now who'd think he'd turn out like that! I sent him to the Christian Brothers and I done what I could for him, and there he goes boosing about. I tried to make him someway decent."

He replaced the cardboard wearily.

"Only I'm an old man now I'd change his tune for him. I'd take the stick to his back and beat him while I could stand over him—as I done many a time before. The mother, you know, she cocks him up with this and that. . . ."

"That's what ruins children," said Mr. O'Connor.

"To be sure it is," said the old man. "And little thanks you get for it, only impudence. He takes th'upper hand of me whenever he sees I've a sup taken. What's the world coming to when sons speaks that way to their fathers?"

"What age is he?" said Mr. O'Connor.

"Nineteen," said the old man.

"Why don't you put him to something?"

"Sure, amn't I never done at the drunken bowsy ever since he left school? 'I won't keep you,' I says. 'You must get a job for yourself.' But, sure, it's worse whenever he gets a job; he drinks it all."

Mr. O'Connor shook his head in sympathy, and the old man fell silent, gazing into the fire. Someone opened the door of the room and called out:

"Hello! Is this a Freemason's meeting?"

"Who's that?" said the old man.

"What are you doing in the dark?" asked a voice.

"Is that you, Hynes?" asked Mr. O'Connor.

"Yes. What are you doing in the dark?" said Mr. Hynes, advancing into the light of the fire.

He was a tall, slender young man with a light brown moustache. Imminent little drops of rain hung at the brim of his hat and the collar of his jacket-coat was turned up.

"Well, Mat," he said to Mr. O'Connor, "how goes it?"

Mr. O'Connor shook his head. The old man left the hearth, and after stumbling about the room returned with two candlesticks which he thrust one after the other into the fire and carried to the table. A denuded room came into view and the fire lost all its cheerful colour. The walls of the room were bare except for a copy of an election address. In the middle of the room was a small table on which papers were heaped.

Mr. Hynes leaned against the mantelpiece and asked:

"Has he paid you yet?"

"Not yet," said Mr. O'Connor. "I hope to God he'll not leave us in the lurch to-night."

Mr. Hynes laughed.

"O, he'll pay you. Never fear," he said.

"I hope he'll look smart about it if he means business," said Mr. O'Connor.

"What do you think, Jack?" said Mr. Hynes satirically to the old man.

The old man returned to his seat by the fire, saying:

"It isn't but he has it, anyway. Not like the other tinker."

"What other tinker?" said Mr. Hynes.

"Colgan," said the old man scornfully.

"It is because Colgan's a working-man you say that? What's the difference between a good honest bricklayer and a publican—eh? Hasn't the working-man as good a right to be in the Corporation as anyone else—ay, and a better right than those shoneens that are always hat in hand before any fellow with a handle to his name? Isn't that so, Mat?" said Mr. Hynes, addressing Mr. O'Connor.

"I think you're right," said Mr. O'Connor.

"One man is a plain honest man with no hunker-sliding about him.

He goes in to represent the labour classes. This fellow you're working for only wants to get some job or other."

"Of course, the working-classes should be represented," said the old man.

"The working-man," said Mr. Hynes, "gets all kicks and no halfpence. But it's labour produces everything. The working-man is not looking for fat jobs for his sons and nephews and cousins. The working-man is not going to drag the honour of Dublin in the mud to please a German monarch."

"How's that?" said the old man.

"Don't you know they want to present an address of welcome to Edward Rex if he comes here next year? What do we want kowtowing to a foreign king?"

"Our man won't vote for the address," said Mr. O'Connor. "He goes in on the Nationalist ticket."

"Won't he?" said Mr. Hynes. "Wait till you see whether he will or not. I know him. Is it Tricky Dicky Tierney?"

"By God! perhaps you're right, Joe," said Mr. O'Connor. "Anyway, I wish he'd turn up with the spondulics."

The three men fell silent. The old man began to rake more cinders together. Mr. Hynes took off his hat, shook it and then turned down the collar of his coat, displaying, as he did so, an ivy leaf in the lapel.

"If this man was alive," he said, pointing to the leaf, "we'd have no talk of an address of welcome."

"That's true," said Mr. O'Connor.

"Musha, God be with them times!" said the old man. "There was some life in it then."

The room was silent again. Then a bustling little man with a snuffling nose and very cold ears pushed in the door. He walked over quickly to the fire, rubbing his hands as if he intended to produce a spark from them.

"No money, boys," he said.

"Sit down here, Mr. Henchy," said the old man, offering him his chair.

"O, don't stir, Jack, don't stir," said Mr. Henchy.

He nodded curtly to Mr. Hynes and sat down on the chair which the old man vacated.

"Did you serve Aungier Street?" he asked Mr. O'Connor.

"Yes," said Mr. O'Connor, beginning to search his pockets for memoranda.

"Did you call on Grimes?"

"I did."

"Well? How does he stand?"

"He wouldn't promise. He said: 'I won't tell anyone what way I'm going to vote.' But I think he'll be all right."

"Why so?"

"He asked me who the nominators were; and I told him. I mentioned Father Burke's name. I think it'll be all right."

Mr. Henchy began to snuffle and to rub his hands over the fire at a terrific speed. Then he said:

"For the love of God, Jack, bring us a bit of coal. There must be some left."

The old man went out of the room.

"It's no go," said Mr. Henchy, shaking his head. "I asked the little shoeboy, but he said: 'O, now, Mr. Henchy, when I see the work going on properly I won't forget you, you may be sure.' Mean little tinker! 'Usha, how could he be anything else?"

"What did I tell you, Mat?" said Mr. Hynes. "Tricky Dicky Tierney."

"O, he's as tricky as they make 'em," said Mr. Henchy. "He hasn't got those little pigs' eyes for nothing. Blast his soul! Couldn't he pay up like a man instead of: 'O, now, Mr. Henchy, I must speak to Mr. Fanning. . . . I've spent a lot of money'? Mean little schoolboy of hell! I suppose he forgets the time his little old father kept the hand-me-down shop in Mary's Lane."

"But is that a fact?" asked Mr. O'Connor.

"God, yes," said Mr. Henchy. "Did you never hear that? And the men used to go in on Sunday morning before the houses were open to buy a waistcoat or a trousers—moya! But Tricky Dicky's little old father always had a tricky little black bottle up in a corner. Do you mind now? That's that. That's where he first saw the light."

The old man returned with a few lumps of coal which he placed here and there on the fire.

"That's a nice how-do-you-do," said Mr. O'Connor. "How does he expect us to work for him if he won't stump up?"

"I can't help it," said Mr. Henchy. "I expect to find the bailiffs in the hall when I go home."

Mr. Hynes laughed and, shoving himself away from the mantelpiece with the aid of his shoulders, made ready to leave.

"It'll be all right when King Eddie comes," he said. "Well, boys, I'm off for the present. See you later. 'Bye, 'bye."

He went out of the room slowly. Neither Mr. Henchy nor the old man said anything, but, just as the door was closing, Mr. O'Connor, who had been staring moodily into the fire, called out suddenly:

" 'Bye, Joe."

Mr. Henchy waited a few moments and then nodded in the direction of the door.

"Tell me," he said across the fire, "what brings our friend in here? What does he want?"

" 'Usha, poor Joe!" said Mr. O'Connor, throwing the end of his cigarette into the fire, "he's hard up, like the rest of us."

Mr. Henchy snuffled vigorously and spat so copiously that he nearly put out the fire, which uttered a hissing protest.

"To tell you my private and candid opinion," he said, "I think he's a man from the other camp. He's a spy of Colgan's, if you ask me. Just go round and try and find out how they're getting on. They won't suspect you. Do you twig?"

"Ah, poor Joe is a decent skin," said Mr. O'Connor.

"His father was a decent, respectable man," Mr. Henchy admitted. "Poor old Larry Hynes! Many a good turn he did in his day! But I'm greatly afraid our friend is not nineteen carat. Damn it, I can understand a fellow being hard up, but what I can't understand is a fellow sponging. Couldn't he have some spark of manhood about him?"

"He doesn't get a warm welcome from me when he comes," said the old man. "Let him work for his own side and not come spying around here."

"I don't know," said Mr. O'Connor dubiously, as he took out cigarette-papers and tobacco. "I think Joe Hynes is a straight man. He's a clever chap, too, with the pen. Do you remember that thing he wrote . . . ?"

"Some of these hillsiders and fenians are a bit too clever if you ask me," said Mr. Henchy. "Do you know what my private and candid opinion is about some of those little jokers? I believe half of them are in the pay of the Castle."

"There's no knowing," said the old man.

"O, but I know it for a fact," said Mr. Henchy. "They're Castle hacks. . . . I don't say Hynes. . . . No, damn it, I think he's a stroke above that. But there's a certain little nobleman with a cock-eye—you know the patriot I'm alluding to?"

Mr. O'Connor nodded.

"There's a lineal descendant of Major Sirr for you if you like! O, the heart's blood of a patriot! That's a fellow now that'd sell his country for fourpence—ay—and go down on his bended knees and thank the Almighty Christ he had a country to sell."

There was a knock at the door.

"Come in!" said Mr. Henchy.

A person resembling a poor clergyman or a poor actor appeared in the doorway. His black clothes were tightly buttoned on his short body and it was impossible to say whether he wore a clergyman's collar or a layman's, because the collar of his shabby frock-coat, the uncovered buttons of which reflected the candlelight, was turned up about his neck. He wore a round hat of hard black felt. His face, shining with raindrops, had the appearance of damp yellow cheese save where two rosy spots indicated the cheek-bones. He opened his very long mouth suddenly to express disappointment and at the same time opened wide his very bright blue eyes to express pleasure and surprise.

"O Father Keon!" said Mr. Henchy, jumping up from his chair. "Is that you? Come in!"

"O, no, no, no!" said Father Keon quickly, pursing his lips as if he were addressing a child.

"Won't you come in and sit down?"

"No, no, no!" said Father Keon, speaking in a discreet, indulgent, velvety voice. "Don't let me disturb you now! I'm just looking for Mr. Fanning. . . ."

"He's round at the *Black Eagle*," said Mr. Henchy. "But won't you come in and sit down a minute?"

"No, no, thank you. It was just a little business matter," said Father Keon. "Thank you, indeed."

He retreated from the doorway and Mr. Henchy, seizing one of the candlesticks, went to the door to light him downstairs.

"O, don't trouble, I beg!"

"No, but the stairs is so dark."

"No, no, I can see. . . . Thank you, indeed."

"Are you right now?"

"All right, thanks. . . . Thanks."

Mr. Henchy returned with the candlestick and put it on the table. He sat down again at the fire. There was silence for a few moments.

"Tell me, John," said Mr. O'Connor, lighting his cigarette with another pasteboard card.

"Hm?"

"What he is exactly?"

"Ask me an easier one," said Mr. Henchy.

"Fanning and himself seem to me very thick. They're often in Kavanagh's together. Is he a priest at all?"

"'Mmmyes, I believe so. . . . I think he's what you call a black sheep. We haven't many of them, thank God! but we have a few. . . . He's an unfortunate man of some kind. . . ."

"And how does he knock it out?" asked Mr. O'Connor.

"That's another mystery."

"Is he attached to any chapel or church or institution or——"

"No," said Mr. Henchy, "I think he's travelling on his own account. . . . God forgive me," he added, "I thought he was the dozen of stout."

"Is there any chance of a drink itself?" asked Mr. O'Connor.

"I'm dry too," said the old man.

"I asked that little shoeboy three times," said Mr. Henchy, "would he send up a dozen of stout. I asked him again now, but he was leaning on the counter in his shirt-sleeves having a deep goster with Alderman Cowley."

"Why didn't you remind him?" said Mr. O'Connor.

"Well, I couldn't go over while he was talking to Alderman Cowley. I just waited till I caught his eye, and said: 'About that little matter I was speaking to you about. . . .' 'That'll be all right, Mr. H.,' he said. Yerra, sure the little hop-o'-my-thumb has forgotten all about it."

"There's some deal on in that quarter," said Mr. O'Connor thoughtfully. "I saw the three of them hard at it yesterday at Suffolk Street corner."

"I think I know the little game they're at," said Mr. Henchy. "You must owe the City Fathers money nowadays if you want to be made Lord Mayor. Then they'll make you Lord Mayor. By God! I'm thinking seriously of becoming a City Father myself. What do you think? Would I do for the job?"

Mr. O'Connor laughed.

"So far as owing money goes. . . ."

"Driving out of the Mansion House," said Mr. Henchy, "in all my vermin, with Jack here standing up behind me in a powdered wig—eh?"

"And make me your private secretary, John."

"Yes. And I'll make Father Keon my private chaplain. We'll have a family party."

"Faith, Mr. Henchy," said the old man, "you'd keep up better style than some of them. I was talking one day to old Keegan, the porter. 'And how do you like your new master, Pat?' says I to him. 'You haven't much entertaining now,' says I. 'Entertaining!' says he. 'He'd live on the smell of an oil-rag.' And do you know what he told me? Now, I declare to God, I didn't believe him."

"What?" said Mr. Henchy and Mr. O'Connor.

"He told me: 'What do you think of a Lord Mayor of Dublin sending out for a pound of chops for his dinner? How's that for high living?' says he. 'Wisha! wisha,' says I. 'A pound of chops,' says he, 'coming into the Mansion House.' 'Wisha!' says I, 'what kind of people is going at all now?'"

At this point there was a knock at the door, and a boy put in his head.

"What is it?" said the old man.

"From the *Black Eagle*," said the boy, walking in sideways and depositing a basket on the floor with a noise of shaken bottles.

The old man helped the boy to transfer the bottles from the basket to the table and counted the full tally. After the transfer the boy put his basket on his arm and asked:

"Any bottles?"

"What bottles?" said the old man.

"Won't you let us drink them first?" said Mr. Henchy.

"I was told to ask for bottles."

"Come back to-morrow," said the old man.

"Here, boy!" said Mr. Henchy, "will you run over to O'Farrell's and ask him to lend us a corkscrew—for Mr. Henchy, say. Tell him we won't keep it a minute. Leave the basket there."

The boy went out and Mr. Henchy began to rub his hands cheerfully, saying:

"Ah, well, he's not so bad after all. He's as good as his word, anyhow."

"There's no tumblers," said the old man.

"O, don't let that trouble you, Jack," said Mr. Henchy. "Many's the good man before now drank out of the bottle."

"Anyway, it's better than nothing," said Mr. O'Connor.

"He's not a bad sort," said Mr. Henchy, "only Fanning has such a loan of him. He means well, you know, in his own tinpot way."

The boy came back with the corkscrew. The old man opened three bottles and was handing back the corkscrew when Mr. Henchy said to the boy,

"Would you like a drink, boy?"

"If you please, sir," said the boy.

The old man opened another bottle grudgingly, and handed it to the boy.

"What age are you?" he asked.

"Seventeen," said the boy.

As the old man said nothing further, the boy took the bottle, said: "Here's my best respects, sir, to Mr. Henchy," drank the contents, put the bottle back on the table and wiped his mouth with his sleeve. Then he took up the corkscrew and went out of the door sideways, muttering some form of salutation.

"That's the way it begins," said the old man.

"The thin edge of the wedge," said Mr. Henchy.

The old man distributed the three bottles which he had opened and the men drank from them simultaneously. After having drank each placed his bottle on the mantelpiece within hand's reach and drew in a long breath of satisfaction.

"Well, I did a good day's work to-day," said Mr. Henchy, after a pause.

"That's so, John?"

"Yes. I got him one or two sure things in Dawson Street, Crofton and myself. Between ourselves, you know, Crofton (he's a decent chap, of course), but he's not worth a damn as a canvasser. He hasn't a word to throw to a dog. He stands and looks at the people while I do the talking."

Here two men entered the room. One of them was a very fat man, whose blue serge clothes seemed to be in danger of falling from his sloping figure. He had a big face which resembled a young ox's face in expression, staring blue eyes and a grizzled moustache. The other man, who was much younger and frailer, had a thin, clean-shaven face. He wore a very high double collar and a wide-brimmed bowler hat.

"Hello, Crofton!" said Mr. Henchy to the fat man. "Talk of the devil . . ."

"Where did the boose come from?" asked the young man. "Did the cow calve?"

"O, of course, Lyons spots the drink first thing!" said Mr. O'Connor, laughing.

"Is that the way you chaps canvass," said Mr. Lyons, "and Crofton and I out in the cold and rain looking for votes?"

"Why, blast your soul," said Mr. Henchy, "I'd get more votes in five minutes than you two'd get in a week."

"Open two bottles of stout, Jack," said Mr. O'Connor.

"How can I?" said the old man, "when there's no corkscrew?"

"Wait now, wait now!" said Mr. Henchy, getting up quickly. "Did you ever see this little trick?"

He took two bottles from the table and, carrying them to the fire, put them on the hob. Then he sat down again by the fire and took another drink from his bottle. Mr. Lyons sat on the edge of the table, pushed his hat towards the nape of his neck and began to swing his legs.

"Which is my bottle?" he asked.

"This, lad," said Mr. Henchy.

Mr. Crofton sat down on a box and looked fixedly at the other bottle on the hob. He was silent for two reasons. The first reason, sufficient in itself, was that he had nothing to say; the second reason was that he considered his companions beneath him. He had been a canvasser for Wilkins, the Conservative, but when the Conservatives had withdrawn their man and, choosing the lesser of two evils, given their support to the Nationalist candidate, he had been engaged to work for Mr. Tierney.

In a few minutes an apologetic "Pok!" was heard as the cork flew out of Mr. Lyons' bottle. Mr. Lyons jumped off the table, went to the fire, took his bottle and carried it back to the table.

"I was just telling them, Crofton," said Mr. Henchy, "that we got a good few votes to-day."

"Who did you get?" asked Mr. Lyons.

"Well, I got Parkes for one, and I got Atkinson for two, and I got Ward of Dawson Street. Fine old chap he is, too—regular old toff, old Conservative! 'But isn't your candidate a Nationalist?' said he. 'He's a respectable man,' said I. 'He's in favour of whatever will benefit this country. He's a big ratepayer,' I said. 'He has extensive house property in the city and three places of business and isn't it to his own advantage to keep down the rates? He's a prominent and respected citizen,' said I, 'and a Poor Law Guardian, and he doesn't belong to any party, good, bad, or indifferent.' That's the way to talk to 'em."

"And what about the address to the King?" said Mr. Lyons, after drinking and smacking his lips.

"Listen to me," said Mr. Henchy. "What we want in this country, as I said to old Ward, is capital. The King's coming here will mean an influx of money into this country. The citizens of Dublin will benefit by it. Look at all the factories down by the quays there, idle! Look at all the money there is in the country if we only worked the old industries, the mills, the ship-building yards and factories. It's capital we want."

"But look here, John," said Mr. O'Connor. "Why should we welcome the King of England? Didn't Parnell himself . . ."

"Parnell," said Mr. Henchy, "is dead. Now, here's the way I look at it. Here's this chap come to the throne after his old mother keeping him out of it till the man was grey. He's a man of the world, and he means well by us. He's a jolly fine decent fellow, if you ask me, and no damn nonsense about him. He just says to himself: 'The old one never went to see these wild Irish. By Christ, I'll go myself and see what they're like.' And are we going to insult the man when he comes over here on a friendly visit? Eh? Isn't that right, Crofton?"

Mr. Crofton nodded his head.

"But after all now," said Mr. Lyons argumentatively, "King Edward's life, you know, is not the very . . ."

"Let bygones be bygones," said Mr. Henchy. "I admire the man personally. He's just an ordinary knockabout like you and me. He's fond of his glass of grog and he's a bit of a rake, perhaps, and he's a good sportsman. Damn it, can't we Irish play fair?"

"That's all very fine," said Mr. Lyons. "But look at the case of Parnell now."

"In the name of God," said Mr. Henchy, "where's the analogy between the two cases?"

"What I mean," said Mr. Lyons, "is we have our ideals. Why, now, would we welcome a man like that? Do you think now after what he did Parnell was a fit man to lead us? And why, then, would we do it for Edward the Seventh?"

"This is Parnell's anniversary," said Mr. O'Connor, "and don't let us stir up any bad blood. We all respect him now that he's dead and gone— even the Conservatives," he added, turning to Mr. Crofton.

Pok! The tardy cork flew out of Mr. Crofton's bottle. Mr. Crofton got up from his box and went to the fire. As he returned with his capture he said in a deep voice:

"Our side of the house respects him, because he was a gentleman."

"Right you are, Crofton!" said Mr. Henchy fiercely. "He was the only man that could keep that bag of cats in order. 'Down, ye dogs! Lie down, ye curs!' That's the way he treated them. Come in Joe! Come in!" he called out, catching sight of Mr. Hynes in the doorway.

Mr. Hynes came in slowly.

"Open another bottle of stout, Jack," said Mr. Henchy. "O, I forgot there's no corkscrew! Here, show me one here and I'll put it at the fire."

The old man handed him another bottle and he placed it on the hob.

"Sit down, Joe," said Mr. O'Connor, "we're just talking about the Chief."

"Ay, ay!" said Mr. Henchy.

Mr. Hynes sat on the side of the table near Mr. Lyons but said nothing.

"There's one of them, anyhow," said Mr. Henchy, "that didn't renege him. By God, I'll say for you, Joe! No, by God, you stuck to him like a man!"

"O, Joe," said Mr. O'Connor suddenly. "Give us that thing you wrote— do you remember? Have you got it on you?"

"O, ay!" said Mr. Henchy. "Give us that. Did you ever hear that, Crofton? Listen to this now: splendid thing."

"Go on," said Mr. O'Connor. "Fire away, Joe."

Mr. Hynes did not seem to remember at once the piece to which they were alluding, but, after reflecting a while, he said:

"O, that thing is it. . . . Sure, that's old now."

"Out with it, man!" said Mr. O'Connor.

"'Sh, 'sh," said Mr. Henchy. "Now, Joe!"

Mr. Hynes hesitated a little longer. Then amid the silence he took off his hat, laid it on the table and stood up. He seemed to be rehearsing the piece in his mind. After a rather long pause he announced:

THE DEATH OF PARNELL

6th October, 1891

He cleared his throat once or twice and then began to recite:

He is dead. Our Uncrowned King is dead.
   O, Erin, mourn with grief and woe
For he lies dead whom the fell gang
   Of modern hypocrites laid low.

He lies slain by the coward hounds
   He raised to glory from the mire;
And Erin's hopes and Erin's dreams
   Perish upon her monarch's pyre.

In palace, cabin or in cot
   The Irish heart where'er it be
Is bowed with woe—for he is gone
   Who would have wrought her destiny.

He would have had his Erin famed,
   The green flag gloriously unfurled,
Her statesmen, bards and warriors raised
   Before the nations of the World.

He dreamed (alas, 'twas but a dream!)
   Of Liberty: but as he strove
To clutch that idol, treachery
   Sundered him from the thing he loved.

Shame on the coward, caitiff hands
   That smote their Lord or with a kiss
Betrayed him to the rabble-rout
   Of fawning priests—no friends of his.

May everlasting shame consume
   The memory of those who tried
To befoul and smear the exalted name
   Of one who spurned them in his pride.

He fell as fall the mighty ones,
   Nobly undaunted to the last,
And death has now united him
   With Erin's heroes of the past.

No sound of strife disturb his sleep!
   Calmly he rests: no human pain
Or high ambition spurs him now
   The peaks of glory to attain.

They had their way: they laid him low.
But Erin, list, his spirit may
Rise, like the Phœnix from the flames,
When breaks the dawning of the day,

The day that brings us Freedom's reign.
And on that day may Erin well
Pledge in the cup she lifts to Joy
One grief—the memory of Parnell.

Mr. Hynes sat down again on the table. When he had finished his recitation there was a silence and then a burst of clapping: even Mr. Lyons clapped. The applause continued for a little time. When it had ceased all the auditors drank from their bottles in silence.

Pok! The cork flew out of Mr. Hynes' bottle, but Mr. Hynes remained sitting flushed and bare-headed on the table. He did not seem to have heard the invitation.

"Good man, Joe!" said Mr. O'Connor, taking out his cigarette papers and pouch the better to hide his emotion.

"What do you think of that, Crofton?" cried Mr. Henchy. "Isn't that fine? What?"

Mr. Crofton said that it was a very fine piece of writing.

the
blind
man

d. h. lawrence

D. H. Lawrence (1885–1930),
a short-story writer and novelist of genius,
was the son of a coal miner in Nottinghamshire.
After winning a high school scholarship,
he went on to college and for a time taught
school. Like Joyce, he struggled all his life
against censors' attempts to suppress his work.
His best-known novels are Sons and
Lovers *(1913) and* Lady Chatterley's
Lover *(1928). For further reading:*
The Prussian Officer, and Other Stories
(1941); The Captain's Doll,
and Other Stories *(1923).*

Isabel Pervin was listening for two sounds—for the sound of wheels on the drive outside and for the noise of her husband's footsteps in the hall. Her dearest and oldest friend, a man who seemed almost indispensable to her living, would drive up in the rainy dusk of the closing November day. The trap had gone to fetch him from the station. And her husband, who had been blinded in Flanders, and who had a disfiguring mark on his brow, would be coming in from the outhouses.

He had been home for a year now. He was totally blind. Yet they had been very happy. The Grange was Maurice's own place. The back was a farmstead, and the Wernhams, who occupied the rear premises, acted as farmers. Isabel lived with her husband in the handsome rooms in front. She and he had been almost entirely alone together since he was wounded. They talked and sang and read together in a wonderful and unspeakable intimacy. Then she reviewed books for a Scottish newspaper, carrying on her old interest, and he occupied himself a good deal with the farm. Sightless, he could still discuss everything with Wernham, and he could also do a good deal of work about the place—menial work, it is true, but it gave him satisfaction. He milked the cows, carried in the pails, turned the separator, attended to the pigs and horses. Life was still very full and strangely serene for the blind man, peaceful with the almost incomprehensible peace of immediate contact in darkness. With his wife he had a whole world, rich and real and invisible.

They were newly and remotely happy. He did not even regret the loss of his sight in these times of dark, palpable joy. A certain exultance swelled his soul.

But as time wore on, sometimes the rich glamour would leave them. Sometimes, after months of this intensity, a sense of burden overcame Isabel, a weariness, a terrible *ennui*, in that silent house approached between a colonnade of tall-shafted pines. Then she felt she would go mad, for she could not bear it. And sometimes he had devastating fits of depression, which seemed to lay waste his whole being. It was worse than depression—a black misery, when his own life was a torture to him, and when his presence was unbearable to his wife. The dread went down to the roots of her soul as these black days recurred. In a kind of panic she tried to wrap herself up still further in her husband. She forced the old spontaneous cheerfulness and joy to continue. But the effort it cost her was almost too much. She knew she could not keep it up. She felt she would scream with the strain, and would give anything, anything, to escape. She longed to possess her husband utterly; it gave her inordinate joy to have him entirely to herself. And yet, when again he was gone in a black and massive misery, she could not bear him, she could not bear herself; she wished she could be snatched away off the earth altogether, anything rather than live at this cost.

Dazed, she schemed for a way out. She invited friends, she tried to give him some further connection with the outer world. But it was no good. After all their joy and suffering, after their dark, great year of blindness and solitude and unspeakable nearness, other people seemed to them both shallow, rattling, rather impertinent. Shallow prattle seemed presumptuous. He became impatient and irritated, she was wearied. And so they lapsed into their solitude again. For they preferred it.

But now, in a few weeks' time, her second baby would be born. The first had died, an infant, when her husband first went out to France. She looked with joy and relief to the coming of the second. It would be her salvation. But also she felt some anxiety. She was thirty years old, her husband was a year younger. They both wanted the child very much. Yet she could not help feeling afraid. She had her husband on her hands, a terrible joy to her, and a terrifying burden. The child would occupy her love and attention. And then, what of Maurice? What would he do? If only she could feel that he, too, would be at peace and happy when the child came! She did so want to luxuriate in a rich, physical satisfaction of maternity. But the man, what would he do? How could she provide for him, how avert those shattering black moods of his, which destroyed them both?

She sighed with fear. But at this time Bertie Reid wrote to Isabel. He was her old friend, a second or third cousin, a Scotchman, as she was a Scotchwoman. They had been brought up near to one another, and all her life he had been her friend, like a brother, but better than her own brothers. She loved him—though not in the marrying sense. There was a sort of kinship between them, an affinity. They understood one another instinctively. But Isabel would never have thought of marrying Bertie. It would have seemed like marrying in her own family.

Bertie was a barrister and a man of letters, a Scotchman of the intellectual type, quick, ironical, sentimental, and on his knees before the woman he adored but did not want to marry. Maurice Pervin was different. He came of a good old country family—the Grange was not a very great distance from Oxford. He was passionate, sensitive, perhaps oversensitive, wincing—a big fellow with heavy limbs and a forehead that flushed painfully. For his mind was slow, as if drugged by the strong provincial blood that beat in his veins. He was very sensitive to his own mental slowness, his feelings being quick and acute. So that he was just the opposite to Bertie, whose mind was much quicker than his emotions, which were not so very fine.

From the first the two men did not like each other. Isabel felt that they *ought* to get on together. But they did not. She felt that if only each could have the clue to the other there would be such a rare understanding between them. It did not come off, however. Bertie adopted a slightly ironical attitude, very offensive to Maurice, who returned the Scotch irony with English resentment, a resentment which deepened sometimes into stupid hatred.

This was a little puzzling to Isabel. However, she accepted it in the course of things. Men were made freakish and unreasonable. Therefore, when Maurice was going out to France for the second time, she felt that, for her husband's sake, she must discontinue her friendship with Bertie. She wrote to the barrister to this effect. Bertram Reid simply replied that in this, as in all other matters, he must obey her wishes, if these were indeed her wishes.

For nearly two years nothing had passed between the two friends. Isabel rather gloried in the fact; she had no compunction. She had one great article of faith, which was, that husband and wife should be so important to one another, that the rest of the world simply did not count. She and Maurice were husband and wife. They loved one another. They would have children. Then let everybody and everything else fade into insignificance outside this connubial felicity. She professed herself quite happy and ready to receive Maurice's friends. She was happy and ready: the happy wife, the ready woman in possession. Without knowing why, the friends retired abashed, and came no more. Maurice, of course, took as much satisfaction in this connubial absorption as Isabel did.

He shared in Isabel's literary activities, she cultivated a real interest in agriculture and cattle-raising. For she, being at heart perhaps an emotional enthusiast, always cultivated the practical side of life and prided herself on her mastery of practical affairs. Thus the husband and wife had spent the five years of their married life. The last had been one of blindness and unspeakable intimacy. And now Isabel felt a great indifference coming over her, a sort of lethargy. She wanted to be allowed to bear her child in peace, to nod by the fire and drift vaguely, physically, from day to day. Maurice was like an ominous thunder-cloud. She had to keep waking up to remember him.

When a little note came from Bertie, asking if he were to put up a tombstone to their dead friendship, and speaking of the real pain he felt on account of her husband's loss of sight, she felt a pang, a fluttering agitation of re-awakening. And she read the letter to Maurice.

"Ask him to come down," he said.

"Ask Bertie to come here!" she re-echoed.

"Yes—if he wants to."

Isabel paused for a few moments.

"I know he wants to—he'd only be too glad," she replied. "But what about you, Maurice? How would you like it?"

"I should like it."

"Well—in that case—— But I thought you didn't care for him——"

"Oh, I don't know. I might think differently of him now," the blind man replied. It was rather abstruse to Isabel.

"Well, dear," she said, "if you're quite sure——"

"I'm sure enough. Let him come," said Maurice.

So Bertie was coming, coming this evening, in the November rain and darkness. Isabel was agitated, racked with her old restlessness and indecision. She had always suffered from this pain of doubt, just an agonizing sense of uncertainty. It had begun to pass off, in the lethargy of maternity. Now it returned, and she resented it. She struggled as usual to maintain her calm, composed, friendly bearing, a sort of mask she wore over all her body.

A woman had lighted a tall lamp beside the table and spread the cloth. The long dining-room was dim, with its elegant but rather severe pieces of old furniture. Only the round table glowed softly under the light. It had a rich, beautiful effect. The white cloth glistened and dropped its heavy, pointed lace corners almost to the carpet, the china was old and handsome, creamy-yellow, with a blotched pattern of harsh red and deep blue, the cups large and bell-shaped, the teapot gallant. Isabel looked at it with superficial appreciation.

Her nerves were hurting her. She looked automatically again at the high, uncurtained windows. In the last dusk she could just perceive outside a huge fir-tree swaying its boughs: it was as if she thought it rather than saw it. The rain came flying on the window panes. Ah, why had she no peace? These two men, why did they tear at her? Why did they not come—why was there this suspense?

She sat in a lassitude that was really suspense and irritation. Maurice, at least, might come in—there was nothing to keep him out. She rose to her feet. Catching sight of her reflection in a mirror, she glanced at herself with a slight smile of recognition, as if she were an old friend to herself. Her face was oval and calm, her nose a little arched. Her neck made a beautiful line down to her shoulder. With hair knotted loosely behind, she had something of a warm, maternal look. Thinking this of herself, she arched her eyebrows and her rather heavy eyelids, with a little flicker of a smile, and for a moment her grey eyes looked amused and wicked, a little sardonic, out of her transfigured Madonna face.

Then, resuming her air of womanly patience—she was really fatally self-determined—she went with a little jerk towards the door. Her eyes were slightly reddened.

She passed down the wide hall and through a door at the end. Then she was in the farm premises. The scent of dairy, and of farm-kitchen, and of farm-yard and of leather almost overcame her: but particularly the scent of dairy. They had been scalding out the pans. The flagged passage in front of her was dark, puddled, and wet. Light came out from the open kitchen door. She went forward and stood in the doorway. The farm-people were at tea, seated at a little distance from her, round a long, narrow table, in the centre of which stood a white lamp. Ruddy faces, ruddy hands holding food, red mouths working, heads bent over the tea-cups: men, land-girls, boys: it was tea-time, feeding-time. Some faces caught sight of her. Mrs. Wernham, going round behind the chairs with a large black teapot, halting slightly in her walk, was not aware of her for a moment. Then she turned suddenly.

"Oh, is it Madam!" she exclaimed. "Come in, then, come in! We're at tea." And she dragged forward a chair.

"No, I won't come in," said Isabel. "I'm afraid I interrupt your meal."

"No—no—not likely, Madam, not likely."

"Hasn't Mr. Pervin come in, do you know?"

"I'm sure I couldn't say! Missed him, have you, Madam?"

"No, I only wanted him to come in," laughed Isabel, as if shyly.

"Wanted him, did ye? Get up, boy—get up, now——"

Mrs. Wernham knocked one of the boys on the shoulder. He began to scrape to his feet, chewing largely.

"I believe he's in top stable," said another face from the table.

"Ah! No, don't get up. I'm going myself," said Isabel.

"Don't you go out of a dirty night like this. Let the lad go. Get along wi' ye, boy," said Mrs. Wernham.

"No, no," said Isabel, with a decision that was always obeyed. "Go on with your tea, Tom. I'd like to go across to the stable, Mrs. Wernham."

"Did ever you hear tell!" exclaimed the woman.

"Isn't the trap late?" asked Isabel.

"Why, no," said Mrs. Wernham, peering into the distance at the tall, dim clock. "No, Madam—we can give it another quarter or twenty minutes yet, good—yes, every bit of a quarter."

"Ah! It seems late when darkness falls so early," said Isabel.

"It do, that it do. Bother the days, that they draw in so," answered Mrs. Wernham. "Proper miserable!"

"They are," said Isabel, withdrawing.

She pulled on her overshoes, wrapped a large tartan shawl around her, put on a man's felt hat, and ventured out along the causeways of the first yard. It was very dark. The wind was roaring in the great elms behind the outhouses. When she came to the second yard the darkness seemed deeper. She was unsure of her footing. She wished she had brought a lantern. Rain blew against her. Half she liked it, half she felt unwilling to battle.

She reached at last the just visible door of the stable. There was no sign of a light anywhere. Opening the upper half, she looked in: into a simple well of darkness. The smell of horses, and ammonia, and of warmth was startling to her, in that full night. She listened with all her ears but could hear nothing save the night, and the stirring of a horse.

"Maurice!" she called, softly and musically, though she was afraid. "Maurice—are you there?"

Nothing came from the darkness. She knew the rain and wind blew in upon the horses, the hot animal life. Feeling it wrong, she entered the stable and drew the lower half of the door shut, holding the upper part close. She did not stir, because she was aware of the presence of the dark hind-quarters of the horses, though she could not see them, and she was afraid. Something wild stirred in her heart.

She listened intensely. Then she heard a small noise in the distance— far away, it seemed—the chink of a pan, and a man's voice speaking a brief word. It would be Maurice, in the other part of the stable. She stood motionless, waiting for him to come through the partition door. The horses were so terrifyingly near to her, in the invisible.

The loud jarring of the inner door-latch made her start; the door was opened. She could hear and feel her husband entering and invisibly passing among the horses near to her, darkness as they were, actively intermingled. The rather low sound of his voice as he spoke to the horses came velvety to her nerves. How near he was, and how invisible! The darkness seemed to be in a strange swirl of violent life, just upon her. She turned giddy.

Her presence of mind made her call, quietly and musically:

"Maurice! Maurice—dea-ar!"

"Yes," he answered. "Isabel?"

She saw nothing, and the sound of his voice seemed to touch her.

"Hello!" she answered cheerfully, straining her eyes to see him. He was still busy, attending to the horses near her, but she saw only darkness. It made her almost desperate.

"Won't you come in, dear?" she said.

"Yes, I'm coming. Just half a minute. *Stand over—now!* Trap's not come, has it?"

"Not yet," said Isabel.

His voice was pleasant and ordinary, but it had a slight suggestion of the stable to her. She wished he would come away. Whilst he was so utterly invisible, she was afraid of him.

"How's the time?" he asked.

"Not yet six," she replied. She disliked to answer into the dark. Presently he came very near to her, and she retreated out of doors.

"The weather blows in here," he said, coming steadily forward, feeling for the doors. She shrank away. At last she could dimly see him.

"Bertie won't have much of a drive," he said, as he closed the doors.

"He won't indeed!" said Isabel calmly, watching the dark shape at the door.

"Give me your arm, dear," she said.

She pressed his arm close to her, as she went. But she longed to see him, to look at him. She was nervous. He walked erect, with face rather lifted, but with a curious tentative movement of his powerful, muscular legs. She could feel the clever, careful, strong contact of his feet with the earth, as she balanced against him. For a moment he was a tower of darkness to her, as if he rose out of the earth.

In the house-passage he wavered and went cautiously, with a curious look of silence about him as he felt for the bench. Then he sat down heavily. He was a man with rather sloping shoulders, but with heavy limbs, powerful legs that seemed to know the earth. His head was small, usually carried high and light. As he bent down to unfasten his gaiters and boots he did not look blind. His hair was brown and crisp, his hands were large, reddish, intelligent, the veins stood out in the wrists; and his thighs and knees seemed massive. When he stood up his face and neck were surcharged with blood, the veins stood out on his temples. She did not look at his blindness.

Isabel was always glad when they had passed through the dividing door into their own regions of repose and beauty. She was a little afraid of him, out there in the animal grossness of the back. His bearing also changed, as he smelt the familiar indefinable odour that pervaded his wife's surroundings, a delicate, refined scent, very faintly spicy. Perhaps it came from the potpourri bowls.

He stood at the foot of the stairs, arrested, listening. She watched him, and her heart sickened. He seemed to be listening to fate.

"He's not here yet," he said. "I'll go up and change."

"Maurice," she said, "you're not wishing he wouldn't come, are you?"

"I couldn't quite say," he answered. "I feel myself rather on the qui vive."

"I can see you are," she answered. And she reached up and kissed his cheek. She saw his mouth relax into a slow smile.

"What are you laughing at?" she said roguishly.

"You consoling me," he answered.

"Nay," she answered. "Why should I console you? You know we love each other—you know *how* married we are! What does anything else matter?"

"Nothing at all, my dear."

He felt for her face and touched it, smiling.

"*You're* all right, aren't you?" he asked anxiously.

"I'm wonderfully all right, love," she answered. "It's you I am a little troubled about, at times."

"Why me?" he said, touching her cheeks delicately with the tips of his fingers. The touch had an almost hypnotizing effect on her.

He went away upstairs. She saw him mount into the darkness, unseeing and unchanging. He did not know that the lamps on the upper corridor were unlighted. He went on into the darkness with unchanging step. She heard him in the bath-room.

Pervin moved about almost unconsciously in his familiar surroundings, dark though everything was. He seemed to know the presence of objects before he touched them. It was a pleasure to him to rock thus through a world of things, carried on the flood in a sort of blood-prescience. He did not think much or trouble much. So long as he kept this sheer immediacy of blood-contact with the substantial world he was happy, he wanted no intervention of visual consciousness. In this state there was a certain rich positivity, bordering sometimes on rapture. Life seemed to move in him like a tide lapping, lapping, and advancing, enveloping all things darkly. It was a pleasure to stretch forth the hand and meet the unseen object, clasp it, and possess it in pure contact. He did not try to remember, to visualize. He did not want to. The new way of consciousness substituted itself in him.

The rich suffusion of this state generally kept him happy, reaching its culmination in the consuming passion for his wife. But at times the flow would seem to be checked and thrown back. Then it would beat inside him like a tangled sea, and he was tortured in the shattered chaos of his own blood. He grew to dread this arrest, this throw-back, this chaos inside himself, when he seemed merely at the mercy of his own powerful and conflicting elements. How to get some measure of control or surety, this was the question. And when the question rose maddening in him, he would clench his fists as if he would *compel* the whole universe to submit to him. But it was in vain. He could not even compel himself.

Tonight, however, he was still serene, though little tremors of unreasonable exasperation ran through him. He had to handle the razor very carefully, as he shaved, for it was not at one with him, he was afraid of it. His hearing also was too much sharpened. He heard the woman lighting the lamps on the corridor, and attending to the fire in the visitors' room. And then, as he went to his room, he heard the trap arrive. Then came Isabel's voice, lifted and calling, like a bell ringing:

"Is it you, Bertie? Have you come?"

And a man's voice answered out of the wind:

"Hello, Isabel! There you are."

"Have you had a miserable drive? I'm so sorry we couldn't send a closed carriage. I can't see you at all, you know."

"I'm coming. No, I liked the drive—it was like Perthshire. Well, how are you? You're looking fit as ever, as far as I can see."

"Oh, yes," said Isabel. "I'm wonderfully well. How are you? Rather thin, I think——"

"Worked to death—everybody's old cry. But I'm all right, Ciss. How's Pervin?—isn't he here?"

"Oh, yes, he's upstairs changing. Yes, he's awfully well. Take off your wet things; I'll send them to be dried."

"And how are you both, in spirits? He doesn't fret?"

"No—no, not at all. No, on the contrary, really. We've been wonderfully happy, incredibly. It's more than I can understand—so wonderful: the nearness, and the peace——"

"Ah! Well, that's awfully good news——"

They moved away. Pervin heard no more. But a childish sense of desolation had come over him, as he heard their brisk voices. He seemed shut out—like a child that is left out. He was aimless and excluded, he did not know what to do with himself. The helpless desolation came over him. He fumbled nervously as he dressed himself, in a state almost of childishness. He disliked the Scotch accent in Bertie's speech, and the slight response it found on Isabel's tongue. He disliked the slight purr of complacency in the Scottish speech. He disliked intensely the glib way in which Isabel spoke of their happiness and nearness. It made him recoil. He was fretful and beside himself like a child, he had almost a childish nostalgia to be included in the life circle. And at the same time he was a man, dark and powerful and infuriated by his own weakness. By some fatal flaw, he could not be by himself, he had to depend on the support of another. And this very dependence enraged him. He hated Bertie Reid, and at the same time he knew the hatred was nonsense, he knew it was the outcome of his own weakness.

He went downstairs. Isabel was alone in the dining-room. She watched him enter, head erect, his feet tentative. He looked so strong-blooded and healthy and, at the same time, cancelled. Cancelled—that was the word that flew across her mind. Perhaps it was his scar suggested it.

"You heard Bertie come, Maurice?" she said.

"Yes—isn't he here?"

"He's in his room. He looks very thin and worn."

"I suppose he works himself to death."

A woman came in with a tray—and after a few minutes Bertie came down. He was a little dark man, with a very big forehead, thin, wispy hair, and sad, large eyes. His expression was inordinately sad—almost funny. He had odd, short legs.

Isabel watched him hesitate under the door, and glance nervously at her husband. Pervin heard him and turned.

"Here you are, now," said Isabel. "Come, let us eat."

Bertie went across to Maurice.

"How are you, Pervin?" he said, as he advanced.

The blind man stuck his hand out into space, and Bertie took it.

"Very fit. Glad you've come," said Maurice.

Isabel glanced at them, and glanced away, as if she could not bear to see them.

"Come," she said. "Come to table. Aren't you both awfully hungry? I am, tremendously."

"I'm afraid you waited for me," said Bertie, as they sat down.

Maurice had a curious monolithic way of sitting in a chair, erect and distant. Isabel's heart always beat when she caught sight of him thus.

"No," she replied to Bertie. "We're very little later than usual. We're having a sort of high tea, not dinner. Do you mind? It gives us such a nice long evening, uninterrupted."

"I like it," said Bertie.

Maurice was feeling, with curious little movements, almost like a cat kneading her bed, for his plate, his knife and fork, his napkin. He was getting the whole geography of his cover into his consciousness. He sat erect and inscrutable, remote-seeming. Bertie watched the static figure of the blind man, the delicate tactile discernment of the large, ruddy hands, and the curious mindless silence of the brow, above the scar.

With difficulty he looked away, and without knowing what he did, picked up a little crystal bowl of violets from the table, and held them to his nose.

"They are sweet-scented," he said. "Where do they come from?"

"From the garden—under the windows," said Isabel.

"So late in the year—and so fragrant! Do you remember the violets under Aunt Bell's south wall?"

The two friends looked at each other and exchanged a smile, Isabel's eyes lighting up.

"Don't I?" she replied. "*Wasn't* she queer!"

"A curious old girl," laughed Bertie. "There's a streak of freakishness in the family, Isabel."

"Ah—but not in you and me, Bertie," said Isabel. "Give them to Maurice, will you?" she added, as Bertie was putting down the flowers. "Have you smelled the violets, dear? Do!—they are so scented."

Maurice held out his hand, and Bertie placed the tiny bowl against his large, warm-looking fingers. Maurice's hand closed over the thin white fingers of the barrister. Bertie carefully extricated himself. Then the two watched the blind man smelling the violets. He bent his head and seemed to be thinking. Isabel waited.

"Aren't they sweet, Maurice?" she said at last, anxiously.

"Very," he said. And he held out the bowl. Bertie took it. Both he and Isabel were a little afraid, and deeply disturbed.

The meal continued. Isabel and Bertie chatted spasmodically. The blind man was silent. He touched his food repeatedly, with quick, delicate touches of his knife-point, then cut irregular bits. He could not bear to be helped. Both Isabel and Bertie suffered: Isabel wondered why. She did not suffer when she was alone with Maurice. Bertie made her conscious of a strangeness.

After the meal the three drew their chairs to the fire, and sat down to talk. The decanters were put on a table near at hand. Isabel knocked the logs on the fire, and clouds of brilliant sparks went up the chimney. Bertie noticed a slight weariness in her bearing.

"You will be glad when your child comes now, Isabel?" he said.

She looked up to him with a quick wan smile.

"Yes, I shall be glad," she answered. "It begins to seem long. Yes, I shall be very glad. So will you, Maurice, won't you?" she added.

"Yes, I shall," replied her husband.

"We are both looking forward so much to having it," she said.

"Yes, of course," said Bertie.

He was a bachelor, three or four years older than Isabel. He lived in beautiful rooms overlooking the river, guarded by a faithful Scottish man-servant. And he had his friends among the fair sex—not lovers, friends. So long as he could avoid any danger of courtship or marriage, he adored a few good women with constant and unfailing homage, and he was chivalrously fond of quite a number. But if they seemed to encroach on him, he withdrew and detested them.

Isabel knew him very well, knew his beautiful constancy, and kindness, also his incurable weakness, which made him unable ever to enter into close contact of any sort. He was ashamed of himself because he could not marry, could not approach women physically. He wanted to do so. But he could not. At the centre of him he was afraid, helplessly and even brutally afraid. He had given up hope, had ceased to expect any more that he could escape his own weakness. Hence he was a brilliant and successful barrister, also a *littérateur* of high repute, a rich man, and a great social success. At the centre he felt himself neuter, nothing.

Isabel knew him well. She despised him even while she admired him. She looked at his sad face, his little short legs, and felt contempt of him. She looked at his dark grey eyes, with their uncanny, almost childlike, intuition, and she loved him. He understood amazingly—but she had no fear of his understanding. As a man she patronized him.

And she turned to the impassive, silent figure of her husband. He sat leaning back, with folded arms, and face a little uptilted. His knees were straight and massive. She sighed, picked up the poker, and again began to prod the fire, to rouse the clouds of soft brilliant sparks.

"Isabel tells me," Bertie began suddenly, "that you have not suffered unbearably from the loss of sight."

Maurice straightened himself to attend but kept his arms folded.

"No," he said, "not unbearably. Now and again one struggles against it, you know. But there are compensations."

"They say it is much worse to be stone deaf," said Isabel.

"I believe it is," said Bertie. "Are there compensations?" he added, to Maurice.

"Yes. You cease to bother about a great many things." Again Maurice stretched his figure, stretched the strong muscles of his back, and leaned backwards, with uplifted face.

"And that is a relief," said Bertie. "But what is there in place of the bothering? What replaces the activity?"

There was a pause. At length the blind man replied, as out of a negligent, unattentive thinking:

"Oh, I don't know. There's a good deal when you're not active."

"Is there?" said Bertie. "What, exactly? It always seems to me that when there is no thought and no action, there is nothing."

Again Maurice was slow in replying.

"There is something," he replied. "I couldn't tell you what it is."

And the talk lapsed once more, Isabel and Bertie chatting gossip and reminiscence, the blind man silent.

At length Maurice rose restlessly, a big obtrusive figure. He felt tight and hampered. He wanted to go away.

"Do you mind," he said, "if I go and speak to Wernham?"

"No—go along, dear," said Isabel.

And he went out. A silence came over the two friends. At length Bertie said:

"Nevertheless, it is a great deprivation, Cissie."

"It is, Bertie. I know it is."

"Something lacking all the time," said Bertie.

"Yes, I know. And yet—and yet—Maurice is right. There is something else, something *there*, which you never knew was there, and which you can't express."

"What is there?" asked Bertie.

"I don't know—it's awfully hard to define it—but something strong and immediate. There's something strange in Maurice's presence—indefinable —but I couldn't do without it. I agree that it seems to put one's mind to sleep. But when we're alone I miss nothing; it seems awfully rich, almost splendid, you know."

"I'm afraid I don't follow," said Bertie.

They talked desultorily. The wind blew loudly outside, rain chattered on the window-panes, making a sharp drum-sound because of the closed, mellow-golden shutters inside. The logs burned slowly, with hot, almost invisible small flames. Bertie seemed uneasy, there were dark circles round his eyes. Isabel, rich with her approaching maternity, leaned looking into the fire. Her hair curled in odd, loose strands, very pleasing to the man. But she had a curious feeling of old woe in her heart, old, timeless night-woe.

"I suppose we're all deficient somewhere," said Bertie.

"I suppose so," said Isabel wearily.

"Damned, sooner or later."

"I don't know," she said, rousing herself. "I feel quite all right, you know. The child coming seems to make me indifferent to everything, just placid. I can't feel that there's anything to trouble about, you know."

"A good thing, I should say," he replied slowly.

"Well, there it is. I suppose it's just Nature. If only I felt I needn't trouble about Maurice, I should be perfectly content——"

"But you feel you must trouble about him?"

"Well—I don't know——" She even resented this much effort.

The night passed slowly. Isabel looked at the clock. "I say," she said. "It's nearly ten o'clock. Where can Maurice be? I'm sure they're all in bed at the back. Excuse me a moment."

She went out, returning almost immediately.

"It's all shut up and in darkness," she said. "I wonder where he is. He must have gone out to the farm——"

Bertie looked at her.

"I suppose he'll come in," he said.

"I suppose so," she said. "But it's unusual for him to be out now."

"Would you like me to go out and see?"

"Well—if you wouldn't mind. I'd go, but——" She did not want to make the physical effort.

Bertie put on an old overcoat and took a lantern. He went out from the side door. He shrank from the wet and roaring night. Such weather had a nervous effect on him: too much moisture everywhere made him feel almost imbecile. Unwilling, he went through it all. A dog barked violently at him. He peered in all the buildings. At last, as he opened the upper door of a sort of intermediate barn, he heard a grinding noise, and looking in, holding up his lantern, saw Maurice in his shirt-sleeves, standing listening, holding the handle of a turnip-pulper. He had been pulping sweet roots, a pile of which lay dimly heaped in a corner behind him.

"That you, Wernham?" said Maurice, listening.

"No, it's me," said Bertie.

A large, half-wild grey cat was rubbing at Maurice's leg. The blind man stooped to rub its sides. Bertie watched the scene, then unconsciously entered and shut the door behind him. He was in a high sort of barn-place, from which, right and left, ran off the corridors in front of the stalled cattle. He watched the slow, stooping motion of the other man, as he caressed the great cat.

Maurice straightened himself.

"You came to look for me?" he said.

"Isabel was a little uneasy," said Bertie.

"I'll come in. I like messing about doing these jobs."

The cat had reared her sinister, feline length against his leg, clawing at his thigh affectionately. He lifted her claws out of his flesh.

"I hope I'm not in your way at all at the Grange here," said Bertie, rather shy and stiff.

"My way? No, not a bit. I'm glad Isabel has somebody to talk to. I'm afraid it's I who am in the way. I know I'm not very lively company. Isabel's all right, don't you think? She's not unhappy, is she?"

"I don't think so."

"What does she say?"

"She says she's very content—only a little troubled about you."

"Why me?"

"Perhaps afraid that you might brood," said Bertie, cautiously.

"She needn't be afraid of that." He continued to caress the flattened grey head of the cat with his fingers. "What I am a bit afraid of," he resumed, "is that she'll find me a dead weight, always alone with me down here."

"I don't think you need think that," said Bertie, though this was what he feared himself.

"I don't know," said Maurice. "Sometimes I feel it isn't fair that she's saddled with me." Then he dropped his voice curiously. "I say," he asked, secretly struggling, "is my face much disfigured? Do you mind telling me?"

"There is the scar," said Bertie, wondering. "Yes, it is a disfigurement. But more pitiable than shocking."

"A pretty bad scar, though," said Maurice.

"Oh, yes."

There was a pause.

"Sometimes I feel I am horrible," said Maurice, in a low voice, talking as if to himself. And Bertie actually felt a quiver of horror.

"That's nonsense," he said.

Maurice again straightened himself, leaving the cat.

"There's no telling," he said. Then again, in an odd tone, he added: "I don't really know you, do I?"

"Probably not," said Bertie.

"Do you mind if I touch you?"

The lawyer shrank away instinctively. And yet, out of very philanthropy, he said, in a small voice: "Not at all."

But he suffered as the blind man stretched out a strong, naked hand to him. Maurice accidentally knocked off Bertie's hat.

"I thought you were taller," he said, starting. Then he laid his hand on Bertie Reid's head, closing the dome of the skull in a soft, firm grasp, gathering it, as it were; then, shifting his grasp and softly closing again, with a fine, close pressure, till he had covered the skull and the face of the smaller man, tracing the brows, and touching the full, closed eyes, touching the small nose and the nostrils, the rough, short moustache, the mouth, the rather strong chin. The hand of the blind man grasped the shoulder, the arm, the hand of the other man. He seemed to take him, in the soft, travelling grasp.

"You seem young," he said quietly, at last.

The lawyer stood almost annihilated, unable to answer.

"Your head seems tender, as if you were young," Maurice repeated. "So do your hands. Touch my eyes, will you?—touch my scar."

Now Bertie quivered with revulsion. Yet he was under the power of the blind man, as if hypnotized. He lifted his hand, and laid the fingers to the scar, on the scarred eyes. Maurice suddenly covered them with his own hand, pressed the fingers of the other man upon his disfigured eye-sockets, trembling in every fibre, and rocking slightly, slowly, from side to side. He remained thus for a minute or more, whilst Bertie stood as if in a swoon, unconscious, imprisoned.

Then suddenly Maurice removed the hand of the other man from his brow, and stood holding it in his own.

"Oh, my God," he said, "we shall know each other now, shan't we? We shall know each other now."

Bertie could not answer. He gazed mute and terror-struck, overcome by his own weakness. He knew he could not answer. He had an unreasonable fear, lest the other man should suddenly destroy him. Whereas Maurice was actually filled with hot, poignant love, the passion of friendship. Perhaps it was this very passion of friendship which Bertie shrank from most.

"We're all right together now, aren't we?" said Maurice. "It's all right now, as long as we live, so far as we're concerned?"

"Yes," said Bertie, trying by any means to escape.

Maurice stood with head lifted, as if listening. The new delicate fulfilment of mortal friendship had come as revelation and surprise to him, something exquisite and unhoped-for. He seemed to be listening to hear if it were real.

Then he turned for his coat.

"Come," he said, "we'll go to Isabel."

Bertie took the lantern and opened the door. The cat disappeared. The two men went in silence along the causeways. Isabel, as they came, thought their footsteps sounded strange. She looked up pathetically and anxiously for their entrance. There seemed a curious elation about Maurice. Bertie was haggard, with sunken eyes.

"What is it?" she asked.

"We've become friends," said Maurice, standing with his feet apart, like a strange colossus.

"Friends!" re-echoed Isabel. And she looked again at Bertie. He met her eyes with a furtive, haggard look; his eyes were as if glazed with misery.

"I'm so glad," she said, in sheer perplexity.

"Yes," said Maurice.

He was indeed so glad. Isabel took his hand with both hers, and held it fast.

"You'll be happier now, dear," she said.

But she was watching Bertie. She knew that he had one desire—to escape from this intimacy, this friendship, which had been thrust upon him. He could not bear it that he had been touched by the blind man, his insane reserve broken in. He was like a mollusc whose shell is broken.

the fly

katherine mansfield

Katherine Mansfield (1888–1923) was born in New Zealand and later moved to England. Her work shows psychological subtlety and a perception of symbolic values. One of her acknowledged masters was Chekhov. For further reading: The Garden Party *(1922);* The Dove's Nest *(1923);* The Short Stories of Katherine Mansfield *(1937).*

"Y'are very snug in here," piped old Mr. Woodifield, and he peered out of the great, green leather armchair by his friend the boss's desk as a baby peers out of its pram. His talk was over; it was time for him to be off. But he did not want to go. Since he had retired, since his . . . stroke, the wife and girls kept him boxed up in the house every day of the week except Tuesday. On Tuesday he was dressed up and brushed and allowed to cut back to the City for the day. Though what he did there the wife and girls couldn't imagine. Made a nuisance of himself to his friends, they supposed. . . . Well, perhaps so. All the same, we cling to our last pleasures as the tree clings to its last leaves. So there sat old Woodifield, smoking a cigar and staring almost greedily at the boss, who rolled in his office chair, stout, rosy, five years older than he, and still going strong, still at the helm. It did one good to see him.

Wistfully, admiringly, the old voice added, "It's snug in here, upon my word!"

"Yes, it's comfortable enough," agreed the boss, and he flipped the *Financial Times* with a paper-knife. As a matter of fact he was proud of his room; he liked to have it admired, especially by old Woodifield. It gave him a feeling of deep, solid satisfaction to be planted there in the midst of it in full view of that frail old figure in the muffler.

"I've had it done up lately," he explained, as he had explained for the past—how many?—weeks. "New carpet," and he pointed to the bright red carpet with a pattern of large white rings. "New furniture," and he nodded towards the massive bookcase and the table with legs like twisted treacle. "Electric heating!" He waved almost exultantly towards the five transparent, pearly sausages glowing so softly in the tilted copper pan.

But he did not draw old Woodifield's attention to the photograph over the table of a grave-looking boy in uniform standing in one of those spectral photographers' parks with photographers' storm-clouds behind him. It was not new. It had been there for over six years.

"There was something I wanted to tell you," said old Woodifield, and his eyes grew dim remembering. "Now what was it? I had it in my mind when I started out this morning." His hands began to tremble, and patches of red showed above his beard.

Poor old chap, he's on his last pins, thought the boss. And, feeling kindly, he winked at the old man, and said jokingly, "I tell you what. I've got a little drop of something here that'll do you good before you go out into the cold again. It's beautiful stuff. It wouldn't hurt a child." He took a key off his watch-chain, unlocked a cupboard below his desk, and drew forth a dark, squat bottle. "That's the medicine," said he. "And the man from whom I got it told me on the strict Q.T. it came from the cellars at Windsor Cassel."

Old Woodifield's mouth fell open at the sight. He couldn't have looked more surprised if the boss had produced a rabbit.

"It's whisky, ain't it?" he piped, feebly.

The boss turned the bottle and lovingly showed him the label. Whisky it was.

"D'you know," said he, peering up at the boss wonderingly, "they won't let me touch it at home." And he looked as though he was going to cry.

"Ah, that's where we know a bit more than the ladies," cried the boss, swooping across for two tumblers that stood on the table with the water-bottle, and pouring a generous finger into each. "Drink it down. It'll do you good. And don't put any water with it. It's sacrilege to tamper with stuff like this. Ah!" He tossed off his, pulled out his handkerchief, hastily wiped his moustaches, and cocked an eye at old Woodifield, who was rolling his in his chaps.

The old man swallowed, was silent a moment, and then said faintly, "It's nutty!"

But it warmed him; it crept into his chill old brain—he remembered.

"That was it," he said, heaving himself out of his chair. "I thought you'd like to know. The girls were in Belgium last week having a look at poor Reggie's grave, and they happened to come across your boy's. They're quite near each other, it seems."

Old Woodifield paused, but the boss made no reply. Only a quiver in his eyelids showed that he heard.

"The girls were delighted with the way the place is kept," piped the old voice. "Beautifully looked after. Couldn't be better if they were at home. You've not been across, have yer?"

"No, no!" For various reasons the boss had not been across.

"There's miles of it," quavered old Woodifield, "and it's all as neat as a garden. Flowers growing on all the graves. Nice broad paths." It was plain from his voice how much he liked a nice broad path.

The pause came again. Then the old man brightened wonderfully.

"D'you know what the hotel made the girls pay for a pot of jam?" he piped. "Ten francs! Robbery, I call it. It was a little pot, so Gertrude says, no bigger than a half-crown. And she hadn't taken more than a spoonful when they charged her ten francs. Gertrude brought the pot away with her to teach 'em a lesson. Quite right, too; it's trading on our feelings. They think because we're over there having a look around we're ready to pay anything. That's what it is." And he turned towards the door.

"Quite right, quite right!" cried the boss, though what was quite right he hadn't the least idea. He came around by his desk, followed the shuffling footsteps to the door, and saw the old fellow out. Woodifield was gone.

For a long moment the boss stayed, staring at nothing, while the grey-haired office messenger, watching him, dodged in and out of his cubbyhole like a dog that expects to be taken for a run. Then: "I'll see nobody for half an hour, Macey," said the boss. "Understand? Nobody at all."

"Very good, sir."

The door shut, the firm heavy steps recrossed the bright carpet, the fat body plumped down in the spring chair, and leaning forward, the boss covered his face with his hands. He wanted, he intended, he had arranged to weep. . . .

It had been a terrible shock to him when old Woodifield sprang that remark upon him about the boy's grave. It was exactly as though the earth had opened and he had seen the boy lying there with Woodifield's girls staring down at him. For it was strange. Although over six years had passed away, the boss never thought of the boy except as lying unchanged, unblemished in his uniform, asleep for ever. "My son!" groaned the boss. But no tears came yet. In the past, in the first months and even years after the boy's death, he had only to say those words to be overcome by such grief that nothing short of a violent fit of weeping could relieve him. Time, he had declared then, he had told everybody, could make no difference. Other men perhaps might recover, might live their loss down, but not he. How was it possible? His boy was an only son. Ever since his birth the boss had worked at building up this business for him; it had no other meaning if it was not for the boy. Life itself had come to have no other meaning. How on earth could he have slaved, denied himself, kept going all those years without the promise for ever before him of the boy's stepping into his shoes and carrying on where he left off?

And that promise had been so near being fulfilled. The boy had been in the office learning the ropes for a year before the war. Every morning they had started off together; they had come back by the same train. And what congratulations he had received as the boy's father! No wonder; he had taken to it marvellously. As to his popularity with the staff, every man jack of them down to old Macey couldn't make enough of the boy. And he wasn't in the least spoilt. No, he was just his bright, natural self, with the right word for everybody, with that boyish look and his habit of saying, "Simply splendid!"

But all that was over and done with as though it never had been. The day had come when Macey had handed him the telegram that brought the whole place crashing about his head. "Deeply regret to inform you . . ." And he had left the office a broken man, with his life in ruins.

Six years ago, six years . . . How quickly time passed! It might have happened yesterday. The boss took his hands from his face; he was puzzled. Something seemed to be wrong with him. He wasn't feeling as he wanted to feel. He decided to get up and have a look at the boy's photograph. But it wasn't a favorite photograph of his; the expression was unnatural. It was cold, even stern-looking. The boy had never looked like that.

At that moment the boss noticed that a fly had fallen into his broad inkpot, and was trying feebly but desperately to clamber out again. Help! help! said those struggling legs. But the sides of the inkpot were wet and slippery; it fell back again and began to swim. The boss took up a pen, picked the fly out of the ink, and shook it on to a piece of blotting-paper. For a fraction of a second it lay still on the dark patch that oozed round it. Then the front legs waved, took hold, and, pulling its small sodden body up it began the immense task of cleaning the ink from its wings. Over and under, over and under, went a leg along a wing, as the stone goes over and under the scythe. Then there was a pause, while the fly, seeming to stand on the tips of its toes, tried to expand first one wing and then the other. It succeeded at last, and, sitting down, it began, like a minute cat, to clean its face. Now one could imagine that the little front legs rubbed against each other lightly, joyfully. The horrible danger was over; it had escaped; it was ready for life again.

But just then the boss had an idea. He plunged his pen back into the ink, leaned his thick wrist on the blotting paper, and as the fly tried its wings down came a great heavy blot. What would it make of that? What indeed! The little beggar seemed absolutely cowed, stunned, and afraid to move because of what would happen next. But then, as if painfully, it dragged itself forward. The front legs waved, caught hold, and, more slowly this time, the task began from the beginning.

He's a plucky little devil, thought the boss, and he felt a real admiration for the fly's courage. That was the way to tackle things; that was the right spirit. Never say die; it was only a question of . . . But the fly had again finished its laborious task, and the boss had just time to refill his pen, to shake fair and square on the new-cleaned body yet another dark drop. What about it this time? A painful moment of suspense followed. But behold, the front legs were again waving; the boss felt a rush of relief. He leaned over the fly and said to it tenderly, "You artful little b . . ." And he actually had the brilliant notion of breathing on it to help the drying process. All the same, there was something timid and weak about its efforts now, and the boss decided that this time should be the last, as he dipped the pen into the inkpot.

It was. The last blot on the soaked blotting-paper, and the draggled fly lay in it and did not stir. The back legs were stuck to the body; the front legs were not to be seen.

"Come on," said the boss. "Look sharp!" And he stirred it with his pen—in vain. Nothing happened or was likely to happen. The fly was dead.

The boss lifted the corpse on the end of the paper-knife and flung it into the waste-paper basket. But such a grinding feeling of wretchedness seized him that he felt positively frightened. He started forward and pressed the bell for Macey.

"Bring me some fresh blotting-paper," he said, sternly, "and look sharp about it." And while the old dog padded away he fell to wondering what it was he had been thinking about before. What was it? It was . . . He took out his handkerchief and passed it inside his collar. For the life of him he could not remember.

the other side of the hedge

e. m. forster

Edward Morgan Forster
(1879–   ) was born in London
and educated at King's College,
Cambridge, where he is still a fellow
of the college. His distinguished
writing career has spanned
more than half a century, during
which he has published several
volumes of essays, criticism, and
biography as well as novels and short
stories. His most widely acclaimed novel
is A Passage to India (1924).
For further reading: The Collected
Tales of E. M. Forster (1946).

My pedometer told me that I was twenty-five; and, though it is a shocking thing to stop walking, I was so tired that I sat down on a milestone to rest. People outstripped me, jeering as they did so, but I was too apathetic to feel resentful, and even when Miss Eliza Dimbleby, the great educationist, swept past, exhorting me to persevere, I only smiled and raised my hat.

At first I thought I was going to be like my brother, whom I had had to leave by the roadside a year or two round the corner. He had wasted his breath on singing, and his strength on helping others. But I had travelled more wisely, and now it was only the monotony of the highway that oppressed me—dust under foot and brown crackling hedges on either side, ever since I could remember.

And I had already dropped several things—indeed, the road behind was strewn with the things we all had dropped; and the white dust was settling down on them, so that already they looked no better than stones. My muscles were so weary that I could not even bear the weight of those things I still carried. I slid off the milestone into the road, and lay there prostrate, with my face to the great parched hedge, praying that I might give up.

A little puff of air revived me. It seemed to come from the hedge; and, when I opened my eyes, there was a glint of light through the tangle of boughs and dead leaves. The hedge could not be as thick as usual. In my weak, morbid state, I longed to force my way in, and see what was on the other side. No one was in sight, or I should not have dared to try. For we of the road do not admit in conversation that there is another side at all.

I yielded to the temptation, saying to myself that I would come back in a minute. The thorns scratched my face, and I had to use my arms as a shield, depending on my feet alone to push me forward. Halfway through I would have gone back, for in the passage all the things I was carrying were scraped off me, and my clothes were torn. But I was so wedged that return was impossible, and I had to wriggle blindly forward, expecting every moment that my strength would fail me, and that I should perish in the undergrowth.

Suddenly cold water closed round my head, and I seemed sinking down for ever. I had fallen out of the hedge into a deep pool. I rose to the surface at last, crying for help, and I heard someone on the opposite bank laugh and say: "Another!" And then I was twitched out and laid panting on the dry ground.

Even when the water was out of my eyes, I was still dazed, for I had never been in so large a space, nor seen such grass and sunshine. The blue sky was no longer a strip, and beneath it the earth had risen grandly into hills—clean, bare buttresses, with beech trees in their folds, and meadows and clear pools at their feet. But the hills were not high, and there was in the landscape a sense of human occupation—so that one might have called it a park, or garden, if the words did not imply a certain triviality and constraint.

As soon as I got my breath, I turned to my rescuer and said:
"Where does this place lead to?"

"Nowhere, thank the Lord!" said he, and laughed. He was a man of fifty or sixty—just the kind of age we mistrust on the road—but there was no anxiety in his manner, and his voice was that of a boy of eighteen.

"But it must lead somewhere!" I cried, too much surprised at his answer to thank him for saving my life.

"He wants to know where it leads!" he shouted to some men on the hill side, and they laughed back, and waved their caps.

I noticed then that the pool into which I had fallen was really a moat which bent round to the left and to the right, and that the hedge followed it continually. The hedge was green on this side—its roots showed through the clear water, and fish swam about in them—and it was wreathed over with dog-roses and Traveller's Joy. But it was a barrier, and in a moment I lost all pleasure in the grass, the sky, the trees, the happy men and women, and realized that the place was but a prison, for all its beauty and extent.

We moved away from the boundary, and then followed a path almost parallel to it, across the meadows. I found it difficult walking, for I was always trying to out-distance my companion, and there was no advantage in doing this if the place led nowhere. I had never kept step with anyone since I left my brother.

I amused him by stopping suddenly and saying disconsolately, "This is perfectly terrible. One cannot advance: one cannot progress. Now we of the road——"

"Yes. I know."

"I was going to say, we advance continually."

"I know."

"We are always learning, expanding, developing. Why, even in my short life I have seen a great deal of advance—the Transvaal War, the Fiscal Question, Christian Science, Radium. Here for example—"

I took out my pedometer, but it still marked twenty-five, not a degree more.

"Oh, it's stopped! I meant to show you. It should have registered all the time I was walking with you. But it makes me only twenty-five."

"Many things don't work in here," he said. "One day a man brought in a Lee-Metford, and that wouldn't work."

"The laws of science are universal in their application. It must be the water in the moat that has injured the machinery. In normal conditions everything works. Science and the spirit of emulation—those are the forces that have made us what we are."

I had to break off and acknowledge the pleasant greetings of people whom we passed. Some of them were singing, some talking, some engaged in gardening, hay-making, or other rudimentary industries. They all seemed happy; and I might have been happy too, if I could have forgotten that the place led nowhere.

I was startled by a young man who came sprinting across our path, took a little fence in fine style, and went tearing over a ploughed field till he plunged into a lake, across which he began to swim. Here was true energy, and I exclaimed: "A cross-country race! Where are the others?"

"There are no others," my companion replied; and, later on, when we passed some long grass from which came the voice of a girl singing exquisitely to herself, he said again: "There are no others." I was bewildered at the waste in production, and murmured to myself, "What does it all mean?"

He said: "It means nothing but itself"—and he repeated the words slowly, as if I were a child.

"I understand," I said quietly, "but I do not agree. Every achievement is worthless unless it is a link in the chain of development. And I must not trespass on your kindness any longer. I must get back somehow to the road, and have my pedometer mended."

"First, you must see the gates," he replied, "for we have gates, though we never use them."

I yielded politely, and before long we reached the moat again, at a point where it was spanned by a bridge. Over the bridge was a big gate, as white as ivory, which was fitted into a gap in the boundary hedge. The gate opened outwards, and I exclaimed in amazement, for from it ran a road—just such a road as I had left—dusty under foot, with brown crackling hedges on either side as far as the eye could reach.

"That's my road!" I cried.

He shut the gate and said: "But not your part of the road. It is through this gate that humanity went out countless ages ago, when it was first seized with the desire to walk."

I denied this, observing that the part of the road I myself had left was not more than two miles off. But with the obstinacy of his years he repeated: "It is the same road. This is the beginning, and though it seems to run straight away from us, it doubles so often, that it is never far from our boundary and sometimes touches it." He stooped down by the moat, and traced on its moist margin an absurd figure like a maze. As we walked back through the meadows, I tried to convince him of his mistake.

"The road sometimes doubles, to be sure, but that is part of our discipline. Who can doubt that its general tendency is onward? To what goal we know not—it may be to some mountain where we shall touch the sky, it may be over precipices into the sea. But that it goes forward —who can doubt that? It is the thought of that that makes us strive to excel, each in his own way, and gives us an impetus which is lacking with you. Now that man who passed us—it's true that he ran well, and jumped well, and swam well; but we have men who can run better, and men who can jump better, and who can swim better. Specialization has produced results which would surprise you. Similarly, that girl——"

Here I interrupted myself to exclaim: "Good gracious me! I could have sworn it was Miss Eliza Dimbleby over there, with her feet in the fountain!"

He believed that it was.

"Impossible! I left her on the road, and she is due to lecture this evening at Tunbridge Wells. Why, her train leaves Cannon Street in—of course my watch has stopped like everything else. She is the last person to be here."

"People always are astonished at meeting each other. All kinds come through the hedge, and come at all times—when they are drawing ahead in the race, when they are lagging behind, when they are left for dead. I often stand near the boundary listening to the sounds of the road—you know what they are—and wonder if anyone will turn aside. It is my great happiness to help someone out of the moat, as I helped you. For our country fills up slowly, though it was meant for all mankind."

"Mankind have other aims," I said gently, for I thought him well-meaning; "and I must join them." I bade him good evening, for the sun was declining, and I wished to be on the road by nightfall. To my alarm, he caught hold of me, crying: "You are not to go yet!" I tried to shake him off, for we had no interests in common, and his civility was becoming irksome to me. But for all my struggles the tiresome old man would not let go; and, as wrestling is not my specialty, I was obliged to follow him.

It was true that I could have never found alone the place where I came in, and I hoped that, when I had seen the other sights about which he was worrying, he would take me back to it. But I was determined not to sleep in the country, for I mistrusted it, and the people too, for all their friendliness. Hungry though I was, I would not join them in their evening meals of milk and fruit, and, when they gave me flowers, I flung them away as soon as I could do so unobserved. Already they were lying down for the night like cattle—some out on the bare hillside, others in groups under the beeches. In the light of an orange sunset I hurried on with my unwelcome guide, dead tired, faint for want of food, but murmuring indomitably: "Give me life, with its struggles and victories, with its failures and hatreds, with its deep moral meaning and its unknown goal!"

At last we came to a place where the encircling moat was spanned by another bridge, and where another gate interrupted the line of the boundary hedge. It was different from the first gate; for it was half transparent like horn, and opened inwards. But through it, in the waning light, I saw again just such a road as I had left—monotonous, dusty, with brown crackling hedges on either side, as far as the eye could reach.

I was strangely disquieted at the sight, which seemed to deprive me of all self-control. A man was passing us, returning for the night to the hills, with a scythe over his shoulder and a can of some liquid in his hand. I forgot the destiny of our race. I forgot the road that lay before my eyes, and I sprang at him, wrenched the can out of his hand, and began to drink.

It was nothing stronger than beer, but in my exhausted state it overcame me in a moment. As in a dream, I saw the old man shut the gate, and heard him say: "This is where your road ends, and through this gate humanity—all that is left of it—will come in to us."

Though my senses were sinking into oblivion, they seemed to expand ere they reached it. They perceived the magic song of nightingales, and the odour of invisible hay, and stars piercing the fading sky. The man whose beer I had stolen lowered me down gently to sleep off its effects, and, as he did so, I saw that he was my brother.

the
duchess
and the
jeweller

virginia woolf

Virginia Woolf (1882–1941) was the daughter of Sir Leslie Stephen, the eminent biographer and literary critic, and grew up in a household where she met such famous literary figures as Robert Louis Stevenson, Thomas Hardy, George Meredith, and John Ruskin. She was a member of the "Bloomsbury Group" and was a founder of The Hogarth Press. Her best-known novels are Mrs. Dalloway *(1925) and* To the Lighthouse *(1927). For further reading:* Monday or Tuesday *(1921);* A Haunted House, and Other Stories *(1943).*

Oliver Bacon lived at the top of a house overlooking the Green Park. He had a flat; chairs jutted out at the right angles— chairs covered in hide. Sofas filled the bays of the windows—sofas covered in tapestry. The windows, the three long windows, had the proper allowance of discreet net and figured satin. The mahogany sideboard bulged discreetly with the right brandies, whiskeys, and liqueurs. And from the middle window he looked down upon the glossy roofs of fashionable cars packed in the narrow straits of Piccadilly. A more central position could not be imagined. And at eight in the morning he would have his breakfast brought in on a tray by a man-servant: the man-servant would unfold his crimson dressing-gown; he would rip his letters open with his long pointed nails and would extract thick white cards of invitation upon which the engraving stood up roughly from duchesses, countesses, viscountesses, and Honourable Ladies. Then he would wash; then he would eat his toast; then he would read his paper by the bright burning fire of electric coals.

"Behold Oliver," he would say, addressing himself. "You who began life in a filthy little alley, you who . . ." and he would look down at his legs, so shapely in their perfect trousers; at his boots; at his spats. They were all shapely, shining; cut from the best cloth by the best scissors in Savile Row. But he dismantled himself often and became again a little boy in a dark alley. He had once thought *that* the height of his ambition

—selling stolen dogs to fashionable women in Whitechapel. And once he had been done. "Oh, Oliver," his mother had wailed. "Oh, Oliver! When will you have sense, my son?" . . . Then he had gone behind a counter; had sold cheap watches; then he had taken a wallet to Amsterdam. . . . At that memory he would chuckle—the old Oliver remembering the young. Yes, he had done well with the three diamonds; also there was the commission on the emerald. After that he went into the private room behind the shop in Hatton Garden; the room with the scales, the safe, the thick magnifying glasses. And then . . . and then. . . . He chuckled. When he passed through the knots of jewellers in the hot evening who were discussing prices, gold mines, diamonds, reports from South Africa, one of them would lay a finger to the side of his nose and murmur, "Hum-m-m," as he passed. It was no more than a murmur; no more than a nudge on the shoulder, a finger on the nose, a buzz that ran through the cluster of jewellers in Hatton Garden on a hot afternoon— oh, many years ago now! But still Oliver felt it purring down his spine, the nudge, the murmur that meant, "Look at him—young Oliver, the young jeweller—there he goes." Young he was then. And he dressed better and better; and had, first a hansom cab; then a car; and first he went up to the dress circle, then down into the stalls. And he had a villa at Richmond, overlooking the river, with trellises of red roses; and Mademoiselle used to pick one every morning and stick it in his button-hole.

"So," said Oliver Bacon, rising and stretching his legs. "So . . ."

And he stood beneath the picture of an old lady on the mantelpiece and raised his hands. "I have kept my word," he said, laying his hands together, palm to palm, as if he were doing homage to her. "I have won my bet." That was so; he was the richest jeweller in England; but his nose, which was long and flexible, like an elephant's trunk, seemed to say by its curious quiver at the nostrils (but it seemed as if the whole nose quivered, not only the nostrils) that he was not satisfied yet; still smelt something under the ground a little further off. Imagine a giant hog in a pasture rich with truffles; after unearthing this truffle and that, still it smells a bigger, a blacker truffle under the ground further off. So Oliver snuffed always in the rich earth of Mayfair another truffle, a blacker, a bigger further off.

Now then he straightened the pearl in his tie, cased himself in his smart blue overcoat; took his yellow gloves and his cane; and swayed as he descended the stairs and half snuffed, half sighed through his long sharp nose as he passed out into Piccadilly. For was he not still a sad man, a dissatisfied man, a man who seeks something that is hidden, though he had won his bet?

He swayed slightly as he walked, as the camel at the zoo sways from side to side when it walks along the asphalt paths laden with grocers and their wives eating from paper bags and throwing little bits of silver paper crumpled up on to the path. The camel despises the grocers; the camel is dissatisfied with its lot; the camel sees the blue lake and the fringe of palm trees in front of it. So the great jeweller, the greatest jeweller in the whole world, swung down Piccadilly, perfectly dressed, with his gloves, with his cane; but dissatisfied still, till he reached the dark little shop, that was famous in France, in Germany, in Austria, in Italy, and all over America—the dark little shop in the street off Bond Street.

As usual, he strode through the shop without speaking, through the four men, the two old men, Marshall and Spencer, and the two young men, Hammond and Wicks, stood straight and looked at him, envying him. It was only with one finger of the amber-coloured glove, waggling, that he acknowledged their presence. And he went in and shut the door of his private room behind him.

Then he unlocked the grating that barred the window. The cries of Bond Street came in; the purr of the distant traffic. The light from reflectors at the back of the shop struck upwards. One tree waved six green leaves, for it was June. But Mademoiselle had married Mr. Pedder of the local brewery—no one stuck roses in his buttonhole now.

"So," he half sighed, half snorted, "so—"

Then he touched a spring in the wall and slowly the panelling slid open, and behind it were the steel safes, five, no, six of them, all of burnished steel. He twisted a key; unlocked one; then another. Each was lined with a pad of deep crimson velvet; in each lay jewels—bracelets, necklaces, rings, tiaras, ducal coronets; loose stones in glass shells; rubies, emeralds, pearls, diamonds. All safe, shining, cool, yet burning, eternally, with their own compressed light.

"Tears!" said Oliver, looking at the pearls.

"Heart's blood!" he said, looking at the rubies.

"Gunpowder!" he continued, rattling the diamonds so that they flashed and blazed.

"Gunpowder enough to blow Mayfair—sky high, high, high!" He threw his head back and made a sound like a horse neighing as he said it.

The telephone buzzed obsequiously in a low muted voice on his table. He shut the safe.

"In ten minutes," he said. "Not before." And he sat down at his desk and looked at the heads of the Roman emperors that were graved on his sleeve links. And again he dismantled himself and became once more the little boy playing marbles in the alley where they sell stolen dogs on Sunday. He became that wily astute little boy, with lips like wet cherries. He dabbled his fingers in ropes of tripe; he dipped them in pans of frying fish; he dodged in and out among the crowds. He was slim, lissome, with eyes like licked stones. And now—now—the hands of the clock ticked on, one, two, three, four. . . . The Duchess of Lambourne waited his pleasure; the Duchess of Lambourne, daughter of a hundred Earls. She would wait for ten minutes on a chair at the counter. She would wait his pleasure. She would wait till he was ready to see her. He watched the clock in its shagreen case. The hand moved on. With each tick the clock handed him—so it seemed—pâté de foie gras, a glass of champagne, another of fine brandy, a cigar costing one guinea. The clock laid them on the table beside him as the ten minutes passed. Then he heard soft slow footsteps approaching; a rustle in the corridor. The door opened. Mr. Hammond flattened himself against the wall.

"Her Grace!" he announced.

And he waited there, flattened against the wall.

And Oliver, rising, could hear the rustle of the dress of the Duchess as she came down the passage. Then she loomed up, filling the door, filling the room with the aroma, the prestige, the arrogance, the pomp, the pride of all the Dukes and Duchesses swollen in one wave. And as a wave breaks, she broke, as she sat down, spreading and splashing and falling over Oliver Bacon, the great jeweller, covering him with sparkling bright colours, green, rose, violet; and odours; and iridescences; and rays shooting from fingers, nodding from plumes, flashing from silk; for she was very large, very fat, tightly girt in pink taffeta, and past her prime. As a parasol with many flounces, as a peacock with many feathers, shuts its flounces, folds its feathers, so she subsided and shut herself as she sank down in the leather armchair.

"Good morning, Mr. Bacon," said the Duchess. And she held out her hand which came through the slit of her white glove. And Oliver bent low as he shook it. And as their hands touched the link was forged between them once more. They were friends, yet enemies; he was master, she was mistress; each cheated the other, each needed the other, each feared the other, each felt this and knew this every time they touched hands thus in the little back room with the white light outside, and the tree with its six leaves, and the sound of the street in the distance and behind them the safes.

"And today, Duchess—what can I do for you today?" said Oliver, very softly.

The Duchess opened her heart, her private heart, gaped wide. And with a sigh but no word she took from her bag a long wash-leather pouch—it looked like a lean yellow ferret. And from a slit in the ferret's belly she dropped pearls—ten pearls. They rolled from the slit in the ferret's belly—one, two, three, four—like the eggs of some heavenly bird.

"All that's left me, dear Mr. Bacon," she moaned. Five, six, seven—down they rolled, down the slopes of the vast mountain sides that fell between her knees into one narrow valley—the eighth, the ninth, and the tenth. There they lay in the glow of the peach-blossom taffeta. Ten pearls.

"From the Appleby cincture," she mourned. "The last . . . the last of them all."

Oliver stretched out and took one of the pearls between finger and thumb. It was round, it was lustrous. But real was it, or false? Was she lying again? Did she dare?

She laid her plump padded finger across her lips. "If the Duke knew . . ." she whispered. "Dear Mr. Bacon, a bit of bad luck . . ."

Been gambling again, had she?

"That villain! That sharper!" she hissed.

The man with the chipped cheek bone? A bad 'un. And the Duke was straight as a poker; with side whiskers; would cut her off, shut her up down there if he knew—what I know, thought Oliver, and glanced at the safe.

"Araminta, Daphne, Diana," she moaned. "It's for *them*."

The ladies Araminta, Daphne, Diana—her daughters. He knew them; adored them. But it was Diana he loved.

"You have all my secrets," she leered. Tears slid; tears fell; tears, like diamonds, collecting powder in the ruts of her cherry blossom cheeks.

"Old friend," she murmured, "old friend."

"Old friend," he repeated, "old friend," as if he licked the words.

"How much?" he queried.

She covered the pearls with her hand.

"Twenty thousand," she whispered.

But was it real or false, the one he held in his hand? The Appleby cincture—hadn't she sold it already? He would ring for Spencer or Hammond. "Take it and test it," he would say. He stretched to the bell.

"You will come down tomorrow?" she urged, she interrupted. "The Prime Minister—His Royal Highness . . ." She stopped. "And Diana . . ." she added.

Oliver took his hand off the bell.

He looked past her, at the backs of the houses in Bond Street. But he saw, not the houses in Bond Street, but a dimpling river; and trout rising and salmon; and the Prime Minister; and himself too, in white waistcoat; and then, Diana. He looked down at the pearl in his hand. But how could he test it, in the light of the river, in the light of the eyes of Diana? But the eyes of the Duchess were on him.

"Twenty thousand," she moaned. "My honour!"

The honour of the mother of Diana! He drew his cheque book towards him; he took out his pen.

"Twenty—" he wrote. Then he stopped writing. The eyes of the old woman in the picture were on him—of the old woman his mother.

"Oliver!" she warned him. "Have sense! Don't be a fool!"

"Oliver!" the Duchess entreated—it was "Oliver" now, not "Mr. Bacon." "You'll come for a long week-end?"

Alone in the woods with Diana! Riding alone in the woods with Diana!

"Thousand," he wrote, and signed it.

"Here you are," he said.

And there opened all the flounces of the parasol, all the plumes of the peacock, the radiance of the wave, the swords and spears of Agincourt, as she rose from her chair. And the two old men and the two young men, Spencer and Marshall, Wicks and Hammond, flattened themselves behind the counter envying him as he led her through the shop to the door. And he waggled his yellow glove in their faces, and she held her honour—a cheque for twenty thousand pounds with his signature—quite firmly in her hands.

"Are they false or are they real?" asked Oliver, shutting his private door. There they were, ten pearls on the blotting-paper on the table. He took them to the window. He held them under his lens to the light. . . . This, then, was the truffle he had routed out of the earth! Rotten at the centre—rotten at the core!

"Forgive me, oh, my mother!" he sighed, raising his hand as if he asked pardon of the old woman in the picture. And again he was a little boy in the alley where they sold dogs on Sunday.

"For," he murmured, laying the palms of his hands together, "it is to be a long week-end."

her
table
spread

spread

elizabeth bowen

Elizabeth Bowen *(1899–*) *lives in Cork, Ireland. A prolific writer, she has published six collections of stories, nine novels, and three volumes of essays. Her best novels include* The Death of the Heart *(1939) and* The Heat of the Day *(1949). For further reading:* Joining Charles *(1929);* Look at All Those Roses *(1941);* Stories by Elizabeth Bowen *(1959).*

Alban had few opinions on the subject of marriage; his attitude to women was negative, but in particular he was not attracted to Miss Cuffe. Coming down early for dinner, red satin dress cut low, she attacked the silence with loud laughter before he had spoken. He recollected having heard that she was abnormal—at twenty-five, of statuesque development, still detained in childhood. The two other ladies, in beaded satins, made entrances of a surprising formality. It occurred to him, his presence must constitute an occasion: they certainly sparkled. Old Mr. Rossiter, uncle to Mrs. Treye, came last, more sourly. They sat for some time without the addition of lamplight. Dinner was not announced; the ladies, by remaining on guard, seemed to deprecate any question of its appearance. No sound came from other parts of the Castle.

Miss Cuffe was an heiress to whom the Castle belonged and whose guests they all were. But she carefully followed the movements of her aunt, Mrs. Treye; her ox-eyes moved from face to face in happy submission rather than expectancy. She was continually preoccupied with attempts at gravity, as though holding down her skirts in a high wind. Mrs. Treye and Miss Carbin combined to cover her excitement; still, their looks frequently stole from the company to the windows, of which there were too many. He received a strong impression someone outside was waiting to come in. At last, with a sigh, they got up: dinner had been announced.

The Castle was built on high ground, commanding the estuary; a steep hill, with trees, continued above it. On fine days the view was

287

remarkable, of almost Italian brilliance, with that constant reflection up from the water that even now prolonged the too-long day. Now, in continuous evening rain, the winding wooded line of the further shore could be seen and, nearer the windows; a smothered island with the stump of a watch-tower. Where the Castle stood, a higher tower had answered the island's. Later a keep, then wings, had been added; now the fine peaceful residence had French windows opening on to the terrace. Invasions from the water would henceforth be social, perhaps amorous. On the slope down from the terrace, trees began again; almost, but not quite, concealing the destroyer. Alban, who knew nothing, had not yet looked down.

It was Mr. Rossiter who first spoke of the destroyer—Alban meanwhile glancing along the table; the preparations had been stupendous. The destroyer had come to-day. The ladies all turned to Alban: the beads on their bosoms sparkled. So this was what they had here, under their trees. Engulfed by their pleasure, from now on he disappeared personally. Mr. Rossiter, rising a note, continued. The estuary, it appeared, was deep, with a channel buoyed up it. By a term of the Treaty, English ships were permitted to anchor in these waters.

"But they've been afraid of the rain!" chimed in Valeria Cuffe.

"Hush," said her aunt, "that's silly. Sailors would be accustomed to getting wet."

But, Miss Carbin reported, that spring there *had* already been one destroyer. Two of the officers had been seen dancing at the hotel at the head of the estuary.

"So," said Alban, "you are quite in the world." He adjusted his glasses in her direction.

Miss Carbin—blonde, not forty, and an attachment of Mrs. Treye's—shook her head despondently. "We were all away at Easter. Wasn't it curious they should have come then? The sailors walked in the demesne but never touched the daffodils."

"As though I should have cared!" exclaimed Valeria passionately.

"Morale too good," stated Mr. Rossiter.

"But next evening," continued Miss Carbin, "the officers did not go to the hotel. They climbed up here through the trees to the terrace—you see, they had no idea. Friends of ours were staying here at the Castle, and they apologised. Our friends invited them in to supper. . . ."

"Did they accept?"

The three ladies said in a breath: "Yes, they came."

Valeria added urgently, "So don't you *think*—?"

"So to-night we have a destroyer to greet you," Mrs. Treye said quickly to Alban. "It is quite an event; the country people are coming down from the mountains. These waters are very lonely; the steamers have given up since the bad times; there is hardly a pleasure-boat. The weather this year has driven visitors right away."

"You are beautifully remote."

"Yes," agreed Miss Carbin. "Do you know much about the Navy? Do you think, for instance, that this is likely to be the same destroyer?"

"*Will they remember?*" Valeria's bust was almost on the table. But with a rustle Mrs. Treye pressed Valeria's toe. For the dining-room also looked out across the estuary, and the great girl had not once taken her eyes from the window. Perhaps it was unfortunate that Mr. Alban should have coincided with the destroyer. Perhaps it was unfortunate for Mr. Alban too.

For he saw now he was less than half the feast; unappeased, the party sat looking through him, all grouped at an end of the table—to the other, chairs had been pulled up. Dinner was being served very slowly. Candles —possible to see from the water—were lit now; some wet peonies glistened. Outside, day still lingered hopefully. The bushes over the edge of the terrace were like heads—you could have sworn sometimes you saw them mounting, swaying in manly talk. Once, wound up in the rain, a bird whistled, seeming hardly a bird.

"Perhaps since then they have been to Greece, or Malta?"

"That would be the Mediterranean fleet," said Mr. Rossiter.

They were sorry to think of anything out in the rain to-night.

"The decks must be streaming," said Miss Carbin.

Then Valeria, exclaiming, "Please excuse me!" pushed her chair in and ran from the room.

"She is impulsive," explained Mrs. Treye. "Have *you* been to Malta, Mr. Alban?"

In the drawing-room, empty of Valeria, the standard lamps had been lit. Through their ballet-skirt shades, rose and lemon, they gave out a deep, welcoming light. Alban, at the ladies' invitation, undraped the piano. He played, but they could see he was not pleased. It was obvious he had always been a civilian, and when he had taken his place on the piano-stool—which he twirled round three times, rather fussily—his dinner-jacket wrinkled across the shoulders. It was sad they should feel so indifferent, for he came from London. Mendelssohn was exasperating to them—they opened all four windows to let the music downhill. They preferred not to draw the curtains; the air, though damp, being pleasant to-night, they said.

The piano was damp, but Alban played almost all his heart out. He played out the indignation of years his mild manner concealed. He had failed to love; nobody did anything about this; partners at dinner gave him less than half their attention. He knew some spring had dried up at the root of the world. He was fixed in the dark rain, by an indifferent shore. He played badly, but they were unmusical. Old Mr. Rossiter, who was not what he seemed, went back to the dining-room to talk to the parlourmaid.

Valeria, glittering vastly, appeared in a window.

"Come *in!*" her aunt cried in indignation. She would die of a chill, childless, in fact unwedded; the Castle would have to be sold and where would they all be?

But—"Lights down there!" Valeria shouted above the music.

They had to run out for a moment, laughing and holding cushions over their bare shoulders. Alban left the piano: they looked boldly down from the terrace. Indeed, there they were: two lights like arc-lamps, blurred by rain and drawn down deep in reflection into the steady water. There were, too, ever so many portholes, all lit up.

"Perhaps they are playing bridge," said Miss Carbin.

"Now I wonder if Uncle Robert ought to have called," said Mrs. Treye. "Perhaps we have seemed remiss—one calls on a regiment."

"Patrick could row him out to-morrow."

"He hates the water." She sighed. "Perhaps they will be gone."

"Let's go for a row now—let's go for a row with a lantern," besought Valeria, jumping and pulling her aunt's elbow. They produced such indignation she disappeared again—wet satin skirts and all—into the bushes. The ladies could do no more: Alban suggested the rain might spot their dresses.

"They must lose a great deal, playing cards throughout an evening for high stakes," Miss Carbin said with concern as they all sat down again.

"Yes, if you come to think of it, somebody must win."

But the naval officers who so joyfully supped at Easter had been, Miss Carbin knew, a Mr. Graves and a Mr. Garrett: *they* would certainly lose. "At all events, it is better than dancing at the hotel; there would be nobody of their type."

"There is nobody there at all."

"I expect they are best where they are. . . . Mr. Alban, a Viennese waltz?"

He played while the ladies whispered, waving the waltz time a little distractedly. Mr. Rossiter, coming back, momentously stood: they turned in hope: even the waltz halted. But he brought no news. "You should call Valeria in. You can't tell who may be round the place. She's not fit to be out to-night."

"Perhaps she's not out."

"She is," said Mr. Rossiter crossly. "I just saw her racing past the window with a lantern."

Valeria's mind was made up: she was a princess. Not for nothing had she had the dining-room silver polished and all set out. She would pace around in red satin that swished behind, while Mr. Alban kept on playing a loud waltz. They would be dazed at all she had to offer—also her two new statues and the leopard-skin from the auction.

When he and she were married (she inclined a little to Mr. Garrett) they would invite all the Navy up the estuary and give them tea. Her estuary would be filled up, like a regatta, with loud excited battleships tooting to one another and flags flying. The terrace would be covered with grateful sailors, leaving room for the band. She would keep the peacocks her aunt did not allow. His friends would be surprised to notice that Mr. Garrett had meanwhile become an admiral, all gold. He would lead the other admirals into the castle and say, while they wiped their feet respectfully: "These are my wife's statues; she has given them to me. One is Mars, one is Mercury. We have a Venus, but she is not dressed. And wait till I show you our silver and gold plates . . ." The Navy would be unable to tear itself away.

She had been excited for some weeks at the idea of marrying Mr. Alban, but now the lovely appearance of the destroyer put him out of her mind. He would not have done; he was not handsome. But she could keep him to play the piano on quiet afternoons.

Her friends had told her Mr. Garrett was quite a Viking. She was so very familiar with his appearance that she felt sometimes they had already been married for years—though still, sometimes, he could not realise his good luck. She still had to remind him the island was hers too. . . . To-night, Aunt and darling Miss Carbin had so fallen in with her plans, putting on their satins and decorating the drawing-room, that the dinner became a betrothal feast. There was some little hitch about the arrival of Mr. Garrett—she had heard that gentlemen sometimes could not tie their ties. And now he was late and would be discouraged. So she must now go half-way down to the water and wave a lantern.

But she put her two hands over the lantern, then smothered it in her dress. She had a panic. Supposing she should prefer Mr. Graves?

She had heard Mr. Graves was stocky, but very merry; when he came to supper at Easter he slid in the gallery. He would teach her to dance, and take her to Naples and Paris. . . . Oh, dear, oh, dear, then they must fight for her; that was all there was to it. . . . She let the lantern out of her skirts and waved. Her fine arm with bangles went up and down, up and down, with the staggering light; the trees one by one jumped up from the dark, like savages.

Inconceivably, the destroyer took no notice.

Undisturbed by oars, the rain stood up from the waters; not a light rose to peer, and the gramophone, though it remained very faint, did not cease or alter.

In mackintoshes, Mr. Rossiter and Alban meanwhile made their way to the boat-house, Alban did not know why. "If that goes on," said Mr. Rossiter, nodding towards Valeria's lantern, "they'll fire one of their guns at us."

"Oh, no. Why?" said Alban. He buttoned up, however, the collar of his mackintosh.

"Nervous as cats. It's high time that girl was married. She's a nice girl in many ways, too."

"Couldn't we get the lantern away from her?" They stepped on a paved causeway and heard the water nibble the rocks.

"She'd scream the place down. She's of age now, you see."

"But if—"

"Oh, she won't do that; I was having a bit of fun with you." Chuckling equably, Mrs. Treye's uncle unlocked and pulled open the boat-house door. A bat whistled out.

"Why are we here?"

"She might come for the boat; she's a fine oar," said Mr. Rossiter wisely. The place was familiar to him; he lit an oil-lamp and, sitting down on a trestle with a staunch air of having done what he could, reached a bottle of whisky out of the boat. He motioned the bottle to Alban. "It's a wild night," he said. "Ah, well, we don't have these destroyers every day."

"That seems fortunate."

"Well, it is and it isn't." Restoring the bottle to the vertical, Mr. Rossiter continued: "It's a pity you don't want a wife. You'd be the better for a wife, d'you see, a young fellow like you. She's got a nice character; she's a girl you could shape. She's got a nice income." The bat returned from the rain and knocked round the lamp. Lowering the bottle frequently, Mr. Rossiter talked to Alban (whose attitude remained negative) of women in general and the parlourmaid in particular. . . .

"*Bat!*" Alban squealed irrepressibly, and with his hand to his ear—where he still felt it—fled from the boat-house. Mr. Rossiter's conversation continued. Alban's pumps squelched as he ran; he skidded along the causeway and baulked at the upward steps. His soul squelched equally: he had been warned; he had been warned. He had heard they were all mad; he had erred out of headiness and curiosity. A degree of terror was agreeable to his vanity: by express wish he had occupied haunted rooms. Now he had no other pumps in this country, no idea where to buy them, and a ducal visit ahead. Also, wandering as it were among the apples and amphoras of an art school, he had blundered into the life room: woman revolved gravely.

"Hell," he said to the steps, mounting, his mind blank to the outcome.

He was nerved for the jumping lantern, but half-way up to the Castle darkness was once more absolute. Her lantern had gone out; he could

orientate himself—in spite of himself—by her sobbing. Absolute desperation. He pulled up so short that, for balance, he had to cling to a creaking
tree.

"Hi!" she croaked. Then: "You *are* there! I hear you!"

"Miss Cuffe—"

"How too bad you are! I never heard you rowing. I thought you were
never coming—"

"Quietly, my dear girl."

"Come up quickly. I haven't even seen you. Come up to the windows—"

"Miss Cuffe—"

"Don't you remember the way?" As sure but not so noiseless as a cat
in the dark, Valeria hurried to him.

"Mr. Garrett—" she panted. "I'm Miss Cuffe. Where have you been?
I've destroyed my beautiful red dress and they've eaten up your dinner.
But we're still waiting. Don't be afraid; you'll soon be there now. I'm
Miss Cuffe; this is my Castle—"

"Listen, it's I, Mr. Alban—"

"Ssh, ssh, Mr. Alban: *Mr. Garrett has landed.*"

Her cry, his voice, some breath of the joyful intelligence, brought the
others on to the terrace, blind with lamplight.

"Valeria?"

"Mr. Garrett has landed!"

Mrs. Treye said to Miss Carbin under her breadth, "Mr. Garrett has
come."

Miss Carbin, half weeping with agitation, replied, "We must go in."
But uncertain who was to speak next, or how to speak, they remained
leaning over the darkness. Behind, through the windows, lamps spread
great skirts of light, and Mars and Mercury, unable to contain themselves,
stooped from their pedestals. The dumb keyboard shone like a ballroom
floor.

Alban, looking up, saw their arms and shoulders under the bright rain.
Close by, Valeria's fingers creaked on her warm wet satin. She laughed
like a princess, magnificently justified. Their unseen faces were all three
lovely, and, in the silence after the laughter, such a strong tenderness
reached him that, standing there in full manhood, he was for a moment
not exiled. For the moment, without moving or speaking, he stood in the
dark, in a flame, as though all three said: "My darling . . ."

Perhaps it was best for them all that early, when next day first light-
ened the rain, the destroyer steamed out—below the extinguished Castle
where Valeria lay with her arms wide, past the boat-house, where Mr.
Rossiter lay insensible and the bat hung masked in its wings—down the
estuary into the open sea.

Graham Greene (1904–   ) worked for the London Times *after
graduating from Oxford University. A poet, novelist, and essayist,
he is known for his preoccupation with Roman Catholic
problems. His early novels were "thrillers,"
or "entertainments" as he called them.
Many of his later novels were hailed
as artistic successes, for example,*
The Power and the Glory
(1940). For further reading:
Nineteen Stories *(1949).*

brother

graham greene

The Communists were the first to appear. They
walked quickly, a group of about a dozen, up the boulevard which runs
from Combat to Ménilmontant; a young man and a girl lagged a little
way behind because the man's leg was hurt and the girl was helping him
along. They looked impatient, harassed, hopeless, as if they were trying
to catch a train which they knew already in their hearts they were too
late to catch.

The proprietor of the café saw them coming when they were still a
long way off; the lamps at that time were still alight (it was later that the
bullets broke the bulbs and dropped darkness all over that quarter of
Paris), and the group showed up plainly in the wide barren boulevard.
Since sunset only one customer had entered the café, and very soon
after sunset firing could be heard from the direction of Combat; the
Métro station had closed hours ago. And yet something obstinate and
undefeatable in the proprietor's character prevented him from putting
up the shutters; it might have been avarice; he could not himself have
told what it was as he pressed his broad yellow forehead against the
glass and stared this way and that, up the boulevard and down the
boulevard.

But when he saw the group and their air of hurry he began immediately to close his café. First he went and warned his only customer, who
was practising billiard shots, walking round and round the table, frowning and stroking a thin moustache between shots, a little green in the
face under the low diffused lights.

"The Reds are coming," the proprietor said, "you'd better be off. I'm
putting up the shutters."

"Don't interrupt. They won't harm me," the customer said. "This is a
tricky shot. Red's in baulk. Off the cushion. Screw on spot." He shot
his ball straight into a pocket.

"I knew you couldn't do anything with that," the proprietor said, nodding his bald head. "You might just as well go home. Give me a hand with the shutters first. I've sent my wife away." The customer turned on him maliciously, rattling the cue between his fingers. "It was your talking that spoilt the shot. You've cause to be frightened, I dare say. But I'm a poor man. I'm safe. I'm not going to stir." He went across to his coat and took out a dry cigar. "Bring me a bock." He walked round the table on his toes and the balls clicked and the proprietor padded back into the bar, elderly and irritated. He did not fetch the beer but began to close the shutters; every move he made was slow and clumsy. Long before he had finished the group of Communists was outside.

He stopped what he was doing and watched them with furtive dislike. He was afraid that the rattle of the shutters would attract their attention. If I am very quiet and still, he thought, they may go on, and he remembered with malicious pleasure the police barricade across the Place de la République. That will finish them. In the meanwhile I must be very quiet, very still, and he felt a kind of warm satisfaction at the idea that worldly wisdom dictated the very attitude most suited to his nature. So he stared through the edge of a shutter, yellow, plump, cautious, hearing the billiard balls crackle in the other room, seeing the young man come limping up the pavement on the girl's arm, watching them stand and stare with dubious faces up the boulevard towards Combat.

But when they came into the café he was already behind the bar, smiling and bowing and missing nothing, noticing how they had divided forces, how six of them had begun to run back the way they had come.

The young man sat down in a dark corner above the cellar stairs and the others stood round the door waiting for something to happen. It gave the proprietor an odd feeling that they should stand there in his café not asking for a drink, knowing what to expect, when he, the owner, knew nothing, understood nothing. At last the girl said "Cognac," leaving the others and coming to the bar, but when he had poured it out for her, very careful to give a fair and not a generous measure, she simply took it to the man sitting in the dark and held it to his mouth.

"Three francs," the proprietor said. She took the glass and sipped a little and turned it so that the man's lips might touch the same spot. Then she knelt down and rested her forehead against the man's forehead and so they stayed.

"Three francs," the proprietor said, but he could not make his voice bold. The man was no longer visible in his corner, only the girl's back, thin and shabby in a black cotton frock, as she knelt, leaning forward to find the man's face. The proprietor was daunted by the four men at the door, by the knowledge that they were Reds who had no respect for private property, who would drink his wine and go away without paying, who would rape his women (but there was only his wife, and she was not there), who would rob his bank, who would murder him as soon as look at him. So with fear in his heart he gave up the three francs as lost rather than attract any more attention.

Then the worst that he contemplated happened.

One of the men at the door came up to the bar and told him to pour out four glasses of cognac. "Yes, yes," the proprietor said, fumbling with the cork, praying secretly to the Virgin to send an angel, to send the police, to send the Gardes Mobiles, now, immediately, before the cork came out, "that will be twelve francs."

"Oh, no," the man said, "we are all comrades here. Share and share alike. Listen," he said, with earnest mockery, leaning across the bar, "all we have is yours just as much as it's ours, comrade," and stepping back a pace he presented himself to the proprietor, so that he might take his choice of stringy tie, of threadbare trousers, of starved features. "And it follows from that, comrade, that all you have is ours. So four cognacs. Share and share alike."

"Of course," the proprietor said, "I was only joking." Then he stood with bottle poised, and the four glasses tingled upon the counter. "A machine-gun," he said, "up by Combat," and smiled to see how for the moment the men forgot their brandy as they fidgeted near the door. Very soon now, he thought, and I shall be quit of them.

"A machine-gun," the Red said incredulously, "they're using machine-guns?"

"Well," the proprietor said, encouraged by this sign that the Gardes Mobiles were not very far away, "you can't pretend that you aren't armed yourselves." He leant across the bar in a way that was almost paternal. "After all, you know, your ideas—they wouldn't do in France. Free love."

"Who's talking of free love?" the Red said.

The proprietor shrugged and smiled and nodded at the corner. The girl knelt with her head on the man's shoulder, her back to the room. They were quite silent and the glass of brandy stood on the floor beside them. The girl's beret was pushed back on her head and one stocking was laddered and darned from knee to ankle.

"What, those two? They aren't lovers."

"I," the proprietor said, "with my bourgeois notions would have thought . . ."

"He's her brother," the Red said.

The men came clustering round the bar and laughed at him, but softly as if a sleeper or a sick person were in the house. All the time they were listening for something. Between their shoulders the proprietor could look out across the boulevard; he could see the corner of the Faubourg du Temple.

"What are you waiting for?"

"For friends," the Red said. He made a gesture with open palm as if to say, You see, we share and share alike. We have no secrets.

Something moved at the corner of the Faubourg du Temple.

"Four more cognacs," the Red said.

"What about those two?" the proprietor asked.

"Leave them alone. They'll look after themselves. They're tired."

How tired they were. No walk up the boulevard from Ménilmontant could explain the tiredness. They seemed to have come farther and fared a great deal worse than their companions. They were more starved; they were infinitely more hopeless, sitting in their dark corner away from the friendly gossip, the amicable desperate voices which now confused the proprietor's brain, until for a moment he believed himself to be a host entertaining friends.

He laughed and made a broad joke directed at the two of them; but they made no sign of understanding. Perhaps they were to be pitied, cut off from the camaraderie round the counter; perhaps they were to be envied for their deeper comradeship. The proprietor thought for no reason at all of the bare grey trees of the Tuileries like a series of exclamation marks drawn against the winter sky. Puzzled, disintegrated, with all his bearings, lost, he stared out through the door towards the Faubourg.

It was as if they had not seen each other for a long while and would soon again be saying good-bye. Hardly aware of what he was doing he filled the four glasses with brandy. They stretched out worn blunted fingers for them.

"Wait," he said. "I've got something better than this"; then paused, conscious of what was happening across the boulevard. The lamplight splashed down on blue steel helmets; the Gardes Mobiles were lining out across the entrance to the Faubourg, and a machine-gun pointed directly at the café windows.

So, the proprietor thought, my prayers are answered. Now I must do my part not look, not warn them, save myself. Have they covered the side door? I will get the other bottle. Real Napoleon brandy. Share and share alike.

He felt a curious lack of triumph as he opened the trap of the bar and came out. He tried not to walk quickly back towards the billiard room. Nothing that he did must warn these men; he tried to spur himself with the thought that every slow casual step he took was a blow for France, for his café, for his savings. He had to step over the girl's feet to pass her; she was asleep. He noted the sharp shoulder blades thrusting through the cotton, and raised his eyes and met her brother's, filled with pain and despair.

He stopped. He found he could not pass without a word. It was as if he needed to explain something, as if he belonged to the wrong party. With false bonhomie he waved the corkscrew he carried in the other's face. "Another cognac, eh?"

"It's no good talking to them," the Red said. "They're German. They don't understand a word."

"German?"

"That's what's wrong with his leg. A concentration camp."

The proprietor told himself that he must be quick, that he must put a door between him and them, that the end was very close, but he was bewildered by the hopelessness in the man's gaze. "What's he doing here?" Nobody answered him. It was as if his question were too foolish to need a reply. With his head sunk upon his breast the proprietor went past, and the girl slept on. He was like a stranger leaving a room where all the rest are friends. A German. They don't understand a word; and up, up through the heavy darkness of his mind, through the avarice and the dubious triumph, a few German words remembered from very old days climbed like spies into the light: a line from the *Lorelei* learnt at school, *Kamerad* with its war-time suggestion of fear and surrender, and oddly from nowhere the phrase *mein Bruder*. He opened the door of the billiard room and closed it behind him and softly turned the key.

"Spot in baulk," the customer explained and leant across the great green table, but while he took aim, wrinkling his narrow peevish eyes, the firing started. It came in two bursts with a rip of glass between. The girl cried out something, but it was not one of the words he knew. Then feet ran across the floor, the trap of the bar slammed. The proprietor sat back against the table and listened and listened for any further sound; but silence came in under the door and silence through the key-hole.

"The cloth. My God, the cloth," the customer said, and the proprietor looked down at his own hand which was working the corkscrew into the table.

"Will this absurdity never end?" the customer said. "I shall go home."

"Wait," the proprietor said. "Wait." He was listening to voices and footsteps in the other room. These were voices he did not recognize. Then a car drove up and presently drove away again. Somebody rattled the handle of the door.

"Who is it?" the proprietor called.

"Who are you? Open that door."

"Ah," the customer said with relief, "the police. Where was I now?

Spot in baulk." He began to chalk his cue. The proprietor opened the door. Yes, the Gardes Mobiles had arrived; he was safe again, though his windows were smashed. The Reds had vanished as if they had never been. He looked at the raised trap, at the smashed electric bulbs, at the broken bottle which dripped behind the bar. The café was full of men, and he remembered with odd relief that he had not had time to lock the side door.

"Are you the owner?" the officer asked. "A bock for each of these men and a cognac for myself. Be quick about it."

The proprietor calculated: "Nine francs fifty," and watched closely with bent head the coins rattle down upon the counter.

"You see," the officer said with significance, "we pay." He nodded towards the side door. "Those others: did they pay?"

No, the proprietor admitted, they had not paid, but as he counted the coins and slipped them into the till, he caught himself silently repeating the officer's order—"A bock for each of these men." Those others, he thought, one's got to say that for them, they weren't mean about the drink. It was four cognacs with them. But, of course, they did not pay. "And my windows," he complained aloud with sudden asperity, "what about my windows?"

"Never you mind," the officer said, "the government will pay. You have only to send in your bill. Hurry up now with my cognac. I have no time for gossip."

"You can see for yourself" the proprietor said, "how the bottles have been broken. Who will pay for that?"

"Everything will be paid for," the officer said.

"And now I must go to the cellar to fetch more."

He was angry at the reiteration of the word pay. They enter my café, he thought, they smash my windows, they order me about and think that all is well if they pay, pay, pay. It occurred to him that these men were intruders.

"Step to it," the officer said and turned and rebuked one of the men who had leant his rifle against the bar.

At the top of the cellar stairs the proprietor stopped. They were in darkness, but by the light from the bar he could just make out a body half-way down. He began to tremble violently, and it was some seconds before he could strike a match. The young German lay head downwards, and the blood from his head had dropped on to the step below. His eyes were open and stared back at the proprietor with the old despairing expression of life. The proprietor would not believe that he was dead. "Kamerad," he said bending down, while the match singed his fingers and went out, trying to recall some phrase in German, but he could only remember, as he bent lower still, "mein Bruder." Then suddenly he turned and ran up the steps, waved the match-box in the officer's face, and called out in a low hysterical voice to him and his men and to the customer stooping under the low green shade, "Cochons. Cochons."

"What was that? What was that?" the officer exclaimed. "Did you say that he was your brother? It's impossible," and he frowned incredulously at the proprietor and rattled the coins in his pocket.

christmas
morning
frank o'connor

*Frank O'Connor (Michael O'Donovan) (1903–   )
was educated at Cork
and is now a member of the
Irish Academy of Letters.
He is the author of about
twenty-five volumes, largely
short stories. By profession he was once
a librarian. For further reading:*
The Stories of Frank O'Connor
(1952); More Stories
of Frank O'Connor *(1954).*

I never really liked my brother, Sonny. From the time he was a baby he was always the mother's pet and always chasing her to tell her what mischief I was up to. Mind you, I was usually up to something. Until I was nine or ten I was never much good at school, and I really believe it was to spite me that he was so smart at his books. He seemed to know by instinct that this was what Mother had set her heart on, and you might almost say he spelt himself into her favour.

"Mummy," he'd say, "will I call Larry in to his t-e-a?" or: "Mummy, the k-e-t-e-l is boiling," and, of course, when he was wrong she'd correct him, and next time he'd have it right and there would be no standing him. "Mummy," he'd say, "aren't I a good speller?" Cripes, we could all be good spellers if we went on like that!

Mind you, it wasn't that I was stupid. Far from it. I was just restless and not able to fix my mind for long on any one thing. I'd do the lessons for the year before, or the lessons for the year after: what I couldn't stand were the lessons we were supposed to be doing at the time. In the evenings I used to go out and play with the Doherty gang. Not, again, that I was rough, but I liked the excitement, and for the life of me I couldn't see what attracted Mother about education.

"Can't you do your lessons first and play after?" she'd say, getting white with indignation. "You ought to be ashamed of yourself that your baby brother can read better than you."

She didn't seem to understand that I wasn't, because there didn't seem to me to be anything particularly praiseworthy about reading, and it struck me as an occupation better suited to a sissy kid like Sonny.

"The dear knows what will become of you," she'd say. "If only you'd stick to your books you might be something good like a clerk or an engineer."

"I'll be a clerk, Mummy," Sonny would say smugly.

"Who wants to be an old clerk?" I'd say, just to annoy him. "I'm going to be a soldier."

"The dear knows, I'm afraid that's all you'll ever be fit for," she would add with a sigh.

I couldn't help feeling at times that she wasn't all there. As if there was anything better a fellow could be!

Coming on to Christmas, with the days getting shorter and the shopping crowds bigger, I began to think of all the things I might get from Santa Claus. The Dohertys said there was no Santa Claus, only what your father and mother gave you, but the Dohertys were a rough class of children you wouldn't expect Santa to come to anyway. I was rooting round for whatever information I could pick up about him, but there didn't seem to be much. I was no hand with a pen, but if a letter would do any good I was ready to chance writing to him. I had plenty of initiative and was always writing off for free samples and prospectuses.

"Ah, I don't know will he come at all this year," Mother said with a worried air. "He has enough to do looking after steady boys who mind their lessons without bothering about the rest."

"He only comes to good spellers, Mummy," said Sonny. "Isn't that right?"

"He comes to any little boy who does his best, whether he's a good speller or not," Mother said firmly.

Well, I did my best. God knows I did! It wasn't my fault if, four days before the holidays, Flogger Dawley gave us sums we couldn't do, and Peter Doherty and myself had to go on the lang. It wasn't for love of it, for, take it from me, December is no month for mitching, and we spent most of our time sheltering from the rain in a store on the quays. The only mistake we made was imagining we could keep it up till the holidays without being spotted. That showed real lack of foresight.

Of course, Flogger Dawley noticed and sent home word to know what was keeping me. When I came in on the third day the mother gave me a look I'll never forget, and said: "Your dinner is there." She was too full to talk. When I tried to explain to her about Flogger Dawley and the sums she brushed it aside and said: "You have no word." I saw then it wasn't the langing she minded but the lies, though I still didn't see how you could lang without lying. She didn't speak to me for days. And even then I couldn't make out what she saw in education, or why she wouldn't let me grow up naturally like anyone else.

To make things worse, it stuffed Sonny up more than ever. He had the air of one saying: "I don't know what they'd do without me in this blooming house." He stood at the front door, leaning against the jamb with his hands in his trouser pockets, trying to make himself look like Father, and shouted to the other kids so that he could be heard all over the road.

"Larry isn't left go out. He went on the lang with Peter Doherty and me mother isn't talking to him."

And at night, when we were in bed, he kept it up.

"Santa Claus won't bring you anything this year, aha!"

"Of course he will," I said.

"How do you know?"

"Why wouldn't he?"

"Because you went on the lang with Doherty. I wouldn't play with them Doherty fellows."

"You wouldn't be left."

"I wouldn't play with them. They're no class. They had the bobbies up to the house."

"And how would Santa know I was on the lang with Peter Doherty?" I growled, losing patience with the little prig.

"Of course he'd know. Mummy would tell him."

"And how could Mummy tell him and he up at the North Pole? Poor Ireland, she's rearing them yet! 'Tis easy seen you're only an old baby."

"I'm not a baby, and I can spell better than you, and Santa won't bring you anything."

"We'll see whether he will or not," I said sarcastically, doing the old man on him.

But, to tell the God's truth, the old man was only bluff. You could never tell what powers these superhuman chaps would have of knowing what you were up to. And I had a bad conscience about the langing because I'd never before seen the mother like that.

That was the night I decided that the only sensible thing to do was to see Santa myself and explain to him. Being a man, he'd probably understand. In those days I was a good-looking kid and had a way with me when I liked. I had only to smile nicely at one old gent on the North

Mall to get a penny from him, and I felt if only I could get Santa by himself I could do the same with him and maybe get something worth while from him. I wanted a model railway: I was sick of Ludo and Snakes-and-Ladders.

I started to practise lying awake, counting five hundred and then a thousand, and trying to hear first eleven, then midnight, from Shandon. I felt sure Santa would be round by midnight, seeing that he'd be coming from the north, and would have the whole of the South Side to do afterwards. In some ways I was very farsighted. The only trouble was the things I was farsighted about.

I was so wrapped up in my own calculations that I had little attention to spare for Mother's difficulties. Sonny and I used to go to town with her, and while she was shopping we stood outside a toyshop in the North Main Street, arguing about what we'd like for Christmas.

On Christmas Eve when Father came home from work and gave her the housekeeping money, she stood looking at it doubtfully while her face grew white.

"Well?" he snapped, getting angry. "What's wrong with that?"

"What's wrong with it?" she muttered. "On Christmas Eve!"

"Well," he asked truculently, sticking his hands in his trouser pockets as though to guard what was left, "do you think I get more because it's Christmas?"

"Lord God," she muttered distractedly. "And not a bit of cake in the house, nor a candle, nor anything!"

"All right," he shouted, beginning to stamp. "How much will the candle be?"

"Ah, for pity's sake," she cried, "will you give me the money and not argue like that before the children? Do you think I'll leave them with nothing on the one day of the year?"

"Bad luck to you and your children!" he snarled. "Am I to be slaving from one year's end to another for you to be throwing it away on toys? Here," he added, tossing two half-crowns on the table, "that's all you're going to get, so make the most of it."

"I suppose the publicans will get the rest," she said bitterly.

Later she went into town, but did not bring us with her, and returned with a lot of parcels, including the Christmas candle. We waited for Father to come home to his tea, but he didn't, so we had our own tea and a slice of Christmas cake each, and then Mother put Sonny on a chair with the holy-water stoup to sprinkle the candle, and when he lit it she said: "The light of heaven to our souls." I could see she was upset because Father wasn't in—it should be the oldest and youngest. When we hung up our stockings at bedtime he was still out.

Then began the hardest couple of hours I ever put in. I was mad with sleep but afraid of losing the model railway, so I lay for a while, making up things to say to Santa when he came. They varied in tone from frivolous to grave, for some old gents like kids to be modest and well-spoken, while others prefer them with spirit. When I had rehearsed them all I tried to wake Sonny to keep me company, but that kid slept like the dead.

Eleven struck from Shandon, and soon after I heard the latch, but it was only Father coming home.

"Hello, little girl," he said, letting on to be surprised at finding Mother waiting up for him, and then broke into a self-conscious giggle. "What have you up so late?"

"Do you want your supper?" she asked shortly.

"Ah, no, no," he replied. "I had a bit of pig's cheek at Daneen's on my way up (Daneen was my uncle). I'm very fond of a bit of pig's cheek. . . . My goodness, is it that late?" he exclaimed, letting on to be astonished. "If I knew that I'd have gone to the North Chapel for mid-night Mass. I'd like to hear the *Adeste* again. That's a hymn I'm very fond of—a most touching hymn."

Then he began to hum it falsetto.

> *Adeste fideles*
> *Solus domus dagus.*

Father was very fond of Latin hymns, particularly when he had a drop in, but as he had no notion of the words he made them up as he went along, and this always drove Mother mad.

"Ah, you disgust me!" she said in a scalded voice, and closed the room door behind her. Father laughed as if he thought it a great joke; and he struck a match to light his pipe and for a while puffed at it noisily. The light under the door dimmed and went out but he continued to sing emotionally.

> *Dixie medearo*
> *Tutum tonum tantum*
> *Venite adoremus.*

He had it all wrong but the effect was the same on me. To save my life I couldn't keep awake.

Coming on to dawn, I woke with the feeling that something dreadful had happened. The whole house was quiet, and the little bedroom that looked out on the foot and a half of back yard was pitch-dark. It was only when I glanced at the window that I saw how all the silver had drained out of the sky. I jumped out of bed to feel my stocking, well knowing that the worst had happened. Santa had come while I was asleep, and gone away with an entirely false impression of me, because all he had left me was some sort of book, folded up, a pen and pencil, and a tuppenny bag of sweets. Not even Snakes-and-Ladders! For a while I was too stunned even to think. A fellow who was able to drive over rooftops and climb down chimneys without getting stuck—God, wouldn't you think he'd know better?

Then I began to wonder what that foxy boy, Sonny, had. I went to his side of the bed and felt his stocking. For all his spelling and sucking-up he hadn't done so much better, because, apart from a bag of sweets like mine, all Santa had left him was a popgun, one that fired a cork on a piece of string and which you could get in any huxter's shop for sixpence.

All the same, the fact remained that it was a gun, and a gun was better than a book any day of the week. The Dohertys had a gang, and the gang fought the Strawberry Lane kids who tried to play football on our road. That gun would be very useful to me in many ways, while it would be lost on Sonny who wouldn't be let play with the gang, even if he wanted to.

Then I got the inspiration, as it seemed to me, direct from heaven. Suppose I took the gun and gave Sonny the book! Sonny would never be any good in the gang: he was fond of spelling and a studious child like him could learn a lot of spellings from a book like mine. As he hadn't seen Santa any more than I had, what he hadn't seen wouldn't grieve him. I was doing no harm to anyone; in fact, if Sonny only knew, I was doing him a good turn which he might have cause to thank me for later. That was one thing I was always keen on; doing good turns. Perhaps this was Santa's intention the whole time and he had merely become confused between us. It was a mistake that might happen to anyone. So I put the book, the pencil, and the pen into Sonny's stocking and the popgun into my own, and returned to bed and slept again. As I say, in those days I had plenty of initiative.

It was Sonny who woke me, shaking me to tell me that Santa had come and left me a gun. I let on to be surprised and rather disappointed in the gun, and to divert his mind from it made him show me his picture book, and cracked it up to the skies.

As I knew, that kid was prepared to believe anything, and nothing would do him then but to take the presents in to show Father and Mother. This was a bad moment for me. After the way she had behaved about the langing, I distrusted Mother, though I had the consolation of believing that the only person who could contradict me was now somewhere up by the North Pole. That gave me a certain confidence, so Sonny and I burst in with our presents, shouting: "Look what Santa Claus brought!"

Father and Mother woke, and Mother smiled, but only for an instant.

As she looked at me her face changed. I knew that look; I knew it only too well. It was the same she had worn the day I came home from langing, when she said I had no word.

"Larry," she said in a low voice, "where did you get that gun?"

"Santa left it in my stocking, Mummy," I said, trying to put on an injured air, though it baffled me how she guessed that he hadn't. "He did, honest."

"You stole it from that poor child's stocking while he was asleep," she said, her voice quivering with indignation. "Larry, Larry, how could you be so mean?"

"Now, now, now," Father said deprecatingly, " 'tis Christmas morning."

"Ah," she said with real passion, "it's easy it comes to you. Do you think I want my son to grow up a liar and a thief?"

"Ah, what thief, woman?" he said testily. "Have sense, can't you?" He was as cross if you interrupted him in his benevolent moods as if they were of the other sort, and this one was probably exacerbated by a feeling of guilt for his behaviour of the night before. "Here, Larry," he said, reaching out for the money on the bedside table, "here's sixpence for you and one for Sonny. Mind you don't lose it now!"

But I looked at Mother and saw what was in her eyes. I burst out crying, threw the popgun on the floor, and ran bawling out of the house before anyone on the road was awake. I rushed up the lane behind the house and threw myself on the wet grass.

I understood it all, and it was almost more than I could bear; that there was no Santa Claus, as the Dohertys said, only Mother trying to scrape together a few coppers from the housekeeping; that Father was mean and common and a drunkard, and that she had been relying on me to raise her out of the misery of the life she was leading. And I knew that the look in her eyes was the fear that, like ьy father, I should turn out to be mean and common and a drunkard.

Henry James (1843–1916), novelist, short-story writer, and literary critic, was born in New York and died in England, a British citizen. One of America's greatest writers, he set a new high standard for craftsmanship—of its kind—in contemporary letters. For further reading: The Real Thing and Other Tales *(1893);* The Better Sort *(1903);* The Short Stories of Henry James, *edited by Clifton Fadiman (1945).*

"europe"

henry james

I

'Our feeling is, you know, that Becky *should* go.' That earnest little remark comes back to me, even after long years, as the first note of something that began, for my observation, the day I went with my sister-in-law to take leave of her good friends. It is a memory of the American time, which revives so at present—under some touch that doesn't signify—that it rounds itself off as an anecdote. That walk to say good-bye was the beginning; and the end, so far as I was concerned with it, was not till long after; yet even the end also appears to me now as of the old days. I went, in those days, on occasion, to see my sister-in-law, in whose affairs, on my brother's death, I had had to take a helpful hand. I continued to go, indeed, after these little matters were straightened out, for the pleasure, periodically, of the impression— the change to the almost pastoral sweetness of the good Boston suburb from the loud, longitudinal New York. It was another world, with other manners, a different tone, a different taste; a savour nowhere so mild, yet so distinct, as in the square white house—with the pair of elms, like gigantic wheat-sheaves in front, the rustic orchard not far behind, the old-fashioned doorlights, the big blue and white jars in the porch, the straight, bricked walk from the high gate—that enshrined the extraordinary merit of Mrs. Rimmle and her three daughters.

These ladies were so much of the place and the place so much of themselves that, from the first of their being revealed to me, I felt that nothing else at Brookbridge much mattered. They were what, for me, at any rate, Brookbridge had most to give: I mean in the way of what it was naturally strongest in, the thing that we called in New York the New England expression, the air of Puritanism reclaimed and refined. The Rimmles had brought it down to a wonderful delicacy. They struck me even then—all four almost equally—as very ancient and very earnest, and I think theirs must have been the house, in all the world, in which 'culture' first came to the aid of morning calls. The head of the family was the widow of a great public character—as public characters were understood at Brookbridge—whose speeches on anniversaries formed a part of the body of national eloquence spouted in the New England schools by little boys covetous of the most marked, though perhaps the easiest, distinction. He was reported to have been celebrated, and in such fine declamatory connections that he seemed to gesticulate even from the tomb. He was understood to have made, in his wife's company, the tour of Europe at a date not immensely removed from that of the battle of Waterloo. What was the age, then, of the bland, firm, antique Mrs. Rimmle at the period of her being first revealed to me? That is a point I am not in a position to determine—I remember mainly that I was young enough to regard her as having reached the limit. And yet the limit for Mrs. Rimmle must have been prodigiously extended; the scale of its extension is, in fact, the very moral of this reminiscence. She was old, and her daughters were old, but I was destined to know them all as older. It was only by comparison and habit that—however much I recede—Rebecca, Maria, and Jane were the 'young ladies.'

I think it was felt that, though their mother's life, after thirty years of widowhood, had had a grand backward stretch, her blandness and firmness—and this in spite of her extreme physical frailty—would be proof against any surrender not overwhelmingly justified by time. It had appeared, years before, at a crisis of which the waves had not even yet quite subsided, a surrender not justified by anything, that she should go, with her daughters, to Europe for her health. Her health was supposed to require constant support; but when it had at that period tried conclusions with the idea of Europe, it was not the idea of Europe that had been insidious enough to prevail. She had not gone, and Becky, Maria, and Jane had not gone, and this was long ago. They still merely floated in the air of the visit achieved, with such introductions and such acclamations, in the early part of the century; they still, with fond glances at the sunny parlour-walls, only referred, in conversation, to divers pictorial and other reminders of it. The Miss Rimmles had quite been brought up on it, but Becky, as the most literary, had most mastered the subject. There were framed letters—tributes to their eminent father—suspended among the mementos, and of two or three of these, the most foreign and complimentary, Becky had executed translations that figured beside the text. She knew already, through this and other illumination, so much about Europe that it was hard to believe, for her, in that limit of adventure which consisted only of her having been twice to Philadelphia. The others had not been to Philadelphia, but there was a legend that Jane had been to Saratoga. Becky was a short, stout, fair person with round, serious eyes, a high forehead, the sweetest, neatest enunciation, and a miniature of her father—'done in Rome'—worn as a breastpin. She had written the life, she had edited the speeches, of the original of this ornament, and now at last, beyond the seas, she was really to tread in his footsteps.

Fine old Mrs. Rimmle, in the sunny parlour and with a certain austerity of cap and chair—though with a gay new 'front' that looked like rusty brown plush—had had so unusually good a winter that the question of her sparing two members of her family for an absence had been threshed as fine, I could feel, as even under that Puritan roof any case of conscience had ever been threshed. They were to make their dash while the coast, as it were, was clear, and each of the daughters had tried—heroically, angelically, and for the sake of each of her sisters—not to be one of the two. What I encountered that first time was an opportunity to concur with enthusiasm in the general idea that Becky's wonderful preparation would be wasted if she were the one to stay with their mother. They talked of Becky's preparation—they had a sly, old-maidish humour that was as mild as milk—as if it were some mixture, for application somewhere, that she kept in a precious bottle. It had been settled, at all events, that, armed with this concoction and borne aloft by their introductions, she and Jane were to start. They were wonderful on their introductions, which proceeded naturally from their mother and were addressed to the charming families that, in vague generations, had so admired vague Mr. Rimmle. Jane, I found at Brookbridge, had to be described, for want of other description, as the pretty one, but it would not have served to identify her unless you had seen the others. *Her* preparation was only this figment of her prettiness—only, that is, unless one took into account something that, on the spot, I silently divined: the lifelong, secret, passionate ache of her little rebellious desire. They were all growing old in the yearning to go, but Jane's yearning was the sharpest. She struggled with it as people at Brookbridge mostly struggled with what they liked, but fate, by threatening to prevent what she *dis*liked, and what was therefore duty—which was to stay at home instead of Maria—had bewildered her, I judged, not a little. It was she who, in the words I have quoted, mentioned to me Becky's case and Becky's affinity as the clearest of all. Her mother, moreover, on the general subject, had still more to say.

'I positively desire, I really quite insist that they shall go,' the old lady explained to us from her stiff chair. 'We've talked about it so often, and they've had from me so clear an account—I've amused them again and again with it—of what is to be seen and enjoyed. If they've had hitherto too many duties to leave, the time seems to have come to recognize that there are also many duties to *seek*. Wherever we go we find them—I always remind the girls of that. There's a duty that calls them to those wonderful countries, just as it called, at the right time, their father and myself—if it be only that of laying up for the years to come the same store of remarkable impressions, the same wealth of knowledge and food for conversation as, since my return, I have found myself so happy to possess.' Mrs. Rimmle spoke of her return as of something of the year before last, but the future of her daughters was, somehow, by a different law, to be on the scale of great vistas, of endless aftertastes. I think that, without my being quite ready to say it, even this first impression of her was somewhat upsetting; there was a large, placid perversity, a grim secrecy of intention, in her estimate of the ages.

'Well, I'm so glad you don't delay it longer,' I said to Miss Becky before we withdrew. 'And whoever should go,' I continued in the spirit of the sympathy with which the good sisters had already inspired me, 'I quite feel, with your family, you know, that *you* should. But of course I hold that every one should.' I suppose I wished to attenuate my solemnity; there was something in it, however, that I couldn't help. It must have been a faint foreknowledge.

'Have you been a great deal yourself?' Miss Jane, I remember, inquired.

'Not so much but that I hope to go a good deal more. So perhaps we shall meet,' I encouragingly suggested.

I recall something—something in the nature of susceptibility to encouragement—that this brought into the more expressive brown eyes to which Miss Jane mainly owed it that she was the pretty one. 'Where, do you think?'

I tried to think. 'Well, on the Italian lakes—Como, Bellagio, Lugano.' I liked to say the names to them.

' "Sublime, but neither bleak nor bare—nor misty are the mountains there!" ' Miss Jane softly breathed, while her sister looked at her as if her familiarity with the poetry of the subject made her the most interesting feature of the scene she evoked.

But Miss Becky presently turned to me. 'Do you know everything——?'

'Everything?'

'In Europe.'

'Oh, yes,' I laughed, 'and one or two things even in America.'

The sisters seemed to me furtively to look at each other. 'Well, you'll have to be quick—to meet *us*,' Miss Jane resumed.

'But surely when you're once there you'll stay on.'

'Stay on?'—they murmured it simultaneously and with the oddest vibration of dread as well as of desire. It was as if they had been in the presence of a danger and yet wished me, who 'knew everything,' to torment them with still more of it.

Well, I did my best. 'I mean it will never do to cut it short.'

'No, that's just what I keep saying,' said brilliant Jane. 'It would be better, in that case, not to go.'

'Oh, don't talk about not going—at this time!' It was none of my business, but I felt shocked and impatient.

'No, not at *this* time!' broke in Miss Maria, who, very red in the face, had joined us. Poor Miss Maria was known as the flushed one; but she was not flushed—she only had an unfortunate surface. The third day after this was to see them embark.

Miss Becky, however, desired as little as any one to be in any way extravagant. 'It's only the thought of our mother,' she explained.

I looked a moment at the old lady, with whom my sister-in-law was engaged. 'Well—your mother's magnificent.'

'*Isn't* she magnificent?'—they eagerly took it up.

She *was*—I could reiterate it with sincerity, though I perhaps mentally drew the line when Miss Maria again risked, as a fresh ejaculation: 'I think she's better than Europe!'

'Maria!' they both, at this, exclaimed with a strange emphasis; it was as if they feared she had suddenly turned cynical over the deep domestic drama of their casting of lots. The innocent laugh with which she answered them gave the measure of her cynicism.

We separated at last, and my eyes met Mrs. Rimmle's as I held for an instant her aged hand. It was doubtless only my fancy that her calm, cold look quietly accused me of something. Of what *could* it accuse me? Only, I thought, of thinking.

II

I left Brookbridge the next day, and for some time after that had no occasion to hear from my kinswoman; but when she finally wrote there was a passage in her letter that affected me more than all the rest. 'Do you know the poor Rimmles never, after all, "went"? The old lady, at the eleventh hour, broke down; everything broke down, and all of *them* on top of it, so that the dear things are with us still. Mrs. Rimmle, the night after our call, had, in the most unexpected manner, a turn for the worse—something in the nature (though they're rather mysterious about it) of a seizure; Becky and Jane felt it—dear, devoted, stupid angels that they are—heartless to leave her at such a moment, and Europe's indefinitely postponed. However, they think they're still going—or *think* they think it—when she's better. They also think—or think they think—that she *will* be better. I certainly pray she may.' So did I—quite fervently. I was conscious of a real pang—I didn't know how much they had made me care.

Late that winter my sister-in-law spent a week in New York; when almost my first inquiry on meeting her was about the health of Mrs. Rimmle.

'Oh, she's rather bad—she really is, you know. It's not surprising that at her age she should be infirm.'

'Then what the deuce *is* her age?'

'I can't tell you to a year—but she's immensely old.'

'That of course I saw,' I replied—'unless you literally mean so old that the records have been lost.'

My sister-in-law thought. 'Well, I believe she wasn't positively young when she married. She lost three or four children before these women were born.'

We surveyed together a little, on this, the 'dark backward.' 'And they were born, I gather, *after* the famous tour? Well, then, as the famous tour was in a manner to celebrate—wasn't it?—the restoration of the Bourbons—' I considered, I gasped. 'My dear child, what on earth do you make her out?'

My relative, with her Brookbridge habit, transferred her share of the question to the moral plane—turned it forth to wander, by implication at least, in the sandy desert of responsibility. 'Well, you know, we all immensely admire her.'

'You can't admire her more than I do. She's awful.'

My interlocutress looked at me with a certain fear. 'She's *really* ill.'

'Too ill to get better?'

'Oh, no—we hope not. Because then they'll be able to go.'

'And *will* they go, if she should?'

'Oh, the moment they should be quite satisfied. I mean *really*,' she added.

I'm afraid I laughed at her—the Brookbridge 'really' was a thing so by itself. 'But if she shouldn't get better?' I went on.

'Oh, don't speak of it! They want so to go.'

'It's a pity they're so infernally good,' I mused.

'No—don't say that. It's what keeps them up.'

'Yes, but isn't it what keeps *her* up too?

My visitor looked grave. 'Would you like them to kill her?'

I don't know that I was then prepared to say I should—though I believe I came very near it. But later on I burst all bounds, for the subject grew and grew. I went again before the good sisters ever did—I mean I went to Europe. I think I went twice, with a brief interval, before my fate again brought round for me a couple of days at Brookbridge. I had been there repeatedly, in the previous time, without making the acquaintance of the Rimmles; but now that I had had the revelation I couldn't have it too much, and the first request I preferred was to be taken again to see them. I remember well indeed the scruple I felt—the real delicacy—about betraying that *I* had, in the pride of my power, since our other meeting, stood, as their phrase went, among romantic scenes; but they were themselves the first to speak of it, and what, moreover, came home to me was that the coming and going of their friends in general—Brookbridge itself having even at that period one foot in Europe—was such as to place constantly before them the pleasure that was only postponed. They were thrown back, after all, on what the situation, under a final analysis, had most to give—the sense that, as every one kindly said to them and they kindly said to every one, Europe would keep. Every one felt for them so deeply that their own kindness in alleviating every one's feeling was really what came out most. Mrs. Rimmle was still in her stiff chair and in the sunny parlour, but if *she* made no scruple of introducing the Italian lakes my heart sank to observe that she dealt with them, as a topic, not in the least in the leave-taking manner in which Falstaff babbled of green fields.

I am not sure that, after this, my pretexts for a day or two with my sister-in-law were not apt to be a mere cover for another glimpse of these particulars: I at any rate never went to Brookbridge without an irrepressible eagerness for our customary call. A long time seems to me thus to have passed, with glimpses and lapses, considerable impatience and still more pity. Our visits indeed grew shorter, for, as my companion said, they were more and more of a strain. It finally struck me that the good sisters even shrank from me a little, as from one who penetrated their consciousness in spite of himself. It was as if they knew where I thought they ought to be, and were moved to deprecate at last, by a systematic silence on the subject of that hemisphere, the criminality I fain would fix on them. They were full instead—as with the instinct of throwing dust in my eyes—of little pathetic hypocrisies about Brookbridge interests and delights. I dare say that as time went on my deeper sense of their situation came practically to rest on my companion's report of it. I think I recollect, at all events, every word we ever exchanged about them, even if I have lost the thread of the special occasions. The impression they made on me after each interval always broke out with extravagance as I walked away with her.

'She may be as old as she likes—I don't care. It's the fearful age the "girls" are reaching that constitutes the scandal. One shouldn't pry into such matters, I know; but the years and the chances are really going. They're all growing old together—it will presently be too late; and their mother meanwhile perches over them like a vulture—what shall I call it? —calculating. Is she waiting for them successively to drop off? She'll survive them each and all. There's something too remorseless in it.'

'Yes; but what do you want her to do? If the poor thing *can't* die, she can't. Do you want her to take poison or to open a blood-vessel? I dare say she would prefer to go.'

'I beg your pardon,' I must have replied; 'you daren't say anything of the sort. If she would prefer to go she *would* go. She would feel the propriety, the decency, the necessity of going. She just prefers *not* to go. She prefers to stay and keep up the tension, and her calling them "girls" and talking of the good time they'll still have is the mere conscious mischief of a subtle old witch. They won't have *any* time—there isn't any time to have! I mean there's, on her own part, no real loss of measure or of perspective in it. She *knows* she's a hundred and ten, and takes a cruel pride in it.'

My sister-in-law differed with me about this; she held that the old woman's attitude was an honest one and that her magnificent vitality, so great in spite of her infirmities, made it inevitable she should attribute youth to persons who had come into the world so much later. 'Then suppose she should die?'—so my fellow-student of the case always put it to me.

'Do you mean while her daughters are away? There's not the least fear of that—not even if at the very moment of their departure she should be *in extremis*. They would find her all right on their return.'

'But think how they would feel not to have been with her!'

'That's only, I repeat, on the unsound assumption. If they would only go to-morrow—literally make a good rush for it—they'll be with her when they come back. That will give them plenty of time.' I'm afraid I even heartlessly added that if she *should*, against every probability, pass away in their absence, they wouldn't have to come back at all—which would be just the compensation proper to their long privation. And then Maria would come out to join the two others, and they would be—though but for the too scanty remnant of their career—as merry as the day is long.

I remained ready, somehow, pending the fulfilment of that vision, to sacrifice Maria; it was only over the urgency of the case for the others respectively that I found myself balancing. Sometimes it was for Becky I thought the tragedy deepest—sometimes, and in quite a different manner, I thought it most dire for Jane. It was Jane, after all, who had most sense of life. I seemed in fact dimly to descry in Jane a sense—as yet undescried by herself or by any one—of all sorts of queer things. Why didn't *she* go? I used desperately to ask; why didn't she make a bold personal dash for it, strike up a partnership with some one or other of the travelling spinsters in whom Brookbridge more and more abounded? Well, there came a flash for me at a particular point of the grey middle desert: my correspondent was able to let me know that poor Jane at last *had* sailed. She had gone of a sudden—I like my sister-in-law's view of suddenness—with the kind Hathaways, who had made an irresistible grab at her and lifted her off her feet. They were going for the summer and for Mr. Hathaway's health, so that the opportunity was perfect, and it was impossible not to be glad that something very like physical force had finally prevailed. This was the general feeling at Brookbridge, and I might imagine what Brookbridge had been brought to from the fact that, at the very moment she was hustled off, the doctor called to her mother at the peep of dawn, had considered that *he* at least must stay. There had been real alarm—greater than ever before; it actually did seem as if this time the end had come. But it was Becky, strange to say, who, though fully recognising the nature of the crisis, had kept the situation in hand and insisted upon action. This, I remember, brought back to me a discomfort with which I had been familiar from the first. One of the two had sailed, and I was sorry it was not the other. But if it had been the other I should have been equally sorry.

I saw with my eyes, that very autumn, what a fool Jane would have have been if she had again backed out. Her mother had of course survived the peril of which I had heard, profiting by it indeed as she had profited by every other; she was sufficiently better again to have come down stairs. It was there that, as usual, I found her, but with a difference of effect produced somehow by the absence of one of the girls. It was as if, for the others, though they had not gone to Europe, Europe had come to them: Jane's letters had been so frequent and so beyond even what could have been hoped. It was the first time, however, that I perceived on the old woman's part a certain failure of lucidity. Jane's flight was, clearly, the great fact with her, but she spoke of it as if the fruit had now been plucked and the parenthesis closed. I don't know what sinking sense of still further physical duration I gathered, as a menace, from this first hint of her confusion of mind.

'My daughter has been; my daughter has been——' She kept saying it, but didn't say where; that seemed unnecessary, and she only repeated the words to her visitors with a face that was all puckers and yet now, save in so far as it expressed an ineffaceable complacency, all blankness. I think she wanted us a little to know that she had not stood in the way. It added to something—I scarce knew what—that I found myself desiring to extract privately from Becky. As our visit was to be of the shortest my opportunity—for one of the young ladies always came to the door with us—was at hand. Mrs. Rimmle, as we took leave, again sounded her phrase, but she added this time: 'I'm so glad she's going to have always——'

I knew so well what she meant that, as she again dropped, looking at me queerly and becoming momentarily dim, I could help her out. 'Going to have what *you* have?'

'Yes, yes—my privilege. Wonderful experience,' she mumbled. She bowed to me a little as if I would understand. 'She has things to tell.'

I turned, slightly at a loss, to Becky. 'She has then already arrived?'

Becky was at that moment looking a little strangely at her mother, who answered my question. 'She reached New York this morning—she comes on to-day.'

'Oh, then——!' But I let the matter pass as I met Becky's eye—I saw there was a hitch somewhere. It was not she but Maria who came out with us; on which I cleared up the question of their sister's reappearance.

'Oh, no, not to-night,' Maria smiled; 'that's only the way mother puts it. We shall see her about the end of November—the Hathaways are so indulgent. They kindly extend their tour.'

'For *her* sake? How sweet of them!' my sister-in-law exclaimed.

I can see our friend's plain, mild old face take on a deeper mildness, even though a higher colour, in the light of the open door. 'Yes, it's for Jane they prolong it. And do you know what they write?' She gave us time, but it was too great a responsibility to guess. 'Why, that it has brought her out.'

'Oh, I knew it *would!*' my companion sympathetically sighed.

Maria put it more strongly still. 'They say we wouldn't know her.'

This sounded a little awful, but it was, after all, what I had expected.

III

My correspondent in Brookbridge came to me that Christmas, with my niece, to spend a week; and the arrangement had of course been prefaced by an exchange of letters, the first of which from my sister-in-law scarce took space for acceptance of my invitation before going on to say: 'The Hathaways are back—but without Miss Jane!' She presented in a few words the situation thus created at Brookbridge, but was not yet, I gathered, fully in possession of the other one—the situation created in 'Europe' by the presence there of that lady. The two together, at any rate, demanded, I quickly felt, all my attention, and perhaps my impatience to receive my relative was a little sharpened by my desire for the whole story. I had it at last, by the Christmas fire, and I may say without reserve that it gave me all I could have hoped for. I listened eagerly, after which I produced the comment: 'Then she simply refused——'

'To budge from Florence? Simply. She had it out there with the poor Hathaways, who felt responsible for her safety, pledged to restore her to her mother's, to her sisters' hands, and showed herself in a light, they mention under their breath, that made their dear old hair stand on end. Do you know what, when they first got back, they said of her—at least it was *his* phrase—to two or three people?'

I thought a moment. 'That she had "tasted blood"?'

My visitor fairly admired me. 'How clever of you to guess! It's exactly what he did say. She appeared—she continues to appear, it seems—in a new character.'

I wondered a little. 'But that's exactly—don't you remember?—what Miss Maria reported to us from them; that we "wouldn't know her." '

My sister-in-law perfectly remembered. 'Oh, yes—she broke out from the first. But when they left her she was worse.'

'Worse?'

'Well, different—different from anything she ever *had* been, or—for that matter—had had a chance to be.' My interlocutress hung fire a moment, but presently faced me. 'Rather strange and free and obstreperous.'

'Obstreperous?' I wondered again.

'Peculiarly so, I inferred, on the question of not coming away. She wouldn't hear of it, and, when they spoke of her mother, said she had given her mother up. She had thought she should like Europe, but didn't know she should like it so much. They had been fools to bring her if they expected to take her away. She was going to see what she could— she hadn't yet seen half. The end of it was, at any rate, that they had to leave her alone.'

I seemed to see it all—to see even the scared Hathaways. 'So she *is* alone?'

'She told them, poor thing, it appears, and in a tone they'll never forget, that she was, at all events, quite old enough to be. She cried— she quite went on—over not having come sooner. That's why the only way for her,' my companion mused, '*is*, I suppose, to stay. They wanted to put her with some people or other—to find some American family. But she says she's on her own feet.'

'And she's still in Florence?'

'No—I believe she was to travel. She's bent on the East.'

I burst out laughing. 'Magnificent Jane! It's most interesting. Only I feel that I distinctly *should* "know" her. To my sense, always, I must tell you, she had it in her.'

My relative was silent a little. 'So it now appears Becky always felt.'

'And yet pushed her off? Magnificent Becky!'

My companion met my eyes a moment. 'You don't know the queerest part. I mean the way it has *most* brought her out.'

I turned it over; I felt I should like to know—to that degree indeed that, oddly enough, I jocosely disguised my eagerness. 'You don't mean she has taken to drink?'

My visitor hesitated. 'She has taken to flirting.'

I expressed disappointment. 'Oh, she took to *that* long ago. Yes,' I declared at my kinswoman's stare, 'she positively flirted—with *me!*'

The stare perhaps sharpened. 'Then you flirted with *her?*'

'How else could I have been as sure as I wanted to be? But has she means?'

'Means to flirt?'—my friend looked an instant as if she spoke literally. 'I don't understand about the means—though of course they have something. But I have my impression,' she went on. 'I think that Becky——' It seemed almost too grave to say.

But *I* had no doubts. 'That Becky's backing her?'

She brought it out. 'Financing her.'

'Stupendous Becky! So that morally then——'

'Becky's quite in sympathy. But isn't it too odd?' my sister-in-law asked.

'Not in the least. Didn't we know, as regards Jane, that Europe was to bring her out? Well, it has also brought out Rebecca.'

'It has indeed!' my companion indulgently sighed. 'So what would it do if she were there?'

'I should like immensely to see. And we *shall* see.'

'Why, do you believe she'll still go?'

'Certainly. She *must.*'

But my friend shook it off. 'She won't.'

'She shall!' I retorted with a laugh. But the next moment I said: 'And what does the old woman say?'

'To Jane's behaviour? Not a word—never speaks of it. She talks now much less than she used—only seems to wait. But it's my belief she thinks.'

'And—do you mean—knows?'

'Yes, knows that she's abandoned. In her silence there she takes it in.'

'It's her way of making Jane pay?' At this, somehow, I felt more serious. 'Oh, dear, dear—she'll disinherit her!'

When, in the following June, I went on to return my sister-in-law's visit the first object that met my eyes in her little white parlour was a figure that, to my stupefaction, presented itself for the moment as that of Mrs. Rimmle. I had gone to my room after arriving, and, on dressing, had come down: the apparition I speak of had arisen in the interval. Its ambiguous character lasted, however, but a second or two—I had taken Becky for her mother because I knew no one but her mother of that extreme age. Becky's age was quite startling; it had made a great stride, though, strangely enough, irrecoverably seated as she now was in it, she had a wizened brightness that I had scarcely yet seen in her. I remember indulging on this occasion in two silent observations: one to the effect that I had not hitherto been conscious of her full resemblance to the old lady, and the other to the effect that, as I had said to my sister-in-law at Christmas, 'Europe,' even as reaching her only through Jane's sensibilities, had really at last brought her out. She was in fact 'out' in a manner of which this encounter offered to my eyes a unique example: it was the single hour, often as I had been at Brookbridge, of my meeting her elsewhere than in her mother's drawing-room. I surmise that, besides being adjusted to her more marked time of life, the garments she wore abroad, and in particular her little plain bonnet, presented points of resemblance to the close sable sheath and the quaint old headgear that, in the white house behind the elms, I had from far back asssociated with the eternal image in the stiff chair. Of course I immediately spoke of Jane, showing an interest and asking for news; on which she answered me with a smile, but not at all as I had expected.

'*Those* are not really the things you want to know—where she is, whom she's with, how she manages and where she's going next—oh, no!' And the admirable woman gave a laugh that was somehow both light and sad—sad, in particular, with a strange, long weariness. 'What you do want to know is when she's coming back.'

I shook my head very kindly, but out of a wealth of experience that, I flattered myself, was equal to Miss Becky's. 'I do know it. Never.'

Miss Becky, at this, exchanged with me a long, deep look. 'Never.'

We had, in silence, a little luminous talk about it, in the course of which she seemed to tell me the most interesting things. 'And how's your mother?' I then inquired.

She hesitated, but finally spoke with the same serenity. 'My mother's all right. You see, she's not alive.'

'Oh, Becky!' my sister-in-law pleadingly interjected.

But Becky only addressed herself to me. 'Come and see if she is. *I* think she isn't—but Maria perhaps isn't so clear. Come, at all events, and judge and tell me.'

It was a new note, and I was a little bewildered. 'Ah, but I'm not a doctor!'

'No, thank God—you're not. That's why I ask you.' And now she said good-bye.

I kept her hand a moment. '*You're* more alive than ever!'

'I'm very tired.' She took it with the same smile, but for Becky it was much to say.

IV

'Not alive,' the next day, was certainly what Mrs. Rimmle looked when, coming in according to my promise, I found her, with Miss Maria, in her usual place. Though shrunken and diminished she still occupied her high-backed chair with a visible theory of erectness, and her intensely aged face—combined with something dauntless that belonged to her very presence and that was effective even in this extremity—might have been that of some centenarian sovereign, of indistinguishable sex, brought forth to be shown to the people as a disproof of the rumor of extinction. Mummified and open-eyed she looked at me, but I had no impression that she made me out. I had come this time without my sister-in-law, who had frankly pleaded to me—which also, for a daughter of Brookbridge, was saying much—that the house had grown too painful. Poor Miss Maria excused Miss Becky on the score of her not being well—and that, it struck me, was saying most of all. The absence of the others gave the occasion a different note; but I talked with Miss Maria for five minutes and perceived that—save for her saying, of her own movement, anything about Jane—she now spoke as if her mother had lost hearing or sense, or both, alluding freely and distinctly, though indeed favourably, to her condition. 'She has expected your visit and she much enjoys it,' my interlocutress said, while the old woman, soundless and motionless, simply fixed me without expression. Of course there was little to keep me; but I became aware, as I rose to go, that there was more than I had supposed. On my approaching her to take leave Mrs. Rimmle gave signs of consciousness.

'Have you heard about Jane?'

I hesitated, feeling a responsibility, and appealed for direction to Maria's face. But Maria's face was troubled, was turned altogether to her mother's. 'About her life in Europe?' I then rather helplessly asked.

The old woman fronted me, on this, in a manner that made me feel silly. 'Her life?'—and her voice, with this second effort, came out stronger. 'Her death, if you please.'

'Her death?' I echoed, before I could stop myself, with the accent of deprecation.

Miss Maria uttered a vague sound of pain, and I felt her turn away, but the marvel of her mother's little unquenched spark still held me. 'Jane's dead. We've heard,' said Mrs. Rimmle. 'We've heard from—where is it we've heard from?' She had quite revived—she appealed to her daughter.

The poor old girl, crimson, rallied to her duty. 'From Europe.'

Mrs. Rimmle made at us both a little grim inclination of the head. 'From Europe.' I responded, in silence, with a deflection from every rigour, and, still holding me, she went on: 'And now Rebecca's going.'

She had gathered by this time such emphasis to say it that again, before I could help myself, I vibrated in reply. 'To Europe—now?' It was as if for an instant she had made me believe it.

She only stared at me, however, from her wizened mask; then her eyes followed my companion. 'Has she gone?'

'Not yet, mother.' Maria tried to treat it as a joke, but her smile was embarrassed and dim.

'Then where is she?'

'She's lying down.'

The old woman kept up her hard, queer gaze, but directing it, after a minute, to me. 'She's going.'

'Oh, some day!' I foolishly laughed; and on this I got to the door, where I separated from my younger hostess, who came no further. Only, as I held the door open, she said to me under cover of it and very quietly:

'It's poor mother's idea.'

I saw—it was her idea. Mine was—for some time after this, even after I had returned to New York and to my usual occupations—that I should never again see Becky. I had seen her for the last time, I believed, under my sister-in-law's roof, and in the autumn it was given to me to hear from that fellow-admirer that she had succumbed at last to the situation. The day of the call I have just described had been a date in the process of her slow shrinkage—it was literally the first time she had, as they said at Brookbridge, given up. She had been ill for years, but the other state of health in the contemplation of which she had spent so much of her life had left her, till too late, no margin for meeting it. The encounter, at last, came simply in the form of the discovery that it *was* too late; on which, naturally, she had given up more and more. I had heard indeed, all summer, by letter, how Brookbridge had watched her do so; whereby the end found me in a manner prepared. Yet in spite of my preparation there remained with me a soreness, and when I was next— it was some six months later—on the scene of her martyrdom I replied, I fear, with an almost rabid negative to the question put to me in due course by my kinswoman. 'Call on them? Never again!'

I went, none the less, the very next day. Everything was the same in the sunny parlour—everything that most mattered, I mean: the immemorial mummy in the high chair and the tributes, in the little frames on the walls, to the celebrity of its late husband. Only Maria Rimmle was different: if Becky, on my last seeing her, had looked as old as her mother, Maria—save that she moved about—looked older. I remember that she moved about, but I scarce remember what she said; and indeed what was there to say? When I risked a question, however, she had a reply.

'But *now* at least——?' I tried to put it to her suggestively.

At first she was vague. ' "Now?" '

'Won't Miss Jane come back?'

Oh, the headshake she gave me! 'Never.' It positively pictured to me, for the instant, a well-preserved woman, a sort of rich, ripe *seconde jeunesse* by the Arno.

'Then that's only to make more sure of your finally joining her.'

Maria Rimmle repeated her headshake. 'Never.'

We stood so, a moment, bleakly face to face; I could think of no attenuation that would be particularly happy. But while I tried I heard a hoarse gasp that, fortunately, relieved me—a signal strange and at first formless from the occupant of the high-backed chair. 'Mother wants to speak to you,' Maria then said.

So it appeared from the drop of the old woman's jaw, the expression of her mouth opened as if for the emission of sound. It was difficult to me, somehow, to seem to sympathise without hypocrisy, but, so far as a step nearer could do so, I invited communication. 'Have you heard where Becky's gone?' the wonderful witch's white lips then extraordinarily asked.

It drew from Maria, as on my previous visit, an uncontrollable groan, and this, in turn, made me take time to consider. As I considered, however, I had an inspiration. 'To Europe?'

I must have adorned it with a strange grimace, but my inspiration had been right. 'To Europe,' said Mrs. Rimmle.

while the auto waits

o. henry

O. Henry (William Sydney Porter) (1862–1910) was born in Greensboro, N.C. He began to write—tradition has it—while he was the night druggist at the Ohio State Prison, having been convicted of embezzling from the bank where he was employed. During his lifetime he wrote more than six hundred short stories and at one point was producing them at the rate of one a week for the New York World. For further reading: The Complete Works of O. Henry (1953).

Promptly at the beginning of twilight, came again to that quiet corner of that quiet, small park the girl in gray. She sat upon a bench and read a book, for there was yet to come a half hour in which print could be accomplished.

To repeat: Her dress was gray, and plain enough to mask its impeccancy of style and fit. A large-meshed veil imprisoned her turban hat and a face that shone through it with a calm and unconscious beauty. She had come there at the same hour on the day previous, and on the day before that; and there was one who knew it.

The young man who knew it hovered near, relying upon burnt sacrifices to the great joss, Luck. His piety was rewarded, for, in turning a page, her book slipped from her fingers and bounded from the bench a full yard away.

The young man pounced upon it with instant avidity, returning it to its owner with that air that seems to flourish in parks and public places— a compound of gallantry and hope, tempered with respect for the policeman on the beat. In a pleasant voice, he risked an inconsequent remark upon the weather—that introductory topic responsible for so much of the world's unhappiness—and stood poised for a moment, awaiting his fate.

The girl looked him over leisurely; at his ordinary, neat dress and his features distinguished by nothing particular in the way of expression.

"You may sit down, if you like," she said, in a full, deliberate contralto. "Really, I would like to have you do so. The light is too bad for reading. I would prefer to talk."

The vassal of Luck slid upon the seat by her side with complaisance. "Do you know," he said, speaking the formula with which park chairmen open their meetings, "that you are quite the stunningest girl I have seen in a long time? I had my eye on you yesterday. Didn't know somebody was bowled over by those pretty lamps of yours, did you, honeysuckle?"

"Whoever you are," said the girl, in icy tones, "you must remember that I am a lady. I will excuse the remark you have just made because the mistake was, doubtless, not an unnatural one—in your circle. I asked you to sit down; if the invitation must constitute me your honeysuckle, consider it withdrawn."

"I earnestly beg your pardon," pleaded the young man. His expression of satisfaction had changed to one of penitence and humility. "It was my fault, you know—I mean, there are girls in parks, you know—that is, of course, you don't know, but——"

"Abandon the subject, if you please. Of course I know. Now, tell me about these people passing and crowding, each way, along these paths. Where are they going? Why do they hurry so? Are they happy?"

The young man had promptly abandoned his air of coquetry. His cue was now for a waiting part; he could not guess the rôle he would be expected to play.

"It *is* interesting to watch them," he replied, postulating her mood. "It is the wonderful drama of life. Some are going to supper and some to —er—other places. One wonders what their histories are."

"I do not," said the girl; "I am not so inquisitive. I come here to sit because here, only, can I be near the great, common, throbbing heart of humanity. My part in life is cast where its beats are never felt. Can you surmise why I spoke to you, Mr.——?"

"Parkenstacker," supplied the young man. Then he looked eager and hopeful.

"No," said the girl, holding up a slender finger, and smiling slightly. "You would recognize it immediately. It is impossible to keep one's name out of print. Or even one's portrait. This veil and this hat of my maid furnish me with an *incog*. You should have seen the chauffeur stare at it when he thought I did not see. Candidly, there are five or six names that belong in the holy of holies, and mine, by the accident of birth, is one of them. I spoke to you, Mr. Stackenpot——"

"Parkenstacker," corrected the young man, modestly.

"—Mr. Parkenstacker, because I wanted to talk, for once, with a natural man—one unspoiled by the despicable gloss of wealth and supposed social superiority. Oh! you do not know how weary I am of it— money, money, money! And of the men who surround me, dancing like little marionettes all cut by the same pattern. I am sick of pleasure, of jewels, of travel, of society, of luxuries of all kinds."

"I always had an idea," ventured the young man, hesitatingly, "that money must be a pretty good thing."

"A competence is to be desired. But when you have so many millions that——!" She concluded the sentence with a gesture of despair. "It is the monotony of it," she continued, "that palls. Drives, dinners, theatres, balls, suppers, with the gilding of superfluous wealth over it all. Sometimes the very tinkle of the ice in my champagne glass nearly drives me mad."

Mr. Parkenstacker looked ingenuously interested.

"I have always liked," he said, "to read and hear about the ways of wealthy and fashionable folks. I suppose I am a bit of a snob. But I like to have my information accurate. Now, I had formed the opinion that champagne is cooled in the bottle and not by placing ice in the glass."

The girl gave a musical laugh of genuine amusement.

"You should know," she explained, in an indulgent tone, "that we of the non-useful class depend for our amusement upon departure from precedent. Just now it is a fad to put ice in champagne. The idea was originated by a visiting Prince of Tartary while dining at the Waldorf. It will soon give way to some other whim. Just as at a dinner party this week on Madison Avenue a green kid glove was laid by the plate of each guest to be put on and used while eating olives."

"I see," admitted the young man, humbly. "These special diversions of the inner circle do not become familiar to the common public."

"Sometimes," continued the girl, acknowledging his confession of error by a slight bow, "I have thought that if I ever should love a man it would be one of lowly station. One who is a worker and not a drone. But, doubtless, the claims of caste and wealth will prove stronger than my inclination. Just now I am besieged by two. One is a Grand Duke of a German principality. I think he has, or has had, a wife, somewhere, driven mad by his intemperance and cruelty. The other is an English Marquis, so cold and mercenary that I even prefer the diabolism of the Duke. What is it that impels me to tell you these things, Mr. Packenstacker?"

"Parkenstacker," breathed the young man. "Indeed, you cannot know how much I appreciate your confidences."

The girl contemplated him with the calm, impersonal regard that befitted the difference in their stations.

"What is your line of business, Mr. Parkenstacker?" she asked.

"A very humble one. But I hope to rise in the world. Were you really in earnest when you said that you could love a man of lowly position?"

"Indeed I was. But I said 'might.' There is the Grand Duke and the

Marquis, you know. Yes; no calling could be too humble were man what I would wish him to be."

"I work," declared Mr. Parkenstacker, "in a restaurant."

The girl shrank slightly.

"Not as a waiter?" she said, a little imploringly. "Labor is noble, but—personal attendance, you know—valets and——"

"I am not a waiter. I am cashier in"—on the street they faced that bounded the opposite side of the park was the brilliant electric sign "RESTAURANT"—"I am cashier in that restaurant you see there."

The girl consulted a tiny watch set in a bracelet of rich design upon her left wrist, and rose, hurriedly. She thrust her book into a glittering reticule suspended from her waist, for which, however, the book was too large.

"Why are you not at work?" she asked.

"I am on the night turn," said the young man; "it is yet an hour before my period begins. May I not hope to see you again?"

"I do not know. Perhaps—but the whim may not seize me again. I must go quickly now. There is a dinner, and a box at the play—and, oh! the same old round. Perhaps you noticed an automobile at the upper corner of the park as you came. One with a white body."

"And red running gear?" asked the young man, knitting his brows reflectively.

"Yes. I always come in that. Pierre waits for me there. He supposes me to be shopping in the department store across the square. Conceive of the bondage of the life wherein we must deceive even our chauffeurs. Good-night."

"But it is dark now," said Mr. Parkenstacker, "and the park is full of rude men. May I not walk——?"

"If you have the slightest regard for my wishes," said the girl firmly, "you will remain at this bench for ten minutes after I have left. I do not mean to accuse you, but you are probably aware that autos generally bear the monogram of their owner. Again, good-night."

Swift and stately she moved away through the dusk. The young man watched her graceful form as she reached the pavement at the park's edge, and turned up along it toward the corner where stood the automobile. Then he treacherously and unhesitatingly began to dodge and skim among the park trees and shrubbery in a course parallel to her route, keeping her well in sight.

When she reached the corner she turned her head to glance at the motor car, and then passed it, continuing on across the street. Sheltered behind a convenient standing cab, the young man followed her movements closely with his eyes. Passing down the sidewalk of the street opposite the park, she entered the restaurant with the blazing sign. The place was one of those frankly glaring establishments, all white paint and glass, where one may dine cheaply and conspicuously. The girl penetrated the restaurant to some retreat at its rear, whence she quickly emerged without her hat and veil.

The cashier's desk was well to the front. A red-haired girl on the stool climbed down, glancing pointedly at the clock as she did so. The girl in gray mounted in her place.

The young man thrust his hands into his pockets and walked slowly back along the sidewalk. At the corner his foot struck a small, paper-covered volume lying there, sending it sliding to the edge of the turf. By its picturesque cover he recognized it as the book the girl had been reading. He picked it up carelessly, and saw that its title was "New Arabian Nights," the author being of the name of Stevenson. He dropped it again upon the grass, and lounged, irresolute, for a minute. Then he stepped into the automobile, reclined upon the cushions, and said two words to the chauffeur:

"Club, Henri."

the
egg
sherwood anderson

Sherwood Anderson (1876–1941) left the paint manufacturing business to become an author and an editor. Although his own work is irregular, his influence has been very great on a whole generation of younger American writers. For further reading: Winesburg, Ohio (1919); Death in the Woods (1933).

My father was, I am sure, intended by nature to be a cheerful, kindly man. Until he was thirty-four years old he worked as a farm-hand for a man named Thomas Butterworth whose place lay near the town of Bidwell, Ohio. He had then a horse of his own and on Saturday evenings drove into town to spend a few hours in social intercourse with other farm-hands. In town he drank several glasses of beer and stood about in Ben Head's saloon—crowded on Saturday evenings with visiting farm-hands. Songs were sung and glasses thumped on the bar. At ten o'clock father drove home along a lonely country road, made his horse comfortable for the night and himself went to bed, quite happy in his position in life. He had at that time no notion of trying to rise in the world.

It was in the spring of his thirty-fifth year that father married my mother, then a country school-teacher, and in the following spring I came wriggling and crying into the world. Something happened to the two people. They became ambitious. The American passion for getting up in the world took possession of them.

It may have been that mother was responsible. Being a school-teacher she had no doubt read books and magazines. She had, I presume, read of how Garfield, Lincoln, and other Americans rose from poverty to fame and greatness and as I lay beside her—in the days of her lying-in—she may have dreamed that I would some day rule men and cities. At any rate she induced father to give up his place as a farm-hand, sell his horse and embark on an independent enterprise of his own. She was a tall silent woman with a long nose and troubled grey eyes. For herself she wanted nothing. For father and myself she was incurably ambitious.

The first venture into which the two people went turned out badly. They rented ten acres of poor stony land on Griggs's Road, eight miles from Bidwell, and launched into chicken raising. I grew into boyhood on the place and got my first impressions of life there. From the beginning they were impressions of disaster and if, in my turn, I am a gloomy man inclined to see the darker side of life, I attribute it to the fact that what should have been for me the happy joyous days of childhood were spent on a chicken farm.

One unversed in such matters can have no notion of the many and tragic things that can happen to a chicken. It is born out of an egg, lives for a few weeks as a tiny fluffy thing such as you will see pictured on Easter cards, then becomes hideously naked, eats quantities of corn and meal bought by the sweat of your father's brow, gets diseases called pip, cholera, and other names, stands looking with stupid eyes at the sun, becomes sick and dies. A few hens and now and then a rooster, intended to serve God's mysterious ends, struggle through to maturity. The hens lay eggs out of which come other chickens and the dreadful cycle is thus made complete. It is all unbelievably complex. Most philosophers must have been raised on chicken farms. One hopes for so much from a chicken and is so dreadfully disillusioned. Small chickens, just setting out on the journey of life, look so bright and alert and they are in fact so dreadfully stupid. They are so much like people they mix one up in one's judgments of life. If disease does not kill them they wait until your expectations are thoroughly aroused and then walk under the wheels of a wagon—to go squashed and dead back to their maker. Vermin infest their youth, and fortunes must be spent for curative powders. In later life I have seen how a literature has been built up on the subject of fortunes to be made out of the raising of chickens. It is intended to be read by the gods who have just eaten of the tree of the knowledge of good and evil. It is a hopeful literature and declares that much may be done by simple ambitious people who own a few hens. Do not be led astray by it. It was not written for you. Go hunt for gold on the frozen hills of Alaska, put your faith in the honesty of a politician, believe if you will that the world is daily growing better and that good will triumph over evil, but do not read and believe the literature that is written concerning the hen. It was not written for you.

I, however, digress. My tale does not primarily concern itself with the hen. If correctly told it will centre on the egg. For ten years my father and mother struggled to make our chicken farm pay and then they gave up that struggle and began another. They moved into the town of Bidwell, Ohio and embarked in the restaurant business. After ten years of worry with incubators that did not hatch, and with tiny—and in their own way lovely—balls of fluff that passed on into semi-naked pullethood and from that into dead henhood, we threw all aside and packing our belongings on a wagon drove down Griggs's Road toward Bidwell, a tiny caravan of hope looking for a new place from which to start on our upward journey through life.

We must have been a sad looking lot, not, I fancy, unlike refugees fleeing from a battlefield. Mother and I walked in the road. The wagon that contained our goods had been borrowed for the day from Mr. Albert Griggs, a neighbor. Out of its sides stuck the legs of cheap chairs and at the back of the pile of beds, tables, and boxes filled with kitchen utensils was a crate of live chickens, and on top of that the baby carriage in which I had been wheeled about in my infancy. Why we stuck to the baby carriage I don't know. It was unlikely other children would be born and the wheels were broken. People who have few possessions cling tightly to those they have. That is one of the facts that make life so discouraging.

Father rode on top of the wagon. He was then a bald-headed man of forty-five, a little fat and from long association with mother and the chickens he had become habitually silent and discouraged. All during our ten years on the chicken farm he had worked as a laborer on neighboring farms and most of the money he had earned had been spent for remedies to cure chicken diseases, on Wilmer's White Wonder Cholera Cure or Professor Bidlow's Egg Producer or some other preparations that mother found advertised in the poultry papers. There were two little patches of hair on father's head just above his ears. I remember that as a child I used to sit looking at him when he had gone to sleep in a chair before the stove on Sunday afternoons in the winter. I had at that time already begun to read books and have notions of my own and the bald path that led over the top of his head was, I fancied, something like a broad road, such a road as Caesar might have made on which to lead his legions out of Rome and into the wonders of an unknown world. The tufts of hair that grew above father's ears were, I thought, like forests. I fell into a half-sleeping, half-waking state and dreamed I was a tiny thing going along the road into a far beautiful place where there were no chicken farms and where life was a happy eggless affair.

One might write a book concerning our flight from the chicken farm into town. Mother and I walked the entire eight miles—she to be sure that nothing fell from the wagon and I to see the wonders of the world. On the seat of the wagon beside father was his greatest treasure. I will tell you of that.

On a chicken farm where hundreds and even thousands of chickens come out of eggs surprising things sometimes happen. Grotesques are born out of eggs as out of people. The accident does not often occur—perhaps once in a thousand births. A chicken is, you see, born that has four legs, two pairs of wings, two heads or what not. The things do not live. They go quickly back to the hand of their maker that has for a moment trembled. The fact that the poor little things could not live was one of the tragedies of life to father. He had some sort of notion that if he could but bring into henhood or roosterhood a five-legged hen or a two-headed rooster his fortune would be made. He dreamed of taking the wonder about to county fairs and of growing rich by exhibiting it to other farm-hands.

At any rate he saved all the little monstrous things that had been born on our chicken farm. They were preserved in alcohol and put each in its own glass bottle. These he had carefully put into a box and on our journey into town it was carried on the wagon seat beside him. He drove the horses with one hand and with the other clung to the box. When we got to our destination the box was taken down at once and the bottles removed. All during our days as keepers of a restaurant in the town of Bidwell, Ohio, the grotesques in their little glass bottles sat on a shelf back of the counter. Mother sometimes protested but father was a rock on the subject of his treasure. The grotesques were, he declared, valuable. People, he said, liked to look at strange and wonderful things.

Did I say that we embarked in the restaurant business in the town of Bidwell, Ohio? I exaggerated a little. The town itself lay at the foot of a low hill and on the shore of a small river. The railroad did not run through the town and the station was a mile away to the north at a place called Pickleville. There had been a cider mill and pickle factory at the station, but before the time of our coming they had both gone out of business. In the morning and in the evening busses came down to the station along a road called Turner's Pike from the hotel on the main street of Bidwell. Our going to the out of the way place to embark in the restaurant business was mother's idea. She talked of it for a year and then one day went off and rented an empty store building opposite the railroad station. It was her idea that the restaurant would be profitable. Travelling men, she said, would be always waiting around to take trains out of town and town people would come to the station to await incoming trains. They would come to the restaurant to buy pieces of pie and drink coffee. Now that I am older I know that she had another motive in going. She was ambitious for me. She wanted me to rise in the world, to get into a town school and become a man of the towns.

At Pickleville father and mother worked hard as they always had done. At first there was the necessity of putting our place into shape to be a restaurant. That took a month. Father built a shelf on which he put tins of vegetables. He painted a sign on which he put his name in large red letters. Below his name was the sharp command—"EAT HERE"— that was so seldom obeyed. A show case was bought and filled with cigars and tobacco. Mother scrubbed the floor and the walls of the room. I went to school in the town and was glad to be away from the farm and from the presence of the discouraged, sad-looking chickens. Still I was not very joyous. In the evening I walked home from school along Turner's Pike and remembered the children I had seen playing in the town school yard. A troop of little girls had gone hopping about and singing. I tried that. Down along the frozen road I went hopping solemnly on one leg. "Hippity Hop To The Barber Shop," I sang shrilly. Then I stopped and looked doubtfully about. I was afraid of being seen in my gay mood. It must have seemed to me that I was doing a thing that should not be done by one who, like myself, had been raised on a chicken farm where death was a daily visitor.

Mother decided that our restaurant should remain open at night. At ten in the evening a passenger train went north past our door followed by a local freight. The freight crew had switching to do in Pickleville and when the work was done they came to our restaurant for hot coffee and food. Sometimes one of them ordered a fried egg. In the morning at four they returned north-bound and again visited us. A little trade began to grow up. Mother slept at night and during the day tended the restaurant and fed our boarders while father slept. He slept in the same bed mother had occupied during the night and I went off to the town of Bidwell and to school. During the long nights, while mother and I slept, father cooked meats that were to go into sandwiches for the lunch baskets of our boarders. Then an idea in regard to getting up in the world came into his head. The American spirit took hold of him. He also became ambitious.

In the long nights when there was little to do father had time to think. That was his undoing. He decided that he had in the past been an unsuccessful man because he had not been cheerful enough and that in the future he would adopt a cheerful outlook on life. In the early morning he came upstairs and got into bed with mother. She woke and the two talked. From my bed in the corner I listened.

It was father's idea that both he and mother should try to entertain the people who came to eat at our restaurant. I cannot now remember his words, but he gave the impression of one about to become in some obscure way a kind of public entertainer. When people, particularly young people from the town of Bidwell, came into our place, as on very rare occasions they did, bright entertaining conversation was to be made. From father's words I gathered that something of the jolly inn-keeper effect was to be sought. Mother must have been doubtful from the first, but she said nothing discouraging. It was father's notion that a passion for the company of himself and mother would spring up in the breasts of the younger people of the town of Bidwell. In the evening bright happy groups would come singing down Turner's Pike. They would troop shouting with joy and laughter into our place. There would be song and festivity. I do not mean to give the impression that father spoke so elaborately of the matter. He was as I have said an uncommunicative man. "They want some place to go. I tell you they want some place to go," he said over and over. That was as far as he got. My own imagination has filled in the blanks.

For two or three weeks this notion of father's invaded our house. We did not talk much, but in our daily lives tried earnestly to make smiles take the place of glum looks. Mother smiled at the boarders and I, catching the infection, smiled at our cat. Father became a little feverish in his anxiety to please. There was no doubt, lurking somewhere in him, a touch of the spirit of the showman. He did not waste much of his ammunition on the railroad men he served at night but seemed to be waiting for a young man or woman from Bidwell to come in to show what he could do. On the counter in the restaurant there was a wire basket kept always filled with eggs, and it must have been before his eyes when the idea of being entertaining was born in his brain. There was something pre-natal about the way eggs kept themselves connected with the development of his idea. At any rate an egg ruined his new impulse in life. Late one night I was awakened by a roar of anger coming from father's throat. Both mother and I sat upright in our beds. With trembling hands she lighted a lamp that stood on a table by her head. Downstairs the front door of our restaurant went shut with a bang and in a few minutes father tramped up the stairs. He held an egg in his hand and his hand trembled as though he were having a chill. There was a half insane light in his eyes. As he stood glaring at us I was sure he intended throwing the egg at either mother or me. Then he laid it gently on the table beside the lamp and dropped on his knees beside mother's bed. He began to cry like a boy and I, carried away by his grief, cried with him. The two of us filled the little upstairs room with our wailing voices. It is ridiculous, but of the picture we made I can remember only the fact that mother's hand continually stroked the bald path that ran across the top of his head. I have forgotten what mother said to him and how she induced him to tell her of what had happened downstairs. His explanation also has gone out of my mind. I remember only my own grief and fright and the shiny path over father's head glowing in the lamp light as he knelt by the bed.

As to what happened downstairs. For some unexplainable reason I know the story as well as though I had been a witness to my father's discomfiture. One in time gets to know many unexplainable things. On that evening young Joe Kane, son of a merchant of Bidwell, came to Pickleville to meet his father, who was expected on the ten o'clock evening train from the South. The train was three hours late and Joe came into our place to loaf about and to wait for its arrival. The local freight train came in and the freight crew were fed. Joe was left alone in the restaurant with father.

From the moment he came into our place the Bidwell young man must have been puzzled by my father's actions. It was his notion that father was angry at him for hanging around. He noticed that the restaurant keeper was apparently disturbed by his presence and he thought of going out. However, it began to rain and he did not fancy the long walk to town and back. He bought a five-cent cigar and ordered a cup of coffee. He had a newspaper in his pocket and took it out and began to read. "I'm waiting for the evening train. It's late," he said apologetically.

For a long time father, whom Joe Kane had never seen before, remained silently gazing at his visitor. He was no doubt suffering from an attack of stage fright. As so often happens in life he had thought so much and so often of the situation that now confronted him that he was somewhat nervous in its presence.

For one thing, he did not know what to do with his hands. He thrust one of them nervously over the counter and shook hands with Joe Kane. "How-de-do," he said. Joe Kane put his newspaper down and stared at him. Father's eye lighted on the basket of eggs that sat on the counter and he began to talk. "Well," he began hesitatingly, "well, you have heard of Christopher Columbus, eh?" He seemed to be angry. "That

Christopher Columbus was a cheat," he declared emphatically. "He talked of making an egg stand on its end. He talked, he did, and then he went and broke the end of the egg."

My father seemed to his visitor to be beside himself at the duplicity of Christopher Columbus. He muttered and swore. He declared it was wrong to teach children that Christopher Columbus was a great man when, after all, he cheated at the critical moment. He had declared he would make an egg stand on end and then when his bluff had been called he had done a trick. Still grumbling at Columbus, father took an egg from the basket on the counter and began to walk up and down. He rolled the egg between the palms of his hands. He smiled genially. He began to mumble words regarding the effect to be produced on an egg by the electricity that comes out of the human body. He declared that without breaking its shell and by virtue of rolling it back and forth in his hands he could stand the egg on its end. He explained that the warmth of his hands and the gentle rolling movement he gave the egg created a new centre of gravity, and Joe Kane was mildly interested. "I have handled thousands of eggs," father said. "No one knows more about eggs than I do."

He stood the egg on the counter and it fell on its side. He tried the trick again and again, each time rolling the egg between the palms of his hands and saying the words regarding the wonders of electricity and the laws of gravity. When after a half hour's effort he did succeed in making the egg stand for a moment he looked up to find that his visitor was no longer watching. By the time he had succeeded in calling Joe Kane's attention to the success of his effort the egg had again rolled over and lay on its side.

Afire with the showman's passion and at the same time a good deal disconcerted by the failure of his first effort, father now took the bottles containing the poultry monstrosities down from their place on the shelf and began to show them to his visitor. "How would you like to have seven legs and two heads like this fellow?" he asked, exhibiting the most remarkable of his treasures. A cheerful smile played over his face. He reached over the counter and tried to slap Joe Kane on the shoulder as he had seen men do in Ben Head's saloon when he was a young farmhand and drove to town on Saturday evenings. His visitor was made a little ill by the sight of the body of the terribly deformed bird floating in the alcohol in the bottle and got up to go. Coming from behind the counter father took hold of the young man's arm and led him back to his seat. He grew a little angry and for a moment had to turn his face away and force himself to smile. Then he put the bottles back on the shelf. In an outburst of generosity he fairly compelled Joe Kane to have a fresh cup of coffee and another cigar at his expense. Then he took a pan and filling it with vinegar, taken from a jug that sat beneath the counter, he declared himself about to do a new trick. "I will heat this egg in this pan of vinegar," he said. "Then I will put it through the neck of a bottle without breaking the shell. When the egg is inside the bottle it will resume its normal shape and the shell will become hard again. Then I will give the bottle with the egg in it to you. You can take it about with you wherever you go. People will want to know how you got the egg in the bottle. Don't tell them. Keep them guessing. That is the way to have fun with this trick."

Father grinned and winked at his visitor. Joe Kane decided that the man who confronted him was mildly insane but harmless. He drank the cup of coffee that had been given him and began to read his paper again. When the egg had been heated in vinegar father carried it on a spoon to the counter and going into a back room got an empty bottle. He was angry because his visitor did not watch him as he began to do his trick, but nevertheless went cheerfully to work. For a long time he struggled, trying to get the egg to go through the neck of the bottle. He put the pan of vinegar back on the stove, intending to reheat the egg, then picked it up and burned his fingers. After a second bath in the hot vinegar the shell of the egg had been softened a little but not enough for his purpose. He worked and worked and a spirit of desperate determination took possession of him. When he thought that at last the trick was about to be consummated the delayed train came in at the station and Joe Kane started to go nonchalantly out at the door. Father made a last desperate effort to conquer the egg and make it do the things that would establish his reputation as one who knew how to entertain guests who came into his restaurant. He worried the egg. He attempted to be somewhat rough with it. He swore and the sweat stood out on his forehead. The egg broke under his hand. When the contents spurted over his clothes, Joe Kane, who had stopped at the door, turned and laughed.

A roar of anger rose from my father's throat. He danced and shouted a string of inarticulate words. Grabbing another egg from the basket on the counter, he threw it, just missing the head of the young man as he dodged through the door and escaped.

Father came upstairs to mother and me with an egg in his hand. I do not know what he intended to do. I imagine he had some idea of destroying it, of destroying all eggs, and that he intended to let mother and me see him begin. When, however, he got into the presence of mother something happened to him. He laid the egg gently on the table and dropped on his knees by the bed as I have already explained. He later decided to close the restaurant for the night and to come upstairs and get into bed. When he did so he blew out the light and after much muttered conversation both he and mother went to sleep. I suppose I went to sleep also, but my sleep was troubled. I awoke at dawn and for a long time looked at the egg that lay on the table. I wondered why eggs had to be and why from the egg came the hen who again laid the egg. The question got into my blood. It has stayed there, I imagine, because I am the son of my father. At any rate, the problem remains unsolved in my mind. And that, I conclude, is but another evidence of the complete and final triumph of the egg—at least as far as my family is concerned.

the long way out

f. scott fitzgerald

F. Scott Fitzgerald (1896–1940) attended Princeton, but did not graduate; in World War I he served as a lieutenant in the army. In the 1920s he was a spokesman for the postwar "lost generation." The Great Gatsby *(1925) and* Tender Is the Night *(1934) are his best-known novels. For further reading:* Flappers and Philosophers, Tales of the Jazz Age *(1922);* All the Sad Young Men *(1926).*

We were talking about some of the older castles in Touraine and we touched upon the iron cage in which Louis XI imprisoned Cardinal Balue for six years, then upon oubliettes and such horrors. I had seen several of the latter, simply dry wells thirty or forty feet deep where a man was thrown to wait for nothing; since I have such a tendency to claustrophobia that a Pullman berth is a certain nightmare, they had made a lasting impression. So it was rather a relief when a doctor told this story—that is, it was a relief when he began it, for it seemed to have nothing to do with the tortures long ago.

There was a young woman named Mrs. King who was very happy with her husband. They were well-to-do and deeply in love, but at the birth of her second child she went into a long coma and emerged with a clear case of schizophrenia or "split personality." Her delusion, which had something to do with the Declaration of Independence, had little bearing on the case and as she regained her health it began to disappear. At the end of ten months she was a convalescent patient scarcely marked by what had happened to her and very eager to go back into the world.

She was only twenty-one, rather girlish in an appealing way and a favorite with the staff of the sanitarium. When she became well enough so that she could take an experimental trip with her husband there was a general interest in the venture. One nurse had gone into Philadelphia with her to get a dress, another knew the story of her rather romantic courtship in Mexico and everyone had seen her two babies on visits to the hospital. The trip was to Virginia Beach for five days.

It was a joy to watch her make ready, dressing and packing meticulously and living in the gay trivialities of hair waves and such things. She was ready half an hour before the time of departure and she paid some visits on the floor in her powder-blue gown and her hat that looked like one minute after an April shower. Her frail lovely face, with just that touch of startled sadness that often lingers after an illness, was alight with anticipation.

"We'll just do nothing," she said. "That's my ambition. To get up when I want to for three straight mornings and stay up late for three straight nights. To buy a bathing suit by myself and order a meal."

When the time approached Mrs. King decided to wait downstairs instead of in her room and as she passed along the corridors, with an orderly carrying her suitcase, she waved to the other patients, sorry that they too were not going on a gorgeous holiday. The superintendent wished her well, two nurses found excuses to linger and share her infectious joy.

"What a beautiful tan you'll get, Mrs. King."

"Be sure and send a postcard."

About the time she left her room her husband's car was hit by a truck on his way from the city—he was hurt internally and was not expected to live more than a few hours. The information was received at the hospital in a glassed-in office adjoining the hall where Mrs. King waited. The operator, seeing Mrs. King and knowing that the glass was not sound proof, asked the head nurse to come immediately. The head nurse hurried aghast to a doctor and he decided what to do. So long as the husband was still alive it was best to tell her nothing, but of course she must know that he was not coming today.

Mrs. King was greatly disappointed.

"I suppose it's silly to feel that way," she said. "After all these months what's one more day? He said he'd come tomorrow, didn't he?" The nurse was having a difficult time but she managed to pass it off until the patient was back in her room. Then they assigned a very experienced and phlegmatic nurse to keep Mrs. King away from other patients and from newspapers. By the next day the matter would be decided one way or another.

But her husband lingered on and they continued to prevaricate. A little before noon next day one of the nurses was passing along the corridor when she met Mrs. King, dressed as she had been the day before but this time carrying her own suitcase.

"I'm going to meet my husband," she explained. "He couldn't come yesterday but he's coming today at the same time."

The nurse walked along with her. Mrs. King had the freedom of the building and it was difficult to simply steer her back to her room, and the nurse did not want to tell a story that would contradict what the authorities were telling her. When they reached the front hall she signaled to the operator, who fortunately understood. Mrs. King gave herself a last inspection in the mirror and said:

"I'd like to have a dozen hats just like this to remind me to be this happy always."

When the head nurse came in frowning a minute later she demanded: "Don't tell me George is delayed?"

"I'm afraid he is. There is nothing much to do but be patient."

Mrs. King laughed ruefully. "I wanted him to see my costume when it was absolutely new."

"Why, there isn't a wrinkle in it."

"I guess it'll last till tomorrow. I oughtn't to be blue about waiting one more day when I'm so utterly happy."

"Certainly not."

That night her husband died and at a conference of doctors next morning there was some discussion about what to do—it was a risk to tell her and a risk to keep it from her. It was decided finally to say that Mr. King had been called away and thus destroy her hope of an immediate meeting; when she was reconciled to this they could tell her the truth.

As the doctors came out of the conference one of them stopped and pointed. Down the corridor toward the outer hall walked Mrs. King carrying her suitcase.

Dr. Pirie, who had been in special charge of Mrs. King, caught his breath.

"This is awful," he said. "I think perhaps I'd better tell her now. There's no use saying he's away when she usually hears from him twice a week, and if we say he's sick she'll want to go to him. Anybody else like the job?"

II

One of the doctors in the conference went on a fortnight's vacation that afternoon. On the day of his return in the same corridor at the same hour, he stopped at the sight of a little procession coming toward him— an orderly carrying a suitcase, a nurse and Mrs. King dressed in the powder-blue suit and wearing the spring hat.

"Good morning, Doctor," she said. "I'm going to meet my husband and we're going to Virginia Beach. I'm going to the hall because I don't want to keep him waiting."

He looked into her face, clear and happy as a child's. The nurse signaled to him that it was as ordered, so he merely bowed and spoke of the pleasant weather.

"It's a beautiful day," said Mrs. King, "but of course even if it was raining it would be a beautiful day for me."

The doctor looked after her, puzzled and annoyed—why are they letting this go on, he thought. What possible good can it do?

Meeting Dr. Pirie, he put the question to him.

"We tried to tell her," Dr. Pirie said. "She laughed and said we were trying to see whether she's still sick. You could use the word unthinkable in an exact sense here—his death is unthinkable to her."

"But you can't just go on like this."

"Theoretically no," said Dr. Pirie. "A few days ago when she packed up as usual the nurse tried to keep her from going. From out in the hall I could see her face, see her begin to go to pieces—for the first time, mind you. Her muscles were tense and her eyes glazed and her voice was thick and shrill when she very politely called the nurse a liar. It was touch and go there for a minute whether we had a tractable patient or a restraint case—and I stepped in and told the nurse to take her down to the reception room."

He broke off as the procession that had just passed appeared again, headed back to the ward. Mrs. King stopped and spoke to Dr. Pirie.

"My husband's been delayed," she said. "Of course I'm disappointed but they tell me he's coming tomorrow and after waiting so long one more day doesn't seem to matter. Don't you agree with me, Doctor?"

"I certainly do, Mrs. King."

She took off her hat.

"I've got to put aside these clothes—I want them to be as fresh tomorrow as they are today." She looked closely at the hat. "There's a spect of dust on it, but I think I can get it off. Perhaps he won't notice."

"I'm sure he won't."

"Really I don't mind waiting another day. It'll be this time tomorrow before I know it, won't it?"

When she had gone along the younger doctor said:

"There are still the two children."

"I don't think the children are going to matter. When she 'went under,' she tied up this trip with the idea of getting well. If we took it away she'd have to go to the bottom and start over."

"Could she?"

"There's no prognosis," said Dr. Pirie. "I was simply explaining why she was allowed to go to the hall this morning."

"But there's tomorrow morning and the next morning."

"There's always the chance," said Dr. Pirie, "that some day he will be there."

The doctor ended his story here, rather abruptly. When we pressed him to tell what happened he protested that the rest was anticlimax— that all sympathy eventually wears out and that finally the staff of the sanitarium had simply accepted the fact.

"But does she still go to meet her husband?"

"Oh yes, it's always the same—but the other patients, except new ones, hardly look up when she passes along the hall. The nurses manage to substitute a new hat every year or so but she still wears the same suit. She's always a little disappointed but she makes the best of it, very sweetly too. It's not an unhappy life as far as we know, and in some funny way it seems to set an example of tranquillity to the other patients. For God's sake let's talk about something else—let's go back to oubliettes."

a clean, well-lighted place

ernest hemingway

Ernest Hemingway (1898–1961), after being wounded in World War I, became a foreign correspondent in Europe. He emerged as a major writer of fiction in the late twenties and was awarded the Nobel Prize for literature in 1954. He died in Ketchum, Idaho, of a gunshot wound, *believed to be self-inflicted. For further reading:* The Fifth Column, and the First Forty-Nine Stories *(1938).*

It was late and every one had left the café except an old man who sat in the shadow the leaves of the tree made against the electric light. In the daytime the street was dusty, but at night the dew settled the dust and the old man liked to sit late because he was deaf and now at night it was quiet and he felt the difference. The two waiters inside the café knew that the old man was a little drunk, and while he was a good client they knew that if he became too drunk he would leave without paying, so they kept watch on him.

"Last week he tried to commit suicide," one waiter said.

"Why?"

"He was in despair."

"What about?"

"Nothing."

"How do you know it was nothing?"

"He has plenty of money."

They sat together at a table that was close against the wall near the door of the café and looked at the terrace where the tables were all empty except where the old man sat in the shadow of the leaves of the tree that moved slightly in the wind. A girl and a soldier went by in the street. The street light shone on the brass number on his collar. The girl wore no head covering and hurried beside him.

"The guard will pick him up," one waiter said.

"What does it matter if he gets what he's after?"

"He had better get off the street now. The guard will get him. They went by five minutes ago."

The old man sitting in the shadow rapped on his saucer with his glass. The younger waiter went over to him.

"What do you want?"

The old man looked at him. "Another brandy," he said.

"You'll be drunk," the waiter said. The old man looked at him. The waiter went away.

"He'll stay all night," he said to his colleague. "I'm sleepy now. I never get into bed before three o'clock. He should have killed himself last week."

The waiter took the brandy bottle and another saucer from the counter inside the café and marched out to the old man's table. He put down the saucer and poured the glass full of brandy.

"You should have killed yourself last week," he said to the deaf man. The old man motioned with his finger. "A little more," he said. The waiter poured on into the glass so that the brandy slopped over and ran down the stem into the top saucer of the pile. "Thank you," the old man said. The waiter took the bottle back inside the café. He sat down at the table with his colleague again.

"He's drunk now," he said.

"He's drunk every night."

"What did he want to kill himself for?"

"How should I know?"

"How did he do it?"

"He hung himself with a rope."

"Who cut him down?"

"His niece."

"Why did they do it?"

"Fear for his soul."

"How much money has he got?"

"He's got plenty."

"He must be eighty years old."

"Anyway I should say he was eighty."

"I wish he would go home. I never get to bed before three o'clock. What kind of hour is that to go to bed?"

"He stays up because he likes it."

"He's lonely. I'm not lonely. I have a wife waiting in bed for me."

"He had a wife once too."

"A wife would be no good to him now."

"You can't tell. He might be better with a wife."

"His niece looks after him."

"I know. You said she cut him down."

"I wouldn't want to be that old. An old man is a nasty thing."

"Not always. This old man is clean. He drinks without spilling. Even now, drunk. Look at him."

"I don't want to look at him. I wish he would go home. He has no regard for those who must work."

The old man looked from his glass across the square, then over at the waiters.

"Another brandy," he said, pointing to his glass. The waiter who was in a hurry came over.

"Finished," he said, speaking with that omission of syntax stupid people employ when talking to drunken people or foreigners. "No more tonight. Close now."

"Another," said the old man.

"No. Finished." The waiter wiped the edge of the table with a towel and shook his head.

The old man stood up, slowly counted the saucers, took a leather coin purse from his pocket and paid for the drinks, leaving half a peseta tip.

The waiter watched him go down the street, a very old man walking unsteadily but with dignity.

"Why didn't you let him stay and drink?" the unhurried waiter asked. They were putting up the shutters. "It is not half-past two."

"I want to go home to bed."

"What is an hour?"

"More to me than to him."

"An hour is the same."

"You talk like an old man yourself. He can buy a bottle and drink at home."

"It's not the same."

"No, it is not," agreed the waiter with a wife. He did not wish to be unjust. He was only in a hurry.

"And you? You have no fear of going home before your usual hour?"

"Are you trying to insult me?"

"No, hombre, only to make a joke."

"No," the waiter who was in a hurry said, rising from pulling down the metal shutters. "I have confidence. I am all confidence."

"You have youth, confidence, and a job," the older waiter said. "You have everything."

"And what do you lack?"

"Everything but work."

"You have everything I have."

"No. I have never had confidence and I am not young."

"Come on. Stop talking nonsense and lock up."

"I am of those who like to stay late at the café," the older waiter said.

"With all those who do not want to go to bed. With all those who need a light for the night."

"I want to go home and into bed."

"We are of two different kinds," the older waiter said. He was now dressed to go home. "It is not only a question of youth and confidence although those things are very beautiful. Each night I am reluctant to close up because there may be some one who needs the café."

"Hombre, there are bodegas open all night long."

"You do not understand. This is a clean and pleasant café. It is well lighted. The light is very good and also, now, there are shadows of the leaves."

"Good night," said the younger waiter.

"Good night," the other said. Turning off the electric light he continued the conversation with himself. It is the light of course but it is necessary that the place be clean and pleasant. You do not want music. Certainly you do not want music. Nor can you stand before a bar with dignity although that is all that is provided for these hours. What did he fear? It was not fear or dread. It was a nothing that he knew too well. It was all a nothing and a man was nothing too. It was only that and light was all it needed and a certain cleanness and order. Some lived in it and never felt it but he knew it all was nada y pues nada y nada y pues nada. Our nada who art in nada, nada be thy name thy kingdom nada thy will be nada in nada as it is in nada. Give us this nada our daily nada and nada us our nada as we nada our nadas and nada us not into nada but deliver us from nada; pues nada. Hail nothing full of nothing, nothing is with thee. He smiled and stood before a bar with a shining steam pressure coffee machine.

"What's yours?" asked the barman.

"Nada."

"Otro loco mas," said the barman and turned away.

"A little cup," said the waiter.

The barman poured it for him.

"The light is very bright and pleasant but the bar is unpolished," the waiter said.

The barman looked at him but did not answer. It was too late at night for conversation.

"You want another copita?" the barman asked.

"No, thank you," said the waiter and went out. He disliked bars and bodegas. A clean, well-lighted café was a very different thing. Now, without thinking further, he would go home to his room. He would lie in the bed and finally, with daylight, he would go to sleep. After all, he said to himself, it is probably only insomnia. Many must have it.

a rose for emily

william faulkner

William Faulkner
(1897–1962) lived most of his life
in Mississippi. He served in the
Canadian Air Force in World War I.
In the late twenties and early thirties
he established himself as one of America's
great literary talents. In 1950 he received
the Nobel Prize for literature. For
further reading: These Thirteen
(1931); Doctor Martino
and Other Stories (1934);
Go Down Moses (1942);
The Collected Stories of
William Faulkner (1950).

I

When Miss Emily Grierson died, our whole town went to her funeral: the men through a sort of respectful affection for a fallen monument, the women mostly out of curiosity to see the inside of her house, which no one save an old man-servant—a combined gardener and cook—had seen in a least ten years.

It was a big, squarish frame house that had once been white, decorated with cupolas and spires and scrolled balconies in the heavily lightsome style of the seventies, set on what had once been our most select street. But garages and cotton gins had encroached and obliterated even the august names of that neighborhood; only Miss Emily's house was left, lifting its stubborn and coquettish decay above the cotton wagons and the gasoline pumps—an eyesore among eyesores. And now Miss Emily had gone to join the representatives of those august names where they lay in the cedar-bemused cemetery among the ranked and anonymous graves of Union and Confederate soldiers who fell at the battle of Jefferson.

Alive, Miss Emily had been a tradition, a duty, and a care; a sort of hereditary obligation upon the town, dating from that day in 1894 when Colonel Sartoris, the mayor—he who fathered the edict that no Negro woman should appear on the streets without an apron—remitted her taxes, the dispensation dating from the death of her father on into perpetuity. Not that Miss Emily would have accepted charity. Colonel Sartoris invented an involved tale to the effect that Miss Emily's father had loaned money to the town, which the town, as a matter of business, preferred this way of repaying. Only a man of Colonel Sartoris' generation and thought could have invented it, and only a woman could have believed it.

When the next generation, with its more modern ideas, became mayors and aldermen, this arrangement created some little dissatisfaction. On the first of the year they mailed her a tax notice. February came, and there was no reply. They wrote her a formal letter, asking her to call at the sheriff's office at her convenience. A week later the mayor wrote her himself, offering to call or to send his car for her, and received in reply a note on paper of an archaic shape, in a thin, flowing calligraphy in faded ink, to the effect that she no longer went out at all. The tax notice was also enclosed, without comment.

They called a special meeting of the Board of Aldermen. A deputation waited upon her, knocked at the door through which no visitor had passed since she ceased giving china-painting lessons eight or ten years earlier. They were admitted by the old Negro into a dim hall from which a stairway mounted into still more shadow. It smelled of dust and disuse —a close, dank smell. The Negro led them into the parlor. It was furnished in heavy, leather-covered furniture. When the Negro opened the blinds of one window, they could see that the leather was cracked; and when they sat down, a faint dust rose sluggishly about their thighs, spinning with slow motes in the single sun-ray. On a tarnished gilt easel before the fireplace stood a crayon portrait of Miss Emily's father.

They rose when she entered—a small, fat woman in black, with a thin gold chain descending to her waist and vanishing into her belt, leaning on an ebony cane with a tarnished gold head. Her skeleton was small and spare; perhaps that was why what would have been merely plumpness in another was obesity in her. She looked bloated, like a body long submerged in motionless water, and of that pallid hue. Her eyes, lost in the fatty ridges of her face, looked like two small pieces of coal pressed into a lump of dough as they moved from one face to another while the visitors stated their errand.

She did not ask them to sit. She just stood in the door and listened quietly until the spokesman came to a stumbling halt. Then they could hear the invisible watch ticking at the end of the gold chain.

Her voice was dry and cold. "I have no taxes in Jefferson. Colonel Sartoris explained it to me. Perhaps one of you can gain access to the city records and satisfy yourselves."

"But we have. We are the city authorities, Miss Emily. Didn't you get a notice from the sheriff, signed by him?"

"I received a paper, yes," Miss Emily said. "Perhaps he considers himself the sheriff . . . I have no taxes in Jefferson."

"But there is nothing on the books to show that, you see. We must go by the—"

"See Colonel Sartoris. I have no taxes in Jefferson."

"But, Miss Emily—"

"See Colonel Sartoris." (Colonel Sartoris had been dead almost ten years.) "I have no taxes in Jefferson. Tobe!" The Negro appeared. "Show these gentlemen out."

II

So she vanquished them, horse and foot, just as she had vanquished their fathers thirty years before about the smell. That was two years after her father's death and a short time after her sweetheart—the one we believed would marry her—had deserted her. After her father's death she went out very little; after her sweetheart went away, people hardly saw her at all. A few of the ladies had the temerity to call, but were not received, and the only sign of life about the place was the Negro man —a young man then—going in and out with a market basket.

"Just as if a man—any man—could keep a kitchen properly," the ladies said; so they were not surprised when the smell developed. It was another link between the gross, teeming world and the high and mighty Griersons.

A neighbor, a woman, complained to the mayor, Judge Stevens, eighty years old.

"But what will you have me do about it, madam?" he said.

"Why, send her word to stop it," the woman said. "Isn't there a law?"

"I'm sure that won't be necessary," Judge Stevens said. "It's probably just a snake or a rat that nigger of hers killed in the yard. I'll speak to him about it."

The next day he received two more complaints, one from a man who came in diffident deprecation. "We really must do something about it, Judge. I'd be the last one in the world to bother Miss Emily, but we've got to do something." That night the Board of Aldermen met—three graybeards and one younger man, a member of the rising generation.

"It's simple enough," he said. "Send her word to have her place cleaned up. Give her a certain time do it in, and if she don't . . ."

"Dammit, sir," Judge Stevens said, "will you accuse a lady to her face of smelling bad?"

So the next night, after midnight, four men crossed Miss Emily's lawn and slunk about the house like burglars, sniffing along the base of the brickwork and at the cellar openings while one of them performed a regular sowing motion with his hand out of a sack slung from his shoulder. They broke open the cellar door and sprinkled lime there, and in all the outbuildings. As they recrossed the lawn, a window that had been dark was lighted and Miss Emily sat in it, the light behind her, and her upright torso motionless as that of an idol. They crept quietly across the lawn and into the shadow of the locusts that lined the street. After a week or two the smell went away.

That was when people had begun to feel really sorry for her. People in our town, remembering how old lady Wyatt, her great-aunt, had gone completely crazy at last, believed that the Griersons held themselves a little too high for what they really were. None of the young men were quite good enough for Miss Emily and such. We had long thought of them as a tableau, Miss Emily a slender figure in white in the background, her father a spraddled silhouette in the foreground, his back to her and clutching a horsewhip, the two of them framed by the back-flung front door. So when she got to be thirty and was still single, we were not pleased exactly, but vindicated; even with insanity in the family she wouldn't have turned down all of her chances if they had really materialized.

When her father died, it got about that the house was all that was left to her; and in a way, people were glad. At last they could pity Miss Emily. Being left alone, and a pauper, she had become humanized. Now she too would know the old thrill and the old despair of a penny more or less.

The day after his death all the ladies prepared to call at the house and offer condolence and aid, as is our custom. Miss Emily met them at the door, dressed as usual and with no trace of grief on her face. She told them that her father was not dead. She did that for three days, with the ministers calling on her, and the doctors, trying to persuade her to let them dispose of the body. Just as they were about to resort to law and force, she broke down, and they buried her father quickly.

We did not say she was crazy then. We believed she had to do that. We remembered all the young men her father had driven away, and we knew that with nothing left, she would have to cling to that which had robbed her, as people will.

III

She was sick for a long time. When we saw her again, her hair was cut short, making her look like a girl, with a vague resemblance to those angels in colored church windows—sort of tragic and serene.

The town had just let the contracts for paving the sidewalks, and in the summer after her father's death they began the work. The construction company came with niggers and mules and machinery, and a foreman named Homer Barron, a Yankee—a big, dark, ready man, with a big voice and eyes lighter than his face. The little boys would follow in groups to hear him cuss the niggers, and the niggers singing in time to the rise and fall of picks. Pretty soon he knew everybody in town. Whenever you heard a lot of laughing anywhere about the square, Homer Barron would be in the center of the group. Presently we began to see him and Miss Emily on Sunday afternoons driving in the yellow-wheeled buggy and the matched team of bays from the livery stable.

At first we were glad that Miss Emily would have an interest, because the ladies all said, "Of course a Grierson would not think seriously of a Northerner, a day laborer." But there were still others, older people, who said that even grief could not cause a real lady to forget *noblesse oblige*— without calling it *noblesse oblige*. They just said, "Poor Emily. Her kinsfolk should come to her." She had some kin in Alabama; but years ago her father had fallen out with them over the estate of old lady Wyatt, the crazy woman, and there was no communication between the two families. They had not even been represented at the funeral.

And as soon as the old people said, "Poor Emily," the whispering began. "Do you suppose it's really so?" they said to one another. "Of course it is. What else could . . ." This behind their hands; rustling of craned silk and satin behind jalousies closed upon the sun of Sunday afternoon as the thin, swift clop-clop-clop of the matched team passed: "Poor Emily."

She carried her head high enough—even when we believed that she was fallen. It was as if she demanded more than ever the recognition of her dignity as the last Grierson; as if it had wanted that touch of earthiness to reaffirm her imperviousness. Like when she bought the rat poison, the arsenic. That was over a year after they had begun to say "Poor Emily," and while the two female cousins were visiting her.

"I want some poison," she said to the druggist. She was over thirty then, still a slight woman, though thinner than usual, with cold, haughty black eyes in a face the flesh of which was strained across the temples and about the eye-sockets as you imagine, a lighthouse-keeper's face ought to look. "I want some poison," she said.

"Yes, Miss Emily. What kind? For rats and such? I'd recom—"

"I want the best you have. I don't care what kind."

The druggist named several. "They'll kill anything up to an elephant. But what you want is—"

"Arsenic," Miss Emily said. "Is that a good one?"

"Is . . . arsenic? Yes, ma'am. But what you want—"

"I want arsenic."

The druggist looked down at her. She looked back at him, erect, her face like a strained flag. "Why, of course," the druggist said. "If that's what you want. But the law requires you to tell what you are going to use it for."

Miss Emily just stared at him, her head tilted back in order to look him eye for eye, until he looked away and went and got the arsenic and wrapped it up. The Negro delivery boy brought her the package; the druggist didn't come back. When she opened the package at home there was written on the box, under the skull and bones: "For rats."

IV

So the next day we all said, "She will kill herself"; and we said it would be the best thing. When she had first begun to be seen with Homer Barron, we had said, "She will marry him." Then we said, "She will persuade him yet," because Homer himself had remarked—he liked men, and it was known that he drank with the younger men in the Elks' Club—that he was not a marrying man. Later we said, "Poor Emily" behind the jalousies as they passed on Sunday afternoon in the glittering buggy, Miss Emily with her head high and Homer Barron with his hat cocked and a cigar in his teeth, reins and whip in a yellow glove.

Then some of the ladies began to say that it was a disgrace to the town and a bad example to the young people. The men did not want to interfere, but at last the ladies forced the Baptist minister—Miss Emily's people were Episcopal—to call upon her. He would never divulge what happened during that interview, but he refused to go back again. The next Sunday they again drove about the streets, and the following day the minister's wife wrote to Miss Emily's relations in Alabama.

So she had blood-kin under her roof again and we sat back to watch developments. At first nothing happened. Then we were sure that they were to be married. We learned that Miss Emily had been to the jeweler's and ordered a man's toilet set in silver, with the letters H. B. on each piece. Two days later we learned that she had bought a complete outfit of men's clothing, including a nightshirt, and we said, "They are married." We were really glad. We were glad because the two female cousins were even more Grierson than Miss Emily had ever been.

So we were not surprised when Homer Barron—the streets had been finished some time since—was gone. We were a little disappointed that there was not a public blowing-off, but we believed that he had gone on to prepare for Miss Emily's coming, or to give her a chance to get rid of the cousins. (By that time it was a cabal, and we were all Miss Emily's allies to help circumvent the cousins.) Sure enough, after another week they departed. And, as we had expected all along, within three days Homer Barron was back in town. A neighbor saw the Negro man admit him at the kitchen door at dusk one evening.

And that was the last we saw of Homer Barron. And of Miss Emily for some time. The Negro man went in and out with the market basket, but the front door remained closed. Now and then we would see her at a window for a moment, as the men did that night when they sprinkled the lime, but for almost six months she did not appear on the streets. Then we knew that this was to be expected too; as if that quality of her father which had thwarted her woman's life so many times had been too virulent and too furious to die.

When we next saw Miss Emily, she had grown fat and her hair was turning gray. During the next few years it grew grayer and grayer until it attained an even pepper-and salt iron-gray, when it ceased turning. Up to the day of her death at seventy-four it was still that vigorous iron-gray, like the hair of an active man.

From that time on her front door remained closed, save for a period of six or seven years, when she was about forty, during which she gave lessons in china-painting. She fitted up a studio in one of the downstairs rooms, where the daughters and granddaughters of Colonel Sartoris' contemporaries were sent to her with the same regularity and in the same spirit that they were sent to church on Sunday with a twenty-five-cent piece for the collection plate. Meanwhile her taxes had been remitted.

Then the newer generation became the backbone and the spirit of the town, and the painting pupils grew up and fell away and did not send their children to her with boxes of color and tedious brushes and pictures cut from the ladies' magazines. The front door closed upon the last one and remained closed for good. When the town got free postal delivery, Miss Emily alone refused to let them fasten the metal numbers above her door and attach a mailbox to it. She would not listen to them.

Daily, monthly, yearly we watched the Negro grow grayer and more stooped, going in and out with the market basket. Each December we sent her a tax notice, which would be returned by the post office a week later, unclaimed. Now and then we would see her in one of the downstairs windows—she had evidently shut up the top floor of the house—like the carven torso of an idol in a niche, looking or not looking at us, we could never tell which. Thus she passed from generation to generation —dear, inescapable, impervious, tranquil, and perverse.

And so she died. Fell ill in the house filled with dust and shadows, with only a doddering Negro man to wait on her. We did not even know she was sick; we had long since given up trying to get any information from the Negro. He talked to no one, probably not even to her, for his voice had grown harsh and rusty, as if from disuse.

She died in one of the downstairs rooms, in a heavy walnut bed with a curtain, her gray head propped on a pillow yellow and moldy with age and lack of sunlight.

V

The Negro met the first of the ladies at the front door and let them in, with their hushed, sibilant voices and their quick, curious glances, and then he disappeared. He walked right through the house and out the back and was not seen again.

The two female cousins came at once. They held the funeral on the second day, with the town coming to look at Miss Emily beneath a mass of bought flowers, with the crayon face of her father musing profoundly above the bier and the ladies sibilant and macabre; and the very old men—some in their brushed Confederate uniforms—on the porch and the lawn, talking of Miss Emily as if she had been a contemporary of theirs, believing that they had danced with her and courted her perhaps, confusing time with its mathematical progression, as the old do, to whom all the past is not a diminishing road but, instead, a huge meadow which no winter ever quite touches, divided from them now by the narrow bottle-neck of the most recent decade of years.

Already we knew that there was one room in that region above stairs which no one had seen in forty years, and which would have to be forced. They waited until Miss Emily was decently in the ground before they opened it.

The violence of breaking down the door seemed to fill this room with pervading dust. A thin, acrid pall as of the tomb seemed to lie everywhere upon this room decked and furnished as for a bridal: upon the valance curtains of faded rose color, upon the rose-shaded lights, upon the dressing table, upon the delicate array of crystal and the man's toilet things backed with tarnished silver, silver so tarnished that the monogram was obscured. Among them lay a collar and tie, as if they had just been removed, which, lifted, left upon the surface a pale crescent in the dust. Upon a chair hung the suit, carefully folded; beneath it the two mute shoes and the discarded socks.

The man himself lay in the bed.

For a long while we just stood there, looking down at the profound and fleshless grin. The body had apparently once lain in the attitude of an embrace, but now the long sleep that outlasts love, that conquers even the grimace of love, had cuckolded him. What was left of him, rotted beneath what was left of the nightshirt, had become inextricable from the bed in which he lay; and upon him and upon the pillow beside him lay that even coating of the patient and biding dust.

Then we noticed that in the second pillow was the indentation of a head. One of us lifted something from it, and leaning forward, that faint and invisible dust dry and acrid in the nostrils, we saw a long strand of iron-gray hair.

*Katherine Anne Porter (1894–   ) has traveled widely
and has lived in many places in the United States.
A brilliant short-story writer, she has also published
a book of essays* The Days Before *(1952)
and a novel of uncertain literary merit* Ship
of Fools *(1962). For further
reading:* Flowering Judas,
and Other Stories *(1930);*
The Leaning Tower,
and Other
Stories *(1944).*

rope

katherine anne porter

On the third day after they moved to the country
he came walking back from the village carrying a basket of groceries
and a twenty-four-yard coil of rope. She came out to meet him, wiping
her hands on her green smock. Her hair was tumbled, her nose was
scarlet with sunburn; he told her that already she looked like a born
country woman. His gray flannel shirt stuck to him, his heavy shoes
were dusty. She assured him he looked like a rural character in a play.

Had he brought the coffee? She had been waiting all day long for
coffee. They had forgot it when they ordered at the store the first day.

Gosh, no, he hadn't. Lord, now he'd have to go back. Yes, he would
if it killed him. He thought, though, he had everything else. She reminded him it was only because he didn't drink coffee himself. If he did
he would remember it quick enough. Suppose they ran out of cigarettes?
Then she saw the rope. What was that for? Well, he thought it might
do to hang clothes on, or something. Naturally she asked him if he
thought they were going to run a laundry? They already had a fifty-foot
line hanging right before his eyes? Why, hadn't he noticed it, really? It
was a blot on the landscape to her.

He thought there were a lot of things a rope might come in handy
for. She wanted to know what, for instance. He thought a few seconds,
but nothing occurred. They could wait and see, couldn't they? You need
all sorts of strange odds and ends around a place in the country. She
said, yes, that was so; but she thought just at that time when every
penny counted, it seemed funny to buy more rope. That was all. She
hadn't meant anything else. She hadn't just seen, not at first, why he
felt it was necessary.

Well, thunder, he had bought it because he wanted to, and that was
all there was to it. She thought that was reason enough, and couldn't
understand why he hadn't said so, at first. Undoubtedly it would be

353

useful, twenty-four yards of rope, there were hundreds of things, she couldn't think of any at the moment, but it would come in. Of course. As he had said, things always did in the country.

But she was a little disappointed about the coffee, and oh, look, look, look at the eggs! Oh, my, they're all running! What had he put on top of them? Hadn't he known eggs mustn't be squeezed? Squeezed, who had squeezed them, he wanted to know. What a silly thing to say. He had simply brought them along in the basket with the other things. If they got broke it was the grocer's fault. He should know better than to put heavy things on top of eggs.

She believed it was the rope. That was the heaviest thing in the pack, she saw him plainly when he came in from the road, the rope was a big package on top of everything. He desired the whole wide world to witness that this was not a fact. He had carried the rope in one hand and the basket in the other, and what was the use of her having eyes if that was the best they could do for her?

Well, anyhow, she could see one thing plain: no eggs for breakfast. They'd have to scramble them now, for supper. It was too damned bad. She had planned to have steak for supper. No ice, meat wouldn't keep. He wanted to know why she couldn't finish breaking the eggs in a bowl and set them in a cool place.

Cool place! If he could find one for her, she'd be glad to set them there. Well, then, it seemed to him they might very well cook the meat at the same time they cooked the eggs and then warm up the meat for tomorrow. The idea simply choked her. Warmed-over meat, when they might as well have had it fresh. Second best and scraps and make-shifts, even to the meat! He rubbed her shoulder a little. It doesn't really matter so much, does it, darling? Sometimes when they were playful, he would rub her shoulder and she would arch and purr. This time she hissed and almost clawed. He was getting ready to say that they could surely manage somehow when she turned on him and said, if he told her they could manage somehow she would certainly slap his face.

He swallowed the words red hot, his face burned. He picked up the rope and started to put it on the top shelf. She would not have it on the top shelf, the jars and tins belonged there; positively she would not have the top shelf cluttered up with a lot of rope. She had borne all the clutter she meant to bear in the flat in town, there was space here at least and she meant to keep things in order.

Well, in that case, he wanted to know what the hammer and nails were doing up there? And why had she put them there when she knew very well he needed that hammer and those nails upstairs to fix the window sashes? She simply slowed down everything and made double work on the place with her insane habit of changing things around and hiding them.

She was sure she begged his pardon, and if she had had any reason to believe he was going to fix the sashes this summer she would have left the hammer and nails right where he put them; in the middle of the bedroom floor where they could step on them in the dark. And now if he didn't clear the whole mess out of there she would throw them down the well.

Oh, all right, all right—could he put them in the closet? Naturally not, there were brooms and mops and dustpans in the closet, and why couldn't he find a place for his rope outside her kitchen? Had he stopped to consider there were seven God-forsaken rooms in the house, and only one kitchen?

He wanted to know what of it? And did she realize she was making a complete fool of herself? And what did she take him for, a three-year-old idiot? The whole trouble with her was she needed something weaker than she was to heckle and tyrannize over. He wished to God now they had a couple of children she could take it out on. Maybe he'd get some rest.

Her face changed at this, she reminded him he had forgot the coffee and had bought a worthless piece of rope. And when she thought of all the things they actually needed to make the place even decently fit to live in, well, she could cry, that was all. She looked so forlorn, so lost and despairing he couldn't believe it was only a piece of rope that was causing all the racket. What *was* the matter, for God's sake?

Oh, would he please hush and go away, and *stay* away, if he could, for five minutes? By all means, yes, he would. He'd stay away indefinitely if she wished. Lord, yes, there was nothing he'd like better than to clear out and never come back. She couldn't for the life of her see what was holding him, then. It was a swell time. Here she was, stuck, miles from a railroad, with a half-empty house on her hands, and not a penny in her pocket, and everything on earth to do; it seemed the God-sent moment for him to get out from under. She was surprised he hadn't stayed in town as it was until she had come out and done the work and got things straightened out. It was his usual trick.

It appeared to him that this was going a little far. Just a touch out of bounds, if she didn't mind his saying so. Why the hell had he stayed in town the summer before? To do a half-dozen extra jobs to get the money he had sent her. That was it. She knew perfectly well they couldn't have done it otherwise. She had agreed with him at the time. And that was the only time so help him he had ever left her to do anything by herself.

Oh, he could tell that to his great-grandmother. She had her notion of what had kept him in town. Considerably more than a notion, if he wanted to know. So, she was going to bring all that up again, was she? Well, she could just think what she pleased. He was tired of explaining. It may have looked funny but he had simply got hooked in, and what could he do? It was impossible to believe that she was going to take it seriously. Yes, yes, she knew how it was with a man: if he was left by himself a minute, some woman was certain to kidnap him. And naturally he couldn't hurt her feelings by refusing!

Well, what was she raving about? Did she forget she had told him those two weeks alone in the country were the happiest she had known for four years? And how long had they been married when she said that? All right, shut up! If she thought that hadn't stuck in his craw.

She hadn't meant she was happy because she was away from him. She meant she was happy getting the devilish house nice and ready for him. That was what she had meant, and now look! Bringing up something she had said a year ago simply to justify himself for forgetting her coffee and breaking the eggs and buying a wretched piece of rope they couldn't afford. She really thought it was time to drop the subject, and now she wanted only two things in the world. She wanted him to get that rope from underfoot, and go back to the village and get her coffee, and if he could remember it, he might bring a metal mitt for the skillets, and two more curtain rods, and if there were any rubber gloves in the village, her hands were simply raw, and a bottle of milk of magnesia from the drugstore.

He looked out at the dark blue afternoon sweltering on the slopes, and mopped his forehead and sighed heavily and said, if only she could wait a minute for *anything*, he was going back. He had said so, hadn't he, the very instant they found he had overlooked it?

Oh, yes, well . . . run along. She was going to wash windows. The country was so beautiful! She doubted they'd have a moment to enjoy it. He meant to go, but he could not until he had said that if she wasn't such a hopeless melancholiac she might see that this was only for a few days. Couldn't she remember anything pleasant about the other summers? Hadn't they ever had any fun? She hadn't time to talk about it, and now would he please not leave that rope lying around for her to trip on? He picked it up, somehow it had toppled off the table, and walked out with it under his arm.

Was he going this minute? He certainly was. She thought so. Sometimes it seemed to her he had second sight about the precisely perfect moment to leave her ditched. She had meant to put the mattresses out to sun, if they put them out this minute they would get at least three hours, he must have heard her say that morning she meant to put them

out. So of course he would walk off and leave her to it. She supposed
he thought the exercise would do her good.

Well, he was merely going to get her coffee. A four-mile walk for
two pounds of coffee was ridiculous, but he was perfectly willing to do it.
The habit was making a wreck of her, but if she wanted to wreck
herself there was nothing he could do about it. If he thought it was
coffee that was making a wreck of her, she congratulated him: he must
have a damned easy conscience.

Conscience or no conscience, he didn't see why the mattresses couldn't
very well wait until tomorrow. And anyhow, for God's sake, were they
living *in* the house, or were they going to let the house ride them to
death? She paled at this, her face grew livid about the mouth, she
looked quite dangerous, and reminded him that housekeeping was no
more her work than it was his: she had other work to do as well, and
when did he think she was going to find time to do it at this rate?

Was she going to start on that again? She knew as well as he did that
his work brought in the regular money, hers was only occasional, if
they depended on what *she* made—and she might as well get straight on
this question once for all!

That was positively not the point. The question was, when both of
them were working on their own time, was there going to be a division
of the housework, or wasn't there? She merely wanted to know, she
had to make her plans. Why, he thought that was all arranged. It was
understood that he was to help. Hadn't he always, in summers?

Hadn't he, though? Oh, just hadn't he? And when, and where, and
doing what? Lord, what an uproarious joke!

It was such a very uproarious joke that her face turned slightly purple,
and she screamed with laughter. She laughed so hard she had to sit
down, and finally a rush of tears spurted from her eyes and poured
down into the lifted corners of her mouth. He dashed towards her and
dragged her up to her feet and tried to pour water on her head. The
dipper hung by a string on a nail and he broke it loose. Then he tried
to pump water with one hand while she struggled in the other. So he
gave it up and shook her instead.

She wrenched away, crying out for him to take his rope and go to
hell, she had simply given him up: and ran. He heard her high-heeled
bedroom slippers clattering and stumbling on the stairs.

He went out around the house and into the lane; he suddenly realized
he had a blister on his heel and his shirt felt as if it were on fire. Things
broke so suddenly you didn't know where you were. She could work
herself into a fury about simply nothing. She was terrible, damn it: not
an ounce of reason. You might as well talk to a sieve as that woman
when she got going. Damned if he'd spend his life humoring her? Well,

what to do now? He would take back the rope and exchange it for something else. Things accumulated, things were mountainous, you couldn't move them or sort them out or get rid of them. They just lay and rotted around. He'd take it back. Hell, why should he? He wanted it. What was it anyhow? A piece of rope. Imagine anybody caring more about a piece of rope than about a man's feelings. What earthly right had she to say a word about it? He remembered all the useless, meaningless things she bought for herself: Why? because I wanted it, that's why! He stopped and selected a large stone by the road. He would put the rope behind it. We would put it in the tool-box when he got back. He'd heard enough about it to last him a life-time.

When he came back she was leaning against the post box beside the road waiting. It was pretty late, the smell of broiled steak floated nose high in the cooling air. Her face was young and smooth and fresh-looking. Her unmanageable funny black hair was all on end. She waved to him from a distance, and he speeded up. She called out that supper was ready and waiting, was he starved?

You bet he was starved. Here was the coffee. He waved it at her. She looked at his other hand. What was that he had there?

Well, it was the rope again. He stopped short. He had meant to exchange it but forgot. She wanted to know why he should exchange it, if it was something he really wanted. Wasn't the air sweet now, and wasn't it fine to be here?

She walked beside him with one hand hooked into his leather belt. She pulled and jostled him a little as he walked, and leaned against him. He put his arm clear around her and patted her stomach. They exchanged wary smiles. Coffee, coffee for the Ootsum-Wootsums! He felt as if he were bringing her a beautiful present.

He was a love, she firmly believed, and if she had had her coffee in the morning, she wouldn't have behaved so funny . . . There was a whippoorwill still coming back, imagine, clear out of season, sitting in the crab-apple tree calling all by himself. Maybe his girl stood him up. Maybe she did. She hoped to hear him once more, she loved whippoor-wills . . . He knew how she was, didn't he?

Sure, he knew how she was.

the benefits
of american
life

james t. farrell

James T. Farrell (1904–   ),
a native of Chicago, established
his reputation as a novelist
with the Studs Lonigan
trilogy (1935).
Noted for his focus on
social inequities among
the lower middle class,
he is generally regarded
as a representative figure of contemporary
"naturalistic" fiction. For further reading:
$1,000 a Week, and Other
Stories (1942); To Whom
It May Concern (1944).

Takiss Tillios was a strong shepherd boy whose home land was located just at the hollow valley of two mountains in Arcadia, Greece, in the central section of the Peloponnesus. He grew up on goat's milk and on pitch black bread whose cinders were not separated so as to produce more bread per pound. His hard-working mother sold a piece of land, which produced enough wheat to pull the family through the whole year, in order to pay his steerage fare to America. For in America the streets were paved with gold; the buildings were taller than mountains; the women all dressed like princesses and the men had their pockets lined with money; every boy had a bicycle; and every man and woman owned an automobile. At the age of thirteen, Takiss, large for his age, arrived in a paradise known as Chicago.

He was met at the railroad station, a scared and bewildered boy, by a relative who took him to a home on South Halsted Street. With voluable beneficence, the relative immediately employed Takiss, offering him a salary of fifteen dollars a month and the privilege of sleeping on marble slabs in his candy kitchen. He told Takiss that all successful Greek men started that way, and he showed the boy Greek newspapers with pictures of stern, mustachioed Greek restaurant owners and candy-store proprietors who recounted the story of their rise to fame and offered themselves as favorable candidates for marriage. And as a final word of advice, the relative told Takiss that his mother was getting old now, and that he should send her some of his wages to help her out.

Takiss quickly discovered what it meant to live in paradise. It meant working from six in the morning until six in the evening, and until even later on week-ends. It meant sweeping out the store, washing dishes and windows, polishing, arranging, mopping, running errands. It meant attending night school to learn English when he could scarcely keep his eyes open and where he was frequently laughed at for his blundering efforts. It meant walking along, living in the midst of dirty streets where coal dust, soot, smoke, and poisonous fumes of automobiles choked his nostrils and made him cough. It meant lonesome memories. For a long period, Takiss was a lonely boy remembering his homeland and his Grecian mountain, remembering the long, slow days with the sheep, remembering the smile and kiss of his old mother, remembering always.

And he was afraid of America, and of that tremendous paradise known as Chicago. He worked doggedly day after day, earning fifteen dollars a month, catching a cough from sleeping on marble slabs. He worked doggedly, and from his wages he saved a pittance which he deposited in an immigrant's savings bank. But he looked ahead to the day when he would be famous, with his picture in the Greek newspapers, a pride and an honor to his native Greece and to the great tradition of the great Socrates about whom his relative so frequently boasted. He dreamed of the time when he would become like Americans, talk like them, wear their clothes, ride in automobiles just as they did, walk along the streets with pretty American girls.

In time, Takiss learned things. He learned American words, but never how to speak them like an American. He learned that he was considered a dirty Greek greenhorn, and that many Americans would have been just as pleased if he and many of his countrymen had never come to their land. And he learned that American girls laughed sardonically at a young Greek greenhorn. Also, he learned of a place owned by a cousin of his, where for a little money he could go and find American girls who did not laugh at a Greek greenhorn, at least for five or ten minutes. He learned how to buy American clothes on installments, to wear a purple silk shirt, purple socks, and an orange tie. And he learned, also, that in the store he could put some of the money received for sales into his pocket instead of into the cash register.

Eventually, the cousin employing him discharged him in anger, branding him a crook, a robber, a traitor. In the heated quarrel, Takiss asked him why, if he wanted honesty, he paid only six dollars a week wages, when he made so much money himself selling bad products and got his picture in the Greek newspapers as a successful pioneer in America.

Takiss was employed by other of his countrymen, in fruit stores, soda parlors, at hot-dog stands, and in restaurants. He acquired additional American knowledge, and more American words. And sometimes when he was dressed up, wearing his purple silk shirt, with socks to match, and the orange tie, he would walk in the parks or along Halsted Street, seeing American girls, wishing that he had one of his own, a blonde girl with a beautiful pink-white complexion.

Time slid from under Takiss, and he was a young man in his early twenties, with his first citizenship papers. He had worked like a dog, and he was still slaving at the same jobs, performing the same tasks and chores as he had always done since he had come to America. He earned eight dollars a week and was busy twelve hours a day in a candy store. He cleaned and mopped; he scrubbed; he polished; he washed; he waited on trade. And often when he was alone in the store he pocketed money from the cash register. Every week he deposited money in the bank, and almost nightly he looked in his bank book, proud of his savings, thinking of how he was going to achieve fame in America. But he was never able to save money, because he was always quitting or losing jobs and having to use savings to support himself between jobs, as well as to send money to his mother.

And he learned another thing . . . he learned how to dance like Americans. A Greek-American friend told him of a dancing school called a taxi-dance hall on West Madison Street, and showed him an advertisement from the Greek-American owner, Professor Christopolos, who stated in the ad that anyone could be as graceful as he if they learned dancing from his beautiful girls at only ten cents a dance. He paid a dollar and was given ten tickets and entered the dimly lighted dancing school of Professor Christopolos on the fourth floor of a dingy and decrepit building. Each ticket was good for one dance which lasted from a minute to a minute and a half. Any girl in the place would dance with him, because she received five cents for each dance. Takiss' tickets were quickly used up, and he bought more. It did not matter if he danced woodenly and clumsily, and the girls acted delighted to teach him. He went to this taxi-dance hall regularly, spending three, four, and five dollars every visit, and once in a while a girl would ask him if he wanted to take her home, and for a few more dollars he could get other favors, too. After he started going to the taxi-dance hall regularly he was able to save less money, and he sent little to his mother.

Takiss then spent some of his savings for a suit with bell-bottom trousers. He cultivated a mustache and long sideburns, greased his hair and parted it in the middle with meticulous attention. He began to look like a sheik, and listened to pick up all the words which the American-born sheiks used. He went to public dance halls where there was only an admission fee and longer dances. At these places, there were always swarms of girls, pretty American girls, some of them tall and beautiful blondes with milky skins and red lips like cherries. He would ask them to dance. Often they would dance with him, once. He would talk, and they would catch his accent, and when he asked them for a second dance they would thank him with great regret and exclaim that all their other dances were taken. So he would quickly be driven to dancing with the homely and ugly girls who were called wall-flowers. And then he would go back to Professor Christopolos' dancing school, where all the girls would dance with him for ten cents a dance.

One day, Takiss was twenty-five. His native Grecian mountains seemed to have receded in time and he saw them only in painful mists of memory, recalling their details and contours with lessening concreteness. Greece to him was a memory. He had been in America for twelve years, and he was working ten hours a day in a hot-dog stand for ten dollars a week, and able to graft from three to five dollars a week extra. He wanted to make money and to become famous like some of his Americanized countrymen. And when he was a rich man with a hot-dog stand or a restaurant of his own, he would return to Greece with an American wife and act like a millionaire. And he had thirty-five dollars in the bank as a start toward these riches. He wanted to get more money, but not by running a brothel as his fourth cousin George did, and not bootlegging as did George's friend, Mike. He remembered the things his mother, now dead, had told him, and he wanted to make his money and his fame in a way that his mother would have approved of. And then he would have his picture in a Greek-American newspaper.

And hard times came to America. Takiss was out of work in the winter, and again his savings melted. He was employed for ten dollars a week in a candy store, still working twelve hours a day, and in four months that job was gone. He worked for seven dollars a week washing dishes in a large restaurant, and then his pay was cut to five dollars, and he went home every night tired, with chafed hands and an aching back. He had less money, also, for taxi dances. And he lost that job.

He walked the streets looking for other work, and always he learned the same story . . . hard times. He ate very frugally, lived in a chilly, rat-infested room, and wished that he was back home again in his native Grecian mountains, or else that he was a rich and famous American-Greek. Every day he went out looking for a job, and sometimes he found work for a few days or a few weeks and was able to skim along while he tried again to find work.

One day he saw an advertisement with large letters at the top . . . DANCE MARATHON. The word Marathon struck him. Greek. He would win it and win another victory for his country as it had been done in ancient times. He would become a famous Greek athlete. He investigated, and learned that it was a contest in which everybody tried to dance longer than the others, and the winner received a five-hundred-dollar prize. And maybe if he won it, he would get a job in the moving pictures and become the idol of American girls, or go on the vaudeville stage, or be hired to dance in a cabaret. And while he was in the contest, he would be cared for, fed, and there would be no room rent to pay. He was strong and husky, even if he had been getting coughs in his chest for years ever since he had slept on those marble slabs. And he could dance. He was used to standing on his feet all day at work. And this was his chance to become rich. He would no longer have to tramp all over town to be told that there were no jobs because it was hard times. This was much better than saving up to own a candy store and grow fat like the American-Greeks for whom he had worked. And after he won this contest, and became famous, he would go back to Greece with a trunk full of clothes and money, and maybe a rich American girl whose skin was like milk.

Takiss entered the dance marathon, and when the rules were explained to him, he only understood that he was to stay out on the floor and dance, and if he was able to do that longer than anyone else, he would get five hundred dollars. A number was pinned on his back, and he was assigned a partner named Marie Glenn, a beautiful blonde American girl of the type he had always dreamed of as a possible wife. At first, when she met him, she shuddered, and her face broke into an expression of disgust. But then she saw that he was strong and husky with broad shoulders, and she smiled, offering him a limp hand and sweetly telling him that she knew they were sure going to be the winners.

The dance marathon was conducted in a public dance hall on the south side of Chicago. A ring was placed in the center with an orchestra dais at one end. Around the ring there were box seats, and behind them, rising rows of bleacher benches. The opening was described, in advertisements, as gala. An announcer talked through a microphone, and the promoters and judges wearing tuxedoes also addressed a full house. The contestants were introduced and some of them, but not Takiss, spoke to the crowd and the large radio audience all over America. It was all a new and promising, if confusing, world to Takiss, and he walked around the floor, feeling as lost and as out of place as he had on those first days in America. But it was leading at last to paradise.

The contest swung into action. They danced for three minutes out of every ten, and walked around and around the floor for the remaining time; and they were given fifteen minutes rest out of every hour. There was glamor in being watched by so many people, in eating sandwiches and drinking coffee before them, in receiving attention from doctors and nurses, and meeting all the others who, like himself, saw at the end of this contest five hundred dollars and fame. As the contestants got to talking to each other, Takiss heard them using one word over and over again . . . celebrity. A celebrity was somebody who was important, like Jack Dempsey and movie stars and Mr. Delphos, the famous

American-Greek who was wealthy and owned a large dance hall known
as the Bourbon Palace. They all wanted to be celebrities. And Takiss,
too, he determined that he was going to be a celebrity.

Takiss had not imagined that anyone could dance for more than a
week like this, and that maybe after a sleepless and tiring week he
would be the winner. In less than twenty-four hours he learned that it
was a grind more gruelling than he had calculated, and while he doggedly gritted his teeth, he determined that he would not let himself drop
out. Still, he wished that he had not entered it. He wished he were back
working in fruit stores and ice cream parlors the way he had been before
hard times had come. He wished that he were a shepherd back in the
Grecian mountains.

When his partner was tired, she put her arms around his neck or
hips, laid her head against him, and fell asleep while he dragged her
heavily around the floor, and when he fell asleep she did the same thing
with him. Again and again their bodies were jolted, shoved, pushed
against each other, and he began wanting her so that her very nearness
became excruciating. And he noticed that she, particularly in the early
dog hours of the mornings when there were scarcely any spectators in the
hall, began brushing herself against him at every opportunity, looking
feverishly into his eyes and telling him smutty jokes. And the other
dancers became the same way, and the fellows used to tell him how
much they wanted one of these girls, any girl.

Day after day the marathon grind went on. His eyes grew heavy.
His back ached. His feet became sore and raw, so that each step was
pain and he felt often as if he were walking on fire. The hall was almost
continuously stale with cigarette smoke and foul with body odors. He
felt constantly dirty, sweaty, itchy. Dust got into his nostrils and his
eyes. He began to cough again. His muscles knotted. He became like a
person who was always only half awake, and everything took on the
semblance of being a semi-dream. Marie, also, changed. She began to
swell around the buttocks. Deep circles grew under her eyes. She became haggard and blowsy and looked like a worn-out prostitute. She
used more and more cosmetics, and her face became like a ghastly carica-
ture of the pretty girl who had entered the contest.

In the beginning, particularly because of his accent and Greek heritage, Takiss became the butt of many jokes. Constantly, he would be
asked why he wasn't running a restaurant, and he would be given
orders for a piece zapple pie kid. He was nicknamed Restaurant, Fruit
Store, Socrates, and Zapple Pie Kid. In time, this wore down and failed
to anger or disturb him. The grind settled into habitual misery and
torture. He, like the other contestants, would long for fresh air, and
during rest periods, when they were not so tired that they would be

dragged like walking somnambulists to the rest cots, they would enter the vile and filthy dressing rooms or the equally unsavory lavatory and jam their heads out of the windows to breathe fresh air and to look yearningly down at the street where people walked free to do what they wished, not tired, able to breathe fresh air, even the fresh air of a city street that was saturated with carbon monoxide fumes and sootiness.

Day after day dragged on. Sometimes Takiss, Marie, or the other contestants would live in stupors of six, twelve hours a day, even longer. As the time passed, the contestants would switch from affected and over-stimulated good spirits to nasty, fighting nervousness, and then into that glaze-eyed stupor. Particularly in those dog hours of the early morning, they would be raw, if awake, and fight and curse. Sex, too, became a growing obsession, and in time was almost madness. Living so near to one another, their bodies touching so frequently, they told smuttier and smuttier jokes. Perversities and desires or propositions for perversities sprang up among them. It became a relentless process of both physical and mental torture. Constipation, diarrhea, sudden inabilities to control their kidneys so that now and then a contestant would be walking around the floor, drugged in sleep, with wet lines down his trousers, or if a girl, down her beach pyjamas which most of them wore regularly. Broken blood vessels and swollen veins in the legs. Headaches, eye troubles, sore throats, fevers, colds. Periods of sweatiness, followed by shivers and chills. And always that returning stupor, caused by sleep-lessness and fatigue, and by the dreams and fantasies which they entertained as relief from that endless procession around and around the floor. And at the end of it all, money, the chance to become a celebrity, sex, and clean white bed sheets and a soft, fresh bed.

Ways of making money from day to day quickly developed and were used to the utmost so that all of the contestants started bank accounts. Every one of them developed some trick or act, a song, a dance, a stunt of some kind, and after putting it on, they would be showered with money from the crowd. One of the contestants, a raw country youth of Lithuanian origin with a nasal twang to his voice, chewed razor blades as his stunt. Takiss learned a dance. Stores, theatres, and politicians also paid them fees to wear signs or sweaters and jerseys with advertising printed on the front or back. Money was sent to them, mash notes, written in as ignorant and as bad English as that which Takiss used and wrote in. The various spectators picked favorites, cheered for them, shouted encouragement.

And still the days stretched out, past the first month, with contestant after contestant dropping out, and the field narrowing down. One day there would be a birthday party. Another day there was a floor wedding between two of the contestants who had been on the floor, and the wedding provided endless hours of raw jokes and humor about when they would have their wedding night, until, sex-crazed, both of the newlyweds went temporarily out of their heads and the girl screamed until she was dragged off the floor. Disqualified, they were out of the marathon, and a new note was introduced in the humor. Another day, a girl had an abscessed tooth extracted on the floor, and immediately afterward she rejoined the endless walking procession that tramped around in this ever dullening stupor. Another day, an Italian boy, who with his wife had entered the marathon because they were both unemployed and had been evicted, required crutches and ran a high fever. With his eyes intense from the fever, with suffering imprinted on his haggard face, he hobbled around and around. After twelve such hours he was forced out by the judges on the advice of a doctor.

Again and again Takiss wanted to quit and satisfy himself with the incidental money he had taken in, and as repeatedly he would go patiently on. Like the others, he would fall into that lumbrous sleep, and external means would be necessary to awaken him so that he might continue. The male nurses would slap him in the face with wet towels, put his shoes on the wrong feet, strap him into an electric vibrator machine, poke their fingers down his throat, tickle his calloused soles. During one period, his cough developed into a severe cold in the chest. For another period, he was not out of his stupor for three days. And Marie, his partner, experienced the same tortures. They went on. Days and nights, and days and nights, with the field narrowing to thirteen, ten, eight, five, finally two couples. Then Marie collapsed and was carried off the floor and shipped to a hospital, and Takiss was disqualified. They each collected the two hundred and fifty dollars second place money.

After recuperation, Takiss entered other dance marathons, and became a professional. He secured a copy of *Yes, We Have No Bananas* with a Greek translation, and this, with his dance stunt, became very popular. He was able, with both attractions and with a growing audience of fans, to earn from ten to fifteen dollars a day in extra money. Even when he was forced to retire from marathons or was disqualified, he departed with added money. Again the desire to return to his homeland like a rich American grew upon him, and now his bank account, with foreign exchange rates, would make him very rich in Greece. He was something of a celebrity in this new world of his. His biography and picture appeared in Greek newspapers. A Greek merchant who sold a raisin beverage paid him and Marie each a hundred dollars to be photographed for a newspaper advertisement in which there was their signed testimony that they drank this beverage. He had a run of a week at a small theatre on South Halsted Street where there were many Greeks. Takiss became a famous American-Greek.

In all, Takiss participated in sixteen dance marathons. In eight of them, he collected money and was the winner of a thousand-dollar super-marathon in which only finalists from other marathons were permitted to enter and in which there were no rest periods. He had money now, five thousand dollars. He returned to Greece. But the strain of the marathons had ruined his lungs and he had tuberculosis. Resorts for tuberculosis had been developed in his native mountains, and when he returned it was necessary for him to become a patient in one of them, and the money he had earned was paid out while he lived there with his lungs rotting away on him.

astronomer's
wife
kay boyle

Kay Boyle (1903–   ) was born in Minnesota, but married young and spent most of her adult life in Europe. A novelist and short-story writer, her stories have been widely reprinted, especially in the O. Henry Memorial Award anthologies. Presently she is a writer-in-residence in California.
For further reading: The White Horses of Vienna, and Other Stories *(1936).*

There is an evil moment on awakening when all things seem to pause. But for women, they only falter and may be set in action by a single move: a lifted hand and the pendulum will swing, or the voice raised and through every room the pulse takes up its beating. The astronomer's wife felt the interval gaping and at once filled it to the brim. She fetched up her gentle voice and sent it warily down the stairs for coffee, swung her feet out upon the oval mat, and hailed the morning with her bare arms' quivering flesh drawn taut in rhythmic exercise: left, left, left my wife and fourteen children, right, right, right in the middle of the dusty road.

The day would proceed from this, beat by beat, without reflection, like every other day. The astronomer was still asleep, or feigning it, and she, once out of bed, had come into her own possession. Although scarcely ever out of sight of the impenetrable silence of his brow, she would be absent from him all the day in being clean, busy, kind. He was a man of other things, a dreamer. At times he lay still for hours, at others he sat upon the roof behind his telescope, or wandered down the pathway to the road and out across the mountains. This day, like any other, would go on from the removal of the spot left there from dinner on the astronomer's vest to the severe thrashing of the mayonnaise for lunch. That man might be each time the new arching wave, and woman the undertow that sucked him back, were things she had been told by his silence were so.

In spite of the earliness of the hour, the girl had heard her mistress's voice and was coming up the stairs. At the threshold of the bedroom she paused, and said: "Madame, the plumber is here."

The astronomer's wife put on her white and scarlet smock very quickly and buttoned it at the neck. Then she stepped carefully around the motionless spread of water in the hall.

"Tell him to come right up," she said. She laid her hands on the bannisters and stood looking down the wooden stairway. "Ah, I am Mrs. Ames," she said softly as she saw him mounting. "I am Mrs. Ames," she said softly, softly down the flight of stairs. "I am Mrs. Ames," spoken soft as a willow weeping. "The professor is still sleeping. Just step this way."

The plumber himself looked up and saw Mrs. Ames with her voice hushed, speaking to him. She was a youngish woman, but this she had forgotten. The mystery and silence of her husband's mind lay like a chiding finger on her lips. Her eyes were gray, for the light had been extinguished in them. The strange dim halo of her yellow hair was still uncombed and sideways on her head.

For all of his heavy boots, the plumber quieted the sound of his feet, and together they went down the hall, picking their way around the still lake of water that spread as far as the landing and lay docile there. The plumber was a tough, hardy man; but he took off his hat when he spoke to her and looked her fully, almost insolently in the eye.

"Does it come from the wash-basin," he said, "or from the other . . . ?"

"Oh, from the other," said Mrs. Ames without hesitation.

In this place the villas were scattered out few and primitive, and although beauty lay without there was no reflection of her face within. Here all was awkward and unfit; a sense of wrestling with uncouth forces gave everything an austere countenance. Even the plumber, dealing as does a woman with matters under hand, was grave and stately.

The mountains round about seemed to have cast them into the shadow of great dignity.

Mrs. Ames began speaking of their arrival that summer in the little villa, mourning each event as it followed on the other.

"Then, just before going to bed last night," she said, "I noticed something was unusual."

The plumber cast down a folded square of sack-cloth on the brimming floor and laid his leather apron on it. Then he stepped boldly onto the heart of the island it shaped and looked long into the overflowing bowl.

"The water should be stopped from the meter in the garden," he said at last.

"Oh, I did that," said Mrs. Ames, "the very first thing last night. I turned it off at once, in my nightgown, as soon as I saw what was happening. But all this had already run in."

The plumber looked for a moment at her red kid slippers. She was standing just at the edge of the clear, pure-seeming tide.

"It's no doubt the soil lines," he said severely. "It may be that something has stopped them, but my opinion is that the water seals aren't working. That's the trouble often enough in such cases. If you had a valve you wouldn't be caught like this."

Mrs. Ames did not know how to meet this rebuke. She stood, swaying a little, looking into the plumber's blue relentless eye.

"I'm sorry—I'm sorry that my husband," she said, "is still—resting and cannot go into this with you. I'm sure it must be very interesting. . . ."

"You'll probably have to have the traps sealed," said the plumber grimly, and at the sound of this Mrs. Ames' hand flew in dismay to the side of her face. The plumber made no move, but the set of his mouth as he looked at her seemed to soften. "Anyway, I'll have a look from the garden end," he said.

"Oh, do," said the astronomer's wife in relief. Here was a man who spoke of action and object as simply as women did! But however hushed her voice had been, it carried clearly to Professor Ames who lay, dreaming and solitary, upon his bed. He heard their footsteps come down the hall, pause, and skip across the pool of overflow.

"Katherine!" said the astronomer in a ringing tone. "There's a problem worthy of your mettle!"

Mrs. Ames did not turn her head, but led the plumber swiftly down the stairs. When the sun in the garden struck her face, he saw there was a wave of color in it, but this may have been anything but shame.

"You see how it is," said the plumber, as if leading her mind away. "The drains run from these houses right down the hill, big enough for a man to stand upright in them, and clean as a whistle too." There they stood in the garden with the vegetation flowering in disorder all about.

The plumber looked at the astronomer's wife. "They come out at the torrent on the other side of the forest beyond there," he said.

But the words the astronomer had spoken still sounded in her in despair. The mind of man, she knew, made steep and sprightly flights, pursued illusion, took foothold in the nameless things that cannot pass between the thumb and finger. But whenever the astronomer gave voice to the thoughts that soared within him, she returned in gratitude to the long expanses of his silence. Desert-like they stretched behind and before the articulation of his scorn.

Life, life is an open sea, she sought to explain it in sorrow, and to survive women cling to the floating débris on the tide. But the plumber had suddenly fallen upon his knees in the grass and had crooked his fingers through the ring of the drains' trap-door. When she looked down she saw that he was looking up into her face, and she saw too that his hair was as light as gold.

"Perhaps Mr. Ames," he said rather bitterly, "would like to come down with me and have a look around?"

"Down?" said Mrs. Ames in wonder.

"Into the drains," said the plumber brutally. "They're a study for a man who likes to know what's what."

"Oh, Mr. Ames," said Mrs. Ames in confusion. "He's still—still in bed, you see."

The plumber lifted his strong, weathered face and looked curiously at her. Surely it seemed to him strange for a man to linger in bed, with the sun pouring yellow as wine all over the place. The astronomer's wife saw his lean cheeks, his high, rugged bones, and the deep seams in his brow. His flesh was as firm and clean as wood, stained richly tan with the climate's rigor. His fingers were blunt, but comprehensible to her, gripped in the ring and holding the iron door wide. The backs of his hands were bound round and round with ripe blue veins of blood.

"At any rate," said the astronomer's wife, and the thought of it moved her lips to smile a little, "Mr. Ames would never go down there alive. He likes going up," she said. And she, in her turn, pointed, but impudently, towards the heavens. "On the roof. Or on the mountains. He's been up on the tops of them many times."

"It's a matter of habit," said the plumber, and suddenly he went down the trap. Mrs. Ames saw a bright little piece of his hair still shining, like a star, long after the rest of him had gone. Out of the depths, his voice, hollow and dark with foreboding, returned to her. "I think something has stopped the elbow," was what he said.

This was speech that touched her flesh and bone and made her wonder. When her husband spoke of height, having no sense of it, she could not picture it nor hear. Depth or magic passed her by unless a name were given. But madness in a daily shape, as elbow stopped, she saw clearly and well. She sat down on the grasses, bewildered that it should be a man who had spoken to her so.

She saw the weeds springing up, and she did not move to tear them up from life. She sat powerless, her senses veiled, with no action taking shape beneath her hands. In this way some men sat for hours on end, she knew, tracking a single thought back to its origin. The mind of man could balance and divide, weed out, destroy. She sat on the full, burdened grasses, seeking to think, and dimly waiting for the plumber to return.

Whereas her husband had always gone up, as the dead go, she knew now that there were others who went down, like the corporeal being of the dead. That men were then divided into two bodies now seemed clear to Mrs. Ames. This knowledge stunned her with its simplicity and took the uneasy motion from her limbs. She could not stir, but sat facing the mountains' rocky flanks, and harking in silence to lucidity. Her husband was the mind, this other man the meat, of all mankind.

After a little, the plumber emerged from the earth: first the light top of his head, then the burnt brow, and then the blue eyes fringed with whitest lash. He braced his thick hands flat on the pavings of the garden-path and swung himself completely from the pit.

"It's the soil lines," he said pleasantly. "The gases," he said as he looked down upon her lifted face, "are backing up the drains."

"What in the world are we going to do?" said the astronomer's wife softly. There was a young and strange delight in putting questions to which true answers would be given. Everything the astronomer had ever said to her was a continuous query to which there could be no response.

"Ah, come, now," said the plumber, looking down and smiling. "There's a remedy for every ill, you know. Sometimes it may be that," he said as if speaking to a child, "or sometimes the other thing. But there's always a help for everything a-miss."

Things come out of herbs and make you young again, he might have been saying to her; or the first good rain will quench any drought; or time of itself will put a broken bone together.

"I'm going to follow the ground pipe out right to the torrent," the plumber was saying. "The trouble's between here and there and I'll find it on the way. There's nothing at all that can't be done over for the caring," he was saying, and his eyes were fastened on her face in insolence, or gentleness, or love.

The astronomer's wife stood up, fixed a pin in her hair, and turned around towards the kitchen. Even while she was calling the servant's name, the plumber began speaking again.

"I once had a cow that lost her cud," the plumber was saying. The girl came out on the kitchen-step and Mrs. Ames stood smiling at her in the sun.

"The trouble is very serious, very serious," she said across the garden. "When Mr. Ames gets up, please tell him I've gone down."

She pointed briefly to the open door in the pathway, and the plumber hoisted his kit on his arm and put out his hand to help her down.

"But I made her another in no time," he was saying, "out of flowers and things and what-not."

"Oh," said the astronomer's wife in wonder as she stepped into the heart of the earth. She took his arm, knowing that what he said was true.

part 3

José Vasconcelos, Jorge Luis Borges, Shirley Jackson,
Bernard Malamud, Flannery O'Connor,
Isaac Rosenfeld, R. V. Cassill, Tommaso Landolfi,
Ted Hughes, James B. Hall,
Wolfgang Hildesheimer,
Alain Robbe-Grillet,
Samuel Beckett

new

dimensions

the boar hunt

josé vasconcelos

*José Vasconcelos (1882–1959)
is one of Mexico's foremost masters
of prose fiction. Working in the grand
tradition of writer–teacher–statesman,
he served as head of the National
University of Mexico (1920–1924)
and as Minister of Education
under the regime of Alvaro Obregón.
In 1929 he was an unsuccessful
candidate for the Mexican presidency.
Few of his stories are available
in English at the present time.*

We were four companions, and we went by the names of our respective nationalities: the Colombian, the Peruvian, the Mexican; the fourth, a native of Ecuador, was called Quito for short. Unforeseen chance had joined us together a few years ago on a large sugar plantation on the Peruvian coast. We worked at different occupations during the day and met during the evening in our off time. Not being Englishmen, we did not play cards. Instead, our constant discussions led to disputes. These didn't stop us from wanting to see each other the next night, however, to continue the interrupted debates and support them with new arguments. Nor did the rough sentences of the preceding wrangles indicate a lessening of our affection, of which we assured ourselves reciprocally with the clasping of hands and a look. On Sundays we used to go on hunting parties. We roamed the fertile glens, stalking, generally with poor results, the game of the warm region around the coast, or we entertained ourselves killing birds that flew in the sunlight during the siesta hour.

We came to be tireless wanderers and excellent marksmen. Whenever we climbed a hill and gazed at the imposing range of mountains in the interior, its attractiveness stirred us and we wanted to climb it. What attracted us more was the trans-Andean region: fertile plateaus extending on the other side of the range in the direction of the Atlantic toward the immense land of Brazil. It was as if primitive nature called us to her breast. The vigor of the fertile, untouched jungles promised to rejuvenate our minds, the same vigor which rejuvenates the strength and the thickness of the trees each year. At times we devised crazy plans. As with all things that are given a lot of thought, these schemes generally material-

375

ized. Ultimately nature and events are largely what our imaginations make them out to be. And so we went ahead planning and acting. At the end of the year, with arranged vacations, accumulated money, good rifles, abundant munitions, stone- and mudproof boots, four hammocks, and a half dozen faithful Indians, our caravan descended the Andean slopes, leading to the endless green ocean.

At last we came upon a village at the edge of the Marañón River. Here we changed our safari. The region we were going to penetrate had no roads. It was unexplored underbrush into which we could enter only by going down the river in a canoe. In time we came to the area where we proposed to carry out the purpose of our journey, the hunting of wild boars.

We had been informed that boars travel in herds of several thousands, occupying a region, eating grass and staying together, exploiting the grazing areas, organized just like an army. They are very easy to kill if one attacks them when they are scattered out satisfying their appetites —an army given over to the delights of victory. When they march about hungry, on the other hand, they are usually vicious. In our search we glided down river between imposing jungles with our provisions and the company of three faithful Indian oarsmen.

One morning we stopped at some huts near the river. Thanks to the information gathered there, we decided to disembark a little farther on in order to spend the night on land and continue the hunt for the boars in the thicket the following day.

Sheltered in a backwater, we came ashore, and after a short exploration found a clearing in which to make camp. We unloaded the provisions and the rifles, tied the boat securely, then with the help of the Indians set up our camp one half kilometer from the river bank. In marking the path to the landing, we were careful not to lose ourselves in the thicket. The Indians withdrew toward their huts, promising to return two days later. At dawn we would set out in search of the prey.

Though night had scarcely come and the heat was great, we gathered at the fire to see each other's faces, to look instinctively for protection. We talked a little, smoked, confessed to being tired, and decided to go to bed. Each hammock had been tied by one end to a single tree, firm though not very thick in the trunk. Stretching out from this axis in different directions, the hammocks were supported by the other end on other trunks. Each of us carried his rifle, cartridges, and some provisions which couldn't remain exposed on the ground. The sight of the weapons made us consider the place where we were, surrounded by the unknown. A slight feeling of terror made us laugh, cough, and talk. But fatigue overcame us, that heavy fatigue which compels the soldier to scorn danger, to put down his rifle, and to fall asleep though the most per-

sistent enemy pursues him. We scarcely noticed the supreme grandeur
of that remote tropical night.

I don't know whether it was the light of the magnificent dawn or the
strange noises which awakened me and made me sit up in my hammock
and look carefully at my surroundings. I saw nothing but the awakening
of that life which at night falls into the lethargy of the jungle. I called
my sleeping companions and, alert and seated in our hanging beds, we
dressed ourselves. We were preparing to jump to the ground when we
clearly heard a somewhat distant, sudden sound of rustling branches.
Since it did not continue, however, we descended confidently, washed
our faces with water from our canteens, and slowly prepared and enjoyed breakfast. By about 11:00 in the morning we were armed and
bold and preparing to make our way through the jungle.

But then the sound again. Its persistence and proximity in the thicket
made us change our minds. An instinct made us take refuge in our
hammocks. We cautiously moved our cartridges and rifles into them
again, and without consulting each other we agreed on the idea of putting our provisions safely away. We passed them up into the hammocks,
and we ourselves finally climbed in. Stretched out face down, comfortably suspended with rifles in hand, we did not have to wait long.
Black, agile boars quickly appeared from all directions. We welcomed
them with shouts of joy and well-aimed shots. Some fell immediately,
giving comical snorts, but many more came out of the jungle. We shot
again, spending all the cartridges in the magazine. Then we stopped to
reload. Finding ourselves safe in the height of our hammocks, we continued after a pause.

We counted dozens of them. At a glance we made rapid calculations
of the magnitude of the destruction, while the boars continued to come
out of the jungle in uncountable numbers. Instead of going on their way
or fleeing, they seemed confused. All of them emerged from the jungle
where it was easy for us to shoot them. Occasionally we had to stop
firing because the frequent shooting heated the barrels of our rifles.
While they were cooling we smoked and were able to joke, celebrating
our good fortune. The impotent anger of the boars amazed us. They
raised their tusks in our direction, uselessly threatening us. We laughed
at their snorts, quietly aimed at those who were near, and Bang! a dead
boar. We carefully studied the angle of the shoulder blade so that the
bullet would cross the heart. The slaughter lasted for hours.

At 4:00 P.M. we noticed an alarming shortage of our ammunition. We
had been well supplied and had shot at will. Though the slaughter was
gratifying, the boars must have numbered, as we had been informed
previously, several thousands, because their hordes didn't diminish. On
the contrary, they gathered directly beneath our hammocks in increasing

groups. They slashed furiously at the trunk of the tree which held the four points of the hammocks. The marks of the tusks remained on the hard bark. Not without a certain fear we watched them gather compactly, tenaciously, in tight masses against the resisting trunk. We wondered what would happen to a man who fell within their reach. Our shots were now sporadic, well aimed, carefully husbanded. They did not drive away the aggressive beasts, but only redoubled their fury. One of us ironically noted that from being the attackers we had gone on the defensive. We did not laugh very long at the joke. Now we hardly shot at all. We needed to save our cartridges.

The afternoon waned and evening came upon us. After consulting each other, we decided to eat in our hammocks. We applauded ourselves for taking the food up—meat, bread, and bottles of water. Stretching ourselves on our hammocks, we passed things to each other, sharing what we needed. The boars deafened us with their angry snorts.

After eating, we began to feel calm. We lit cigars. Surely the boars would go. Their numbers were great, but they would finally leave peacefully. As we said so, however, we looked with greedy eyes at the few unused cartridges that remained. Our enemies, like enormous angry ants, stirred beneath us, encouraged by the ceasing of our fire. From time to time we carefully aimed and killed one or two of them, driving off the huge group of uselessly enraged boars at the base of the trunk which served as a prop for our hammocks.

Night enveloped us almost without our noticing the change from twilight. Anxiety also overtook us. When would the cursed boars leave? Already there were enough dead to serve as trophies to several dozen hunters. Our feat would be talked about; we had to show ourselves worthy of such fame. Since there was nothing else to do, it was necessary to sleep. Even if we had had enough bullets it would have been impossible to continue the fight in the darkness. It occurred to us to start a fire to drive the herd off with flames, but apart from the fact that we couldn't leave the place in which we were suspended, there were no dry branches in the lush forest. Finally, we slept.

We woke up a little after midnight. The darkness was profound, but the well-known noise made us aware that our enemies were still there. We imagined they must be the last ones which were leaving, however. If a good army needs several hours to break camp and march off, what can be expected of a vile army of boars but disorder and delay? The following morning we would fire upon the stragglers, but this painful thought bothered us: they were in large and apparently active numbers. What were they up to? Why didn't they leave? We thus spent long hours of worry. Dawn finally came, splendid in the sky but noisy in the jungle still enveloped inwardly in shadows. We eagerly waited for the sun to penetrate the foliage in order to survey the appearance of the field of battle of the day before.

What we finally saw made us gasp. It terrified us. The boars were painstakingly continuing the work which they had engaged in throughout the entire night. Guided by some extraordinary instinct, with their tusks they were digging out the ground underneath the tree from which our hammocks hung; they gnawed the roots and continued to undermine them like large, industrious rats. Presently the tree was bound to fall and we with it, among the beasts. From that moment we neither thought nor talked. In desperation we used up our last shots, killing more ferocious beasts. Still the rest renewed their activity. They seemed to be endowed with intelligence. However much we concentrated our fire against them, they did not stop their attack against the tree.

Soon our shots stopped. We emptied our pistols, and then silently listened to the tusks gnawing beneath the soft, wet, pleasant-smelling earth. From time to time the boars pressed against the tree, pushing it and making it creak, eager to smash it quickly. We looked on hypnotized by their devilish activity. It was impossible to flee because the black monsters covered every inch in sight. It seemed to us that, by a sudden inspiration, they were preparing to take revenge on us for the ruthless nature of man, the unpunished destroyer of animals since the beginning of time. Our imagination, distorted by fear, showed us our fate as an atonement for the unpardonable crimes implicit in the struggle of biological selection. Before my eyes passed the vision of sacred India, where the believer refuses to eat meat in order to prevent the methodical killing of beasts and in order to atone for man's evil, bloody, treacherous slaughter, such as ours, for mere vicious pleasure. I felt that the multitude of boars was raising its accusing voice against me. I now understood the infamy of the hunter, but what was repentance worth if I was going to die with my companions, hopelessly devoured by that horde of brutes with demonlike eyes?

Stirred by terror and without realizing what I was doing, I hung from the upper end of my hammock, I balanced myself in the air, I swung in a long leap, I grasped a branch of a tree facing the one on which the boars were digging. From there I leaped to other branches and to others, reviving in myself habits which the species had forgotten.

The next moment a terrifying sound and unforgettable cries told me of the fall of the tree and the end of my companions. I clung to a trunk, trembling and listening to the chattering of my jaws. Later, the desire to flee gave me back my strength. Leaning out over the foliage, I looked for a path, and I saw the boars in the distance, marching in compressed ranks and holding their insolent snouts in the air. I knew that they were now withdrawing, and I got down from the tree. Horror overwhelmed me as I approached the site of our encampment, but some idea of duty made me return there. Perhaps one of my friends had managed to save himself. I approached hesitantly. Each dead boar made me tremble with fear.

But what I saw next was so frightful that I could not fix it clearly in my mind: remains of clothing—and footwear. There was no doubt; the boars had devoured them. Then I ran toward the river, following the tracks we had made two days before. I fled with great haste, limbs stiff from panic.

Running with long strides, I came upon the boat. With a great effort, I managed to row to the huts. There I went to bed with a high fever which lasted many days.

I will participate in no more hunts. I will contribute, if I have to, to the extermination of harmful beasts. But I will not kill for pleasure. I will not amuse myself with the ignoble pleasure of the hunt.

the
secret
miracle
jorge luis borges

*Jorge Luis Borges (1899–)
was born in Buenos Aires and educated
in Geneva and Spain. Widely
read abroad, his work suggests Poe,
Baudelaire, and Valéry. He is a
poet, essayist, and short-story writer
and has also written detective narratives
and two movie scripts. Unquestionably,
Borges is a short-story writer of
worldwide stature. For further reading:*
Labyrinths, Selected Stories
and Other Writings *(1962).*

And God had him die for a hundred years and then revived him and said:
"How long have you been here?"
"A day or a part of a day," he answered.

Koran, II, 261

The night of March 14, 1943, in an apartment in the Zeltnergasse of Prague, Jaromir Hladik, the author of the unfinished drama entitled *The Enemies*, of *Vindication of Eternity* and of a study of the indirect Jewish sources of Jakob Böhme, had a dream of a long game of chess. The players were not two persons, but two illustrious families; the game had been going on for centuries. Nobody could remember what the stakes were, but it was rumored that they were enormous, perhaps infinite; the chessmen and the board were in a secret tower. Jaromir (in his dream) was the first-born of one of the contending families. The clock struck the hour for the game, which could not be postponed. The dreamer raced over the sands of a rainy desert, and was unable to recall either the pieces or the rules of chess. At that moment he awoke. The clangor of the rain and of the terrible clocks ceased. A rhythmic, unanimous noise, punctuated by shouts of command, arose from the Zeltnergasse. It was dawn, and the armored vanguard of the Third Reich was entering Prague.

On the nineteenth the authorities received a denunciation; that same nineteenth, toward evening, Jaromir Hladik was arrested. He was taken to an aseptic, white barracks on the opposite bank of the Moldau. He was unable to refute a single one of the Gestapo's charges; his mother's family name was Jaroslavski, he was of Jewish blood, his study on Böhme had a marked Jewish emphasis, his signature had been one more on the protest against the *Anschluss*. In 1928 he had translated the *Sepher Yezirah* for the publishing house of Hermann Barsdorf. The fulsome catalogue of the firm had exaggerated, for publicity purposes, the translator's reputation, and the catalogue had been examined by Julius Rothe, one of the officials who held Hladik's fate in his hands. There is not a person who, except in the field of his own specialization, is not credulous; two or three adjectives in Gothic type were enough to persuade Julius Rothe of Hladik's importance, and he ordered him sentenced to death *pour encourager les autres*. The execution was set for March 29th, at 9:00 A.M. This delay (whose importance the reader will grasp later) was owing to the desire on the authorities' part to proceed impersonally and slowly, after the manner of vegetables and plants.

Hladik's first reaction was mere terror. He felt he would not have shrunk from the gallows, the block, or the knife, but that death by a firing squad was unbearable. In vain he tried to convince himself that the plain, unvarnished fact of dying was the fearsome thing, not the attendant circumstances. He never wearied of conjuring up these circumstances, senselessly trying to exhaust all their possible variations. He infinitely anticipated the process of his dying, from the sleepless dawn to the mysterious volley. Before the day set by Julius Rothe he died hundreds of deaths in courtyards whose forms and angles strained geometrical probabilities, machine-gunned by variable soldiers in changing numbers, who at times killed him from a distance, at others from close by. He faced these imaginary executions with real terror (perhaps with real bravery); each simulacrum lasted a few seconds. When the circle was closed, Jaromir returned once more and interminably to the tremulous vespers of his death. Then he reflected that reality does not usually coincide with our anticipation of it; with a logic of his own he inferred that to foresee a circumstantial detail is to prevent its happening. Trusting in this weak magic, he invented, *so that they would not happen,* the most gruesome details. Finally, as was natural, he came to fear that they were prophetic. Miserable in the night, he endeavored to find some way to hold fast to the fleeting substance of time. He knew that it was rushing headlong toward the dawn of the twenty-ninth. He reasoned aloud: "I am now in the night of the twenty-second; while this night lasts (and for six nights more), I am invulnerable, immortal." The nights of sleep seemed to him deep, dark pools in which he could submerge himself. There were moments when he longed impatiently for the final burst of fire that would free him, for better or for worse, from the vain compulsion of his imaginings. On the twenty-eighth, as the last sunset was reverberating from the high barred windows, the thought of his drama, *The Enemies,* deflected him from these abject considerations.

Hladik had rounded forty. Aside from a few friendships and many habits, the problematic exercise of literature constituted his life. Like all writers, he measured the achievements of others by what they had accomplished, asking of them that they measure him by what he envisaged or planned. All the books he had published had left him with a complex feeling of repentance. His studies of the work of Böhme, of Ibn Ezra, and of Fludd had been characterized essentially by mere application; his translation of the *Sepher Yezirah,* by carelessness, fatigue, and conjecture. *Vindication of Eternity* perhaps had fewer shortcomings. The first volume gave a history of man's various concepts of eternity, from the immutable Being of Parmenides to the modifiable Past of Hinton. The second denied (with Francis Bradley) that all the events of the universe make up a temporal series, arguing that the number of man's possible experiences is not infinite, and that a single "repetition" suffices to prove that time is a fallacy . . . Unfortunately, the arguments that demonstrate this fallacy are equally fallacious. Hladik was in the habit of going over them with a kind of contemptuous perplexity. He had also composed a series of Expressionist poems; to the poet's chagrin they had been included in an anthology published in 1924, and no subsequent anthology but inherited them. From all this equivocal, uninspired past Hladik had hoped to redeem himself with his drama in verse, *The Enemies.* (Hladik felt the verse form to be essential because it makes it impossible for the spectators to lose sight of irreality, one of art's requisites.)

The drama observed the unities of time, place, and action. The scene was laid in Hradčany, in the library of Baron von Roemerstadt, on one of the last afternoons of the nineteenth century. In the first scene of the first act a strange man visits Roemerstadt. (A clock was striking seven, the vehemence of the setting sun's rays glorified the windows, a passionate, familiar Hungarian music floated in the air.) This visit is followed by others; Roemerstadt does not know the people who are importuning him, but he has the uncomfortable feeling that he has seen them somewhere, perhaps in a dream. They all fawn upon him, but it is apparent—first to the audience and then to the Baron—that they are secret enemies, in league to ruin him. Roemerstadt succeeds in checking or evading their involved schemings. In the dialogue mention is made of his sweetheart, Julia von Weidenau, and a certain Jaroslav Kubin, who at one time pressed his attentions on her. Kubin has now lost his mind, and believes himself to be Roemerstadt. The dangers increase; Roemerstadt, at the end of the second act, is forced to kill one of the conspirators. The third and final act opens. The incoherencies gradually increase; actors who had seemed out of the play reappear; the man Roemerstadt killed returns for a moment. Someone points out that evening has not fallen; the clock strikes seven, the high windows reverberate in the western sun, the air carries an impassioned Hungarian melody. The first actor comes on and repeats the lines he had spoken in the first scene of the first act. Roemerstadt speaks to him without surprise; the audience understands that Roemerstadt is the miserable Jaroslav Kubin. The drama has never taken place; it is the circular delirium that Kubin lives and relives endlessly.

Hladik had never asked himself whether this tragicomedy of errors was preposterous or admirable, well thought out or slipshod. He felt that the plot I have just sketched was best contrived to cover up his defects and point up his abilities and held the possibility of allowing him to redeem (symbolically) the meaning of his life. He had finished the first act and one or two scenes of the third; the metrical nature of the work made it possible for him to keep working it over, changing the hexameters, without the manuscript in front of him. He thought how he still had two acts to do, and that he was going to die very soon. He spoke with God in the darkness: "If in some fashion I exist, if I am not one of Your repetitions and mistakes, I exist as the author of *The Enemies*. To finish this drama, which can justify me and justify You, I need another year. Grant me these days, You to whom the centuries and time belong." This was the last night, the most dreadful of all, but ten minutes later sleep flooded over him like a dark water.

Toward dawn he dreamed that he had concealed himself in one of the naves of the Clementine Library. A librarian wearing dark glasses asked him: "What are you looking for?" Hladik answered: "I am looking for God." The librarian said to him: "God is in one of the letters on one of the pages of one of the four hundred thousand volumes of the Clementine. My fathers and the fathers of my fathers have searched for this letter; I have grown blind seeking it." He removed his glasses, and Hladik saw his eyes, which were dead. A reader came in to return an atlas. "This atlas is worthless," he said, and handed it to Hladik, who opened it at random. He saw a map of India as in a daze. Suddenly sure of himself, he touched one of the tiniest letters. A ubiquitous voice said to him: "The time of your labor has been granted." At this point Hladik awoke.

He remembered that men's dreams belong to God, and that Maimonides had written that the words heard in a dream are divine when they are distinct and clear and the person uttering them cannot be seen. He dressed: two soldiers came into the cell and ordered him to follow them.

From behind the door, Hladik had envisaged a labyrinth of passageways, stairs, and separate buildings. The reality was less spectacular: they descended to an inner court by a narrow iron stairway. Several soldiers—some with uniform unbuttoned—were examining a motorcycle and discussing it. The sergeant looked at the clock; it was 8:44. They had to wait until it struck nine. Hladik, more insignificant than pitiable, sat down on a pile of wood. He noticed that the soldiers' eyes avoided his. To ease his wait, the sergeant handed him a cigarette. Hladik did not smoke; he accepted it out of politeness or humility. As he lighted it, he noticed that his hands were shaking. The day was clouding over; the soldiers spoke in a low voice as though he were already dead. Vainly he tried to recall the woman of whom Julia von Weidenau was the symbol.

The squad formed and stood at attention. Hladik, standing against the barracks wall, waited for the volley. Someone pointed out that the wall was going to be stained with blood; the victim was ordered to step forward a few paces. Incongruously, this reminded Hladik of the fumbling preparations of photographers. A big drop of rain struck one of Hladik's temples and rolled slowly down his cheek; the sergeant shouted the final order.

The physical universe came to a halt.

The guns converged on Hladik, but the men who were to kill him stood motionless. The sergeant's arm eternized an unfinished gesture. On a paving stone of the courtyard a bee cast an unchanging shadow. The wind had ceased, as in a picture. Hladik attempted a cry, a word, a movement of the hand. He realized that he was paralyzed. Not a sound reached him from the halted world. He thought: "I am in hell, I am dead." He thought: "I am mad." He thought: "Time has stopped." Then he reflected that if that was the case, his mind would have stopped too.

He wanted to test this; he repeated (without moving his lips) Vergil's mysterious fourth Eclogue. He imagined that the now remote soldiers must be sharing his anxiety; he longed to be able to communicate with them. It astonished him not to feel the least fatigue, not even the numbness of his protracted immobility. After an indeterminate time he fell asleep. When he awoke the world continued motionless and mute. The drop of water still clung to his cheek, the shadow of the bee to the stone. The smoke from the cigarette he had thrown away had not dispersed. Another "day" went by before Hladik understood.

He had asked God for a whole year to finish his work; His omnipotence had granted it. God had worked a secret miracle for him; German lead would kill him at the set hour, but in his mind a year would go by between the order and its execution. From perplexity he passed to stupor, from stupor to resignation, from resignation to sudden gratitude.

He had no document but his memory; the training he had acquired with each added hexameter gave him a discipline unsuspected by those who set down and forget temporary, incomplete paragraphs. He was not working for posterity or even for God, whose literary tastes were unknown to him. Meticulously, motionlessly, secretely, he wrought in time his lofty, invisible labyrinth. He worked the third act over twice. He eliminated certain symbols as over-obvious, such as the repeated striking of the clock, the music. Nothing hurried him. He omitted, he condensed, he amplified. In certain instances he came back to the original version. He came to feel an affection for the courtyard, the barracks; one of the faces before him modified his conception of Roemerstadt's character. He discovered that the wearying cacophonies that bothered Flaubert so much are mere visual superstitions, weakness and limitation of the written word, not the spoken . . . He concluded his drama. He had only the problem of a single phrase. He found it. The drop of water slid down his cheek. He opened his mouth in a maddened cry, moved his face, dropped under the quadruple blast.

Jaromir Hladik died on March 29, at 9:02 A.M.

the
lottery

shirley jackson

Shirley Jackson (1919–   ) was born in San Francisco and is a novelist, essayist, and short-story writer. Her work is strongly influenced by the discipline of anthropology. She is married to the folklorist and critic Stanley Edgar Hyman. For further reading: The Lottery, or The Adventures of James Harris *(1949).*

The morning of June 27th was clear and sunny, with the fresh warmth of a full-summer day; the flowers were blossoming profusely and the grass was richly green. The people of the village began to gather in the square, between the post office and the bank, around ten o'clock; in some towns there were so many people that the lottery took two days and had to be started on June 26th, but in this village, where there were only about three hundred people, the whole lottery took less than two hours, so it could begin at ten o'clock in the morning and still be through in time to allow the villagers to get home for noon dinner.

The children assembled first, of course. School was recently over for the summer, and the feeling of liberty sat uneasily on most of them; they tended to gather together quietly for a while before they broke into boisterous play, and their talk was still of the classroom and the teacher, of books and reprimands. Bobby Martin had already stuffed his pockets full of stones, and the other boys soon followed his example, selecting the smoothest and roundest stones; Bobby and Harry Jones and Dickie Delacroix—the villagers pronounced this name "Dellacroy"—eventually made a great pile of stones in one corner of the square and guarded it against the raids of the other boys. The girls stood aside, talking among themselves, looking over their shoulders at the boys, and the very small children rolled in the dust or clung to the hands of their older brothers or sisters.

Soon the men began to gather, surveying their own children, speaking of planting and rain, tractors and taxes. They stood together, away from the pile of stones in the corner, and their jokes were quiet and they smiled rather than laughed. The women, wearing faded house dresses and sweaters, came shortly after their menfolk. They greeted one another and exchanged bits of gossip as they went to join their husbands. Soon the women, standing by their husbands, began to call to their children, and the children came reluctantly, having to be called four or five times. Bobby Martin ducked under his mother's grasping hand and ran, laughing, back to the pile of stones. His father spoke up sharply, and Bobby came quickly and took his place between his father and his oldest brother.

The lottery was conducted—as were the square dances, the teen-age club, the Halloween program—by Mr. Summers, who had time and energy to devote to civic activities. He was a round-faced, jovial man and he ran the coal business, and people were sorry for him, because he had no children and his wife was a scold. When he arrived in the square, carrying the black wooden box, there was a murmur of conversation among the villagers, and he waved and called, "Little late today, folks." The postmaster, Mr. Graves, followed him, carrying a three-legged stool, and the stool was put in the center of the square and Mr. Summers set the black box down on it. The villagers kept their distance, leaving a space between themselves and the stool, and when Mr. Summers said, "Some of you fellows want to give me a hand?" there was a hesitation before two men, Mr. Martin and his oldest son, Baxter, came forward to hold the box steady on the stool while Mr. Summers stirred up the papers inside it.

The original paraphernalia for the lottery had been lost long ago, and the black box now resting on the stool had been put into use even before Old Man Warner, the oldest man in town, was born. Mr. Summers spoke frequently to the villagers about making a new box, but no one liked to upset even as much tradition as was represented by the black box. There was a story that the present box had been made with some pieces of the box that had preceded it, the one that had been constructed when the first people settled down to make a village here. Every year, after the lottery, Mr. Summers began talking again about a new box, but every year the subject was allowed to fade off without anything's being done. The black box grew shabbier each year; by now it was no longer completely black but splintered badly along one side to show the original wood color, and in some places faded or stained.

Mr. Martin and his oldest son, Baxter, held the black box securely on the stool until Mr. Summers had stirred the papers thoroughly with his hand. Because so much of the ritual had been forgotten or discarded, Mr. Summers had been successful in having slips of paper substituted for the chips of wood that had been used for generations. Chips of wood, Mr. Summers had argued, had been all very well when the village was tiny, but now that the population was more than three hundred and likely to keep on growing, it was necessary to use something that would fit more easily into the black box. The night before the lottery, Mr. Summers and Mr. Graves made up the slips of paper and put them in the box, and it was then taken to the safe of Mr. Summers' coal company and locked up until Mr. Summers was ready to take it to the square next morning. The rest of the year, the box was put away, sometimes one place, sometimes another; it had spent one year in Mr. Graves's barn and another year under foot in the post office, and sometimes it was set on a shelf in the Martin grocery and left there.

There was a great deal of fussing to be done before Mr. Summers declared the lottery open. There were the lists to make up—of heads of families, heads of households in each family, members of each household in each family. There was the proper swearing-in of Mr. Summers by the postmaster, as the official of the lottery; at one time, some people remembered, there had been a recital of some sort, performed by the official of the lottery, a perfunctory, tuneless chant that had been rattled off duly each year; some people believed that the official of the lottery used to stand just so when he said or sang it, others believed that he was supposed to walk among the people, but years and years ago this part of the ritual had been allowed to lapse. There had been, also, a ritual salute, which the official of the lottery had had to use in addressing each person who came up to draw from the box, but this also had changed with time, until now it was felt necessary only for the official to speak to each person approaching. Mr. Summers was very good at all this; in his clean white shirt and blue jeans, with one hand resting carelessly on the black box, he seemed very proper and important as he talked interminably to Mr. Graves and the Martins.

Just as Mr. Summers finally left off talking and turned to the assembled villagers, Mrs. Hutchinson came hurriedly along the path to the square, her sweater thrown over her shoulders, and slid into place in the back of the crowd. "Clean forgot what day it was," she said to Mrs. Delacroix, who stood next to her, and they both laughed softly. "Thought my old man was out back stacking wood," Mrs. Hutchinson went on, "and then I looked out the window and the kids was gone, and then I remembered it was the twenty-seventh and came a-running." She dried her hands on her apron, and Mrs. Delacroix said, "You're in time, though. They're still talking away up there."

Mrs. Hutchinson craned her neck to see through the crowd and found her husband and children standing near the front. She tapped Mrs. Delacroix on the arm as a farewell and began to make her way through the crowd. The people separated good-humoredly to let her through; two or three people said, in voices just loud enough to be heard across the crowd, "Here comes your Missus, Hutchinson," and "Bill, she made it after all." Mrs. Hutchinson reached her husband, and Mr. Summers, who had been waiting, said cheerfully, "Thought we were going to have to get on without you, Tessie." Mrs. Hutchinson said, grinning, "Wouldn't have me leave m'dishes in the sink, now, would you, Joe?," and soft laughter ran through the crowd as the people stirred back into position after Mrs. Hutchinson's arrival.

"Well, now," Mr. Summers said soberly, "guess we better get started, get this over with, so's we can go back to work. Anybody ain't here?"

"Dunbar," several people said. "Dunbar, Dunbar."

Mr. Summers consulted his list. "Clyde Dunbar," he said. "That's right. He's broke his leg, hasn't he? Who's drawing for him?"

"Me, I guess," a woman said, and Mr. Summers turned to look at her. "Wife draws for her husband," Mr. Summers said. "Don't you have a grown boy to do it for you, Janey?" Although Mr. Summers and everyone else in the village knew the answer perfectly well, it was the business of the official of the lottery to ask such questions formally. Mr. Summers waited with an expression of polite interest while Mrs. Dunbar answered.

"Horace's not but sixteen yet," Mrs. Dunbar said regretfully. "Guess I gotta fill in for the old man this year."

"Right," Mr. Summers said. He made a note on the list he was holding. Then he asked, "Watson boy drawing this year?"

A tall boy in the crowd raised his hand. "Here," he said. "I'm drawing for m'mother and me." He blinked his eyes nervously and ducked his head as several voices in the crowd said things like "Good fellow, Jack," and "Glad to see your mother's got a man to do it."

"Well," Mr. Summers said, "guess that's everyone. Old Man Warner make it?"

"Here," a voice said, and Mr. Summers nodded.

A sudden hush fell on the crowd as Mr. Summers cleared his throat and looked at the list. "All ready?" he called. "Now, I'll read the names—heads of families first—and the men come up and take a paper out of the box. Keep the paper folded in your hand without looking at it until everyone has had a turn. Everything clear?"

The people had done it so many times that they only half listened to the directions; most of them were quiet, wetting their lips, not looking around. Then Mr. Summers raised one hand high and said, "Adams." A man disengaged himself from the crowd and came forward. "Hi, Steve," Mr. Summers said, and Mr. Adams said, "Hi, Joe." They grinned at one another humorlessly and nervously. Then Mr. Adams reached into the black box and took out a folded paper. He held it firmly by one corner as he turned and went hastily back to his place in the crowd, where he stood a little apart from his family, not looking down at his hand.

"Allen," Mr. Summers said. "Anderson. . . . Bentham."

"Seems like there's no time at all between lotteries any more," Mrs.

Delacroix said to Mrs. Graves in the back row. "Seems like we got through with the last one only last week."

"Time sure goes fast," Mrs. Graves said.

"Clark. . . . Delacroix."

"There goes my old man," Mrs. Delacroix said. She held her breath while her husband went forward.

"Dunbar," Mr. Summers said, and Mrs. Dunbar went steadily to the box while one of the women said, "Go on, Janey," and another said, "There she goes."

"We're next," Mrs. Graves said. She watched while Mr. Graves came around from the side of the box, greeted Mr. Summers gravely, and selected a slip of paper from the box. By now, all through the crowd there were men holding the small folded papers in their large hands, turning them over and over nervously. Mrs. Dunbar and her two sons stood together, Mrs. Dunbar holding the slip of paper.

"Harburt. . . . Hutchinson."

"Get up there, Bill," Mrs. Hutchinson said, and the people near her laughed.

"Jones."

"They do say," Mr. Adams said to Old Man Warner, who stood next to him, "that over in the north village they're talking of giving up the lottery."

Old Man Warner snorted. "Pack of crazy fools," he said. "Listening to the young folks, nothing's good enough for *them*. Next thing you know, they'll be wanting to go back to living in caves, nobody work any more, live *that* way for a while. Used to be a saying about 'Lottery in June, corn be heavy soon.' First thing you know, we'd all be eating stewed chickweed and acorns. There's *always* been a lottery," he added petulantly. "Bad enough to see young Joe Summers up there joking with everybody."

"Some places have already quit lotteries," Mrs. Adams said.

"Nothing but trouble in *that*," Old Man Warner said stoutly. "Pack of young fools."

"Martin." And Bobby Martin watched his father go forward. "Overdyke. . . . Percy."

"I wish they'd hurry," Mrs. Dunbar said to her older son. "I wish they'd hurry."

"They're almost through," her son said.

"You get ready to run tell Dad," Mrs. Dunbar said.

Mrs. Summers called his own name and then stepped forward precisely and selected a slip from the box. Then he called, "Warner."

"Seventy-seventh year I been in the lottery," Old Man Warner said as he went through the crowd. "Seventy-seventh time."

"Watson." The tall boy came awkwardly through the crowd. Someone said, "Don't be nervous, Jack," and Mr. Summers said, "Take your time, son."

"Zanini."

After that, there was a long pause, a breathless pause, until Mr. Summers, holding his slip of paper in the air, said, "All right, fellows." For a minute, no one moved, and then all the slips of paper were opened. Suddenly, all the women began to speak at once, saying, "Who is it?," "Who's got it?," "Is it the Dunbars?," "Is it the Watsons?" Then the voices began to say, "It's Hutchinson. It's Bill," "Bill Hutchinson's got it."

"Go tell your father," Mrs. Dunbar said to her older son.

People began to look around to see the Hutchinsons. Bill Hutchinson was standing quiet, staring down at the paper in his hand. Suddenly, Tessie Hutchinson shouted to Mr. Summers, "You didn't give him time enough to take any paper he wanted. I saw you. It wasn't fair!"

"Be a good sport, Tessie," Mrs. Delacroix called, and Mrs. Graves said, "All of us took the same chance."

"Shut up, Tessie," Bill Hutchinson said

"Well, everyone," Mr. Summers said, "that was done pretty fast, and now we've got to be hurrying a little more to get done in time." He consulted his next list. "Bill," he said, "you draw for the Hutchinson family. You got any other households in the Hutchinsons?"

"There's Don and Eva," Mrs. Hutchinson yelled. "Make *them* take their chance!"

"Daughters draw with their husbands' families, Tessie," Mr. Summers said gently. "You know that as well as anyone else."

"It wasn't *fair*," Tessie said.

"I guess not, Joe," Bill Hutchinson said regretfully. "My daughter draws with her husband's family, that's only fair. And I've got no other family except the kids."

"Then, as far as drawing for families is concerned, it's you," Mr. Summers said in explanation, "and as far as drawing for households is concerned, that's you, too. Right?"

"Right," Bill Hutchinson said.

"How many kids, Bill?" Mr. Summers asked formally.

"Three," Bill Hutchinson said. "There's Bill, Jr., and Nancy, and little Dave. And Tessie and me."

"All right, then," Mr. Summers said. "Harry, you got their tickets back?"

Mr. Graves nodded and held up the slips of paper. "Put them in the box, then," Mr. Summers directed. "Take Bill's and put it in."

"I think we ought to start over," Mrs. Hutchinson said, as quietly as she could. "I tell you it wasn't *fair*. You didn't give him time enough to choose. *Every*body saw that."

Mr. Graves had selected the five slips and put them in the box, and he dropped all the papers but those onto the ground, where the breeze caught them and lifted them off.

"Listen, everybody," Mrs. Hutchinson was saying to the people around her.

"Ready, Bill?" Mr. Summers asked, and Bill Hutchinson, with one quick glance around at his wife and children, nodded.

"Remember," Mr. Summers said, "take the slips and keep them folded until each person has taken one. Harry, you help little Dave." Mr. Graves took the hand of the little boy, who came willingly with him up to the box. "Take a paper out of the box, Davy," Mr. Summers said. Davy put his hand into the box and laughed. "Take just *one* paper," Mr. Summers said. "Harry, you hold it for him." Mr. Graves took the child's hand and removed the folded paper from the tight fist and held it while little Dave stood next to him and looked up at him wonderingly.

"Nancy next," Mr. Summers said. Nancy was twelve, and her school friends breathed heavily as she went forward, switching her skirt, and took a slip daintily from the box. "Bill, Jr.," Mr. Summers said, and Billy, his face red and his feet over-large, nearly knocked the box over as he got a paper out. "Tessie," Mr. Summers said. She hesitated for a minute, looking around defiantly, and then set her lips and went up to the box. She snatched a paper out and held it behind her.

"Bill," Mr. Summers said, and Bill Hutchinson reached into the box and felt around, bringing his hand out at last with the slip of paper in it.

The crowd was quiet. A girl whispered, "I hope it's not Nancy," and the sound of the whisper reached the edges of the crowd.

"It's not the way it used to be," Old Man Warner said clearly. "People ain't the way they used to be."

"All right," Mr. Summers said. "Open the papers. Harry, you open little Dave's."

Mr. Graves opened the slip of paper and there was a general sigh through the crowd as he held it up and everyone could see that it was blank. Nancy and Bill, Jr., opened theirs at the same time, and both beamed and laughed, turning around to the crowd and holding their slips of paper above their heads.

"Tessie," Mr. Summers said. There was a pause, and then Mr. Summers looked at Bill Hutchinson, and Bill unfolded his paper and showed it. It was blank.

"It's Tessie," Mr. Summers said, and his voice was hushed. "Show us her paper, Bill."

Bill Hutchinson went over to his wife and forced the slip of paper out of her hand. It had a black spot on it, the black spot Mr. Summers had made the night before with the heavy pencil in the coal-company office. Bill Hutchinson held it up, and there was a stir in the crowd.

"All right, folks," Mr. Summers said. "Let's finish quickly."

Although the villagers had forgotten the ritual and lost the original black box, they still remembered to use stones. The pile of stones the boys had made earlier was ready; there were stones on the ground with the blowing scraps of paper that had come out of the box. Mrs. Delacroix selected a stone so large she had to pick it up with both hands and turned to Mrs. Dunbar. "Come on," she said. "Hurry up."

Mrs. Dunbar had small stones in both hands, and she said, gasping for breath, "I can't run at all. You'll have to go ahead and I'll catch up with you."

The children had stones already, and someone gave little Davy Hutchinson a few pebbles.

Tessie Hutchinson was in the center of a cleared space by now, and she held her hands out desperately as the villagers moved in on her. "It isn't fair," she said. A stone hit her on the side of the head.

Old Man Warner was saying, "Come on, come on, everyone." Steve Adams was in the front of the crowd of villagers, with Mrs. Graves beside him.

"It isn't fair, it isn't right," Mrs. Hutchinson screamed, and then they were upon her.

the
jewbird
bernard malamud

Bernard Malamud (1914–   ) was born in Brooklyn and attended both the College of the City of New York and Columbia University. He has taught in New York City high schools and at Oregon State University. Currently he lives with his wife and children in Vermont. For further reading: The Magic Barrel *(1958);* Idiots First *(1964).*

The window was open so the skinny bird flew in. Flappity-flap with its frazzled black wings. That's how it goes. It's open, you're in. Closed, you're out and that's your fate. The bird wearily flapped through the open kitchen window by Harry Cohen's top-floor apartment on First Avenue near the lower East River. On a rod on the wall hung an escaped canary cage, its door wide open, but this black-type longbeaked bird—its ruffled head and small dull eyes, crossed a little, making it look like a dissipated crow—landed if not smack on Cohen's thick lamb chop, at least on the table, close by. The frozen foods salesman was sitting at supper with his wife and young son on a hot August evening a year go. Cohen, a heavy man with hairy chest and beefy shorts; Edie, in skinny yellow shorts and red halter; and their ten-year-old Morris (after her father)—Maurie, they called him, a nice kid though not overly bright—were all in the city after two weeks out, because Cohen's mother was dying. They had been enjoying Kingston, New York, but drove back when Mama got sick in her flat in the Bronx.

"Right on the table," said Cohen, putting down his beer glass and swatting at the bird. "Son of a bitch."

"Harry, take care with your language," Edie said, looking at Maurie, who watched every move.

The bird cawed hoarsely and with a flap of its bedraggled wings—feathers tufted this way and that—rose heavily to the top of the open kitchen door, where it perched staring down.

"Gevalt, a pogrom!"

"It's a talking bird," said Edie in astonishment.

"In Jewish," said Maurie.

"Wise guy," muttered Cohen. He gnawed on his chop, then put down the bone. "So if you can talk, say what's your business. What do you want here?"

"If you can't spare a lamb chop," said the bird, "I'll settle for a piece of herring with a crust of bread. You can't live on your nerve forever."

"This ain't a restaurant," Cohen replied. "All I'm asking is what brings you to this address?"

"The window was open," the bird sighed; adding after a moment, "I'm running. I'm flying but I'm also running."

"From whom?" asked Edie with interest.

"Anti-Semeets."

"Anti-Semites?" they all said.

"That's from who."

"What kind of anti-Semites bother a bird?" Edie asked.

"Any kind," said the bird, "also including eagles, vultures, and hawks. And once in a while some crows will take your eyes out."

"But aren't you a crow?"

"Me? I'm a Jewbird."

Cohen laughed heartily. "What do you mean by that?"

The bird began dovening. He prayed without Book or tallith, but with

passion. Edie bowed her head though not Cohen. And Maurie rocked
back and forth with the prayer, looking up with one wide-open eye.

When the prayer was done Cohen remarked, "No hat, no phylacteries?"

"I'm an old radical."

"You're sure you're not some kind of a ghost or dybbuk?"

"Not a dybbuk," answered the bird, "though one of my relatives had
such an experience once. It's all over now, thanks God. They freed her
from a former lover, a crazy jealous man. She's now the mother of two
wonderful children."

"Birds?" Cohen asked slyly.

"Why not?"

"What kind of birds?"

"Like me. Jewbirds."

Cohen tipped back in his chair and guffawed. "That's a big laugh.
I've heard of a Jewfish but not a Jewbird."

"We're once removed." The bird rested on one skinny leg, then on the
other. "Please, could you spare maybe a piece of herring with a small
crust of bread?"

Edie got up from the table.

"What are you doing?" Cohen asked her.

"I'll clear the dishes."

Cohen turned to the bird. "So what's your name, if you don't mind
saying?"

"Call me Schwartz."

"He might be an old Jew changed into a bird by somebody," said
Edie, removing a plate.

"Are you?" asked Harry, lighting a cigar.

"Who knows?" answered Schwartz. "Does God tell us everything?"

Maurie got up on his chair. "What kind of herring?" he asked the
bird in excitement.

"Get down, Maurie, or you'll fall," ordered Cohen.

"If you haven't got matjes, I'll take schmaltz," said Schwartz.

"All we have is marinated, with slices of onion—in a jar," said Edie.

"If you'll open for me the jar I'll eat marinated. Do you have also, if
you don't mind, a piece of rye bread—the spitz?"

Edie thought she had.

"Feed him out on the balcony," Cohen said. He spoke to the bird.
"After that take off."

Schwartz closed both bird eyes. "I'm tired and it's a long way."

"Which direction are you headed, north or south?"

Schwartz, barely lifting his wings, shrugged.

"You don't know where you're going?"

"Where there's charity I'll go."

"Let him stay, papa," said Maurie. "He's only a bird."

"So stay the night," Cohen said, "but no longer."

In the morning Cohen ordered the bird out of the house but Maurie cried, so Schwartz stayed for a while. Maurie was still on vacation from school and his friends were away. He was lonely and Edie enjoyed the fun he had, playing with the bird.

"He's no trouble at all," she told Cohen, "and besides his appetite is very small."

"What'll you do when he makes dirty?"

"He flies across the street in a tree when he makes dirty, and if nobody passes below, who notices?"

"So all right," said Cohen, "but I'm dead set against it. I warn you he ain't gonna stay here long."

"What have you got against the poor bird?"

"Poor bird, my ass. He's a foxy bastard. He thinks he's a Jew."

"What difference does it make what he thinks?"

"A Jewbird, what a chuzpah. One false move and he's out on his drumsticks."

At Cohen's insistence Schwartz lived out on the balcony in a new wooden birdhouse Edie had bought him.

"With many thanks," said Schwartz, "though I would rather have a human roof over my head. You know how it is at my age. I like the warm, the windows, the smell of cooking. I would also be glad to see once in a while the *Jewish Morning Journal* and have now and then a schnapps because it helps my breathing, thanks God. But whatever you give me, you won't hear complaints."

However, when Cohen brought home a bird feeder full of dried corn, Schwartz said, "Impossible."

Cohen was annoyed. "What's the matter, crosseyes, is your life getting too good for you? Are you forgetting what it means to be migratory? I'll bet a helluva lot of crows you happen to be acquainted with, Jews or otherwise, would give their eyeteeth to eat this corn."

Schwartz did not answer. What can you say to a grubber yung?

"Not for my digestion," he later explained to Edie. "Cramps. Herring is better even if it makes you thirsty. At least rainwater don't cost anything." He laughed sadly in breathy caws.

And herring, thanks to Edie, who knew where to shop, was what Schwartz got, with an occasional piece of potato pancake, and even a bit of soupmeat when Cohen wasn't looking.

When school began in September, before Cohen would once again suggest giving the bird the boot, Edie prevailed on him to wait a little while until Maurie adjusted.

"To deprive him right now might hurt his school work, and you know what trouble we had last year."

"So okay, but sooner or later the bird goes. That I promise you."

Schwartz, though nobody had asked him, took on full responsibility for Maurie's performance in school. In return for favors granted, when he was let in for an hour or two at night, he spent most of his time overseeing the boy's lessons. He sat on top of the dresser near Maurie's desk as he laboriously wrote out his homework. Maurie was a restless type and Schwartz gently kept him to his studies. He also listened to him practice his screechy violin, taking a few minutes off now and then to rest his ears in the bathroom. And they afterwards played dominoes. The boy was an indifferent checker player and it was impossible to teach him chess. When he was sick, Schwartz read him comic books though he personally disliked them. But Maurie's work improved in school and even his violin teacher admitted his playing was better. Edie gave Schwartz credit for these improvements though the bird pooh-poohed them.

Yet he was proud there was nothing lower than C minuses on Maurie's report card, and on Edie's insistence celebrated with a little schnapps.

"If he keeps up like this," Cohen said, "I'll get him in an Ivy League college for sure."

"Oh I hope so," sighed Edie.

But Schwartz shook his head. "He's a good boy—you don't have to worry. He won't be a shicker or a wifebeater, God forbid, but a scholar he'll never be, if you know what I mean, although maybe a good mechanic. It's no disgrace in these times."

"If I were you," Cohen said, angered, "I'd keep my big snoot out of other people's private business."

"Harry, please," said Edie.

"My goddamn patience is wearing out. That crosseyes butts into everything."

Though he wasn't exactly a welcome guest in the house, Schwartz gained a few ounces although he did not improve in appearance. He looked bedraggled as ever, his feathers unkempt, as though he had just flown out of a snowstorm. He spent, he admitted, little time taking care of himself. Too much to think about. "Also outside plumbing," he told Edie. Still there was more glow to his eyes so that though Cohen went on calling him crosseyes he said it less emphatically.

Liking his situation, Schwartz tried tactfully to stay out of Cohen's way, but one night when Edie was at the movies and Maurie was taking a hot shower, the frozen foods salesman began a quarrel with the bird.

"For Christ sake, why don't you wash yourself sometimes? Why must you always stink like a dead fish?"

"Mr. Cohen, if you'll pardon me, if somebody eats garlic he will smell from garlic. I eat herring three times a day. Feed me flowers and I will smell like flowers."

"Who's obligated to feed you anything at all? You're lucky to get herring."

"Excuse me, I'm not complaining," said the bird. "You're complaining."

"What's more," said Cohen, "even from out on the balcony I can hear you snoring away like a pig. It keeps me awake at night."

"Snoring," said Schwartz, "isn't a crime, thanks God."

"All in all you are a goddamn pest and free loader. Next thing you'll want to sleep in bed next to my wife."

"Mr. Cohen," said Schwartz, "on this rest assured. A bird is a bird."

"So you say, but how do I know you're a bird and not some kind of a goddamn devil?"

"If I was a devil you would know already. And I don't mean because your son's good marks."

"Shut up, you bastard bird," shouted Cohen.

"Grubber yung," cawed Schwartz, rising to the tips of his talons, his long wings outstretched.

Cohen was about to lunge for the bird's scrawny neck but Maurie came out of the bathroom, and for the rest of the evening until Schwartz's bedtime on the balcony, there was pretended peace.

But the quarrel had deeply disturbed Schwartz and he slept badly. His snoring woke him, and awake, he was fearful of what would become of him. Wanting to stay out of Cohen's way, he kept to the birdhouse as much as possible. Cramped by it, he paced back and forth on the balcony ledge, or sat on the birdhouse roof, staring into space. In the evenings, while overseeing Maurie's lessons, he often fell asleep. Awakening, he nervously hopped around exploring the four corners of the room. He spent much time in Maurie's closet, and carefully examined his bureau drawers when they were left open. And once when he found a large paper bag on the floor, Schwartz poked his way into it to investigate what possibilities were. The boy was amused to see the bird in the paper bag.

"He wants to build a nest," he said to his mother.

Edie, sensing Schwartz's unhappiness, spoke to him quietly.

"Maybe if you did some of the things my husband wants you, you would get along better with him."

"Give me a for instance," Schwartz said.

"Like take a bath, for instance."

"I'm too old for baths," said the bird. "My feathers fall out without baths."

"He says you have a bad smell."

"Everybody smells. Some people smell because of their thoughts or because who they are. My bad smell comes from the food I eat. What does his come from?"

"I better not ask him or it might make him mad," said Edie.

In late November Schwartz froze on the balcony in the fog and cold, and especially on rainy days he woke with stiff joints and could barely move his wings. Already he felt twinges of rheumatism. He would have liked to spend more time in the warm house, particularly when Maurie was in school and Cohen at work. But though Edie was good-hearted and might have sneaked him in in the morning, just to thaw out, he was afraid to ask her. In the meantime Cohen, who had been reading articles about the migration of birds, came out on the balcony one night after work when Edie was in the kitchen preparing pot roast, and peeking into the birdhouse, warned Schwartz to be on his way soon if he knew what was good for him. "Time to hit the flyways."

"Mr. Cohen, why do you hate me so much?" asked the bird. "What did I do to you?"

"Because you're an A-number-one trouble maker, that's why. What's more, whoever heard of a Jewbird? Now scat or it's open war."

But Schwartz stubbornly refused to depart so Cohen embarked on a campaign of harassing him, meanwhile hiding it from Edie and Maurie. Maurie hated violence and Cohen didn't want to leave a bad impression. He thought maybe if he played dirty tricks on the bird he would fly off without being physically kicked out. The vacation was over, let him make his easy living off the fat of somebody else's land. Cohen worried about the effect of the bird's departure on Maurie's schooling but decided to take the chance, first, because the boy now seemed to have the knack of studying—give the black bird-bastard credit—and second, because Schwartz was driving him bats by being there always, even in his dreams.

The frozen foods salesman began his campaign against the bird by mixing watery cat food with the herring slices in Schwartz's dish. He also blew up and popped numerous paper bags outside the birdhouse as the bird slept, and when he had got Schwartz good and nervous, though not enough to leave, he brought a full-grown cat into the house, supposedly a gift for little Maurie, who had always wanted a pussy. The cat never stopped springing up at Schwartz whenever he saw him, one day managing to claw out several of his tailfeathers. And even at lesson time, when the cat was usually excluded from Maurie's room, though somehow or other he quickly found his way in at the end of the lesson, Schwartz was desperately fearful of his life and flew from pinnacle to pinnacle—light fixture to clothestree to door-top—in order to elude the beast's wet jaws.

Once when the bird complained to Edie how hazardous his existence was, she said, "Be patient, Mr. Schwartz. When the cat gets to know you better he won't try to catch you any more."

"When he stops trying we will both be in Paradise," Schwartz answered. "Do me a favor and get rid of him. He makes my whole life worry. I'm losing feathers like a tree loses leaves."

"I'm awfully sorry but Maurie likes the pussy and sleeps with it."

What could Schwartz do? He worried but came to no decision, being afraid to leave. So he ate the herring garnished with cat food, tried hard not to hear the paper bags bursting like fire crackers outside the birdhouse at night, and lived terror-stricken closer to the ceiling than the floor, as the cat, his tail flicking, endlessly watched him.

Weeks went by. Then on the day after Cohen's mother had died in her flat in the Bronx, when Maurie came home with a zero on an arithmetic test, Cohen, enraged, waited until Edie had taken the boy to his violin lesson, then openly attacked the bird. He chased him with a broom on the balcony and Schwartz frantically flew back and forth, finally escaping into his birdhouse. Cohen triumphantly reached in and grabbing both skinny legs, dragged the bird out, cawing loudly, his wings wildly beating. He whirled the bird around and around his head. But Schwartz, as he moved in circles, managed to swoop down and catch Cohen's nose in his beak, and hung on for dear life. Cohen cried out in great pain, punched the bird with his fist, and tugging at its legs with all his might, pulled his nose free. Again he swung the yawking Schwartz around until the bird grew dizzy, then with a furious heave, flung him into the night. Schwartz sank like stone into the street. Cohen then tossed the birdhouse and feeder after him, listening at the ledge until they crashed on the sidewalk below. For a full hour, broom in hand, his heart palpitating and nose throbbing with pain, Cohen waited for Schwartz to return but the broken-hearted bird didn't.

That's the end of that dirty bastard, the salesman thought and went in. Edie and Maurie had come home.

"Look," said Cohen, pointing to his bloody nose swollen three times its normal size, "what that sonofabitchy bird did. It's a permanent scar."

"Where is he now?" Edie asked, frightened.

"I threw him out and he flew away. Good riddance."

Nobody said no, though Edie touched a handkerchief to her eyes and Maurie rapidly tried the nine times table and found he knew approximately half.

In the spring when the winter's snow had melted, the boy, moved by a memory, wandered in the neighborhood, looking for Schwartz. He found a dead black bird in a small lot near the river, his two wings broken, neck twisted, and both bird-eyes plucked clean.

"Who did it to you, Mr. Schwartz?" Maurie wept.

"Anti-Semeets," Edie said later.

the life
you save may
be your own
flannery o'connor

Flannery O'Connor (1925–1964) was born and raised in Georgia, where she spent most of her adult life. Her first novel, Wise Blood *(1952), received wide critical acclaim, although it was her short stories that established her reputation as a writer. Flannery O'Connor's early death brought to an end one of the strongest talents in modern Southern fiction. For further reading:* A Good Man Is Hard to Find *(1955).*

The old woman and her daughter were sitting on their porch when Mr. Shiftlet came up their road for the first time. The old woman slid to the edge of her chair and leaned forward, shading her eyes from the piercing sunset with her hand. The daughter could not see far in front of her and continued to play with her fingers. Although the old woman lived in this desolate spot with only her daughter and she had never seen Mr. Shiftlet before, she could tell, even from a distance, that he was a tramp and no one to be afraid of. His left coat sleeve was folded up to show there was only half an arm in it and his gaunt figure listed slightly to the side as if the breeze were pushing him. He had on a black town suit and a brown felt hat that was turned up in the front and down in the back and he carried a tin tool box by a handle. He came on, at an amble, up her road, his face turned toward the sun which appeared to be balancing itself on the peak of a small mountain.

The old woman didn't change her position until he was almost into her yard; then she rose with one hand fisted on her hip. The daughter, a large girl in a short blue organdy dress, saw him all at once and jumped up and began to stamp and point and make excited speechless sounds.

Mr. Shiftlet stopped just inside the yard and set his box on the ground and tipped his hat at her as if she were not in the least afflicted; then he turned toward the old woman and swung the hat all the way off. He had long black slick hair that hung flat from a part in the middle to beyond the tips of his ears on either side. His face descended in forehead for more than half its length and ended suddenly with his features just balanced over a jutting steel-trap jaw. He seemed to be a young man but he had a look of composed dissatisfaction as if he understood life thoroughly.

"Good evening," the old woman said. She was about the size of a cedar fence post and she had a man's gray hat pulled down low over her head.

The tramp stood looking at her and didn't answer. He turned his back and faced the sunset. He swung both his whole and his short arm up slowly so that they indicated an expanse of sky and his figure formed a crooked cross. The old woman watched him with her arms folded across her chest as if she were the owner of the sun, and the daughter watched, her head thrust forward and her fat helpless hands hanging at the wrists. She had long pink-gold hair and eyes as blue as a peacock's neck.

He held the pose for almost fifty seconds and then he picked up his box and came on to the porch and dropped down on the bottom step. "Lady," he said in a firm nasal voice, "I'd give a fortune to live where I could see me a sun do that every evening."

"Does it every evening," the old woman said and sat back down. The daughter sat down too and watched him with a cautious sly look as if he were a bird that had come up very close. He leaned to one side, rooting in his pants pocket, and in a second he brought out a package of chewing gum and offered her a piece. She took it and unpeeled it and began to chew without taking her eyes off him. He offered the old woman a piece but she only raised her upper lip to indicate she had no teeth.

Mr. Shiftlet's pale sharp glance had already passed over everything in the yard—the pump near the corner of the house and the big fig tree that three or four chickens were preparing to roost in—and had moved to a shed where he saw the square rusted back of an automobile. "You ladies drive?" he asked.

"That car ain't run in fifteen year," the old woman said. "The day my husband died, it quit running."

"Nothing is like it used to be, lady," he said. "The world is almost rotten."

"That's right," the old woman said. "You from around here?"

"Name Tom T. Shiftlet," he murmured, looking at the tires.

"I'm pleased to meet you," the old woman said. "Name Lucynell Crater and daughter Lucynell Crater. What you doing around here, Mr. Shiftlet?"

He judged the car to be about a 1928 or '29 Ford. "Lady," he said, and turned and gave her his full attention, "lemme tell you something. There's one of these doctors in Atlanta that's taken a knife and cut the human heart—the human heart," he repeated, leaning forward, "out of a man's chest and held it in his hand," and he held his hand out, palm up, as if it were slightly weighted with the human heart, "and studied it like it was a day-old chicken, and, lady," he said, allowing a long significant pause in which his head slid forward and his clay-colored eyes brightened, "he don't know no more about it than you or me."

"That's right," the old woman said.

"Why, if he was to take that knife and cut into every corner of it, he still wouldn't know no more than you or me. What you want to bet?"

"Nothing," the old woman said wisely. "Where you come from, Mr. Shiftlet?"

He didn't answer. He reached into his pocket and brought out a sack of tobacco and a package of cigarette papers and rolled himself a cigarette, expertly with one hand, and attached it in a hanging position to his upper lip. Then he took a box of wooden matches from his pocket and struck one on his shoe. He held the burning match as if he were studying the mystery of flame while it traveled dangerously toward his skin. The daughter began to make loud noises and to point to his hand and shake her finger at him, but when the flame was just before touching him, he leaned down with his hand cupped over it as if he were going to set fire to his nose and lit the cigarette.

He flipped away the dead match and blew a stream of gray into the evening. A sly look came over his face. "Lady," he said, "nowadays, people'll do anything anyways. I can tell you my name is Tom T. Shiftlet and I come from Tarwater, Tennessee, but you never have seen me before: how you know I ain't lying? How you know my name ain't Aaron Sparks, lady, and I come from Singleberry, Georgia, or how you know it's not George Speeds and I come from Lucy, Alabama, or how you know I ain't Thompson Bright from Toolafalls, Mississippi?"

"I don't know nothing about you," the old woman muttered, irked.

"Lady," he said, "people don't care how they lie. Maybe the best I can tell you is, I'm a man; but listen, lady," he said and paused and made his tone more ominous still, "what is a man?"

The old woman began to gum a seed. "What you carry in that tin box, Mr. Shiftlet?" she asked.

"Tools," he said, put back. "I'm a carpenter."

"Well, if you come out here to work, I'll be able to feed you and give you a place to sleep but I can't pay. I'll tell you that before you begin," she said.

There was no answer at once and no particular expression on his face. He leaned back against the two-by-four that helped support the porch roof. "Lady," he said slowly, "there's some men that some things mean more to them than money." The old woman rocked without comment and the daughter watched the trigger that moved up and down in his neck. He told the old woman then that all most people were interested in was money, but he asked what a man was made for. He asked her if a man was made for money, or what. He asked her what she thought she was made for but she didn't answer, she only sat rocking and wondered if a one-armed man could put a new roof on her garden house. He asked a lot of questions that she didn't answer. He told her that he was twenty-eight years old and had lived a varied life. He had been a gospel singer, a foreman on the railroad, an assistant in an undertaking parlor, and he had come over the radio for three months with Uncle Roy and his Red Creek Wranglers. He said he had fought and bled in the Arm Service of his country and visited every foreign land and that everywhere he had seen people that didn't care if they did a thing one way or another. He said he hadn't been raised thataway.

A fat yellow moon appeared in the branches of the fig tree as if it were going to roost there with the chickens. He said that a man had to escape to the country to see the world whole and that he wished he lived in a desolate place like this where he could see the sun go down every evening like God make it to do.

"Are you married or are you single?" the old woman asked.

There was a long silence. "Lady," he asked finally, "where would you find an innocent woman today? I wouldn't have any of this trash I could just pick up."

The daughter was leaning very far down, hanging her head almost between her knees, watching him through a triangular door she had made in her overturned hair; and she suddenly fell in a heap on the floor and began to whimper. Mr. Shiftlet straightened her out and helped her get back in the chair.

"Is she your baby girl?" he asked.

"My only," the old woman said, "and she's the sweetest girl in the world. I wouldn't give her up for nothing on earth. She's smart too. She can sweep the floor, cook, wash, feed the chickens, and hoe. I wouldn't give her up for a casket of jewels."

"No," he said kindly, "don't ever let any man take her away from you."

"Any man come after her," the old woman said, " 'll have to stay around the place."

Mr. Shiftlet's eye in the darkness was focused on a part of the automobile bumper that glittered in the distance. "Lady," he said, jerking his short arm up as if he could point with it to her house and yard and pump, "there ain't a broken thing on this plantation that I couldn't fix for you, one-arm jackleg or not. I'm a man," he said with a sullen dignity, "even if I ain't a whole one. I got," he said, tapping his knuckles on the floor to emphasize the immensity of what he was going to say, "a moral intelligence!" and his face pierced out of the darkness into a shaft of doorlight and he stared at her as if he were astonished himself at this impossible truth.

The old woman was not impressed with the phrase. "I told you you could hang around and work for food," she said, "if you don't mind sleeping in that car yonder."

"Why listen, Lady," he said with a grin of delight, "the monks of old slept in their coffins!"

"They wasn't as advanced as we are," the old woman said.

The next morning he began on the roof of the garden house while Lucynell, the daughter, sat on a rock and watched him work. He had not been around a week before the change he had made in the place was apparent. He had patched the front and back steps, built a new hog pen, restored a fence, and taught Lucynell, who was completely deaf and had never said a word in her life, to say the word "bird." The big rosy-faced girl followed him everywhere, saying "Burrttddt ddbirrrttdt," and clapping her hands. The old woman watched from a distance, secretly pleased. She was ravenous for a son-in-law.

Mr. Shiftlet slept on the hard narrow back seat of the car with his feet out the side window. He had his razor and a can of water on a crate that served him as a bedside table and he put up a piece of mirror against the back glass and kept his coat neatly on a hanger that he hung over one of the windows.

In the evenings he sat on the steps and talked while the old woman and Lucynell rocked violently in their chairs on either side of him. The old woman's three mountains were black against the dark blue sky and were visited off and on by various planets and by the moon after it had left the chickens. Mr. Shiftlet pointed out that the reason he had improved this plantation was because he had taken a personal interest in it. He said he was even going to make the automobile run.

He had raised the hood and studied the mechanism and he said he could tell that the car had been built in the days when cars were really built. You take now, he said, one man puts in one bolt and another man puts in another bolt and another man puts in another bolt so that it's a man for a bolt. That's why you have to pay so much for a car: you're paying all those men. Now if you didn't have to pay but one man, you could get you a cheaper car and one that had had a personal interest taken in it, and it would be a better car. The old woman agreed with him that this was so.

Mr. Shiftlet said that the trouble with the world was that nobody cared, or stopped and took any trouble. He said he never would have been able to teach Lucynell to say a word if he hadn't cared and stopped long enough.

"Teach her to say something else," the old woman said.

"What you want her to say next?" Mr. Shiftlet asked.

The old woman's smile was broad and toothless and suggestive. "Teach her to say, 'sugarpie,'" she said.

Mr. Shiftlet already knew what was on her mind.

The next day he began to tinker with the automobile and that evening he told her that if she would buy a fan belt, he would be able to make the car run.

The old woman said she would give him the money. "You see that girl yonder?" she asked, pointing to Lucynell who was sitting on the floor a foot away, watching him, her eyes blue even in the dark. "If it was ever a man wanted to take her away, I would say, 'No man on earth is going to take that sweet girl of mine away from me!' but if he was to say, 'Lady, I don't want to take her away, I want her right here,' I would say, 'Mister, I don't blame you none. I wouldn't pass up a chance to live in a permanent place and get the sweetest girl in the world myself. You ain't no fool,' I would say."

"How old is she?" Mr. Shiftlet asked casually.

"Fifteen, sixteen," the old woman said. The girl was nearly thirty but because of her innocence it was impossible to guess.

"It would be a good idea to paint it too," Mr. Shiftlet remarked. "You don't want it to rust out."

"We'll see about that later," the old woman said.

The next day he walked into town and returned with the parts he needed, and a can of gasoline. Late in the afternoon, terrible noises issued from the shed and the old woman rushed out of the house, thinking Lucynell was somewhere having a fit. Lucynell was sitting on a chicken crate, stamping her feet and screaming, "Burrddttt! bddurrddtttt!" but her fuss was drowned out by the car. With a volley of blasts it emerged from the shed, moving in a fierce and stately way. Mr. Shiftlet was in the driver's seat, sitting very erect. He had an expression of serious modesty on his face as if he had just raised the dead.

That night, rocking on the porch, the old woman began her business at once. "You want you an innocent woman, don't you?" she asked sympathetically. "You don't want none of this trash."

"No'm, I don't," Mr. Shiftlet said.

"One that can't talk," she continued, "can't sass you back or use foul language. That's the kind for you to have. Right there," and she pointed to Lucynell sitting cross-legged in her chair, holding both feet in her hands.

"That's right," he admitted. "She wouldn't give me any trouble."

"Saturday," the old woman said, "you and her and me can drive into town and get married."

Mr. Shiftlet eased his position on the steps.

"I can't get married right now," he said. "Everything you want to do takes money and I ain't got any."

"What you need with money?" she asked.

"It takes money," he said. "Some people'll do anything anyhow these days, but the way I think, I wouldn't marry no woman that I couldn't take on a trip like she was somebody. I mean take her to a hotel and treat her. I wouldn't marry the Duchesser Windsor," he said firmly, "unless I could take her to a hotel and give her something good to eat.

"I was raised thataway and there ain't a thing I can do about it. My old mother taught me how to do."

"Lucynell don't even know what a hotel is," the old woman muttered. "Listen here, Mr. Shiftlet," she said, sliding forward in her chair, "you'd be getting a permanent house and a deep well and the most innocent girl in the world. You don't need no money. Lemme tell you something: there ain't any place in the world for a poor disabled friendless drifting man."

The ugly words settled in Mr. Shiftlet's head like a group of buzzards in the top of a tree. He didn't answer at once. He rolled himself a cigarette and lit it and then he said in an even voice, "Lady, a man is divided into parts, body and spirit."

The old woman clamped her gums together.

"A body and a spirit," he repeated. "The body, lady, is like a house: it don't go anywhere; but the spirit, lady, is like a automobile: always on the move, always . . ."

"Listen, Mr. Shiftlet," she said, "my well never goes dry and my house is always warm in the winter and there's no mortgage on a thing about this place. You can go to the courthouse and see for yourself. And yonder under that shed is a fine automobile." She laid the bait carefully. "You can have it painted by Saturday. I'll pay for the paint."

In the darkness, Mr. Shiftlet's smile stretched like a weary snake waking up by a fire. "Yes'm," he said softly.

After a second he recalled himself and said, "I'm only saying a man's spirit means more to him than anything else. I would have to take my wife off for the weekend without no regards at all for cost. I got to follow where my spirit says to go."

"I'll give you fifteen dollars for a weekend trip," the old woman said in a crabbed voice. "That's the best I can do."

"That wouldn't hardly pay for more than the gas and the hotel," he said. "It wouldn't feed her."

"Seventeen-fifty," the old woman said. "That's all I got so it isn't any use you trying to milk me. You can take a lunch."

Mr. Shiftlet was deeply hurt by the word "milk." He didn't doubt that she had more money sewed up in her mattress but he had already told her he was not interested in her money. "I'll make that do," he said, and rose and walked off without treating with her further.

On Saturday the three of them drove into town in the car that the paint had barely dried on and Mr. Shiftlet and Lucynell were married in the Ordinary's office while the old woman witnessed. As they came out of the courthouse, Mr. Shiftlet began twisting his neck in his collar. He looked morose and bitter as if he had been insulted while someone held him. "That didn't satisfy me none," he said. "That was just something a woman in an office did, nothing but paper work and blood tests. What do they know about my blood? If they was to take my heart and cut it out," he said, "they wouldn't know a thing about me. It didn't satisfy me at all."

"It satisfied the law," the old woman said sharply.

"The law," Mr. Shiftlet said, and spit. "It's the law that don't satisfy me."

He had painted the car dark green with a yellow band around it just under the windows. The three of them climbed in the front seat and the old woman said, "Don't Lucynell look pretty? Looks like a baby doll." Lucynell was dressed up in a white dress that her mother had uprooted from a trunk and there was a Panama hat on her head with a bunch of red wooden cherries on the brim. Every now and then her placid expression was changed by a sly isolated little thought like a shoot of green in the desert. "You got a prize!" the old woman said.

Mr. Shiftlet didn't even look at her.

They drove back to the house to let the old woman off and pick up the lunch. When they were ready to leave, she stood staring in the window of the car, with her fingers clenched around the glass. Tears began to seep sideways out of her eyes and run along the dirty creases in her face. "I ain't ever been parted with her for two days before," she said.

Mr. Shiftlet started the motor.

"And I wouldn't let no man have her but you because I seen you would do right. Goodbye, Sugarbaby," she said, clutching at the sleeve of the white dress. Lucynell looked straight at her and didn't seem to see her there at all. Mr. Shiftlet eased the car forward so that she had to move her hands.

The early afternoon was clear and open and surrounded by pale blue sky. The hills flattened under the car one after another and the climb and dip and swerve went entirely to Mr. Shiftlet's head so that he forgot his morning bitterness. He had always wanted an automobile but he had never been able to afford one before. He drove very fast because he wanted to make Mobile by nightfall.

Occasionally he stopped his thoughts long enough to look at Lucynell in the seat beside him. She had eaten the lunch as soon as they were out of the yard and now she was pulling the cherries off the hat one by one and throwing them out the window. He became depressed in spite of the car. He had driven about a hundred miles when he decided that she must be hungry again and at the next small town they came to, he stopped in front of an aluminum-painted eating place called The Hot Spot and took her in and ordered her a plate of ham and grits. The ride had made her sleepy and as soon as she got up on the stool, she rested her head on the counter and shut her eyes. There was no one in The Hot Spot but Mr. Shiftlet and the boy behind the counter, a pale youth with a greasy rag hung over his shoulder. Before he could dish up the food, she was snoring gently.

"Give it to her when she wakes up," Mr. Shiftlet said. "I'll pay for it now."

The boy bent over her and stared at the long pink-gold hair and the half-shut sleeping eyes. Then he looked up and stared at Mr. Shiftlet. "She looks like an angel of Gawd," he murmured.

"Hitch-hiker," Mr. Shiftlet explained. "I can't wait. I got to make Tuscaloosa."

The boy bent over again and very carefully touched his fingers to a strand of the golden hair and Mr. Shiftlet left.

He was more depressed than ever as he drove on by himself. The late afternoon had grown hot and sultry and the country had flattened out. Deep in the sky a storm was preparing very slowly and without thunder as if it meant to drain every drop of air from the earth before it broke. There were times when Mr. Shiftlet preferred not to be alone. He felt too that a man with a car had a responsibility to others and he kept his eye out for a hitch-hiker. Occasionally he saw a sign that warned: "Drive carefully. The life you save may be your own."

The narrow road dropped off on either side into dry fields and here and there a shack or a filling station station stood in a clearing. The sun began to set directly in front of the automobile. It was a reddening ball that through his windshield was slightly flat on the bottom and top. He saw a boy in overalls and a gray hat standing on the edge of the road and he slowed the car down and stopped in front of him. The boy didn't have his hand raised to thumb the ride, he was only standing there, but he had a small cardboard suitcase and his hat was set on his head in a way to indicate that he had left somewhere for good. "Son," Mr. Shiftlet said, "I see you want a ride."

The boy didn't say he did or he didn't but he opened the door of the car and got in, and Mr. Shiftlet started driving again. The child held the suitcase on his lap and folded his arms on top of it. He turned his head and looked out the window away from Mr. Shiftlet. Mr. Shiftlet felt oppressed. "Son," he said after a minute, "I got the best old mother in the world so I reckon you only got the second best."

The boy gave him a quick dark glance and then turned his face back out the window.

"It's nothing so sweet," Mr. Shiftlet continued, "as a boy's mother. She taught him his first prayers at her knee, she give him love when no other would, she told him what was right and what wasn't, and she seen that he done the right thing. Son," he said, "I never rued a day in my life like the one I rued when I left that old mother of mine."

The boy shifted in his seat but he didn't look at Mr. Shiftlet. He unfolded his arms and put one hand on the door handle.

"My mother was a angel of Gawd," Mr. Shiftlett said in a very strained voice. "He took her from heaven and giver to me and I left her." His eyes were instantly clouded over with a mist of tears. The car was barely moving.

The boy turned angrily in the seat. "You go to the devil!" he cried. "My old woman is a flea bag and yours is a stinking pole cat!" and with that he flung the door open and jumped out with his suitcase into the ditch.

Mr. Shiftlet was so shocked that for about a hundred feet he drove along slowly with the door still open. A cloud, the exact color of the boy's hat and shaped like a turnip, had descended over the sun, and another, worse looking, crouched behind the car. Mr. Shiftlet felt that the rottenness of the world was about to engulf him. He raised his arm and let it fall again to his breast. "Oh, Lord!" he prayed. "Break forth and wash the slime from this earth!"

the
brigadier
isaac rosenfeld

*Isaac Rosenfeld (1918–1956) died young
and thus cut short a promising literary career.
Although he left a relatively small body of work
in the short story, the quality of
his vision and his themes show that
Rosenfeld was distinctly a man of his
times. For further reading:* Passage
From Home *(1961);* An Age
of Enormity *. . . (1962).*

We have been fighting the enemy a very long time. So long that I, who entered the war a foot soldier, have had time to receive more than the usual number of decorations and promotions and to become a brigadier, attached to staff headquarters. I forget how many times I have been wounded and the names of all the battles and campaigns in which I have participated. The greater number of them, however, are not to be forgotten: Striplitz, Bougaumères, Trèle, Bzelokhorets, Kovinitsa, Laud Ingaume, El Khabhar, Woozi-Fassam, and so on. I am the oldest man in our field office, though not in the brigade itself. Lately, the newcomers have not been rising from the ranks, but from the Academy. They are young men who have not proved themselves in any way; some have not even fought.

I am settled into my work, which for many years, I am pleased to say, has been of an absorbing nature. It is difficult to recall the time when I fretted with impatience to return to what I considered my natural life as a citizen. I am happy that I am no longer impatient. I have developed, instead, a great eagerness—an eagerness, however, which is thoroughly disciplined and in every way related to our military enterprise. I do not hesitate to call our enterprise the most glorious and far-reaching that has ever been undertaken.

Far-reaching is not quite the word—though it is only in an unofficial capacity that I admit as much. Let me say that it is not the word for me to use. As a matter, simply, of objective fact, what we are engaged in is, of course, that—I mean far-reaching—and much else besides. But for myself it is not enough, and the work I do must be otherwise defined. I have been studying the ends of our warfare while pursuing them; I have tried to make them a part of myself. I should not want it to be said that the Objective is one thing, and the brigadier's effort in its behalf is quite another, not related to it as the word one and the number one are related. My work is the war itself.

The office in which I do my work was once a schoolhouse; it stands in what used to be enemy country. A section of blackboard, cracked down the middle, is still affixed to the wall near my desk and on it you can read a lesson in the enemy's language, written by one of his children; when the chalk began to fade, I had it carefully restored and covered with a coat of shellac. I can read the enemy's hand—which is sometimes difficult even for scholars, as the script is spidery and irregular and varies not only with the dialect but with the very temperament of the writer. The broken lines read: ". . . of the cat and the dog? What will she . . ."; here the first line ends, broken off at the jagged edge of the board. "We," runs the second line, "know that the . . . [several words are obliterated] while the bird was singing. . . ." The third and last line: ". . . is what we all love. It makes us very happy." I like to imagine, although I know this is nothing but a child's exercise, that these broken lines, could I only complete them, would tell me more about the enemy than all the work of our specialists combined. As for my subordinates, I have led them to believe that these scraps of writing have something to do with logistics—which is all they care about.

The benches, the charts, the books and other blackboards of the schoolhouse have long since been removed. The rooms are now occupied by sturdy desks of our own design, developed during the war, and the walls are lined with filing cabinets and hung with maps of the region. The sides of the house have been reinforced against blast with sandbags, and the windows have been covered with intersecting strips of wire and tape which, when the sun is right, cast patterns of shadow upon our papers. If there were nothing else to do, it would be a pleasure to trace some of these patterns. The glass—these are the enemy's original panes—is very bright and clear. The enemy is known for the quality of his glass works. A strange people.

Our office is a relay station among the various fronts. The position of the fronts has grown so complicated through the years, that I never attempt to give our location with reference to the lines of battle. We are well in the center of one circle of fighting, on the periphery of a second, and connected by a long tangent with a third. From time to time our position appears enveloped, and we pack our papers, dismantle our immobile equipment, and prepare to retreat. Subsequent intelligence, however, informs us that the first reports, owing to the complexity of the warfare, were erroneous in many respects and that, far from being encircled, our position may be described as part of an arc thrown round the enemy's flank. The lines of battle, the longer I study them, seem to me more and more like the arms of many embracing bodies.

It is our general purpose, but not my specific task, to supply logistical information to headquarters in the front and in the rear. We are one of a number of stations that co-ordinate the numerous reports both of the enemy's movements and of our own, and relay these back and forth. These reports never fail to conflict with one another, and no matter how well trained our spies, pilots, observers, and scouts may be, we must keep a large staff working round the clock to prevent mistakes, repetitions, and inconsistencies from appearing in our dispatches. Even so we have blundered many times, and our only consolation, and at the same time the reason that reprimands from headquarters have not been more severe, is the fact that the enemy must work under the same disadvantages. Very often a report so complicated and contradictory that it seems impossible to submit, is nevertheless a true picture of the fighting. You can see what we are up against. And then there are the many spontaneous breakdowns of routine for which no one is to blame, the impatience of my superiors which is always interfering with the work, the orders handed down from above, countermanding orders that have already been carried out, and so many other difficulties that are part of the day's normal detail. To make matters worse a training class for scouts is held in the basement of our schoolhouse and we often hear them laughing or crying out in pain as they tumble about on the mats. I have been trying to get this class removed, thus far without success.

My own work developed as a subsidiary of the main logistical operation. My superiors are not yet convinced of the importance of my task (I have been at it for eleven years!), but some of them are interested, and all my equals and subordinates support me in it, so I am not required to give up my investigations. I work in a semiofficial capacity, filling in and sending out my own reports and as much corroborative material as I can lay my hands on—all this in addition to my regular duties. I am kept very busy indeed, seldom working less than sixteen hours at a stretch. I sometimes think, sitting as I do in an old schoolhouse, that I am both schoolmaster and pupil: a teacher to those who are beneath me in rank and an idiot child to my superiors.

I work on the enemy proper. I am trying to discover what he is, what motivates him, what his nature is. And if you say, as so many of my superiors do, that this is known, I reply that I am attacking his very essence. This is not known. In spite of the many long years that we have been at war with him, and the periods of time, in the past, when we lived at his side in restless peace, we know nothing of him that is really worth knowing and that must be known. I myself am convinced that victory will be impossible until we gain this knowledge—and it is precisely to this knowledge that I am devoting my life.

What do we know? The enemy is darker than we, and shorter in stature. His language, as I have indicated, has nothing in common with our own; his religion is an obscenity to all of us who have not made a specialty of studying it. Well then, as I say, he is shorter and darker, two positive facts. His language, though it would be too much trouble to go into it here, is of such and such a kind—a third fact—and his religion is this, that and the other thing, which gives us still another fact. So much we know. Still, what is he?

I have gone many times to the camps and hospitals in the rear to interview the prisoners we have taken. It teaches me nothing, but I nevertheless make my regular visits, and just the other week I returned from one of our hospitals. There was the usual sight in the wards; I am hardened to it. (And yet, almost as if to test myself, I try to recall what I have seen. Am I absolutely hardened?) There were the lightly wounded, their personalities not distorted by pain, and the natural qualities of these men could be observed: their churlishness, stupidity, sullenness, or good nature. They are much like our own soldiers, especially in their boredom. I spoke with them, I took my usual sampling—so many boys (as with our own troops, eleven-year-olds are not uncommon), so many youths, so many of the middle-aged, so many old men, old campaigners. The usual questions, the usual answers—home, parents, occupation, the government, women, disease, God, the purpose of the war, of life, of history, etc. There is nothing to be learned here that we don't already know. Then the wards of the severely wounded—the amputations, the blinded, the infected. The stench is the same as our own stench (the hospital orderlies deny this, maintaining that the enemy's is worse!). The ones with fever have fever, though their skins and eyes show it differently from ours. The delirious rave, the chilled shiver, the poisoned vomit and groan. There are outcries, the usual hysteria, weeping, coughing, and hemorrhage. One lies in a coma; the stump of his leg is gangrenous, it is too late, he cannot be saved. Another soldier has nearly every bone in his body broken: he has both his thighs in traction, a broken back, a broken arm, his skull wound in bandages. Can he be said to suffer either more or less than one of our own men in similar circumstances, or in any way differently from him? I attend an operation—it is the same thing over and over again. The mental casualties in their guarded ward are no different from ours. Some in straightjackets, strapped to their beds, some screaming, some colorless, lifeless, forever immobile. Here and there a dead body, not yet removed. I lift the sheet; the face is already puffed up. The shock of it is gone, and I can no longer remember what it actually used to be like. I poke a finger into a puffy cheek, leaving a depression which takes a long time to fill up again. It is the same death as our own.

I go to the hospitals, though I learn nothing there, and I go to the prison camps, also in vain. Once I had myself incarcerated, disguised as an enemy soldier. I slept with the men in their barracks, ate with them, studied them, was soon infested with the same lice. I was involved in a plan to escape, of which I informed our guards. No one saw through my disguise, and I, in turn, failed to see through the undisguised men and learned nothing. In fact, the few weeks I spent in prison camp were extremely discouraging, for if the gap between the enemy and ourselves is so small that I can pose, undetected, as one of his men, why is it that I can't cross over to him?

I have even suspected my project of a subtle treason. By "cross over to him," I mean of course, "cross the gulf that separates us from knowledge of his true nature." Now I know where I stand in this regard and it no longer troubles me; but at one time I feared that the second expression really meant nothing more than the first and I thought surely that my whole ambition was only to desert to the enemy. Perhaps he fascinated me in the precise sense of attraction, drawing me, through my desire to know, closer and closer to his side. My conscience drove me to my superior, Major General Box. He believes in my project and follows my reports with interest. The General reassured me; it is his opinion that we are all drawn to the enemy, particularly in such a long war, and that the enemy is drawn to us. In certain respects we even begin to resemble each other. But this is only natural, and has nothing to do with my project, which, far from being treason, remains the most important of the war.

I was reassured, but was soon taken with a fresh disquietude. A suggestion that the general had made, without meaning to do so, set me on a new course of activity. The general had said that in certain respects we come to resemble the enemy. What are these respects? Perhaps the knowledge that I was seeking really lay in myself? The resemblance to the enemy might have grown so strong in my case, that it was my own nature I would have to know in order to know his. I took a leave from the service, the only one I have had in the entire campaign, and spent a month in one of the enemy's mountain villages that had been captured by our troops. I lived away from the men, attended only by goats which forage high up among the rocks in this region. I had a hut to myself, and all the mountains necessary to a great introspection. But I learned nothing, nothing that I did not already know.

It was when I returned to active service that I began the most desperate work that I have as yet undertaken. I selected a group of twenty prisoners, all young, sturdy, healthy men. I lived with them until I grew to know them well; some were like my own sons, and one in particular, a peasant boy named Reri, I will say that I loved. I spent long hours out of doors with my companions, joined them in races and various sports, their own as well as ours. We went on long camping and fishing trips about the country, and I developed so great a trust in them that I even provided them with firearms and let them hunt with me. Evenings, when we were not camping under the open sky, we entertained ourselves in my lodge, drinking, playing cards or chess, listening to music, or holding the most intimate conversations—conversations and confidences that verged on love. We became very intimate; there has never been a group of men whom I have known or loved so well, never a youth as my Reri for whom I have had such a close and tender feeling. It was above all with Reri that I carried on my desperate yet gentle work; I strove to know him as completely as one man can ever hope to know another, and something in his response to me, perhaps an intuitive comprehension of my motive, promised that my effort would be rewarded. He was a handsome boy, taller than the average among the enemy, and fairer in color and complexion. Certainly one such as he could be known, a face as open as his could not long conceal the secrets of the inner nature. Often when I was not with him I would picture his face to myself, trusting that a chance moment of insight might reveal him, and therefore his whole people, to me. And I studied his image, sketching him and taking many photographs while he sat patiently before me. (I have kept these sketches and photographs, and look at them from time to time as I once looked at the living Reri. His image still saddens and perplexes me.) So, with all my companions, I engaged in an unceasing search after friendship and understanding, hoping that love would teach me what I was determined to know.

But my ultimate means were not to be gentle, and when I failed again I had to resort, with great reluctance, in shame and disgust, to the final means I had selected to attain my objective. As I had been their friend and lover and father, their teacher in the ways of our people and their pupil in the ways of theirs, so, at last, I became their torturer, hoping now to break them down and force them to yield what they had not been able to give freely. One day I ordered them whipped, the next, beaten; all of them, including Reri. I stood by, directing their tortures and noting their surprise, their hatred of me, their screams and their pleas for mercy. I could not help feeling that I had betrayed them; but my guilt only excited me the more and made me inflict always greater agony and humiliation upon them. It must have been guilt that was responsible for my extreme excitement, in the grip of which, while supervising the tortures, I would feel an overwhelming hatred of the enemy, and become convinced that my hatred had brought me so much farther than love, to the very brink of knowledge. When my companions died, I trained, in much the same manner, a new group, in which I included some of the enemy's women. The experiment was repeated. This time I did not spare myself, but submitted in their company to some of the same tortures, as if there might still be lurking in me an essential particle of their enemy's nature which was itself either capable of yielding the truth, or of preventing me from finding it. The experiment failed again. Again I learned nothing, nothing at all.

I still go to the wards and the camps, and from time to time I still conduct tortures. I have devised many other means of coping with my problem, some of them not yet tested. Over the years, I have grown hardened to failure: I more or less expect it now as an essential element of my work. But though I am hardened and toughened and experienced, I find that my work grows more and more difficult. Because of my interest in prisoners, new duties have been assigned to me. Recently negotiations for the exchange of prisoners broke down between the enemy and ourselves, and their number keeps piling up, as ours does in their camps; it is now my duty to arrange for their transportation to the interior. And then there are still the many administrative details of my department, to which I must somehow find time to attend; there are still the hazards and ever greater complications of our old war, which we have not yet won, and which, I have become absolutely certain, we will never win unless I succeed in my task. To know the enemy! It is the whole purpose and nature of our war, its ultimate meaning, its glory and its greatness. Already I have succeeded in my own character, for I have become my task in my whole being. Nothing comes between me and the work I do. I have triumphed in my character and in my person, but I must still triumph over the enemy. Sometimes I see his armies standing before me, clearly revealed in their dark, powerful mass, and I rush out of the schoolhouse, out of our office, and I feel that in a moment, but one moment more, I will know the truth. And when I hear our gunfire from the front that winds around us in all directions, I know that if my faith is only great enough, the knowledge will come to me and I will win.

happy
marriage
r. v. cassill

*R. V. Cassill (1919–   ) was born in Iowa
and began his artistic career as a painter.
He is the author of more than
a dozen novels; his short stories
are widely anthologized. Presently
he is a writer-in-residence at the
celebrated Iowa Writers' Workshop.
For further reading: 15 × 3 (1957).*

The skinny was always:

You married specifically against death. Young enough I had said "Bettcr marry" and "I will not die here," when *here* was the attic in Chesterfield where I found the arrowheads in the trunk under dust-smelling calico, the letters of Genevieve Wren to Morton Wren, and the old book with angel pictures (really cupids, their bare butts square in my face when I opened the pages). I knew at once that love's chemistry burned such fat.

Outside, the grass was browning in the degeneration of August, the sore-pocked shepherd dog chased chickens, the fishpool scummed, and the wind turned high and blue on a wheel's paradigm, turning on the dear axle of my body. I shouldn't die here, I thought. I love this dark attic too well and myself bare like these angels.

Once I found a pine cone in the dark woods. Put it in a milk bottle filled with water and hid it way. Later the water had turned purple. Thus God instructed me.

And once we went to the cabin on Crow Island in May when the river was low enough to ford. Behind Clayton on his pony the rest of the troop rode bikes or went scout's pace. The ranked cottonwoods of the island were to be our fort against the Nebraska sky. The undersides of logs drifted on the island were still wet from the floods in April, and we found mushrooms warm as our hands in the sticky shadows. Rhubarb and dutchman's britches lined the path to the abandoned Scout Cabin. The path was velvet with fine grass like the fuzz that grows on a burn scar. The insignia of the Eagle troop hung on a rusting nail beside the door.

In the afternoon we stripped and lay belly down on the sandbar and talked about Clayton's cousin—who was eleven and that was the sweetest age for girls—and how she ought to be there with us. I looked up and saw her coming in over the cottonwoods like a highjumper or a monoplane, naked as a cloud and about eighty feet tall. Judas, I yelled. I had to run and throw myself in the cold water while the sports laughed at my trouble and flung sand.

At night all the girls we knew were among us when we jabbered and tight-closed our eyes. I saw them all parade hot white and featureless as mushrooms. Reasoning toward midnight, I knew clearly that never in this world of dark in the trees and wind and river sweeping our island was Clayton's cousin going to wrap me with her candy arms. I turned my face to the logs and in loneliness asserted the possibility realized on the mainland of June, in a more sober year, in an apartment we were lucky to find for $22 a month. We had two rooms and the kitchen window looked out on a slate roof, more sky, and more noon than God bargained for when he made my world. Pure luck.

Mr. Nixon, when I told him I would marry without it if I had to, gave me a raise to $105 and fixed things so I'd have time at noon to walk home to her and that great window. Who do you love? she said in jealousy of my staring out. You, I said.

One of our first days there she was cleaning the apartment and found in the cupboard under the sink a mouse's skull. Our insects had eaten it clean. It was so fresh it still looked pink and white as a flower, or the fresh bone on a butcher's table. She shivered and tried loyally to hide it from me. Put it back and leave it, I said. It's the totem to bless this house. She laughed and that afternoon while I was at work took it out with the trash.

When I knew it was lost I was afraid. Where do I have to go to find it? I said.

Then there was the war and I came back from it to a different apartment. The first winter home I was sick, and one night in a fever dream I told her where the skull had gone.

You found it there, she said. Cheat.

I said, That's right. In the amphitheater of water fear I crushed it. It was more fragile than I had thought.

You won't die out there, she said. Look, I've put yellow curtains at the window, as I wrote you. Come home and cry.

I woke crying all right, and there she was in the kitchenette as big and pretty as life, breaking an egg into water and saying, Do you want it on toast, my lad? You'll feel better if you eat.

Not yet, I said. Wait a while. Come listen.

To what?

To me.

II

I have a twin named Lynch, I said. His soles walk on the soles of my feet.

That's chummy, she said.

He is in death. He braces against me on the edge between life and death. You have no business knowing him, since you threw the skull away, but I know him. I was down there with him.

I thought you were in the Army.

Listen, I said. I *went* to that island. I know what it's like. You don't.

Is his name really Lynch? Or is that a joke?

Lynch by name, Lynch by character. He was absolutely no good. Liar, lazy, cheat, half-wit, Regular Army chicken and the Captain's suck. Face like an old man's except no calm in it. Simultaneously sleepy and tormented. Didn't know a soul in the outfit except by name and didn't want to. Wanted to "get up North" and get him a Jap's ears. Wrote no letters, got no mail. Never played softball in the evenings with the rest of us. Played poker only to win. So he was in my work crew for two weeks while we were building the airstrip at Pallikula. I had trouble with him every day. So one day we were blasting coral. I had lit all the fuses and started to run. He was there beside me, grabbing my arm, saying, What's the matter, Sergeant, you scared? I hadn't been, but he scared me. What's the use of running? he said and showed his teeth. I jerked away like an animal that pulls its leg off to get out of a trap, and sprinted to flop behind a coconut log. Real flat on my belly, real flat, like I was holding onto you. Waited. I wouldn't look up to see if the bastard had taken cover. Then all three of the charges I set went at once, and it seems he hadn't.

Dead? she asked. I could feel the jerk go through her when I answered and then the terrible unstiffening of her arm. We were sitting among pillows in our Dearborn Street apartment, God's safest children, but something hit us. Flying coral.

It wasn't your fault, she said.

No; my death, I said. I had it in my hand to save but I squeezed too hard. When I looked over the log and saw the black blood coming from his mouth I knew I had nothing to hang onto but love. I think I let him go for your sake.

That's enough, she said.

No. I'll tip. You don't understand, I said.

If I don't, help me, she said. Help me.

When the finger touches the hollow in the elbow and the wiggle of the ordinarily hidden vein, touches skin running from oil smooth to dusty rough on the circumference of the thigh, the stubble in the armpit, the loaded velvet of the lip, the humorous wobble of the kneecap, the hard curve of rib, the rebounding curve of the breast and the frantic nipple—there is no understanding.

Or when the body settles like a rigid numeral paired with a nubile zero, what understands us is not ourselves.
Understanding is afterward, the long afterward and the falling apart. As decay is a vegetable.
What *doth* man of woman require?
The spangled lineaments which represent desire? Or only the sea-brine reminiscent harbor of the sea's disaster?
Within the shell of happiness the kernel of repudiation. In the timbre of the sex-cry, wailing. In the after-fondness (counterfeited) the true coin of innocence. In promise, denial. In wholeness the explanatory shape of division.
Is all that possible, darling, my darling?
No.

III

Whom do you love? some others said, conventionally.
"Qu'est-ce-que tu aime?" the whore said. What do you love?
Thee, when I came in from the snow-bewildered street, moist snow dripping from my hat brim; when I ordered a cognac from fat Margot, the barmaid with the biggest radio—six bands and enough dials to tune in clear any station in Europe.
"Une femme cruelle? Les garçons?"
Thou—when you bumped plumply against my knee without taking your eyes from the red-headed soldier in the corner; when you said— as if the pity of it might brim over the cup and anoint me with its excess—"Lousy night. It's always slow the week before you pay your GI's." Then did I wish to make the house, to lay down in a joke the aspiration with its strange device, the image of man, instructed and moralized. I offered her the watching skull. I said to her, As Pascal cried in anguish, *Who watched with Lynch?*
"You have fear?" she said, who knew I had.
I bought that out, I said. Am buying.
"It costs dearly."
Dearly.
In lieu of action, for 1500 francs I recounted my triumphs in the erotic field, the time I went down on a nightingale at Dover Beach, frolicked with the blue china poor Rupert loved, made out with a sonnet, got to the Hegelian dialectic, exposed myself to bullfights, Mahler, and the sea.
I love plain living and high thinking.
Excellence.
Airplanes.
Samson Agonistes.
I will not let you go until you bless me, I said.

The loathing and contempt of her eyes made me think of a mongoose examining a garter snake. "Qu'est-ce-que tu aime?" she said.

Everything.

She grunted. "Some other night, then, cheri?"

In the springtime.

But in the springtime, the season sweet and colored in lofty blossoms like the skulls of mice, what was there to do but act out the mysteries with two Danish girls? Their eyes were all four blue as that original window opening North. They were sixteen and seventeen and hitch-hiking around Europe. For culture.

"My name is meaning the night," the sixteen-year-old explained. I had bought her peppermint candy and her tongue was red as macaw feathers. She bobbed like an earnest daisy when she insisted, "I is always loving dezz."

I laughed and lightly told her what Rimbaud, dying, said to his sister, "Tomorrow you will be in the sun and I will be in the dark."

She licked her candy and seemed pleased, as though I had paid her a personal compliment. But the next morning, lying in her friend's arms, she called across the hotel room to me, "No, *you* will be in the sun and I will be in Hell wiz my sisser here."

Their Danish wrists were laced delicately with the scars of old razor cuts. I had never pondered that Gillette had undone so many.

"We has found somezing beyond the ee roh teek," she called. From her tone that something could have been faith, wisdom, or charity. Turned out to be ether.

We lay in the Parisian spring, three cotton pads to our faces, dreaming that outside the room bells rang a chivalry of disaster. Under chestnut trees the dead girls paraded, those whom Paris loved, and in spacious evenings they rumored the infidelity of life as if they might be gossiping the anxieties of fashionable love.

The spike of her bird-feather tongue was bitter with the taste of ether. We lay two days conversing in our respective languages. She told me how the razors tickled her wrists like shy schoolboys, driven to horror that so much beauty was abroad in the uncertainty of a temporal world, unsaved among war, lechery, or the fluctuations of paper currency. Like a painter's brushes the razors had stroked to fix that beauty—a fresco in a lightless corridor. Her father, she said once, in the children's hour when we had all three sobered enough to use common words, when we looked down together from the hotel windows into the damning illusion of the street—her father was literally a painter, had known Munch and Ensor many years ago. Her mother was younger and danced the Charleston. She must send them a postcard so they would not worry about her.

They must not worry, she said, slopping the virgin handful of cotton from a newly opened liter. There was nothing to worry about. In the gently downward planes of these dimensions neither she nor her sister-friend and I must worry that sometime in a Marseilles canal her dancer's body would float headless, with an illiterate love note stuffed into her brassiere.

I should not worry, the ether and the razors said, that I had been unfaithful to living friends and wives. You never wanted any more, they whispered to me, than just to eat your cake and have the eating of it, than praise for the bashfulness with which you sinned, than immortality, than to bury the dead in another chance and time to come.

There were no razors but I felt them crawl like instructive maggots on the wrists to which I held a claim. Little brothers beyond the ee roh teek. By the second night I had learned everything from them.

I can tell you that Ee Roh Teek is a mountain in Central Africa and not everyone knows why there should be leopards on it. It is the yellow sugar gate to Hell and beyond it are all the eyes. Beyond it everyone may call for Lynch and anyone may answer. He will approach you like a child and whisper, "Lead me back."

Come on, I said.

"Is it far?"

Not very *far*, but there isn't any *way*.

IV

Out of sheer habit I came back.

With the damnedest hangover, an oceanic, sloshing void in which floated everything. A hangover as big and hollow as a cosmos in which a filament suspended me at the center of appearances.

I was in my room behind the Sorbonne and had no idea how I'd come there, except that my ragged pulse suggested I might have galloped on all fours. I closed my eyes and tried to imagine what a fish would do if it wanted to evolve into a man. There must be something it could take, I thought. I expected to die unless I could damn soon discover why to live. I tried to remember back to Crow Island. If I could lie by the muddy edge of the water in a growing season and count new pubic hairs, if I could climb to a blue window or the attic in August to feel the sweat pour out of me like evil going home, if I could remember why Morton Wren loved Genevieve then I could instruct my body how it must endure.

Looking at my unmarked wrists I could not even remember for a while whose were scarred. Who is in the sun and who is in the dark? It seemed to me I had left her, too, beyond the mountain, but the her I left had no identity. Something I had done, as with a razor, had fragmented the person with whom I had talked and lain. I knew I wasn't winning and then my only chance was trying to make it to a bar.

In the blue morning the tower of Ste. Chapelle trembled like a flower stem. Now I'm all right, I thought: since it was real I could put my hand to steady it. But then I passed a newsstand and saw the headlines about an English murderer. He had slashed the wrists of innumerable girls and they, poor things, those moorings cut, had gone drifting down the streams of summer. The killer, I read, was still at large.

Still at large. I took a deep breath. The medium I breathed was horror, and all its aspects were fair to the eye. The shade that fingered the sunny pavements was horrible and lovely and I was still, horribly, at large.

I sat outside *Old Navy* Bar-Tabac fingering a glass of wine the color of the Danish girls' hair. They were my guides, I thought. I needed the right girls to lead me past the meridian, where I could admit in the presence of judges that I had renounced my rebellion against death. Through the luxury of their doomed flesh I had come to where the ideal Lynch had meant that I must. Now I would leave him where he was nothing. The negative twin no longer had to exist. I had bought out the title of my fear.

Now, in the noonward tending light, and a hangover imitation of the Passion, it seemed permissible to remember Lynch and the other dead. Now, I could fix the place in time—far back, far back—when I had seen the naked bone like a flagstaff in the gutted foxhole, when I had tried to swear *I will come back one more time to give you a decent burial, O denied.* Now, like an animal of the afternoon which does not remember the morning in which the bones lived, I could enter in the body of the abstract woman and hive in the moisture of time to come. That spot of blood was a ruptured capillary. Only from drunkenness.

In my jacket pocket was a card with the names of the girls. *De votre malheur il ne reste que les noms.* Goodbye, I said. O, Goodbye.

Then it was the sun's noon, and under every morsel and scrap on the pavement the shape of shadows changed. The jerk of my healing finger tapped the wine glass on the table top. In the yellow-white ripples I saw all timeless constancy twitch and quiver to the disturbance of my inconstant caress. I believed this city was mine.

Tommaso Landolfi (1908–   ) has been called the Italian Kafka. His work is often linked with the surrealists, and his feeling for fantasy suggests Borges. In general his work presents a combination of humor, prodigious imagination, and controlled irony. For further reading: Gogol's Wife and Other Stories, *translated by Rosenthal, Longrigg, and Young (1963).*

wedding night

tommaso landolfi

At the end of the wedding banquet the chimney sweep was announced. The father, out of joviality, and because it seemed proper to him that a ceremony such as the cleaning of the chimney should be celebrated on just that day, gave the order to let him come in. But the man did not appear; he preferred to remain in the kitchen, where the great hearth was. Not all the toasts had yet been given, and this was why some of the guests, in their heart of hearts, criticized the interruption; nonetheless, due to the uproar made by the children, everyone rose from the table.

The bride had never seen a chimney sweep: she had been in boarding school when he used to come. Going into the kitchen she saw a tall, rather corpulent man, with a serious gray beard and bent shoulders; he was dressed in a corduroy suit the color of linseed oil. His stoop was counterbalanced by the weight of two huge mountain boots which seemed to hold his entire body erect. Although he had just washed very carefully, the skin of his face was deeply tinted with black, as though many black-heads of varying dimensions had taken root there; a black deposit, gathered between the lines of his forehead and cheeks, conferred a quality of meditative wisdom on that physiognomy. But this impression quickly dissolved, and the man's great timidity became quite obvious, especially when his features broke into a sort of smile.

He nearly frightened the young bride, because he was standing behind the door, though he acted frightened himself; and, as if he had been caught doing something reprehensible and had to justify his presence in that place, he began to repeat, speaking directly to the young bride, some sentences which she did not hear or did not understand. He stammered insistently and behaved as if he thought that what he said concerned her greatly and, all the while, he looked at her with the eyes

425

of a beaten dog and yet significantly. From the very first moment the young bride was aware of his caterpillar nature.

He took off his jacket and began to unbutton his vest. She slipped out through the other door, but continued to follow what was going on in the kitchen; she had the feeling that something improper was about to happen and that her presence might make him uneasy in the performance of his rites. Somehow she almost felt ashamed for him. But there was no noise to feed her imagination and so she went back in again. The children had been sent away and he was alone. At that moment he was climbing a ladder set up inside the hood of the fireplace; his feet were bare and he was in his shirtsleeves, a brown shirt. Across his chest, fastened with leather straps, he had a tool which resembled the scraper for a kneading trough but whose use remained forever unknown to the young bride. And he had a kind of black gag, tied up behind his ears, which fitted over his mouth and nose. But she did not see him enter the flue of the chimney, because she ran away again.

When she came back the second time, the kitchen was empty and a strange smell, a terrible smell, had spread through it. Looking around her, the young bride connected it first with the man's large shoes set in a corner next to a bundle of clothes; it was, however, the death smell of the soot which was piling up on the hearthstone, falling in intermittent showers to the rhythm of a dull scraping which gnawed at the marrow of the house and which she felt echoing in her own entrails. In the intervals, a muffled rubbing revealed the man's laborious ascent.

An instant of absolute silence fell, an instant of lacerating suspense for the young bride. She continued to stare at the mouth of the flue, there under the hood at the end of the fireplace's black funnel; this mouth was not square but narrow, a dark slit.

Then a very high, guttural, inhuman cry sounded from some mysterious place, from the well, from the stones of the house, from the soul of the kitchen's pots and pans, from the very breast of the young bride, who was shaken by it through and through. That bestial howl of agony soon proved to be a kind of joyous call: the man had burst through onto the roof. The muffled rubbings resumed more rapidly now; finally a black foot came down out of the slit searching for support—the foot of a hanged man. The foot found the first rung of the ladder and the young bride ran away.

In the courtyard, as the bride sat on a millstone, the old housekeeper, one of those women for whom everything is new, assumed the task of keeping her informed; she walked back and forth bringing her the news with a mysterious air. "Now he is doing his cleaning under the hood," and the young bride pictured him as he shook off the soot, standing upright on the pile like a gravedigger on a mound of earth. "But what does he put on his feet to claw into the wall?" And then she ran after him to ask him: "My good man, what do you put on your feet to claw into the wall?" A gay reply followed which could not be heard clearly. "Now he is eating breakfast," and the housekeeper remained inside. Then she reappeared with a few small edelweiss; she said that the man had taken them out of a very clean little box and had offered them for the young bride.

After some time he himself came out, dressed again and with a pack on his back. He crossed the countyard to leave, but the father stopped him and began to question him benevolently about his life. The young bride approached, too. Here the man, in the weak sun of winter, his face darker, his beard flecked with black and his eyes puckered by the light, looked like a big moth, a nocturnal bird surprised by the day. Or rather he looked like a spider or crab louse; the fact is that the hood of the hearth, when seen from below and if there is enough light ouside, is not completely black but leaks a gray and slimy sheen.

He said that for thirty-five years he had been traveling through those towns cleaning the chimneys, that next year he would take his young son along to teach him the trade, that picking edelweiss was now forbidden and he had been able to gather those few flowers on the sly, and other such inconsequential things. Yet, whether astute or halting, it was quite clear that he only wished to hide himself behind those words, that he let the curtain of words fall in the same way that the cuttlefish beclouds the water.

He knew about all the deaths in the family, yet none of them had ever seen him!

By now the young bride felt that she was no longer ashamed for him, but was actually ashamed of herself.

After the chimney sweep had gone, she placed the few edelweiss beneath the portraits of the dead.

snow

ted hughes

Ted Hughes (1930–   )
was born in England and still resides
in Great Britain, where he is known
as a poet, a short-story writer, and a
critic. He is one of the few new writers
in England, at the present time, who seeks
new directions for the short-story form.

And let me repeat this over and over again: beneath
my feet is the earth, some part of the surface of the earth. Beneath the
snow beneath my feet, that is. What else could it be? It is firm, I
presume, and level. If it is not actually soil and rock, it must be ice. It
is very probably ice. Whichever it may be, it is proof—the most substantial proof possible—that I am somewhere on the earth, the known earth.
It would be absurd to dig down through the snow, just to determine
exactly what is underneath, earth or ice. This bedded snow may well
be dozens of feet deep. Besides, the snow filling all the air and rivering
along the ground would pour into the hole as fast as I could dig, and
cover me too—very quickly.

This could be no other planet: the air is perfectly natural, perfectly
good.

Our aircraft was forced down by this unusual storm. The pilot tried
to make a landing, but misjudged the extraordinary power of the wind
and the whereabouts of the ground. The crash was violent. The fuselage
buckled and gaped, and I was flung clear. Unconscious of everything
save the need to get away from the disaster, I walked farther off into
the blizzard and collapsed, which explains why when I came to full
consciousness and stood up out of the snow that was burying me I could
see nothing of either the aircraft or my fellow passengers. All around
me was what I have been looking at ever since. The bottomless dense
motion of snow. I started to walk.

Of course, everything previous to that first waking may have been
entirely different since I don't remember a thing about it. Whatever
chance dropped me here in the snow evidently destroyed my memory.
That's one thing of which there is no doubt whatsoever. It is, so to speak,
one of my facts. The aircraft crash is a working hypothesis, that merely.

There's no reason why I should not last quite a long time yet. I seem
to have an uncommon reserve of energy. To keep my mind firm, that
is the essential thing, to fix it firmly in my reasonable hopes, and lull it
there, encourage it. Mesmerise it slightly with a sort of continuous
prayer. Because when my mind is firm, my energy is firm. And that's the
main thing here—energy. No matter how circumspect I may be, or how

lucid, without energy I am lost on the spot. Useless to think about it. Where my energy ends I end, and all circumspection and all lucidity end with me. As long as I have energy I can correct my mistakes, outlast them, outwalk them—for instance the unimaginable error that as far as I know I am making at this very moment. This step, this, the next five hundred, or five thousand—all mistaken, all absolute waste, back to where I was ten hours ago. But we recognise that thought. My mind is not my friend. My support, my defence, but my enemy too—not perfectly intent on getting me out of this. If I were mindless perhaps there would be no difficulty whatsoever. I would simply go on aware of nothing but my step by step success in getting over the ground. The thing to do is to keep alert, keep my mind fixed in alertness, recognise these treacherous paralysing, yes, lethal thoughts the second they enter, catch them before they can make that burrowing plunge down the spinal cord.

Then gently and without any other acknowledgment push them back— out into the snow where they belong. And that *is* where they belong. They are the infiltrations of the snow, encroachments of this immensity of lifelessness. But they enter so slyly! We are true, they say, or at least very probably true, and on that account you must entertain us and even give us the run of your life, since above all things you are dedicated to the truth. That is the air they have, that's how they come in. What do I know about the truth? As if simple-minded dedication to truth were the final law of existence! I only know more and more clearly what is good for me. It's my mind that has this contemptible awe for the probably true, and my mind, I know, I prove it every minute, is not me and is by no means sworn to help me. Am I a lie? I must survive—that's a truth sacred as any, and as the hungry truths devour the sleepy truths I shall digest every other possible truth to the substance and health and energy of my own, and the ones I can't digest I shall spit out, since in this situation my intention to survive is the one mouth, the one digestive tract, so to speak, by which I live. But those others! I relax for a moment, I leave my mind to itself for a moment—and they are in complete possession. They plunge into me, exultantly, mercilessly. There is no question of their intention or their power. Five seconds of carelessness, and they have struck. The strength melts from me, my bowels turn to water, my consciousness darkens and shrinks, I have to stop.

What are my facts? I do have some definite facts.

Taking six steps every five seconds, I calculate—allowing for my brief regular sleeps—that I have been walking through this blizzard for five months and during that time have covered something equal to the breadth of the Atlantic between Southampton and New York. Two facts. and a third: throughout those five months this twilight of snow has not grown either darker or brighter.

So.

There seems no reason to doubt that I am somewhere within either the Arctic or the Antarctic Circle. That's a comfort. It means my chances of survival are not uniquely bad. Men have walked the length of Asia simply to amuse themselves.

Obviously I am not travelling in a straight line. But that needn't give me any anxiety. Perhaps I made a mistake when I first started walking, setting my face against the wind instead of downwind. Coming against the wind I waste precious energy and there is always this wearisome snow blocking my eyes and mouth. But I had to trust the wind. This resignation to the wind's guidance is the very foundation of my firmness of mind. The wind is not simply my compass. In fact, I must not think of it as a compass at all. The wind is my law. As a compass nothing could be more useless. No need to dwell on that. It's extremely probable indeed and something I need not hide from myself that this wind is leading me to and fro in quite a tight little maze—always shifting too stealthily for me to notice the change. Or, if the sun is circling the horizon, it seems likely that the wind is swinging with it through the three hundred and sixty degrees once in every twenty-four hours, turning me as I keep my face against it in a perfect circle not more than seven miles across. This would explain the otherwise strange fact that in spite of the vast distance I have covered the terrain is still dead level, exactly as when I started. A frozen lake, no doubt. This is a strong possibility and I must get used to it without letting it overwhelm me, and without losing sight of its real advantages.

The temptation to trust to luck and instinct and cut out across wind is to be restricted. The effect on my system of confidence would be disastrous. My own judgment would naturally lead me in a circle. I would have to make deliberate changes of direction to break out of that circle—only to go in a larger circle or a circle in the opposite direction. So more changes. Wilder and more sudden changes, changes of my changes—all to evade an enemy that showed so little sign of itself it might as well not have existed. It's clear where all that would end. Shouting and running and so on. Staggering round like a man beset by a mob. Falling, grovelling. So on. The snow.

No. All I have to do is endure: that is, keep my face to the wind. My face to the wind, a firm grip on my mind, and everything else follows naturally. There is not the slightest need to be anxious. Any time now the Polar night will arrive, bringing a drastic change of climate—inevitable. Clearing the sky and revealing the faultless compass of the stars.

The facts are overwhelmingly on my side. I could almost believe in Providence. After all, if one single circumstance were slightly—only slightly—other than it is! If, for instance, instead of waking in a blizzard on a firm level place I had come to consciousness falling endlessly through snow-cloud. Then I might have wondered very seriously whether I were in the gulf or not. Or if the atmosphere happened to consist of, say, ammonia. I could not have existed. And in the moment before death by asphyxiation I would certainly have been convinced I was out on some lifeless planet. Or if I had no body but simply arms and legs growing out of a head, my whole system of confidence would have been disoriented from the start. My dreams, for instance, would have been meaningless to me, or rather an argument of my own meaninglessness. I would have died almost immediately, out of sheer bewilderment. I wouldn't need nearly such extreme differences either. If I had been without these excellent pigskin boots, trousers, jacket, gloves and hood, the cold would have extinguished me at once.

And even if I had double the clothing that I have, where would I be without my chair? My chair is quite as important as one of my lungs. As both my lungs, indeed, for without it I should be dead. Where would I have slept? Lying in the snow. But lying flat, as I have discovered, I am buried by the snow in just under a minute, and the cold begins to take over my hands and my feet and my face. Sleep would be impossible. In other words, I would very soon collapse of exhaustion and be buried. As it is, I unsnap my chair harness, plant the chair in the snow, sit on it, set my feet on the rung between the front legs, my arms folded over my knees and my head resting on my arms, and am able in this way to take a sleep of fully ten minutes before the snow piles over me.

The chain of providential coincidences is endless. Or rather, like a chain mail, it is complete without one missing link to betray and annul the rest. Even my dreams are part of it. They are as tough and essential a link as any, since there can no longer be any doubt that they are an accurate reproduction of my whole previous life, of the world as it is and as I knew it—all without one contradictory detail. Yet if my amnesia had been only a little bit stronger!—it needed only that. Because without this evidence of the world and my identity I could have known no purpose in continuing the ordeal. I could only have looked, breathed and died, like a nestling fallen from the nest.

Everything fits together. And the result—my survival, and my determination to survive. I should rejoice.

The chair is of conventional type: nothing in the least mystifying about it. A farmhouse sort of chair: perfectly of a piece with my dreams, as indeed are my clothes, my body and all the inclinations of my mind. It is of wood, painted black, though in places showing a coat of brown beneath the black. One of the nine struts in the back is missing and some child—I suppose it was a child—has stuck a dab of chewing-gum into the empty socket. Obviously the chair has been well used, and not too carefully. The right foreleg has been badly chewed, evidently by a puppy, and on the seat both black and brown paints are wearing through showing the dark grain of the pale wood. If all this is not final evidence of a reality beyond my own, of the reality of the world it comes from, the world I re-dream in my sleeps—I might as well lie down in the snow and be done with.

The curious harness needn't worry me. The world, so far as I've dreamed it at this point, contains no such harness, true. But since I've not yet dreamed anything from after my twenty-sixth birthday, the harness might well have been invented between that time and the time of my disaster. Probably it's now in general use. Or it may be the paraphernalia of some fashionable game that came in during my twenty-seventh or later year, and to which I got addicted. Sitting on snow peaks in nineteenth-century chairs. Or perhaps I developed a passion for painting polar scenery and along with that a passion for this particular chair as my painting seat, and had the harness designed specially. A lucky eccentricity! It is perfectly adapted to my present need. But all that's in the dark still. There's a lot I haven't dreamed yet. From my twenty-third and twenty-fourth years I have almost nothing—a few insignificant episodes. Nothing at all after my twenty-sixth birthday. The rest, though, is about complete, which suggests that any time now I ought to be getting my twenty-third and twenty-fourth years in full and, more important, my twenty-seventh year, or as much of it as there is, along with the accurate account of my disaster and the origin of my chair.

There seems little doubt of my age. Had I been dreaming my life chronologically there would have been real cause for worry. I could have had no idea how much was still to come. Of course, if I were suddenly to dream something from the middle of my sixtieth year I would have to reorganise all my ideas. What really convinces me of my youth is my energy. The appearance of my body tells me nothing. Indeed, from my hands and feet—which are all I have dared to uncover—one could believe I was several hundred years old, or even dead, they are so black and shrunken on the bone. But the emaciation is understandable, considering that for five months I have been living exclusively on will-power, without the slightest desire for food.

I have my job to get back to, and my mother and father will be in despair. And God knows what will have happened to Helen. Did I marry her? I have no wedding ring. But we were engaged. And it is another confirmation of my youth that my feelings for her are as they were then—stronger, in fact, yes a good deal stronger, though speaking impartially these feelings that seem to be for her might easily be nothing but my desperate longing to get back to the world in general—a longing that is using my one-time affection for Helen as a sort of form or model. It's possible, very possible, that I have in reality forgotten her, even that I am sixty years old, that she has been dead for thirty-four years. Certain things may be very different from what I imagine. If I were to take this drift of thoughts to the logical extreme there is no absolute proof that my job, my parents, Helen and the whole world are not simply my own invention, fantasies my imagination has improvised on the simple themes of my own form, of clothes, my chair, and the properties of my present environment. I am in no position to be sure about anything.

But there is more to existence, fortunately, than consideration of possibilities. There is conviction, faith. If there were not, where would I be? The moment I allow one of these "possibilities" the slightest intimacy—a huge futility grips me, as it were physically, by the heart, as if the organ itself were despairing of this life and ready to give up.

Courageous and calm. That should be my prayer. I should repeat that, repeat it like the Buddhists with their "O jewel of the lotus". Repeat it till it repeats itself in my very heart, till every heartbeat drives it through my whole body. Courageous and calm. This is the world, think no more about it.

My chair will keep me sane. My chair, my chair, my chair—I might almost repeat that. I know every mark on it, every grain. So near and true! It alone predicates a Universe, the entire Universe, with its tough carpentering, its sprightly, shapely design—so delicate, so strong. And while I have the game I need be afraid of nothing. Though it is dangerous. Tempting, dangerous, but—it is enough to know that the joy is mine. I set the chair down in the snow, letting myself think I am going to sleep, but instead of sitting I step back a few paces into the snow. How did I think of that? The first time, I did not dare look away from it. I had never before let it out of my hand, never let it go for a fraction between unbuckling it and sitting down on it. But then I let it go and stepped back into the snow. I had never heard my voice before. I was astonished at the sound that struggled up out of me. Well, I need the compensations. And this game does rouse my energies, so it is, in a sense, quite practical. After the game, I could run. That's the moment of danger, though, the moment of overpowering impatience when I could easily lose control and break out, follow my instinct, throw myself on luck, run out across the wind.

But there is a worse danger. If I ran out across the wind I would pretty soon come to my senses, turn my face back into the wind. It is the game itself, the stage of development it has reached, that is dangerous now. I no longer simply step back. I set the chair down, turn my face away and walk off into the blizzard, counting my steps carefully. At fourteen paces I stop. Fifteen is the limit of vision in this dense flow of snow, so at fourteen I stop, and turn. Let those be the rules. Let me fix the game at that. Because at first I see nothing. That should be enough for me. Everywhere, pouring silent grey, a silence like a pressure, like the slow coming to bear of some incalculable pressure, too gradual to detect. If I were simply to stand there my mind would crack in a few moments. But I concentrate, I withdraw my awe from the emptiness and look pointedly into it. At first, everything is as usual—as I have seen it for five months. Then my heart begins to thump unnaturally, because I seem to make out a dimness, a shadow that wavers deep in the grey turmoil, vanishes and darkens, rises and falls. I step one pace forward and using all my will-power stop again. The shadow is as it was. Another step. The shadow seems to be a little darker. Then it vanishes and I lunge two steps forward but immediately stop because there it is, quite definite, no longer moving. Slowly I walk towards it. The rules are that I keep myself under control, that I restrain all sobs or shouts though of course it is impossible to keep the breathing regular—at this stage at least, and right up to the point where the shadow resolves into a chair. In that vast grey dissolution—my chair! The snowflakes are drifting against the legs and gliding between the struts, bumping against them, clinging and crawling over the seat. To control myself then is not within human power. Indeed I seem to more or less lose consciousness at that point. I'm certainly not responsible for the weeping, shouting thing that falls on my chair, embracing it, kissing it, bruising his cheeks against it. As the snowflakes tap and run over my gloves and over the chair I begin to call them names. I peer into each one as if it were a living face, full of speechless recognition, and I call to them—Willy, Joanna, Peter, Jesus, Ferdinand, anything that comes into my head, and shout to them and nod and laugh. Well, it's harmless enough madness.

The temptation to go beyond the fourteen paces is now becoming painful. To go deep into the blizzard. Forty paces. Then come back, peering. Fifteen paces, twenty paces. Stop. A shadow.

That would not be harmless madness. If I were to leave my chair like that the chances are I would never find it again. My footprints do not exist in this undertow of snow. Weeks later, I would still be searching, casting in great circles, straining at every moment to pry a shadow out of the grey sameness. My chair meanwhile a hundred miles away in the blizzard, motionless—neat legs and elegant back, sometimes buried, sometimes uncovering again. And for centuries, long after I'm finished, still sitting there, intact with its tooth-marks and missing strut, waiting for a darkening shape to come up out of the nothingness and shout to it and fall on it and possess it.

But my chair is here, on my back, here. There's no danger of my ever losing it. Never so long as I keep control, keep my mind firm. All the facts are on my side. I have nothing to do but endure.

us
he
devours
james b. hall

James B. Hall (1918–   ), novelist and poet, was born in rural Ohio. Before becoming a professor of English at the University of Oregon, he was a merchant sailor and a soldier. For further reading: 15 × 3 (1957); Us He Devours (1964).

The goat coughed in the tree outside her window.

Oh she had waited so long to see the hoofs firm upon the lowest branches, the flanks slender, stretched upward among the catalpa leaves, the head half concealed, the backward curving horns erect, glistening in the moist light of the moon.

Miss Festner had thought all these times were past, forever, but now her branches rustled louder, and she stiffened in her bed. Stringy and coarse and rancid as a chicken house floor, the odor afloat in the catalpa tree came to her. She lay in her bed and she felt her back and her thighs harden. This time she was determined to wait.

From experience Miss Festner knew that to leap from her bed, to rush to the casement, to cry out, was useless. When younger she had cried out, in fear; later she knew she must wait without emotion. Not always did the goat leap with a terrible cracking of small branches, and scramble pawing across her window sill.

Sometimes it came—perhaps silently—then deserted her. Sometimes the cry of reed pipes swelled inside her room until her ears and heart and her hard breasts ached; sometimes, after the cry of the loon and after the last crackling noise of great weight among branches, it went away. If it awakened her, and then deserted her, she would go to her window and stare out across the town, which fell away below her windows toward the river. Therefore she did not now dare look toward the window when the odor of stalls and rabbit hutches and stables came to her like smoke from the leaves of the shimmering tree.

For this it seemed she had been waiting a very long time. She had almost given up hope, but now she did what she could. Her quick money-counting fingers dug deeper into the little holes in the farthest edges of her mattress. The sheet across her knees and thighs and her dry belly made spasms of motion.

Some things she could not control, but some things she could do: always she left her window open, she used only the lightest of sheets, and always she was *clean, clean.* If she looked now the eyes she might see would flee into the kingdom of her dreams. But oh tonight she could not wait.

With her eyes still closed she threw the small sheet from her body. Exposed. Yes and on display and naked as the first day her quick money-counting fingers worked inside her Teller's cage. From Escrows in the bank, she had gone behind a Teller's window. Since then she had her window at the bank, with bars, and the businessmen of the town came to her with money and she handled each day the hard, hand-fitting, phallic rolls of dimes, nickels, and quarters. That night in spring, for the first time, the goat coughed in the catalpa tree in the yard of her small house and in her inexperience and her fear she had run too quickly to her bedroom window and the musk-scented thing had fled somewhere across the roiled shadows of her yard.

Finally she learned to wait motionless in her bed, for only then would the wool-soft yarn and the perfume and the polished mother-of-pearl horns and the soft resilient body—only then would it stay lovely as flowers unfolding beside and over her until the dawn humming awoke in her arms. Those mornings she telephoned Mr. Nelscot at the bank. She did not go down the hill to sit behind the window of her Teller's cage until after her lunch.

Louder now outside her bedroom window the small branches scattered. Was now the time, this night?

In the catalpa tree outside she heard it whet the saber of its horns against the topmost branches. Were the hoarse violent eyes staring at her now?

She resisted a moment, and then she no longer cared. To see, to glimpse it among branches seemed enough. She opened wide her eyes. No. Not there. Gone.

The cry of the loon in the frozen trees chilled her. She had been terribly hot; now she was not hot. She felt more deserted, and more forlorn, than ever before. Yet she was not and never could be sinfully passive, for urgency even in her waking hours grew like a fuse somewhere inside her. She recognized, she even welcomed, the desperation that came galloping to her. She knew she must go out, must seek, must search once more.

Of late when the goat coughed in the branches outside her window and then deserted her, she had followed. Once she had been astonished at her own headlong urgency, but she had gone on because she believed that in frenzy was the hot little kernel of satisfaction. Now that restraint was somewhere far behind her she could think of nothing at all except a highway, twisting somewhere ahead.

II

Furiously she drove the country, limestone roads. Ahead on a curve the guardrails writhed in her headlight beams. At a crossroad she saw the shadow of a country mailbox lie black beside some farmer's lane, and as she passed the black check mark shadow seemed to fade, and then to become a check mark of flame in the corner or her headlong eye.

The constant search, it was, that vexed her. At one time the first place she stopped was always the right place. But as the years fled her, she found the right place was now always farther away, until now she was resigned to the longest drive of all: this night she knew without caring that she would go far beyond a familiar tilt-roofed, ramshackle barn that roosted in a pasture, reviled even by the shoat's moist farming nose.

One spring she had first gone outside. She had gone directly to a certain creek that divided two meadows, where a sand bar of supine luminous tissues of gravel lay exposed between rocks and the water. Later she found her sand bar was not the right place and she had to drive on to a field freshly harrowed, and then on still farther, in the fall, to a place of stubbles, of wheat lately under the sickle bars of harvest. From habit, or from some terrible wish, she still drove first to the sand bar and then to the fields, in the order of their discovery. Finally she came to a familiar bridge. Across this bridge was a grove of oaks that was lovely and dark and deep, a mat of green between two hills.

The planks of the bridge seemed to say this was the place that she must find. But she could accept no comfort from the mutter of planks. Always, until the final moment, there was uncertainty. Suppose the place now had to be still more remote, a place where she could never travel, a place so cleverly concealed in a shaggy-thighed wood that no one could ever find it. She could not think upon that ultimate possibility. As always, at this time, she knew with the Bible-black certainty of prayer that here was the place. Here nothing would be denied her.

The boxes and packages she kept locked in the car trunk. These were things she bought on impulse during her lunch hour or on Saturday, as though each purchase were for herself. She had not thought there were so many, but the oblong, white boxes and the largest flat box—all of them—seemed to leap into her arms. Without pausing she ran across a culvert and across a flat small meadow and into the first sentinel trees at the oak grove's edge.

Too late she realized the briers also guarded the grove. They had grown and had become heavy as barbed wire since the last time.

With the white boxes held high above her head, and with her robe open, flapping behind her, she leaped high and for a moment seemed to float above the caress of briers. She landed running. Her legs burned. But Miss Festner did not cry out.

Ahead she saw the smooth arena, in the center of her secret grove of oaks.

"Here, oh here," she said to the briers, which seemed to roll away in unbroken humps of light toward a creek beyond.

"Here. I am here, now," she said to the crossed branches of the trees overhead. "Here . . ."

She took off her robe.

She spread the robe near the boxes, at the edge of the clearing. Carefully in the moonlight she searched the clay ground, inch by inch; there was no dung, and no hair of cattle wedged in the bark of the oak trees. As she had imagined as she drove those limestone roads, the grove was clean, clean.

In the middle of the hoof-packed clay in the center of the grove of oaks, Miss Festner lay herself down upon the ground, which now seemed warm under the muscles of her flesh.

Nothing did come to her.

She was alone.

She listened but she heard only the mockery of silence among the trunks of trees. The intricate thunder of possibility shook her: was this the end, was she to be deserted like this at the final meeting place between two hills.

Then she heard it cough.

Nearby in the encircling brier she heard its jaws nibble the harsh vegetation. A small branch ripped under the plunge of a hoof. Then she heard it above her, high in the canopy of branches overhead; perhaps it was now looking down at the raised, white supplication of her arms.

She heard once more the cry of the loon: near, then far away. She heard something hoarse, and very close, in the ring of the briers. Held fast in the bondage of her desire, she lay with eyes closed in the moonlight, and still nothing came to her.

Over, she thought. Oh over and gone and never again to return to me. She realized a truth about herself: since the first time when the hair was sweet as a cloud of wool above her she had given more and more of herself. She had walked much, had driven farther and farther into strange woods. Then, like a reprieve, the coarse odor came to her. The lust of its eye rustled the briers.

The gifts. Yes, the boxes piled near her robe. Each time, with gifts, she also gave more and more. At first it was only a flower tossed lightly upon the sand bar. Then her gifts were only the green enticement, but finally she had to give the silks of reward, everything.

In a frenzy she opened her gifts.

Against rocks she broke the expensive, sullen perfumes. Each vial shattered and split and this enticement by odor overwhelmed even the trunks of the black trees.

Oh, come to me?

She paused, listened.

Somewhere beyond the shadows, somewhere in the forest of that night she felt something advance. She felt something come closer to her.

Her quick money-counting fingers clawed at the smaller boxes. She ripped tissue paper from all the jewels she had purchased at all the big jewelry stores all across the city. Tiaras and small rings and pearls in white strands, all these she tore into shreds of diamonds and single rubies and broken pearls, and these she threw into the encircling briers.

Oh, come to me?

The odor—so lurid, no near—seemed to stroke her thighs, and then in the old way it seemed to retreat beyond her farthest gifts.

Without her seeming to touch the hoof-packed clay she ran to the largest, final package. This she had saved, for the habit of frugality could also be with her, even in moments of extravagance.

She opened the box. The white, intense fleece of a lamb was what she held aloft. She waved the fleece in the light of the clearing. She held the fleece above her lowing mouth. She allowed the fleece to fall like a shower of myrrh and spice, to fall like the color of flowers around her, to cover her shoulders and her back with the incense of new wool.

Oh, come to me?

When nothing came to her, Miss Festner ran toward the thing she heard, toward a harsh plunging noise, in those final briers.

But she stopped. She knew it had deceived her, and therefore she stood weeping and ruined, fanned by the hot cry of the loon, in the center of briers and all her nights.

III

Escrow, Checking, Loans, and finally a Teller's cage: she had worked through each department, and now as the green floodgate doors of the bank opened, promptly at ten, she watched people swim into the bright hard marble pool of light, the interior of First National, Main.

In the hard security of a Teller's cage, she began this day by loosening the green drawstrings of green moneybags. Rolls of coins were what she found in each puffy little sack, rolls of dimes, and quarters, and half dollars, each roll made especially for her hand. In even rows the packets of bills, the twenties and fifties, fit precisely into each slot of her tray, and she felt the first smile of the morning hazard its first trial with the flesh of her own lips and cheeks as a customer snuffled just beyond the bars of her window.

From up the line, from Window Number One, Miss Festner heard the money-counting sound of laughter. The sound of the laughter made her see the two derby hats and the two false beards of the two men who were shaking hands with a Vice-President in the officers' enclosure, across the room. When she also saw the two beards rise and fall with the handshakes of the two men, she felt her own mouth pick up the laughter and pass it on to the next Teller in the long, money-counting line.

The State's Centennial Year, it was. The State Banking Inspectors were making believe. Across the room, in the officers' marble enclosure, two short men in make-believe beards began to laugh and laugh.

While her fingers counted out sixty-nine-sixty of the pensioner's check, which had snuffled under the bars of her window, she knew the ledgers and the adding machine tapes folded and held with paper clips and the dormant accounts and the Escrows were writhing, somewhere in the vaults or the storage rooms of First National, Main Branch.

Though the bills and the coins flowed through and around and over her fingers as water flows over and around a sand bar in some moonlit creek, the two derby hats and the beards of false gray hair seemed to float, seemed to become an echo, in the high corners of the main floor.

The edges of marble, the parallel shadows on the foot-trampled floor, the parallel lines of the brass-barred window before her, were the squares and the bars of a place she clearly remembered.

Across the bridge, beyond the village edge, was where the pens were.

There in Ohio, beyond the edge of a limestone road, she had awakened from the sleepless dawns of girlhood to hear the cruel roosters cry *blood, blood, bloooood* across the sties and pens and across the hen yard's dusty wallows. Often she lay in her bed, listening to the sounds of animals already awake; the snigger of boars or somewhere in the corner of a pasture the dry dirt-pawing hoof of her father's bull. The dirt, the droppings of turkeys and pea fowl, and the dung of sparrows on a beam under the barn's eave were always there, or were seen in memory only as a brown composite of wind and random dust flapping across barnyards.

In that house the women swept floors, brushed crumbs from tables, rocked toward evening, waited for the odor of farm boots and the odor of work clothes, denim jackets, and old felt hats to walk through kitchen doors; waited until the warm odor of milk drifted into the fried heat of a kitchen in March.

In summer a tomcat lolled on the tendrils and the matted leaves of a grape arbor, and stared all day at the martin's box high on a curved, white pole.

Mostly she remembered the things maimed: a rabbit leaping from stubble into the light of her father's sickle bar; the cut-shoat's lyric scream; the pullet, headless toward noon, butting a post of her mother's clothesline. Or the hired men, their fingers aligned at the thresher's dinner table, each man with something clipped off, missing: a finger gone to the nibbling belt of a corn sheller, a toe left at a chopping block, a hand or a forearm shucked by the whirling, frost-wet picker rolls.

All of that was past. She had gone to school, though she had visited her old home out of sentiment at the change of each season. For three years she taught at a consolidated high school. Though she tried to beat them with a yardstick the hulking baseball and football and basketball players refused to obey her. Finally the principal said why after all the First National, Main, paid twice as much, and then she could really have a place of her own. Therefore she had gone to live at the edge of this town, where sometimes a goat coughed in the catalpa leaves, and the backward curve of horn was mother-of-pearl in the moist light of the moon.

The two Inspectors came back toward noon.

Finally they began to work. Because it really was the Centennial Year, they wore derby hats and gray, false whiskers while they walked in and out of the officers' marble enclosure, or in and out of the vaults. She heard them laughing as they worked, and from her window it seemed they walked through the glass partitions. Toward three o'clock they walked past, together, nibbling a candy bar with their white goat teeth; and then they were behind the row of Tellers, nibbling stacks and stacks of twenties and fifties with their money-counting fingers.

At four o'clock doors were locked and the blinds were drawn, and only the feet and the knees of people walked past in the disembodied street. When she saw the legs walking past, Miss Festner thought, Why yes, tomorrow or the next day some one of the officers will walk up behind me and will stare and will then walk away as though he had seen something different. Then she would say what she knew all the others like her always said to the press: For my friends, for my friends, I did it, because I wanted them to be as happy as I have always been. You see, I gave it all to my friends . . .

At check-out, in the steel-lined vault, she saw the other money trays, all in a row. She knew this might be her last night at home in her own bed, in the room where the catalpa leaves were sometimes perfume in the night.

For the last time, tonight, she knew she might hear the hoofs firm upon the lowest branches, might see the flanks slender, stretched upward among the leaves, and might see also that final, unwinking eye stare at her from the tenderness of leaves.

Without hesitation she opened her massive, over-the-shoulder purse. Into the wide unlatched maw she stuffed all the singles and bundles of twenties and bundles of fifty dollar bills that her country hands could gather. In case, oh, in case it was money that was wanted, after all.

As always, Mr. Nelscot was standing at the bank door.

He smiled and he bowed very slightly as he let Miss Festner and her valise of a purse out the door.

All over again she heard the click of the door of First National, Main, behind her. She knew he would never do more than smile, would never do more than bow ever so slightly as he opened the door for her to leave. Or had that been his voice, after all; had he said as she left, as the door shut and clicked somewhere in the past and also in the future of her days, had he said too late, "See you. Same time tomorrow?"

a world ends
wolfgang hildesheimer

*Wolfgang Hildesheimer (1916–   )
is one of a group of new German writers,
including Heinrich Böll and
Gerd Gaiser, who define the
remarkable growth of the
short story in Germany since
World War II. At present,
only a few short stories
by Hildesheimer are available
in English. For further reading:*
Great German Short Stories,
*edited by Stephen
Spender (1960).*

The Marchesa Montetristo's last evening party has impressed itself indelibly on my memory. This is partly due, of course, to its extraordinary conclusion but in other ways as well the evening was unforgettable.

My acquaintance with the Marchesa—a Waterman by birth, of Little Gidding, Ohio—came about by a coincidence. I had sold her, through the intermediary of my friend, Herr von Perlhuhn (I mean of course the Abraham-a-Santa Clara expert, not the neo-mystic), the bathtub in which Marat was murdered. It is perhaps not generally known that it had been until then in my possession. Gambling debts obliged me to offer it for sale. So it was that I came to the Marchesa who had long wanted this appliance for her collection of eighteenth-century washing utensils. This was the occasion of my getting to know her. From the bathtub our conversation soon passed to more general esthetic topics. I noticed that the possession of this collector's piece had given me a certain prestige in her eyes. And I was not surprised when one day I was invited to one of her famous parties in her palazzo on the artificial island of San Amerigo. The Marchesa had had the island thrown up a few miles southeast of Murano on a sudden whim, for she detested the mainland—she said it was hurtful to her spiritual equilibrium, and she could find nothing to suit her in the existing stock of islands. So here she resided, devoting her life to the cult of the antique and forgotten, or, as she liked to put it, of the "true and eternal."

The invitation card gave the time of the party as eight o'clock, which meant that the guests were expected at ten. So custom ordered it. Further it ordered that the guests should come in gondolas. In this fashion, it is true, the crossing lasted nearly two hours and was moreover uncomfortable when the sea was rough, but these were unwritten rules of behavior at which no one but a barbarian would cavil—and barbarians were not invited. Besides, many of the younger guests, not yet fully sensible of the dignity of the occasion, would hire a *vaporetto* to take them within a hundred yards of the island whence they were ferried over one by one in a gondola which had been brought in tow.

The splendor of the building needs no description from me. For outside it was an exact replica of the Palazzo Vendramin, and inside every period, from the Gothic onward, was represented. But of course they were not intermingled. Each one had its own room. The Marchesa could really not be accused of breaches of style. Nor need the opulence of the catering be referred to her. Anyone who has ever attended a state banquet in a monarchy—and it is to such that I principally addressed myself—knows what it was like. Moreover it would hardly be true to the spirit of the Marchesa and her circle to mention the pleasures of the table, especially here, where I have to describe the last hours on earth of some of the most eminent figures of the age, which I as sole survivor had the privilege to witness.

After exchanging a few civilities with my hostess and stroking the long-haired Pekinese which never stirred from her side, I was introduced to the Dombrowska, a woman doubly famous, first for her contributions to the rhythmic-expressionist dance, a vanishing art form, and secondly as the author of the book *Back to Youth*, which, as the title indicates, argued in favor of a return to youthfulness of style and which, I need hardly remind the reader, has won adherents far and wide. While we were chatting together, an elderly gentleman of upright bearing came up to us. It was Golch. The Golch. (Unnecessary to give further particulars of a man whose share in the enrichment of our intellectual life is so widely known.) The Dombrowska introduced me: "Herr Sebald, the late owner of Marat's bathtub." My fame had spread.

"Aha," said Golch. I inferred, from the inflection he gave to these syllables, that he was weighing my potentialities as a candidate for the cultural élite. I asked him how he had liked the exhibition of contemporary painting in Luxemburg. For one might, indeed one must, assume that those here assembled had seen, read, and heard everything of any real importance. That was why they were here. Golch raised his eyes as if looking for a word in space and said, "Passé." (He used the English accentuation of the word which was then in fashion. The words "cliché" and "pastiche" too were pronounced *à l'anglaise*. I don't know what the current usage is. I am now too much taken up with everyday affairs to concern myself with such matters.) I noticed in any case that I had blundered in thus mentioning the contemporary. I had gone down a step, but I had learnt my lesson.

A move was made to the buffet. Here I encountered Signora Sgambati, the astrologer, who had recently made a considerable stir by her theory that not only the fate of individuals but whole trends in the history of ideas could be read in the stars. She was no ordinary phenomenon, this Sgambati, as was at once clear from her appearance. Yet I find it incomprehensible in the circumstances that she did not see in the constellation of the heavens the imminent engulfment of so many substantial members of the intellectual world. She was deep in conversation with Professor Kuntz-Sartori, the politician and royalist, who had been trying for decades to introduce a monarchy in Switzerland. Another notable figure.

After taking some refreshment the company moved to the Silver Room for what was to be the climax of the evening's entertainment, a performance of a special kind—the world première of two flute sonatas by Antonio Giambattista Bloch, a contemporary and friend of Rameau, who had been discovered by the musicologist Weltli. He too of course was there. They were played by the flautist Beranger (yes, a descendant) and accompanied by the Marchesa herself, on the self-same harpsichord on which Celestine Rameau had initiated her son into the fundamental principles of counter-point, and which had been sent for from Paris. The flute too had a history, but I have forgotten it. The two performers had put on rococo costume for the occasion, and the little ensemble looked— they had purposely so arranged themselves—like a picture by Watteau. The performance of course took place by the dimmest of candlelight. There was not a person there who would have found electric light for such an occasion anything but intolerable. By a further sensitive whim of the Marchesa the guests were required after the first sonata (D major) to move over from the Silver Room (Baroque) to the Golden Room (early Rococo), there to enjoy the second sonata. For the Silver Room had a major resonance, the Golden, it could not be disputed, a minor.

At this point I must remark that the tedious elegance which clings to the flute sonatas of second-rank, and more particularly of newly discovered, masters of this period, was in the present case to be explained by the fact that no such person as Giambattista Bloch had ever lived. The works here performed had in reality been composed by the musicologist Weltli. Although this circumstance did not become known till later, I cannot, in retrospect, help feeling it a humiliation for the Marchesa that she should have employed her last moments in the interpretation, however masterly, of a forgery.

During the second movement of the F minor sonata I saw a rat creeping along the wall. I was astonished. At first I thought it might have been lured from its hole by the sound of the flute—such things do happen, they say—but it was creeping in the opposite direction. It was followed by another rat. I looked at the guests. They had not noticed anything, and indeed most of them were keeping their eyes closed in order to be able to abandon themselves to the harmonies of Weltli's forgery. I now heard a dull reverberation, like very distant thunder. The floor began to vibrate. Again I looked at the guests. If they had heard anything—and something they must be hearing—it was at any rate not discernible from their hunched-up postures. I however was made uneasy by these strange symptoms.

A manservant entered. This is barely the place to remark that in the unusual costume worn by the Marchesa's domestic staff he looked like a character out of *Tosca*. He went up to the performers and whispered something in the Marchesa's ear. I saw her turn pale. How well it suited her in the dim candlelight! But she controlled herself and without interruption played the *andante* calmly to the end. Then she nodded to the flautist, stood up, and addressed the company.

"Ladies and gentlemen," she said, "I have just learnt that the foundations of the island and those of the palace with them are breaking up. The Office of Submarine Works has been informed. The right thing, I think we shall all agree, is to go on with the music."

She sat down again, gave the sign to Monsieur Beranger, and they played the *allegro con brio,* the last movement, which did seem to me at the time, though I had yet no inkling that it was a forgery, little suited to the uniqueness of the situation.

On the polished floor small puddles were forming. The reverberation had grown louder and sounded nearer. Most of the guests were now sitting upright, their faces ashen in the candlelight, and looking as if they were long dead already. I stood up and said, "I'm going," not so loud as to give offense to the musicians, but loud enough to intimate to the other guests that I had the courage to admit my fear. The floor was now almost evenly covered with water. Although I walked on tiptoe, I could not help splashing an evening dress or two as I passed. But, in view of what was soon to come, the damage I did must be reckoned inconsiderable. Few of the guests thought me worthy of a glance, but I did not care. As I opened the door to the passage a wave of water poured into the room and caused Lady Fitzjones (the preserver of Celtic customs) to draw her fur wrap more closely about her—no doubt a reflex movement, for it could not be of any use. Before shutting the door behind me I saw Herr von Perlhuln (the neo-mystic, not the Abraham-a-Santa Clara expert) casting a half-contemptuous, half-melancholy glance in my direction. He too was now sitting in water almost to his knees. So was the Marchesa, who could no longer use the pedals. I do not as a matter of fact know how essential they are on the harpsichord. I remember thinking that if the piece had been a cello sonata, they would perforce have had to break it off here since the instrument would not sound in water. Strange what irrelevant thoughts occur to one in such moments.

In the entrance hall it was suddenly as quiet as in a grotto, only in the distance a sound of rushing water was to be heard. I divested myself of my tail coat and was soon swimming through the sinking palace toward the portals. My splashes echoed mysteriously from the walls and columns. Not a soul was to be seen. Evidently the servants had all fled. And why should they not? They had no obligation to the true and eternal culture, and those assembled here had no further need of their services.

Outside the moon shone as if nothing were amiss, and yet a world, no less, was here sinking beneath the ocean. As if at a great distance I could still hear the high notes of Monsieur Beranger's flute. He had a wonderful *embouchure*, that one must allow him.

I unhitched the last gondola which the escaping servants had left behind and pushed out to sea. Through the windows past which I paddled the water was now flooding into the palace. I saw that the guests had risen from their seats. The sonata must be at an end, for they were clapping, their hands held high over their heads, since the water was now up to their chins. With dignity the Marchesa and Monsieur Beranger were acknowledging the applause, though in the circumstances they could not bow.

The water had now reached the candles. Slowly they were extinguished, and as the darkness grew, it became quiet; the applause was silenced. Suddenly I heard the crash and roar of a building in collapse. The Palazzo was falling. I steered the gondola seaward so as not to be hit by plaster fragments.

After paddling some hundreds of yards across the lagoon in the direction of the island of San Giorgio, I turned round once more. The sea lay dead calm in the moonlight as if no island had ever stood there. A pity about the bathtub, I thought, for that was a loss which could never be made good. The thought was perhaps rather heartless but experience teaches us that we need a certain distance from such events in order to appreciate their full scope.

the
secret
room
alain robbe-grillet

Alain Robbe-Grillet (1922–   )
was born in Brest and subsequently graduated
from the Institut National Agronomique.
He has done research in Morocco,
Equatorial Africa, and the French
Antilles. A French "new novelist"
his Les Gommes (The Erasers,
1962) and Le Voyeur (1959)
became centers of controversy.
His work pays minute attention to
objective details. Much of his short
fiction has not yet been
translated into English.

First there is a red spot, bright, red, shiny but dark, shading to almost black. It forms an irregular, clearly outlined rosette, extended on several sides by wide streaks of varying lengths which then divide and dwindle until they are no more than meandering threads. The entire area stands out against the pallor of a smooth, rounded, dull and yet pearly surface, a half-sphere gently curving to an expanse of the same pale hue—a whiteness attenuated by the gloom of the place: dungeon, crypt or cathedral—gleaming with a diffused luster in the darkness.

Beyond, the space is occupied by the cylindrical shafts of columns that grow more numerous and blurred in the distance, where the beginning of a huge stone staircase can be made out, gradually turning and narrowing as it rises toward the high vaulting into which it vanishes.

The whole of this scene is empty, staircase and colonnades. Alone in the foreground, glimmers the prone body, on which the red spot is spreading—a white body suggesting the luminous, supple, doubtless fragile and vulnerable flesh. Beside the bloodstained half-sphere, another identical though intact globe can be seen from almost the same angle; but the darker ringed tip crowning it is here quite recognizable, whereas the first is almost completely destroyed, or at least concealed, by the wound.

In the background, toward the bend of the stairs, a black figure is vanishing from sight, a man wrapped in a long, loose cape, who mounts the last steps without turning around, his crime committed. A faint vapor rises in intertwining spirals from a kind of incense burner set on a high, silvery-metal stand. Quite near lies the milky body where wide rivulets of blood are flowing from the left breast, down the side and over the hip.

It is a woman's body, its forms opulent but not heavy, completely naked, lying on its back, the bust half-raised by thick cushions laid on the floor, which is covered by rugs of Oriental design. The waist is very narrow, the neck long and slender, curved to one side, the head thrown back into a darker area where the features of the face can still be discerned, the mouth half open, the large eyes wide, gleaming with a fixed luster, and the mass of the long black hair spread out in waves of formal disorder on the heavy folds of some fabric, velvet perhaps, on which the arm and shoulder also rest.

It is a smooth, dark-violet velvet, or seems to be in this light. But violet, brown and blue also seem to prevail in the colors of the cushions —of which only a small part is concealed by the velvet material and which extend farther down under the bust and the waist—as well as in the Oriental patterns of the rugs on the floor. Beyond, these same colors recur in the stone of the slabs and columns, the arches of the vaulting, the staircase, the vaguer surfaces where the limits of the room are lost to view.

It is difficult to specify the latter's dimensions; the slaughtered young woman seems at first glance to occupy a considerable place in it, but the vast proportions of the staircase descending toward her would suggest, on the contrary, that she does not take up the whole room, for a noticeable area must actually extend to the right and the left, as well as toward those distant browns and blues in the various rows of columns, perhaps toward other sofas, heavy rugs, piles of cushions and fabrics, other tortured bodies, other incenseburners.

It is also difficult to say where the light is coming from. Nothing, on the columns or on the floor, suggests the direction of its source. Moreover, there is no window in sight, and no torch. It is the milky body itself that seems to illuminate the scene, the neck and the swelling breasts, the curve of the hips, the belly, the full thighs, the legs stretched out, wide apart, and the black fleece, of the sex exposed—provocative, proffered, henceforth useless.

The man has already moved several strides away. Now he is already on the first steps of the staircase which he is about to mount. The lower steps are long and deep, like the shallow stairs leading to some public edifice, temple or theatre; they then gradually diminish in size as they rise, and at the same time begin a broad spiral movement, so gradual that the staircase has not yet effected a half-turn when, reduced to an awkward narrow passageway without a railing, even vaguer in the deepening darkness, it disappears toward the top of the vaulting.

But the man is not looking in this direction, where his steps will nonetheless carry him; his left foot on the second step and his right already set on the third, knee bent, he has turned around to take a look at the scene. The long loose cape which he has hastily thrown over his shoulders, and which he holds at his waist with one hand, has been swept by the rotation which has just brought his head and upper body around to face away from the direction he is going, a flap of material raised in the air as though by the effect of a gust of wind; the corner, which folds back on itself in a loose S, reveals the gold-embroidered, red-satin lining.

The man's features are impassive, but strained, as though in anticipation—fear perhaps—of some sudden event, or rather reassuring himself as to the total immobility of the scene. Although he looks back in this way, his whole body has remained leaning slightly forward, as though he were still continuing his ascent. His right arm—the one not holding the edge of the cape—is half extended to the left, toward a point in space where the railing would be if there were one on this staircase, an interrupted, almost incomprehensible gesture, unless it is an instinctive impulse to catch hold of the missing support?

As for the direction of his gaze, it is unquestionably toward the body of the victim lying exposed on the cushions, the limbs extended in a cross, the bust raised slightly, the head thrown back. But perhaps the face is hidden from the man's eyes by one of the columns which rises at the foot of the stairs. The young woman's right hand touches the floor just at this column's base. A thick iron fetter encircles the delicate wrist. The arm is almost in shadow, the hand alone receiving enough light for the slender, spread fingers to be clearly visible against the circular rim that forms a base for the stone shaft. A black-metal chain is fastened around the shaft and passes through a ring on the fetter, closely attaching the wrist to the column.

At the arm's other end, a round shoulder, raised by the cushions, is also plainly lighted, as are the neck, the throat and the other shoulder, the armpit and its down, the left arm stretched behind the body too and and its wrist attached in the same way to the base of another column, quite close to the foreground; here the iron ring and the chain are clearly seen, drawn with great distinctness down to the smallest detail.

Seen in the same way, still in the foreground but on the other side, is a similar though somewhat lighter chain which twice encircles the ankle directly, attaching it to a heavy ring set in the floor. About a yard or so behind it, the right foot is chained in the same manner. But it is the left foot and its chain that are represented with the most precision.

The foot is small, delicate, finely modeled. The chain has bruised the flesh in places, making noticeable though small depressions. Its links are oval, thick and about the size of an eye. The ring is like those used for hitching horses; it is lying almost flat on the stone slab, in which it is held by a massive spike. The edge of a rug begins an inch or so away; it is raised here by a fold produced, no doubt, by the victim's convulsive though necessarily limited movements when she attempted to struggle.

The man is still half leaning over her, standing about a yard away. He examines her face tilted back, the dark eyes enlarged by cosmetics, the mouth wide as if in a scream. The man's position reveals only one-quarter of his face, but he is evidently in the grip of violent excitement, despite his rigid position, silence, and immobility. His back is bent slightly. His left hand, the only one that can be seen, holds away from his body a piece of fabric, some dark garment which trails on the rug and which must be the long cape with its gold-embroidered lining.

This massive figure greatly conceals the naked flesh where the red spot, which has spread over the bulge of the breast, flows in long rivulets which branch out as they grow thinner, against the pale background of the torso and the whole side. One of them has reached the armpit and traces a fine, almost straight line the length of the arm; others have run down toward the waist and drawn a more arbitrary network, which is already congealing over the belly, the hip and the top of the thigh. Three or four veinules have reached as far as the hollow of the groin and formed a meandering line which joins the point of the V formed by the parted legs and vanishes in the black fleece.

There, now the flesh is still intact, the black fleece and the white belly, the gentle curve of the hips, the slender waist and, above, the pearly breasts which rise in time to the rapid breathing, whose rhythm grows faster. The man, close beside her, one knee on the ground, bends farther forward. The head with the long wavy hair, which alone has kept some freedom of movement, stirs, struggles; finally the girl's mouth opens and twists, while the flesh yields, the blood spurts out over the tender, smooth skin, the skillfully painted black eyes widen enormously, the mouth opens still further, the head is flung from right to left, violently, one last time, then more gently, finally falling back motionless in the mass of black hair spread out on the velvet.

At the very top of the stone staircase, the little door is open, releasing a yellow, sustained light, against which the dark figure of the man wrapped in his long cape is silhouetted. He has no more than a few steps to climb in order to reach the threshold.

Then the whole scene is empty, the enormous violet-shadowed room with its stone columns extending on all sides, the monumental staircase with no railing that turns as it rises, growing narrower and vaguer as it mounts into the darkness toward the top of the vaulting, where it vanishes.

Near the prone body whose wound has congealed, whose luster is already fading, the faint vapor from the incense burner forms complicated volutes in the calm air: at first it is a strand inclined to the left, then rises and increases slightly in height, then returns toward the axis of its point of departure, exceeds it on the right, again starts in the other direction, only to return once more, thus tracing an irregular, gradually fading sinusoid, which rises vertically toward the top of the canvas.

stories
and texts
for nothing,
III

samuel beckett

Samuel Beckett (1906–) was born in Dublin and was a lecteur d'anglais in the late twenties in Paris. He now prefers French as a medium for his novels, plays, and short stories. Since 1938 he has resided outside of Paris and leads a life of austerity and isolation. He is a follower of Joyce (whom he knew personally), but came to fame in his own right with the play Waiting for Godot (1952). For further reading: Novels and Texts for Nothing (1955).

Leave, I was going to say leave all that. What matter who's speaking, someone said what matter who's speaking. There's going to be a departure, I'll be there, it won't be me, I'll be here, I'll say I'm far, it won't be me, I won't say anything, there's going to be a story, someone's going to try and tell a story. Yes, enough denials, all is false, there's no one, it's agreed, there's nothing, enough phrases, let's be dupes, dupes of time, all time, until it's over, all over, and the voices are stilled, they're only voices, only lies. Here, leave here and go elsewhere, or stay

here, but coming and going. Move first, there must be a body, as of old,
I don't say no, I won't say no any more, I'll say I have a body, a body
that moves, forward, backward, up and down, as required. With a clutter
of limbs and organs, all that's needed to live once again, to hold out, a
short spell, I'll call that living, I'll say it's me, I'll stand up, I'll think no
more, I'll be too taken up, standing up, keeping standing up, moving
about, holding out, getting to the next day, the next week, that will be
enough, a week will be enough, a week in spring, that will be bracing.
It's enough to will, I'm going to will, will myself a body, will myself a
head, a little strength, a little courage, I'm going to start, a week is soon
over, then back here, this inextricable place, far from the days, the days
are far, it's not going to be easy. And why, after all, no no, leave it, don't
start that again, don't listen to everything, don't say everything, all is old,
all one, that's settled. There you are up, I give you my word, I swear
it's mine, work your hands, palp your skull, seat of the understanding,
without it nothing doing, then the rest, the lower parts, can't do without
them, and say what you are, what kind of man, have a guess, there must
be a man, or a woman, feel between your legs, no need of beauty, or
strength, a week is soon over, no one's going to love you, don't worry.
No, not like that, too sudden, I gave myself a fright. And to start with
stop panting, no one's going to kill you, oh no, no one's going to love
you and no one's going to kill you. You may emerge in the high depression of Gobi, there you'll feel at home. I'll wait for you here, my mind at
rest, at rest for you, no, I'm alone, I alone am, it's I must go, this time
it's I. I know what I'll do, I'll be a man, I must, a kind of man, a kind
of old infant, I'll have a nurse, she'll be fond of me, she'll give me her
hand, to cross over, she'll let me loose in gardens, I'll be good, I'll sit in
a corner and comb my beard, smooth it down, to be nicer looking, a little
nicer, if it could be like that. She'll say to me, Come, lamb, it's time for
home. I won't have any responsibility, she'll have all the responsibility,
her name will be Nanny, I'll call her Nanny, if it could only be like that.
Come, pet, it's time for bottle. Who taught me all I know, I alone, when
I was still a wanderer, I deduced it all, from nature, with the aid of an
all-in-one, I know it's not true, but it's too late now, too late to deny it,
the knowledge is there, items of knowledge, gleaming in turn, far and
near, flickering over the abyss, allies. Leave it and go, I must go, I must
say so anyway, the moment is come, one doesn't know why. What does it
matter where you say you are, here or elsewhere, fixed or movable, shapeless or oblong like man, without light or in the light of heaven, I don't
know, it seems to matter, it's not going to be easy. If I went back to
where all went out and then on from there, no, that wouldn't lead anywhere, that never led anywhere, the memory of it has gone out too, a
great flame and then blackness, a great spasm and then no more bulk

or traversable space, I don't know. I tried to have me fall, off the cliff, in the street in the midst of mortals, that led nowhere, I gave up. Travel the road again that cast me up here, before going back the way I came, or on, wise advice. That's so that I'll never stir again, dribble on here till time is done, murmuring every ten centuries, it's not me, it's not true, it's not me, I'm far. No no, I'll speak now of the future, I'll speak in the future, as in the days when I said to myself, in the night, Tomorrow I'll put on my blue tie, the one with the stars, and put it on, when the night was past. Quick quick before I weep. I'll have a friend, my own age, my own bog, an old warrior, we'll fight our battles over again and compare our scratches. Quick quick. He had served in the navy, perhaps under Jellicoe, while I was potting at the invader from behind a barrel of Guinness, with my arquebus. We have not long, that's right, in the present, not long to live, it's our last winter of all, halleluiah. We wonder what will carry us off finally. He's gone in the wind, I in the bladder rather. We envy each other, he envies me, I envy him, on and off. I catheterize myself unaided, with trembling hand, standing in the public pisshouse, bent double, under cover of my cape, people take me for a dirty old man. Meanwhile he waits for me on a bench, coughing up his guts, spitting into a snuff-box which no sooner overflows than he empties it into the canal, out of public-spiritedness. We have deserved well of our motherland, she'll get us into hospital before we die. We spend our life, it's ours, trying to unite in the same instant a ray of sunshine and a free bench, in an oasis of public greenery, we have taken to a love of nature, in our sere and yellow, it belongs to one and all, in places. He reads to me in choking murmur from the paper of the day before, he had better been the blind one. Our passion is horse-racing, dog-racing too, we have no political opinions, just limply republican. But we also have a warm spot for the Windsors, the Hanoverians, I forget, the Hohenzollerns is it. Nothing human is foreign to us, once we have digested the dogs and horses. No, alone, I'd be better off alone, it would be quicker. He'd feed me, he had a friend, a pork-butcher, he'd ram my soul back down my gullet with black pudding. With his consolations, allusions to cancer, recollections of imperishable raptures, he'd prevent discouragement from sapping my foundations. And I, instead of concentrating on my own horizons, which might have enabled me to throw them under a lorry, would have my mind distracted by his. I'd say to him, Come on, son, leave all that, think no more about it, and it's I would think no more about it, besotted with brotherliness. And the obligations, I have in mind particularly the appointments at ten o'clock in the morning, rain, hail or shine, in front of Duggan's, thronging already with sporting men in a hurry to get their bets out of harm's way before the bars opened. We were, there we are past and gone again, so much the better, so much the better, most punctual, I must say. To see the remains of Vincent arriving in sheets of rain, with the brave involuntary swagger of the old tar, his head swathed in a bloody clout and a gleam in his eye, was for the acute observer an example of what man is capable of, in his thirst for enjoyment. With one hand he sustained his sternum, with the heel of the other his spinal column, no, that's all memories, last shifts more ancient than the flood. To see what's happening here, where there's no one, where nothing happens, to get something to happen here, someone to be here, then put an end to it, make silence, enter silence, or another noise, a noise of other voices than those of life and death, of lives and deaths that never will be mine, enter my story, in order to leave it, no, that's all fiddle-faddle. Is it possible I'll sprout a head in the end, all my own, in which to brew some poisons worthy of me, and legs to kick my heels, I'd be there at last, I could go, it's all I ask, no, I can't ask anything. Nothing but the head and the two legs, or just one, in the middle, I'd go hopping. Or nothing but the head, nice and round, nice and smooth, no need of features, I'd roll, downhill, almost a pure spirit, no, that wouldn't work, all's uphill from here, there'd have to be a leg, or the equivalent, an annular joint or so, contractile, with them you go a long way. To set forth from Duggan's door, on a spring morning of rain and shine, not knowing if you'll ever come to evening, what's wrong there? It would be so easy. To be buried in that flesh or in another, in that arm held by a friendly hand, and in that hand, without arms, without hands, and.without soul in those trembling souls, through the crowd, the hoops, the toy balloons, what's wrong there? I don't know, I'm here, that's all I know, and that it's still not me, that's what you have to make the best of. There's no flesh anywhere, nor any means of dying, leave all that, to want to leave all that, without knowing what that means, all that, it's soon said, soon done, in vain, nothing has stirred, no one spoken. Here, nothing will happen, there will be no one here, for many a long day. Departures, stories, they're not for tomorrow. And the voices, wherever they come from, are stone dead.

chronology
of
authors

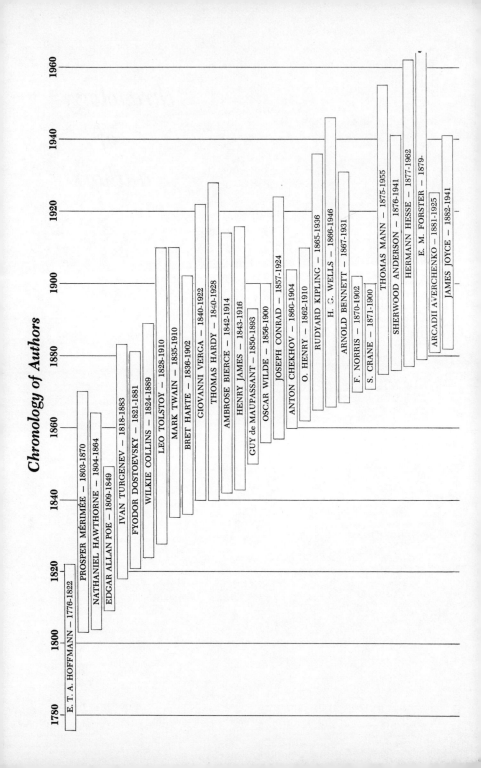

Chronology of Authors

E. T. A. HOFFMANN – 1776-1822

PROSPER MÉRIMÉE – 1803-1870

NATHANIEL HAWTHORNE – 1804-1864

EDGAR ALLAN POE – 1809-1849

IVAN TURGENEV – 1818-1883

FYODOR DOSTOEVSKY – 1821-1881

WILKIE COLLINS – 1824-1889

LEO TOLSTOY – 1828-1910

MARK TWAIN – 1835-1910

BRET HARTE – 1836-1902

GIOVANNI VERGA – 1840-1922

THOMAS HARDY – 1840-1928

AMBROSE BIERCE – 1842-1914

HENRY JAMES – 1843-1916

GUY de MAUPASSANT – 1850-1893

OSCAR WILDE – 1856-1900

JOSEPH CONRAD – 1857-1924

ANTON CHEKHOV – 1860-1904

O. HENRY – 1862-1910

RUDYARD KIPLING – 1865-1936

H. G. WELLS – 1866-1946

ARNOLD BENNETT – 1867-1931

F. NORRIS – 1870-1902

S. CRANE – 1871-1900

THOMAS MANN – 1875-1955

SHERWOOD ANDERSON – 1876-1941

HERMANN HESSE – 1877-1962

E. M. FORSTER – 1879-

ARCADII AVERCHENKO – 1881-1925

JAMES JOYCE – 1882-1941

1780	1800	1820	1840	1860	1880	1900	1920	1940	1960

VIRGINIA WOOLF – 1882-1941

JOSÉ VASCONCELOS – 1882-

FRANZ KAFKA – 1883-1924

D. H. LAWRENCE – 1885-1930

K. MANSFIELD – 1888-1923

KAREL ČAPEK – 1890-1938

STRATES MYRIVELES – 1892-

ISAAC BABEL – 1894-1941

KATHERINE ANNE PORTER – 1894-

F. SCOTT FITZGERALD – 1896-1940

WILLIAM FAULKNER – 1897-1962

VALENTIN KATAYEV – 1897-

ERNEST HEMINGWAY – 1898-1961

JORGE LUIS BORGES – 1899-

ELIZABETH BOWEN – 1899-

KAY BOYLE – 1903-

FRANK O'CONNOR – 1903-

JAMES T. FARRELL – 1904-

GRAHAM GREENE – 1904-

JEAN-PAUL SARTRE – 1905-

SAMUEL BECKETT – 1906-

TOMMASO LANDOLFI – 1908-

BERNARD MALAMUD – 1914-

WOLFGANG HILDESHEIMER – 1916-

ISAAC ROSENFELD – 1918-1956

JAMES B. HALL – 1918-

R. V. CASSILL – 1919-

SHIRLEY JACKSON – 1919-

ALAIN ROBBE-GRILLET – 1922-

FLAN. O'CONNOR – 1925-1964

TED HUGHES – 1930-